High in the Bavarian Alps

A Novel

*"One's destination is never a place,
but a new way of seeing things."*
Henry Miller

High in the Bavarian Alps

A Novel

JAMES EARL

High in the Bavarian Alps: A Novel. Copyright 2019 by James Earl.

Published by Bits of Time Publishing, Carmel, California.

Bits of Time Publishing, PO Box 223502, Carmel, CA 93922-3502.
https://www.bitsoftimepublishing.com

Published in the United States of America.

The Library of Congress Cataloging-in-Publication Data
Names: Earl, James, [1938] author.
Title: High in the Bavarian Alps / James Earl.
ISBN: 978-0-9997552-0-4 (hardback book with jacket).

Author's Note: This novel is a work of historical fiction. Names, characters, businesses, organizations, places and incidents either are the product of the author's imagination or are used fictitiously. Any resemblance to actual events, locales or persons, living or dead, is entirely coincidental.

Main subjects: Local cultures and history in Bavaria, Germany, Austria, Munich, Garmisch, Oberammergau, Berchtesgaden, Lake Chiemsee and Obersalzberg; 1971-1972; Armed Forces Recreation Center (AFRC); Castles of King Ludwig II; Adolf Hitler; Nazi influence on cultures in Bavaria and other areas of Europe; Red Army Faction (RAF); Andreas Baader; Ulrike Meinhof; Gudrun Ensslin.

Cover logos and emblems: Bavarian Coat of Arms; Emblem of Nazi Party; Logo of Red Army Faction (RAF); Logo of Armed Forces Recreation Center (AFRC).

Our books may be purchased in bulk.
Contact your local bookseller or send your request to:
Bits of Time Publishing, PO Box 223502, Carmel, CA 93922-3502.
https://www.bitsoftimepublishing.com
sales@bitsoftimepublishing.com

First Edition: May 2019

Preface

In the early 70s, Bavaria offered adventure, fabulous skiing and other fun activities in fairy-tale settings.

Many of the characters are civilian employees, privileged to work for the American military at facilities of the Armed Forces Recreation Center. These young men and women frolic and travel through Bavaria, Austria, Germany, Spain, Italy and other countries in Europe. Among other things, they explore castles of King Ludwig II, ski on the most beautiful glaciers and mountains, learn about the local cultures, enjoy fabulous cuisine, follow the 1972 Munich Olympics and attend the Austrian Grand Prix.

Native characters tell their stories about the Nazi Party and its history. Some of them were around Hitler, up close and personal.

Acts of terrorism occur in the story, inspired by real-life events, including attacks by the Red Army Faction, a group also known as the Baader-Meinhof Gang.

Intended for adult reading, this novel is a work of historical fiction.

CHAPTER 1

Europe: Touching Down

Lucas felt nervous upon arriving at the airport. He kept looking over his shoulder, expecting police to stop him from boarding the plane because they had told him not to leave the Los Angeles area. He almost fainted when he heard the loudspeaker announcement, "Paging: Mr. Lucas Gary. Will you please report to the information desk?"

He was tempted to ignore the page. When he arrived at the desk, he received a phone call. His attorney, Mark Olson, advised him to not go on this trip. Lucas wondered if the attorney had somehow learned he bought a one-way plane ticket. All Lucas said was, "Goodbye Mark." Then, he boarded the plane with his good friend, George Bennett, both ready for a beer and happy to be on a new adventure.

Lucas Gary ducked his head as he boarded Flight 279 at LAX going to Frankfurt, Germany. On a beautiful September morning, he followed George down the aisle of the Continental Airlines Boeing 727.

This was only the 2nd time the 30-year-old had flown. Lucas was in the ROTC Program at Fresno State when he flew on a C-47 Air Force plane from Fresno to Nellis Air Force Base on the outskirts of Las Vegas. He remembered wearing a parachute, seated on a hardwood bench in the transport plane.

The cost of this charter flight from Los Angeles to Frankfurt was only $200. Lucas did not expect free beer and a tasty sauerbraten lunch which was served somewhere over Illinois. Most of the passengers were German and enrolled in the Continental Travel Club. Lucas and George joined the club for $20 each to get such a cheap flight.

They fit right in with the Germans, drank beer, joked and laughed all the way to Bangor, Maine. Both were disappointed when they discovered there was no bar at this airport. It was only a hanger. During a 45-minute stopover, they sat on uncomfortable, hard chairs.

The flight across the Atlantic was quieter. Most of the passengers stayed in their seats, and some were taking naps. George and Lucas talked for a while and enjoyed another in-flight meal. Then, George closed his eyes and drifted off. This gave Lucas a chance to reflect on how and why he was flying to Europe on this particular day, September 9, 1971. He first thought of Jodie.

It is now seven months since I lost my fiancée, Jodie Conover, a busty blonde with a cute turned-up nose and very kissable lips.

Jodie was murdered, and the presumed culprit was Bruno, a former boyfriend who had mob connections and fled to Europe to escape arrest. Bruno Castignoli stood six foot two and weighed two hundred twenty-five pounds. Jodie was petite and 8 inches shorter. He physically abused her on multiple occasions. It appeared the last time was fatal for her.

She and I were a couple, planning to be married. Bruno phoned her one night and told her he was sorry for his abuse; he hoped they could work out their problems and get back together. When Jodie told Bruno she was seeing someone, she felt happy and comfortable in her new relationship, and she didn't wish to see him again, Bruno got upset on the phone. Then, he told her he would be around if she changed her mind.

It was only three days later when Jodie's beaten and battered body was discovered in the water at a canal in Naples, a district of Long Beach near Belmont Shore. Cement blocks were tied to her body. The coroner's report stated she was brutally beaten and noted the assailant must have been crazed with extreme anger, based on the severity of her injuries.

I remember the first time I saw Jodie: she walked into my Anaheim Street restaurant, located in the outskirts of Long Beach, and sat by herself in a booth by a window. It was hard not to stare at this woman who was in her late twenties. She looked amazing with short blonde hair, big blue eyes and a cleavage which caught my eye. After she finished her lunch, I grabbed a piece of lemon meringue plus a piece of cherry pie and took those with me to her table. I had to restrain myself and not look down at her breasts. As I stared into those big blue eyes, I almost choked on my words, but I said, "Hi. I'm Lucas Gary, the owner and chef of this restaurant. Could I interest you in a piece of pie? We have apple, peach, blueberry, apricot, coconut cream, chocolate cream, custard or pecan pie. We also have rice pudding, bread pudding and baked apples."

Jodie laughed, took the lemon meringue and asked me to join her. She shocked me by saying someone had told her to come there for lunch and check me out. I was not sure how to respond, feeling embarrassed at first. I asked, "In that case, would you like to go out with me sometime soon?" Then, she asked, "Would Friday night be okay with you?"

Friday night, Jodie picked me up at my house behind the restaurant, and we drove to Hennessey's, a seaside tavern in Manhattan Beach. I had several beers and Jodie had several glasses of white wine. We spent the evening talking and getting to know each other. When we walked outside, Jodie's green, nineteen sixty-eight Volkswagen "Bug" was nowhere in sight. I was mistaken when I told Jodie it was okay to park in a motel lot on the side street. We inquired at the motel desk, learned it was towed and got the address of the impound lot.

By the time we got back to Long Beach, it was late. She kissed me goodnight and agreed to go out with me again, maybe the following night, if she could cancel a meeting to talk with her former boyfriend.

Jodie telephoned me at work on Saturday morning. She told me she had canceled her meeting with Bruno, and we planned to go out in the evening. After dinner, she asked me if I would spend the night at her home which was two blocks from my restaurant on Anaheim Street. Jodie's place was the last split-level condominium on a quiet side street. She met me at the door with a sexy outfit on, and we spent the rest of the evening getting to know each other.

The next day, Jodie surprised me. On her way to work, she walked in my restaurant kitchen, wearing her nurse's uniform and looking great. Handing me a front door key to her place, Jodie said, "This is the key to my house, and you are welcome anytime." I recall thinking I liked this lady, more every minute, and I wondered what other surprises she had in store for me.

Many times, at her place or mine, if I became upset for any reason, Jodie would take off her clothes. In an instant, the possibility of argument or any sort of issue ended. Within a very short time, we developed a conflict-free relationship.

Both wanting to avoid feeling tied down, we were happy with the unspoken commitment we had. Many of my friends partied with us. Some Saturday nights, I would close the restaurant at nine p.m. and hire a local rock band. We enjoyed those evenings with the Long Beach group until all hours. Then, I would spend Sunday morning in bed with Jodie. Those mornings were special times together.

We enjoyed eating out and often went for breakfast at Hof's Hut in Lakewood. Another favorite was Joe Jost's Restaurant on Anaheim Street, famous for a delicious polish sausage sandwich on rye bread with mustard and provolone cheese, served with pickled eggs and pretzels. It had a bar with pool and billiards. Jodie was a good sport, and I taught her how to play the British game of Snooker there.

We also enjoyed going to Long Beach State basketball games. The 49ers had a great team with Jerry Tarkanian as the head coach. He went out across the country and signed players who were not eligible for some top universities. He was also becoming famous for chewing on a towel while he sat on the sideline and coached the game.

All things considered; life was going well for me. I had two restaurants and even found a buyer for my Fourth Street restaurant if I wanted to sell.

Located in downtown Long Beach across the street from Sears, it was a busy restaurant. I drank Coors beer all day and night when I wanted to, and I had lots of friends. Some Friday nights, I went out with the guys. When I was not working, on weekends and during the week, I shot pool and played basketball. My beautiful girlfriend always wanted sex when I did; and I never felt so secure in life and in a relationship during my thirty years on earth.

I loved to play basketball. When my game was on, I could shoot with the best of them. I had been playing for ten years in the Long Beach City League. I also played pick-up games at the YMCA and on the courts at Belmont Shore Beach.

One February evening, my team won a basketball game at Wilson High School, and I had a season-high twenty-nine points. I showered in the gym and headed to Jodie's place for a late snack and some TV.

When I arrived, a police car was blocking the driveway, and a police officer stopped me before I could reach the front door. The officer was Mike Fletcher who worked for the Long Beach Police Department. He had been to parties at my restaurant and had become a regular along with my beer buddies. Mike gave me the gruesome news: someone found Jodie's body in the water at a canal in the Naples area of Belmont Shore. She had been badly beaten and weighted down with cement blocks. I immediately thought of Bruno. Next, I thought of Darrell Langley, Jodie's ex-husband who had also physically abused her.

Mike questioned me as to my whereabouts during the day. He told me Jodie had left work at seven a.m. Since then, no one had seen her until someone spotted her body in the canal.

I recounted my day to the police: I worked at my restaurant all day, left about seven p.m., went to the gym and played basketball. After the game, I showered and dressed, then picked up a large combination pizza at Shakey's on Pacific Coast Highway near Atlantic. I had two Coors beers while I waited and talked to people who I knew. Last, I got to Jodie's house about ten thirty p.m. The police knew the rest.

I was never a real suspect, only a person of interest. So, it boiled down to Bruno, Darrell, or who knows who. As it turned out, Darrell also had an iron-clad alibi, leaving Bruno as the main suspect. Since his previous abuse of Jodie was known to the police, and she had broken off their relationship, it did not look good for Bruno. But, before they could charge him, he disappeared. For some reason, the police did not seem too eager to go looking for him.

Later, Mike Fletcher told me the Long Beach Police Department had a lead: Bruno might have gone to Germany, and he might be in a town called Garmisch-Partenkirchen which is in Bavaria. Fletcher had a friend in Bavaria, who worked for the Armed Forces Recreation Center. His friend thought Bruno might be a bartender at a hotel in Garmisch.

Months later, I was making pies at the end of a hard day at work, and my friend George Bennett walked into the kitchen. George was a high school volleyball coach, a math teacher, a world class volleyball player, an all-around good athlete and a beer-drinking buddy. George was complaining to me about the kids at school.

I listened for a minute and asked, "Do you want to go to Europe?"

Without hesitation, George said, "Yeah!"

Although the Long Beach Police told me to stick around, in case they need to reach me about the investigation into Jodie's death, George and I made travel plans. We went to Los Angeles, got our passports, joined the Continental Club and reserved tickets for the charter flight to Frankfurt, leaving at 8 a.m. on September 9th.

When I heard Bruno may be working in Garmisch, Germany, for the Armed Forces Recreation Center, known as AFRC, I was told to look up a housemaid at the Green Arrow Hotel, a young lady named Gail. By coincidence, Gail knew Bruno from the bar scene around Manhattan Beach. Fletcher told me his friend Gail described Garmisch as a resort area for the military, and a lot of civilians worked there. They came from all over the world. According to Gail, anyone who was interested could get a job with the AFRC.

I did some research and got information about military bases and civilian benefits, offered to persons who work for the American military in Germany. They issue ID cards for use at any military base in Europe, and Class Six shopping privileges included alcohol and cigarettes. We could purchase gasoline from any military stations, and we would have commissary and PX privileges plus access to military hotels and other facilities, such as movie theaters and bowling alleys.

Fletcher's friend Gail told him we could get jobs right away at the Abrams Kaserne in Frankfurt and work there until snow falls. Winter is when the military will hire new people in Garmisch for a busy ski season. Or, we could work a short while in Frankfurt, and then travel around Europe, using military IDs for access to military facilities while we waited until the snow falls.

When I shared this information with George, we devised a plan. We will get jobs at the American military base in Frankfurt and stay there long enough to get our ID cards. Then, we will take off and go to the Green Arrow in Garmisch, find Gail and look for Bruno.

Lucas got comfortable and fell asleep. George poked him at 6:12 a.m. and said, "Wake up, Lucas, we are arriving in Europe!"

Looking out the window from his aisle seat, Lucas saw an overcast sky. The plane descended in what seemed like a normal approach. Then, the moment he could see the runway, the plane accelerated and climbed back into the clouds. This being only his 2nd time in a plane and his 1st international flight, Lucas got nervous. The plane made a wide circle, then came down and again pulled out of the landing approach and back into the clouds. This time the pilot made an announcement: a warning light came on when they lowered the landing gear. Their last 2 approaches allowed ground crew to do a visual inspection of the landing gear which appeared to be in place.

Now, coming in for the 3rd time, Lucas' palms were sweating and his knuckles turned white from gripping the armrests so tightly. He looked over at a concerned George Bennett, and said, "It looks like we may never see Europe, after all."

He looked out the window again and saw lines of ambulances and fire trucks on the runway. This was a definite reason for concern. When the wheels hit the runway, the plane bounced, and it seemed to go on forever before it began to slow down.

When the plane finally stopped at the end of the runway, all the passengers applauded and let out a simultaneous sigh of relief.

CHAPTER 2
Frankfurt

He was still shaking after what happened on the landing. Lucas also felt overwhelmed as he realized he was in Europe for the first time. They passed through customs without delay, no one asked questions, and no one searched anything. They each lugged 3 pieces of baggage to the taxi stand and found an unoccupied taxi. When they asked the driver if he spoke English, he replied, "A little."

Lucas told the driver to find a cheap hotel in downtown Frankfurt. He replied, "Okay," then set the meter, pulled onto the autobahn and was going 80+ miles per hour (128+ kilometers per hour) in no time. It was a white-knuckle time again for Lucas because he liked to be in control, and he was a nervous passenger, anyway.

What seemed like only a few minutes passed, and the driver dropped them off at the Intercontinental Frankfurt Hotel on Wilhelm-Leuschner Strasse. It was not what they had in mind and not a cheap hotel. They were so tired, they stayed there, but only for 1 night.

It was almost lunchtime when they got to their room, and Lucas asked George, "Are you hungry?"

"I'm starving. Let's go have lunch," replied George.

After asking at the front desk, they got directions to the Main Mizza Restaurant, right on the Main River and only a 10-minute walk to get lunch and beer. Going out of the hotel, they turned right and walked along Wilhelm-Leuschner Strasse to Mosel Strasse, onto Untermainkai Strasse for 2 blocks, and arrived at the restaurant. It was a beautiful day in Frankfurt, so they asked to sit on the patio and got a table overlooking the river. George ordered the Rump Steak with herb butter, roasted potatoes and green beans. Lucas had to try the original Weiner Schnitzel with cranberries and lemon, potato and cucumber salad. They each had 2 half-liter glasses of Veltins Pils draft beer.

Their 1st meal in Germany was fun and delicious, especially the beer. Lucas said to George, "I've been drinking Coors beer for years. Now, it tastes like carbonated water compared with German beer."

After lunch, Lucas and George felt exhausted as they walked back to the Intercontinental. They crashed until 6 p.m., showered, put on casual clothes and went downstairs to ask about the nearest beer hall. The desk clerk told them to try the Kaiser Karl Bierstube on Baseler Strasse which was across the autobahn, and he suggested they take a taxi.

When they walked out to the taxi stand, 2 young women, both blonde and tanned, stood waiting for a taxi. Lucas didn't hesitate to ask them if they knew of a beer hall nearby. They said they were going to the Kaiser Karl Bierstube on Baseler Strasse.

"Would you ladies like to share a cab?" asked Lucas.

One lady looked Lucas in the eye and said, "Yes, we would." As they all introduced themselves, Cindy and Barbara told the guys they were from Manhattan Beach, California.

Lucas said, "Come on, you must be kidding. We flew clear across the USA and Atlantic Ocean from Long Beach, and who are the first people we meet? Two ladies from Manhattan Beach, only a few miles up the road from home."

Cindy and Barbara told the guys they were airline stewardesses for United Airlines, and they came to Germany often. The 4 of them paired into couples: Lucas with Cindy and George with Barbara.

When they arrived at the beer hall, they stood in line and each got a heavy, liter-size glass mug of German beer. They found a place to sit together at a long wooden table with bench seats, then tried to carry on a conversation over the oompah music, loud singing and talking. This Bierstube was busy. It felt like a circus atmosphere. The bandstand was in the middle of the large hall, and the long tables extended out and around the bandstand.

Cindy and Lucas talked about Southern California beach towns, his restaurants and her job traveling.

After some "fest" food and beer, they walked along the Main River on a beautiful, star studded night. When they all left the Bierstube, George and Barbara had gone their own direction after their light meal of bratwurst, pommes frites and Henninger Kaiser Pilsner beer.

Cindy had on a knee-length, light blue skirt which showed off her shapely, tanned legs. She had an athletic build, blonde hair which fell to her shoulders, a thin face and nose, penetrating blue eyes and a mischievous smile. They held hands which felt natural, and they kissed several times. After midnight, they were both tired, so they walked back to the Intercontinental. As they rode the elevator to her floor, they kissed goodnight and agreed to talk the next day. They both wanted to make plans for another time together.

The following day (their 2nd day in Germany), Lucas and George checked out cheaper hotels. They chose the Hotel Rossija in Frankfurt. By taxi, it was a short ride along Moselstrasse from the Intercontinental. The rate at Hotel Rossija was $54 a night for a room, and it was convenient to public transportation.

Lucas and George found the hotel clean and well-maintained. It was in the heart of Frankfurt, 100 meters from Central Station and about 500 meters from the exhibition center. Every morning, the hotel offered a breakfast buffet which varied. At the front desk, snacks and drinks were available for purchase, anytime.

The next thing they had to do was go to Abrams Kaserne and apply for jobs. They took a bus. After a 24-minute ride from their hotel, the guard at the gate told them where the personnel office was. He pointed to a beige-colored building which was about 100 yards inside the fence which surrounded the kaserne. At the office, they filled out applications and waited for interviews.

A pleasant-looking man, wearing an army uniform, approached them and called out, "Lucas Gary?"

Lucas followed him down the hall to a small office. By a hand signal, the soldier directed Lucas to a chair in front of a tidy desk. Then, he sat and asked, "Mr. Gary, why are you in Frankfurt?"

"I would like to study the German language, learn about German culture and history, and go to cooking school," he replied.

The soldier introduced himself as Sergeant Harrison. When he asked Lucas about his cooking experience, he seemed very impressed by Lucas' background, considering he was only 30 years old.

Sergeant Harrison interviewed George next. When he finished, he told them he would need about 2 hours to find open jobs, and he promised to let them know, either way. He suggested they wait in the PX where they could have lunch and a beer. They both ordered a hamburger with fries and asked for a beer. The German cook pointed to a beer machine and told them it was for the employees.

"Are employees allowed to drink at work?" asked Lucas.

"Welcome to Germany," replied the cook.

They each bought a half-liter of Henninger beer for 70 pfennigs. A pfennig is 100th part of a deutschemark which was 2 for 1 dollar which made each half-liter of beer cost 35 cents.

Lucas thought: *Welcome to Germany, a beer drinker's paradise.*

Exactly 2 hours later, the Sergeant came in the PX and sat at their table. He said, "We have a cook's job open for you, Lucas. All we have available for you, George, is a dishwasher job."

George looked upset as if he was going to throw up or cry, but he quickly regained his composure.

They both agreed to take the jobs and start as soon as they could. The Sergeant told them it would be 4 days before their military IDs would be issued, but they could start work the next day. This meant they would be on their way to Garmisch in less than a week, they could find Gail at the Green Arrow Hotel and see if Bruno was in the area.

Lucas still did not have a clue what he would do about Bruno if he found him. Maybe he started to doubt his motive for coming to Europe. So far, he was having a great time, away from the pressures of running his restaurants in Long Beach.

Lucas and George worked the day shift together and rode the trolley car together, between the kaserne and the hotel. They went out and drank every night; but the nightlife took a toll on them and made the 4-day-wait seem longer. At work, Lucas was glad he could drink great German beer to make his hangover go away.

The day before Lucas and George expected to receive their military ID cards, Cindy and Barbara got back in town. They all met in the lobby of the Intercontinental Hotel where the ladies were staying.

Rather than sitting somewhere for several hours, listening to oompah music and drinking beer, they planned for an evening of fun and hoped for some frolic.

George asked, "How about going to the red-light district?"

After the ladies exchanged bewildered looks, Barbara replied, "I think we should go to Sachsenhausen, drink Apfelwein, eat local food and go dancing. You guys can go to the red-light district without us. We have been there and seen enough."

"We can ride twenty-five minutes in a stinky trolley, or we can walk forty-minutes in fresh air," said Cindy.

Lucas thought: *Trollies are fine, if you can stand the body odor smell. Don't Germans know about deodorant?*

Deciding to stroll around and see the sights, they walked out the front entrance of the Intercontinental Hotel, turned right, walked on Wilhelm-Leuschner-Strasse for 15 minutes, and took a side street onto Mankai. They strolled along the Main River to a bridge which crossed over the river and into the Sachsenhausen district of Frankfurt, an area packed with Apfelwein pubs.

Barbara told them about the bridge, "Built in eighteen sixty-eight, this old bridge is called the Eiserner Steg (Iron Bridge). At the end of World War Two, the Wehrmacht (German armed forces) destroyed it. In nineteen forty-six, wealthy private citizens paid for reconstruction of the bridge. There was not enough room to build a ramp and allow access to automobiles, so they constructed it only for pedestrians. It took three years to build this bridge, and they charged a toll when it opened. Then, the city took over control and did away with the toll. I guess you have noticed all the locks in the fence along the bridge. Lovers have engraved their names on the locks. As you can see, the locks are different colors and shapes. This bridge looks fantastic when they turn the lights on. You will see it during our walk back."

Lucas studied his surroundings. He had never visualized Frankfurt as a beautiful and scenic place until now.

Looking at the Main River which was about 55 meters wide (180 feet), they saw river taxis, cruise ships and a barge-restaurant, packed with people who were dining in a big outdoor patio. There were many pedestrians strolling along the river path. Looking back across the river, there were modern skyscrapers on the other side.

Cindy and Barbara led them down a stairway, through a residential area, along Schulstrasse, across several intersections and finally turned right onto a cobblestone street. Both sides of the street had narrow brick sidewalks. Cindy pointed out a light magenta-colored building with pale green trim on their left.

"Here is the Apfelwein-Wirtschaft Fichtekranzi," said Cindy. "This place was founded around eighteen fifty, and it's one of the oldest apple wine houses in Sachsenhausen."

The entrance was in the rear, through a light-green gate. There was a handwritten menu in a glass case next to the gate, and Lucas saw a large chalkboard menu mounted on a sandwich board at the restaurant entrance. In front of the restaurant, there were picnic tables with wood benches, placed randomly under some oak trees in a patio area. It was a comfortable evening, so they wanted to sit outside. They joined a group of 4 young, fit-looking German men who spoke broken English as they introduced themselves. They were German policemen, and it was obvious they had a head-start on drinking the apple wine.

Cindy and Barbara were quite familiar with the Old Sachsenhausen festivities, due to many layovers in Frankfurt as stewardesses. They told the guys about Rippchen mit Kraut und Brot (pork rib with sauerkraut and a bread roll), the traditional meal which goes best with apple wine. But Lucas wanted to try the Gebratene Schweinshaxe mit Kraut und Brot (roasted pork hock with sauerkraut and bread). George chose the Gekochte Haspel mit Kraut und Brot (pickled knuckle of pork with sauerkraut and bread). Cindy had Schweinemedaillons mit Pfeffersauce, Bratkartoffeln & Salat (medallions of pork with green pepper sauce, pan fried potatoes and salad). Barbara was eager to order the Frankfurter Schnitzel mit Grüner Sauce & Bratkartoffeln (breaded schnitzel with frankfurter, green sauce and pan-fried potatoes). She claimed it was delightful and a local favorite; then she explained how they made the green sauce with seven herbs and yogurt.

While they were eating their dinner, 1 of the 4 tipsy policemen sat next to Lucas. He introduced himself as Luther, and he told them they were drinking *Stöffche from Gerippten (Stoffche* is German for apple wine*)*. "A Gerippten is a glass with a rhombus (diamond) cut which refracts light. A full Gerippten is called a Schoppen. If you drink more than a glass or you're in a group, you order a Bembel (a specific Apfelwein jug). Most establishments only offer a single choice of apple wine, their house wine, which is often made on the property."

"How do they go about making the apple wine?" asked Lucas.

"Apple wine is made with apples picked up after falling off the tree," said Luther. "Through a slow process, the apples are pressed, and the juice is fermented, resulting in alcohol content between four and nine percent.

"In the sixteen hundreds, a local council adopted strict regulations and specifications for the process of making apple wine. Those are still in effect to this day, much like the regulations for making beer in Germany."

"How is this different from the hard cider we have in the U.S. and in other countries?" asked George.

"German apple wine is refreshing, with a tart, sour taste. Fermented ciders, at least those I have tried, are sweet and bland," replied Luther.

He added, "True cider houses which produce their own Apfelwein can be spotted by a wreath of evergreen branches at the entrance. As required by local law, Apfelwein must be the cheapest alcoholic beverage for sale in any public place. The Gerippten (ribbed apple wine glass) in front of you has a diamond cut which allowed a person to grip the glass with greasy hands, before eating utensils came into use. You can see the unique colors as light becomes a spectrum through degrees of refraction, caused by the unfiltered apple wine inside the Gerippten."

After dinner, the ladies wanted to show them more and see the rest of Old Sachsenhausen. Throughout this area, the walkways were narrow and made of cobblestones. Lucas felt as if he had been transported to a previous time in history.

Pointing to the houses across the street, Lucas asked Cindy, "What is the architectural style of those old houses?"

They kept walking, as Cindy replied, "Half-timbered construction was popular in the eighteenth century, along with what is called Gothic stone buildings. Nowadays, we have Tudor Revival architecture which is similar in appearance to half-timbered buildings. The originals were timber-framed to support the whole weight of the building or house. Tudor Revival uses other methods of support."

Walking out of the restaurant's front entrance, they turned right to Paradiesgass, took a short walk on the cobblestone walkway, and made another right turn onto Klappergasse which had apple wine bars lining both sides of the narrow street. Each bar had wooden picnic tables, filled with partiers who were eating the local food and drinking apple wine. Some people were standing around, all with a Gerippten or a Bembel in their hands, talking and listening to the music.

The 4 of them sat and drank more apple wine. The ladies told Lucas and George about the beverage and some local customs.

They each got a Gerippten, raised their glasses and said, "Prost." The waitress left a Bembel (pitcher), filled with the local drink of choice.

"Why did apple wine become so popular?" asked Lucas "I never heard of it before we came here."

"According to the story I heard, it happened four or five centuries ago in this area of Frankfurt," said Barbara. "They had a terribly cold year and the grape crop failed, but they found apples could grow in the cold winters, so they switched from grapes to apples. The wine made from crushed, fermented apples became popular, and many apple wine bars opened. These new bars needed government approval. Once the bars got approved, they were required to hang an evergreen wreath on the front door, and it is still done."

Cindy said, "We came to Klappergasse for a reason. There is a funny story, famous around this area, about an old woman who liked to drink the apple wine. The title is, *Fraa Rauscher from the Klappergasse has a Beul at the Egg*." Seeing puzzled looks on Lucas' and George's faces, Cindy said, "The story is about a market woman, found lying on the ground at the end of this street, unconscious, with a bump on her head. Young boys were making fun of her, and a policeman came. The story goes on about whether she was drunk, then fell and hit her head, or her husband hit her and caused the bump. Somehow, details from the police report reached the newspaper. Afterward, the story became a local legend. In the early sixties, someone wrote a song about the incident, and the song became part of the legend."

Barbara added, "In fact, the word *Rauscher* means half-fermented apple wine, or wine which is too young and is still fermenting. It has less alcohol content, and it gives people diarrhea and headaches. I do not understand the dialect in the song, but a local Frankfurt sculptor created a bronze statue to represent Fraa Rauscher in the early sixties. It perpetuated the story. I think she is fictitious anyway, but we'll see the statue when we go further down the street."

The atmosphere was like a festival since the streets and cider houses were full of partiers. Lucas had fun, talking with the well-traveled ladies from Southern California. The more apple wine they drank, the more they were laughing and enjoying each other's company.

After Lucas paid the check, Cindy and Barbara led them along the cobbled-stone street, holding hands and winding through the crowd.

When they got to the bronze statue, they made their way to the front of the crowd of people who were admiring the sculpture. The ladies positioned Lucas and George in front of it, and Cindy was telling Lucas about many famous fountains and wells around old Sachsenhausen.

Suddenly, a stream of water spewed from the statue's mouth. George got very wet because he could not duck soon enough. Some of the water hit Lucas, so he turned around and got back at Cindy by giving her a big hug and a long, lingering kiss. The surrounding crowd's laughter changed into cheers for the lovers.

They walked back to the Old Iron Bridge and admired the view. Looking at central Frankfurt, the lights on the bridge and lights coming from the tall buildings of the city was a spectacular sight. Lucas was holding Cindy's hand and said, "Would you like to come back to my hotel room and spend the night?"

"In case you asked, Barbara and I already discussed the possibility," said Cindy. "I would love to spend what is left of the night and morning with you, Lucas."

When they reached the far side of the bridge, the couples split up. Following the tree-lined river path, Lucas and Cindy walked past a children's playground, turned north on Moselstrasse, and then got back into central Frankfurt.

As they were about to cross Wilhelm-Leuschner Strasse, George ran up behind them and said, "I'm sorry to tell you this, Cindy, but Barbara is sick and is going back to your room at the Intercontinental."

"Rauscher," said Lucas.

Cindy offered a slight smile, kissed Lucas and said, "Well Lucas, perhaps another time."

"We are going to Garmisch tomorrow," said Lucas. "Maybe you can come and visit. You have our contact information, so I hope we see you there." Lucas and Cindy kissed again. Then, he and George headed back to their hotel.

They were 2 long blocks from their hotel and passing a little bar when George said, "I'm disappointed. Hey, Lucas, do you want to go in here and get a beer or something?"

"Okay. We can sleep in tomorrow since we're off for two days," said Lucas. "Then, we can pick up our ID cards and get train tickets."

The bar was empty except for a big guy, behind the bar, and an older gentleman, sitting at the end of the bar with papers in front of him and a glass of beer, half-full. They sat on bar stools, and the bartender walked over to them. He offered no greeting, but looked at George.

"Two glasses of apple wine please," George requested.

The bartender said, "No apple wine here."

George looked at Lucas and said, "Two glasses of beer, please."

When the bartender set their beers on the bar, George said to Lucas, "Let's sit in the booth against the wall at the end of the bar."

Lucas and George were discussing events of the evening and making plans for their trip to Garmisch. George had his leg up on the bench which he was sitting on, turned sideways and leaning halfway against the wall, very relaxed.

He was talking to Lucas when the older guy came over from the end of the bar and kicked George's leg off the bench, yelling, "What are you, stupid Americans?" Then, he yelled more, but in German.

Lucas and George had no idea what the German was saying, and they jumped up—not with an intention to hit the guy or anything. It was more like, *"What's going on?"*

The big guy must have thought differently. He came out around the bar with a 2-foot steel bar in his hand and a menacing look.

Lucas held his hand in front of his face as if it was a stop sign. He pulled out his wallet and paid for the beers. Then, he and George hurried out of the bar.

Walking into their hotel, Lucas said, "I'm sure glad we are leaving Frankfurt. I hope the natives in Bavaria are a little friendlier."

CHAPTER 3

First Trip to Garmisch

The train for Garmisch left at 12:15 p.m. Lucas and George found the small bar on the train and settled in. Each had a Henninger beer and a brotchen (German roll) with ham and cheese. Then, both sat back to enjoy the 6-hour train ride. They had purchased a German language book, a mystery novel and a deck of cards when they were at the Abrams PX. They had also bought good-sized backpacks, so their hands were free, and they did not have to drag luggage everywhere they went.

It seemed like they had not had a full night's sleep since their arrival in Germany. They both fell asleep and did not awake until the train arrived in Garmisch-Partenkirchen at 6:25 p.m. Lucas and George put on their large backpacks and stepped off the train.

Gazing at the mountains, green hills, endless fields of wildflowers and 2-story houses with colorful planters on the balconies, Lucas thought: *I will never want to leave here.*

Lucas had read about Garmisch in a travel book which he got from the Abrams PX in Frankfurt. He learned the train station is located between 2 districts, Garmisch in the west and Partenkirchen in the east. He also read the Partnach River flows between the train station and Partenkirchen.

Showing their new ID cards, Lucas and George boarded a military shuttle bus at the front of the train station and got off at the Sheridan, a military hotel. They checked in, set down their backpacks, went to the hotel bar and ordered a half-liter of Augustiner beer for 75 cents, plus a hot dog for 25 cents. They asked the bartender about the local night life, and he gave them a brochure which had a lot of information about the military facilities in Bavaria. He also told them the International Bar and Grill has a discotheque with live music, and when the band takes a break, a disc jockey spins records until 2 a.m.

After putting their backpacks in their room, showering and changing clothes, Lucas and George got back on the shuttle bus and headed for the discotheque. During the ride over to the International Bar and Grill, George read to Lucas from *The Stars and Stripes*, a military newspaper,

"Locals call it The Grill. It opened last November, and it already has become very popular. The steaks and other delicious cuisine are a factor. But what pulls 'em in is the discotheque where snow bunnies and their escorts join in the latest après-ski exercises: the frug, the swim, the monkey or the bunny hop. The action swirls around a 60-seat bar, shaped in a semi-circle, with a raised bandstand in the center. When the band is away, the spotlight centers on the opposite end of the room where a disc jockey—most often a female—keeps them spinning into the wee hours. American military owns and manages The Grill discotheque, so they require a military ID at the door, or you must be a guest of someone who has proper ID. However, it seems any female can get in without one."

"Wow. It sounds like Heaven on Earth. I can't wait to see this place," said Lucas.

A big guy was checking IDs while he was talking to 2 attractive young ladies at the entrance to The Grill. Once inside, the size of the bar and grill surprised Lucas. As they walked through the double doors, the huge semi-circular bar was on their left, with 60 seats around it. Behind the bar, a raised bandstand had musical instruments placed on the stage. Below the bandstand, the bartenders' work area wrapped all the way around the half-circle and required multiple bartenders to handle the crowd. There was a very large dance floor. Tables and chairs sat along each side of the dance floor and along the back wall.

It was early in the evening, but the place was already busy. Lucas and George bought a couple half-liters of draft beer for 75 cents each and grabbed 2 seats at the bar.

"Is it always this crowded?" asked Lucas. He saw the bartender's name tag identified him as John.

John shouted back, "Every night."

Lucas saw attractive young ladies, scattered around the dance floor, and many seemed to be unattached.

After another half-liter of beer, Lucas was ready to move with the music. So, he asked a young lady to dance. She was tall, blonde and wearing very-short shorts. They danced to a few fast songs. Then, Lucas shouted over the noise and pointed toward an empty table, "Would you like to sit, and I'll buy you a drink?"

"Yes, I would, and I am drinking beer," she answered.

While she sat, Lucas went to get 2 Augustiner beers from John, the bartender. When he came back and got seated, he said, "My name is Lucas Gary. I came from California and arrived in Garmisch today."

She replied, "My name is Sonya von Dusseldorf Anderson, and I live here in Garmisch."

Lucas and Sonya talked about her life in Garmisch. She told him she was born and raised in Garmisch. Her mother was German and had married an American Army Colonel who was stationed at Rhein-Main Air Force Base, near Frankfurt. Lucas told her of his restaurants and life in Long Beach.

They talked and danced to live rock music, performed by a local group who played a lot of current rock songs until The Grill closed at 2 a.m. Then, they walked to the Sheridan Hotel.

As they passed by a sleepy-looking desk clerk, they both said, "Good morning," in unison.

When they got to his room, Sonya pulled out a pipe and said she had hashish. So, they lit the pipe, passed it back and forth and started kissing. Their encounter became heated as they undressed each other. They tumbled over into bed and had great sex. In the morning, Sonya said she had to leave and get home because she lived with her mother who would worry about her.

"Would you like to have breakfast with me at the PX?" asked Lucas. "We can take the shuttle to town."

"I'll ride with you, but I'll pass on breakfast," replied Sonya.

When Lucas walked into the PX coffee shop, he noticed a big guy who he had seen at The Grill, carrying glasses out to the bartenders.

Lucas went over to his table and said, "Hi. I'm Lucas Gary. I arrived from California, a short time ago. Do you mind if I sit with you?"

After he spoke, Lucas thought: *Maybe, I don't want people to know I'm from Long Beach. Bruno might get suspicious if he heard about me. Although, I don't think he knows of me or knows what I look like.*

The guy looked at Lucas and said, "Sure. Please, have a seat. My name is Bob Ostergaard."

Bob was sitting by himself and reading a newspaper. He put it aside to talk with Lucas. While they exchanged information about themselves, Lucas learned a lot about Bob. His evening job, washing glasses at The Grill, allowed him to get an ID card which made military facilities available to him. He said he had a degree in Marine Biology from the University of Maryland, but ran a business of refurbishing old, rusted-out VW vans. They slap on some fiberglass to cover the holes, then sand and paint the vans, sometimes using a paint brush or a roller. Bob and his partner, a GI named Steve Dobson, build cabinets and a bed in the back, then sell them to GIs for traveling around Europe. They made an excellent profit. But Bob said he always got in trouble with the military police for not having the proper license plates on his vans. He would switch the plates so he would not have to register the vans before he sold them.

Lucas did not realize how big Bob was until he stood. Lucas shook his large, rough and very-strong hand. Bob Ostergaard did not look muscular; he was just a huge guy.

After breakfast, Lucas walked to the Green Arrow Hotel, hoping to locate Gail, the maid who may have information about Bruno.

It was 1 p.m. when he arrived. He took a seat at the bar and ordered a half-liter draft of Augustiner beer. Lucas looked around the cozy bar which had a fire going in the fireplace. There were only 3 other people in the bar, all seated at a table, and they asked Lucas to join them. He tried his best to remember people's names the 1st time around.

Sitting on Lucas' left, Eric was a muscular, blonde-haired guy who had an easy smile. On Eric's left, a young brunette with long hair and a great tan, introduced herself as Susie from Newport Beach, 20 miles south of Long Beach, California.

Thinking Susie looked familiar, Lucas searched his brain, trying to recall when and where he had seen her before. He remembered. It was a Friday night at Feliciano's, a discothèque in Newport Beach, where he and George met Susie and her girlfriend, Kathy. Later in the evening, Lucas had taken Kathy to her house in Seal Beach where they spent a delightful, sexy night together. When they left the disco, George and Susie were sitting together and remained there.

Lucas told her, "Susie, I believe I met you and your girlfriend at Feliciano's in Newport Beach, this past summer, and I gave your friend Kathy a ride home."

"Oh yeah, I remember you," said Susie. "Who was the creepy guy who gave me a ride home? I asked him to drop me off at my boyfriend's house in Anaheim, where I pounded on the door for ten minutes because I knew he was in there. He was with another woman, and I was furious with him."

Lucas informed Susie she rode home with his friend George who was now skiing in Garmisch, and he would be around later. He asked her, "Who was your boyfriend then?"

The guy sitting to her left said, "That would be me. Hi, my name is Jordan Lewis. I'm from Long Beach, California, and I'm the bouncer and doorman at The Grill. Where are you from, Lucas?"

They all had a big laugh when Lucas said, "I don't believe this. I got to Germany a week ago, coming from Long Beach."

This is amazing, thought Lucas. *We all come clear across the United States and the Atlantic Ocean, and we end up together in this little bar in Garmisch, Germany.*

A short, cute, red-headed maid came in, and they asked her to sit and have a beer. She said, "Okay," and introduced herself as Gail.

Lucas thought: *Bingo!* But he did not want to talk about Bruno in front of the others, and he figured he could talk to Gail later. So, as everyone else had done, he only gave his name.

Bob Ostergaard came in and took a seat. Bob knew everyone as did Gino who was a bartender at The Grill. When Gino came in, he told them he had the day off and was ready to party.

They were all ready to party, and everyone agreed to meet at The Grill, later in the evening.

On the way out, Lucas followed Gail out the back entrance of the bar. He got her attention and said, "Gail, I'm Mike Fletcher's friend from Long Beach. He suggested you might know a guy named Bruno Castignoli."

Although Gail was surprised, she said, "Yes, I know Bruno. He tends bar at the Von Steuben Hotel, here in Garmisch. But I heard he went to Ibiza for a vacation."

Arriving back at the Sheridan, Lucas knocked on George's door. When George let him in, Lucas asked, "How was skiing?"

"It was some of the best skiing I've ever done. You should have gone with me," said George.

Lucas then told George about his day and all the people he had met, including Gail at the Green Arrow; she claimed Bruno had taken off for Ibiza, but she did not know for how long.

"I've always wanted to go to Ibiza," said Lucas. "Where is it?"

"Let's look it up," replied George.

Later, everyone met at The Grill and partied until 2 a.m. Sonya arrived at 9 p.m. and sat on Lucas' lap, most of the evening, except when they were dancing. George was tired from skiing all day, so he left early. Lucas and Sonya walked back to the Sheridan. They undressed, climbed into bed and had sex which was beyond expectation again.

In the morning, Sonya took the shuttle back downtown to her house. Lucas stayed at the hotel because he wanted to talk to George. They went into the hotel restaurant for a big breakfast of ham, eggs, wheat toast and hash browns. George drank orange juice, and Lucas had a bottle of Hacker-Pschorr beer to get the day going.

They discussed the earlier talk at The Grill where they learned there would not be any job openings until it snows.

It was only September, so Lucas and George decided to buy a new VW camper and go traveling in style. They went to the VW dealer in Garmisch and picked out a new cream-colored Westphalia pop-top van. It will sleep 4 people if needed and depending on the situation. After they did all the paperwork and arranged for payments, they drove it to the PX commissary and stocked it with food and supplies.

With transportation handled, they were ready to party at The Grill in the evenings. It would only be a few days until they left for Spain. The Grill was jumping every night. George and Lucas were meeting a lot of new and interesting people. Although George had not hooked up with a lady yet, things were getting hot and heavy between Sonya and Lucas.

Sonya told Lucas about her mother, Victoria, who had a fixation with King Ludwig. She invited him for dinner at their house to meet her mother and her mother's friend, Lawrence. He was also a King Ludwig fanatic who even dressed the part.

Lucas said he was sorry, but it would have to wait until he and George returned from Spain, assuming the invitation was still open. Lucas thought Sonya was okay with his explanation because she said nothing more about it. They danced, drank and laughed the night away. When they got back to Lucas' room, they made love like there was no tomorrow.

The next morning, Sonya went to work, and Lucas met George for breakfast. George told Lucas he spoke to some Germans last night at The Grill. They told him about a glacier in Italy which had snow almost year around. It was above a small village called Gomagoi.

"Okay, but if we're going there, I want to buy new skis, boots and gear," said Lucas.

George thought new skis was a good idea for Lucas. George planned to use the rental Völkl skis. He had used them at the Zugspitze, and he really liked them.

In the afternoon, they went to the PX ski shop. Lucas bought Atomic skis and Salomon boots for a reasonable price. On their way out of town, they stopped at a local store and bought extra beer for the trip.

Leaving Garmisch, George was driving. Lucas opened a Paulaner beer as they headed for Fern Pass, Austria, a mountain pass in the Tyrolean Alps. Then, it would be a 2-hour drive to Gomagoi, Italy.

CHAPTER 4

Austria

Lucas and George went southwest on the highway to Fern Pass. The weather was cloudy, and it started to rain.

George drove 19 kilometers to Lermoos. By then, light snow was falling, but not sticking to the road. They had not yet bought chains or snow tires because it was only September.

Passing on the highway between Lermoos and Nassereith was not possible. So, Lucas sat back, relaxed in his seat, enjoyed the beautiful surroundings and drank his beer. With no commitments, he felt free and void of any stress.

As they went by the turnoff for Biberwier, Lucas remembered reading about it. The longest T-bar ski lift in Europe is at Biberwier; and Austria has many of those T-bar lifts. Passing Weissensee and Mittersee Lakes, near the southern part of Blindsee, they were on the back side of the Zugspitze, the highest mountain in Germany. They reached the summit of Fern Pass and pulled into the parking lot at the Zugspitzblick Rasthaus. Lucas had read about it in the Frommer's travel book.

Lucas and George climbed the wooden steps to the rasthaus dining room and bar. The restaurant was busy, but the hostess seated them at a table by a window with a wonderful view of the Zugspitze and Mittersee Lake. The incredible beauty of these surroundings mesmerized Lucas.

Their waiter spoke enough English to describe menu items to them. Lucas went for the Wildragout mit Semmelknoedel und Preiselbeeren (Game Ragout with bread dumpling and cranberries). George ordered Jägerschnitzel and Knödel (a lean pork cutlet pan-seared and sautéed in a savory mushroom sauce, served with a large bread dumpling). They each ordered a half-liter glass of Stiegl Bier and marveled at how much fun everyone was having.

One man played an accordion while Austrians and Germans drank beer in half-liter glasses. Everyone was laughing, joking and singing. The benches had cushioned seats and backs, covered in blue and white plaid fabric. Matching lamp shades adorned the tables.

After lunch, they walked outside and saw it had been snowing while they ate. Pulling out of the parking lot, they saw piles of fluffy snow where moving traffic pushed it to the sides of the road.

George was still driving, but the going was slow and downhill now, so he used a lower gear. It helped to slow them down and reduced excessive braking on many sharp curves in the road. Coming around one bend, it surprised them to see a man and a woman standing by the side of the road. When they got closer, they saw a BMW stuck in the snow bank and the front end wrapped around a tree.

George stopped to see if they could help the man and woman. He parked as far off the side of the road as he could. Although, there was no other traffic in sight.

Lucas and George walked over to the couple who stood and watched their approach. “Are you okay?” asked Lucas.

Before they answered, George asked where they wanted to go. The young women asked him, “Where are you going?”

“We are going skiing in Gomagoi,” George replied.

“My name is Lucas Gary, and this fellow is George Bennett.”

With a heavy accent, the man said, “What are you, Americans?”

Noticing a somewhat unfriendly tone to the question and seeing the German license plate on the BMW, Lucas said, “Yes, we are Americans. Are you German?”

The man pulled a pistol from his parka pocket. Aiming it at Lucas and George, he said, “Yah, we are German. We are taking your van.”

Lucas looked him in the eye as he declared, “You don’t need the gun and you must be cold. Let’s get in the van, have a beer and talk this over. Perhaps we can help you.”

The German looked over at the woman, then put the gun back in his coat pocket and said, “Okay, we will do that. But remember, I still have the gun in my pocket.” The Germans walked back to the BMW and retrieved their backpacks. Then, they got into the back of the VW van and sat on the padded bench.

The German man asked, “Why do you have American military license plates? Are you American military?”

“No,” Lucas answered. “We are American civilians, but we work for the military. We came from California to have fun, here in Europe. Now, would you care for a beer?”

The German man said, “I don’t like American beer.”

Lucas got 4 bottles of Paulaner beer from a cabinet behind the front seat, opened and passed them around as he replied, “I don’t either, not after I tasted true German beer.”

The German man laughed before he said, "My name is Andreas Baader and this is Ulrike Meinhof. Do you know who we are? Do you read local newspapers or watch television?"

"Lucas and I haven't watched TV or read the news since we left California, two weeks ago," replied George. "Why do you ask?"

"We are leaders of the Red Army Faction, well-known to the press and on television as The Baader-Meinhof Gang," said Ulrike.

"It sounds like you're wanted by police. Why?" asked Lucas.

"The most recent reason is I escaped from prison," replied Andreas. "I was placed there because of my political beliefs."

Ulrike added, "The authorities believe we manage terrorist attacks and bank robberies."

"How did you escape from prison? Where was this?" asked Lucas.

Andreas looked at Ulrike, then he answered Lucas, by saying, "It is a long story. If we could have another beer, I will tell you."

Lucas handed him another beer, and Andreas said, "I was doing four years for arson, but Ulrike and some other RAF (Red Army Faction) members devised a plan. Ulrike and I told prison officials we needed to do research at the library for a book I was writing about helping young people on the fringes of society. When we arrived at the library, they took off my handcuffs, gave me a cup of coffee and put us in the reading room with doors and windows locked. While Ulrike and I sat at a table and talked, two young gals knocked at the door. The librarian let them in and told them to stay in the hallway. Then, the front doorbell rang, the gals tripped the door lock, and two comrades came in wearing wool masks and holding guns. All the ruckus distracted the guards and the librarian. Ulrike opened a window, we climbed out and drove away in an Alpha Romeo which was waiting for us. You saw we now drive a BMW as do many of our comrades. The 'pigs' like to say BMW (the abbreviation for Bavarian Motor Works) is now slang for Baader-Meinhof Wagen."

"Where does your money come from?" asked Lucas.

Without a second thought, Ulrike answered, "We rob banks."

The snow fell a little heavier and piled higher on the road.

Maybe we should have gotten chains, thought Lucas.

Lucas got beers for Andreas and Ulrike, plus one for himself, and he asked, "What did you do before you robbed banks?"

Ulrike responded, "I studied philosophy, sociology and the German language at the University of Münster. I became a journalist and wrote articles for *Konkret* magazine where I was Editor-in-Chief. I married Klaus Röhl, the founder of *Konkret* magazine. In nineteen sixty-two, we had twin girls, Regine and Bettina. Klaus and I separated in nineteen sixty-seven and divorced in nineteen sixty-eight.

"I met Andreas while he was in prison, and we planned to collaborate on the book about young people who live on the fringes of society. We worked on the book for a while. Then, we planned the escape, and here we are—on the run."

Lucas wanted to ask what their group's main goal was, but the van skidded on the snow-covered road. It was in the center of the road, skidding sideways as the back slid around, and the right side of the van was on the downhill side.

Thinking fast, as trees on the road flashed by, Lucas yelled out to George, "Slowly turn the wheel to your right and gently step on the brake—easy—lightly!"

George reacted properly. He got the front of the van facing downhill again, and then he eased it over to the side of the road.

Finally, George stopped the van, got out, took a deep breath and said, "I need another beer!"

Lucas took over driving and continued down the slippery slope while everyone else caught their breath.

When their conversation resumed, George began by asking, "What does the Red Army Faction hope to gain by burning buildings, robbing banks, opposing authority and terrorizing the state?"

Baader thought about this for a few seconds, and he replied, "We, members of the RAF, believe attacking the state will force the state to respond with massive retaliation; and the state's action will provoke and inspire an enormous number of German people to take up our cause. Then, we will overthrow the state which is our ultimate goal."

Ulrike said, "We believe our righteous cause justifies violence."

They were above the town as they got close to Nassereith, Austria. Below and to their right another fairy-tale village was nestled close to the mountain in a green valley. All the rooftops were red and gray. There was a beautiful lake on the south side of the village. Driving by the Tyrolean-style houses, flower boxes were bursting with colorful flowers. An old church stood in the center of town. Its tall steeple and onion-shaped dome rose above the other buildings.

They stopped in Nassereith, filled the gas tank and went across the street to an old gasthaus. The dining room was rustic with blonde-colored wood panels and checkered tablecloths. The owners had mounted all sizes of deer heads on the walls, and a stuffed mountain lion sat on a shelf above the entrance.

Lucas and George were new to German and Austrian food, so they let Andreas and Ulrike do the ordering for them.

George and Andreas wanted the Pfeffersteak mit Bauernpommes und Speckbohnen (pepper steak with fries and green beans with bacon). Ulrike ordered Schnitte vom Lachsfilet mit Safransauce auf Ruccola risotto (cuts of salmon fillet with saffron sauce on a bed of arugula risotto). Lucas got Steak vom Jungschweinrücken mit Tomaten Mozzarella überbacken auf Penne Spinaci a Gorgonzola-Rahmsauce (pork sirloin steak, made with tomato, mozzarella, penne pasta, gorgonzola cheese and spinach).

Andreas called his comrades in Innsbruck and agreed to meet them in Landeck at the Hotel Schwarzer Adler on Malserstraße. Lucas got a case of Stiegl beer from the store, and they headed for Landeck.

Behind the wheel again, Lucas hollered back at Andreas and Ulrike, "If you are being hunted so much, how will you avoid arrest?"

"We have many followers who support our cause and help us escape capture in Europe," said Andreas.

Ulrike looked at Andreas as if she was asking his permission, and he nodded. She told Lucas and George about RAF members' plan: they will go to Jordan and train in the desert at a Palestinian training camp. She added, "My two daughters are already on their way there."

Wow. Since they are sharing their plan with us, they must trust us, thought Lucas. *Or, they plan to kill us. We'd better be nice to them.*

Lucas asked George to hand them all a beer.

Driving through the little town of Imst, green checkerboard fields of farms surrounded them. They drove along the Gurglbach River at the foot of the Northern Limestone Alps, a mountain range which George had read about in their Frommer's travel guide. They could see the double chairlift and the typical church steeple which towered above all the other buildings. Andreas told them he was familiar with the area, and the Gurglbach River originates in Mount Heiterwand which is near Nassereith.

"Where are you going next?" asked Andreas.

Lucas thought: *Good question. Maybe they don't plan to kill us.*

Then, he answered, "After we go skiing for a few days in Gomagoi, we will make our way to Ibiza, Spain, where we will search for the man who killed my girlfriend last February in Long Beach, California."

"What will you do if you find him?" asked Ulrike.

"We have no plan yet," said Lucas. "Have you any suggestions?"

"No," said Andreas. "But, if you have trouble and need help, I'll give you a phone number to call. Maybe they can assist you."

"Who are they?" asked George.

Ulrike answered, "They are various members of our left-wing radical movement, willing to help good people in trouble and the underdogs, as you Americans would put it."

Handing Lucas a paper with a phone number on it, Andreas said, "Your secrets are safe with us. We hope ours are safe with you. You have been kind to us, and we wish you Viel Glück (Good Luck)!"

"Thank you," George replied.

At the same time, Lucas said, "Thank you. We wish the best of luck to you as well."

In Landeck, they found Hotel Schwarzer Adler on Malserstraße. Waiting in the parking lot, 2 young men were in a new BMW.

"There is no need for you to meet our friends," said Andreas. "So, we will say goodbye now." Then, they all hugged.

Driving away, Lucas thought: *I wonder if we'll see them again.*

It stopped snowing, and the roads had been plowed and salted. On this somewhat clear road, George would take over the driving.

But, before they got started, and with a big, "Whew," George said, "Lucas, let's have a beer!"

CHAPTER 5

Trafoi Ski Area

They made good time since the road was clear of snow. Along the way, there were even bits of blue skies. After 1 hour and 45 minutes, driving from Landeck to Gomagoi, George parked in front of the Hotel Gomagoi Hof where they had reserved a room for 3 nights.

Lucas was thinking how wonderful it will be to get up the mountain, enjoy the cool, fresh air and the fabulous views, then ski all the way to the bottom. Skiing was a time Lucas could feel free, away from the pressures and responsibilities of everyday life, especially here in this remote Italian ski village.

While they were waiting to check in, they could not help but notice 2 attractive women who were speaking German and checking into the hotel. They were both about 5'7". One was blonde, and the other had auburn-colored hair. They both looked athletic, wearing figure-hugging ski pants and sweaters.

George was reading aloud from a travel book about Gomagoi and Stelvio Pass Road which they would drive tomorrow, *"The pass road, built in the early eighteen hundreds, has a height difference of over six thousand feet and forty-eight hairpin turns."* He added, "Fortunately, I do not expect to see snow on the road tomorrow."

George kept reading, *"A fortress which was built in the mid-eighteen hundreds is. now used as a depot for the Highway Administration offices. After World War Two when the Allies took charge, they decided this area would stay a part of Italy. The German-speaking population and the Italians have been at odds, including recent terrorist attacks by an anti-government group."*

Lucas was joking when he said in a quiet voice, "It wasn't the Red Army Faction was it? We know they are in the area."

When the 2 German hotties finished checking in, they both gave Lucas and George a nice smile. The redhead said something which sounded like, "Chris Dick." When Lucas asked the desk clerk what the lady said, he explained: *Grüss dich* means "Greet you" or just "Hello." It is less formal than *Grüss Gott*. The word *Servus* also means "Hello." And, *Grüss Gott* means "May God greet you."

After they got settled into their 3rd floor room, Lucas and George were hungry, so they headed downstairs to eat.

The hotel had a large, open dining room. There was a band playing Tyrolean music, and everyone seemed cheerful. Most of the patrons were drinking out of 1-liter mugs, filled with beer. Seated in a booth, Lucas and George asked for a dinner menu and ordered 2 of the 1-liter mugs of beer. At the far end of the dining room, there was a small dance floor where some colorful Bavarian dancers were enjoying the music in front of the stage and musicians.

When beers and menus arrived, Lucas saw the 2 German ladies from hotel registration, waiting for a table. He did not hesitate to jump up.

Lucas walked over to the ladies and said, "Grüss Gott."

The redhead answered, "Grüss Gott."

Lucas then asked them in English, "Would you ladies care to join us for dinner?"

The ladies looked at each other and nodded. The blonde said, "Yes we would, thank you."

They all took seats in the round booth with the ladies on the inside. The lady who had dark red hair sat next to Lucas.

Lucas introduced himself, "My name is Lucas Gary; here from Long Beach, California. I'm in Europe to have fun."

George went next, "I'm George Bennett, and I am from Manhattan Beach, California. I came here to travel, see the sights and ski."

The blonde spoke English with a delightful German accent, "My name is Sabine Bloch. I live in Seefeld, Austria. I'm a ski instructor."

It was the redhead's turn, and she offered with a sexy accented voice, "I am Inga Mueller. I live in Oberammergau, Germany, work as a woodcarver, and own a small shop there."

Looking at her, Lucas thought: *I sure love redheads.*

Inga asked, looking at him, "What is your occupation, Lucas?"

"I am a chef and restaurant owner. I hope to learn some European styles of cooking while I'm here," he replied.

George answered the same question, saying, "I'm a volleyball coach and math teacher at a Long Beach High School in California."

Then, the topic changed to ordering dinner, and the ladies translated the menu for Lucas and George. They both chose the Krustenbraten mit Dunkelbiersosse (roast pork, served with a dark beer sauce). Inga ordered Tafelspitz, (boiled beef, roast potatoes, horseradish and root vegetables: carrots, leeks and celery root). Sabine decided to have Trancio di sella di cervo con finferli e polenta (a slice of roast venison with fresh chanterelle mushrooms and polenta). They all agreed on a bottle of Fritsch Zweigelt which the waitress described as a dry, red Austrian wine, with hints of red plums and cherries.

After eating, Lucas and Inga joined other dancers on the crowded floor, and they danced to polka music, played by the Tyrolean band. George and Sabine sat at the table, drank wine and talked.

Instead of dessert, the ladies wanted shots of Jägermeister which was something new for Lucas and George. Inga described it as an herbal liqueur which goes well with beer. So, they ordered 4 shots, and the guys enjoyed it so much, they ordered 4 more.

This is fantastic, thought Lucas. *We need a bottle of Jägermeister in the van. It does taste great, with or without beer.*

He paid the check and left a token tip. He had learned to tip less in Europe since restaurants usually added a tip into the checks.

They all rode the kind-of-creaky elevator to the 3rd floor. Their rooms were down the hall from each other. After they agreed to meet for breakfast and go skiing together, everyone said goodnight and went to their respective rooms.

At 7 a.m., they met in the dining room and enjoyed a nice, Austrian breakfast buffet. Sabine explained what food was offered: Schwarzbrot (a black bread made of rye and wheat flour), and bread rolls called Semmeln (a single roll is a Semmel), served with butter and marmelade (Austrians call it jam). Muesli is raw, rolled oats and other ingredients, such as grains, fresh or dried fruits, seeds and nuts, all mixed together with milk, yogurt or fruit juice. Hard-boiled eggs, Danish pastry, schinken (sliced ham), speck (bacon), coffee and orange juice are also available.

After breakfast, they piled into the VW van with Lucas driving and Inga riding shotgun. George and Sabine were getting comfortable in the back, as they all started the fantastic, hour-long drive up the famous Stelvio Pass Road.

Lucas had seen an aerial map of the Stelvio Pass Road. It zig-zags on the side of the mountain as it rises from the ravine. Stelvio Pass Road has 48 hairpin turns and spectacular views. It begins in forest land and climbs the mountain, much like giant steps, to a glacier at over 2,780 meters (9,000 feet) above sea level.

It was a bright sun-shiny day. With the van parked, they were putting on sun screen, and Inga said, "Just one more thing." She pulled out a wooden pipe in the shape of a swan and passed it around for two hits of hashish each. They grabbed their skis and poles and headed to the cable car for a day of fun on the slopes in September.

Mid-morning, they stopped at the top of the cable car run to drink beer in the restaurant. Sabine wanted to ski a black diamond runs, and George said he would ski with her. Lucas and Inga wanted to stay on the blue runs. They all agreed to meet at 12:30 p.m. for lunch in the restaurant.

Lucas realized Inga was a better skier than he was. It made him more determined to ski his best and keep pace with her. Most of the morning, they skied on the cable car runs, but they tried some T-bar runs, a little higher on the mountain.

The tree-line stopped about halfway up the cable car run, and the slopes above were wide open. Lucas gave Inga his take on glacier skiing, "It differs from other places I've skied. Everything is spread out here with so many T-bars to ride and only two cable cars."

Lucas and Inga enjoyed being together, laughing, kissing and skiing. Late morning, they stopped after getting off the cable car. As they stood and scanned the view of the valley below, Lucas marveled over his recent activities—only 3 days ago, he was waterskiing in Lake Eibsee, near Garmisch; and now, he is snow skiing with a beautiful lady on this glorious mountain. He told Inga how great he felt and how much fun he was having in Europe.

"I'm also having a fabulous time, Lucas. You are fun to be with, and you look very handsome," said Inga.

She leaned over her skis and kissed him. Then, they headed downhill for another run before lunch, and they were both flying high.

Meeting at the restaurant, everyone had what Lucas now considered the traditional, local-skiers' lunch: mugs of Stiegl beer, goulash soup and semmeln (bread rolls).

Skiing as a group in the afternoon, the 4 of them went behind a shed and took turns on the swan pipe, full of brown-red hashish. They all enjoyed the rest of the day and had a great time together, laughing and joking around.

On the way back to Gomagoi, Sabine asked, "Where are we having dinner? Inga and I are buying."

Lucas responded, "Okay, but we'll be easy on you. I read about a pizza restaurant. How about going there?" Everyone agreed.

At the hotel, they had more beer and smoked some of Inga's hashish. Now, they were ready to eat. The pizza restaurant was a 10-minute drive from the hotel, and it offered 20 different choices of pizza. Following a long decision-making process, they selected a combination pizza with tomato sauce, mozzarella cheese, ham, Tyrolean bacon and mushrooms, sprinkled with gorgonzola on top.

Being a native Austrian, Sabine entertained them with some local history of South Tyrol and the Passo dello Stelvio. She told them about the area around Gomagoi. Over the years, several governments had ruled since it is so close to the Italian, Swiss and Austrian borders.

She said, "Italian-speaking and German-speaking populations of the area were always at odds about who should govern who. During World War One, there were many battles fought in this area. They still celebrate one of the most famous Germans, General Erwin Rommel, as one of the top military strategists of all time. During World War Two, he was called The Dessert Fox. He led his mountain battalion through several strategic captures of fortresses, right here on this mountain-top, where Austria is separate from Italy.

"Also, you may not know Rommel committed suicide by taking a cyanide pill; however, they gave him a state funeral with all the honors of a military genius and hero."

"Why did he commit suicide?" Lucas asked Sabine.

She replied, "At the end of World War Two, he realized Germany would lose the war, and he recommended they make a deal with the Allies for peace. Rommel associated with a group which attempted to murder Hitler. When Hitler discovered this, he did not want to see bad publicity, or see a most respected general in the German military labeled as a traitor. So, he gave Rommel the suicide choice. Rommel's battles will always be a part of world history. The same is true for battles of your American General Patton. Worldwide, people remember him as a great general."

"Did they ever agree on something to make both the Italians and Austrians happy? And, what about the Swiss? Isn't their border also involved?" asked George.

"Well, the Swiss will always try to remain neutral and not get involved," replied Sabine. "In nineteen sixty-seven and nineteen sixty-eight, there were several local terrorist attacks by South Tyrol liberation supporters against the immigration and governing situations. Last year, an International Committee reviewed the problem, and their plan has gone into effect. So far, it seems to be working for all parties concerned. The new self-governing program began this year, and it should provide more financial resources because these provinces will keep 90% of all the money they have raised. From what I have read about it, everyone seems okay with it."

It had been a great day, but a long one, and everyone seemed tired. When they got to their floor at the hotel, no one had to say anything about where they were going. Lucas and Inga went to his room, and George and Sabine went to her room. They all said, "Gute nacht," and they closed their doors.

Lucas and Inga smoked hashish and made love for what seemed like hours. They enjoyed each other's bodies, talked and laughed afterward, and then went to sleep in each other's arms.

The next morning during breakfast, everyone talked about the intimidating road and the difficulty of the drive, going from 910 meters above sea level to 2,780 meters, a climb of 1,870 meters.

When they discussed what runs they should ski for the rest of the day, George said, "It's nice to ride the cable cars, but we must use the T-bar lifts if we want to get more variety."

After a morning toke on the pipe, they were off for another day of autumn skiing.

Stopping along the way, Lucas purchased some cheap shot glasses and a bottle of Jägermeister to enjoy after skiing.

Maybe I do not want to go to Ibiza to find Bruno, thought Lucas. *I hate to see Inga get away, but she may not feel the same way. And, I do not have time to become tied down in a relationship, right now.*

It was a little cooler on their 2nd day of skiing, and a cross-wind was blowing as they skied the runs. It made carving a little more difficult, so they all skied hard. Around 3 p.m., they were ready to go back to the hotel for a hot tub, some beer and Jägermeister.

They all ate in the hotel again. After dinner, they had another shot of Jägermeister, and they agreed to meet for breakfast. Inga and Sabine would be leaving in the morning.

With little conversation, Lucas and Inga headed for Lucas' room, while George and Sabine went to Sabine's room.

Sex for Lucas was even better than before. This was their 2nd time in bed, they knew exactly where they wanted to go with each other, and it was fantastic. The 1st night had involved a lot of exploration.

In the morning, Lucas was feeling a little sad about he and Inga going their separate ways for now. He also thought George had enjoyed being with Sabine. As everyone said goodbye, they all agreed to get together after Lucas and George got back to Garmisch.

Inga said, "Lucas, Oberammergau is only twenty kilometers (12.4 miles) from Garmisch; and Seefeld, where Sabine lives, is about two hours south from Oberammergau."

This sounds like an invitation which I may pursue, thought Lucas.

CHAPTER 6

Italy

Deciding to take a side trip, Lucas and George headed to a place named Santa Caterina di Valfurva where they would check out the ski area. It was 12 kilometers southeast of Bormio.

They were close to the Italian village of Sant'Antonio (SO) when they saw 2 ladies standing on the side of the highway in a downhill section. Lucas pulled the van over as far as he could. The guys got out and saw the problem. Off the road and down a little slope of grass and weeds, a Fiat was stuck with the front end on a big boulder. Both ladies were attractive and well-dressed. Their clothing appeared to be evening wear, not travel garments. Lucas guessed they were about 45 years old.

This could be interesting, thought Lucas.

Remembering when they met the Baader-Meinhof leaders, he said to George, "What are these two, PLO?"

Lucas walked over to the blonde who was the shorter of the two, maybe 5'5". She introduced herself as Ulla Burns. Her friend was a brunette, maybe 5'7", named Francie Burkmier. Both ladies were trim and had good figures. The guys introduced themselves, and George suggested the ladies get in the van where they could have a beer, or a shot of Jägermeister, and decide what to do. The ladies managed a smile and agreed they needed a ride. When they found a phone, they could call the rental company to handle the Fiat.

George said he would take over the driving. The brunette climbed into the front passenger seat and buckled up. The blonde got in back with Lucas. He handed everyone a Stiegl beer, and off they went.

Well, that was easy, thought Lucas. *So much for the need to choose who will be with whom.*

Since they had individual tastes, it was interesting how he and George paired off when they met new women.

George liked cute, athletic, quiet women. Francie was an American yoga instructor from Tampa Bay, Florida.

Lucas preferred buxom, sexy women who like to have fun and laugh. It was a bonus if they were also athletic and played tennis or other sports. However, Lucas never felt the need to win in a competition against his bed partner. His new companion, Ulla, seemed more his type. She was born in Sweden, divorced and living in Tampa Bay where she attended Francie's yoga class.

"What else do you do in Tampa Bay, Ulla?" asked Lucas.

"I sell real estate to very wealthy people," she replied.

He asked, "Do you have an itinerary for seeing Europe?"

"I have been to Europe several times, always with a schedule for everything," she replied. "However, Francie and I agreed to do something more adventurous on this trip. We rented a car, and we drive to where it takes us, so to speak."

"What are you guys doing in Europe?" she asked Lucas.

"This is a great adventure," he replied. "I am a chef, looking to get some European cooking experience while I'm here. Right now, we have no agenda, but we are having fun as we learn about the lifestyles and customs of Europeans."

While they all drank beer, they snacked on grapes and peanut butter on crackers. They told stories about their lives in general, and each shared their experiences in Europe.

Lucas left out the Baader-Meinhof incident, keeping his promise to Andreas and Ulrike. He told Ulla about Garmisch, the AFRC, how much fun they had at the International Bar and Grill, how great the people were and what a beautiful place it was. Ulla was excited to hear Garmisch and things to do there; she had only been to Munich.

"You must come to Garmisch when I get settled," said Lucas. "I plan to work there with military privileges and use of military facilities."

He thought: *Oh, yeah! George and I still have our ID cards. We can use those at U.S. military bases, all over Europe.*

They had turned around and driven back to Bormio where Francie called the rental company to take care of the Fiat. Lucas suggested the ladies accompany them to Milan, then see what happens from there. They would have plenty of time to find a hotel, check in and go have dinner. The ladies were agreeable.

Before they left Bormio, Lucas said to George, "We should look for an American military base where can eat a real hamburger or a steak and enjoy some activities, like a movie or bowling."

George saw a policeman talking to some men on a street corner, and he pulled the van over. Lucas got out to ask where an American military base might be. The policeman did not speak English, but he was talking to someone who acted as an interpreter.

"I'm looking for the nearest American military base," said Lucas.

The man translated to the policeman who said, "Aviano."

Lucas said, "Thank you," and he walked back to the van.

He told George, Francie and Ulla about the military base in Aviano. He and George had not planned to be on a long trip, but they had time for some R&R and could travel wherever they wanted to go. George passed another round of Stiegl beers to the group, and Lucas spread a map of Europe on the table in the van. From their current location, a 6-hour drive would get them to Aviano, and Venice is only 1 1/2 hours south of Aviano. Lucas felt excited about the possibility of going to such a romantic city with these 2 beauties. He asked the group, "Shall we change course?"

George nodded and said, "I'm ready, let's go!"

"There's more," said Lucas. "From Venice, we can drive south to Genoa, then west along the coast of the Riviera and go to Barcelona."

The ladies got out to discuss it. They decided R&R was a great idea, and they looked forward to being with Americans for a while. Both came back to the van with enthusiasm, and Ulla said, "It sounds delightful and exciting. Let's go!"

Without delay, Lucas found a phone and called a hotel in Venice which he read about in a travel book. Although it was expensive, he reserved 2 rooms at the Santa Chiara Hotel. He chose this hotel because it had an underground parking garage where the van would be secure while they explored Venice.

Meanwhile, they headed to Aviano and stopped at Albergo Ristorante Borghese, a hotel with a restaurant and bar, located north of the base. It was an old, white, 3-story building with maroon shutters on the windows. They checked into 2 rooms on the 3rd floor. The ladies took 1 room, and the men were down the hallway.

After they changed clothes, Lucas drove them to the base where he expected a good hamburger or steak. He also wanted to see if they could buy whiskey at the Class Six Store because he heard a bottle of whiskey might be useful to have.

I will get a bottle and keep it on hand, in case we need to bribe border guards for any reason, thought Lucas. *Except, I know it will not be for drugs because I do not want to get caught with hashish while I am crossing a border.*

He did not know the penalty, but he figured it would be prison time in a foreign prison. It was something Lucas wanted no part of.

When they arrived at Aviano Military Base, there was a line of about twenty cars ahead of them at the main gate, and guards were searching every vehicle. After waiting 30 minutes, a military policeman came over to the van and told them all to get out.

"What's going on? Are you looking for someone?" asked Lucas.

The MP answered, "All the U.S. and NATO bases are on alert because of a terrorist threat, made by the Red Army Faction, also known as the Baader-Meinhof Gang."

Lucas and George caught each other's eye, wondering if they might run into their new friends, Andreas and Ulrike; but they did not let on any recognition of the gang. The MPs searched the van. After studying each person's passport plus Lucas and George's military IDs, the MPs gave them a map and let them onto the base.

Lucas pulled into a parking place about 100 yards from the gate and studied the map. He did not see a bowling alley, but he located the PX, the commissary, and the officers' club for drinks and dinner. Before the stores closed, they all went shopping at the PX to purchase personal items and some food for the trip to Spain. Lucas and George did not need much since they had stocked the van at the commissary in Garmisch. Here, they bought whiskey, Jägermeister and more beer.

After shopping, they went to the officers' club where the ladies got noticed, by most of the men in the bar area. They walked through and sat in a corner booth of the dining room, away from the noisy bar. They each ordered a burger with fries and a bottle of Peroni beer. Playing foosball after they ate, each had 2 shots of Jägermeister plus several beers. Ulla and Lucas were getting very friendly, exchanging a few kisses and touching each other.

They drove back to the hotel, and Ulla led Lucas to her room while George and Francie were still in the van. Lucas opened 2 beers, and they shared a toast, "To destiny," for meeting the way they did. Then, Ulla set her glass on an end table, and she seduced Lucas—like he had never been seduced before.

Lucas thought: *Man, if this is how older women act in bed, I have really been missing out.*

When they were all together for breakfast, Lucas declared, "Next stop Venice, Italy—a beautiful, romantic city."

"Yeah and also lots of pigeons," said George.

"Don't knock the pigeons," Lucas replied. "In the nineteen twenties, many people survived during the depression in Europe because of pigeons. I read Hemingway would wheel a baby carriage through the park, grab a pigeon, wring its neck and throw it into his baby carriage."

"Ewww, that's gross," said Ulla.

"Well, I understand many French restaurants serve pigeon, but those are not from the park," said Lucas.

During the 1 1/2-hour trip from Aviano to Venice, they were all in a festive mood, talking, laughing and getting more acquainted. Arriving at the hotel, Lucas pulled into the last open parking spot. It relieved him to have secure parking, his main reason for choosing this place.

The Hotel Santa Chiara is located on the far side of the Ponte Della Liberta (Bridge of Liberty) which connects the mainland to the center of Venice. It overlooks the Grand Canal and Piazzale Roma at the city's historic center which is the only area reachable by car.

Having read about the hotel, Lucas shared some of what he learned, "Five hundred years ago, this building was part of a Monastery for the Sisters of St. Clare (Poor Clare Nuns). When this area developed into residential and farming, most of the Monastery disappeared and St. Clare Garden took over the space next to the hotel. The Santa Lucia Train Station, built nearby, and the bridge to the mainland made this area a hub of activity. All means of public transportation are available, and it is only a twenty-minute walk to San Marcos Square."

Looking around the Piazzale Roma, Lucas thought: *After we crossed over the bridge, coming from the mainland, and walked away from the van, we entered a whole new world of water living. I spent a little time in Venice, California, a town with a small canal section near Los Angeles. By comparison, Venice in Italy is a huge city of islands, and it seems to have hundreds of canals instead of streets.*

The Hotel Santa Chiara was twice as old as the United States. Seeing the front of the pink, four-story building with light blue shutters and doors, Lucas appreciated the charm of this hotel and other historic buildings in Europe. They entered the lobby, walked past a lounge on the left, then past the main bar and the dining room. At the reception desk, a young Italian gentleman said their rooms would not be ready for an hour; the bar and restaurant were open, and they could wait in there. They sat at a table, overlooking the Grand Canal, and ordered 4 Peroni beers.

George had found a small brochure about the history of Venice, and he shared some of the information with the others, "Do you know there are around three hundred arched bridges in Venice, and most of them are made of stone?"

Not waiting for an answer, George said, "Only three bridges cross the Grand Canal. The oldest one, the Ponte de Rialto, is an arched-stone bridge. It replaced an original bridge made of wood. Ponte dei Scalzi, meaning 'Bridge of the Barefoot [monks]', is also an arched-stone bridge. It replaced an iron bridge. The third bridge, the Ponte dell'Accademia, is a wooden structure which replaced a steel bridge, despite local desire for another stone bridge."

After checking into the hotel, they went to their rooms, dressed for a fun evening, and all met in the bar. It was time to have another Peroni beer before looking around this old city on the water.

Lucas had also read about Venice. He said, "Fifteen hundred years ago, people from the mainland escaped hostile invaders to come and live on the 118 islands which now form the city of Venice. They built bridges as needed, to cross the waterways (canals) and access the islands."

Francie suggested, "We should get lost in Venice. At least, we should wander around, drink lots of wine and eat pizza with pasta."

Lucas added, "Or, maybe we should have a great dinner and wine at the Hotel Antica Locanda Montin which we heard about." He turned and whispered into Ulla's ear, "Then, you and I will make wild, passionate love after midnight."

Ulla kissed him on the cheek and pressed her body against him. Using her sexy Swedish accent, she said, "It sounds delightful, Lucas."

"What sounds delightful?" asked George.

"Lucas has a great plan for dinner," replied Ulla.

George, Francie, Lucas and Ulla were eager to get started. It was 7:15 p.m. when they walked out of the hotel, onto Fondamenta Santa Chiara, dressed for a beautiful autumn evening.

I am in Venice, Italy with my best friend and two sexy ladies, getting lost on purpose. It's unbelievable, thought Lucas.

They were not really lost because the hotel concierge recommended having dinner at Hotel Antica Locanda Montin on Fondamenta Borgo. He also gave them a map and directions. They turned onto Fondamenta Papadopoli and walked across the bridge at Rio Dei Tolentini (canal), then walked alongside the Giardino Papadopoli (a terraced, garden park), surrounded by water on 3 sides. They strolled along a wide cement walkway with the Rio Dei Tolentini on the right and the park on the left. About every 100 yards, old-fashioned lamp posts lined the main walkway they were on.

They could see into the park, through window-shaped openings in the high, stone wall around it. The park was full of tall trees and many varieties of plants. Stone pathways led people who wandered through the lovely gardens, studded with statues and benches.

At the canal, boats crowded the docks, and many powerboats cruised through the murky water. Their walk continued along the canal and past the Hotel Moresco where they turned right, crossed another bridge and went past the Fondamenta Rio Nuovo. They continued walking on Calle Larga Raqusei to Calle Contarini where the street took a 45-degree angle to the left, went straight to Calle Del Cristo, across another bridge and over Rio Dei Tolentini. Then, they made a left onto Fondamenta Soccorso and a right onto Calle de la Pazienza. After a short walk and left onto Rio Terra de la Scoazzera, they got on Calle de la Pazienza again, walked across the bridge at Rio de San Barnaba, turned left on Calle Lunga San Barnaba and right onto Fondamenta de Borgo.

Going across another bridge at Rio de Malpaga, they continued to Hotel Antica Locanda Montin, and they arrived at 8:15 p.m.

The entrance was a long hall with glossy wood floors and a wood-beamed, vaulted ceiling. In frames of all sizes, colorful works of art lined the walls, and a dark wood-framed doorway led them to the dining room. A waiter with a great smile, his thick black hair combed straight back, escorted them past more artwork in the dining room, as he took them out to the most beautiful and tranquil garden-dining area Lucas could ever remember seeing. A brown-and-red-carpeted aisle went through the center of the space, dividing tables for 4 people on the right and tables for 2 on the left. All the tables were set with white tablecloths. Over this garden area, a rounded arbor was formed by thick vines. Green foliage and flowers covered the whole arbor.

Lucas ordered a bottle of Chianti as they discussed the menu which Ulla translated for them. They settled on the Cozze Aglio Olio (mussels with garlic, olive oil and peperoncino, an Italian chilli pepper) for the 1st course. George and Lucas both ordered the house specialty, Rana Pescatrice Pomodoro fresco e l'aglio (monkfish in tomato-garlic sauce). Both ladies ordered the Filetto Di Branzino con Parmentier Di Patate Viola (sea bass fillet with purple potatoes). They had two bottles of Chardonnay with dinner, and they had another bottle of Chardonnay while deciding on dessert. Their conversation was lively, and no one was in a hurry—they had all night.

For dessert: Ulla chose Tiramisu, George had Cannoli, Francis chose Apple Crostata and Lucas ordered Torta Caprese, a flourless cake made with rich chocolate. The waiter told them it was originally created by mistake when the chef forgot to put the flour in the batter.

While they were waiting for dessert—all hell broke loose outside, and they heard a loud whooshing noise. At the front of the restaurant, people in the main dining room could see all kinds of debris flying around outside. Multi-story buildings protected the patio-dining area on 3 sides of the arbor; however, they could hear the tremendous wind and crashing noises, coming from the street.

The waiter said, "It must be a tornado. However, those are very rare in Italy." At first, everyone in the restaurant was frantic. They were all talking at once and seemed to be shaken.

The owner passed around shots of Frangelico (hazelnut liqueur). The guests calmed down and went on with their evening. Although, many were still wondering what damages had occurred outside.

When dessert arrived, Lucas suggested, "We should walk over to San Marcos Square this evening. Someone told me late evening, from ten to midnight, is the best time to go and avoid big crowds."

They all shared their desserts, so they tasted and enjoyed each one. Lucas paid the check, and they headed out to explore the area.

Outside, they saw several boats upside down, one pushed against a building, and a lot of debris on the walkway. In the open areas, it was a mess. Tables, chairs, awnings, trash cans and other items had blown all over the place, some into the water.

They were glad to have a map of the city which helped them plan a return route to the hotel. Going to San Marcos Square, they had to zig-zag on various walkways and over some canals. The narrow walkways were lined with old buildings and houses on one side and boats in canals on the other side.

Lucas said, "It's hard for me to get used to this, being surrounded by water and seeing canals as the main transportation route. I read about the congestion and amazing navigation of workboats, garbage barges and freight barges, all passing each other in the canals, going about their business day and night, along with the water buses which the locals call Vaporettos."

By the time they got to the square, the crowds had thinned out. They stopped at a café which was still open, sat at an outside table and ordered a pitcher of house red wine.

Sitting across from Lucas, George had his travel book out. He was reading to the others about the Bell Tower, located in the far corner of San Marcos Square.

Lucas noticed a couple at a table in the back corner of the patio, and he did a double take. In a low voice, he said, "George, look at the couple in the far corner without letting them notice you're looking. Tell me if you recognize them."

Discreetly, George looked and said, "It's Andreas and Ulrike."

At the same time, both ladies asked, "Who are they?"

These ladies might think Andreas and Ulrike are celebrities, but I do not want to say they are Celebrity Terrorists, thought Lucas.

"We gave them a ride and enjoyed talking to them," said Lucas. "They're English speaking Germans. Can we invite them to join us?"

"Well, I speak German," said Ulla. "But it is better to speak English, so everyone can understand. Yes, invite them over."

Lucas excused himself and walked over to Andreas and Ulrike. When he approached them, he said, "Hi, do you remember me?"

They looked startled, at first, but then they both smiled. Andreas said, "Of course we do. How are you Lucas?"

"I am doing great," Lucas replied. "What brings you to Venice?"

Calmly, Andreas whispered, "We robbed a bank this evening. Now, we are waiting to meet a boat which will take us out of here. But the boat will not be here until six a.m. And, we are trying to figure out how we can look inconspicuous until then."

Andreas then asked Lucas, "Who are those women with you?"

"They are from the U.S. We met them a few days ago after their car ran off the road in South Tyrol," replied Lucas. "They joined us, and we've been having lots of fun, seeing the country."

Lucas suggested they join his group and walk back to the hotel where they could stay out of sight. Knowing they were probably the subject of a large manhunt, he added, "If you joined us, I think you would be less conspicuous as two happy, drunk people."

Andreas and Ulrike agreed, grabbed their backpacks and walked over to his table. Lucas introduced everyone, and then he asked the waiter to bring 2 more glasses.

"What is your profession, Ulrike?" asked Ulla.

"I am a journalist. Andreas and I are writing a book. We have been enjoying the mountains and countryside," she replied.

Lucas advised his group Andreas and Ulrike would walk back to the hotel with them. Lucas bought 2 bottles of house red and got plastic glasses from the waiter, so they could drink during their walk.

They put on a good show, acting like 3 drunk couples who got lost along the canals of Venice. Drunk tourists were a common sight in this city. No one took notice of their behavior, or people laughed it off.

Falling back from the others, Lucas said to Andreas, "I think it might be good for you and Ulrike to wait inside our van until you have to leave. It's underground in the parking garage. The desk clerk, or anyone else who could identify you, will not see you in the van."

"Thank you, Lucas. I think it would be best," said Andreas.

Lucas told Andreas to pull the curtains in the back of the van, and they could help themselves to any food and beer in the cupboards.

Andreas spoke with sincerity, "Danke schoen, Lucas. We owe you. Maybe someday we can repay you for your kindness."

"Do you want to tell me about your plans? Are you still going to Jordan?" asked Lucas.

"We were lucky the tornado hit at the same time we robbed the bank," replied Andreas. "There were four of us. We separated and plan to meet at the boat in the morning. Maybe we will look for you when we get back from Jordan. Where did you say you will be? Garmisch?"

"Garmisch will be my home base, and I plan to be there unless I'm traveling," replied Lucas.

They caught up with the rest of the group, and everyone walked to the garage underneath the hotel. Andreas and Ulrike would settle in for a few hours before they left to meet their boat. Appearing to be in a group, made them less likely to be recognized if someone was in the garage, but no one else was there.

At the van, Lucas and George gave them a hug and said good luck.

Finally, Lucas and George escorted the ladies into the hotel, all still happy, laughing and singing.

In the comfort of the hotel room, Lucas and Ulla had a glass of wine. Both toasted to a great evening and slow-danced to music on the radio while they undressed each other. They climbed on the bed and had their way with each other. It was fabulous and thrilling.

At 10:00 a.m., George knocked on the door. Ulla was sound asleep, and Lucas was barely awake. Everyone had agreed to sleep in because they had a 4-hour drive to Genoa, in the afternoon.

Lucas threw on underwear and a T-shirt, then opened the door and let George into the front sitting room. He wondered who looked more hung over, him or George. Lucas went to the closet, grabbed 2 bottles of Peroni beer, opened them and gave 1 to George.

Although George looked like he might be sick to his stomach, he took a long drink and said, "This is the true breakfast of champions. Now, I must know what you and Andreas talked about last night. I never got the chance to find out what's going on with them."

"I'm going to jump in the shower, before I wake Ulla," said Lucas. "I'll hurry, and you can meet me downstairs in the dining room."

Going back into the bedroom, Lucas realized Ulla was naked. He took off his shirt and jockey shorts, climbed back in bed, snuggled with her and got an erection.

He thought: *Ulla has a great body. I like her shapely, muscular legs, and her breasts are marvelous.*

Ulla opened her eyes and groaned. Lucas asked her if she wanted a beer. She groaned again, reached down and felt Lucas' hardness.

"Oooh, look what I found!" she said. "Do we have to get up now?"

"I told George I would meet him in the dining room. Maybe we can catch some afternoon delight when we get to Genoa," he replied.

Ulla gave him a kiss and said, "Well, then, let's get going."

Lucas took a quick shower and got dressed in blue jeans and a white polo shirt which accented his remaining California tan. He grabbed 2 more Peroni beers and went downstairs while Ulla showered.

Sitting at a window table in the dining room, George was trying to decipher a German newspaper. The article had Andreas and Ulrike's photo on the front page.

"Let's start the day off right," said Lucas, handing George a beer.

"Sounds good to me," he replied.

"I know you're eager to hear about Andreas and Ulrike," said Lucas. "But, let's wait for the ladies. Ulla can translate the newspaper article, and I'll fill in the blanks with what Andreas told me."

George agreed. Then, they talked about the next leg of their trip.

The ladies walked into the dining room, looking fresh and pretty.

What wonders a shower and a little makeup will do for an already beautiful woman, thought Lucas.

When Ulla and Francie saw the front-page photos of Andreas, Ulrike and other RAF members, Lucas noticed the ladies' change in demeanor and mood. Ulla translated the newspaper article which made Andreas, Ulrike and the other Celebrity Terrorists sound like monsters. Ulla and Francie were upset; and it was obvious.

Lucas fueled it even more when he told the ladies Andreas and Ulrike seemed to be very nice people, and they were fun to be around. Both ladies were outraged about being introduced to people who were murderers, bank robbers and terrorists. They decided to take the next train to Rome, fearful of being arrested for associating with known criminals. As soon as possible, they would return to "The States."

Sitting with the ladies became a silent event. Lucas and George kept their heads down, waiting for the lunch menu. It was too late for breakfast which was okay with them. It seems the Italians only eat bread or rolls with their cappuccino, but Americans love big breakfasts.

The waiter arrived and told them they were also a little early for lunch; however, the chef would make them polenta and sausage, or veal liver and sautéed onions, a local favorite of the Venetians. George and Ulla went for the liver. Lucas and Francie ordered polenta and sausage. The guys had Moretti beers, and the ladies had cappuccinos.

After breakfast, they all returned to their respective rooms and packed. Everyone checked out at the front desk, took a five-minute walk to the Ponte degli Scalzi and crossed the bridge. Arriving at the train station, they all said a chilly goodbye with brief kisses, light hugs and empty promises to go visit each other, sometime in the future.

CHAPTER 7

Road to Ibiza: Aftermath of Tornado

Lucas and George walked back to the van, put their backpacks inside and took off for Padua. They did not get far before the traffic stopped. A traffic cop told them trees and power lines were down, all the way through Padua, a result of the tornado which had struck west of there. So, they were driving along the path which the tornado had taken. Hearing this, Lucas and George pulled into the next store and bought a case of Peroni beer. They each opened a beer and toasted to being on the road again. It took a long time to get through Padua, but they breezed through Vicenza and Verona without even stopping.

Turning left off the main highway at Brescia, they headed south past Cremona, curved west toward Piacenza and Voghera, then south at Tortona. They were an hour from Genoa, a port city on the coast of Italy where they might find a hotel room. If they find a campground, or a place to park for the night, they could sleep in the van.

When they arrived in Genoa, they followed the highway as far as they could to the blue Ligurian Sea, parked the van and asked a traffic cop for directions to a campground in Genoa. He told them about Camping Baciccia! It was next to the beach about an hour drive to the west. They thanked the officer, got back to the van and popped another Peroni. Driving along the coast and through the neat little town of Savona, they followed the water to the campground.

They pulled in and found a nice shady spot, not too far from the campground's restaurant and bar, walked to the office and registered, then went to the bar for a beer and a look at the dinner menu.

Lucas and George were pleased to find out they had a tennis court. George was extra pleased to see a volleyball court at the private beach. Lucas thought they should stay a couple of days to unwind before driving on to Barcelona. There were no eligible-looking ladies around yet, but he and George had just arrived.

After learning where all the facilities were, they went back to the van and drank another Peroni while they changed into shorts and tennis shoes.

Then, they went looking for a game. George wanted to see what was happening at the volleyball court. There was a game with young men and women who finished playing a few minutes later.

Most of the players wandered off. It was about the time people get ready for dinner. Lucas watched them take the ball to a hut which was next to the office. So, he and George walked over there and asked if they could use the volleyball. They left an ID at the hut, went back to the court, and hit the ball to each other.

Two tall, dark-haired Italian guys walked over and asked in Italian, "Vuoi giocare una partita?"

"I'm sorry, but we only speak English," said Lucas.

The Italian guy who had spoken before, said in broken English, "Would you like to play a game?"

"Yes, we would. I'm George, and this is Lucas."

The taller Italian said, "My name is Giuseppe, and he is Alberto. You can serve first, and we will play to 11 points per game."

George had a wicked serve and got them off to a 5-0 start. When the Italians came back with a few dinky shots and a good slam, the score went to 6-3. That was as close as the Italians got to the Americans.

Resting for a beer break, Lucas thought: *George was the last man cut in drafts for the 1968 Olympic volleyball team, and he is a high school volleyball coach. Also, I have beach creds for volleyball, basketball, wiffle ball and Frisbee. We should beat these guys.*

They did win, scoring 11-6, 11-8 and 11-3, and the Italians did not look too happy about it.

Several people had gathered around to watch their competitive game. Lucas could not help but notice 2 very attractive young ladies, maybe in their mid-20s, who were trim and athletic-looking. Lucas caught the eye of 1 lady as he gave her a smile, and she did the same.

Then, everyone walked away, going in different directions. George and Lucas wanted to shower and change clothes, then head to the bar and restaurant. Lucas hoped he would see and talk with the young lady who he had smiled at.

Lucas wore a blue polo shirt and tan tennis shorts. George wore crazy looking plaid shorts and a light-yellow T-shirt. They both wore leather sandals which they had bought last May during a lost Cinco de Mayo weekend when they went to Ensenada in Baja California.

The 2 young ladies who had watched the volleyball match were now standing at the bar with a drink in their hands. The 2 Italian guys were standing next to them, but the guys appeared to be waiting for their drinks and not talking to the ladies.

There was just enough room for Lucas to slip in next to the lady who he had smiled at. Noticing her drink was almost empty, he said, “Hi, could I get you a refill?”

Surprised, she turned around and said, “Oh! It’s you!”

“Yes, it is,” replied Lucas. The young lady was now smiling.

He spoke to the bartender and ordered, “Two Moretti beers. Also, please give the ladies whatever they are having.”

As they turned their backs on the 2 Italian guys, the young ladies had Lucas and George’s complete attention. Introducing themselves as Judy and Deanna, they said they were avid skiers from Banff, Canada, and they were planning to return and get jobs after it snows in Garmisch. This added a lot more excitement to the conversation. The ladies had not been to Garmisch yet, and they wanted to know all about it.

The Italian guys wandered away and went over to play foosball, realizing the ladies were more interested in the Americans.

Lucas and Judy were hitting it off, laughing at the funny side of their travels in Europe, such as the different types of restrooms, toilets, showers and toilet paper. Judy was also drinking Moretti beer.

Lucas bought another round, and the 4 of them wandered over by the foosball table where Giuseppe and Alberto were playing each other. Seeing Lucas and George, the Italians asked if they wanted to play a game against them.

These guys might be good, but George and I have played foosball in California for several years, and it has been a long while since we lost to anybody, thought Lucas.

The Italians put up a good battle, but Lucas was a lightning-quick goalie, and George hammered the hardwood ball with such force and precision, it made a loud cracking sound against the back of the other goal. Everyone in the bar gathered around the foosball table to watch the Americans destroy these young Italian machos’ game.

Judy was excited. She gave Lucas a kiss on the cheek and said, “Are you guys this good at everything?”

He replied, “Well, I think I’ll leave that for you to decide.”

She looked at him, out of the corner of her eye, and smiled. They talked about each of their travel plans, and Lucas shared his experience of skiing in Gomagoi. He did not mention the RAF or the Baader-Meinhof Gang since he feared it would scare her away.

The Italian guys stopped playing. So, Judy and Lucas played against George and Deanna, and they each won a game. Then, they got a table together in the dining room, ordered more beers and studied the menu. This place advertised as a pizza restaurant, but it had other interesting menu items, including grilled baby squid, fillet of sea bream with potato crust, spaghetti with seafood and risotto with lobster. The pizza looked so good, they all chose pizza and Moretti beer. They also shared a plate of fried calamari, shrimp and anchovies.

Everyone was full. Lucas thought the pizza was excellent since the restaurant loaded it with gorgonzola, tomato, mozzarella, sausage and onion. They skipped dessert, each had a shot of Jägermeister, and Lucas paid the check.

Outside in the fresh air, the group split up. Lucas and Judy strolled the grounds and talked about their respective lives in North America. Lucas told Judy about his busy life in Long Beach, his two restaurants, waterskiing, basketball, and occasional ski trips to Mammoth Mountain, Lake Tahoe, Heavenly Valley or Squaw Valley. Judy talked about her life in Banff, her skiing, and her job as catering manager of a large resort hotel at Lake Louise, a 1-hour drive north of Banff.

"Would you like to take a walk on the beach?" asked Lucas.

It was a beautiful night, and Judy said, "Yes, if you'll take me home, after our walk."

"Whose home?" he asked.

"I don't care, as long as you are there," said Judy.

"What about George and Deanna?" he asked.

She said, "Deanna and I already worked it out. They can stay in the cabin, and you and I can stay in your van. Okay?"

They headed for the beach which was next to the volleyball court, and they enjoyed being together. By the time they walked back to the van, they were holding hands.

"Do you have a special lady back home?" asked Judy.

"No, I don't," replied Lucas.

He thought about Jodie: *Someone took my special lady from me when she was murdered, last February. Jodie was more than special; she was my fiancée. The prime suspect, Bruno, an ex-boyfriend, fled to Europe. George and I learned Bruno worked in Garmisch as a bartender, but he took time off and went to Ibiza, Spain. Now, we will go there, not so much to find him, but to have fun and see Spain. We have no action planned for Bruno yet. We must figure out what we want to do. I believe we have the advantage since I doubt Bruno knows what I look like; and he would have no reason to think I am looking for him in Europe.*

Lucas realized he should not tell people about Bruno because he did not know how the matter would end.

He changed the subject and spoke about his good friend George, how much they both loved sports, and how well they traveled together.

After Lucas told Judy about getting their ID cards in Frankfurt, and the fun people they met in Garmisch, Judy said, "I look forward to seeing

Garmisch. It sounds like a great place to work, and I hope to get a job there with an ID card too."

When they arrived at the van, things were quiet in the campground, except for loud music. Someone was playing "American Woman" by The Guess Who, a few aisles over from the VW van.

Lucas slid the door open and said, "The bed in my van is a virgin."

"Oh my. We should do something about it," said Judy.

After they climbed inside, Lucas poured shots of Jägermeister, put a Neil Diamond tape in the cassette player, made the bed and turned down the lights. Between kisses, they undressed and explored each other's bodies, using their hands and fingers. Then, they fell into bed together. Judy was quite a physical young lady. Lucas also learned—the lady was very acrobatic.

Lucas got up early, walked to the men's room and ran into George. They talked about plans for their trip and decided to stay at the campground. Both wanted to play there an extra day.

Lucas asked George, "What do you think about inviting Judy and Deanna to go to Barcelona with us?"

"Let's talk to them about it," said George. "It sounds great to me. They are fun ladies."

"What do you expect? They are skiers!" replied Lucas.

When Lucas got to the van, Judy was lying on the bed, blankets barely covering her bottom half. She was moaning about a hangover. He admired what beautiful breasts Judy had as he climbed on the bed and gave her a kiss. Then, he reached in the cabinet, grabbed two Peroni beers, opened them and put a beer in Judy's hand.

To his surprise, she took a big swallow and smiled, then said to him, "You are a lifesaver. What's for breakfast, Chef?"

Lucas could have pulled out the Coleman stove and cooked pancakes, but he suggested they go see what the restaurant offered. George and Deanna were there, sitting at a table by the window. Lucas pulled a chair out for Judy. Then, he went and spoke to the waiter who brought 4 Moretti beers to the table.

When everyone had a fresh beer in hand, Lucas said, "We should celebrate our meeting and maybe discuss travel plans."

"Where are you guys planning to go next?" asked Deanna. "Judy and I were planning on taking a train to Spain."

"Where did you land in Europe?" asked George.

"We flew from Banff to London with two other gals, but we separated in Paris," replied Judy. "The other two are traveling in Germany, and we plan to meet them in Garmisch."

Extending an invitation, Lucas said, "George and I would like it very much if you come with us, at least as far as Barcelona," leaving it open for further discussion when they get there.

The ladies told them they would discuss it and let them know.

"Okay. Meanwhile, let's have fun today," said Lucas.

They all ate cereal, boiled eggs, pannetoni and melon. They also had another round of Moretti beers. After breakfast, they went back to their respective places, the ladies in their cabin, and the men in the van.

Lucas and George put on shorts and tank tops to play basketball.

They were glad to see synthetic, hard-court surfaces which allowed for true bounce of the balls on the basketball and tennis courts.

It was 10 a.m., and nobody was playing on the courts yet. So, Lucas and George checked out a basketball and shot a game of H-O-R-S-E. Using his deadly jump shot, Lucas won. He could make the shot from anywhere within 15 to 25 feet of the hoop.

Giuseppe and Alberto arrived and challenged Lucas and George to a game. Lucas won the free throw shoot-off against Alberto, and he began the game by passing to George who was guarded by the taller Giuseppe. Lucas faked to the right, leaving Alberto in his tracks, then he went left, and George fired the ball back to him for an easy 14-foot jump shot. George and Lucas were off to an 8-0 lead when Alberto threw a long jumper which swished the net. So, Lucas played him tight, making him work hard to receive a pass, and this frustrated Alberto who was quick, but not a great ball handler. Lucas took the ball away from him, or he sagged off when he had the ball. Lucas also intercepted two passes to Giuseppe. He could see Alberto and Giuseppe getting frustrated and angry because they could not do anything on offense against Lucas and George's tenacious defense.

Lucas and George won 2 games, scoring 12-4 and 12-6, then they all broke for lunch. Giuseppe and Alberto abstained from handshakes at the net. They walked off the court, heading toward the bar.

Back at their van, Lucas and George cleaned up, changed clothes and walked over to Judy and Deanna's cabin. Both ladies cleaned up nicely and looked fresh, even after such a late night.

They told the ladies about the basketball game against the Italians. Lucas asked if they wanted to go have a few beers and lunch, then go for dinner and dancing, later in the evening.

"We would love to have lunch and go out this evening, but I need a nap after lunch," said Judy. "I'm getting into the European schedule of a siesta in the afternoon."

"Okay, let's go get a table before it gets crowded," said George.

For lunch, they started with 4 Moretti beers. Lucas chose Sautéed Mussels with tomato sauce. Judy ordered Grilled Salmon with lemon, capers and anchovy. George selected the Grilled Sea Bass with an aromatic herb butter. Deanna wanted to try the local Ligurian Rabbit with rosemary. For starters, the server brought food and placed it in the center of the table to be shared: a large bowl of steaming, house-made Flat Spaghetti with Pesto Genovese, another big bowl of Sautéed Vegetables which included zucchini, eggplant, garlic, tomato and baby artichoke, plus a basket of sliced Focaccia bread.

During lunch, Lucas talked about the origin of pesto and some of the variations, "The word *pesto* means pounded; it's the old-fashioned way they made it. Some cooks still swear by pounding a mixture of aromatic herbs, salt, garlic, olive oil, cheese and sometimes nuts. The ancient Romans used it and ate it with bread. Nowadays, it is used not only for pasta, but as a condiment for many kinds of foods. The Genovese-style Pesto is the most famous. It originated here in the coastal region of Liguria, and they make it with fresh basil leaves, crushed garlic, cheeses and European pine nuts, all blended with olive oil to a soft paste."

"Lucas, how do you know all this stuff?" asked Deanna.

"I've always loved history, and when it relates to food or chefs, I am even more interested," he replied.

Judy announced the ladies' decision about Spain, "We would love to go to Spain with you, but we want to split the cost of gas and food."

Lucas always pays, so he appreciated the offer. He said, "Okay with me. How about you, George?"

"Fine, but we buy the beer and Jägermeister," said George.

The ladies left to take a nap after lunch. Lucas saw the dart board and asked the bartender for darts. The bartender handed him 2 sets with 3 darts in each set. Giuseppe and Alberto were sitting at the bar, and they saw Lucas get the darts.

"Hey, you two want to play a game of cricket?" asked Alberto.

With a straight face, Lucas said, "If you'll show us how to play."

Alberto smiled with confidence and said, "Sure, we'll show you how to play." So, Alberto explained the game, then he and Lucas each threw 1 dart to see who goes 1st. Alberto threw closest to the bullseye, so he went 1st and threw 3 twenties, right off the bat. Lucas could only throw 1 twenty, but got an eighteen. Before he could mark it on the chalkboard, Alberto said, "Your eighteen doesn't count."

Lucas disagreed. "You didn't explain that before we started, and I think it should count. Let's ask the bartender." Alberto hesitated, but agreed, and the bartender told them it should count. Lucas said, "See?"

Alberto looked angry when he said, “Oh, all right, but this means all the lucky shots count.”

Guiseppe made 2 twenties which gave them 40 points. George threw 2 eighteens. Alberto threw 1 more twenty and 1 eighteen. Lucas then threw nothing and Guiseppe got 2 more twenties. George finally closed out twenties, and the score was now in favor of the Italians, 100 to 0.

The Italians closed out eighteens and sixteens. But the Americans managed to score 72 on eighteens and 80 on sixteens for 152. The Italians added to their lead of 100, getting 57 on nineteens and 68 on seventeens for 225. The Americans only closed those numbers out. After Alberto threw 2 fifteens, Lucas threw 4 fifteens, giving the Americans 167. Then, Giuseppe closed out fifteens.

Now, it was down to throwing bulls. Lucas was always able to pull games out of the fire because he was deadly with bullseyes. Guiseppe led off and threw 1 bull. George also threw 1, and then Alberto threw 1. Now, with the Italians 2 bulls and the Americans 1 bull, Lucas needed to throw 2 bulls to stay in the game. He hit the wire with his 1st dart which stayed outside the bull’s ring. His next dart was dead center, double-bulls, closing bulls out for his team. Next, Guiseppe got nothing. George followed with 1 bull, bringing the Americans to 217. Alberto threw 2 darts and missed badly. His 3rd dart hit close, but outside the wire. It was Lucas’ turn; 2 darts missed, but the 3rd dart landed in the green bull’s ring for the win. Game over: Americans 242 to Italians 225.

“I thought you didn’t know how to play,” said Guiseppe.

“Beginners luck, I guess,” said Lucas. Then, he asked the Italians, “Do you guys play tennis?”

“Are you kidding? We are the undefeated Verona City doubles-champions,” said Alberto.

Lucas was not sure he believed their claim. Since he had been playing a lot of tennis, the last 3 years, and George was such a natural athlete, Lucas said, “We’ll do the best we can against you champions.”

On the tennis court, the Italians came out strong with a 4 to 1 game start. Lucas and George held serve the rest of the way, but could not break through the Italians and lost the 1st set 4-6. As they switched sides for the 2nd set, Lucas noticed the Italian guys seemed more energized and confident, but it did matter. Lucas and George were *on fire* in the 2nd set, winning the 1st 4 games.

The Italians tried to come back, but Lucas started to “get in a zone” as he sometimes does, and he was focused. He and George won the set 6-4. It was hot on the court, but heat never bothered Lucas too much. He grew up playing on asphalt courts in Fresno, California, where it was common to play in temperatures over 100 degrees.

Both teams held serve; it was 1 game each. Giuseppe served to Lucas, and he played everything to Lucas' double-handed backhand. It proved to be a mistake because Lucas' backhand was stronger than his forehand. He hit 2 blazing backhand returns, one down the line and the other down the center which seemed to deflate the Italians. Lucas and George went on to win the set 6-3 and the match. Final scores: 4-6, 6-4, 6-3.

Losing the tennis match was the last straw for the 2 Italians. They did not go to the net and shake hands with the Americans. Instead, the Italians walked around the net and began running fast, toward Lucas and George, as if to tackle them.

When Lucas and George saw the Italians coming, they naturally moved closer together.

George said, "Low."

Lucas said, "High."

Then they waited, only 10 feet away from collision with 2 big Italian guys who were barreling toward them.

George threw himself laterally, across the legs of both aggressors. As the Italians fell forward, Lucas leaped and spread his body across the upper-halves of both their bodies, leading with his shoulder and bringing his knee up with force. As a result, the Italian on the left smashed his nose into Lucas' right shoulder, and the other Italian shattered his nose and cheek bone on a Lucas' knee. George jumped and kicked Alberto in the head, and Lucas kicked Giuseppe in the balls. Lucas and George stood there expecting more fight, but the Italians stayed down. The Italians were bleeding all over the tennis court. When they finally stood and walked away, Alberto and Giuseppe were holding their respective noses, and both had their heads hanging down. They had just been humiliated by two California beach guys.

Waiting to meet the ladies for dinner in the campground restaurant, Lucas and George got seated at a table. When the ladies arrived, Deanna said, "On our walk over here, we saw the Italian guys driving out the gate. They both had bandages on their noses. One guy had the whole bottom-half of his head bandaged. Do you know what happened to them?"

Lucas and George both shrugged and extended their arms with palms up as if to say, *"We don't know anything."*

"Oh, come on, tell us what happened," said Deanna.

Lucas looked at George and extended his hand, indicating, *"You tell them, George."*

When George responded, he told the ladies, "All I want to say is—they were very poor losers."

Then, the guys described their day, playing darts and tennis. Their story ended with how the Italians attacked them on the tennis court.

Lucas explained, "The difference in our skirmish was teamwork. Giuseppe and Antonio came at us as individuals; one was going for George, and the other one was going for me. We went after them as a team and took them out."

After dinner and 2 shots of Jägermeister apiece, George and Deanna headed for the cabin. Lucas and Judy walked down to the beach, took off their shoes and waded in the water. Judy turned to Lucas and said, "Oh Lucas, I'm so glad we met here. It has been great fun, and I'm excited about traveling to Barcelona with you. I also look forward to crawling into bed with you in your van. Can we go now?" Judy put her arms around Lucas' neck. She kissed him with great passion, and then they held hands. Both anticipated a fun night together.

It was another acrobatic night, and Judy exhausted Lucas. Before he fell asleep, he thought: *Judy isn't the type who most often attracts me. I like ample-breasted women and dislike skinny legs. Judy has a dancer's legs, and the shape of her breasts is superb, although they are medium-small. So, it is quality over quantity with Judy. Having sex with Judy is almost an out-of-body experience; it makes me want more of her.*

Using a Coleman stove on the table which folds down from the side of a cabinet, Lucas stood outside the van's sliding door and made pancakes with scrambled eggs and ham. Lucas, George and Deanna were all having a Peroni beer. Judy walked over to the restaurant to get coffee and a melon which Lucas would slice for breakfast.

After breakfast, they cleaned up, and Lucas put 4 backpacks in the rear of the van. Each of them grabbed a beer, and off they went for an hour and a half drive to Nice.

Judy exclaimed, "This is so exciting, being able to see these great places which I've always read about. What makes it so special is doing it with such fun, beautiful people."

Lucas raised his beer bottle and said, "Here is to beautiful people, heading for the French Riviera!"

CHAPTER 8

Road to Barcelona

Lucas was driving. Everyone else was enjoying the panoramic views as they passed through many of the beach towns and marinas along the Mediterranean coastline.

"What are we going to do tonight?" Judy asked Lucas.

"Good question. Let's discuss it," he replied.

While turning down the Stones music tape, Lucas hollered to the back, "Hey George, would you hand Judy one of those travel books? We should find a few things to do in Nice tonight. While you're at it, would you hand us two Peronis?"

Lucas told Judy, "I want to get in the hills, or find a high building for a better view of these famous, historic places. These cities and small villages are the playgrounds for the rich and famous. I know we will not be going inside the Casino de Monte-Carlo because the attire is formal there, and I forgot to bring my tux."

Judy handed Lucas a beer, took a drink from hers and said, "There is a club on the promenade in Nice, named The High Club. I wonder if it means people get 'high' in the club."

"Do you smoke dope?" Lucas asked Judy.

"Yes, of course. We are skiers," she replied.

"Yeah, I guess it's true, at least among the young skiers. Okay, your idea sounds like fun," said Lucas.

A few moments later, Lucas suggested, "We should find a hotel first, and then we can plan things to do nearby. I remember reading about Old Town Nice and the promenades."

Looking in the tour book, Judy responded, "There are lots of options, but here is a hotel right in Old Town, the Paradis Hotel. It is near the Promenade des Anglais and close to a place known as Wayne's Bar which is the most popular nightclub in Nice.

"The Paradis Hotel sounds perfect," said Lucas. "Let's stop at the next market or gas station. We can buy more beer, get gas and discuss it with George and Deanna."

They stopped in San Remo, bought a case of Peroni, made their plan of attack for Nice, and called to reserve rooms at the Paradis Hotel.

Driving on the upper highway, they caught some great views from villages overlooking the French Riviera.

Along the way, they found an interesting restaurant for lunch, the Au Rendez vous des Amis. The travel book gave it a fantastic review and offered several photos of a colorful dining room, outdoor patio dining and wonderful views of the blue Mediterranean. This restaurant was in Gairaut near Aire Saint Michel, an exclusive district of Nice. It was a bright sunny day, so they elected to sit on the patio. Walking through a beautiful dining room, Lucas admired a large vase of fresh, bright-yellow sunflowers, displayed on a decorative table. The dining tables were adorned with pink tablecloths, fine cloth napkins, yellow candles, long stemmed wine glasses and yellow-green dishes. Overhead, a green-striped awning went through the dining room and out to the patio area where green umbrellas and large lime trees shaded the guests.

Their waiter introduced himself as Topo. He came from Argentina, and he is working a temporary job here until he can go to Germany. He wants to get a job in Garmisch, working for the American military.

Lucas spoke up, “Well, it looks like we all are planning on the same thing. Are you going there to ski, Topo?”

“Yes, I am,” replied Topo. “I love to ski, and I can’t wait to ski in the Alps. Are you all skiers?”

“Yes,” said Deanna. “Judy and I are from Banff, Canada. Lucas and George are from California. Topo, can you tell us where to go for some nightlife, drinking and dancing?”

Topo smiled a great smile. He was a handsome, dark-complected, tall Latino who answered by saying, “Yes. Go to Wayne’s Bar in Old Town. It rocks there every night, and they have great music.” Then, leaning forward, Topo whispered, “Do you get high?”

“Yes, we do,” Lucas replied, quietly. “However, we have nothing with us, right now.”

Topo flashed his great smile again. Then, he whispered, “I have some killer hashish which I will sell you, three grams for thirty-one thousand and two hundred fifty lira—or fifty American dollars.”

They all laughed and agreed with enthusiasm. Lucas said, “Sounds great. We’ll take it.”

Topo spoke softly, “I’ll come out to your car when you are ready to leave. Now, let’s talk about food. I must get back to work.”

As Topo suggested, they all ordered a 3-course meal from the menu. To start, all four wanted crispy, Fried Calamari as their entrée.

For the main course: George and Deanna had Faux Filet a la Plancha (grilled tenderloin with pickled onions and pine nuts). Judy chose Magret de Canard (breast of duck, grilled with port wine and shallots). Lucas had Filet de Loup (sea bass, sautéed with tomatoes, olives, onion and garlic).

For dessert: Lucas and Judy shared the Blueberry Clafoutis which looked and tasted like a fruit cobbler. George and Deanna had Mousse de Mascarpone et ses Cerises cuites aux Kirsch, parsemé d'éclats de noisettes (mascarpone mousse with cherries cooked in cherry liquor, topped with chopped hazelnuts).

After eating great food, drinking Moretti beers and having fun with the handsome, Argentinean, dope-dealing waiter, Lucas paid the check and left a more-than-generous tip for their new friend. Leaving the restaurant, Topo followed them out to the van and made the deal for hashish. Since Topo had a pipe, he joined them for some hits.

"Being in a real French restaurant is like being in another world. How long has this restaurant been here, Topo?" Lucas asked.

"I understand they built this place in the thirties," replied Topo. "At first, it was a grocery store, then a dancehall, and later it became a hotel. Each new owner changed the decor, but the building and the character of it has remained the same."

"Topo, how did you come to work in France? Do you need a work permit, a visa or something? Do you speak French?" asked George.

"Yes, I speak five languages," he replied. "My parents wanted me to visit Europe, so I prepared by learning the languages. Hey, do you need a hash pipe?"

"Yeah, we sure do, come to think of it," said Lucas.

Topo offered, "Here, you can have this pipe. I have another in my locker." They took turns hugging and thanking Topo, then laughed their way back to the Paradis Hotel.

Following a big lunch and smoking hashish, Lucas and Judy crashed and cuddled together on 1 of the 2 double beds in their hotel room. George and Deanna took a nap in their room next door.

When Lucas and Judy awoke, they grabbed a Peroni beer and showered together. They were not trying to save water; it was more fun together than showering alone. They got dressed and were ready to go find a bar when someone knocked on their door.

Lucas opened the door. As George came in the room, followed by Deanna, he asked, "Where is the hash pipe?"

They each had two hits, and Judy opened Peroni beers for all. Looking on the map for the nearest bar, Lucas showed George where to meet them. Deanna and George headed for their room to shower and dress. Judy and Lucas headed outside. He was feeling good about life in general.

Judy and Lucas walked along Avenue Verdun to the Promenade des Anglais, then along the promenade to Ruhl Plage restaurant. It was owned and operated by the same family since 1950. The terrace overlooked the Mediterranean Sea and the gray, crushed-rock beach.

Being so attracted to Judy surprised Lucas. He thought she was smart, beautiful and sexy. Her body was well-toned. She was attracted to him because he turned her on and made her laugh. She did the same for him, and he enjoyed spending time with her.

When George and Deanna arrived, they all ordered a bottle of Moretti and enjoyed the view.

"I love this place," said Judy. "Why don't we eat here tonight? From here, we can walk over to the casino on the promenade. Then, we can go back to the hotel and smoke dope before it is time to go for drinks and dancing at Wayne's Bar."

Staying at Ruhl Plage, they had a fun dinner and shared bites of the different foods: Crevettes with Sauce Boursin (shrimp sautéed with sun-dried tomatoes, corn and leeks in a garlic, herb cream sauce), Moules Marinieres ou a la Crème (mussels steamed with cream in a garlic wine sauce), Saint-Jacques Sauce Gingembre et Citron Vert (pan-seared sea scallops in a ginger lime sauce) and a plate of Les Petite Farcis a la Nicoise (Nicoise-style stuffed vegetables). They skipped dessert, but all had a shot of Jägermeister, and the ladies paid the check.

Lucas leaned over to whisper in Judy's ear, "I'll thank you later."

Judy smiled. Then, she whispered, "I'll bet you will."

They walked along the Promenade des Anglais to the spectacular facade of the Casino Palais de La Méditerranée.

"I read about this place. It was built in nineteen twenty-nine, and it was the jewel of casinos on the French Riviera," said Judy. "Let's go in, grab a beer and walk around. I also read it has gone downhill in recent years, and it needs a remodel."

As they entered the casino, Lucas said, "I hope they don't demolish this facade. It is magnificent."

They got glasses of Moretti beer at the bar, then wandered around and marveled at many sculptures, the huge staircase, stained glass windows, crystal chandeliers, and a stunning view of the Mediterranean, looking through enormous picture windows. They saw a theater which seated a thousand people. Some of the world's greatest performers had entertained there. No one in their group had any interest in gambling, and Lucas said he was so excited to be in Nice, he did not want to sit still. They all agreed, it would be more fun to wander around and enjoy the sights.

Walking back to the hotel, they held hands and made frequent stops to enjoy the beautiful scenery around them and to share kisses.

In Lucas and Judy's hotel room, Lucas filled the pipe with some crumbled hashish, they all passed it around and drank another beer. Everyone was feeling great and their mood was festive.

Walking out of the hotel, they stepped onto the sidewalk and heard tires screeching. They saw a fast-moving, dark blue BMW crash into a metal lamp post on the sidewalk. It was only 50 feet away from the spot where they all stood.

A man got out of the front passenger seat, looking dazed, bleeding from the forehead and very confused. Lucas ran over to the driver's side and saw the steering wheel pushed into the driver's chest. The young-looking male was groaning and trying to move his legs. However, the steering column pinned him in place. Lucas could see a gash on the driver's right leg and blood gushing out of the wound. In a matter of minutes, an ambulance and a police car arrived.

I don't need this right now, thought Lucas. *I'm high from smoking dope and here come the police.*

The paramedics tried to free the driver, but they needed more help to get him out. George and Lucas stepped in and pulled the steering wheel off the man's chest while the paramedic and a policeman tried to remove him from the front seat. The driver went limp in their arms. Within seconds, he died, right in front of the casino. Lucas, George, Judy and Deanna were so stunned, they could only stand there and watch what happened. Other police cars arrived on the scene.

Since Deanna spoke French, she understood conversation between the ambulance driver and the police. She translated for her friends, "These guys are wanted by the police in Germany. They are members of the notorious Baader-Meinhof Gang. They were fleeing from a local police chase when they drove their BMW onto the promenade. The pedestrians were lucky they were not hit by the BMW."

When the policeman opened the trunk, they saw several automatic rifles and pistols, plus ammunition and plastic explosives. Lucas was not surprised, by the items in the trunk, and he knew the RAF members liked to drive BMWs, based on conversations he had with Andreas.

George and Lucas looked at each other, and Lucas said, "Let's go settle in our room where we have more dope and beer. I do not want to talk with police and answer a bunch of questions."

Walking a little behind the ladies, Lucas asked George, "Do you think we should tell the ladies about Andreas and Ulrike?"

George thought about it for maybe 30 seconds, then he said, "The last time we did that, it didn't work out so well."

"Yeah, but these ladies aren't middle-aged divorcees from Florida," said Lucas. "However, you have a good point. I rarely drop names, and these are not ordinary celebrities; they are not someone you would ask for an autograph."

George was joking when he said, "We could tell them we know the leaders of the RAF, and Andreas and Ulrike aren't so bad, even though they kill people, rob banks and blow up buildings."

Back at the Paradis Hotel again, Lucas said to Judy and Deanna, "George and I want to tell you a story."

Judy asked, "Could you tell us on the way over to Wayne's Bar? I'm too nervous to sit still. I'd like to go dancing and unwind."

"Dancing sounds good," said Lucas, as he handed Judy the pipe.

Exhaling smoke, Deanna said, "Do you realize how close the BMW was to running us down?" They all agreed, but wanted to forget it.

"Yeah, let's finish these beers and go," said George.

It was midnight, so Wayne's should be jumping. As they went out the front entrance of the hotel—this time, they looked both ways before stepping onto the sidewalk. They walked across Avenue de Verdun and turned left onto the sea-front esplanade, paved with brick.

During the walk, they came to Jardin Albert 1, a children's park with a large Ferris wheel and other carnival rides. The park and paths were well-lit, but the rides were closed since it was late at night.

While they were in the park, enjoying the beautiful garden along the walkway, lined with tall sycamore trees and flower beds, Lucas told the ladies how they met Andreas and Ulrike. He told them how they became acquainted, and he said aloud what he thought at the time, "Being friendly was better than being shot." He told them Andreas, Ulrike and other members drove BMWs, and they appeared to be well-educated. Ulrike was a writer for a German magazine. Also, she and Andreas were writing a book, but he did not know the subject.

To summarize his understanding of the RAF and complete the story, Lucas said, "Whatever their reasons may be, Baader-Meinhof Gang members believe if their organization provokes people in large enough numbers, they can overthrow the government. I don't think they are around here anymore, but I don't know where they are, exactly. They might have left Europe."

"You guys sure make strange friendships," said Deanna.

George responded, "Yes, we know. But it's always interesting to see how things plays out."

They crossed Boulevard Jean Jaures, onto Rue de la Prefecture, and then arrived at Wayne's Bar and Restaurant. It looked like any other restaurant in Provence. There was a white awning in front, crowded tables outside and a chalkboard menu beside the front door. However, it was known as the busiest bar on the French Riviera.

At the door, they showed their IDs and stepped into a lively bar where the noise level was high. Being here reminded Lucas of the bars around Long Beach.

A loud trio played "Ob-La-Di, Ob-La-Da" and sounded a lot like the Beatles. They even had the mop-style haircuts. It was too loud to talk. The place was busy, and the long wooden tables with wooden benches all appeared full. Some people even danced on their table. They tried to worm their way to the bar, but gave up and stood to watch the crowd.

When George saw a table, he grabbed it. They ordered 4 shots of Jägermeister and 4 Stella Artois (Belgian beer).

The dance floor was full, and everyone was having a great time. Lucas and Judy were feeling loose and got on the dance floor for 3 long sets of fast songs. Returning to the table, they squeezed onto the wooden bench. George had ordered another round of drinks.

Lucas downed half his beer and told Judy he was going to the restroom. He had to wait in a long line, and it took a while to get back to the table. When he returned, there was a Spanish-looking guy who had his arm around Judy. He was sitting next to her and talking in her ear.

"Oh Lucas, I'm so glad you are back," said Judy. "I asked this guy to leave, but he is a little drunk and very persistent."

Leaning over the Spaniard, Lucas put his hand on the fellow's shoulder and said, "Excuse me, but you are in my seat, and this is my girlfriend. So, please get up."

The Spaniard looked at Lucas, and he got up, slowly. Judy stood, grabbed Lucas by the arm and pulled it, wanting to get away.

"Let's go to the bar. I don't like the company here," said Judy.

The drunk guy grabbed a beer bottle off the table, yelled something in Spanish, pulled his arm back and aimed to hit Lucas in the back of his head. George was standing behind the guy. He grabbed the guy's wrist, yanked his arm back with a sudden jerk downward, and the Spaniard's elbow snapped. The guy screamed out in agony and went down to his knees. George could have finished him, but the guy was done fighting. He moaned in agony, held his crooked arm, and did not try to get up.

Lucas grabbed Judy's hand and headed toward the door. George and Deanna followed them through the crowded bar. When they got close to the entrance, a bouncer stepped in front of Lucas and asked, "Hey, what happened back there?"

Lucas said, "The guy on the floor is drunk, and he tried to hit me from behind. My friend here stopped him, and we thought it best to leave now, so there won't be any more trouble. We had a good time, and you have a great bar."

Instead of asking more questions, the bouncer said, “Okay. I am sorry for the trouble. Thank you for coming.”

Lucas, Judy, George and Deanna walked out into the fresh air.

“Wow, George! You moved fast in there,” Deanna exclaimed.

“It’s all about teamwork, my dear,” he replied.

“I think we’ve had enough negative excitement and challenges for tonight,” said Lucas.

“I think we should walk back to the hotel and all have a nightcap,” Deanna suggested.

In agreement, George said, “You’re my kind of lady.”

Back in the hotel, they all expressed a desire to sleep-in the next morning. They planned to meet at Sarao, a restaurant on the Promenade Anglais for breakfast—or lunch. The desk clerk had told them Sarao had a good selection of food and offered a decent omelette.

Even with today’s excitement behind them, Lucas and Judy were both wound up. They had energetic sex until they fell apart, exhausted, and went to sleep, holding hands.

CHAPTER 9

Barcelona

The next morning at breakfast, Deanna had a *latté* while the others drank Kronenbourg 1664 beers. They all had seen enough of the French Riviera. From here, they would drive straight to Barcelona, more or less.

Judy and Deanna said they both had obligations in Banff, Canada, and they would have to fly home from Barcelona. However, they made it clear they both wanted to see the guys again, and they hoped to get jobs in Garmisch soon.

Lucas was driving. With some hesitation, Judy said to Lucas, "I have not told you this, but I sort of have a boyfriend back home."

He asked her, "Are you bringing him back to Garmisch?"

"No, I won't because I want to be with you," she replied. "I will break it off with him and get out of there, as fast as I can."

Lucas did not know how to respond to Judy. He changed the subject by asking George to hand him and Judy a Peroni from the back.

George gave them each a beer and said, "Since you ladies are leaving us, we only have a short time left to party together. We'd better stop somewhere to finish smoking this hashish and throw away the pipe before we reach the border. We also need more beer."

Lucas advised the others, "Someone told me the automatic penalty for trying to smuggle drugs into Spain is six years plus one day in a Spanish prison—it is not something we want to do."

They drove into Banyuls-sur-Mer, a quaint village on the Bay of Bisque, a few miles north of the Spanish border. After filling the tank with gas, they purchased a case of Kronenbourg 1664, some ham, cheese and bread. Lucas found a quiet spot to park the van, near the promenade, overlooking the bay and the dark-blue Mediterranean Sea. They made small sandwiches, drank beer, smoked hash, laughed and kissed. After tossing the hash pipe in a trash can, they drove to the border crossing without a care in the world.

At the border, Lucas planned to stop at the barrier, but a gendarme waived them through.

"I guess they don't care about you leaving France," said Judy. "But you still must cross over to the Spanish side."

Her observation was right on point because the La Migra (Spanish border guard) took their passports and told them to pull into a parking area on the side of the road. Then, they all had to get out of the van and wait as it was being searched. The La Migra was neat while doing his job. As he moved things around in the van, he put everything back in place. When he finally cleared them to enter Spain, Judy was in the restroom.

Looking at George, Lucas shook his head, saying, "Whew, I'm glad we have nothing illegal."

"I'm paranoid enough. Let's not get caught with drugs," he replied.

Judy came back and said, "I'm starving. Can we stop for lunch soon?"

"Sure, I'm hungry too," replied Lucas. "Let's ask these guys where the locals eat. Although, we have had several good ones, I am tired of eating tourist meals."

Since the La Migra who had searched the van seemed to be a nice guy, Lucas walked over and asked him, "What and where is your favorite restaurant in this area?"

In good English, he replied, "My favorite is the Restaurant Hostel Nou in Girona. If you wait a minute, I'll get you a map."

When he came back, he handed Lucas the map and showed him the way to get there, going south. He said it was about an hour drive on the way to Barcelona.

They all said, "Gracias," and then got in the van.

Leaving the border, George passed out bottles of Kronenbourg 1664, and they drove along the ocean highway, going toward Girona. Lucas told everyone the La Migra also mentioned a place which they should not miss, La Luna Restaurant in Barcelona.

The directions and map worked out well. They did not get lost at all. Restaurant Hostel Nou was on a narrow, well-paved road. Parking was on only 1 side of the street; the other side was lined with trees. This restaurant was 40 years old, and the front of it was not too impressive.

"It has character," said Judy.

Restaurant Hostel Nou was a 1-story building with a long front, shaded by 4 awnings. The dining room had about 10 tables with white tablecloths. Wooden chairs with seat cushions looked comfortable. The back of the dining room opened into a patio dining area which had bare, wood-top tables and wooden chairs without cushion seats.

The patio looked so inviting, they asked to sit out there, although it was a little warm. After studying the menu, they ordered a pitcher of Sangria and Catalan-style seafood paella for everyone. The paella was delightful. The ice-cold Sangria was so good, they ordered another pitcher.

Everyone talked about plans for their last evening together, and where they would stay for the night. Lucas said he would pay for 2 rooms when they get to Barcelona and find a hotel.

Meanwhile, Judy and Deanna made reservations for the next day. They would fly out at 9 p.m. on Air Canada, going first to Frankfurt, then on to Montreal and to Calgary.

Lucas and George made reservations to stay in Sitges campground. It is at the beach and 30 minutes from the airport. They would stay there until they could catch a boat to Ibiza. They hoped to play volleyball, waterski and clean the van while they were at the campground.

Back on the road, they drove 50 miles south to a tourist center at the Plaça de Catalunya (public square in the heart of Barcelona) near Avinguda Diagonal (Diagonal Avenue).

When they stopped, Lucas called the Hotel Medium Prisma on Av. de Josep Tarradellas. He reserved 2 rooms for 1 night.

With the van parked in a nearby garage, they checked into their rooms, showered and dressed for a night out and dinner at La Luna Restaurant.

They met in Lucas and Judy's room, and Lucas offered everyone a Kronenbourg 1664 with a shot of Jägermeister. He suggested, "I think we should roam around, hit a few bars and eat tapas. If we are still hungry, we can go to La Luna for dinner."

Judy said, "It sounds like a good plan; but what is a tapa?"

"Let's go find out. I'm thirsty tonight," said George.

They went into a quaint bar, Taverna Mediterranea. Black-and-white checkered flooring covered the center of the long room. The bar was on the right as you walked in. White tables, draped in black tablecloths, filled the left side of the room. The menu for tapas was on a blackboard, written with chalk. On top of the wooden bar, colorful liquor bottles sat on display. Over the bar, wine glasses hung upside down in a rack. At the end of the dining room, there was a cold case full of great-looking tapas.

Since it was early, this place was not crowded yet. They found seats at the bar and all ordered Pilsner Urquell beers.

The bartender claimed, "This is one of the top-rated beers in the world. It comes from Czechoslovakia."

After discussing the menu, they ordered Fried Calamari, Mussels in a white wine/shallot sauce, and Patatas Blravas (twice-fried Yukon gold potatoes). For side dishes, they chose garlic aioli, spicy tomato sauce, chickpea hummus, grilled flatbread and vegetables.

Next, they moved to the large terrace. In this area, there were aluminum chairs with plastic straps. All the tables were dressed with black tablecloths, white paper napkins in metal holders, and a white candle in the center of each table. Tall palm plants lined the terrace on all sides. Overhead, white awnings gave shade to the tables.

While looking at his map of Barcelona, George suggested, "I think it would be fun to take a walk in the old section of the city, the Barceloneta (small Barcelona). It is right on the water, so we can look around the port. By then, it will be time to go have dinner at La Luna. From the port, the restaurant is only a fifteen-minute walk through the traditional district of sailors and fishermen."

Lucas said, "Great idea." Both ladies agreed, and Lucas called for the check. They left and walked along Carrer Enric Granados.

Rather than walk an hour to the port, they went to Carrer de Balmes and caught a bus to the Barceloneta. On the ride, they circled the Placa de Catalunya, a square in Barcelona which had manicured gardens and impressive fountains, surrounded by white statues.

When they got off the bus at Barceloneta, they turned onto Calle de Balboa and discovered a hidden treasure, a tapas bar, Cerveceria el Vaso de Oro. Here, there were no tables, only stools at the long bar. Glass food cases were filled with tasty-looking tapas. These tapas were made with ingredients such as eggplant, portabellas, whole shrimp, octopus, calamari and dried ham, served on sliced baguettes.

They all ordered the house-made beer and compared it to Italian beers which they had tried before. When they were finished eating tapas, they each had a shot of Jägermeister, and Lucas paid the check.

Back outside, a short walk took them to the water and a marina full of boats, then past the Museu d'Història de Catalunya and along the Pla del Palau to the restaurant.

La Luna Restaurant looked just like Lucas had pictured it. At the front, Lucas saw the cloth LA LUNA sign which hung from an iron rod, attached to the brick facade. Above the doorway, there were 2 windows with iron bars. On their way in, a sandwich board stood at the entrance, and menu specials were handwritten on the chalkboard.

Once inside the doorway, Lucas said, "Wow." He appreciated the layout. This bar and restaurant were well-planned. Brick archways divided the large dining room, and colorful, modern-art paintings hung on all the walls. The dining room was on 2 levels. A wooden staircase led them to the upper level.

Heavy wooden tables and cushioned, wooden chairs were placed along the rail, overlooking the lower dining area. Tall palm plants grew in big pots around the dining room, like those which framed the front entrance. The crowded bar had standing room only. A trio was playing music in the back of the restaurant, and the noise level was very high.

Judy and Deanna looked spectacular, wearing short skirts and colorful blouses. They revealed a proper amount of cleavage which was tasteful and sexy at the same time. Most men paid attention to these lovely Canadian ladies when they walked into a room.

They ordered Red Sangria and the Assorted Tapas Platter—it turned out to be 2 platters. The waiter brought a large Lazy Susan, packed with little white dishes, and loaded with many tapas on big round platters.

"What are all these things? Can you tell us, Lucas?" asked Judy.

"Well, I'll try," he replied.

Pointing to each dish as he spoke, he said, "This is baby octopus, and these are mussels with chorizo. Next, we have fried calamari and a Mediterranean-type salad, roasted tomatoes with fresh mozzarella cheese, potato salad, Spanish olives and meatballs."

After devouring the delicious tapas, those dishes were cleared. Next, they got a big Paellera (paella skillet with 2 handles), full of Barcelona-style Paella, made with chicken, chorizo, shrimp, squid, clams, mussels, piquillo peppers, peas and saffron rice. This food came with crusty, Spanish bread rolls which they ordered another basket of.

After eating, they all felt great and agreed it could have been the best meal of their lives, including Chef Lucas Gary.

Leaving the restaurant, they turned right and walked along Carrer Abaixadors. Lucas and Judy walked quietly, holding hands, kissing and enjoying their evening together. Both were planning for more fun in the privacy of their hotel room.

Lucas and Judy were lagging. Some distance ahead of them, George and Deanna turned right at the next corner, onto Placa de Santa Maria.

When Lucas and Judy got to the corner and turned right, they were shocked. A man, about Lucas' size, stood with his back turned away from them, and facing him were George and Deanna with their hands on their heads. The man was holding something in his right hand.

Lucas did not hesitate, and he moved so fast, neither George nor Deanna saw him coming. Lucas wrapped his left arm around the man's throat, got him in a choke hold, applied pressure, and saw a knife in the man's hand. Lucas said, "Drop the knife, or I'll break your neck."

The man hesitated, a little too long, and Lucas applied even more pressure. Finally, the man dropped the knife, and George kicked it out of the way. To make sure he had no fight left in him, George connected with an elbow to the guy's nose and kicked him in the balls. Lucas let go of his neck, and the guy fell, holding his nose and his crotch as he moaned.

Lucas searched the guy for any more weapons, then looked around and saw a dumpster across the street. George kicked the guy in the crotch again. This time the guy did not moan—he screamed for help, but there was nobody around at this hour of the morning. Lucas told George to grab the guy's feet. They hauled him across the street, heaved him into the dumpster, closed the lid and latched it shut.

When they walked back across the street to the spot where the ladies were waiting, George bent down and grabbed the knife.

"What are you going to do with the knife?" asked Deanna.

George replied, "Let's go catch a bus back to the hotel. I'll dump it on the way to the bus stop."

They got back to the hotel and gathered in Lucas and Judy's room. Lucas set out the Jägermeister and 4 bottles of Kronenbourg 1664 as Judy set out 4 shot glasses. Still shaken, the ladies needed a few minutes to calm down, maybe the guys did too.

"If the guy can't get out of the dumpster, what happens when it is picked up by a garbage truck?" asked Judy.

Lucas smiled at George. Then he said, "Gee, I did not think about it, did you George? What did he want from you, anyway?"

"I don't know. I could not understand him, but I would have reached for my wallet," he replied. "We were isolated from normal business and people as we walked through the port area. So, maybe we should have been more alert about the possibility of a robbery or mugging."

"Let's call it a night," said Lucas. "It's been eventful enough!"

They all agreed to meet for lunch and drinks. Lucas and George would drive the ladies to the airport. Then—off to Banff for the ladies, and—off to Sitges for the men.

The next day at Barcelona airport, Lucas stopped by the travel desk and asked about a boat to Ibiza from Barcelona. He was told to take the boat from Valencia because it was cheaper and a shorter boat ride. So, he and George agreed they would drive to Valencia. They canceled their Sitges campground reservation and made a new reservation for a site at Camping Valencia.

Waiting for Judy and Deanna's flight to board, they all went to the bar in the airport. Each had a shot of Jägermeister and a Pilsner Urquell. Lucas and George said a sad farewell to the Canadian ladies, and they all promised to meet again in Garmisch after Christmas.

Lucas and George went out to the van, opened some Kronenbourg 1664 beers and began a 3-hour drive to Valencia. They had a plan: take a boat to Ibiza and look for Bruno.

CHAPTER 10

Valencia

When they checked into the campground in Valencia, George and Lucas were glad to see a swimming pool, a tennis court and beach volleyball courts. There was also a small store, stocked with all the basics, plus a discothèque which was a welcome bonus.

They found a nice spot under some eucalyptus trees, parked the van, and both headed for the restrooms. There was 1 guy in the restroom. He was about 5'6" and standing in front of the mirror, trimming his hair.

George exclaimed, “It’s Gino!”

Lucas looked closer and said to George, “Yeah, the bartender from The Grill in Garmisch.”

Directing his voice across the room, Lucas said, “Hey, Gino! What are you doing in Valencia?”

Gino recognized the guys and replied, “I’m on my way to Ibiza and Formentera for a week of fun. What are you two doing here?”

“We are also going to Ibiza,” said George, “to look for a guy named Bruno. We heard is a bartender at the Von Steuben Hotel in Garmisch.”

“Bruno?” Gino asked, “Why are you looking for that asshole?”

Looking at George, Lucas said, “I guess we can tell him; he already knows Bruno is a bad guy.”

“Police want Bruno for questioning about the murder of my fiancée last February in Long Beach, California,” Lucas explained. Then, he asked Gino, “Why do you call him an asshole?”

“A waitress who works at The Grill came to work, and her face was all bruised,” said Gino. “She told me Bruno had beaten her for dancing with some other guy. Is he supposed to be in Ibiza? I sure don’t want to be around him.” After pausing for a moment, Gino asked, “What are you going to do when you find him?”

“We don’t have a plan yet,” replied Lucas. “We wanted to go to Ibiza, anyway, and someone told me he was going there.”

George asked Gino, “Why don’t you come over to our van and have a beer with us?”

"Okay. Where is your van?" asked Gino.

"It is in line with the door. You can see it from here, a very dirty, cream-colored VW van," George advised him.

"Great. I'll be over in a few minutes," said Gino.

Returning to the van, they only had 3 Kronenbourg 1664 beers. After Gino gets there, they would go to the campground store and see what beer is available. When Gino knocked on the van door, Lucas slid it open and handed him a beer.

As Gino climbed in, he said, "You might want to close the door while we smoke this joint."

George pulled the door shut, and they all sat at the table.

Gino handed Lucas a perfectly rolled joint, then lit it for him. Lucas took a long hit and handed it to Gino. He took a long hit and handed it to George who did likewise and passed it back to Gino.

Lucas asked, "Gino. Do you know of a good restaurant around here? I think I will be very hungry, pretty soon." They all laughed.

Gino said, "The locals recommend La Luna Valencia."

"We ate at a restaurant in Barcelona which had the same name," said Lucas. "It was maybe the best meal I've ever eaten."

Since Gino already had his reservation for passage to Ibiza, he suggested they call to make theirs when they went to dinner. He thought it would be great if they all went together, and he would bring them a book which describes the island's many activities.

"When does this boat leave?" Lucas asked Gino.

"It's a huge ferry going to Ibiza, and it leaves at eight p.m. tomorrow evening," he replied.

"Perfect," said George. "I can play volleyball in the morning."

Lucas chimed in, "Yeah, and I want to play tennis."

"I don't play tennis, but I can set and dig volleyball," said Gino.

"Okay. We need to buy more beer at the store," Lucas added.

Gino said, "I will clean up and change clothes. When I come back, we can smoke another joint before we go out."

"This is great," said George. "It's like being at home in Manhattan Beach on a Friday night!"

Since George wanted to look around the campground, Lucas walked to the store alone. He considered himself lucky when he found Spaten Munchener beer, so he bought a case.

Lucas got back to an empty van, opened a beer and thought about Gino: *Gino told me he was born and raised in Miami. Later, he lived in the Caribbean, directing movies in the porn industry. He also spent time in New York and Houston, producing TV commercials. Gino has a dark-tan skin color, a large nose, a mustache and a loose-perm hairdo. He can be mistaken for different nationalities and fits in anywhere. He does not arouse suspicion of illegal activity, such as smuggling drugs into the country. Although I am glad Gino has some hashish, it makes me a little nervous. Gino might be a little shady, but he seems to be a friendly and knowledgeable guy who wants to have fun. Besides, he can't be any shadier than Andreas and Ulrike.*

When they were all ready to go, they got back in the van and shared another joint, plus each had a shot of Jägermeister and a Spaten beer. George drove, and Gino sat in the front. Sitting at the back table, Lucas studied the map, and then he said, "It's a forty-minute drive to Puerta de Valencia, then a twenty-minute drive back to the restaurant."

Gino knew right where to go at the port. Lucas and George booked their passage—4th class, sleeping on the deck or in a chair. Driving back north toward La Luna Valencia Restaurant, they decided to put both vans in storage at the port while they went to Ibiza.

The restaurant was inside an old farmhouse, of the sixteenth century. Old-fashioned lamp posts stood out front. The shape of a while crescent moon was high on the building. Below it, a wrought-iron sign had the name, LA LUNA de VALENCIA RESTAURANT. To the left of the wooden double doors, a menu was mounted on the stucco wall. The main dining room had a high ceiling and beige-color, brick walls. Decorations in the restaurant included tapestry art and large oil paintings. Antique clocks filled a fine mahogany shelf which hung on a wall. A candlelit, crystal chandelier hung from the ceiling in the center of the room. Square tables were set with white tablecloths, assorted sizes of wine glasses, silverware and white napkins, folded in a pyramid shape.

Next to their table, a tall rectangular window extended from the top of the wall to within 2 feet of the floor. They got a pitcher of Sangria, and each ordered a 3-course dinner—all different menu choices, except for 1 item: everyone had lemon sorbet after their entrée.

Lucas ordered: Monkfish Medallions with lobster sauce.
Sirloin Steak with Iberian sauce, sweetened with Pedro Ximenez.
Cheese custard tart with blueberries.

George ordered: Hake with chive veloute.
Centre Beef Tenderloin, garnished with foie gras sauce.
Parfait with pistachios and hot chocolate.

Gino ordered: Foie Gras Terrine in Armagnac (brandy).
Lobster Paella (half a lobster, saffron rice and Spanish Chorizo).
Tiramisu with bitter cocoa and raspberry coulis.

Lucas and George agreed this food was as good as what they had eaten at La Luna Barcelona Restaurant. The well-traveled and knowledgeable Gino said his meal was also memorable. They split the check between them after another pitcher of Sangria and a shot of Fundador Brandy which Gino called "Thunderfuck Brandy." It had a real kick.

Arriving back at the campground, they smoked more of Gino's hashish, had shots of Jägermeister and drank several bottles of Spaten beer. They talked about Gino's travels, Andreas and Ulrike, the RAF gang and its future intentions.

"The RAF is considered a threat to all the U.S. bases in Europe," said Gino. "They are all on alert. And now, I think it's time to turn in."

In the morning, Gino joined them for breakfast which Lucas cooked on the Coleman stove. He served ham, tomato and cheese omelettes, plus potato pancakes, Spanish rolls (purchased) and blackberry jelly.

After they washed the breakfast dishes, George said, "I am heading for the beach to play volleyball."

"I'm not a good spiker because I'm too short," said Gino. "But I can set pretty well. Yeah, I think I want to play volleyball too."

They all agreed to meet back at the van, by 3 p.m.

Before Gino and George left for the beach, Lucas told them he would try to play tennis. He also wanted to shower before they drive to the port and ride the ferry to Ibiza.

It was almost noon. When Lucas walked past the swimming pool, it was crowded with people because it was getting hot. No one was on the tennis court.

Lucas went into the white stucco building, next to the tennis court. There were 4 people inside, 2 blonde ladies who looked to be about 25 years old, a Spaniard was behind the counter, and another Spaniard was talking to the ladies.

The guy who was behind the counter looked at Lucas and jerked his head back as if to say, *"What do you want?"*

Lucas said, "Hi, would it be possible to play tennis today?"
The Spaniard asked, "Do you have someone to play with, and do you have your own equipment?"

"No, I don't. I'm hoping to rent a racket and find someone here to play with," replied Lucas.

The other guy who was standing with the ladies said, "I can play, and I think these ladies will play. Do you want to play doubles?"

The taller of the 2 ladies said, "We would love to play. How about mixed-doubles?"

The counter guy pulled 4 Wilson rackets off a rack behind him, and he told them they could pay when they finished playing.

The players introduced themselves and walked over to the court. It was a clay court, something Lucas had never played on. They spun rackets to see who the partners would be. Lucas and the taller lady got W (s) pointed down. The other guy and the shorter lady matched with their W (s) pointing up. Next, they all hit some balls to warm up.

Lucas felt uncomfortable and slightly disoriented which was not his usual, confident demeanor on a tennis court. *It must be the hashish I smoked this morning after breakfast,* he thought.

The more they warmed up, the more Lucas realized this would be a difficult match. Everyone seemed to hit the ball well, like they knew what they were doing.

Lucas' partner gave her name as Emily, and the other lady's name was Abby. They lived in Sydney, Australia. They came here to get jobs and stay for a year. The young guy said his name was Emilio. He was a law student who lived in Madrid, and he was on a holiday.

Serving 1st, Lucas got them off to a good start with well-placed serves and solid strokes. He and Emily won the 1st game 40-15.

Lucas always felt he could cover the court better if he played right inside the service line, and he could move forward easier than he could backward. It was working, so far. Both he and Emily were hitting crisp shots, and they led 4-1. Lucas realized how focused he was, seeing the ball all the way to his racket strings. However, as so often was the case when he got a lead, he seemed to ease off a little. He barely missed a few shots long or wide, and he double-faulted.

They lost the next 4 games, then won 2 games and led 6-5. Emilio hit a cross-court shot which Lucas tried to chase down. He also missed a shot down the right line and over the net post. Lucas thought it hit the end line, but Abby called it out. They played a tie break, and after leading 6-3, they lost 8-6.

When Lucas got behind in a match, he had always regained his concentration and come back. With determination, even if he did not win the match, he could always make it respectable.

He started to make close shots because he got to the ball quicker and set up his powerful topspin shots from both sides. When Emily was at the net, he also got back on several lob shots. They won the 2nd set 6-2.

Emilio asked, "Hey, Lucas. Do you want to wager the winner of this set pays for the court, plus rackets and balls?"

When Lucas turned to Emily, she felt confident and said, "Sure, we'll accept your wager."

Lucas, Abby and Emily all won their serves; and Lucas and Emily led 2 games to 1. It was hot out there in the sun, and Lucas wished he had a beer. Then, he realized what he really wanted was to finish this set and invite these ladies back to the van for a Spaten beer.

Lucas and Emily finally broke Emilio's service and now led 3-1. But Lucas lost concentration somewhat, hit a forehand long, hit a cross-court backhand out, double-faulted his serve and lost his service. In the next game, Abby held her service with well-placed strokes to 3-3. Now, Lucas felt his game was on, and he hit a backhand service return down the middle which broke Abby's serve. Lucas and Emily led the 3rd set 5-3.

Serving in the following game, Lucas' 1st serve went down the middle and hit the line for 15-love. Then, Lucas hit his favorite serve to the add court, perfectly placed and wide enough; Abby could not get a racket on it. It was now 30-love. Emilio hit a nice return, down the line, but Emily could not react in time. It was 30-15.

Lucas served to Abby, she returned it to Emily who hit it down the line to Emilio. He hit it cross-court to Lucas' forehand. Lucas had to hit on the run, and his shot went back cross-court at such a great angle, Emilio could only watch it go by. Now, it was 40-15 which seemed to take the wind out of the opponents' sails. Lucas hit his 1st serve into the net. His 2nd serve went wide to the right, but curved back enough to catch the outside line. Lucas and Emily won the 3rd set, 6-3, and the match.

When everyone shook hands, Emilio seemed upset about losing. On the way back to the clubhouse, Emilio said to Lucas, "What are you, a tennis hustler?"

Lucas replied, "Well, it was your idea to play for who pays. No, I'm not a hustler, but I am flattered to hear you think I'm so good."

Now, Emilio looked irritated and angry.

Here we go again—another hot-headed Spaniard, thought Lucas.

Emilio dropped his racket on the counter, paid his half of the rental fees and stormed out of the building. Everyone else turned in their rackets, and Abby paid the remaining fees.

Lucas was dying for a beer. He asked the ladies if they would like to have a beer and meet his friends at his campsite. When they got to the van, George was back from the beach.

"Where is Gino?" asked Lucas.

"He's getting his stuff together for Ibiza," replied George.

Introducing the ladies, Lucas said, "George, this is Emily and Abby, two excellent tennis players who came from Sydney, Australia."

Emily chimed in, "Are you going to Ibiza?"

"Yes, tonight at eight p.m." said Lucas.

"We wanted to go to Ibiza, but our friends expect us to meet them in Madrid, so we have to leave tomorrow," said Abby. "Then, we plan to look for jobs."

George asked, "Where do you plan to look for work?"

Abby replied, "We're not sure, maybe on a ship or at a Club Med. We have heard some good things about working for the American military in Germany and other places in Europe."

Hearing this, George told them about Garmisch, the great skiing, and how easy it is to find work when winter hiring begins which occurs as soon as it snows. He told them he and Lucas were returning to Garmisch after they see Ibiza, Rome, Florence and Oktoberfest in Munich, plus other places where they might end up.

Gino came over, Lucas made introductions, and they all got in the van. Gino passed around another joint, and George passed around 5 Spaten beers. While Gino and the ladies told funny travel stories, Lucas felt like a traveling newcomer, but he planned to catch up.

Everyone thought they were starving, thanks to Gino's hashish. So, they went to the bar and ordered pizza, plus 5 Pilsner Urquell beers.

Lucas paid the tab. Tennis cost him nothing, and he felt he should buy the beers and pizza.

Gino told the ladies more about Garmisch, the International Bar and Grill, the benefits of working for the military and where to go to apply for jobs. It was almost 6 p.m. and time for the guys to get on the road. Their ship would leave at 8 p.m. So, they walked the ladies out, said goodbye and told them they hoped to see them in Garmisch.

Lucas and George went back to their van. Gino got his van and brought it back to their campsite. He would follow behind them on the drive over to the port.

As he handed Lucas a book about the history, geography and things to do in Ibiza and Formentera, Gino said, "If George is driving to the ferry, you can read about the islands.

"I have heard about the riotous nightlife there," said George.

Gino responded, "That's why we are going there, isn't it?"

"I brought two books to read on the beach," said Lucas. "One is *The Godfather*, by Mario Puzo. The other is *Ball Four*, a baseball book about the Yankees during the time when Mickey Mantle played. It was written by Jim Bouton, a former Yankee pitcher."

"I've read the snorkeling and diving is spectacular around the islands," said Gino.

"We'll be there tomorrow morning to find out," replied George.

It was time to go. They opened 3 Spaten beers, got into their vans and took off for the port.

CHAPTER 11

Ibiza

Lucas, George and Gino boarded the ferry to Ibiza at 7:30 p.m. They each carried several bottles of Spaten beer in their backpacks. Lucas also had a new bottle of Jägermeister. They all brought sleeping bags to sleep on the deck—4th class with the hippies.

At the bar, it pleased them to order Stella Artois, the great Belgian Beer. They had to stand and drink because the bar was crowded. Gino was getting cozy with a hippie-looking lady, named Annie something, who wore a long dress, sandals and a funky wide-brimmed hat. She was friendly; however, she did not look very clean.

Lucas looked for a quiet place on deck where he could read. At the rear of the ferry, he found a spot with a light on the wall over his head. After crawling into his sleeping bag, he opened *The Godfather* and read about 25 pages. He was already hooked on the book, but he dozed off and slept until the sun woke him up. When he stood, Lucas was surprised to see they were still in the Port of Valencia. In his deck area, most of the passengers were sleeping while others were just waking up. He had no idea what caused the delay in departure.

Lucas gathered his things, went to the snack bar and ordered a Spanish omelette. In Long Beach, Spanish omelettes have tomatoes, garlic, onions and bell peppers. Here, however, he got Spain's version: eggs with potatoes, onions and grease. Sitting at the table and gazing at the ocean, he overheard someone say the ferry had engine trouble.

George arrived and asked, "Where did you sleep last night?"

"I was somewhere on the rear deck of the ferry," said Lucas. "Where did you sleep?"

"I slept on a bench in the lounge with about fifty hippies," replied George. "Have you seen Gino?"

"No," replied Lucas. "I just got my breakfast."

When George asked what he was eating, Lucas said, "I ordered a Spanish omelette, but it was a flat omelette with diced potatoes and onion, all mixed with a lot of grease. It came with a chunk of crusty Spanish bread. At least, I washed it down with a Spaten beer."

"It sounds bad," said George. "I think I'll have a sweet roll and a beer. When I last saw Gino, he was carrying his sleeping bag and heading to the deck with the hippie chick who wore the grandma dress."

Suddenly, they heard the engines working. As the sound got louder, the ferry began to move away from the dock. Several people on the ferry had tossed rolls of toilet paper to their friends on the dock. While people on the dock were cheering and waving their hands, the toilet paper was streaming from ship-to-shore. On the ferry, the quiet atmosphere changed to party time!

It was about a 4-hour trip to Ibiza from Valencia. Lucas and George knew they had better grab seats while some were still available. They found two lounge chairs on the rear sundeck, set down their packs and sleeping bags, grabbed two Spatens and got comfortable. Lucas took out *The Godfather,* and George read about the islands in the travel book.

They arrived in Sant Antoni de Portmany, Ibiza, about 6 p.m. Gino caught up with them as they were departing the ferry. He said, "I found a place to stay for a reasonable price. It's convenient to restaurants and clubs in Ibiza Town where the action is."

Lucas asked Gino, "Where is Annie?"

"She left with some people she knows, heading to someplace where there are caves," Gino answered.

They checked into the Hotel Montesol Ibiza, the oldest hotel in Ibiza. It is on Passeig de Vara de Rey, a few minutes away from the port. They got a room with 3 single beds for 1 night. Tomorrow, they would be off to Formentera.

Hotel Montesol is a massive 4-story hotel with a coral-color exterior and white trim, built on a little mountain by the sea. It has a beautiful terrace, with tables and chairs for dining, which overlooks Vara de Rey (central promenade) across from Dalt Vila (upper town). The hotel has 55 rooms, and each room has an outside balcony; many have views of the harbor and the Dalt Vila. Tonight, their room was on the 3rd floor, overlooking the port.

Gazing at the beautiful, panoramic view, Lucas saw the ferry which they had arrived on. While there were other large boats and yachts in the port, the ferry stood out as the biggest vessel, floating in calm water which was clear as crystal. Outward of the cove, he could see the dark-blue Mediterranean Sea with white caps, rolling in the distance. The view was truly remarkable.

Lucas, George and Gino went for a walk on Passeig de Vara de Rey. The restaurant which Gino led them to was an ancient building, painted with Ibiza's standard colors: coral with white trim. The front entrance was a narrow, open doorway. From a tall post at the left of the doorway, a wrought-iron lantern shed light on the entrance. Below the lantern, a white, glass-covered menu cabinet hung on the stucco wall, and the daily specials were hand-written. Right of the doorway, a big wrought-iron sculpture hung on the wall, depicting the black silhouette of a sailing vessel with four sails blowing in the wind. Below it, the name of the restaurant, eL CORSARIO, was also sculpted in wrought-iron, and the black letters cast bold, individual shadows on the stucco.

A young hostess greeted them, inside the open doorway, and Gino asked for seating on the roof terrace. At their table, the view was even more spectacular than the view from their room at the Montesol Hotel. The terrace was about half-full of people dining, most were middle-aged or older, and they all looked conservative. Here, the atmosphere differed greatly from the ferry which carried so many hippies.

None of them wanted a lot of food. They shared a large platter of Fried Calamari and a large bowl of delicious Pisto, a Spanish vegetable stew, made with tomatoes, garlic, onions, bell pepper, eggplant and cumin (similar to Ratatouille). They drank a pitcher of Sangria, Lucas paid the check, and they headed out in search of some nightlife.

As all of them would soon find out, nightlife in Ibiza is almost too wild, even by Lucas' standards for fun.

Back in their hotel room, Gino passed a joint around, and each had a shot of Jägermeister. Then, they went down to the hotel bar, and drank Spanish beer, Estrella Damm. It is a lager beer which they enjoyed; but they all agreed it was not as good as the best German, Belgian or Czech beers. Later in the evening, they found a place called Toto's Bar which had a DJ and loud music. Lucas, George and Gino sat on a bank of cushioned benches with their backs to a wall. They were facing the bar and could see the DJ on stage. Lucas thought about the name of the bar, *Toto's*. It made him think of Topo, the very charming Argentinean waiter who they had met in Nice. He hoped he would see the likeable fellow again. Perhaps, Topo would make it to Garmisch.

As they sat in the crowded bar, watching people and listening to the music, Lucas found 1 song most interesting. He had to ask Gino if he knew what musical group the DJ was playing.

Gino shouted back, "The group is The Moody Blues, a rock group from England, and the album is called *Threshold of a Dream*."

The busy setting and hearing this new sound gave Lucas a cosmic feeling, something seemed outside reality. In his mind, he drifted back to nineteen fifty-seven: In a phone booth on Lakewood Boulevard in Long Beach, California, he read what someone had written on the wall, *"Reality is a hallucination caused by an alcohol and drug deficiency."* He always remembered the writing because he left his wallet in the phone booth.

Lucas heard most bars in Ibiza stayed open until 6 a.m., and some bars never closed, but he and Gino were done about 2 a.m. They went back to their room and fell into beds. Lucas slept until 10 a.m.

When Lucas got up, Gino was gone. George was still asleep because he had stayed at the bar, talking to a young married couple, Scott and Faye, who came from Berkeley and looked like hippies.

Lucas put on cream-colored shorts, a blue T-shirt and sandals, then went to look for Gino. He found Gino sitting at an outdoor café with Scott and Faye. They waved Lucas over, and Scott grabbed him a chair from the next table.

"Wow," said Lucas. "What a night!"

"Every night in Ibiza is like a giant party," replied Scott.

They talked about going to Formentera and things they wanted to do when they got there. All three confirmed their plans to work and ski in Garmisch for the winter. George joined them 30 minutes later, and he looked like hell.

I doubt if I look much better, thought Lucas.

After ordering a Spanish omelette with bread, jelly and a Stella Artois beer, Lucas gobbled his food, ordered a 2nd beer and felt almost decent.

Gino wanted to go shopping for snorkels, masks and fins. He was told the water around Formentera was some of the clearest water you could ever swim in. After shopping, they made their reservations for the ferry to Formentera. When they checked out of the hotel, it was time to head for the port. Loaded down with gear, they grabbed a beer and hamburger at an American café on the way to the ferry. Scott and Faye had a BMW motorcycle which they were taking to Formentera, and they all watched a crane lift it onto the ferry deck. Lucas, George and Gino planned to rent bicycles for transportation on the island.

The cruise to Formentera took an hour and a half. A crew member told them about a cheap place to stay, a small hotel and restaurant which was right on the beach, but it was a 1-hour walk (4 kilometers) from the port. They each rented a bicycle for the week and rode to San Roqueta, carrying all their stuff in backpacks. Lucas fell in love with this place. It was away from the busy-ness of Ibiza Town and only yards from a secluded beach. Based on your preference, they would serve breakfast in your room, or the restaurant, or in the outdoor area. A thatched, overhead structure shaded the outside tables. Built like a carport with stone pillars for support, it was painted white and matched the rest of the building.

Lucas thought he had found a paradise island. He bought 6 bottles of Estrella Damm, the local's favorite beer, according to the bartender. On the sand, he claimed a beach chair and used his towel as a side-table for his book, *The Godfather.* Next, he opened a beer. The smoothness and the taste of this lager impressed him. According to the label, Estrella Damm was brewed in Barcelona.

While Gino and George rode their bikes to a place called Platja d'en Bossa on the other side of the island, Lucas was thrilled to stay and enjoy the special service he was receiving at this little beach-side hotel. He spent a full day and a half, relaxing at this same spot on the beach, going to the restaurant for more beer, eating tapas and going to the restroom. The restaurant served excellent tapas, and they always had a good variety. They offered arroz del día (rice of the day), meat, seafood, albóndigas (meatballs), some very good potato salad, and fried calamari which was his favorite.

Lucas loved being here. In the afternoon of the 2nd day, a dark-haired, well-endowed lady put her beach towel on the sand, not too far from him. He waited until she got settled, then he walked over and said, "Hello! Do you speak English?"

The lady acted startled, at first. Then, she looked into Lucas' blue eyes and replied with a German accent, "Yes, I do."

"Would you care to join me for a beer?" asked Lucas.

"Okay, I'll move over there. It looks like you would have more stuff to move," she replied.

Lucas helped her move things, then he opened a beer for each of them. They introduced themselves before getting seated, and her name was Gabrielle. Lucas learned she was an Air Traffic Controller from Hanover in northwest Germany. She came with a friend who met an Italian guy, but she had not seen her friend for the last 2 days.

"Well, Gabrielle, maybe it was my good luck. Would you have dinner with me tonight?" he asked.

She flashed him a wide smile and said, "Yes. I will."

After getting to know each other on the beach during the afternoon, they had a nice dinner in the hotel restaurant, sitting at a corner table with fresh flowers and a candle in the center.

Lucas had Monkfish with a delightful brandy tomato sauce, similar to Sauce *Américaine.* Gabrielle had Mussels with white wine, shallots and cream. They shared a small loaf of local bread.

For dessert Gabrielle had Crema Catalana, the restaurant's version of crème *brûlée*, and Lucas had a Peach Tarte with almond meringue. They each had a shot of Fundador Brandy with dessert.

Lucas paid the check and left a generous tip because the servers had been taking such good care of him in the restaurant.

They went to Lucas' room, and Gabrielle surprised him. She reached in her bag, pulled out a little case, opened it, pulled out a joint and asked, "Would you like to get high?"

"I sure would. I want to go where you go," said Lucas.

They smoked half of the joint, had a shot of Jägermeister, opened 2 bottles of Estrella Damm and walked out onto the beach. Then, they took off their sandals and waded in the refreshing Mediterranean water where they kissed and explored each other with roaming hands.

Back in his room, they slowly undressed each other. Lucas could see Gabrielle did not shave her armpits, but she shaved her shapely legs. Lucas loved women with medium-large breasts, and Gabrielle's breasts were marvelous.

Before he fell asleep, Lucas thought about how he felt when he made love with Gabrielle: *It was like going to another world.*

They awoke in each other's arms. Gabrielle went to the bathroom. When she got back, Lucas did the same. When he came back, they made love again, each in lust with the other.

Having missed breakfast, Lucas and Gabrielle went to the restaurant for lunch. Both were drinking Estrella Damm. Lucas was looking at the *International Herald*, as he read to Gabrielle, *"Franco's regime is throwing three thousand hippies off Ibiza and Formentera. According to the regime, these hippies give the place a bad name; but the islanders don't agree—locals insist the hippies are simply tourists."*

"Do you think they'll deport us too?" asked Lucas.

"No, you look too straight to pass for a hippie, but they might think I'm a hippie," replied Gabrielle.

Lucas laughed and reassured her; he would say she was with him. Gabrielle thought for a minute, then said, "I should go to the port, and see if my friend Kirstin is leaving today. I was going to leave with her, but I guess she is still with the Italian guy. Would you be willing to go with me and ride our bikes over to the port, so I can look for her?"

Lucas agreed to go. At the port, a mass of people on the dock appeared to be hippies. Some looked angry while most looked sad. Seeing George and Gino, Lucas asked them what was going on.

"Franco wants all the hippies thrown off Formentera and Ibiza," said Gino. "People are trying to find out if they have to leave and when it will happen. Many of these people have been here for months, some even years. Besides, what defines a hippie?"

The 4 of them worked their way closer to the ferry. Gabrielle wanted to check if her friend had used her reservation to leave the island.

"Hey, there's the guy who is dating Kirstin, but I don't see her," said Gabrielle, pointing to a tall, black-haired guy.

“Oh no,” Gino said. “Lucas, he’s the guy we spoke about. He tends bar at the Von Steuben Hotel in Garmisch.”

Lucas exclaimed, “That’s Bruno Castignoli?”

“You know him?” asked Gabrielle.

“I don’t know him, except by reputation, a bad one,” replied Gino.

“Now we know who we’re looking for,” Lucas said to George.

Gabrielle looked surprised when she asked, “You are looking for Kirstin’s boyfriend?”

“I guess so,” said Lucas. Then, he added, “Police in Long Beach, California, suspect Bruno of murdering someone I was close to. But he came to Europe before they could charge him.”

“Well, you found him. What will you do now?” asked Gabrielle.

“We think he will go back to work in Germany for the winter,” said Lucas. “We will probably see him there, and then we can figure out what we want to do.”

There was a short silence before Lucas added, “Well, we are not going to do anything about him here. So, let’s all go back to San Roqueta and have some fun. Okay?”

At once, everyone said, “Yes!”

Quietly, Gabrielle said to Lucas, “I hope Kirstin is in her room.”

Arriving back at the hotel in San Roqueta, Lucas went to the front desk with Gabrielle to ask if Kirsten had checked out. The desk clerk said no one had seen her friend for 2 days; the clerk had asked about her, and the boyfriend claimed she must have left the island because he had not seen her either. Since then, the boyfriend checked out of his room, and there was no sign of Gabrielle’s friend.

After a short discussion, they asked the clerk about larger rooms. Gabrielle turned in her room key. Then, she and Lucas moved into a room with a queen size bed. After settling things in their new room, they went down to the beach, enjoyed the afternoon, watched the sunset and got further acquainted.

While they were eating dinner, Lucas asked Gabrielle, “Have you ever heard of the Baader-Meinhof Gang?”

Gabrielle looked surprised and concerned. “Why do you ask? Are you a police officer?” she asked.

“No way!” said Lucas. “As I told you, I’m a chef and restaurant owner from Long Beach, California. I asked because George and I met Andreas and Ulrike in Austria where we gave them a ride. Then we saw them again in Venice, Italy, and we seemed to become friends.”

Gabrielle looked puzzled, and then thoughtful. She said, “My brother is an RAF member. The police want to find him. I have met Andreas and Ulrike, and I also consider myself their friend.”

Lucas felt dazed during dinner. Events of the day had stunned him. They finished dinner and went back to their room. When Gabrielle pulled out a joint, Lucas said, "Great idea. Please, light it up."

They smoked half of the joint, had shots of Jägermeister, opened Estrella Damm beers and went to the beach for another late-night stroll. Sitting near the water, small waves were splashing on the shore, and the moon was glowing over the sea.

Leaning against each other, Lucas said, "You know, Gabrielle, I'm still in shock about what happened today."

"I am too, Mein Schatze (My Dear). It shows what a small world this big world is," said Gabrielle.

Lucas looked at her and said, "Huh?" They laughed and kissed.

He thought, *I could get used to this!*

However, their time together would end soon because Gabrielle had to go home to Hanover. Talking about what they wanted to do together, both agreed they would leave the next day and return to Ibiza.

Back in their room, making love felt desperate and possessive. Neither wanted to let go of what they found together on Formentera.

The next morning, they had breakfast with George and Gino. Lucas announced he and Gabrielle would catch the ferry and return to Ibiza for 2 days. Then, Gabrielle had to leave for Valencia. George and Gino wanted to stay on Formentera for another day. They would all meet again at the Hotel Montesol on Ibiza. Lucas planned to get a room there for his and Gabrielle's last 2 nights together.

After breakfast, Lucas and Gabrielle checked out of the hotel, ferried to Ibiza, and checked into the Hotel Montesol.

While they were getting settled in the room, Gabrielle said, "I should try to find Kirsten. Let's call the hotel on Formentera again. I want to ask if someone saw her last night or today."

Gabrielle used the phone in the bar, but had no luck finding anyone who had seen Kirsten.

"I want to see the police and report her missing," said Gabrielle.

"Let's go," replied Lucas.

When they asked the bartender how to find the police station, he gave them directions and a map. They did a 20-minute walk across town to the Comisaría De Policía. At the station, they spoke to an officer who assured them the police would do their best to find Kirstin or discover where she may have gone.

The officer said, "Believe it or not, with all the tourists who come in and out of here, we don't lose many." He convinced Gabrielle she had nothing to gain by staying in Ibiza. The police would do everything possible to find her friend.

On their last night in Ibiza, Lucas, Gabrielle, George, Gino, Scott and Faye had dinner as a group. It was their going away party. The following day, they would take the ferry and return to Valencia. From there, everyone would scatter to different places. Gino was headed back to Garmisch, Scott and Faye to Madrid, and Gabrielle to Hanover.

Lucas and George thought about Rome, Florence and Oktoberfest in Munich. They also heard Torremolinos was a happening place. Since Gino told them it was too early to get jobs, there was no hurry in returning to Germany. The winter hiring starts around Thanksgiving or Christmas, depending on when it snows.

Lucas and George figured they were 7 hours from Torremolinos, and they decided to go there. They would leave the next day after they picked up the VW van in Valencia.

Early the next day, the whole group got together, ate Paella and bread, drank Sangria and had shots of Jägermeister.

After the meal, Scott got out his pipe and some Afghan Red hashish. They all walked to the port and sat on a dock. As they watched sailboats move across the water on the other side of the marina, they drank Estrella Damm and passed the hash pipe around.

Lucas felt so free and happy. He enjoyed being with his buddy George and new friends: Gino, Gabrielle, Scott and Faye. But he did not forget his quest to find Bruno Castignoli, keep him from getting away with murder, and maybe keep him from murdering someone else.

George and Lucas were ready for some good beach volleyball, body surfing, and whatever adventures should arise on the Costa del Sol. They learned the temperature is always in the 80s, and it seldom rained in the area. There would be lots of sunshine! Everyone was anxious to leave, but it would be a few hours before the ferry boarded passengers.

Gabrielle took Lucas for a walk while the others stayed on the dock. They went to their room at Hotel Montesol and experienced an intense lovemaking session which seemed perpetual. Lucas wanting this feeling to continue. However, now it was time for them both to get back to reality, whatever that was.

Once again, Lucas remembered the writing he found when he was a teenager. Scribbled on the wall of a phone booth, it read, *"Reality is a hallucination caused by an alcohol and drug deficiency."*

The ferry was packed with expelled hippies who were going back to the mainland. Lucas and Gabrielle found a small alcove on the upper deck and claimed it as their personal spot where they could lie on their sleeping bags or lean against the wall. It had a light on the wall above. They talked, read to one another and drank Estrella Damm until they fell asleep, cuddled up.

Shortly before the ferry docked at Port Valencia, Lucas and Gabrielle woke up. Through an emotional goodbye, both agreed they had a great time together and hoped they would soon meet again. Gabrielle gave him her phone number in Hanover, and she told him he could visit anytime if he was in her area.

Saying goodbye to Gino, both Lucas and George vowed they would see him in Garmisch. They made the same promise as Scott and Faye got onto their BMW bike and headed for Madrid.

Lucas and George got their VW van out of storage and filled the tank with gas. Next, they stopped to get beer and thought they were lucky to find a case of Löwenbräu Pilsner.

Now, they were headed south, toward Malaga and Torremolinos.

CHAPTER 12

Costa del Sol

Driving through Malaga, Lucas and George changed their minds and did not stop. Their prime target was Torremolinos, known for sandy beaches and great nightlife on the southern coast of Spain.

At 6 p.m., coming into Torremolinos, they felt overwhelmed by huge crowds of people on the street, in the cafés and in the plazas.

They drove another 16 minutes, arrived in Fuengirola, and found parking by the port on Paseo Marítimo Rey de España. They walked to Calle Martínez Catena and into the London Pub, a corner bar where they ordered Harps beers and watched 2 guys throwing darts. Standing at the bar, they downed those beers and ordered a couple more.

A guy who had been throwing darts came over to the bar for another beer. He asked Lucas and George, "Are you Yanks?"

George replied, "Yes, we're from California. My name is George, from Manhattan Beach. And, this is my friend Lucas, from Long Beach."

This tall guy had short blonde hair. He said, "My name is David, from Australia, but I've lived in London for three years."

David got his 2 bottles of English Bass beer and asked, "Would you like to play a game of cricket darts with us?"

"Sure, we enjoy playing darts," replied Lucas.

David introduced his friend as a Brit from London, named Cedric, who said, "Do you Yanks want to play for beers?"

"Okay," said George. "Can we warm up a little before we start?"

While they were playing darts, David told them about a bar in Los Boliches, a small beach town which is a short distance away. He said, "This bar, named The Alamo, is also a restaurant, owned by Ty Harden, an American movie actor. They serve Texas barbecue food." Cedric described some of the activity in Los Boliches and said Ty Harden also owns several laundromats in the area.

"It sounds good. Are you going there tonight?" asked Lucas.

"We go every night," said Cedric. "Ty is nice, but watch out for *her highness*, his British royalty girlfriend, or so she says."

"Oh, she's not too bad," said David. "She's a little picky sometimes when we're helping in the bar, the kitchen or the laundromat."

Cedric said, "Ty is a great guy and a fantastic volleyball player. Around here, he and David are one of the best beach volleyball doubles-teams. There are a few local Spanish guys who play well, but they are macho and hot-headed. They hate to lose."

"Oh yeah, we discovered those qualities in some young Spaniards, up close and personal," said Lucas.

They played 2 out of 3 games of cricket. Then, the last game went down to the last bull. David and Cedric won.

"Hey, I didn't know Yanks could play darts so well," said David.

"Yeah, and we also play beach volleyball," replied George.

"Good, maybe we can take on the Spaniards," said David.

He told them about a campground in Cabopino, only 20 kilometers away and on the coast. Lucas told David and Cedric they would meet them at The Alamo, right away, because Texas barbecue food sounded good. Before leaving, Lucas paid for everyone's beer.

They got lucky and found a parking place in Los Boliches on Paseo Marítimo Rey de España. They were 1 block away from 77 Calle Poeta Salvador Rueda, the address of The Alamo.

Lucas made a mental note, looking at the front of the bar/restaurant from across the street: *The building is painted a light brown color. Wood trim, shutters and door frames are all chestnut color. The Alamo Bar and Restaurant occupies two floors, yet it is only a small portion of a large building. The upper floor has large glass doors, leading out to a narrow balcony, all surrounded by a wrought-iron railing about waist high. On the ground floor, the main entrance has double doors, made of solid, dark wood with brass pull-handles which open out toward the street. To the right, a glass case hangs on the wall with a menu inside, illuminated by an iron lantern. There is a 3-by-4-foot window, centered in the front, covered with iron bars. To the right of the window, there is a narrow, arched doorway with an iron gate which looks like private access. It has no handle, only a key lock and hinges.*

As George and Lucas walked into The Alamo, they saw 6 tables on their left and the bar on their right. Behind the bar, bottles and glasses lined the wall. In front of the bar, there were 15 bar stools which were all occupied. The tables were also full. Lucas and George stood by the door way and looked around. The kitchen area was behind the end of the bar. To the right of the open kitchen door, a stairway led upstairs to more restaurant seating. This place was busy, and Lucas recognized Ty Harden from his television shows, *Cheyenne* and *Bronco Lane*.

Lucas thought: *Gino would have loved this since he worked in the movie industry.*

David was sitting at the bar with Cedric, and he saw them come in. As he waved them over, Lucas and George went to the bar.

"What do you two want to drink?" asked David.

"Do they have any German beer?" asked Lucas.

"No, mostly English beer," replied David. "They have Budweiser, Harps, Bass, Alhambra and Estrella Damm, a Spanish beer."

Both Lucas and George went for the Estrella Damm. Then, David introduced them to Ty Harden who said, "Oh yes, David told me about you guys. So, you have a new VW van, huh?"

"Yes. We have a new van," said George. "We plan to sleep in it while we stay at the campground in Cabopino."

Ty excused himself because he was busy. He told them they would talk later after it slows down. David, Cedric, Lucas and George grabbed a table when a foursome left, and they helped clear the table. It was so busy the staff could not keep up. The food from the kitchen looked great, but it was coming out slow. They all had Ty's famous Texas style pork ribs with fries and coleslaw. It was delicious.

This place reminds me of home, thought Lucas. *It's very similar to being in Long Beach, California.*

Lucas figured Ty was about 8 years older than him, maybe 38. He looked tan and had a full well-trimmed beard which was white. His medium-length hair was blonde, but it was almost as white as his beard. He also looked fit.

When they finished eating, Ty came over to their table. He brought Estrella Damm beers for Lucas and George. Sipping on a Budweiser, Ty said, "I can't get used to Spanish beer."

"Since I got to Europe, I have developed a taste for German beer. It's really good," Lucas replied.

"I have tried very little German beer," Ty said. "I made a few movies in Spain and loved it here so much, I bought this place and then some laundromats. Let's go back into my office and talk."

The office was also a small storeroom, but there was room for 3 chairs and a small desk. Ty reached in a drawer, pulled out a small brass pipe, loaded it with hashish, lit it and passed it to Lucas who took a drag and passed it on to George.

"As you can see, I need some good help," said Ty. "Have either of you ever tended bar or cooked in a restaurant?"

"I tended bar when I was in college and Lucas is a chef," said George. "He owns two restaurants, back in Long Beach."

Ty said, "Are you serious? Will you be around here for a while? I need extra help here while I take a few trips." He was smiling now.

Lucas and George looked at each other. George said, "We haven't thought about how long we will stay because we don't have an agenda. We heard you have good beach volleyball games here, so we came to play, and we want to enjoy the night life. We will let you know in a couple days, maybe even tomorrow."

Lucas and George checked into Camping Cabopino, the place which David had recommended. They found a spot under some trees and got a good night's sleep.

Breakfast in the campground restaurant was the usual, somewhat greasy, Spanish omelette, and bread with jelly, plus a couple of beers. They drove back to Los Boliches, got to The Alamo Bar about 11:15 a.m. and sat at the bar, next to David and Cedric.

After ordering Estrella Damm beers, Lucas asked David, "When does lunch start?"

David answered, "You'll know," as he nodded.

Ty Harden walked out of the kitchen and smiled. He had a great smile. He said, "I'm glad to see you guys. I think we'll be extra busy because we had a good write-up in the local newspaper. Would you be willing to help us out today?"

"Sure, I'll be happy to," said Lucas.

George also agreed. He would help, behind the bar.

"Great! Come with me to the office, and we'll get ready for lunch," said Ty. They followed him into the storeroom where he lit the hash pipe again and passed it around.

Ty started the conversation, saying he will pay them by the hour with cash. But, if anyone asks, they should say they were not getting paid, they were only friends, helping him out.

When Lucas and George agreed, Ty said, "When you're here working, you get free beer and food."

Lucas and George thanked Ty, and he continued talking, "I must go to Morocco tomorrow with my son. I hope you will both work for a few days with David, Cedric and Christina, my girlfriend. It will take all of you to keep the place going. If it works out for everyone, maybe you could stay while I go to London and do a play for six weeks. We can talk about it when I get back from Morocco."

After leaving the storeroom/office, Ty showed George around the bar, and David got Lucas started in the kitchen.

"I'll work where I'm needed," David said to Lucas. Then, he handed Lucas a lunch and dinner menu.

The Alamo menus included Ty's favorite foods: Texas chili with cornbread, chicken-fried steak with country gravy, barbecue pork ribs, burgers, fries, baked potato, beef brisket, grilled corn on the cob, and other veggies. For dessert, they offered pecan pie, apple pie or carrot cake.

People in the lunch crowd were mostly Yanks, Aussies and Brits, plus some Spaniards. Many patrons were curious about the Texas food and the restaurant with a movie star owner. Lots of women came in to get a look at the very handsome Ty Hardin in the flesh.

With all the help they had, lunch service was smooth. Although, Lucas and George were new to this setup, they were professionals who knew what to do and when, by instinct. Since they had extra help, Ty and Christina could visit and entertain the patrons. Ty even pulled out his guitar during lunch. He and Christina sang while others ate, drank, clapped, and had a great time.

After lunch when the restaurant was clean, Ty said, "Do you guys want to play volleyball?"

George smiled, then said, "It's the main reason I came here."

Ty, Lucas, George, David, Cedric, Christina and 2 Aussies walked along the beach. When they arrived at the volleyball court, 4 Spaniards were playing doubles.

This was a sand court. Someone used a rope to line the boundaries of the court, and they staked the corners down. Next to the court, they built a snack shop with a wood porch. There were tables and chairs on the porch and on the sand. Large, colorful beach umbrellas shaded the area around The Shack. David told them it was always busy, serving hamburgers, fries, some tapas, beer and Sangria. And, many bikini-clad young ladies were always present.

Ty seemed to know the guys playing volleyball, and he challenged the 4 Spaniards to a game. With 4-man teams, they would play each game to 11 points, and whoever wins 2 out of 3 games is the winner. Ty, David, Lucas and George took on the Spaniards who were younger and looked to be in good shape.

When they began the 1st game, the temperature was about 30 degrees Celsius (86 degrees Fahrenheit). Watching everybody warm up, Lucas thought any of the 8 guys on the court could spike the ball well.

To begin the game, Lucas gave Ty and George excellent sets which they put away, resulting in visible frustration of the Spaniards. The Alamo guys won the 1st game 11-6. People watching from the beach and the people at The Shack were all cheering for Ty's team. The ladies in the crowd got quite excited, watching Ty play.

Losing the 1st game irritated the Spaniards. Also, losing the ladies' support must have gotten to them because they came out for the 2nd game and got off to a 6-0 lead. Then, they missed 2 kills which hit out of bounds on close calls by The Alamo guys. This added a little fuel to the burning anger of the Spaniards. They lost the lead at 6-7, then rallied to a 10-8 lead until Ty put away 2 great kills, tying it at 10-10.

They each got a point. Then, George slammed a shot down the left side, landing just inside the rope. It tied the score at 12-12, and the Spaniards were serving. After a few good digs, off kills by each side, the tallest Spaniard smashed a ball down the line. David called it out. The Spaniards yelled and claimed it looked in, but David said, "I saw it clearly, and the ball was out."

A Spaniard challenged him and said, "Liar, it hit the rope."

David picked up the ball and said, "Let's finish the game."

The Spaniards were fuming, but they went back and got ready for David's serve. His jump-serve got dug out and set to the left side, a Spaniard returned the ball well, but Lucas dove and dug it out, then Ty set George who put away a tremendous spike. The game ended with The Alamo guys winning 14-12. That was the last straw for the Spaniards, and they came after the winners, ready for a fight.

George and Lucas were standing on the side line of the court.

As Lucas saw 2 of the Spaniards coming at them, he looked down at the rope, caught George's eye and mouthed, *"Rope."*

George nodded.

With murder in their eyes, the Spanish guys were almost on them, and George said, "Now!"

As Lucas and George sidestepped the oncoming Spaniards, they bent over, grabbed the rope and jerked it up. The rope caught both guys below the knees and sent them tumbling face down into the sand. George was all over 1 guy; using his elbows, he landed some tremendous blows to the guy's head. Lucas kicked the other guy in the balls; and when he tried to get up, Lucas caught him with a knee to the nose. Before the guy hit the sand, Lucas smashed the guy's nose again with his elbow. With blood all over him, the guy stayed on the sand, holding his nose in agony. Lucas looked over at David who was pounding another Spaniard with his fists. Ty was making hamburger out of the last guy's face—it was all over. Alamo 4, Spaniards 0.

People around the volleyball court were cheering, including the 2 big Australian guys who walked over from the bar with them. All pumped, the winners headed back to have a few beers and relax at The Alamo before they get ready for the dinner rush.

On the way back, Cedric commented to Lucas, "Your clever rope trick really surprised the Spaniards; it was a great move."

"We learned about fighting the hard way," replied Lucas. "After several broken hands and broken noses, George and I decided if we got into a fight together, we would work as a team. We both quit trying to out-box other guys in a damned street fight—it's all about survival, not like going for an Olympic medal. Since we stopped using our fists, we had to invent gimmicks to surprise the opposition. Now, we always look for something to use as a weapon or tool and gain an advantage. We have even rehearsed some scenarios which we may have to deal with."

When their group got to The Alamo, Ty invited Lucas and George into the storeroom. After they got settled with an Estrella Damm beer in hand, Ty passed around the hash pipe and said, "Tomorrow morning, my son and I are going to Morocco in his Ford Transit Van. It has a false bottom, and we will return with twenty-five kilos of hashish the next day.

"You know, you guys can make a lot of money. I could put a false bottom in your VW van and handle the arrangements. You could make the same run my son and I are doing."

"You are nuts, Ty," replied Lucas. "I sure don't want to spend the rest of my life in a Moroccan or Spanish prison."

Ty said, "Okay. But I know from experience, we won't get caught. Will you think about working here while I go to London with Christina? We're going to do a play there for six weeks."

"George and I will talk about it and let you know," said Lucas.

It was a good thing Ty had extra help for the night shift because The Alamo was jumping. Word of the volleyball game and the fight was a hot topic in town. It brought a lot of curious people into the restaurant and bar, even some from Torremolinos.

The crowd drank and ate until 2 a.m., and Ty was eager to close. After Lucas, George, Ty, Christina, David and Cedric finished cleaning, they all had Estrella Damm beers and shots of Jägermeister.

Ty announced it was the busiest night ever for The Alamo. They all cheered before saying goodnight. Ty told them he would see them in a few days. Then, he said, "Hold down the fort," as he pointed over the bar at his sign—THE ALAMO was written in big bold letters.

On the drive back to the campground, Lucas said, "Can you believe it? Ty wanted us to smuggle drugs from Morocco in our van! The payoff might be large, but the risk is too great."

"I think he is crazy to even try it," said George.

"What do you think about staying here and taking care of his restaurant for six weeks?" asked Lucas

"I love the weather, the food is good, and most of the people are great, except for some hotheaded Spaniards," he replied. "But, if we stay here, we will work double shifts; and we will have no time to play volleyball, tennis, body surf and chase women. I would rather head back toward Garmisch and spend time skiing on the Zugspitze."

"I agree. Let's tell Ty, as soon as he gets back," said Lucas.

After a long and eventful day, Lucas and George climbed in the van, crawled in bed and fell asleep. George was in the double bed which unfolded, and Lucas was in a hammock bed above George.

The next day in The Alamo kitchen, Christina was showing Lucas how to scramble eggs in a double boiler which she claimed was the British and French method. He could not help but notice how friendly she was this morning, and she kept pushing her breasts against him as they stood by the stove together. Lunch service was busy again. Everyone knew what to do, so it was a smooth process. Some regular patrons asked why Ty was absent. Christina told them he was out of town on business, and he would be back in a few days.

While they cleaned the kitchen after lunch, Christina asked Lucas if he would come over to her apartment, help get some meat from the freezer and bring it back to The Alamo. Lucas told her he had plans to meet George, David and Cedric at The Shack on the beach, but he would help her before he left.

Christina and Lucas walked 2 blocks to the apartment where she and Ty lived. The place looked very basic: motel-class furniture, clothes scattered around and some dirty dishes in the sink.

While Lucas was pulling frozen ribs out of the freezer, Christina stood behind him as if she was looking over his shoulder. Without warning, she pushed her whole body against him. Christina had very dark, shoulder-length hair. It was usually in a ponytail, but she had removed the hair clip, so it fell on her shoulders. She also had removed her shoes and unbuttoned her blouse which showed ample cleavage.

She turned Lucas around, planted a kiss on his lips, grabbed his butt and said, "You are a handsome man, Lucas. I was attracted to you, the minute I saw you. I want you. Why don't we go into the bedroom?"

Lucas was shocked, and he jumped back like in reflex to danger. He gathered his senses and said, "Oh, Christina, you are a gorgeous woman, and you excite me; but I consider Ty my friend now. I would never fuck my friend's wife or girlfriend. So, can we please forget this happened and keep our relationship friendly, yet professional?"

Christina was flabbergasted, realizing she was not irresistible and Lucas would not jump into bed with her. They transferred meat into a shopping cart on the rear patio of the apartment. The swamp cooler in the window was off, so inside was hot and humid since the apartment had been closed. Lucas could not wait to get out of there. Finally, they pushed the shopping cart along the street and got it to The Alamo. He helped put the meat away, and he left.

Lucas went to the beach and joined the guys. They were on the deck at The Shack, drinking beers.

The 4 Spaniards who they fought yesterday were playing 2-man volleyball. The Spaniards did not even look at the guys on the deck. George, Lucas and others did not want to start anything today, so they finished their beers and returned to The Alamo.

The evening was quiet in the kitchen. Christina looked pissed off, and Lucas had nothing to say to her, so David did most of the talking. The others listened and agreed with whatever David said. The bar was lively, but George and Cedric had it under control, and everyone had a fun time. After closing, they smoked some of Ty's hashish, drank beers, said goodnight and headed for their own places to sleep.

The next day, Lucas and George parked the van in the usual place on Paseo Marítimo Rey de España. They walked to The Alamo and arrived about 10 a.m. Standing out front, they could see something was not right. Strangers, dressed in suits, were in and out of the restaurant, carrying bags and boxes to a black van, parked in front. Lucas and George walked into the bar and spotted more "suits" in the back storeroom/office, going through Ty's desk.

Christina came out of the kitchen and into the bar, looking terrified. When Lucas and George asked her what happened, she said, "Ty and his son got busted by customs officers when they drove off the ferry from Morocco with 25 kilos of hashish in his son's van. Both are in jail, and no bail is set yet."

Lucas looked at George, and they simultaneously turned around. They went out the front door, walked back to their van, drove straight to the campground and checked out.

Back on the road, Lucas said, "I sure don't want to end up like Ty."

"Where should we go next?" asked George.

"Well, you want to go toward Garmisch," he replied. "Let's go west to Tarifa. It's on the coast near Gibraltar. From there, we can go north to Seville, Madrid and Zaragoza, then decide what's next."

"Okay," said George. "We need to stop for beer and gas. Then, we can find a place to grab lunch."

They stopped in Nueva Andalucía, bought gas and a case of Becks beer, forgot about the lunch and drove on toward Tarifa.

While George drove, Lucas read about Tarifa in his travel book.

"What do you think of going to Morocco?" he asked.

"I've never thought about it. Why?" asked George.

"We've been in Spain quite a while, and we've sampled most of the food here," he replied. "It would be fun to see a different culture for a change. From Tarifa, it's thirty-nine kilometers to Tangiers which is only two hours by ferry. If we take the van, we will have it to get around, and we can also sleep in it if we want to."

"Great," said George. "It sounds like a good plan. Now, we might as well go straight to the port and see if we can catch the next ferry. Hand me a Becks and let's celebrate. We're going to another continent!"

They clinked beer bottles together, and Lucas returned to reading.

When George turned on some music, they both recognized the Beatles new album, *Let it Be*. The timing seemed appropriate as they listened to the song playing. It was "The Long and Winding Road."

Arriving at the port of Tarifa, George put the van in line for the next ferry to Tangier.

CHAPTER 13

Tangier

When George drove onto the ferry, his and Lucas' van was the last vehicle to get on. As the ferry moved away from the dock and headed to Tangier, they walked upstairs to the observation car, went straight to the bar and bought Estrella Damm beers.

Lucas talked to an American who had penetrating brown eyes and shoulder-length, black hair. He was wearing worn, Levi cut-off shorts and leather sandals. After Lucas introduced himself, the guy said his name was David, and he was from Fresno, California.

"Hey, David, I grew up in Fresno!" exclaimed Lucas. "What high school did you go to?"

"I went to Fresno High," replied David. "What school did you go to, and what year did you graduate?"

Before Lucas spoke, David said, "Wait a minute, Lucas Gary. We played on the same basketball team. I'm David Burns, and I was a year behind you in school. My brother Del was in your class."

Lucas turned to George and said, "You won't believe this, George. David Burns and I went to high school together."

Ready to carry 3 Foster beers back to his group, David said to Lucas, "Come with me. You can meet my girlfriend and her two friends."

Introducing Lucas and George to the ladies, David said, "This is my girlfriend, Emma, and her friends are Ashleigh and Olivia. They're all from Australia. This is Lucas and George, from California. Lucas and I went to school together in Fresno. Now, it is, what? Fourteen years later, and here we are on the same ferry, going to Morocco."

Emma, David's girlfriend, is about 5'5". She has a bubbly personality, a full figure, a cute face, short red hair, and a great smile.

Olivia impressed Lucas, right away. She has dark brown hair, big blue eyes, a turned-up nose and good-sized breasts. Wearing blue shorts which are mid-thigh length, her shapely and muscular legs are exposed. Only the top button is undone on her white blouse. Lucas felt captivated.

Ashleigh is taller, with an athletic build which suited George just fine. She has a nice tan, and her blonde hair is in a ponytail.

As happened so many times in the past, they seemed to pair off with these ladies. It was automatic with Lucas and George.

Lucas had never been around Australian women. As he talked to Olivia, she seems to be a strong-willed and fun-loving young lady. She is 24 years old, arrived in Europe about 2 months ago, and wants to travel for a while longer. Then, she will go back to Germany or England and get a job. She has never skied; but she is a surfer, tennis player, volleyball player and beer drinker.

David told the guys he had an old postal-van. He did the work himself and converted it to a camper, with a regular four-burner stove, a small porta-potty and a double bed. A friend of David's had spent 2 months in Morocco, and he recommended they stay at the Dar Omar Khayam Hotel on Rue Antaki in Tangier. It's a 15-minute walk from the port. David also had the phone number of a place where they could buy hashish and a pipe. (Morocco supplied hashish to a large part of Europe). From Tangier, he and Emma would drive south to Casablanca and Marrakech.

Lucas and George advised David they had no specific agenda.

George and I talked about staying in campgrounds, thought Lucas. *Maybe, we should rethink those plans. If things work out the way I now picture them, hotel rooms sound a lot better.*

The ferry was close to docking when Lucas said, "Is it okay if we follow you to the hotel and see if they have rooms?"

Olivia and Ashleigh seemed happy and nodded.

David agreed and said, "Let's get to our vans and be ready. The port looks busy."

David's converted German postal-van was painted orange, yellow and white. It made an impression, and people on the streets stopped to look at it when they drove by. Lucas and George followed behind David and the ladies. They drove along the Avenue Mohammed VI and veered off onto Rue Antaki. Parking on the street did not look too promising, so they pulled into the circular driveway and stopped at the entrance.

Since it was early in the week, Dar Omar Khayam Hotel was half-full. They got 3 rooms on the 2nd floor: 1 room for Lucas and George, 1 room for David and Emma, plus 1 room for Olivia and Ashleigh.

We'll start off this way and see how it ends up, thought Lucas.

They all put things in their rooms. Then, Lucas and David went to move the vans into a parking garage, by the port. George wanted to stay at the hotel. Lucas asked Olivia if she wanted to ride with him since Emma was going with David. They would all walk back together.

"Good. Ashleigh and I can have a beer at the bar," said George.

Their hotel was in the heart of Tangier, a 10-minute walk to the old city, and the beach was only 5 minutes away. At the front desk, they got directions to the parking garage, and Olivia took a hotel brochure. She read to Lucas while he drove back on Avenue Mohammed VI which the desk clerk called The Boulevard.

Olivia read, *"Since its construction at the end of the 19th Century, this historical landmark has undergone several changes. During the First World War, it was a hospital for wounded officers. Later, it became a school for Jesuits, and then a convent during the Spanish Colonization. Today, the revived Dar Omar Khayam Hotel unveils all its charm. It offers an amazing architectural treasure to those who are in love with the city of Tangier and those who are passing by."*

On the return walk, David wanted to stop and make a phone call. He would meet them at the hotel. Lucas, Olivia and Emma walked to the hotel and joined George and Ashleigh in the bar. Lucas ordered a round of the local favorite beer, Casablanca, a smooth tasting lager.

About 30 minutes later, David arrived, grinning. He said, "Come to our room." They finished their beers at the bar, and they all headed to the elevator. George grabbed 6 Becks beers which he had brought in from the van, and they all went to David and Emma's room.

David was leaning over the desk, loading a hash pipe. He said, "I got a phone number and address from a guy I know in Malaga. His contact person sold me a little hashish. So, let's try it!"

They all smoked hash and drank their beers. Lucas said, "Let's go see Tangier and try the local food." Everyone went their separate ways to get ready for a night out.

Lucas and George were in the bar, drinking Casablanca beers while waiting for the others. The bartender was not busy, and he told them about Caid's Bar. It was the inspiration for *Rick's Place,* a bar in the movie *Casablanca.* He gave them directions and drew a map on a napkin.

The bartender also told them about a hippie café, located on Avenue Sidi Mohamed Ben Abdellah, named Café Baba. He said they serve the best mint tea, and it is a fun place to go if you can stand the smoke from cigarettes, hashish and whatever else people smoke there. The café is in the Medina (the old walled city) on a narrow alleyway. Some rock 'n' roll stars have been seen there, smoking hashish, such as Bob Marley and Mick Jagger.

The 3 couples walked along Avenue Belgique and turned left onto Avenue d'Angleterre for a short distance. Given the names of streets and different restaurant foods available, a mixed culture of Spanish, Moroccan and French was obvious in Tangier. They followed the map to the Kasbah Museum, walked on a very narrow street, continued across a parking lot and through an arched, stone gateway on their right. They followed a stone path down the hill which veered to the left and finally reached a stone stairway at their destination.

On a metal sign above the entrance, the lettering for Café Baba was scripted in English and Arabic. A stone arch surrounded the narrow doorway. Inside, the air was heavy with smoke. The walls were blue, and the ceiling was white. Throughout the space, there were beautiful wooden chairs with inset upholstered seats and backrests, placed around small tables. Up 3 steps, overlooking the main room, an alcove had more tables and cushioned benches along the walls. The café was crowded. Everyone was talking and laughing. Some people were playing games: dice, backgammon, Parcheesi, and other board games.

Lucas grabbed Olivia's hand to let her know he wanted to sit with her. They settled on a cushioned bench in the alcove and ordered mint tea. Served in a silver pitcher and loaded with fresh mint, the tea was sweet and delicious.

George and Ashleigh were talking to Emma at a table nearby. David sat at a corner table, talking to a guy who looked like a local.

Olivia was giving Lucas news on current events. She shocked him when she said, "The Beatles broke up."

"No way! Say it isn't so, Olivia," he said.

She smiled, then continued, "The United States invaded Cambodia, and there are some violent situations in 'The States' where people are demonstrating against the war in Viet Nam."

"I am against this war," said Lucas. "But I guess we'll always fight to oppose communism. Now, we also have terrorism to consider."

Olivia went on with current events, "Jimi Hendrix died of a drug overdose. And, the PLO tried to assassinate King Hussein."

Hearing the last bit of news made Lucas think of Andreas and Ulrike because he figured they were now in Jordan.

He asked Olivia, "Have you heard anything in the news about the Baader-Meinhof Gang or the RAF?"

"The other day, I read about Ulrike Meinhof's twin girls who were found at the foot of Mount Etna, being cared for by hippies," said Olivia. "They were returned to their father in Italy. Why do you ask?"

"It's a long story. If we have time, I'll tell you later," he replied.

Lucas noticed David walking out, following the Moroccan guy. David motioned for Lucas to follow him, and he also pointed to George. Lucas asked Olivia to wait, and he went to George's table.

"I don't know why," said Lucas, "but David wants us to follow him." George excused himself from Ashleigh, and he followed Lucas.

Outside, Lucas and George saw David and the Moroccan turn right at the end of the building. When they got to the corner, Lucas motioned for George to stop, as he peeked around the building. The Moroccan had his back turned to them, and David was facing them. When he handed money to the guy, David said, "Okay, now give me the package."

The Moroccan reached into his backpack as if he would give David something, or so Lucas thought. But the Moroccan pulled out a knife and said, "Tough luck, sucker," as he backed up.

Lucas looked around and spotted a small round stool, next to the wall. As they went toward the Moroccan guy, he whispered to George, "I'll take the knife arm; you take the head." Then, he grabbed a leg of the stool, took 4 quick steps and swung the stool down, hitting the guy's right arm and hand which held a 6-inch knife.

The Moroccan held the knife as if he was holding a spear. When Lucas brought the stool down, the guy's arm came down fast, he did not loosen his grip, and the knife went about 2 inches into his thigh. At the same time, George used his elbow and hit him in the back of the head, using all his might. The guy went down hard. For good measure, Lucas kicked him in the balls. Barely conscious, the guy made no attempt to get up.

Lucas grabbed the backpack and found a package, containing 2 square pieces of hashish, while George pulled David's money out of the guy's pants pocket. When they gave it all to David, he said, "Thanks, a lot. I guess you can't trust anybody, these days."

"Let's get the ladies and get out of here before we have to answer any questions," said Lucas.

Back inside the café, they told the waiter some guy was lying in the street, around the corner; he was bleeding and needed an ambulance or someone to help him. The guys gathered their ladies, but did not stop to finish their mint tea.

They all walked to the Grande Socco (Grand Square) where they could eat some cous cous. It was only a 10-minute walk from Café Baba. When they arrived, they found many cafés in the large market place which was very colorful and busy.

While most places served Arabic food, there were other options for eating a meal. They chose a small restaurant in a corner of the square, and they sat outside under a blue canvas awning.

Each ordered Casablanca beer, cous cous with lamb, mergez sausage and vegetables. They all ate with their fingers, Moroccan style.

David told them Moroccans only eat with their right hand, because they use their left hand for cleaning, and they do not use toilet paper.

He let them draw their own conclusions about his comments, and they all had a good laugh.

"Actually," David added, "the Moroccans are very meticulous about washing their hands and cleaning under their fingernails because they all eat from the same platters, using their right hand."

Olivia kept her left hand on Lucas' leg during most of the meal, and she whispered in his ear, "I want to sleep with you tonight."

Lucas looked over at her with a happy expression, and he nodded. He thought: *I like this Australian lady. I can't remember when or where I was last in bed with a woman. I think it was in Ibiza with Gabrielle. It seems so long ago.*

At dinner, they exchanged travel stories and drank Casablanca beer. David told of his travels in London when he landed in Europe for the 1st time. From there, he went to Amsterdam where he bought his bus and met the 3 Australian ladies.

Then, they drove to Paris and on to Bordeaux. They wanted to see the Running of the Bulls, a festival in Pamplona, but they were a week early. Instead, they went to Lake Yesa which is nearby, and they met a bunch of crazy Australians. Since it was hot at the lake, they all waterskied and enjoyed drinking big pitchers of ice-cold Sangria.

Being the only American in the group, the Australians taught David how to play cricket. If there was a dispute in play, they would adjourn to the bar and discuss it over a pitcher of Sangria. Those Australians were a close-knit group. David said he counted 12 Australians climbing out of a VW van during his last morning at Lake Yesa.

When he and the ladies arrived at the "fest" in Pamplona, David considered himself lucky when he found a place to park. It was in the main square and next to a large park which had grass and shade trees. However, he was afraid to leave the van because people in the park were getting rowdy. The festival would not start until the following day, so they stayed around the van, drank beer and watched the people.

Then a fight broke out between an Aussie group, the same group they had met at Lake Yesa, and a bunch of hot-headed, young Spaniards. To David's surprise, it was the Spaniards who got the best of the fight.

David said the madness continued throughout the night. A few young women came to David's van, banging and pleading to get in because they saw women being raped in the park. David let them in to sleep in the van although it was crowded.

Early in the morning, a thunder and lightning storm woke everyone. It was the 1st day of the Festival of San Fermin (Running of the Bulls), and the women from the park left the van to attend the event. David and the 3 Australian ladies decided the festival at Pamplona was too crazy for them. From there, they headed south, made their way to Tarifa, and got on the ferry to Tangier.

"Speaking of Tangier," Lucas said to David, "Do you suppose the drug dealer guy will come after us? I have no idea if he did or did not see my face and George's face."

"Maybe not, but we were in Café Baba together," said George.

"Well, I think it would be best if we all left Tangier," replied David. "Emma and I are going to Marrakech. I believe Olivia and Ashleigh are heading back to Europe. What are you guys going to do?"

Lucas looked at George, then said, "We have not yet decided. But we have kicked around some possibilities such as going to Oktoberfest in Munich, or touring the Cervenia/Zermatt area and skiing on the glacier at the Matterhorn."

"Oh, it would be exciting to see the Matterhorn; and I would love to learn how to snow ski," said Olivia.

Lucas looked at George again. They both smiled, and George said, "Okay, we'll talk about it in the morning over breakfast and beers. Let's go find Caid's Bar. We heard it was the model for *Rick's Place* in the movie *Casablanca*."

After Lucas paid the check, they paired up and took a 5-minute walk along Rue de La Liberté to Caid's Bar. It was packed, and a large group of people stood outside waiting for a table.

David asked, "Should we go back to the hotel, smoke hashish, drink beer and have a shot of Jägermeister?" The others agreed.

"Yes. We don't need sleazy tonight," Olivia said to Lucas.

The ladies went to use the restroom in Caid's Bar.

Lucas asked George, "What do you think about asking the ladies to come with us to the Oktoberfest?"

"We only met them this morning," he replied. Then, he asked Lucas, "Do you think they would?"

"Olivia already told me she wants to sleep with me," said Lucas. "She and Ashleigh both want to change the sleeping arrangement."

"Okay then, yes, yes, yes!" he replied.

All gathered in Lucas and George's room, they drank the last of the Becks beer and smoked hashish which David tried to buy.

David and Emma went to their room for the night. George left with Ashleigh and went down the hall to her room.

This was something new to Lucas. He and Olivia had not even kissed yet, but he liked her and wanted to be with her. After showering, Olivia came out of the bathroom, wearing a short, low-cut garment, and she looked amazing. Olivia walked over to Lucas, put her arms around him and kissed him.

Lucas thought: *Wow, she has a better body than advertised. I am so glad I showered already.*

They spent the best part of the night getting to know each other from every angle. When they were not making love, they discussed many subjects and travel plans, such as going to Oktoberfest and skiing the Matterhorn. Lucas told her about Bavarian towns, the Armed Forces Recreation Center in Garmisch, his life in Long Beach and his restaurants. Olivia told him about her life in Melbourne where she practically grew up on a surfboard.

Lucas explained his preference in water sports and many other sports: Although Lucas had tried board surfing, he preferred bodying surfing and waterskiing. He enjoyed playing beach volleyball, basketball, fast-pitch softball and an occasional game of golf. In the winter, he took a few ski trips to Mammoth Mountain or Lake Tahoe. With all his other activities, he did not have much time to learn board surfing.

"Have you seen the movie, *Endless Summer*?" Lucas asked.

"Yes," she replied. "I don't know a surfer who hasn't. Why?"

"I shared a duplex with Robert August and his dad, Blackie, back in nineteen fifty-eight," said Lucas. "Blackie August was one of the first to surf at Redondo Beach. He was a legendary lifeguard at city beaches, even before surfing became so popular in Southern California."

"Where was this duplex?" she asked.

"It was on Seal Beach at Thirteenth Street between the pier and the breakwater," said Lucas. "The surfing was good there, and Robert was about fourteen."

"We made a sand volleyball court in a vacant sandlot, next to the duplex," he added. "Late at night, when the grunion would run, it seemed like the whole town would turn out to party on the beach and catch buckets full of grunion."

"What is a grunion?" she asked.

"A grunion is a silver-colored fish about the same size and shape as a sardine," he said. "They call the event a Grunion Run. It's a mating ritual at very high tides, involving thousands of grunions. The male grunion wraps himself around the female to deposit his sperm. The female grunion finds her way onto the beach, digs her tail into the sand and lays her eggs. The grunion eggs hide in the sand for ten days. When the next set of high tides comes in, the eggs hatch, and newborn fish get washed out to sea where they live happily ever after."

Olivia laughed at his story.

"It sounds fun and just like us Aussies—any excuse for a beach party!" she explained.

The next morning at 11 a.m., they all had sweet bread, cheese, fruit and Casablanca beer for breakfast. David and Emma were in a hurry to get going and travel to Marrakech. Lucas invited them to come visit Garmisch when they get tired of Africa.

"Saying goodbye to people I have come to like makes me sad," said Lucas, "because I wonder if I will ever see them again." Everyone hugged, and the 2 new couples said goodbye to Emma and David.

George said, "You know, we have seen very little of the city, other than the Kasbah area and little back alleys in the old Medina."

"Is there a particular place you want to visit?" asked Lucas.

Pulling his travel book out of his backpack, George replied, "Well, let's see here. We could walk around the port, then have drinks on the patio of the famous Hotel Continental, overlooking the harbor."

"Okay, let's head to the port," said Lucas. "On the way, we can buy more beer, stop by the van and smoke some of this hash."

While they followed George and Ashleigh, Lucas and Olivia talked about what life must be like in Tangier, the way they saw it.

"What type of bus is that blue and white one?" asked Olivia.

"It's a Mercedes. I've seen several around the city, and they all have wild looking advertisements on them," replied Lucas.

Lucas and Olivia caught up with the others to find out if they want to stay here tonight or go back to Spain. When they asked George what he wanted to do, he said, "I want to go back to Spain where we can get Becks beer and more Jägermeister."

"Yeah," said Lucas, "I'm craving tapas and paella."

Both ladies agreed with them. They all got to the van and climbed in. Lucas opened 4 Casablanca beers, Olivia loaded the hash pipe, and George asked the ladies, "Do you think you'll be comfortable, traveling in this van?"

"Are you kidding?" asked Olivia. "You'd be surprised if you saw some of the transportation we've used since we got to Europe. This is a luxury for us, and your van looks brand new. Where did you get this?"

"We bought it in Garmisch," said George. "Then, we stocked it with food and supplies, purchased at the military PX and commissary,"

"Are you guys in the military?" Olivia asked.

"No. We're civilian employees on vacation. I'll tell you about it later," replied Lucas. "Let's finish our beers, then walk around the port and go see the Hotel Continental."

They were amazed to see fleets of fishing boats and their crews who would leave the port to fish all night and bring in their catch the next morning. The docks were crowded with busy fishermen, tending to their nets and getting ready to go out again. They could not help but notice all the cats around the port, such as they saw in the Medina district, but these cats were looking for scraps of leftover fish. They walked along the

Avenue Mohammed VI, made a few turns, passed by assorted small stores and shops, then stayed on Rue Dar el-Baroud to the Hotel Continental, a stately hotel of Moroccan architecture, painted white with gold trim. The building was four stories high and quite large.

The hotel's interior was awesome. Mosaic-tile designs covered many of the fountains, columns, archways and ceilings. Some ceilings were coffered and others were domed. Several archways and windows had stained-glass sections. Walking through a kaleidoscope of colors, there were 2 patios: 1 for breakfast and 1 next to the bar. Both had a fantastic view, overlooking the entire harbor area. Seated in the patio bar, they learned it served no alcohol. So, they all ordered mint tea. This hotel was famous for their mint tea. It was served in a tall glass, and the top 3rd was filled with mint leaves.

"I think this is known as High Tea," said Ashleigh. "Today, we could also call it *High at Tea.*" They all laughed.

Each of them admired the fabulous view and enjoyed being together with newfound friends and lovers. After finishing tea, they marveled at the colorful walls, tiled in a variety of decorative patterns, as they walked back through the hotel.

They strolled through crooked, narrow streets which looked more like alleyways. Beautiful, decorative doorways on many buildings and homes were magnificent; there was something almost royal about them. Other buildings were plain, yet painted in bright colors; above those doorways the electrical wires, strung from building to building, did not look safe. They found their way along a winding path and climbed many stairways, getting to the highest point of the city, the Kasbah, an old military fortress, overlooking the Strait of Gibraltar.

On this beautiful, clear day, they could see all the way to Spain, and Lucas said, "This is great. In a few hours, we'll be over there."

"Eating tapas and drinking Becks beer," added George.

"Where will we be staying?" asked Olivia.

"Good question," replied Lucas. "We have to research it."

They walked beside the fortress wall and gazed at huge old cannons, all scattered around the cliff and pointing at the sea. From the top of the cliff, they went down a long stairway which led to the beach, continued along brick pathways, got to the port and bought their tickets for the ferry. Lots of people were coming and going at the crowded dock.

Suddenly, Lucas said, "Uh oh!"

"What's the matter, Lucas?" asked Olivia.

Speaking in a low voice, only loud enough for his friends to hear, Lucas said, "The Moroccan, the one we left in the alley at Café Baba, is standing next to the kiosk building." Looking over George's shoulder,

Lucas watched the Moroccan and said, "He is with another guy and looking our way. We may have trouble if he recognizes us as the guys who were with David."

Thinking fast, Lucas suggested, "Look out this short pier to our left. Do you see the fish nets lying about halfway down the pier? Maybe we can use those. We outnumber those guys which gives us an advantage. Ladies, would you walk away, as if you are going to the restroom, and look for a length of pipe or wood? We may need to crown these guys after we snarl them in the net.

"Okay. George, when the ladies come back, we split up and walk away in different directions. Whichever couple they might follow can mingle through the crowd, then double back and walk out on the pier. If those guys approach them, the other couple can come from behind and throw the net on them. We can signal by touching our left hand to our right shoulder if we feel threatened."

"It sounds complicated," he replied. "But, it's better than no plan at all. At least, we will have the element of surprise."

Lucas hoped the 2 guys would not jump 4 people. *However, they might not hesitate to jump one guy and one lady,* he thought.

Sure enough, the guys followed George and Ashleigh around and past the fish nets, going toward the end of the pier.

Lucas and Olivia followed the Moroccans, picked up one fish net and got as close as they dared. They did not need a signal. Lucas saw the knives come out. Without hesitation, he ran several steps forward and threw the fishing net over both guys. Olivia hit a guy over the head, using a piece of pipe which she had found in a pile of trash. George took care of the other guy, using his patented elbow smash.

Then, they all pushed together, dumping the Moroccans off the dock and into the bay, still wrapped in the fishing net.

The owner of the net came running and screaming about his net. Lucas pulled out his wallet and handed him 100 dirhams (about $20). First, the fisherman looked at the money. Then, he looked down at the water and the Moroccans tangled in his net. He looked back at the money, and he started yelling instructions to his crew.

Lucas, Olivia, George and Ashleigh walked away as if sightseeing. They got to the van, climbed in and pulled the curtains closed.

George opened 4 Casablanca beers, and Olivia passed the hashish pipe around, saying, "This is the last of the hash, so we should smoke it and dispose of the pipe before we go back to Spain."

They drove to the ferry, got in line behind other cars and held their breath until they left port. Finally, they were heading back to Tarifa.

CHAPTER 14

Cervenia and Zermatt

Lucas, Olivia, George and Ashleigh were all concerned and looking over their shoulders until they reached Tarifa, got off the ferry and drove away from the port.

"We need to stop for gas and get Becks beer. Let's go to the place we stopped last time," said George.

"Good, then I can call Paco, David's buddy," said Olivia. "I want to see if he has any hashish for sale."

"I think we should stay in a hotel tonight, have a nice dinner and get a good night's rest," Lucas suggested.

"Yes. We need some rest," said Olivia. "Where shall we stay?"

"I know about a place in Malaga," said Lucas.

"I wonder if The Alamo is still open," George joked.

Lucas laughed. He knew George was kidding, but he replied, "I think we should go somewhere else. I don't want to see any of those people, especially the Spanish volleyball players."

Lucas and George told the ladies the whole story of Los Boliches and The Alamo. Olivia and Ashleigh both knew about Ty Hardin since they had seen him on television, playing his role as Bronco Lane.

After a scenic drive along the ocean which took about 2 hours, they got to the Castilla Guerrero Hotel, near the Port of Malaga. They arrived right before sunset, parked on the street and checked in. The hotel was a 6-story building on a V-shaped street corner. People accessed its bar and large café through the lobby or an outside street entrance.

Olivia called Paco who said he could sell them some hash and a small pipe. He would meet them at their hotel room because his place is hard to find, and he lived in a bad neighborhood, anyway. When Paco arrived, they handed him a beer, paid for the hashish and smoked some. He told them he heard of 2 Moroccan guys who were looking for 2 American assholes and 2 American bitches in Tarifa.

"Excuse me ladies," said Paco, "I was only repeating what I heard."

To the guys, he said, “The Moroccans returned to Tangier because no one had seen the Americans. You guys wouldn’t know anything about this would you?”

“Gee, Paco, we don’t have an answer for you,” said Lucas. “Maybe you can ask David when he gets back.”

“Where did he go?” asked Paco.

“We don’t know,” replied George. “We haven’t seen him since we had dinner together in Tangier.”

When Paco finished his beer, he stood and said, “Adios y buena suerte” (Goodbye and good luck), as he walked out the door.

After Paco had gone, Lucas said, “He seems like a nice guy.”

“Yeah, but he’s still a drug dealer,” Olivia said, “and I feel a little uncomfortable because he knows our room number.”

“Well, let’s not worry about Paco,” said George. “We have all our essentials covered, and we’re ready for a great time tonight. Where shall we go to eat?”

“I suggest we walk around and ask the locals,” said Lucas.

Each had another hit on the pipe, and they were all ready to paint the town. Downstairs, they walked through the hotel lobby, went across the street to Lis Bar and sat at a table. Lighting in this bar was dim, and the furniture was very worn, scratched-up wood. They ordered Stella Artois beers and inquired about local restaurants. The bartender told them about a fun bodega which he called “El Pimpi”. He described it as a charming old farmhouse with a wine room, cocktail bar and restaurant. A 15-minute walk took them along the Paseo Parkway, past the Plaza de Marina, left onto Calle Molina Lario, right on Calle Santa Maria, left on Calle Santa Augustin and right on Calle Granada.

They stood across the street from “El Pimpi” and Lucas studied the building: *Around the entrance, colorful plants, bushes and potted flowers, blooming in bright pinks and reds, are plentiful. The building is a light pink color. Clinging to the building, a tall green vine with purple flowers shoots from the ground and spreads out at the rooftop. To the left of the entrance, a menu board hangs on the stucco, next to a wrought-iron lantern. Above the doorway, a sign reads BODEGA BAR EL PIMPI. On the second floor, a terrace-style shelf, filled with potted flowers in full bloom, hangs above the entrance. The flowers sit under a shuttered window, and a wrought-iron rail encloses the terrace-style shelf. To the left, there are four identical windows/shelves/flowers/rails above a tall hedge which hides most of the wall. A dining patio extends around the right side and to the back of the building. Umbrellas provide shade to guests at many of the patio tables; other tables are under trees.*

They walked into the bar where all seats were occupied. Continuing into the dining room, a beautiful Spanish hostess greeted them with a great smile, coal-black hair and sparkling brown eyes. She led them toward the far end of a long dining room. Along 1 wall, blue and white cushions covered a wooden bench, and it extended the whole length of the room. Individual tables were placed in front of the long bench-seating, and chairs were on the opposite side of the tables.

The hostess seated them at a table, near the rear door which led outside to patio dining. They could see the patio was a busy area since people occupied most of the outside tables. Many waiters were hustling around, joking and laughing with the customers.

Off to the left of the dining room, there was a wine room which they passed on the way to their table. The hostess had stopped and showed them large wooden wine barrels, stacked along a wall in the room. They saw chalk writings on the end of each barrel which were autographs of famous people. Celebrities who had been there and written on the barrels included Antonio Banderas, Brigitte Bardot, Grace Kelly and the Prince of Monaco. Who knows, prior guests might even include Pablo Picasso who is now 88 years old and living in France.

This old farm house had wood-beamed ceilings and many rooms. Framed posters of flamenco dancers and bullfighters hung on some walls. Throughout the building, there were different style floors, laid in various colors of stone and tile. Several small rooms and nooks served as intimate dining areas. The bar, the barrel room, the patio and the main dining room were separated by arched doorways, covered in vines.

To start, they ordered bottles of Stella Artois beers and shots of Jägermeister. The large menu had many types of food. Wanting to try different things, they all ordered à la carte and shared several items.

They sampled Paella, Iberian Ham, Fried Calamari Rings, Iberian Chestnut-fed Pork Loin, Oxtail, Kid Goat, Monkfish Filet, Spanish Chicken Skillet, and mixed-barbecue-grill items. Throughout dinner, they had more bottles of Stella Artois and shots of Jägermeister.

Lucas thought: *Olivia and Ashleigh sure can drink!*

Dinner conversations covered many topics, including travel and food in different countries. The guys spoke of skiing at the Matterhorn, working for AFRC, living in Bavaria, and Lucas' restaurants in Long Beach. The ladies' talked about their youth and surfing in Melbourne, Australia.

"How long do you plan to stay in Europe? And, who is taking care of things for you in California?" Olivia asked Lucas.

"The way things are now, I could stay here forever," said Lucas. "In both restaurants, I have excellent managers and chefs who I trained. Also, I have a fantastic accountant. In fact, he landed a new client, a fast-food chain, named Wienerschnitzel. It has nothing to do with veal, only hot dogs, and they are selling franchises. I think my accountant, Dennis, might be into something good."

"How about you, Olivia, what are your plans?" Lucas asked.

"I planned to go back in six months unless I can get a good job," Olivia replied. "It depends on a lot of things. Right now, here with you, I am having so much fun. Let's go dancing."

She had spoken loud enough for people around them to hear. Many people stood, raised their glasses, toasted to dancing and laughed.

When the band played a flamenco number, a waiter and waitress danced around the room, clicking their castanets and twirling to the music. At the end of their dance, everyone was standing, clapping and cheering with appreciation. Lucas paid the check, and they left.

It was a short walk to a discothèque on Calle Beatas. Olivia and Lucas held hands, kissed, talked and laughed. They fell behind George and Ashleigh who were half-a-block ahead.

These Aussie ladies are a kick to be around, thought Lucas.

They arrived at Liceo Discoteca, a former palace. There were 2 floors and 4 bars. Loud rock music was playing in each bar. A staircase led to a mezzanine where you could watch the action which took place on a large dance floor below. The club stayed open until wee hours of the morning for the party animals, and it was packed.

They wormed their way to a bar at the back of 1 room, near a crowded dance floor, and ordered Estrella Damm beers, plus shots of Jägermeister. Standing, watching for a table to become vacant and drinking their drinks, they did not even try to talk because the music was so loud. After a short wait, Olivia poked Lucas and motioned to a table where people looked like they would leave. They all moved fast and positioned themselves to take over the table. When those people left, they staked their claim and set down their drinks.

Before Lucas could sit, Olivia pulled him toward the dance floor, as the DJ put on "Cracklin' Rosie" by Neil Diamond. They danced and kept dancing to "Lookin' Out My Back Door" (song by Creedence Clearwater Revival) and "American Woman" (song by The Guess Who). Afterward, they went back to the bar for more beer.

The whole group danced to a few more rock 'n' roll songs. When they were ready to go back to the hotel. They wound their way to Calle Molina Lario, holding hands and kissing along the way.

Lucas and George stayed alert as they walked. Although both were intoxicated, they remembered all the trouble they experienced on the streets of strange countries during early morning hours.

They strolled onto Plaza del Siglo Pito and stopped to look at the Cathedral de la Encarnación de Málaga. The size of the cathedral amazed Lucas. The cathedral's tower was 7 stories high. At the top, it had clocks on all 4 sides. Continuing their walk on Calle Molina Lario, they turned right at Alameda Principal, left at Calle Córdoba, walked 100 meters to the end of the next block, and arrived at their hotel.

In Lucas and Olivia's room, they all smoked hashish and drank another Becks beer before George and Ashleigh went to their room.

This was a day of exciting anticipation for Lucas, and it seemed to be for Olivia too. They undressed, caressed, kissed and explored each other until they could not stand it anymore. Then, they climbed into bed and really got to know about each other's desires—and fantasies.

Before Lucas fell asleep, he thought: *I feel as if I've been to a place I have never been before—and I can't wait to go there again.*

The next afternoon, they all got together for a quick breakfast of bread, Iberian ham, cheese and Becks beer. Everyone was feeling a little slower than usual, yet they were all smiling. After they checked out of the hotel, they smoked hashish in the van while driving north toward Valencia.

"After all the fun and frolic last night, I think we should drive straight through to Cervenia, and go glacier skiing," Lucas suggested.

Lucas was driving. Olivia sat next to him and kept him supplied with Becks beer, music and smiles. George and Ashleigh closed the curtains, turned off the stereo speakers in back, talked a short while and dozed off. In the front, Olivia also turned the music down.

Although tired, Lucas managed a 6 1/2-hour drive to Valencia while everyone else slept. He finally pulled off the road and into a truck stop to fill the gas tank. Lucas went inside and bought a case of Estrella Damm beer, pistachio nuts and grapes, a fresh loaf of bread, yellow cheese and Iberian ham. Earlier, he thought the Iberian ham was great.

Everyone was awake now, so they folded the bed up. Sitting around the table, they drank beer, ate sandwiches and laughed about the great time they had in Malaga. All of them agreed: they had seen enough of Spain, and they were eager to get to Cervenia.

It was George's turn to drive. Lucas and Olivia crawled into bed together, turned on the rear speakers and fell asleep in each other's arms, listening to music. "Close to You" was playing on a cassette tape. This hit song was released last year, by the Carpenters.

They did not stop again until they reached La Jonquera which is still in Spain, but close to the French border. George found a remote spot under some trees near the highway. They smoked the rest of the hashish and threw the pipe in a trash can. The van could now pass inspection.

While showing their passports at the border station, the guards enjoyed flirting with the ladies and waived them through. With George still at the wheel, they buzzed across the border, all joking and laughing as they went into Southern France.

An hour later, they passed through Narbonne which is a commune. Ashleigh read about communes in the travel book. A French commune may be a 10-person hamlet, a town of 10,000 people, or a city of 2,000,000 inhabitants. Large communes have subdivisions, lower administrative divisions which are called municipal arrondissements, and each has its own mayor. An example: The City of Paris has twenty of these municipal arrondissements. Urban neighborhoods in the United States are similar, by comparison.

The next city they would come to is Béziers. Ashleigh was reading to everyone, *"On a small bluff, above the river Orb, sits the town of Béziers. In the year twelve hundred and nine, an army of Catholic Crusaders killed some twenty thousand people in Béziers to eliminate Catharism. They also burned down all the buildings, including the Romanesque Cathedral. Rebuilding of the town and cathedral, lasted from the early thirteenth century until the fifteenth century. Bullfighting became popular here, and the towns' Plaza de Toros has featured some of the world's greatest matadors since eighteen ninety-seven. Every August, Béziers hosts the famous Feria de Béziers, a festival centered on bullfighting. This five-day event attracts one million visitors."*

They were only 10 kilometers from the Mediterranean Sea when they passed through Montpellier. Then, the highway took them inland, through Nimes, due north to Valence, and northeast to Grenoble.

Ashleigh, still reading, said, *"Grenoble is at the foot of the French Alps, where The Drac (river) joins the Isère River... Grenoble hosted the nineteen sixty-eight winter Olympics, in which Jean-Claude Killy won three gold medals, including the slalom. The slalom medal was first given to an Austrian skier, Karl Schranz, after he got to repeat his run because an official was on the course during his initial run. Schranz claimed the official distracted him in the dense fog. On his re-run, he had a faster time than Killy, and he received the gold medal. However, upon further review of Schranz's initial run, they discovered he missed a gate before coming to the official on the course. Schranz was disqualified, and they finally gave the slalom gold medal to Jean-Claude Killy."*

"What a relief it must have been for Killy!" said Lucas.

After traveling northeast for 2 hours, they were still in France, but they were close to a point where borders of 3 countries come together: France, Italy and Switzerland.

As they passed through Chamonix, Ashleigh said, "The highest mountain in Europe is here. It is called Mont Blanc because the top is always covered with white snow."

Reading, Ashleigh said, *"Mont Blanc was the site of the first Winter Olympics in nineteen twenty-four. The highest point of elevation is four thousand eight hundred and eight meters (15,774 ft.), and it has the highest vertical-ascent cable car in the world."*

As he focused on driving along a curvy highway, Lucas was constantly aware of the huge mountain looming above.

"If we weren't on such a mission to get to Cervenia, I would want to look around," said Lucas. "Maybe, some other time."

"Yeah, let's go skiing, but let's have a beer first," said George as he reached in the cabinet and handed them each a Becks beer.

After driving about 20 hours from Malaga, Spain, they rolled into Cervenia, Italy. It was close to 5 a.m. Lucas saw the cable cars and headed toward them. There were several parking lots with tour buses, cars, SUVs and vans. The cable car station would open at 7 a.m.

This early in the morning, the parking lot furthest from the cable car was empty, except for a group of 7 VW vans which had German Zoll license plates or green U.S. Military plates. Although, nobody was stirring around those vans, Lucas had a hunch about them.

"I think we should park here," said Lucas. "Some of these vans might be from Garmisch."

A moment later, the nearest van's door opened, and Gino stepped out. Surprised to see Lucas and George, he walked toward their van and exclaimed, "Oh no, you two again!"

George and Lucas got out and hugged Gino. When Ashleigh and Olivia got out, George introduced the ladies. Gino said he wanted to get a shower, but he figured he would have to sneak into the hotel. Lucas and George decided to rent a room where they could all take a shower, get dressed and figure out what they would do next. Gino knew of a bakery in town with some rooms above it which were cheap to rent.

They all walked over to the bakery where Lucas and George rented the whole upstairs for a very reasonable price. Everyone went to get settled in their rooms. Lucas brought in the Estrella Damm beers and Jägermeister from the van. There were 3 rooms in the upstairs apartment. The largest room had 3 king-size beds. Lucas and Olivia claimed a single room. George and Ashleigh took the other single room which had its own bathroom. Gino said he could sleep anywhere.

As he pulled a hash pipe out of his backpack, Gino asked, "Would anyone care to smoke some good hashish?"

"Yes, we would," said George. "We were afraid to bring any across the French border, coming from Spain. I guess we are in Italy now."

"I think if you relax and don't look guilty, they won't bother you, unless they know something," replied Gino.

Lucas and his group finished their beer and ate the rest of their food: French bread, cheese, Iberian ham and grapes.

"Did you plan on skiing today?" asked Gino. "I am going up. If you want, I can show you around."

Speaking to Olivia, George and Ashleigh, Lucas asked, "What do you think? We must rent skis and boots for the ladies. Whatever else they need, such as gloves and sunglasses, can be purchased."

Everyone agreed, and they were excited about skiing.

"The ski shop is at the bottom of the cable car," said Gino.

"Are all those vans in your group?" Lucas asked him.

"Yes," replied Gino. "We all came from Garmisch, by way of Venice. You'll meet everyone soon enough."

"How long has your group been here, Gino?" Olivia asked.

"Two days. The skiing on the glacier is fantastic, and the weather has been great," he answered.

Gino grabbed his skis and boots, climbed in their van and sat with George and Ashleigh. Lucas dropped everyone off at the entrance of the tram, along with his own skis and poles. He drove back to the lot and parked on the end, next to the rest of the VW vans from Garmisch.

After Lucas put on his boots, hat, gloves, sunglasses and parka, he grabbed his wallet and walked back to the tram. Right on time, the other 4 walked around the corner. Gino and George were in front while the ladies struggled with their ski gear and fell behind.

Riding on the tram, Gino told them a little about the area, "We will ski on Plateau Rosa. The word *Rosa* means frozen in the local French dialect. Plateau Rosa is about thirty-five hundred meters up; and it's on the Swiss side of the border. You can take a cable car down to Zermatt and have lunch in Switzerland, come back up on a cable car, and then ski down the Italian side to Cervenia."

Gino was an expert skier. By lunch time, he had the ladies carving turns. Being surfers, they learned fast and did well, skiing on the gentler slopes. On the Plateau Rosa Glacier, they had to contend with T-bar lifts, but they rode the triple chair until lunch. If you rode with Gino, you got to smoke hashish.

Lucas loved the feeling he had. It was like being on top of the world. He stood there on his skis, looking up at the magnificent Matterhorn peak, and the view took his breath away, or maybe it was the elevation at 3,480 meters (11,417 ft.) above sea level.

At the end of the day, they skied down the mountain until they ran out of snow, took off their skis and walked back to the vans, laughing and talking about their day on the slopes. They had all enjoyed it.

In the parking lot, George passed around Estrella Damm beers to all. Lucas told Gino's friends they could shower at the bakery apartment, even sleep there if they wanted. However, he advised them the 2 smaller rooms were taken.

Lucas and his group left their skis in the van, went to the market across the street and bought a case of Paulaner beer. They returned to their rooms, took showers and got ready for dinner.

The rest of the guys straggled in from the parking lot to shower and have a beer. Someone said Resto Grill Les Clochards was a fun place to eat. Gino reserved tables for their group, now a large party of 16.

Lucas mingled to meet everyone. He recognized Bob Ostergaard and Eric, the tall handsome guy with a great smile who Lucas met in Garmisch. Eric was here with his Minnesota friend, Steve, who now lived in Biberbeir, Austria. Bob brought his girlfriend, Maggie, and his business partner, Steve Dobson, who brought his girlfriend, Judann, and her girlfriend, Shelley. A Texan, Regan Stone, came with his lady, Denise. There were also two Canadian ladies, Leslie and Marnie.

Since they made dinner reservations for 16 people, the restaurant sent 2 jeeps to pick them up. They jammed 9 people into each jeep, including the drivers. It was a cozy 10-minute ride.

Arriving at the restaurant, everyone agreed: this 2-story chalet could be placed anywhere in the Alps, and it would look perfect in each location. A hostess seated them in their own dining area, yet they could still see into the main dining room. There were light-colored wood tables and chairs with rope seats. Copper pots and various kitchen utensils dotted the walls and ceilings.

In the room next to them, a large group of people were drinking and having fun; they were loud. So were the Garmisch people, including Lucas, George and the Aussie ladies. Through an open doorway, Lucas could see into a 3rd room which had a large fire pit and an iron grate. In there, cooks were grilling an assortment of meats, fowl and sausages.

Meals were served family style on platters of grilled meats, polenta, and a potato pancake with cheese, referred to as a Rösti Matterhorn. Lucas loved it. For dessert, everyone had apple strudel, served with warm vanilla sauce and cinnamon ice cream.

After dinner, Lucas paid the check for Olivia, George, Ashleigh, Gino and himself. When the ladies went to the restroom, Lucas said, "We will wait for you outside."

Gino, George and Lucas went out to smoke some of Gino's hashish. They stood at the side the building, out of sight, away from the dining room and any windows.

A woman about 40 years old walked over and said, "Do you mind if I join you?" She had shoulder-length, blonde hair and a shapely figure. Looking straight at Lucas, she added, "I don't like to smoke alone."

Then, she took out a joint, lit it, took a drag and passed it around. She introduced herself, saying, "My name is Rachel Lawson, and I am Cast Recruiter for a movie we are making at this location. *Snow Job* is the name of the movie which George England is directing. The stars are Jean-Claude Killy, Danièle Gaubert, Cliff Potts and Vittorio De Sica. Since we need some extras, I wonder—Will your group be here on Thursday and Friday? We will pay you to work in the movie, and you can have dinner with us on Thursday night, here at this restaurant."

"I don't know. We came here to ski and relax," said Lucas.

"We wouldn't need you until after three p.m., and the tram opens at seven a.m., so you will have all day to ski," replied Rachel.

"How many of us do you need?" Gino asked her.

"I'm sure we can use all sixteen of you," she answered

Rachel handed her card to Lucas. She looked like she wanted to devour him, as she touched his hand and said, "I wrote my room number and hotel on the back of the card. After you talk to the rest of your group, please call me, or come by, and let me know if you want to be in the movie."

When the entire group of 16 finally got together, they piled into the jeeps for the return trip to the bakery apartment. Eric, Steve and the Canadian ladies, Leslie and Marnie, stayed in the biggest room with Gino. The smaller rooms were private: Lucas and Olivia stayed in one. George and Ashleigh got the other.

After unwinding with a shot of Jägermeister, Lucas and Olivia slowly undressed each other and made love for what seemed like hours. They could not get enough of each other. As each day passed, they enjoyed being together even more.

In the early morning hours, they awoke to a wonderful smell of things cooking in the bakery. After they ate breakfast downstairs, everyone grabbed their skis and headed for the tram. Each of them looked forward to another day of skiing on the slopes next to the Matterhorn. The Italians call the mountain *il Cervino*.

Lucas had a wonderful morning in the sunshine, skiing with George, Gino and the Australian ladies. Perfectly groomed slopes seemed to go on forever below the famous mountain peak.

Mid-day, they skied down the Swiss side of the mountain, as far as the Trockener Steg cable car station. Leaving skis and poles at the station, they rode 2 cable cars down to Zermatt and ate lunch. There were many restaurants along Bahnhofstrasse, the main street of Zermatt, plus bars, boutiques, souvenir shops, bakeries and other shops.

Gino had a brochure which described interesting features of this small Swiss village, so he read to the group, *"Zermatt is surrounded by large mountains, including nine of the ten highest mountains in Europe. In this area, twenty mountains are over four thousand meters (13,100 ft.)."*

"Zermatt is so quiet," said Lucas. "It's one of the first things I noticed. I understand they don't allow combustion-engine vehicles."

"Yes, it's true," Gino replied. "Most people either walk or ride a bicycle in the village, but horse-drawn carriages and small electric taxis are used here. If you are not skiing and riding the cable car, the only ways to get in and out of here is by train or walking."

"I love the quaint village with cobblestone streets, the clean air and the friendly people," said Olivia.

Lucas hoped to have Goulash soup for lunch, but it was not on the menu. They all ate delicious vegetable soup and cheese fondue.

When they finished, George said, "We still have time for a couple more runs before become movie stars."

Back up at Plateau Rosa Glacier, they skied a couple more fun runs, then the long run down to Cervenia. As they arrived to meet the film crew at the bank, Rachel greeted them. Assistants divided the group and led them away for their parts in the shoot, except for Lucas.

Rachel guided Lucas to a trailer. She handed him an Italian Alpini uniform and hat, then took him to a group of 10 men, all wearing the same uniform. The men learned about the Alpini, infantry troops who specialize in mountain combat for the Italian Army.

Rachel explained the plot to the Alpini actors, "This movie is about a ski instructor who works at a winter resort in the Italian Alps. He robs the resort with the help of a down-on-his-luck ski racer. You are on a special Alpini training assignment. You will go everywhere Christian goes, thus making him (Jean-Claude Killy) very nervous."

Looking at the tall, balding man who stood beside her, Rachel said, "This is our Assistant Director, Peter Madsen. He will give all of you the instructions about your roles, and he will tell you what to do for the filming of various scenes."

Most of the day, the extras stood around, waiting to learn what they would do and listening to the director say, "Okay, roll 'em."

About sunset, filming for the day was done, and Rachel thanked everyone. She said she would see them all at Resto Grill Les Clochards, the restaurant would be theirs for the evening, starting at 8 p.m., and the studio would pay the tab.

In the restaurant's main dining room, 3 long tables were set with white tablecloths, silverware, cloth napkins, wine glasses, water glasses and candles. All the actors, directors and movie people sat at the table furthest from Lucas' table, except Rachel.

Lucas sat with the Garmisch group, and Rachel made sure she sat next to him for dinner. She said she had another role to discuss with him about the next day's filming.

Their first course was a choice of minestrone soup or a vegetable tarte. Lucas chose the tarte since he had soup for lunch.

Everyone seemed to be laughing and enjoying themselves, yet Lucas thought it was odd for Rachel to sit with his group.

With their main course in front of them, Rachel asked Lucas, "Have you ever driven a snowmobile?"

"No. I think I'll stick to skiing," he replied.

"It doesn't matter," said Rachel. "You can learn fast. I want you to drive a snowmobile in a race scene. Believe me, Lucas, it is safe, it pays well, and it will be fun for you. Please, think about it. We also want to have George drive a snowmobile if he is willing."

"I'll talk it over with George. It does sound like fun," he replied.

For the remaining dinner service, Lucas spent his time talking to Olivia who sat on the other side of him.

When Olivia excused herself and went to the restroom, Rachel asked Lucas, "Is she your girlfriend?"

"We are traveling together," he replied. "We met in Tarifa, Spain. After this, we will head for the Oktoberfest in Munich, and then we will go to Garmisch for the ski season."

Rachel looked disappointed, but she asked, "I don't suppose you could slip away to spend time with me alone?"

He replied, "Rachel, you are a beautiful and sexy woman. In a different situation, I would not hesitate to accept your offer. But I am with Olivia, and we're having a great time together. Now, I must know, do you still want me to drive a snowmobile tomorrow?"

Rachel paused a moment before she said, "I find you so attractive, I had to ask. Although I am very disappointed, I can see you and your Olivia are having a good time together. Yes, Lucas, the offer still stands."

They all had fun at dinner, especially Gino. He loved being back with some movie people, and he even got a speaking part in the movie. Lucas told George they had something to discuss after dinner.

The main course was beef tenderloin fondue with several sauces: béarnaise sauce, aioli, creamed horseradish and an Emmentaler cheese sauce. For dessert, servers came around with trays of delicious small cakes and pastries.

After dinner, people hung around the bar area to drink and talk. Some drifted in and out of the restaurant to smoke hashish or whatever movie people do. The event ended a little after midnight.

Everyone needed to get some rest. They wanted to be on the slopes early and would be shooting movie scenes in the afternoon. George, Ashleigh, Lucas and Olivia skipped nightcaps and retired early.

In their room, Lucas and Olivia smoked a little hashish which Gino gave them. When they made love, it began slow then finished more explosive than ever. Afterward, lying side by side, naked and holding hands, they were reminiscent about their day of skiing and acting.

Lucas told Olivia about the snowmobile race, and she said, "Oh, I hope I'll be able to watch you race."

"Do you know what you will do today?" asked Lucas.

"I'll be part of the bank crowd or maybe a bank teller," she replied. "The bank robbery takes place this afternoon. Jean-Claude Killy, playing the role of Christian, will jump off the roof onto the top of a cable car as it is leaving the shed. He will ride it to the top station, jump off the cable car and ski away with a backpack full of money."

"It sounds spectacular," said Lucas. "Our group is filming at a different location, somewhere with trees and deep snow."

Waiting for a reply, he looked over at Olivia who looked fantastic, but she was now sound asleep. He covered her with the down comforter, and he realized how comfortable it was to be with Olivia. Lucas looked forward to another beautiful day, skiing with her on the slopes. He was smiling when he drifted off to sleep.

George seemed excited about the snowmobile race. So, Lucas called Rachel early and told her they would both drive in the afternoon race. She advised him where they should be at 2 p.m.

Gino went to have breakfast with the movie crew. Lucas, George, Olivia and Ashleigh had breakfast in the bakery. While eating, they agreed to be in Munich on Saturday for the Oktoberfest.

Lucas called the Columbia Hotel, a military hotel in downtown Munich. Since he and George still had military ID cards, he reserved 2 double rooms for 3 nights. The Aussie ladies were impressed because hotel rooms were hard to come by during Oktoberfest in Munich.

On the final day of acting, Lucas and George had 30 minutes of instruction and solo test drives. Both passed and were ready to go.

It was time for the snowmobile races. A total of 16 racers were set to compete in drag races, divided in groups of 4 snowmobiles at a time. Lucas was in the last group of racers. He was standing next to his snowmobile when 2 policemen came running up. They were yelling in

Italian and pointing at men who had just taken off on a snowmobile, going across a wide slope and down to the left, toward Zermatt.

Over the noise of snowmobile motors, Lucas yelled at a policeman and asked him to speak English.

The policeman yelled back, "Bank robbers, follow the snowmobile!"

"Is this part of the movie?" asked Lucas.

The policeman answered, "No movie, we go, hurry," and he jumped on the back of the snowmobile.

To help the policeman, Lucas jumped on the front, put it in gear and followed the bank robbers. George and the other policeman joined the chase, right behind them. They were on the Italy/Switzerland border. Lucas had skied this slope for 2 days. He knew the terrain, and he thought the bank robbers were going too fast. They also did not seem very skillful at driving the snowmobile.

These guys are out of control, and they will crash, thought Lucas.

He slowed down, deciding to keep the robbers in sight and not crash the snowmobile he was on.

The policeman yelled in Lucas' ear, "Più veloce!" (Faster!).

However, Lucas kept driving the same speed, as they approached the Trockener Steg Lift. On this downhill run, he knew about a pile of large rocks which were a few feet beyond a sharp left turn, and he slowed down a little more.

The robbers did not know about the turn or the rock pile. They flew into the field of sharp rocks with the sickening sound of a crash. Above them, people on the chairlift watched and said, "Oooh," all at once.

Lucas stopped close to the crash site, and the policeman got off. George and the other policeman pulled in behind Lucas. They could see the stolen snowmobile was destroyed, and it was obvious 1 robber was dead. With his head smashed in and his face a bloody mess, his limp and battered body hung over a rock. The other robber was not moving, but his head still looked intact. Since the policeman said he could not find a pulse, Lucas helped to roll the guy over.

When he saw the man's face, Lucas looked squarely at George and shook his head which warned George to keep quiet. Lucas recognized this robber, as the man who had come to meet Andreas Baader and Ulrike Meinhof in Landeck, Austria.

Lucas announced, "We have to go back to work. If you need us, you can contact the movie company in Cervenia. Ciao (Goodbye)."

Not waiting for the policemen to respond, Lucas and George climbed on the 2 snowmobiles and headed back up the slope.

They arrived at Plateau Rosa. The movie director and crew were standing at the start line where the snowmobile race was taking place.

Everyone began talking at the same time and there seemed to be a lot of confusion about their arrival.

Lucas had to yell, to be heard, “We helped those policemen chase two criminals—until they crashed. Then, we came right back!”

“We cut you two from the scene, and we’re just finishing up,” said the director. “You can take the snowmobiles down to the Testa Grigia Lift and wait for us at the truck. Or, leave the snowmobiles there and take the cable car back to Cervenia where they are filming the robbery scene. Then, we’ll see you at the bank.”

Lucas and George had a great time riding the snowmobiles, all the way to the truck. The scenery was fantastic, and the visibility was excellent. After dropping off the snowmobiles, they headed toward the bank and hoped to find the rest of their group.

While walking from the cable car to the bank, Lucas said, “Wow, this has been quite a day! Those RAF guys are still robbing banks. I think Andreas and Ulrike might still be in Jordan. Well anyway, they have two fewer members now. The robbers could have followed the movie script and escaped to Zermatt, by riding the lifts. I wonder what made them decide to steal a snowmobile.”

“I guess we’ll never know,” said George. “The robbers are dead, and the snowmobile is beyond repair. For now, I think we should sit on this and not say too much about it, not even to Gino and the ladies.”

“Okay,” said Lucas. “We should probably leave early in the morning, and head to the Oktoberfest. If we stay here, we might get stuck answering questions which we don’t want to answer.”

Streets around the bank were still roped off for filming of the robbery scene. Rachel spotted them and waived them into the crew area.

Olivia and Ashleigh rushed over. Olivia kissed Lucas on the cheek and said, “We worried about you Yanks; we heard there was a snowmobile accident and two men are dead.”

Lucas and George gave them a condensed version of the chase.

Rachel joined them and said, “You are finished filming for the day. You can come by the main trailer to return the uniforms and get your paychecks before noon tomorrow. However, if you want to stay and work for a while, you are all welcome to do so.”

They all declined to stay. Everyone had a great time, being extras in the movie, and each person expressed their appreciation to Rachel.

On the walk back to the apartment, Olivia said to Lucas, “I was so relieved when I saw you at the bank. If you had been in the accident, I would never see you again which would make me very unhappy.”

She stopped in the street, gave Lucas a big hug and a great kiss. Then, they held hands and strutted back to the bakery.

Everyone was back from skiing, yet in various stages of dressing, including the very curvaceous Judann who was running around in only her bra and panties.

The group sent someone to go get more beer. The rest stayed in and ordered pizza from the bakery downstairs.

Everyone shared stories about their experiences as movie extras. It was a fantastic evening with lots of laughter. The highlight of the night was a heated wrestling match between Eric and George, both macho guys until Lucas jumped on top of them. Then, they all started laughing.

Everyone wanted to hear George and Lucas tell their story again. They left out the part about recognizing the real bank robber, a member of the notorious Baader-Meinhof Gang.

After great pizza, several beers, shots of Jägermeister and hits on Gino's hash pipe, Lucas and Olivia snuck out and went to their room for some quality time together.

The next morning, Lucas, Olivia, George and Ashleigh got up early and grabbed sweet rolls, wrapped to go. Saying goodbye to Gino, they thanked him for sharing his hashish, finding the apartment and teaching the ladies to ski. Everyone said they had a great time.

Next, they stopped at the movie's administration trailer, dropped off their uniforms and collected their meager paychecks.

Lucas kept his Alpini hat with a feather in it. When they left, he chuckled as he thought: *I need lederhosen to go with my new hat.*

Everyone looked forward to seeing Gino again in Garmisch. They all agreed: Gino had become a close friend during their short time together in Cervenia.

Before starting the 8-hour drive to Munich, they stopped at the store and bought another case of Paulaner.

CHAPTER 15

Munich

George and Ashleigh crawled into the bed in the van, turned off the back speakers, and slept the next 3 1/2 hours while Lucas drove.

Olivia was reading to Lucas about the Oktoberfest and Munich, *"The Oktoberfest is an annual, sixteen-day festival, held from late September to the first week of October. It began as a wedding celebration when Crown Prince Ludwig, later to become King Ludwig the First, married Princess Therese of Saxe-Hildburghausen in eighteen ten on October twelfth. All citizens of Munich were invited to attend and celebrate the happy, royal event. The festivities took place on grassy fields in front of the city gates. In honor of the Crown Princess, the fields were named Theresienwiese (Meadows of Therese). They kept the name ever since, but the locals refer to the fields as The Wiesn. For the Oktoberfest, all the beer comes from six breweries: Spaten, Löwenbräu, Hacker-Pschorr, Augustiner, Hofbräu and Paulaner."*

Olivia waved her Paulaner beer bottle in the air, saying, "Prost," and continued reading, *"Beer is brewed in March, and then it goes through a slow process of fermentation. The resulting alcohol content is between five and six percent. At Oktoberfest, the most popular beer is a pale lager. Marzen is also popular; it is a darker beer with a slight reddish color. Some people don't realize how strong the festival beer is, and they pass out. The local Germans call them Bierleichen (beer corpses)."*

"I think American beer is between three and five percent for the strongest, but I can't drink American beer anymore," said Lucas. "It's too carbonated and leaves you with a headache if you drink as much as I do, or as much as you do too, Olivia."

Olivia laughed, finished her Paulaner beer and got them another. Then, she said to Lucas, "Ashleigh and I need to get jobs soon. Do you think we can get jobs in Garmisch?"

"Gino told us they won't be hiring until the ski slopes get ready to open, so pray for snow," replied Lucas. "But it might be a good idea to apply while we are in Munich. We can stay in a military hotel. There is a large commissary and PX in town. George and I got jobs right away when we were in Frankfurt."

Stopping in Bern, Switzerland, Lucas got gas. George and Ashleigh woke up, and everyone agreed it was time for lunch.

Lucas loved the layout of Bern. They pulled off Laubeggstrasse, the main highway, onto Ostermundigenstrasse which makes a short jag and becomes Alter Aargauerstaldens, and they found a restaurant named der Rosengarten (the Rose Garden).

Sitting at a table on the terrace, they had a beautiful view of the old town which is on a peninsula. The Aare River surrounds it on 3 sides. The menu was a mixture of German, Italian, local Swiss and even a single Indian dish.

While others were still deciding, Lucas ordered Lamm-Entrecôte mit Oliven-Kräuterkruste, Weissweinrisotto und Gemüse (lamb sirloin steak with olive-herb crust, white wine risotto and vegetables).

Olivia and Ashleigh wanted Black Angus Rinds-Filet mit Markbein, Pommes Frites und Gemüse (Black Angus beef filet with bone marrow, vegetables and French fries).

George asked for Grilliertes Zandersteak auf geschmortem mon Le braised Zitronen-Fenchel, und Kapern (grilled Zander steak with lemon fennel and capers on braised vegetables). The waiter told them Zander was a fish which had similarities to both pike and perch.

After lunch, they walked through a vast rose garden. It also featured other flowers: irises, rhododendrons and azaleas. They saw stone statues, manicured lawns, and a pond where they found a bench to sit on.

Ashleigh got the travel book out and read to the others about Bern, *"The city was first built on a narrow hill where the Aare River makes a one-hundred-and-eighty-degree turn and surrounds the peninsula on three sides. Over the years the city has spread to both sides of the river, and bridges were built, but the old city still has the same medieval charm. Tourists can visit the Bärengraben (Bear Pit), a park enclosure which houses live bears. The bear has been a symbol of Bern for several centuries. According to legend, a local Duke decided they would name the city after the first animal encountered by his hunting party. Since that was a bear, the image for Bern's coat of arms became a black bear, climbing upward on a background of red and gold stripes."*

They walked across the Nydeggbrücke (bridge) over the Aare River and along Kramgasse. Ashleigh said, "The travel book has a small map of places to see. The famous Zytglogge is on this street close to a flat where Albert Einstein lived at Forty-nine Kramgasse."

"What is a Zytglogge?" asked George.

Reading from her travel book, Ashleigh replied, *"The Zytglogge is a medieval tower which was built in the thirteenth century. Over the years, it was used as a guard tower, a prison and a clock tower. It is a big tourist attraction at the center of activity here. The original tower was only sixteen meters (52 ft.) in height, however the Zytglogge has been renovated and made higher, many times, to its current height of fifty-four and one-half meters (179 ft.)."*

When they got to the open, cobblestone square, Lucas studied the famous clock tower. He wondered if it ever stood alone because the tower was attached on 1 side to a 5-story building, and there were many similar, but separate, buildings in the square. The ground floor of the tower was a gigantic, arched walkway which people passed through.

High at the top, under a pointed steeple, was a large bell and a gold bell-striker (an animated, mechanized figure of a person) with a hammer. The striker was the same height as the bell. Every hour on the hour, the striker moved and struck the bell. There were 2 smaller gold bells which rang out every quarter-hour when struck by a smaller bell-striker. Those hung in a carved, ornate section on the face of the tower, located below the large hour-bell.

"What is the smaller clock about, Ashleigh?" asked Lucas.

"I was reading about it. It's an astronomical clock," she said.

Lucas studied the clocks. *The largest clock is protected by a steep shingle roof which extends out 6 feet or more beyond the tower walls below. The big clock is impressive enough with gold hands and numerals. Below it, the smaller clock is a very complicated piece of machinery.*

Seeing the puzzled looks on her friends' faces, Ashleigh read, *"An astronomical clock has special mechanisms and various dials which display astronomical information, such as the relative positions of the sun, moon, zodiacal constellations and sometimes major planets. The term often refers to any clock which provides astronomical information in addition to the time of day."*

"It would take someone like Einstein to figure it out," said George.

Leaving Bern and heading straight to Munich, everyone was wide awake. Lucas drove for 2 hours, then George drove for 2 1/2 hours. They drank beer and sang, while listening to music, performed by Crosby, Stills, Nash and Young, plus another group called Blood, Sweat and Tears.

The Columbia Hotel is at Jagdstraße 8 in Munich. Many American military hotels in Munich are similar; nothing is fancy, but the price is right. Also, they could get a beer and a hot dog for $1. The Aussie ladies could not believe prices were so cheap.

"This is why we want to work for the military," said Lucas.

They checked in, went to their rooms, showered and changed clothes. When they were all ready, they went to the restaurant and got a table near the bar. Looking for a waiter or a waitress, Lucas saw a man come out of a back room. Walking toward them was a handsome Latino who had a great smile.

Lucas could not believe who it was, and he blurted out, “Topo!”

Topo’s smile got broader, and he said, “Lucas and George!” They both got a big hug before Lucas introduced Olivia and Ashleigh.

As Lucas could see, the ladies were spellbound, by Topo’s imposing appearance and fantastic smile. While being introduced, Olivia took Topo’s left hand and Ashleigh took his right hand, both greeting him at the same time.

“Topo, will you please get us all a good German beer and a menu?” asked Lucas. “Then, come back and talk when you have time.”

“Let’s all have a shot of Jägermeister for old time’s sake, as we did in Nice,” said Topo. Before he left, he flashed his great smile again.

When Topo brought the beers, shots and menus, he bent over and whispered into Lucas’ ear, “How are you fixed for hashish?”

“We have none,” Lucas whispered back. “Since we didn’t want to cross any borders with it, we smoked it all before we left Italy.”

“Give me your room number, and I’ll bring some to you during my break,” Topo said, quietly.

“You’re on, my friend,” claimed Lucas, as he raised his shot glass and said a toast, “To the road to Garmisch.” They all raised their glasses, took a sip and laughed.

After dinner, they went back to Lucas and Ashleigh’s room, armed with *The Stars and Stripes* and *International Herald* newspapers. While the others were talking, Lucas took a quick look at the papers. He was disturbed to see news about things happening in Jordan.

When Topo arrived, he produced a new hash pipe and a nice chunk of dark-colored hashish which he said was great stuff.

As they passed the pipe around, Lucas got Topo a beer and he asked, “Topo, how did you get here, and how did you get a job, so fast?”

“I took a train from Nice, got hired here, got an ID card and found a place to live,” said Topo. “As soon as I can, I will transfer to Garmisch, Berchtesgaden or Lake Chiemsee and ski in Bavaria.”

“Olivia and I are from Melbourne,” said Ashleigh. “We’ve been in Europe for a few months, and we’ve been traveling all over, but we need to get jobs now. Do you think we could get jobs here?”

“I’m sure they will find jobs for such pretty, fit-looking ladies,” Topo replied. “This is different, compared to most jobs. Working for the military is fun, and many civilian employees are travelers, like us. Some are locals, leftovers from the war-era. The atmosphere is relaxed here, and you can drink beer while you work. I do, all the time. Employees get to eat free, but the menu is limited unless you work in the kitchen. It's a good place to work, and Americans tip better than anyone."

"Topo, where did you get this stuff? This is great!" asked Lucas.

"If I told you, I'd have to kill you," he said. Everybody laughed.

Then, conversation turned to a recent airplane hijacking in Jordan. It was like he awoke from a dream—Lucas had been reading about the PLO (Palestine Liberation Organization), how they hijacked 4 airplanes and took them to a remote airstrip in Jordan. The conversation triggered Lucas to think of Andreas and Ulrike because they had said they were going to train with the Palestine insurgents in Jordan.

"Based on things I've read, RAF members are active in the same area of Western Asia," said Lucas.

"Yes. I've heard of them," said Topo. "You never know where or when they will appear and kidnap someone, rob a bank or bomb something. What's the deal with those guys?"

"Well, I read about the leaders," said Lucas. "Andreas Baader and his girlfriend, Gudrun Ensslin, started the group nineteen sixty-eight. About the same time, they burned down a store in Frankfurt. They seem to be more serious now. If they are training with the PLO, there is no telling what they will do if they don't get caught."

Lucas thought about his and George's encounters with the RAF. He knew it would be best to keep quiet about any acquaintance with leaders of the terrorist group.

George and Lucas told Topo about their experience in Tangier when the Moroccan pulled a knife and tried to rob their friend, David Burns. They knew the guy was looking for them because they beat him up, took his hashish and took back David's money.

When they finished telling the story, Topo said, "Man, you are lucky to be alive. Those drug dealers don't like to get ripped off. Hey, I must get back to work. Thanks for the beer and shots. It was great to see you. I will also be working here tomorrow. I hope to see you then."

"He is such a nice man," Ashleigh said after he left.

"And, so handsome," Olivia added.

"I agree on both counts," said Lucas.

They were all tired from the drive, so they took showers and changed clothes. They smoked hashish, but did not drink beer since they figured it would be better to pace themselves.

Riding a streetcar to the Oktoberfest, they saw many people on the streets, but nothing compared with crowds at the 'fest' grounds. It was a very busy place with an oompah band playing, people singing and dirndl-clad waitresses carrying 10 glass mugs of beer. Each mug held a full liter of beer. One waitress carried 16 mugs at once. The group bought liters of beer and walked around. At the food stands, there were long lines of hungry people, all carrying mugs of beer and swaying to “Ein Prosit” which was the favorite song of the Oktoberfest.

They saw walls of Hendl (roast chicken) turning on spits. Other food items included Schweinebraten (roast pork), Schweinshaxe (grilled ham hock), Steckerlfisch (grilled fish on a stick), Würstl (sausages), Brezen (pretzel), Knödel (potato or bread dumplings), Käsespäetzle (cheese noodles), Reiberdatschi (potato pancakes), Rotkohl/Blaukraut (red cabbage), Sauerkraut and other Bavarian delicacies such as Obatzda (a spicy cheese-butter spread) and Weisswurst (a white sausage).

With another liter of beer, they all tried and shared the Hendl, Knodel, Reiberdatschi, Rotkohl and Weisswurst. After eating so much food, they all wanted leave; and they rode the tram back to the hotel.

Lucas and Olivia plopped into bed and went right to sleep. However, the next morning Olivia invited Lucas into the shower, and they had a great time massaging each other with the bar of soap. Then, they got back in bed for a very exciting romp.

At noon, George and Ashleigh met Lucas and Olivia in the hotel dining room. They all ordered club sandwiches, French fries and a Spaten beer for breakfast. As they were finishing their food, Topo came in and stopped by their table before he went to work.

“Gruss Gott,” said Topo. “I trust you found the Oktoberfest.”

“Yeah, and we had fun, but it was a long day,” said Lucas.

“When you have time, would you tell us where to apply for a job?” Olivia asked Topo.

“Okay, I have time now,” he replied. “It’s at McGraw Kaserne. Ask the desk clerk for directions and a map. Buena suerte! (Good luck).”

They drove over to McGraw Kaserne, and Lucas got on base, using his military ID card. The guard gave Lucas a map and directions to the civilian personnel office which is in the administration building. As he looked at the map, it amazed him to see the size of the kaserne. There were many large barracks and other buildings. Most structures were 3 or 4 stories and had the cold look of Nazi architecture.

While the ladies went inside, George and Lucas waited in the van, drank beer and listened to a Johnny Rivers tape. Lucas liked the music, but George hated it.

The ladies came back out to the van and said they had finished with their applications. Right now, the personnel office had no specific job information, but they were told to call back daily and get updates on their hiring status.

"Well, rather than hang out in this crowded city, we can ski on the Zugspitze, and we can dance at The Grill in Garmisch," said Lucas.

"You can call from Garmisch, and we can bring you back if you get jobs in Munich," George told the ladies. "You can also apply in Garmisch if you want to."

Olivia and Ashleigh looked at each other, and both nodded.

"Where will we stay in Garmisch?" asked Olivia.

"We can stay in a military hotel or in a German Gasthof," said Lucas. "Both offer reasonable accommodations. There's a gymnasium in town, waterskiing on Lake Eibsee if it isn't too cold now, and there are lots of hiking trails."

"Okay, let's go check out of the Columbia Hotel," said George. "Also, we should tell Topo of our plan."

They drove back to the hotel, parked on the street, went to their rooms, and they all drank a beer while they got their stuff together. Downstairs, saying goodbye to Topo, they told him they would be back soon, and everyone gave Topo a big hug.

When they left and walked out to the van—it was not there.

"It must have been towed, or it was stolen," said Lucas. "Let's go back in the hotel and ask the desk clerk."

They told him about the van, and the first thing the clerk asked was, "Where did you park?"

Lucas described the location. The clerk shook his head and said, "I guess you did not read the sign, posted for NO PARKING in front of the hotel. It is written in German."

After the desk clerk told them where they could locate their van, he phoned for a taxi. The ladies stayed at the hotel while Lucas and George went to get the van.

"We left the hashish in the van, right?" asked George.

"Yeah, but it's in the food cabinet," replied Lucas. "If they search the van and find it, maybe they'll think it is some type of spice. I guess, if they put handcuffs on us, we'll know for sure. Let's find out."

After paying a fine and towing charges, they looked to see if the hashish was still there—it was. They both felt relieved.

We must be more careful with our stash. I sure don't want to go to jail, thought Lucas.

George and Lucas picked up the ladies at the hotel. They stopped for gas, got a case of Löwenbräu and headed toward Garmisch. Driving along the autobahn, they passed many small towns including Penzberg, a coal mining town which is 50 kilometers southwest of Munich. They drove through Ohlstadt, Eschenlohe and Oberau, then drove past the Garmisch Golf Club.

For Lucas, driving into Garmisch-Partenkirchen was like driving into a fairy tale. The massive and beautiful Alps loomed above him and hovered over the magical village where church steeples pointed to the sky, much taller than all the other buildings.

They checked into the Lake Eibsee Hotel, 10 kilometers west of Garmisch, and got rooms overlooking the lake, hoping they would still be able to waterski.

Everyone got cleaned up, and then they drove to The Grill, all eager to see Gino, have dinner, drink beer and maybe dance a little.

As usual, Gino and John Ferrell were behind the bar. They let out a big yell when Lucas, George and the ladies walked in. The band was playing, and the place was crowded, although it was only 8:30 p.m.

Seated in the dining room, everyone had a half-liter of Augustiner beer, grilled rib eye steak, baked potato and red cabbage.

When they finished dinner, they headed into the bar's disco and found an empty table for 6 people. The extra chairs would be handy if people they met in Cervenia were there, and Gino might join them on his break. Lucas wanted to find out if Bruno came back to Garmisch from Ibiza.

Before getting out on the dance floor, Lucas ordered beers and shots of Jägermeister to get everyone going. The music was so loud, Lucas and Olivia spoke directly into each other's ears while they sat at the table. It was difficult to hear what the other was saying.

They gave up talking and decided to dance for a while. Lucas liked the band because they played current pop music.

A young lady sang a Cher song, "Gypsies, Tramps & Thieves." Then, a mop-haired guitarist joined her to sing the Sonny and Cher song, "I Got You Babe." They also did versions of "Close to You" (song by the Carpenters), "River Deep–Mountain High" (a song recorded by Ike and Tina Turner), and "Proud Mary" (a song written by John Fogerty, of Creedence Clearwater Revival).

They went back to their table, and Gino did come by on his break. He asked Lucas, "Where are you staying?"

"At the Eibsee Hotel," Lucas answered.

"I get off at ten, so save me a seat," said Gino. "I have some things to tell you about Bruno."

While Lucas and Olivia danced again, Lucas saw Sonya dancing with a big guy who had black hair. Lucas recognized him when he turned around. It was the same guy he saw at the docks in Formentera and Ibiza. It was Bruno.

His own thoughts surprised Lucas when he saw them together: *I hope Sonya is not dating this mortal enemy of mine. Maybe she is only dancing with him. I might be jumping to conclusions.*

When Lucas and Olivia finished dancing, they returned to their table. A few guys from the Cervenia crowd arrived, including Eric and Steve. Lucas stood and shook hands with them.

Over loud music, Eric shouted to Lucas, "Tomorrow afternoon, can you get together with some Cervenia guys for a few beers?"

"Yeah, but we plan to go waterskiing after lunch," said Lucas. "For us, it will be breakfast. Maybe you guys would like to join us. We can meet at Lake Eibsee Hotel."

"Maybe. I've wanted to try waterskiing, but I never have," said Eric.

"Are you a snow skier, Eric?" asked Lucas.

"Cervenia was my first attempt," said Eric. "But I'll get better,"

Gino came to tell Lucas he was off work and ready to leave. George and Ashleigh wanted to hang around, so Lucas offered to leave the van at The Grill, so they could use it. Since he and Olivia were going back to the hotel, Lucas asked if anyone wanted a ride with Gino; everyone else was staying at the bar.

"I'll try to come see you tomorrow at the lake," Eric said to Lucas.

Before leaving, Lucas scanned the room and spotted Sonya. Sure enough, she was sitting on Bruno's lap. Lucas liked Sonya too much to let this guy abuse her, or kill her. Bruno already murdered Jodie in Long Beach, and Gabrielle's friend, Kirstin, was never found in Formentera. Lucas had to do something about Bruno soon.

Arriving back at the hotel, Gino parked his van and came to their room. Lucas handed out Spaten beers while Olivia lit the hash pipe and passed it around.

"I guess you noticed, Bruno is back," said Gino. "I heard he is working again at the Von Steuben Hotel. Lately, he is spending a lot of time with Sonya, and it is alarming our circle of friends. Here at AFRC, people are aware of his horrible reputation."

"Who are Bruno and Sonya?" asked Olivia.

Lucas did not want people to know he is stalking Bruno. He said to Olivia, "They are just two more Garmisch characters. You will run across them while you're here."

He poured them each a shot of Jägermeister for a "Prost." Then, Lucas asked, "Gino, are you working tomorrow?"

"Yes, I am," he replied. "I have Sunday and Monday off."

Olivia asked Lucas, "If the weather stays nice at the lake, as it is today, could we go waterskiing tomorrow? I really want to ski at the lake."

"Sounds great," said Lucas. "On Friday, I want to go to the Zugspitze and hit the slopes. In fact, if you want to ski on water and snow, we could do both tomorrow. Where else can you do those in one day?"

Gino suggested an option: Instead of using military hotels, Lucas could get a room in a German hotel. They are affordable, priced by the week, and within walking distance of most things in town.

At the moment, Lucas was focused on getting into bed with Olivia, and he said, "I'll keep it in mind. Thanks for the ride to our hotel."

After Gino thanked them for the beers, hashish and Jägermeister, he felt exhausted and headed for his room at the Bayerischer Hof.

"How long have you known Gino?" Olivia asked.

"When George and I got off the train from Frankfurt, Gino and John, the other bartender you saw at The Grill, were the first people we met in Garmisch." Lucas answered.

"It seems like he is an old friend, and he is so nice," said Olivia.

"So far," said Lucas, "I've only met nice people, except for one."

"Who are you referring to?" she asked.

"I'd rather not say, right now," he replied. "Anyway, you don't want to know him. He is a bad man."

"Okay, but now I'm curious," she said.

Lucas smiled. "I'm going to hit the shower," he said. "Would you care to join me?"

Olivia laughed, then answered by pulling off her sweater and pants as she headed toward the bathroom. Lucas followed her, fumbling with the zipper on his pants.

In the morning, Lucas and Olivia had a late breakfast at the hotel with George and Ashleigh. They finished eating, returned to their rooms, put on swimsuits, went down to the dock and got in line to waterski.

Lucas had been waterskiing since he was a teenager. Also, he and George had owned a sleek ski boat. They would launch in the Marine Stadium (a venue for boating, waterskiing and rowing) at Belmont Shore, or they launched at Long Beach Harbor. At the harbor, they skied next to huge naval-aircraft carriers which always docked there.

Olivia and Ashleigh were naturals on the water because of their surfing skills. However, the water was quite chilly, so they each took only 2 laps around the lake.

On the way back to her and Lucas' room, Olivia asked the others, "Did you notice the guy in the boat who looks like a movie star?"

"Yeah, I saw him," said Lucas. "There is something familiar about him, but I don't know where from."

In their room, Olivia phoned the Munich Kaserne to check with the personnel office. She spoke to a woman who told her they were hired as waitresses, and they should come to the office on Monday.

Olivia got off the phone and said to Ashleigh, "They want us to go Monday for orientation. We start work Tuesday as waitresses!"

"Waitress is good, it means tips," said Ashleigh.

George and Ashleigh went to grab an afternoon nap. They would all meet up later and go out for the evening.

Olivia took advantage of this quiet time with Lucas, and she asked about what they would do next.

"We could go skiing on the Zugspitze tomorrow," said Lucas. "Then, if you want to, we can drive to Munich and stay in the Columbia Hotel where we can spend one more night together."

"It sounds perfect," she said. "I'm going to miss you, Lucas. I have had the best time of my life."

"I have had a fabulous time with you, Olivia, and I hope we will have more fun together in the future," he replied.

They went to the bar where Eric, Regan Stone and John Ferrell were sitting at a table with a view, overlooking the lake.

When Lucas and Olivia walked over, Eric said, "Have a seat, you two. Did you ski on the lake today?"

"Yes. We had a late breakfast with George and Ashleigh," said Lucas. "Then, we all had fun waterskiing. It was the ladies' first time, and they did very well. Now, we're all looking forward to a great Saturday night at The Grill. What are you guys up to?"

"We played three-on-three basketball at the gym," replied Regan. "We're also going to The Grill after we have dinner here."

"Oh, you play basketball, huh?" asked Lucas.

"Yes. Regan played point guard at a Texas college," said Eric. "I was a baseball pitcher at the University of Minnesota, but I can hold my own on the basketball court. Lucas, do you play?"

"Yeah. During high school, I played in Fresno. Then, I played for several years in Long Beach with the city's A-League," said Lucas. "I look forward to playing with you guys. George is an All-American Volleyball Player, and he's the volleyball coach at a Long Beach High School. He is a fantastic athlete."

Regan smiled. Speaking with his Texas drawl, he said, "Okay, we'll see about that. Y'all bring some money."

Everyone laughed. *Now, the stage is set for some real fun on the court,* thought Lucas.

At the Eibsee Hotel, Lucas, George, Olivia and Ashleigh enjoyed a nice Prime Rib Dinner with creamed horseradish, scalloped potatoes, and Brussels sprouts cooked with bacon. For dessert, they had apple strudel.

Following dinner, Olivia said, "Lucas, I need to dance all night after such a big meal."

Lucas finished his Spaten beer and said, "Let's go have fun."

At the International Bar and Grill, Lucas, Olivia, George and Ashleigh sat with Eric, Steve and Regan. John Ferrell was working with Gino; both were tending bar.

Lucas and Olivia enjoyed themselves. They sat and drank a beer, danced to a couple of songs, stopped and sat for another beer, then kept repeating the sequence.

Halfway through the evening, Lucas and Olivia were dancing, and a fight broke out on the dance floor. A big, drunk GI attacked an older civilian man who had longer hair and a smaller physique. The bouncer, Jordan Lewis, came behind the big GI and lifted him, as he wrapped his arms and huge hands under the GI's arms and applied pressure on the GI's neck. Then, Lewis walked the GI outside and turned him over to MPs who are usually on duty around The Grill at night. Olivia and Lucas had a ringside view of the whole thing.

After things quieted down, Olivia, pointed to Jordan Lewis and asked, "Lucas, do you know the bouncer? His action was impressive."

"I met him once," he replied. "He's from Long Beach. I didn't know him there, but he knew one of my best friends. Jordan is a lot tougher than he looks. In any street fight, I'd want him on my side."

"I hope it never happens, mate," said Olivia. "I've seen too many of those in Australia."

"Yeah, I saw some of your guys' action in Spain," said Lucas.

They danced the night away, drank Augustiner draft, laughed and had fun with their new friends in Garmisch. Lucas, Olivia, George and Ashleigh left at 2 a.m.

Lucas and Olivia crashed in each other's arms and slept soundly until a maid knocked on the door. It was 10:00 a.m. and time to check out. When they took a quick shower together, Olivia said she would attend to his erection later, at the hotel in Munich.

At breakfast with Olivia, George and Ashleigh, Lucas said, "You know, I am tired of eating hotel and restaurant food. I think I want to find a place with a kitchen where we can cook and eat healthier meals. Anyway, I love to cook."

"If you do, can Olivia and I come back to visit?" asked Ashleigh.

"You have an open invitation, anytime you want," replied Lucas.

The night before, their group had agreed to take Eric and Regan with them to the Oktoberfest.

Lucas went along with the group's plan, although he thought: *I guess skiing on the Zugspitze will have to wait for another day.*

Since Regan was working as a busboy at the Hausberg Restaurant, he also had a military ID. They got 3 rooms at the Columbia Hotel in Munich, using 3 ID cards.

The group had a great time at the Oktoberfest. While finishing their 2nd mug of Oktoberfest beer, Lucas, George, Olivia and Ashleigh decided they all had enough of the crowds.

When they said goodnight to Eric and Regan, the guys were talking to 2 American cuties, young women who were staying in Munich before returning to school in Italy.

Back at the hotel, Lucas and Olivia went to George and Ashleigh's room, smoked a bowl of hash and had a shot of Jägermeister.

Retiring to their own room, Lucas and Olivia made love, as if it was the end of the earth. It was profound.

Saying goodbye to the ladies was difficult for Lucas and George. After an early breakfast, they drove the ladies to McGraw Kaserne for orientation. Lucas and George had each cultivated closeness with these marvelous Australian ladies, and both wanted to see them again.

Arriving back at the Columbia Hotel, they found Eric and Regan waiting outside, and they looked like hell. Lucas climbed into the back of the van and opened the sliding door.

When Eric and Regan got in, Lucas handed each of them a Spaten beer and said, "Prost. How was the Oktoberfest?"

Eric mumbled something about picking up 2 German women, taking them back to their room and not getting much sleep.

"Well, let's get back to Garmisch," said Lucas.

Everyone got their bags and checked out of the hotel. George drove and Regan sat in the front passenger seat, nursing a beer. From Munich, it was a 1-hour drive to Garmisch. During this ride, Lucas learned a few things about Eric and Regan.

Eric was from Minnesota. It has a large Scandinavian population, and his Swedish heritage showed in his appearance. At 6'3" and 220 lbs., he had blonde hair and creamy Scandinavian skin. He had pitched baseball in the College World Series while he was a pitcher for the University of Minnesota. He told them he liked all sports, played golf and basketball, and he wanted to learn how to ski this winter.

Regan Stone was orphaned at birth and later adopted by a man who has one of the largest ranches in West Texas. Regan will inherit the family estate when his adoptive father passes on. He played point guard for a small Texas college. Recently, he passed the Texas bar exam and got his law degree. Before he starts a law practice in Corpus Christi, Texas, he is taking time off. Here in Europe, he works as a busboy at the Hausberg Restaurant, and he drives an old, blue VW Van. Of course, he bought the van from Bob Ostergaard.

While they got closer to Garmisch, everyone sat back, relaxed and listened to music.

As Lucas thought about this group of people, gathering in Garmisch, he realized they had something special going on. He only knew them for a short period, and he already felt like part of the group.

Everyone here had common goals: having a good time, partying, skiing, getting high and getting laid, as much as possible, to name a few. All these activities occurred while working for and mooching off the American military, known here in Bavaria as the AFRC (Armed Forces Recreation Center).

Thinking about the fun he and George had with Olivia and Ashleigh, Lucas remembered his conversation with George, earlier in the day.

After they left Olivia and Ashleigh in Munich and drove away from McGraw Kaserne, Lucas had asked George, "I wonder which one will sleep with Topo?"

George had smiled before he replied, "Maybe both."

CHAPTER 16
Garmisch

Back in Garmisch, Lucas and George checked into the Sheridan, put their stuff in the room, and then headed over to the gym at the American school. Teamed with Bill Stevens who coached for the school, the guys played a pick-up game against some GIs who thought they played great basketball until they got beat, 21 to 10.

Eric, Regan and John Ferrell arrived and challenged the winners. John is 35 years old, and he guarded Lucas. John handled the ball well, plus he played tight and aggressive on defense. He had Lucas well-covered, and he kept Lucas from getting the ball. Then, Lucas got going. He would take a pass from George and dribble around John for a reverse lay-up, or he stepped back and drilled a fall-away, 18-foot jump shot.

Eric and George were going at it. There was rivalry between them, maybe even dislike for each other. Eric was bigger than George, but George was a superb athlete. George could jump and shoot over Eric, allowing him to grab rebounds and fire them back out to Lucas. Then, Lucas could shoot his jumper, or drive while going to the basket, or pass off to either Bill or George if he was double-teamed.

Regan turned out to be a sharpshooter who could also go to the basket. Lucas tightened his defense and smothered him, trying to keep him from getting the ball. However, Regan's shooting got his team ahead 14 to 12. Then, Lucas did what he knew he could do—he took over the game. Stealing the ball from Regan and using a wicked crossover dribble, Lucas drove to the basket for a lay-up. His next score was a 20-foot jump shot. Afterward, he took a pass from Bill on the baseline and made a reverse lay-up. His team now led, 18 to 14.

Eric hit a wild hook shot from 8 feet. Then, Lucas gave Bill a behind-the-back pass in the lane, and Bill laid it in for a 20 to 16 score. John hit a long set shot, making the score 20 to 18.

Lucas passed to George who dribbled at the top of the key and passed to Bill on the left wing. Then, Bill passed right back to George as Lucas was crossing under the basket to the right wing, losing Regan just enough to get the pass from George; Lucas canned a 21-footer which won the game at 22 to 18.

Regan, John and Eric promised to get even, next time. They all showered in the gym and headed to The Grill for dinner, except for Bill who had to work the next day.

While Lucas and George had an early dinner with Regan, John and Eric, they learned about John Ferrell who was born and raised in Boston, Massachusetts. John played basketball in high school and had 2 college degrees: 1 in accounting and 1 in psychology. He spent 2 years in the U.S. Army, stationed in Italy where he learned to speak Italian; he also spoke Russian. John learned to tend bar here at The Grill, and he made great tips from the Americans. John loved to drink beer with the rest of the group, but he seemed to get drunk faster than others.

Lucas saw Sonya cuddling with Bruno in the discothèque, and he felt concern for her safety. Once more, he thought: *I must do something about this guy, before he hurts Sonya again, or kills her.*

Since Lucas and George planned to go skiing on the Zugspitze the next day, they only had two beers. On their way out, they talked to Gino who was busy tending bar. Then, they returned to the Sheridan where they shared a room for the night with no women around.

The next morning, Lucas and George had an early breakfast and went to catch the Zugspitzbahn (railway/cog-train) for a beautiful scenic ride which would take them 18.6 kilometers (11.6 miles) to Zugspitze.

Inside the train's 2nd car, as German skiers were filling it, Lucas spotted a couple in the back of the car. When Lucas recognized them, he thought: *Damn! It's Bruno and Sonya.*

He yanked on George's parka, led him to a vacant double-seat, and they both got seated before Lucas explained his actions to George.

Lucas did not want Sonya to see him there. He thought she might tell Bruno about him and George being from Long Beach. Since Bruno was also from Long Beach, he might connect them with Jodie somehow. When the time came, Lucas hoped he and George could surprise Bruno and see him punished for his crimes in some creative way. For now, they could only dodge any contact with him.

They purchased ski passes earlier, so they climbed off the cog-train, put on their skis and got on the chairlift. George pulled out the hash pipe for a few hits, and they talked as they rode above the slope.

Before they went to Spain, George learned about the Zugspitze when he skied there alone. He told Lucas, "At almost three thousand meters above sea level, the Zugspitze is the highest mountain in the country, it has three glaciers, and it's also Germany's highest ski resort. There are twenty kilometers of ski runs, a deep covering of powdery snow and wide-open runs. The Zugspitze Glacier looks like a big, white bowl. It is well above tree-line and similar to what we saw at the Matterhorn; but the Matterhorn is more of a plateau. At Gomagoi, skiing takes you between large boulders and rock formations. All three glaciers have beautiful snow for skiing."

Lucas and George skied great runs and had a fun day on the slopes. From a distance, they saw Bruno and Sonya who seemed happy.

"I wonder how long their cheerfulness will last," said Lucas.

"Until she does something he doesn't like," replied George.

Lucas loved skiing in Europe. On the mountaintops, overlooking Alpine buildings, green farmlands and blue lakes, he seemed to be standing on top of the world, and those were the most peaceful, solitary moments of his being. Today, riding the cog-train down the mountain was also spectacular; it seemed like they could see forever.

As soon as they got back to their room, Lucas said, "I want to call Inga in Oberammergau to ask if she will come visit and go skiing. Do you think you'd enjoy seeing Sabine again?"

"Are you kidding?" asked George. "Sabine is fantastic, and she's a great skier. I also love her Austrian accent."

Lucas called Inga and George called Sabine. Both ladies agreed to come visit them, next Wednesday. It was only 6 days away, and they would stay for 3 or 4 days. Inga told Lucas she also wanted him to come and visit her, see her woodcarving shop and let her show him the magical town of Oberammergau.

Since he had seen Bruno earlier, Lucas said, "I should also phone Gabrielle and see what's going on with the RAF, Andreas and Ulrike. I'm sure you remember her friend was missing after being with Bruno in Formentera. We think he may have murdered her friend, and Gabrielle might have an idea about what to do with Bruno. I'm not suggesting we murder him, although I have given it some thought. Maybe we could nudge him over the edge of a cliff while he is skiing."

The next morning, Lucas went to join Bob Ostergaard for breakfast at the PX. Before he went inside, Lucas called Gabrielle from a payphone. He told her Bruno was back in Garmisch, dating a local German lady who hung out at The Grill. Gabrielle told Lucas her brother had been in contact with Andreas and Ulrike who left Jordan, came through East Germany and got into West Germany, using false passports. Recently, they took actions against the government, and it appears they have plans to attack American military facilities, here in Germany or in Italy.

Lucas said, "Gabrielle, if you talk to your brother, ask him if he can get a message to Andreas from Lucas and George who he met in Austria and Venice. The message is: Please do not bomb the military facilities in

Garmisch because we are here, and this place is too beautiful to destroy." He added, "I would appreciate ideas from you and your brother about how to deal with Bruno. Also, I would love to see you again. Do you think you could come to Garmisch and ski with us, this winter? George and I skied on the Zugspitze Glacier today, and it was spectacular."

With her sexy German accent, Gabrielle replied, "I would love to see you again. I will plan to come visit after Christmas and stay for a week. Are the holidays a good time for you, Lucas?"

"Yes, I have no other plans," he said. "I will count the days until I see you again. Auf Wiedersehen, Gabrielle."

"Auf Wiedersehen, Mein Schatz (my sweetheart)," she replied.

Lucas felt good when he got off the phone and walked inside. Most mornings, Lucas could find Bob Ostergaard at the PX, eating ham and eggs with toast while he read the *Stars and Stripes* newspaper. This morning, Lucas was reading the sports section of the paper, and Bob noticed what he was reading.

Bob was a business man and part-owner of the "Shifty Sales" VW van refurbishing business. Steve Dobson, a soldier, was his partner. Bob said, "Lucas, you should read the business section, as I do."

Responding, he said, "Bob, I already have two businesses, and I am doing fine, thank you. Well, look at this…" He pointed to the sports section, "the Orioles beat the Big Red Machine in the World Series. The Orioles won one hundred and eight games this year, and the Reds won one hundred and two."

Bob looked at Lucas like he was crazy, and Bob went back to reading the business section. Lucas finished eating, said goodbye to Bob and went to do some shopping.

With their ID cards, Lucas and George had learned they could stay in military hotels, providing they moved around to different locations. These are recreation hotels, not residential hotels. But Lucas and George got to know most of the desk clerks. If they liked you, they would give you a room when one was available. On most weekends, the hotels were full, and civilians had to stay in a German Gasthof. The prices are reasonable at a Gasthof, and the Bavarian owners are usually families who are helpful and very friendly.

For the next few days, Lucas got into a routine while waiting for Inga and Sabine to arrive. He had breakfast in the PX with Ostergaard and sometimes Ferrell. Occasionally, Eric would be there, but Eric partied hard every night, and he usually slept in.

In the afternoons, Lucas went to a local bar where he, his new civilian friends and military personnel, including the ski patrol, drank many half-liter glasses of German beer. It was a way of life here in Bavaria. Lucas could find people he knew at the Green Arrow, the Sheridan, the Eibsee Hotel and the American's favorite German-owned bar—The Last Chance, sometimes referred to as Sonya's Place. Sonya's mother owned the restaurant, and Sonya worked there. The Last Chance got its name because it was the last place to get a beer before leaving town, and it was the last place to stop on the way back to the Sheridan Kaserne, a local housing facility for military personnel.

The Last Chance was usually packed with Americans, Australians, Britons and Bavarians. They served good old-fashioned Bavarian food and several kinds of Schnitzel: Wiener Schnitzel, Wiener Schnitzel a la Holstein (with a fried egg, pickle, tomato and anchovy), Wiener Schnitzel Cordon Bleu (with black forest ham and Swiss cheese), and Hunter's Schnitzel (with sautéed onions and mushrooms in a white wine/cream sauce). They also had Hungarian Goulash, Bavarian Roulade (flank steak stuffed with veggies, egg and sausage, topped with peppercorn gravy) or Sauerbraten (marinated beef in a rich, tart and spicy sauce). At this bar, the atmosphere was always "party time" with loud music, singing and lots of laughter.

While they were in Cervenia, Lucas and George had partied and skied with these people who formed the core of this certain group. They all go to the bars and military hotels, including The Grill and The Last Chance. Most of the people in this group drove one of Bob Ostergaard's used VW Vans, excluding Lucas and George. When they arrived in Garmisch, they purchased a brand-new VW Van.

The International Bar and Grill was the night-time meeting place. Ladies of Garmisch had their own core of women, sometimes referred to as *Grill Queens*.

Lucas called Sonya the *Head Grill Queen* because she was a local, half-German, and she grew up in Garmisch. If Sonya liked you, and you ever needed hashish, she always had some for you. It was evident she was fond of Lucas, but she was still seeing Bruno. Lucas thought of telling her about Bruno, but he did not want Bruno to know who he was or learn about his knowledge of Bruno.

George wanted to ski the Zugspitze every day and bought a week's pass, so he did not play basketball at night.

Many evenings, Lucas was at the gym, playing 3-on-3 basketball. The players were good, but they had found no one to guard Lucas. He could always shoot, and he seemed to favor these rims, or they favored him because he was shooting with more accuracy than ever before. Playing with the military personnel, he had earned their respect on the court. Lucas usually played with Eric and Regan; some nights he played with Bill, the school coach. So far, Lucas was undefeated.

Lucas counted the days until Inga arrived. When he met her at the train station, they hugged, kissed and laughed with joy, both happy to see each other again. Lucas paid for a room at the Eibsee to enjoy a romantic setting, with a view of the lake. When they arrived at the hotel, Lucas closed the door to their room. Inga set down her backpack, took off her coat, wrapped her arms around Lucas and kissed him. She made it very clear she had missed him.

"Got any dope?" asked Inga.

"Of course! Who do you think you're dealing with?" said Lucas.

They shared a bowl of Topo's great hashish and drank Spaten beer, sitting on a private balcony. There were scattered clouds with patches of sunshine, and they felt a cool breeze coming across the water.

Lucas asked Inga if she wanted to ski the Zugspitze while she's here, and she replied, "I would love to ski again with you. We had so much fun skiing in Gomagoi."

Someone knocked on the door. When Lucas opened it, there stood Sabine. Lucas gave her big hug, as did Inga, he handed her a Spaten beer, and they passed around another pipe-full of hashish. They all stood on the balcony, looking out at the beautiful Lake Eibsee, with the Zugspitze looming in the background.

Sabine had skied several times at the Zugspitze Glacier. Now, she was eager to get back to work in Seefeld, as a ski instructor, but she could not work there until the snow falls.

As they finished their beers, there was another knock on the door. It was George, back from skiing. George and Sabine hugged and kissed, then went through the pipe and beer ritual. It was the 3rd time around for Lucas and Inga, so they were relaxed and feeling fine.

Neither Inga nor Sabine had been inside an American military hotel. It amazed them to learn everything was so inexpensive. Lucas told them a pack of cigarettes is 15 cents, and a fifth of whiskey is $5.00 in the Class Six Store. Also, they can get a half-liter of German beer for 75 cents and a hot dog for 25 cents in any of the military bars. He reminded them hotels in Bavaria were taken from the Nazis by allied forces. When the same hotels became part of the Armed Forces Recreation Center, Americans maintained the original charm of the hotels, and they kept many of the key German employees.

They all had New York Steak with Green Peppercorn Sauce for dinner, and it was delicious. After each had a shot of Jägermeister and a glass of Augustiner beer, they piled into the VW van and went to The Grill for some dancing. Everyone had a great time, and the Bavarian ladies were a big hit as Lucas and George introduced them to new friends.

Lucas felt comfortable, being with Inga again. It was as if they had always known each other. They had become very close during only a few days together. In between breaks to drink beer and shots of Jägermeister, Lucas and Inga danced to a local band's versions of hit songs by several popular groups: The Beatles, Elvis, The Rolling Stones, Tony Orlando and Creedence Clearwater Revival.

Later, with only moonlight shining into their room at the Eibsee hotel, Lucas and Inga had enough light to explore each other, visually. They were so tuned into each other while making love, it seemed like nothing else existed in those moments.

Skiing the next day was a challenge for Lucas. It was windy, and there was a heavy overcast which meant the natural light was flat. You could not tell the snow from the sky, and you could not see the bumps.

He simply followed the other 3 who were expert skiers and stayed with the group as best he could. They all had fun, and they stopped for beers a few times. Mid-day, they enjoyed a long lunch of Goulash soup, Paulaner beer and brotchen.

They finished skiing and rode down on the cog-train. Inga invited Lucas, George and Sabine to have dinner at the Post Hotel, her favorite restaurant in Wallgau. Everyone thought it was a great idea.

The Post Hotel was 30 kilometers from Eibsee, and the drive would take about 40 minutes. On the way to dinner, Lucas announced it would be his treat.

Inga said, "Lucas, you always pay for everything. Please, let me pay for dinner this time."

He shrugged and said, "What can I say? Inga, you are an angel."

Lucas drove, and Inga directed him, passing through the villages of Grainau, Schmolz and Breitenau. They got on St Martins Strasse and drove past the Olympic Ice Stadium, then went through Kaltenbrunn, Gerold, Klais and Krün before arriving at the Post Hotel in Wallgau.

As he drove into Wallgau, Lucas thought: *I am in another fairy-tale town. Everything is clean and beautiful, the fields are brilliant green colors, and flowers are blooming in all the window boxes.*

At the Post Hotel, a mural on the front of the building depicted an angel, resting on a cloud and playing a harp. Along with the angel, biblical characters were standing and sitting on clouds. There was a wooden bench next to the entrance, and a covered patio to the right of the Weinstube (small tavern). Wooden tables and benches were filled with Bavarians who were all laughing and cheerful. A band was playing Polka music, and the atmosphere was electric.

Inside the hotel, there were paintings of angels, crystal chandeliers, an inlaid wooden floor, a winding stairway, large wood pillars and wood beams on the ceilings.

A dirndl-clad hostess led Lucas, Inga, George and Sabine upstairs, got them seated and handed each of them a beautiful leather-bound menu. Of course, it was written in German. He and George let the ladies order, and they were glad they did when the food came.

After dinner, Lucas said it was the most impressive dinner service, of any he had experienced. Since Europe was new to him, he did not know what to expect from here on. However, he knew this service was fabulous, and this food was spectacular.

The main course was a saddle of venison which served 4 people. It was beautifully displayed and carved at the table. Cooked medium-rare, the venison was served with sauce Grand Venuer and Lingonberries, along with a large tray of scalloped shells, filled with various Bavarian side dishes: Bayerische Semmelklösse (dumplings), Karottesalat (carrot salad), Rotkohl (red cabbage), Sauerkraut, Späetzle (German-style egg noodles), Wurstsalat (sausage salad), Kartoffelpuffer (potato pancakes), Gurkensalat (cucumber salad) and shredded celery root with lemon mayonnaise. They all drank Hacker-Pschorr draft beer with dinner, and had shots of Jägermeister with dessert, a delightful apple strudel and *crème fraîche*.

From their mezzanine table, overlooking the dining room and dance floor below, they watched colorful Bavarian dancers entertain everyone during dinner.

For Lucas, this was a true culinary experience. Right after dinner, he did something he never had the nerve to do until now. He wandered back into the large kitchen.

It was immaculate and the most organized kitchen he had ever seen in action. Everything seemed fluid and effortless. To the right of the kitchen entrance, there was a long line of 10 different stations, each had a cook or chef preparing and plating meals.

Orders were called out, by the Chef de Partie, seated at the end of the line. He inspected and approved each plate before it was picked up by a waiter or waitress who carried meals to the dining room. Lucas watched the process and took it all in.

Before heading back to his table, Lucas thought: *This evening, I feel as if I'm in a dream. We are in this magical setting of a typical Bavarian village. It's Saturday night, and we're seated at a beautiful, hand-carved wooden table with matching chairs on a mezzanine, overlooking a dining room and dance floor. The band is playing polkas for Bavarian dancers, ladies are dressed in their dirndls, men in lederhosen and Bavarian hats with feathers. Throughout the restaurant, many of the diners are clapping in tune with the music.*

When Lucas returned, Inga said, "It is such a festive evening! I have had dinner here several times, but tonight feels special."

Looking into Inga's blue eyes, he said, "It does feel special, and I must add—I am with the most beautiful lady in the building."

"Being with you, Lucas, makes it special for me," she replied. "I hope you will come with me to Oberammergau. I think you will fall in love with it as I have."

"I am looking forward to it. When do you want me to come for a visit?" asked Lucas.

"Would you give me a ride, when I go home?" she asked.

"I would like nothing better," he replied.

I don't know where this is going, thought Lucas. *But I think it will be a very fun ride.*

"Lucas, I hope you will let me show you around Bavaria," said Inga. "There is so much to see here, and I want you to enjoy it. Being raised here, I know the area well and will be a good tour guide."

"I am sure you will be," he replied, "and I promise you will have my undivided attention."

After a 40-minute drive to the Eibsee Hotel, they went to Lucas and Inga's room, smoked hashish and had another shot of Jägermeister.

Since it was early, and The Grill was still open, they all wanted to go dancing. When they arrived, John Ferrell and Gino were behind the bar, Jordan Lewis, the bouncer, was standing right behind the last 4 stools at the bar where they were sitting.

The ladies took the center 2 stools, between Lucas and George. They ordered draft Augustiner beers for 75 cents apiece, and Gino supplied them with pretzels to snack on.

Lucas and Inga enjoyed dancing to the music of a local rock band. It was a young group, playing popular songs, including a long version of "American Woman," a hit song by The Guess Who. Then, they were both ready for a break and went back to their seats at the bar.

When Inga and Sabine went to the restroom, Sonya came over. She brushed against Lucas and spoke into his ear, "Hi Lucas, I've missed you. I noticed you around town, but did not get a chance to say welcome back. How was your trip?"

"Hi, Sonya. Nice to see you too," he replied. "My trip was great."

"I see you are with Inga Mueller," said Sonya.

"Oh, where do you know Inga from?" asked Lucas.

"We both grew up here; and when we were in school, we used to ski against each other," she replied.

Suddenly, someone bumped Lucas, hard, from behind.

Next, he saw Bruno grab Sonya by the back of her neck, as he yelled at her, "Who are you with, bitch, him or me?"

Before she could answer, bouncer Jordan Lewis chopped down on the arm Bruno extended, causing him to release Sonya's neck. Jordan spun Bruno around, twisted Bruno's arm behind his back, and wrapped his own left arm around Bruno's neck in a choke hold. Then, he marched Bruno out the front door and into the arms of the MPs.

Sonya left the bar and followed them outside.

When Inga and Sabine returned from the restroom, Lucas and George were still on their stools, talking to Gino, as if nothing had happened.

Inga wrapped her arms around Lucas and whispered in a very sexy voice, "Ich will mit dir schlafen (I would like to sleep with you)."

Lucas had been studying German, and he surprised Inga by saying, "Danke, gleichfalls (thank you the same to you)."

They both laughed. Then, they told the others they wanted to leave. George and Sabine agreed; they were also ready to go.

Back at the Eibsee Hotel, both couples retired for the night.

In the privacy of their room, Inga said, "Lucas, a woman came into the restroom and said there was trouble with a big guy and a young lady at the bar. She also noticed you were involved. What was it about, Mein Schatzi (My Treasure)?"

"Well, let's have another toke on the pipe and another beer. Then, I'll tell you a true story," he replied.

Lucas told her the story about Bruno, pertaining to Long Beach and Ibiza. He explained how Bruno had a history of abuse and was more than likely guilty of 2 murders. Tonight, when Sonya stopped to say hello at the bar, Bruno showed his possessiveness and bad temper.

"Oh, you know Sonya?" asked Inga.

"She was one of the first people I met in Garmisch," he replied.

"I know Sonya well," she said. "We used to race against each other in downhill skiing at school. She has always been aggressive in sports and in her relationships with men."

"Yeah, I dubbed her Head Grill Queen," said Lucas.

Inga cracked up. "It's perfect for her." Then, she kissed Lucas and asked, "Want to take a shower with me?"

"Are you kidding?" Lucas asked as he pulled off his pants.

They both enjoyed fooling around and exploring each other in the shower. Still wet, they stood beside the bed, and tenderly dried each other with soft towels. Then, they jumped on the bed and got lost in the experience until they were both completely exhausted.

The next morning, they went out on the balcony to enjoy the view, but it was a rather gloomy, rainy day, so they went back inside.

Sensing Lucas was still bothered about Bruno, Inga suggested it would blow over while he came to her place in Oberammergau.

"It sounds good, but let's talk about it after breakfast," he replied. "I must tell you, Inga, I don't want Bruno to know anything about me or where I am from. He might put two and two together and realize I'm a threat, before I can bring him down."

They went downstairs to join George and Ashleigh for breakfast in the hotel restaurant. George announced he would ski the rest of the week, then go to Frankfurt and fly back to Long Beach on a military flight since he still had his ID card. He told them volleyball season would begin next month, and he wanted a head start at the high school, getting ready for coaching and getting to know his team this year.

Lucas was not even thinking of going back, at least not anytime soon. It made him sad to hear his buddy was leaving. They were close friends for many years before they came to Europe.

In California, Lucas had bought a house, next door to his restaurant. For a while, he and George became roommates there.

Many evenings, Lucas would close his restaurant, go home, wake up George and say, "Hey George, do you want to go shoot pool and have a few beers?"

George would always jump out of bed and put on his clothes, ready for a night of carousing the town.

Now, George was leaving; and Lucas knew he would miss him.

George and Lucas agreed: Lucas would buy out George's half of the van because Lucas was staying in Europe. George and Sabine could use her car until George took the train to Frankfurt.

Lucas and Inga decided: They would go to Oberammergau for a while. So, they said goodbye to George and Sabine.

CHAPTER 17

Oberammergau and King Ludwig

Along the drive, going from Garmisch to Oberammergau, Lucas saw more of the spectacular Bavarian countryside. When they arrived, Inga directed him through the center of the town, and it felt magical. It was a sensation Lucas had throughout Bavaria when he came into towns or villages which were new to him, and each place had its own uniqueness and charm.

He saw Frescos on most of the buildings in Oberammergau. Many of the frescos were of a religious theme. Others depicted Bavarian people, dressed in colorful clothes, going about daily chores of cooking, sewing, tending to their stock, and plowing the fields. As they drove through the streets of Oberammergau, Inga pointed out places they would go to when he comes to visit another time.

Next, she showed him her ranch-style house which sat in a meadow, next to the ski lifts. There was a studio-size cottage, 50 yards down the hill. Below this property, the main highway took people south to Oberau, or north to Unterammergau and beyond.

Inga built a fire in the large tiled-fireplace. Lucas opened 2 Spaten beers, and they went outside.

Inga pointed up the hill and said, "The double chairlift on the right is Wanklift Two. The lift on the left is Wanklift One; and behind it is the Kolbensattel Bahn, a lift which takes you all the way to the top for a nice long run to the bottom. All the lifts are within walking distance, except for the Kolbenalmlift on the far side of the Kolbenbach River.

"Lucas, I want you to come and ski with me, this winter. Better yet, why don't you come and stay here with me? We'll have so much fun. We can ski, cook and keep each other warm at night."

"It sounds perfect. I'll see what I can work out," he replied.

They settled into lounge chairs, and Inga told Lucas the story of the *Passion Play*, "It began in the fifteenth century after a plague ravaged the residents of Oberammergau. People vowed that if God spared them from the plague, they would produce a play for all time, depicting the life and death of Jesus. The play became too expensive to produce every year, so they switched to every ten years. Now, the play involves over a thousand performers, and it lasts all day. Since we had it last year, the next play will happen in nineteen eighty."

Lucas felt relaxed, listening to Inga and looking at a green meadow, surrounded by big trees. The meadow extended all the way to the top of the Wanklift II where the tree-line ended. The lifts were now idle.

Inga offered to tell Lucas all about King Ludwig if he did not already know the story, and she asked him if he might want to visit Ludwig's Linderhof Castle.

"I'm all ears," replied Lucas. "I've heard of him. However, I know nothing about this King Ludwig. Perhaps you can tell me while we eat. I'm getting hungry. What shall we do for dinner?"

Inga suggested they make Hungarian goulash, bread dumplings and celery root salad. Lucas agreed, then said he would make an apple pie. They had to go shopping. So, he followed Inga around town where she introduced him to so many people, Lucas stopped trying to remember anyone's name.

Inga's kitchen impressed Lucas. She did not have a lot of clutter on the counters which allowed them plenty of space to work together. To his surprise, Inga's recipe and her method for making goulash was the same as he made in his Long Beach restaurants, for several years.

They did not have enough time to make brotchen (rolls), so they got fresh rolls at the bakery. Inga peeled and shredded the celery root, added mayonnaise which she made by hand, added extra lemon juice and fresh chopped parsley, then garnished the salad with red beet wedges. She also showed Lucas how she made bread dumplings with bacon.

"Locals serve spaetzle (homemade noodles) with their Hungarian goulash, but I prefer bread dumplings, and I thought you might enjoy them too," said Inga.

After dinner, they drank Spaten beer and listened to German music on the radio while washing dishes. Heading downtown next, they followed Kolbengasse which winds toward town and ends at Bahnhofstrasse. There, they made a sharp right turn across the Ammer River. The street name changed to Dorfstrasse, became narrower and wound through small side streets. They passed the impressive Hotel Wittelsbach and arrived at the Gasthaus zum Stern, but Inga kept walking.

"I want to show you my woodcarving shop. It's on this street behind the Hotel Turmwirt," she said.

She stopped on a corner where trees lined a grassy area around the side and to the rear of the building. Inga's workshop was upstairs. Lucas saw 4 large, shuttered windows above 2 garage doors.

"We won't take time to go into the shop today," said Inga. "We can come back tomorrow. Now, let's go to Gasthaus Stern where you can experience a real Bavarian beer garden."

They got seated at a table and ordered mugs of Spaten beer which arrived with perfect heads on top. The waiter brought traditional white radish curls and pretzels along with their beer. A local Bavarian band was playing music inside, and the rasthaus was packed with people.

Inga said, "In the sixteenth century, the Ettal Monastery built this place and used it as a guest house. There is a fresco on the south facade, known as *Anna Selbdritt,* which dates to about seventeen hundred. It represents Saint Anne and her daughter, the Virgin Mary, holding the child Jesus. It was discovered under seven layers of paint, but remained mostly intact. When the fresco was revealed, they cleaned it and preserved it. On our way out, we'll see the fresco.

"Tomorrow, we can go to Linderhof Castle, and you can learn about our famous King Ludwig. The castle is impressive."

"Based on photos I have seen, I like his castles," Lucas replied.

"Let's go back to my place now, and we'll see how my bed works out for us tonight," said Inga.

Without hesitation, Lucas paid the waiter. As usual, he left a large tip, and Inga said, "You're tipping too much, Lucas. You're not in the United States. Waiters and waitresses don't expect it here, and extra-large tips will insult some of them."

"Thanks for the reminder," he said. "It's an old habit of mine."

Walking back on this beautiful, clear night, Lucas was reminiscing about the first time they met.

"I remember how I felt in Gomagoi," he said, "when we went our separate ways. I wanted to spend more time with you, Inga. Now, I can't believe we are together again in this fantasyland."

"I had similar feelings about leaving you in Gomagoi," she replied. "I was so happy when you phoned me. Come on, Lucas, walk fast. I can't wait to get you into bed and play with your magnificent body!"

Lucas grabbed her hand, and they picked up the pace.

Inga opened her front door, and Lucas asked, "Inga, don't you lock your door?"

"I never have, and I've never had a problem," she said. "But maybe I should start. These days, there are more tourists in town, and this place is isolated. The closest neighbor is a half-mile away."

Once inside, Inga opened 2 Spaten beers, lit her swan-shaped hash pipe, took a big drag and handed it to Lucas. Then, she unbuttoned her blouse and headed to the shower.

About 5 minutes later, Inga poked her head out of the shower and asked Lucas, "Are you going to join me?"

"I thought you would never ask," he replied.

Falling asleep after great sex which was unbelievable, Lucas felt like he was in a dream, from which he never wanted to wake up.

What a wonderful lady Inga is, he thought.

In the morning, Lucas cooked a tasty, American breakfast for Inga: Denver Omelette, made with Bavarian ham, onion, garlic, bell pepper and Emmentaler cheese, plus hash browns and wheat toast with peanut butter and jelly. Inga loved the omelette and hash browns, but she was not too keen on the peanut butter.

While they cleaned the kitchen, Inga's phone rang. She talked for a minute, then said, "It's Sabine. George wants to talk to you."

Lucas took the phone, and George told him about a note. Gabrielle had left it for Lucas at The Grill.

"Gabrielle is in town and has to see you right away," said George.

Lucas told George he would be there in 45 minutes, and he hung up the phone. He turned to Inga and said, "I'm so sorry, Inga, but I have to return to Garmisch and handle some business. I promise I will come back—if you want me to."

"Oh, I'm sorry, too," she replied. "Please, hurry back. There is so much more for me to show you."

He kissed Inga and said, "Thank you, Mein Schatzi."

Then, he grabbed his things, got in the van and headed back to Garmisch-Partenkirchen. He would see George, then meet Gabrielle.

When I asked Gabrielle to come for a visit, I did not think it would be so soon. I hope she has a plan for Bruno, thought Lucas.

George and Sabine were staying at the Sheridan. When Lucas got there, he found George in the bar, sitting alone.

"Here is Gabrielle's note," said George as he handed it to Lucas.

Lucas read it aloud, *"Hello, Lucas. I'm in town, and I want to see you. Sorry I didn't tell you sooner. It was a last-minute thing, and we left in a rush. Here is a map and the house address where we are staying. I hope to see you soon, Gabrielle."*

On his way to see Gabrielle, Lucas stopped at the market and bought a case of Hacker-Pschorr beer. He drove through the countryside to an isolated old house, partially hidden in a grove of birch trees. As he was parking, Gabrielle came running out of the house. She threw her arms around Lucas, gave him a big kiss and said, "Come on inside and visit with some people who you may know."

Lucas, trying not to show alarm, said, "Andreas and Ulrike are here? Why do they want to see me?"

"Because they like you, Lucas. You know they are wanted, and they trust you will not turn them in to the police," she replied.

"I understand they have a cause, and they believe violence is their answer," he said. "I would never turn them in. Let me grab a case of beer and you can carry a bottle of Jägermeister. I want to hear about their experience in Jordan and what is going on now."

"I'm so glad to see you," said Gabrielle. Then, she put her arms around his neck and kissed him like she meant it.

As Gabrielle led Lucas into the living room, he was not expecting the person who he saw next. Gudrun Ensslin was standing in front of the fireplace. Lucas recognized her from photos he had seen in the newspapers. Andreas Baader and Ulrike Meinhof stood on either side of this notorious woman.

"Lucas, I believe you know Andreas and Ulrike, and this lady is Gudrun Ensslin," said Gabrielle. Both Lucas and Gudrun nodded.

Lucas noticed Andreas' appearance. He looked different for some reason. His hair was shorter and combed to the side, his full sideburns ended below his ears, and he had a serious, stern expression. However, when Andreas spoke to Lucas, his manner was calm, and he used a pleasant, low-key voice.

Looking at Andreas and Ulrike, Lucas said, "The last time I saw both of you was in Venice. I've been reading about you, and it appears you have been busy. How was your trip to Jordan?"

Andreas said, "Lucas, thank you again for all the help you gave to Ulrike and me in Austria and in Venice. We want you to know we consider you a friend.

"If we can do anything to help you, please don't hesitate to ask. Gabrielle tells us you have a problem with some bartender, here in Garmisch, and he might have murdered her best friend in Spain. We will take care of him if you need us to. However, I have not discussed it with Gabrielle yet."

Looking at her, Lucas asked, "Have you come up with any ideas about Bruno, Gabrielle?"

"No one here would be served by bringing police into this. They might ask questions which we would rather not answer," she replied.

"We can't bring the police into this because we don't have proof of anything," said Lucas. "One murder happened in Formentera, Spain; and the other one happened in Long Beach, California. I only hope nobody else gets hurt by Bruno. I would feel somewhat responsible if I did nothing, and he kept getting away with it."

"Lucas, do you know of any other incidents, involving Bruno, here in Garmisch?" asked Gabrielle.

"Yes, last week at The Grill," he replied. "Bruno grabbed the throat of a young lady who he has been dating. She was talking to me at the time. It happened right in front of the bouncer who handled Bruno and turned him over to the Military Police. Since then, I've been in Oberammergau and haven't seen him. From now on, I will keep an eye out. One of my new friends will also keep an eye on him."

"Lucas, I guess you know we want to get the American military's attention, and we're looking for possible targets," said Ulrike.

"I hope you don't choose AFRC facilities or their hotels," he replied. Lucas smiled, then added, "The people here are ordinary, fun people, just like the rest of us, and I have made a lot of friends here."

Gabrielle chimed in, "I think it's far too beautiful a place to destroy. Bavaria had enough of its buildings demolished during the war."

"Okay, Lucas," said Andreas, "maybe we will reconsider and let you enjoy this beautiful Bavaria which you chose as your new home."

Lucas felt some relief, thinking Andreas and his group may leave Bavaria alone. He and Gabrielle gave everyone beers. Next, they poured shots of Jägermeister for the group. They all toasted to Bavaria, the RAF, and the undoing of Bruno Castignoli.

"We cannot be seen shopping around town, but we want you to cook us dinner," Andreas said to Lucas. "So, we must also ask you to do the shopping, and we will pay for everything."

"I would love to cook dinner for you," said Lucas. "Do you know what you want for dinner, or should I choose for you?"

"Oh Lucas, you surprise us," said Ulrike.

"I would go with you," said Gabrielle, "but local authorities might connect me to the RAF, with information about my brother Horst."

"It's okay," said Lucas. "I don't need an interpreter. I will shop at the commissary, the PX and Class Six Store. I'll decide on the menu while I am there. Before I get going, are there any special requests?"

Gudrun spoke for the 1st time, "I would enjoy a bottle of vodka and American cigarettes."

"Okay, anyone else?" asked Lucas.

"Can you get Jack Daniels whiskey?" asked Andreas.

"Yes. I'm sure I can," he replied.

Lucas spent 2 hours shopping at 4 different stores. He found most items at military stores, then he stopped at a German economy store for fresh trout, salmon and a large chicken.

Instead of going to the Oktoberfest, he would bring Oktoberfest to them. He planned to serve Kartoffelpuffer (potato pancakes), Rotkohl (red cabbage), roasted chicken, trout stuffed with salmon mousse in puff pastry with béarnaise sauce, fresh asparagus and Baked Alaska dessert. Gabrielle offered to help Lucas with prep work and cooking.

To start, Lucas made a génoise (Italian sponge cake) for the Baked Alaska. Then, he started the puff pastry, by making a détrempe (water, flour and butter mixture). He rolled it into a round and put it in the refrigerator to rest while he worked more butter on a marble slab, using the heel of his hand. He was glad to be in a well-equipped kitchen. Marble is the best surface for making pastry dough. Lucas formed the butter into a perfect square, 1-inch thick, and put it in the refrigerator to rest with the détrempe for 15 minutes.

Doing prep work for the latkes, Gabrielle peeled and grated potatoes, then put them in a colander and rinsed them under cold water; several rinses would keep the potatoes from turning dark.

Making red cabbage, Gabrielle sautéd onions and sliced the cabbage, then combined those with sliced apple, apple cider vinegar, sugar, salt and bay leaf. It simmered for 1 1/2 hours in a large pot with 3 cups of water.

From the refrigerator, Lucas retrieved the détrempe and butter which had rested and chilled. He rolled the détrempe in a circle, set the butter in the center, folded and sealed the détrempe over the top of the butter, rolled it in a rectangle, folded it into 3rds and repeated the process again. Using his fingertips, he poked 2 holes in the dough to remind him he had done 2 turns, and put it in the refrigerator to rest for another 15 minutes.

Lucas boned 3 trout and put them back into the refrigerator as he pulled out the salmon. The butcher had filleted and ground the salmon for him. Now, Lucas pureed the salmon and set it aside. He would use the salmon to make a mousse, and he would stuff the trout with the mousse. Lucas prepared shallots, chopped fine and sautéed in butter, added a little brandy and flamed it. When it cooled, he mashed it to a pulp and added it to the pureed salmon, along with egg white, heavy cream, a little lemon juice, salt and pepper. To test the texture and taste in cooked form, he poached 1 tablespoon of the mousse in some chicken stock. Then, he adjusted the texture and seasoning of the uncooked mousse to get a consistency and flavor he liked.

Going back to the puff pastry, Lucas rolled and folded it again, 2 more turns, then poked it with 4 holes and returned it to the refrigerator to rest again for 15 minutes.

For the Béarnaise sauce, Lucas clarified butter, made a shallot and fresh tarragon reduction, then set it aside until it was time to make the sauce. Next, he separated eggs: whites for meringue on Baked Alaska, and yolks for Béarnaise sauce.

For Baked Alaska, he sliced the génoise into 1/4-inch-thick layers, and he cut those into 3 pieces, each in the shape of a boat. Lucas brushed the génoise pieces with simple syrup which he had flavored with Grand Marnier. He set 1 piece into the bottom of an oval baking dish, then added 2 large scoops of French vanilla ice cream and formed a mound in the shape of the dish. He covered the ice cream with the other 2 pieces of génoise, placing 1 edge of each piece along the sides of the mound and forming them by hand to meet at the top of the mound. Then, the dessert went into the freezer.

To season the chicken, Lucas rubbed it with sea salt and fresh herbs. He put it in the oven to roast at 200 degrees Celsius (392F).

Lucas took out the boned trout and stuffed them with the salmon mousse. These 3 large trout would serve 6 people.

He rolled out the finished puff pastry, making 3 sections big enough to wrap each of the stuffed trout. He shaped the pastry on each fish to look like a whole salmon, brushing the body with egg yolk and using a plain round pastry tip to make fish-scale markings. He outlined a neck, using a strip of puff pastry to create a fish head, made a round eye with the pastry tip, and carved a mouth with the tip of a paring knife which left markings like teeth. Puff pastry was also used to create fins and tails. He would serve these beautiful, sculpted items on a large cutting board with béarnaise sauce and lemon wedges in side dishes.

It was time to make the béarnaise sauce. He whisked the egg yolks with a little water until they were smooth, then added clarified butter and some lemon juice, as needed, to make a thick, smooth emulsion. He stirred the tarragon/shallot reduction into the sauce, cooked it on a medium burner, added salt and a little cayenne to taste. When the sauce was done, he turned off the burner, and the sauce stayed warm over the stove.

When the chicken was done, Lucas set it aside to rest over the stove until he carved it at the table.

He then put the fish/puff pastry in the oven at 220 Celsius (428F). While the fish was baking, Gabrielle fried the Kartoffelpuffer until the pancakes were crispy on the outside, and she laid them on a paper towel to absorb extra grease.

Looking at the results of their hard work in the kitchen, Lucas said, "Gabrielle, timing is everything, and we are ready!"

The rest of the group were out on the back deck. Lucas and Gabrielle grabbed 2 beers and the hash pipe, then went to join the party before they all sat in the dining room for dinner.

With everyone seated, Lucas and Gabrielle brought out the food. Lucas carved the large chicken at the table, and Gabrielle came in with the golden brown, salmon-shaped trout in puff pastry. Everyone gasped with surprise at the beauty of the food, especially the fish. Before eating,

Gudrun said a prayer, blessing all of them and the wonderful meal on the table. She was the most religious of the group.

During dinner, Lucas asked, "How did all of you begin this big crusade of yours?"

"We all had different beginnings," Ulrike answered, "and different reasons to join forces and take serious action against the fascists. I can tell you how I came to be with this group. My father died when I was six years old, and my mother died when I was fourteen. A friend of my mother's raised my sister and me. I went on to study sociology, philosophy and German history at Marburg. Then, I became involved with anti-nuclear protests at a university in Munster, and I wrote for some student newspapers. At the time, I even felt I might have a career in journalism. I joined the German Communist Party in nineteen fifty-seven, although it was outlawed in Germany. In nineteen sixty-two, I had a tumor removed from my brain, and I recovered from it."

"Wow, I'm glad to hear you recovered," said Lucas.

"Lucas, I don't remember if I told you when I met you," said Ulrike, "I was editor of a left-wing magazine, married the publisher, had twin girls, got divorced and planned to meet the twins in Jordan. Since then, their transport to Jordan was interrupted, and their father sent someone to kidnap them before I could get them back. Now, I think they are better off with Klaus because the newspapers call us criminals. We are not criminals; we are political activists. For example, if you set a car on fire, that is a criminal offense. If you set hundreds of cars on fire, that is political action."

"When I was in Tangier, I read about the twins," replied Lucas. "What do you want to accomplish with these political actions?"

"We hope our organization draws enough attention and grows so large the fascist 'pigs' will have to listen," replied Ulrike.

Lucas watched the 5 of them stand and raise their beer glasses.

Andreas said, "Darauf erhebe ich mein Glas. Prost!" (To that I raise my glass. Cheers!).

Seeing Gabrielle get excited by the toast, Lucas wondered if she was a bigger part of their activity, than what he knew about her. She might have been more involved all along.

Lucas excused himself and went to finish the Baked Alaska dessert. He was delighted to find a copper bowl and a new wire whip in the kitchen. Using lemon juice to remove any grease, he cleaned the bowl and dried it well.

For the meringue, he put 4 egg whites, saved earlier, into the bowl and hand-whipped them to soft peaks. He slowly added 1/2 cup of white sugar and continued whipping until the egg whites were shiny and held a firm peak. Using a pastry bag with a star tip, he covered the frozen cake and ice cream with the meringue. Next, he browned it to a golden color, quickly, in a 232 Celsius (450F) oven. Lucas entered the dining room, carrying the Baked Alaska and listening to the sound of "Oohs" and "Aahs," expressed by everyone still seated at the table. He sliced the Baked Alaska and served dessert to each person. At the same time, Gabrielle gave them all shot glasses filled with Jägermeister.

After dessert, Lucas and Gabrielle did the dishes and cleaned the kitchen. The others stayed in the living room, talking business.

"Gabrielle, how involved are you in the RAF?" asked Lucas.

"This is the first trip I've taken with them," she replied. "My brother Horst introduced me to Andreas and his girlfriend, Gudrun. The police want horst, so they are probably aware of me. I am not involved in any planning or actions and not wanted by the police. I came here to see you and help with the Bruno problem. Horst told me if we want Bruno to disappear, they would take care of him."

"I don't want to get involved with murder in any way," said Lucas. "However, I think he should get a warning about abusing women, and he should face a firm hand in the same manner he dishes out."

"I'll talk to them about it," she replied. "For now, let's go for a walk. We have so much to catch up on since we left Ibiza. I have a private room here, so you can stay with me tonight if you want to."

"I hope we don't get raided," he said.

Gabrielle said, "I'm not sure how hard the police are looking for them. RAF members have won over a lot of public opinion with their charisma, and that's what makes them so dangerous. They get a lot of help from people like you and me. To us outsiders, they seem to be fun-loving people who enjoy drinking beer and schnapps, smoke hash and have a good time; however, they all have a dark and ruthless side, including my brother Horst. Many of the young German people admire them, as if they are rock stars, which has romanticized them. The news media dubbed them Celebrity Terrorists. Since they do have public sympathy, I think the police have been a little relaxed in their pursuit of the RAF leaders."

Gabrielle paused for a moment, then she continued, "I must tell you they have all changed since they went to Jordan. They seem more determined than ever to keep robbing banks and bombing buildings, anything to harass the police. Andreas seems intent on taking this all the way to the end, whatever it might be."

"Do you know anything about his background?" asked Lucas.

"Horst is as close to Andreas as anyone," she replied, "except for Gudrun. He has told me a lot about their backgrounds and their beliefs. The Soviets captured and killed Andreas' father during the last war, and

Andreas' mother spoiled him. He was an only child who became a juvenile delinquent. In his youth, police arrested him several times for petty thefts. In the mid-sixties, he got involved with a student movement which was growing fast. Then, he became a spokesman for violence against the state. Andreas was not a good student because he was more interested in chasing the young female students."

"When did he meet Gudrun?" asked Lucas.

"She saw him once at a protest rally in Berlin," replied Gabrielle. "Students were protesting a visit by the Shah of Iran, and Gudrun listened to Andreas' speech, supporting mass violence against the state. Then, the police shot and killed a young, radical student at the rally. Much later, they met at a party in Gudrun's apartment, and she was captivated by his rants against the 'pigs' and the state. She joined in, screaming her own rants against them. At the time, Gudrun was engaged, and she had a baby boy. When she partnered with Andreas, she abandoned her family, in favor of this war against their sworn enemy, the state."

Lucas and Gabrielle held hands as they walked into the kitchen to grab more Hacker-Pschorr beers.

Back in the living room, Lucas felt he had a new point of view about this group. As he looked at Gudrun, he saw a reed-thin lady. Straight, black hair hung to her shoulders, and bangs covered her forehead. She had a square jaw, a somewhat long nose, a rather hard look, and she did not wear makeup. Her pale blue eyes and piercing stare seemed to look right through you.

In Lucas' opinion, Gudrun looked nothing but German. Gabrielle told him Gudrun was smart, well-educated and religious; yet she somehow became a vicious radical for her cause.

Andreas rose from his seat and said, "Lucas, you have convinced us; we will not harm your Americans in Bavaria. But we can't make any promises for the rest of Europe."

"Thank you!" exclaimed Lucas. "This is good news for me and for Bavaria." Then he asked, "Are you all still driving BMWs around and making the cops crazy?"

"We keep a low profile when we visit this house," Ulrike replied. "Our BMW stays parked in the garage because we do not want to attract any unwanted attention."

"Whose house is this, anyway?" asked Lucas.

"We found it through a young lady named Sonya," said Gudrun. "Her mother is the caretaker of the house, and she rents it to us, as a vacation home. We have friends who are willing to help our cause and offer us assistance, all over Europe."

Then, it came to Lucas, the reason he had seen so many paintings of King Ludwig, hanging throughout the house. Sonya's mother, Victoria, worshipped King Ludwig the Second. Sonya told him her mother would raise her wine glass and toast his portrait, every night.

Lucas thought: *I'd better not tell them I know Sonya without talking to her first. I must ask Gabrielle if Sonya is an RAF sympathizer. It's time for Sonya to learn about Bruno, anyway. If I go against him, it would be nice to have her on my side.*

They all passed the hash pipe around again. Gabrielle brought out more Hacker-Pschorr beers and poured shots of Jägermeister. They raised their glasses and shouted, "Prost." Then, they sang something. Lucas could not understand the song.

Before too long, things quieted down and everyone wandered off to their respective rooms.

It seemed like this group felt confident. Since they had no "look out" person at watch during the night, they must assume the police do not know where they are.

Lucas and Gabrielle retired to her room and picked up where they left off in Ibiza. He admired Gabrielle's body; she had gorgeous and substantial breasts. Lucas thought making love with Gabrielle was like going to another world, one of her choice, and it was amazing.

In the morning, Lucas hated to leave Gabrielle, but there were things he wanted to do. Besides, hanging out with Celebrity Terrorists was making him nervous.

Andreas told Lucas they would all leave the next day, and he asked where they might find Herr Bruno, this evening. Andreas did not go into details, except to say some RAF guys would be having a little chat with Herr Bruno.

"He hangs out at The Grill in the evenings," said Lucas, "I heard he's been staying at the Bayerischer Hof, a hotel on Partnachstrasse. It is right on the river."

"I can point him out, so I'll go with Andreas," said Gabrielle.

"We'll have our 'conversation' with him after we check out the location and find the best spot," Andreas declared.

Lucas gave them all hugs and gave Gabrielle a special kiss. Then, he said, "Auf wiedersehen," and he took off.

Heading for the Sheridan, Lucas wanted to see George before he got on the train to Frankfurt. He found George and Sabine, having breakfast in the hotel restaurant, and he joined them. Lucas kept his mouth shut about his time with the RAF people because he did not want Sabine to know or tell Inga about it.

Lucas realized it was not wise to let people know he was hanging out and partying with terrorists. While some people considered them to be national heroes, other people had died because of their actions.

George's train left in 30 minutes. Lucas was headed downtown, and he promised to meet them at the station.

When he arrived, Lucas gave George and Sabine hugs. He also invited Sabine to come back and go skiing with Inga and him. It made him sad to say goodbye to his close friend, not knowing when they would see each other again.

Lucas went to The Grill to have a beer and talk with Gino or John. He sat on the 1st bar stool as he always did when it was available. Today, Gino was behind the bar, and John would be in soon.

"Gino, have you seen Bruno or heard anything about him?" asked Lucas. "I've been in Oberammergau and out of touch for a few days."

"Yeah," said Gino. "I asked George where you had been, and he told me you were out of town. Bruno's been in every night with Sonya. Last night, I swear she had bruises on her face. She had a scared look and a sad demeanor about her. Somebody should get Bruno straightened out before he beats someone to death again."

Lucas nodded in agreement. He thought: *Andreas and his friends will take care of it tonight.*

Eric walked in and sat next to Lucas. After they shook hands, Lucas ordered them both an Augustiner draft beer.

"Where have you been, Lucas?" asked Eric. "We missed you at the gym. We've been playing every night before coming over here."

"I'm itching to play, and I need some exercise," he replied. "Are you playing tonight? I also need to get a hotel room for a few days, or until I figure out what I want to do next."

"Me too," said Eric. "I've been staying at the Bayerischer Hof, but they were full with the out-of-towners this week. I want to get a job, so I can get an ID card. Lucas, how did you get your ID card?"

Lucas told Eric and Gino about how he and George worked in Frankfurt for 4 days, got their ID cards, and then split for Garmisch.

"Won't CID be looking for you?" asked Gino.

"We sent a letter from 'The States' to say we were sorry, but we got called home to Long Beach," he replied. "Actually, George's mom sent the letter from her address. They must have believed us; they sent our paychecks there. I will get a job here, someday. I love being in Bavaria. Eric. If you want to, we can find a room to share, and you would be my guest. Which of the American hotels would you want to stay at?"

Eric didn't hesitate to say, "Lake Eibsee Hotel. It's the best."

"The fun Australian ladies, Olivia and Ashleigh, work in Munich," said Lucas. "I'll call them and ask if they want to go skiing with us."

Lucas and Eric checked into the Eibsee. When Lucas called Olivia, he asked if she and Ashleigh could come to Garmisch and go skiing on the Zugspitze with him and his friend Eric. He also told her George had gone back to California.

"I would love to come see you and ski, Lucas," said Olivia. "Let me talk to Ashleigh, and we'll see if we can get time off, together. How can I phone you?"

"We're staying at Lake Eibsee Hotel," Lucas replied. "Our room number is two fourteen. I hope you can come. If you can make it, call the Eibsee Hotel and reserve a room for all the nights you can stay."

"Okay. I'll call you right back," Olivia promised.

Lucas and Eric sat on the small balcony of their 2nd floor room, overlooking the lake with a view of the Zugspitze. Of all the military hotels in Garmisch, the Eibsee Hotel was Lucas' 1st choice to stay because of the beautiful surroundings.

"Skiing with your friends sounds good," said Eric. "I love Australian women. They are a little crazy though."

"Yeah, fun crazy," replied Lucas.

Leaning back in his chair, drinking a Hacker-Pschorr beer, Lucas said, "You know, Eric. It doesn't get much better than this."

"No, it doesn't," he replied. "Are you free tonight? John Ferrell and I want you to play basketball. There are three guys who have been beating everybody, two big guys and Regan Stone who used to play with John and me. Regan can shoot, and he is fast."

"It sounds fun. Bring them on," said Lucas.

Waiting for Olivia to call back, they opened another Hacker-Pschorr beer. The phone rang and Lucas answered it.

"Hi Lucas," said Olivia. "We will come after work tonight and arrive there at ten o'clock. Will you meet us at the train station?"

"We will be there," he replied. "Hey, Olivia, if you see Topo before you leave, please see if he has any hashish for sale. If he does, buy me fifteen grams, and I'll pay you back when you get here."

"I have plenty of hashish," she said. "But I'll see if he has any to sell. Topo always does. I can't wait to see you, Lucas. It seems like it's been a long time."

"Yes, it does," he said. "I look forward to seeing you this evening." Lucas hung up the phone.

CHAPTER 18

Neuschwanstein Castle

Eric and Lucas walked into the gym, both dressed and ready to play. They stood by the entrance and scanned the court. It was early, and only 2 guys were there. At the far end of the court, Lucas saw Regan with a guy named Duffy who was about 6'5" and a little bulky.

"While we wait for Ferrell to get here," said Eric, "let's go see if they have a 3rd and want to play a game. Oh, there's Ferrell now."

Eric walked over to Regan who was shooting baskets, and he asked if they had another player.

"Yeah," said Regan. "Here he comes behind you. Hey, Bruno!"

A chill ran down Lucas' back when he heard the name. He turned around and stood face-to-face with Bruno. When Regan introduced them, Lucas managed to shake Bruno's hand; but it challenged his composure.

Bruno recognized Eric and said, "How ya doin'?"

Throwing free-throws to see who starts with the ball, each team made 4 in a row until Regan rimmed 1 out, and Lucas' shot sailed through the net. Lucas' team (Ferrell, Eric and himself) took the 1st ball out of bounds, Eric threw in to Lucas, and the match-ups were set.

Ferrell and Duffy had the same build, although Duffy was an inch taller, and both looked strong. Regan and Lucas were about the same size. They played against each other once before, and Lucas got the best of him. Bruno was taller than Eric and a lot heavier, but Eric was very strong. He was unbeaten in arm wrestling at the local bars. He was also quick and a good passer.

Lucas' team began playing a rotating high post to keep Bruno away from the basket. The guys on the wings would stay deep. Sometimes, the high post would pass, set a screen and roll to the basket; or, he would fake one way and go to the basket the other way to look for a pass. This seemed to confuse Bruno and Duffy, so if Regan tried to double-team the ball, it left someone open. Then, Ferrell or Lucas would hit a jumper from the wings, or they would drive the baseline and hit the high post who was coming down the center. Every time Bruno was guarding him, Lucas would hit a jumper over Bruno. If Bruno came after him, Lucas would dribble around him, then lay the ball in the basket, or he would hit the open man if they double-teamed him. After Regan hit two long jumpers, Lucas overplayed him which denied him the ball.

Bruno and Duffy were not scorers. They both muscled their way to the basket. Eric did a great job, pushing Bruno away from the basket. Ferrell lived on the outside and kept Duffy from the basket. Lucas watched Bruno who looked like he wanted to kill somebody, but Bruno did not know who to blame for his frustration. If he did not know who Lucas was before, he sure did now. Lucas made Bruno look clumsy and slow. When Lucas could not drive to the basket, he would step back and bury his jump shot. His team's strategy was to keep the other side away from the basket. It worked well-enough to beat them twice in a row, best 2 out of 3.

Eric, Lucas and Ferrell felt great, walking out of the gym. However, they all knew Bruno was upset.

"Bruno looks like he could eat his horse if he had one," said Ferrell. "He also looks pissed."

"He seems to have a serious anger problem," said Eric.

"Yeah, he and Sonya are dating," Ferrell replied. "I've seen bruises on her face which makeup did not cover up."

Lucas thought: *Bruno is about to learn a lesson about how to treat women—better yet, how not to treat women.*

Meeting the Australian ladies at the train station, Lucas got a big kiss and a hug from Olivia. After Eric greeted Olivia and Ashleigh, they went to the van and smoked some hashish, sent by Topo along with his love.

Everyone was hungry, so they went to The Grill and enjoyed steak dinners in the restaurant. Then, they went into the discothèque and said hello to Gino who was behind the bar. He served an Augustiner draft beer to each, and they looked for a table. The place was packed.

Lucas saw Scott and Faye who he met in Ibiza. They had a table with 2 open chairs. They all said hello, then Eric and Ashleigh sat at their table to get further acquainted. Lucas was not surprised to see Eric and Ashleigh hit it off. Although they had met before, this was a personal encounter. Now, they were both single.

If you don't get along with Eric, you don't get along with anybody, thought Lucas. *I imagine Eric's sparking smile and muscular build would impress any woman.*

Olivia took Lucas to the dance floor, and they moved to the music of a local rock band. The young band members did a good job performing The Rolling Stones' song "Honky Tonk Woman." Next, they played "Proud Mary" by Creedence Clearwater Revival.

Leaving the dance floor, Lucas found 2 empty chairs, and he carried those back to join the group at Scott and Faye's table. Scott majored in Political Science while Faye majored in Journalism; both graduated from UC Berkeley. They planned to stay in Garmisch and needed jobs. They also wanted to travel and see more of Europe. Scott seemed like a nice guy, although Lucas remembered Scott was slow to pull his wallet out when it was his turn to buy a round of drinks.

Lucas jested in thought: *I guess it takes all kinds. They seem to be good people, but they are anti-government. Maybe I should introduce them to Andreas, Gudrun and Ulrike.*

Around midnight, Jordan Lewis, the bouncer, came to their table and pulled Lucas aside. He knew Lucas and Sonya were friends. Lewis said MPs found Bruno Castignoli, lying on a side street near the Bayerischer Hof Hotel and close to the Ammer River. Bruno was conscious, but he sustained quite a beating.

"Was it a robbery?" asked Lucas.

"They don't think so," he replied. "He still had his wallet."

"Well, he must have made someone angry," said Lucas. "Thanks for letting me know. I'll follow up with Sonya."

Since he set it up, Lucas had mixed feelings when he heard the scumbag got beaten. Yet, he knew it was justified. He hoped this would help to protect women who get involved with Bruno in the future.

Feeling energized, Lucas danced to 3 more songs with Olivia. He bought a round of Jägermeister for everyone at the table, and then he headed to the Eibsee Hotel with Olivia, Eric and Ashleigh.

Sitting on the balcony of Lucas and Olivia's room, they passed the hash pipe, drank Hacker-Pschorr beers and had another shot of Jägermeister. They were all feeling good.

"Who got beaten up? Do you know him?" asked Olivia.

"We played basketball with him tonight," replied Lucas. "His team lost, and he was in a very bad mood when we all left the gym."

Ashleigh said to Eric, "We better get out of here. It's been a while since these two have seen each other."

Lucas thought: *I can see why Eric enjoys Australian women. They know what they want, and they will tell you what that is.*

Eric stood and said, "Goodnight all." Grinning and following Ashleigh out, he looked like a cat about to eat a canary.

Olivia and Lucas took advantage of the private time. Their passion was extreme and lovemaking was intense. Lucas felt more excited than ever before and wondered if their behavior was borderline illegal.

He thought: *Chalk up another gold star for Australian women.*

In the morning, Lucas and Olivia were tired. But they put on their ski gear, grabbed 2 beers and knocked at their friends' room. Eric and Ashleigh were dressed and ready to go.

Eating ham and eggs with toast and Augustiner beer, they all sat on the restaurant deck. They could see the cable cars operating on the Zugspitze. The cable spanned the mountain's rock face at a vertical angle to the top. Soon, they would be there at 2,962 meters (9,718 ft.) elevation.

After breakfast, they went to their rooms and gathered their stuff. They piled into the van, drove a short distance and parked near the bottom of the cable car lift. In this foursome, Lucas was the only person who had been to the Zugspitze. He acted as a tour guide, pointing out many landmarks which they saw from the cable car.

The views were spectacular, riding through the forest at tree-line, and then up the steep, rocky mountainside. At the top, an observation platform offered a 360-degree panorama of 400 mountain peaks in 4 different countries. Everyone was awestruck by the absolute beauty of their surroundings. It was hard to take it all in at once.

At the mountain-top restaurant, tables and umbrellas filled a sun-splashed deck where they each had a Spaten beer. Next, they took the cable car down to Zugspitzplatt where they would enjoy a sunny day, use ski lifts and ski on the glacier. They shared a pipe-full of hashish at the top of the lift, but out of sight. Then, both couples started to ski.

Eric and Ashleigh stayed on the easier slopes. This being only his 2nd time on skis, Eric seemed to do great. Ashleigh was also skiing well, and it was only her 2nd time out.

Everyone had agreed to meet for lunch in the cafeteria-style restaurant at the Zugspitzplatt. Eric skied to the lodge, looking confident. However, as he got closer, Lucas noticed Eric was bleeding from his forehead.

"What happened to you?" asked Lucas.

"I had a conflict with a little hut," he replied. "It got in my way."

"Well, how did you do, besides clashing with a hut?" asked Lucas.

"He learns fast," said Ashleigh. "He's carving smooth turns."

"I'm enjoying it now," said Eric.

"Good," said Lucas. "Then, we can ski together this afternoon."

Lucas went with Eric to the First Aid Station where Eric got his head bandaged. When they returned to the restaurant, everyone had a traditional Bavarian skier's lunch: Spaten beer, goulash soup and brotchen.

After lunch, Lucas told Eric, "The blue runs are gentle, but they offer you enough slope to make it fun."

They rode the lifts and went off to the side, out of the wind, where they passed the pipe around. Lucas led them down the mountain, going a little slower than his normal pace which kept everyone together. An hour later, they stopped for a beer and restroom break, then went to ski more runs.

After they finished skiing, they all rode the cable car to the top and enjoyed another Spaten beer in the restaurant.

Riding back down the mountain and looking at fabulous views of Lake Eibsee, cable-car passengers shared a lot of "Oohs" and "Aahs."

When they got to the hotel, the 2 couples agreed to meet in the bar later, then decide where they would have dinner.

In the privacy of their room, Lucas and Olivia got out of their ski clothes and relaxed. They smoked hashish and opened Hacker-Pschorr beers. Wearing only her bra and panties, Olivia wrapped her arms around him. Lucas was completely naked, and she kissed him so passionately, it was intoxicating.

"Let's shower together, then mess up the bed," she suggested.

"I'm putty in your hands, my dear," he replied.

Lucas followed her as she pulled off her bra, and Olivia turned to kiss him again, giving him a view of those sumptuous breasts. He took her in his arms and slowly slid his hands down her back, inside her white panties, and explored the curves of her nearly perfect ass. Lucas was tingling with excitement.

As he got into the shower with the delightful Olivia who came from the Gold Coast, Lucas thought: *Aussie ladies rule.*

After their passionate session of "love in the afternoon," Lucas and Olivia dressed and went downstairs to meet their friends.

Eric and Ashleigh were already in the bar. They had Augustiner beers waiting on the table for Lucas and Olivia.

"Lucas, have you eaten at The Last Chance?" asked Eric.

"No, but I went there twice for a beer," he replied. "It is a lively place. Lots of ski patrol guys hang out there which means lots of young ladies will be there." Everyone chuckled.

Ashleigh said, "Good, then Olivia and I won't be the only ladies. I get uncomfortable in a room full of men."

"I will warn you it gets noisy there every night, also during some afternoons, especially Friday afternoons," said Eric.

"I think I'd better speak now," said Olivia. "Ashleigh and I want to go see the Disneyland Castle. Would you take us there?"

"It's on my list of things to do in Bavaria," said Lucas. "I'm ready to go and see it. Have you been to the castle, Eric?"

"No, I have not," he replied. "I would love to go with all of you. Now, if you will excuse me, I'll call The Last Chance and find out when we can get a table."

Lucas said to the ladies, "When we go to the castle, I think we should take a guided tour. It will be more informative, and I'm very interested in this King Ludwig character."

Eric came back and said the restaurant had a 1-hour wait before their group would get a table.

"Why don't we go to The Grill and have a beer first?" suggested Lucas. "I want to talk to Gino, anyway."

When they got to The Grill, Gino was working behind the bar. Sonya was sitting alone at the end of the bar. She looked sad.

Lucas, Eric and their ladies sat at a table with Bob Ostergaard and John Ferrell. While the rest of the group chatted, Eric went to the bar and brought back beers for everyone. Then, Lucas asked Bob about the status of his VW van restoration business.

Bob's reply was, "I can't buy, restore and paint them fast enough. I have back orders from many GIs who want vans."

"Lucas told me about you, Bob," said Olivia. "He told me you put cabinets and a fold-up bed in each of them. Ashleigh and I are looking to buy one of your vans."

While Olivia was busy talking to Bob, Lucas excused himself. He went to the bar, sat next to Sonya and asked, "Am I intruding?"

"Hi, Lucas," said Gino who was talking to Sonya while he worked. "We were just discussing what happened to Bruno last night."

"I went to see the asshole in the hospital," said Sonya. "He actually blamed me for his beating. I had nothing to do with it. But I did ask him how it felt to be beaten which really pissed him off."

"What sort of injuries does he have?" Lucas asked Sonya.

"He has horrible bruises all over his body," she replied. "The doctors will be checking his head to see if he has any brain damage."

"I hope he recovers; and I hope he learned his lesson," said Lucas.

Gino and Sonya looked at Lucas with odd expressions, and they wanted to hear more; but Lucas changed the subject. He ordered 6 draft Augustiner beers which Gino would bring to their table.

By the time Lucas got back to the table, Olivia had charmed Bob into selling his own van to her for a very reasonable price. Since she now worked in Munich, she had offered to pay him in installments. Bob had agreed, and Lucas was surprised.

He thought: *She also has me eating out of her hand, but I don't mind. The end reward is well worth a little humbleness.*

They finished their beers, and everyone waived goodbye to Gino.

Arriving at the entrance of The Last Chance which Americans call Sonya's Place, Lucas noticed a bright neon sign mounted above the doorway, a heavy wood railing around the balcony, and large windows with curtains on both sides of the wood entry door. Below the railing, colorful flowers filled a planter box. One side of the balcony overlooked the highway, Zugspitzstrasse; the other side overlooked the Sheridan Barracks. The neon sign read PSCHORRQUELLE, and Lucas imagined it had something to do with beer.

Since Lucas had been here and driven by many times, he expected The Last Chance to be overflowing with ski patrol and young women. Inside, everyone was drinking half-liter glasses of beer, talking, singing, kissing, laughing, dancing and even groping. The Bavarian music was loud, and the place looked like a madhouse.

Passing through the happy groups of ski patrol people, they were escorted to a table in the rear, a short distance away from the mayhem. After being seated, they received menus from the Bavarian hostess who was young, pretty and wearing a dirndl.

"I saw the word *Pschorrquelle* on the sign over the door. What does it stand for?" asked Lucas, speaking to no one in particular.

"I have a limited understanding of German and Bavarian dialect," said Eric. "I think it means this place is a source for Pschorr beer."

Everyone ordered Pschorr beer and studied a menu. The Last Chance featured several versions of schnitzel and classic Bavarian dishes.

Lucas ordered Sauerbraten (marinated beef in a rich, tart and spicy sauce). Olivia chose the Jäger Hühnerschnitzel (boneless chicken breasts in white wine/mushroom cream sauce). Lucas had noticed Eric was a big eater. True to form, Eric ordered the Schweins Hax'n (boiled, 2-pound pork shank, served with crispy skin left on). Ashleigh wanted to try the Bavarian Roulade (flank steak stuffed with veggies, egg and sausage, served with peppercorn gravy).

Portions were large, and the food was excellent. Everyone cleaned their plates, and they emptied a big bowl of fresh brotchen rolls. They skipped dessert, but all had shots of Jägermeister before Lucas paid the check.

Everyone wanted a good night's sleep to be fresh in the morning for a tour of Neuschwanstein Castle. Lucas had called from The Grill, to make their tour reservation, and he requested a private guide.

The next day, they had breakfast outside at the hotel restaurant. From the patio, the view was fabulous, overlooking the lake. Lucas knew it was something he would never get tired of seeing.

"What's the deal with the beer coasters and the lines drawn on them at The Last Chance?" Lucas asked Eric.

"It is her method to keep track of what you owe," he replied. "On one side of the coaster, they mark each beer you drink; shots of schnapps get marked on the other side. Catering to AFRC employees and the American military keeps them very busy."

"When it snows and winter hiring starts, Ashleigh and I hope we can transfer from Munich to Garmisch, and ski here," said Olivia.

"Yeah, Eric and I will both apply for jobs soon," said Lucas. "Up to this point, we've been too busy—having fun."

Leaving from Lake Eibsee Hotel, the drive on a winding mountain highway would take about an hour, going to the Neuschwanstein Castle. Lucas drove toward Garmisch to Grainau. A sharp left turn put them onto Zugspitzstrasse and across the Austrian border. They passed Ehrwald and Lermoos, small local ski areas, then passed a few more. A sharp right onto Weisshaus Landesstrasse took them northeast, over the Lech River, across the border again, and back into Bavaria. The highway goes through the town of Füssen which is on the Lech River, then it winds through the Lech Gorge which is 5 kilometers north of the Austrian Border.

Arriving early at the tourist parking area, they left the van and went for beers at a restaurant near Hohenschwangau Castle. From this lower castle, they would walk uphill 2 kilometers (1.24 miles) to reach Neuschwanstein Castle, a climb in elevation of 125 meters (410 ft.) which would take them about 40 minutes.

A long, winding pathway led them to the top where a young man greeted them. He wore a gray Bavarian hat with the front brim turned down and a blue ribbon around the crown. He said, "My name is Oliver, and I will be your private tour guide at Neuschwanstein Castle."

Oliver wore a white shirt with blue stripes, suspenders on lederhosen pants, plaid knee-length socks and black loafer shoes. He spoke excellent English. With a prominent nose, thin lips and an easy smile, Oliver was charming and handsome, attracting the attention of both Aussie ladies, although they were with Lucas and Eric.

They walked to the Queen Mary's Bridge (Marienbrücke) which spans a gorge. Oliver explained, "If you want to, you can get photos of a very impressive view. A waterfall cascades to a river below in *Pöllat Gorge*. This bridge is quite high, and the structure is iron with wood planks. They bend a little when you walk on them. It is always crowded, and I apologize for this, but anyone is free to go out on this bridge. Please, do not go if you suffer from vertigo; you will not enjoy it."

They discovered Oliver was right about crowds on the bridge. They pushed their way through some large groups, tourists of all nationalities, to get to the center of the bridge where Olivia could take photos and capture the moment. After fighting their way off the bridge, they found Oliver, and he led them back to the castle.

Oliver said, "Now, we begin the tour of Neuschwanstein Castle. Before we go in, I want to tell you a little about the Hohenschwangau Castle and King Ludwig the Second.

"Construction of Hohenschwangau Castle was finished in eighteen thirty-seven. It became his family's summer residence, and Ludwig spent a large part of his childhood there.

"Later, New Hohenschwangau Castle got built. After Ludwig the Second's death, it was renamed as Neuschwanstein Castle.

A confusing result occurred when Hohenschwangau and Schwanstein swapped names. Hohenschwangau Castle replaced the ruins of Schwanstein Castle, and Neuschwanstein Castle replaced the ruins of the two Hohenschwangau Castles.

"The Neuschwanstein Castle is one of the most visited castles in Germany, and a popular tourist destination in Europe. Ludwig admired Richard Wagner, and Neuschwanstein pays homage to the German composer. The interior of the castle depicts many scenes of Wagner's operas. In fact, Neuschwanstein shares the same name as the castle in *Lohengrin*, one of Wagner's operas.

"Contrary to the castle's medieval appearance, Ludwig included modern technologies of the day such as running hot and cold water, flush toilets and heating. Water comes from a nearby spring, situated two hundred meters above the castle.

"Neuschwanstein means New Swan Stone, and the castle's name comes from The Swan Knight, one of the characters in Wagner's opera, *Lohengrin*. This castle was built for only one person—King Ludwig the Second. Since Ludwig was Richard Wagner's patron, Wagner's operas inspired many rooms of the castle. Despite this, Wagner never visited the castle because he died before its completion. Also, Ludwig slept only eleven nights in the castle."

Next, Lucas was awestruck by the splendor of the Throne Room.

Oliver said, "Welcome to the Thronsaal. It is twenty meters long and twelve meters wide (66 ft. by 39 ft.). The Throne Room is also thirteen meters (43 ft.) in height, and it occupies the third and fourth floors. As you can see, there are colorful arcades on three sides of the room. At the end of the room, the semi-dome should exhibit Ludwig's throne above the wide stairs. He died before it was built; and the order was canceled.

"Surrounding the throne dais are paintings of Jesus, the Twelve Apostles and six canonized Kings: Saint Louis of France, Saint Stephen of Hungary, Saint Edward the Confessor of England, Saint Wenceslaus of Bohemia, Saint Olaf of Norway and Saint Henry the Holy Roman Emperor. The floor mosaic was completed after King Ludwig's death. The intricate mosaic designs depict different animals in the wild. The chandelier is fashioned after a Byzantine crown. At the other end of the hall, you see a mural of Saint George, slaying the dragon.

"We will now go to the largest room of the palace, based on area. The Hall of the Singers is twenty-seven meters long by ten meters wide (89 ft. by 33 ft.). The reclusive King never used the Hall of the Singers because it was not designed for court festivities. It only served as a monument, representing the culture of knights and the courtly love of the aristocracy which occurred during the Middle Ages. It was one of the King Ludwig's favorite projects.

"In nineteen thirty-three, the first performance took place in this hall. It was a concert, commemorating the fiftieth anniversary of Richard Wagner's death. He died when he was forty-one years old.

"The King had this room decorated with themes from two of Wagner's operas, *Lohengrin* and *Parsifal,* the latter includes the Arthurian knight's quest for the Holy Grail. On the western side of the room, they separated the Singers' Bower (alcove) from the main room, using steps to three arcades and a small gallery above it. The Singers' Bower is painted with a forest scene, ending with Parsifal's son who was The Swan Knight in *Lohengrin.* Signs of the zodiac are drawn on the coffered ceiling.

"Okay, let's move on. By the time of Ludwig's death, only fourteen rooms were completed, out of about two hundred rooms which had been planned for the castle. Remember, King Ludwig only spent eleven nights in the castle. Yet, his all the King's loves and longings come to life here, through his murals and decorations.

"Apart from the large, ceremonial rooms, there are smaller rooms, created for Ludwig the Second's personal use. Royal lodging is on the third floor of the palace where his living space comprises eight rooms in the east wing. There are also smaller anti-rooms.

"Despite the gaudy décor, the King's living space has moderate room sizes and suites with sofas. Representative requirements of former times when a monarch's life was public, were not important to King Ludwig.

"Many of this castle's interior decorations include mural paintings, tapestry, furniture and other handicraft which relate to King Ludwig's favorite themes: The Grail Legend, works of Wolfram von Eschenbach, and their interpretations by Richard Wagner.

"Now, we are in the Eastern Drawing Room. Decorations here are legendary themes from the opera, *Lohengrin.* The sofa, table, armchairs and seats in this room, plus the furniture in the alcove on the north end, make the space comfortable and homelike."

Next to the drawing room, they entered a small, artificial grotto which forms a passage to the study. Another passage connects it to a small conservatory. Oliver said, "King Ludwig loved this grotto, a stalactite cavern with an artificial waterfall. Mechanical illumination from above creates the effect of a rainbow as you can see. They used Oakum to build the grotto. It is a loose fiber which comes from twisted hemp. The oakum was infused with tar, or a tar derivative, and combined with plaster-of-Paris. The mixture was formed to structure the unusual walls and ceiling of the grotto, then used to caulk the seams and pack all the joints."

The group followed Oliver, as he said, "Opposite the study, we will see the King's Dining Room, adorned with themes of courtly love."

From the dining room, they entered the King's Bedroom. Oliver said, "King Ludwig was arrested here on June 12, 1886. This bedroom and the adjacent house chapel remain in neo-Gothic style (19th century Gothic Revival). A huge bed, decorated with carvings, dominates the King's Bedroom. It took fourteen carvers over four years to make the bed canopy, its many pinnacles and oak panels. Ludwig installed an electrical bell system to summon servants. As in all the residences of King Ludwig the Second, the King's Bedroom is extravagant. The seat coverings are blue silk with embroidered lions, swans, crowns, lilies and the Bavarian Coat of Arms. As you can see, the swan theme is obvious in this bedroom. One of the most unusual features is the washstand; it has a fountain in the form of a silver-plated swan. Small swans also decorate the washstand set, water jug, sponge and soap containers. While the swan represents the character of The Swan Knight in Wagner's opera, it also represents purity in Christian literature. King Ludwig identified with The Swan Knight character whose tragedy and downfall was his everlasting loneliness.

"During construction of the castle, the emblem of the swan was an important image. In the castle's living room, you will see an entire corner dedicated to this magnificent bird."

Lucas asked, "Is it true, Ludwig committed suicide?"

"There are many theories about what happened to the King," said Oliver. "After the King was arrested and diagnosed as insane, he and his doctor were found dead in waist-deep water at Lake Starnberg."

"Oliver, are we going to see the kitchen?" asked Lucas.

"Yes, after we see the dressing room and living room," he replied.

They entered the Dressing Room and Oliver said, "This room has simple oak paneling. The image of trellis-work, painted on the ceiling, creates an illusion of the room being open to the sky."

Next, they entered the Living Room, full of beautiful decorations. Pointing to an extension chamber, Oliver said, "The Swan's Corner is dedicated to the legend of The Swan Knight in *Lohengrin*—a story of great meaning and importance for King Ludwig the Second."

Oliver led them to a stairway, and they went to the fourth floor for a quick look at unfinished Guest Rooms.

Back on the third floor, there were Servants' Quarters. They looked at one of the completed rooms. It was used by a servant when King Ludwig stayed at the castle. The room had oak wood furniture, walls paneled in oak wood and polished wood floors. The furnishings were simple, but the room looked comfortable.

Going down another stairway, Oliver said, "Most of the rooms on the second floor were unfinished: service rooms, a small kitchen, an anti-room and offices. Other spaces in the castle were also never completed: A Knight's Bath, a Knight's House and a Ladies' House."

Arriving on the second floor, Oliver led them into the Main Kitchen. What caught Lucas' eye were the awesome marble pillars, supporting a massive, vaulted ceiling which comprised many arched sections. Oliver stood quietly and gave everyone time to view this massive space.

Lucas stood near the kitchen doorway and studied the kitchen: *In the center of the back wall is a rotisserie with a five-foot spit. To the right is a plate warmer. The kitchen itself is gigantic. The central prep table is twenty feet long. Along one wall, wood cupboards sit below a long, granite slab counter. On the wall above the counter, open shelves are made of heavy wrought-iron. The counter and shelves display copper cookware of all types and sizes, perhaps 45 to 50 pieces. Throughout the kitchen, additional pieces of copper cookware, too many to count, hang from large hooks and rest on other shelves.*

Oliver broke the silence, "Builders equipped this kitchen with the latest technology of the day. It included a large stove and a sideboard, a large and a small spit, a built-in roasting oven, a plate warmer, a baking oven, a large mortar, and a fish tank, among other things. Adjacent to the kitchen are the pantry with a built-in crockery cupboard, a glass-partitioned room for the Chef de Cuisine, and the scullery area which I might call a general housekeeping space.

"In Neuschwanstein, this kitchen is three stories below the dining room; therefore, it was impossible to install a wishing table (dining table which lowers into the kitchen by mechanical means), such as you would see at Herrenchiemsee Palace and Linderhof Castle. Instead, the kitchen staff sent items up to the King's Dining Room, using a service lift.

"Let's go outside. The tour is almost over, but I want to add a few of my own observations." Everyone followed him to a lower courtyard. They stood behind the gatehouse, but still inside the gate.

Oliver said, "We are not supposed to talk about a certain use of this castle during World War Two. However, it is a known fact Nazis used it as headquarters for the Reichsleiter Rosenberg Taskforce. We also know the Nazi Party confiscated artwork and valuables from many places in Nazi-occupied countries, especially France.

"There is no record of Hitler ever visiting this castle, or even commenting on it. Yet, Nazi plunder was stored here and cataloged. In nineteen forty-five, it was obvious they had lost the war, and the SS considered bombing the castle to prevent the castle and artwork from falling into the hands of their enemy. However, the SS-Gruppenführer (Group Commander) was unaware of the order, and he surrendered it all to the Allies, undamaged. The allied forces found stolen artwork and other valuables, plus thirty-nine photo albums of documentation.

"Now, I will bore you with some statistics about the castle. Then, we will be finished, and you can all go to lunch.

"In eighteen sixty-nine, the King wrote a letter to Richard Wagner." Oliver read a portion of the letter, *"It is my intention to rebuild the old castle ruin of Hohenschwangau near the Pöllat Gorge, in the authentic style of the old German knights' castles, and I must confess to you, I am looking forward very much to living there one day."*

"King Ludwig died in eighteen eighty-six which was sixteen years after construction began. If Neuschwanstein Castle had been completed, it would have over two hundred interior rooms, including housing for guests and servants.

"Since the Middle Ages, two small castles sat on this hill where Neuschwanstein Castle is today. King Ludwig knew and loved the two castle ruins since his childhood. After all, nearby Hohenschwangau Castle was the royal family's summer residence.

"Okay, here are a few interesting statistics for you. The castle is one hundred and thirty meters long (426.5 feet). It is built on top of a sheer hill which is two hundred meters (656 feet) high. Its main tower is sixty-five meters high (213 feet). During construction of this castle, twenty thousand workers used four hundred sixty-five tons of Salzburg marble, four thousand tons of sandstone, four hundred thousand bricks, six hundred tons of cement, fifty tons of hard coal and thirty-six hundred cubic meters of sand."

The tour ended when Oliver said, "Auf wiedersehen. Thank you for coming." They all thanked him for a great tour, and Lucas gave him a good tip. Going down the hill, they had another 40-minute walk.

Back at the parking lot, they sat in the van and smoked hashish while they drank Spaten beers and talked about the impressive castle tour. Lucas moved to the front seat, put on some music and started the hour-long drive, heading back to Garmisch.

CHAPTER 19

NATO Officers Club

Lucas, Olivia, Eric and Ashleigh arrived at Hotel Eibsee and went into the lobby. A guy, about Lucas' size, was talking to the desk clerk.

When the man turned around, he walked over to Lucas and said, "My name is Robinson. I'm with the U.S. Military Criminal Investigation Division. Mr. Gary, do you have a military ID?"

"Yes, I do," said Lucas.

"Would you hand it to me, please?" asked Robinson.

Lucas took his ID out of his wallet and handed it to the officer.

"I'm confiscating this ID card," said Robinson. "You were supposed to turn it in when you terminated employment in Frankfurt. Now, you cannot use any military facilities without a sponsor.

"I found out about your ID card because your name came up in another matter. I want to talk to you about an attack on Bruno Castignoli which happened the night before last. I understand you played basketball with him during the evening. Could you tell me where you went after you left the gym?"

"Sure," said Lucas. "My friend Eric and I met these young ladies at the train station, then we all went to The Grill. We had dinner in the restaurant, and we were in the bar until after midnight."

"Gary, do you know Bob Ostergaard?" asked Robinson.

"Yes. I do," he replied.

"Are you involved in his business, or can you tell me anything about the operation?" asked Robinson.

"No. I know nothing about it," said Lucas.

"We are looking into his used vehicle business," Robinson said, "to see if he is doing anything illegal, under military law or German law." He hesitated as if he wanted to ask more questions, however he said, "Okay, you all have a nice day now."

"What was all his fuss about?" asked Olivia.

"It's a long story," said Lucas. "Bottom line—Now, I need a job with the military to get another ID card."

He turned to Eric. "I think I'll go over to administration and apply now. Do you want to go with me?"

"No time like the present—if we must," he replied.

"We have to get back to Munich, anyway. Will you drop us off at the train station?" asked Olivia.

"Sure, let's get your stuff together and go," said Lucas. "I want to be in Garmisch before the personnel office closes."

After an emotional goodbye to the fantastic Australian ladies, Lucas and Eric went to the personnel office and filled out applications.

Lucas gave his resume to Sergeant Masterson. After reading it, the sergeant whistled and told Lucas he would be right back. He was gone about 10 minutes.

The sergeant returned, sat at his desk and said, "Lucas, your resume is great. The NATO Officers Club in Oberammergau has an opening for a chef. They need you immediately. If you are interested, they want you to see the manager this afternoon for an interview. What do you think? Can you go there today?"

"Yes. I will gladly go today for an interview," he replied.

"Good," said the sergeant. "I'll make copies of your resume and application which you can take to your interview."

The sergeant turned to Eric and said, "Eric, we need a bartender at the Von Steuben Hotel in Garmisch. Their bartender got transferred to NATO Officers Club in Oberammergau."

A little startled by this information, Lucas inquired if the sergeant knew the name of the bartender who got transferred. He replied, "Bruno Castignoli. He's also from Long Beach, California." Then, he asked Lucas, "Do you know him?"

Almost choking on his words, Lucas replied, "We played basketball with him in Garmisch."

"I have always thought bartenders and chefs seem to bond with each other," said the sergeant.

"Yeah, bartenders like to eat, and chefs like to drink," said Lucas.

All the men laughed. Then, the sergeant gave Lucas directions to NATO Officers Club in Oberammergau. Next, he called and made an appointment for Eric to interview for the bartender job. Eric did not need directions to the Von Steuben Hotel in Garmisch.

Lucas and Eric were very close to becoming government employees. It was time to check out of the Eibsee Hotel. After this, Eric would find his own lodging.

Meanwhile, Eric wanted a ride to The Grill. When they arrived, both went to the bar and told Gino and John about their job interviews.

Lucas mentioned how CID Robinson forced him to look for work, sooner than he expected, but his friends just laughed.

"Welcome back to the working class, Lucas," said John.

"Thank you. I'd better get going for my interview," he replied.

Before leaving The Grill, Lucas phoned Inga at her shop. When she answered, he told her he would be in Oberammergau this evening, and he asked if she wanted to have dinner at a place of her choice.

Sounding excited, Inga said, "Yes, I would love to have dinner with you, but why don't we cook at my house? It is such a nice day, and we can barbecue something."

"I have exciting news. Tell me what I can bring," he said.

"Oh Lucas, I've been thinking about you and wondering if I should come find you," she replied. "Just bring your amazing body and a smile. Come any time you want. I'll shop for food and go home early. I can't wait to hear your exciting news. Bis spatter (See you later)."

After Lucas said goodbye to Inga, he enjoyed the 30-minute drive to Oberammergau. He had positive thoughts and felt like all was going well for him. He also hoped Bruno would behave himself. If not, Lucas still must figure out what to do about Bruno.

Following directions from an MP at the gate, Lucas arrived at the NATO Officers Club. He found the German manager who was drinking a beer at the bar, and he introduced himself.

As the manager shook his hand, he told Lucas to call him Helmut and asked, "May I call you Lucas?"

"Of course, Helmut, please do," he replied.

"Would you like a beer?" asked Helmut.

"I sure would, thank you," he replied.

Helmut introduced Lucas to the bartender, Karin, a sexy, blonde German. She poured him a beer and gave him a come-on smile. Then, Helmut led him to a table and said, "Watch out for Karin and her twin sister, Margo. They play tricks because we can't tell them apart."

When they got seated, Helmut said, "You have quite an impressive resume, Lucas. What brings you to Bavaria?"

"I needed a break from the fast pace of Southern California," he said. "I want to learn European ways of cooking and travel in Europe to get acquainted with the people and the German language."

"I think the best way for a man like you to learn a language is to find a nice German lady to live with," replied Helmut.

"Well, I don't know, but you may be right," said Lucas.

Lucas thought of his new relationship with Inga: *I don't know where it is going. I enjoy being with her, and we have a great time together. I also think we have a lot in common. We both enjoy cooking, skiing, drinking beer and having fabulous sex.*

"We are in a bind, Lucas, and we could use you right away. Can you start tomorrow?" asked Helmut.

"Yes. What time should I be here?" he asked.

"I think eight a.m. is a good time to start tomorrow," replied Helmut. "You can set your own hours and here is a copy of our menu. Our two cooks will arrive early in the morning. Herr Becker is a good cook and a character; however, he does not speak much English. He is also seventy years old and not very strong, but he's worked here since this place opened. The other cook is a local guy who was born and raised here. He is forty years old, speaks good English and will be a big help to you. His name is Kurt.

"I can get you a room in the barracks within walking distance. It is always nice to have a room, a quiet place to go after a long day at work. The only drawback is the barracks are only for men. They do not allow women, and it is a strict rule. There is a gymnasium shower downstairs, and you are welcome to use the facilities in the gym, weight room and library. You can drink beer and eat anything you want here at the club. If you need anything or have questions, please come and see me. Do you have a place to stay tonight?"

"Yes. I have a friend who lives in the area," Lucas answered.

"Very good," said Helmut. "If you have no other questions, I will see you tomorrow."

After they shook hands, Lucas walked back to his van with a spring in his step. He was smiling as he drove to Inga's house.

Inga was sitting in the backyard next the barbecue, drinking a beer. Seeing Lucas, she came to him with a big kiss and great hug. Then, she went to the kitchen and brought out 2 more Paulaner beers.

Lucas told Inga about his afternoon—He surrendered his military ID to a CID official; He applied for a job at the personnel office in Garmisch; Personnel sent him here; He is now the new chef at NATO Officers Club; He will get a rent-free room in the barracks, and there is a gymnasium where he can shower and play basketball.

"Congratulations!" said Inga. "This is good news, and I'm so excited to see you. We should talk about your living quarters later. For dinner, I bought pork ribs to cook on the charcoal grill, plus yellow potatoes, celery root, carrots and beets for a salad. Yesterday, I made Rotkohl, and I have plenty of Paulaner beer."

Then, she reached into her bag, pulled out her wooden, swan-shaped hash pipe, lit the pipe and handed it to Lucas.

"Inga, I know this is a dumb question, but did you make this beautiful pipe?" he asked.

"Of course," she said. "Did you know the swan was King Ludwig's favorite bird? In all his castles, it is displayed as a main theme."

"Yes, I toured Neuschwanstein Castle, and I learned a little about him." he replied. "I want to learn more about his life and his castles."

"Growing up in Bavaria, I've heard and read most everything there is to know on the subject of King Ludwig. I will be happy to share with you what I have learned," she offered.

Inga paused for a moment, then said, "Tonight, however, all I want to share with you is my body and my bed."

After dinner, they went for a short walk through the beautiful grassy meadow behind Inga's house. Heading uphill toward the ski lift, they held hands as they walked and talked in the moonlight.

Inga told Lucas about King Ludwig the Second, "Ludwig was born in eighteen forty-five at Nymphenburg Palace in a suburb of Munich. He spent most of his childhood at Hohenschwangau Castle, built by his father, Maximilian the Second, on the same site where Neuschwanstein Castle is today. It's close to the town of Füssen near the Schwansee (Swan Lake). Young Ludwig and his cousin, Duchess Elisabeth of Bavaria, grew up together. Both were interested in poetry and nature. She called him Eagle, and he called her Dove. They were lifelong friends. She later became Empress of Austria. When Ludwig's father died in eighteen sixty-four, Ludwig became King. But he was only eighteen, and he was not prepared for the responsibility.

"Well, this is only a little background, but I think it is enough about Ludwig for tonight. We'll get to other good stuff about the King when we have more time."

Arriving back at her kitchen, Inga said, "You have to work tomorrow, and I'm going to do the dishes while you take a shower. Or, if you prefer, we can both do the dishes and shower together afterward."

"You choose," said Lucas.

Handing him a dish towel, she said, "Let's get these dishes done."

Each time Lucas and Inga made love, it seemed to be more exciting than the time before. Lucas was having a great time with Inga. She was mellow and comfortable to be with.

The next morning, they had a quick cup of coffee and brotchen. When Lucas said goodbye to Inga, he promised to call her and let her know what time he would get off work; he would also give her the phone number for the officers' club.

On his way to work, Lucas stopped at the store and bought a case of Spaten beer.

After he got on the base and parked, Lucas put 6 bottles of beer in his backpack. At 10 minutes before 8 a.m., he walked in the front door of NATO Officers Club. He saw the dining room was bustling with breakfast service. To the left of the entrance, the bar was closed.

Lucas went in the kitchen and introduced himself to Kurt and Herr Becker. He left his backpack in his new office, put on an apron and a chef's hat, then jumped right into breakfast service and worked with Kurt. Herr Becker was making soup and doing other prep-work. When things slowed down, Lucas went into the bakery and introduced himself to the pastry chef, Dieter, a short, heavy-set Bavarian who was rolling puff pastry dough. It seemed like Dieter did not talk much, or he was not comfortable speaking English. Maybe, he did not like Americans.

Everyone did their own thing in this kitchen.

They all seem happy, except perhaps Dieter, and I sure don't want to upset the apple cart, thought Lucas.

He went back into the kitchen and opened 2 Spaten beers. He handed one to Kurt and one to Herr Becker who poured the beer in his coffee mug and placed it under the counter.

I guess, Herr Becker wants no one to know he drinks beer while he works, thought Lucas.

Kurt noticed Lucas was watching Herr Becker. He said, "Dieter and Herr Becker have a personal battle going on, and they play childish games on each other."

Lucas shook his head and laughed. The day went by fast, and kitchen employees were good at their jobs. While Lucas followed Kurt around, he asked questions and took notes. Then, he helped with prep-work.

In Germany, the normal shift for cooks is a split shift, and they work 6 days a week. After owning 2 restaurants and working in kitchens since he was 19 years old (the past 11 years), Lucas was used to long hours. Although this kitchen was ruled by Garmisch military command, it seemed to be running with German efficiency and Bavarian festivity.

Lucas went behind the kitchen and introduced himself to Arno, a young, husky Bavarian teenager who was scraping and spraying dishes. He offered a beer to Arno who replied in English, "Yes please." As Lucas opened it for him, Arno smiled. He took a sip and said, "Danke sehr."

After lunch, Lucas called Inga to let her know he would be off work at 9 p.m. He suggested she come to the bar for a beer, and said he would fix them something to eat. Inga told Lucas she would be there, and she would be prompt.

Most of the menu was American, but daily specials were Bavarian. Lucas hoped he would learn how to prepare the Bavarian meals which Kurt said his grandmother taught him to cook.

After cleaning in the kitchen, Lucas wandered into the bar. It was 10 minutes before 9 p.m. when he sat, and Karin set a half-liter glass of Augustiner beer in front of him.

Karin gave him a big smile and asked, "Well, Herr Gary, how was your first day at work?"

"Well, Karin, it was fantastic! How was your day?" he asked.

"It was not so fantastic," she replied. "This was the first day for the new guy, Bruno. He seems rather lazy and moody. I'm used to working with my twin sister, Margo, and she is not lazy or moody."

"Maybe you can train him to be more efficient. He is an American, you know," said Lucas.

"So are you. Do I get to train you too?" asked Karin.

Lucas laughed, but he did not quite know how to take her remark.

The door opened, and Inga walked in. She hesitated, but said, "Oh, what the hell." She planted a big kiss on Lucas' lips, and then she said, "Gruss Gott, Chef. I'll have a beer."

Lucas smiled. He introduced her to Karin and to Kurt who had come in moments before. Karin poured Inga and Kurt an Augustiner beer.

"Thank you for leaving my name at the guard hut," said Inga.

"You are welcome. Have you been here before?" asked Lucas.

"No. I've never been here," she replied. "It looks nice, and I hear it's popular with the military guys. I can see they have plenty of indoor sports: foosball and pool tables, darts, and even dice cups at the bar. Do you play foosball or darts, Lucas?"

"I have played lots of pool and darts, but only some foosball. What do you like to play?" he asked.

"I grew up playing foosball and skiing. I also played Bavarian football, a game you Americans call soccer," she replied.

"Uh oh. Then, it looks like I'm in trouble," said Lucas.

Inga walked over to the foosball table, grabbed two handles and said to Lucas, "Okay, Chef. Show me what you've got."

Lucas was no match for Inga, but she assured him he would be great, and soon, since he had very good hand/eye coordination.

"My basketball coaches told me the same thing," said Lucas.

In a low voice, Inga said, "I love how you use your hands, how your eyes look at me, and how you coordinate them so well."

"In that case," he replied, "let's go into the kitchen and get our dinner. I prepared Sauerbraten with Kartoffelpuffer and salad, all ready to go."

"Is it okay if you take this food home?" asked Inga.

"Well, I am the chef, and I manage the food cost," said Lucas. "Based on what I've seen, working for the military, they waste so much money, no one will care about two dinners. Shall we go?"

After dinner and a shower, they made love. Lucas figured their earlier foosball competition may have helped to fuel their passion.

Lucas felt content, bonding with Inga. Physical attraction between them was increasing, and a true friendship was evolving.

After working for three weeks at the officers' club and spending so much time with Inga, Lucas was feeling a bit overwhelmed by these sudden changes in his life. However, he was having a great time at work, and his relationship with Inga seemed to get better, each time they were together. He had taken a room in the barracks, but he stayed at Inga's house when it was convenient for them. Some days, if they were both working, he would go downtown and have lunch with her. When he and Inga had something to do, he could always take an extra day off.

The job was so much fun for Lucas, time at work flew by. On breaks and after work, he spent a fair amount of time in the bar with Helmut, drinking Augustiner beer and working on his foosball game. Since Helmut played almost as good as Inga, Lucas' game improved fast.

The downside at the club was seeing Bruno, the guy who murdered his fiancée, back in Long Beach, and probably murdered another young lady in Formentera, Spain.

When Bruno worked, he kept to himself, except with Margo; they seemed to hit it off. Seeing them together made Lucas nervous because he liked her and her twin sister. Lucas could not blame Margo; women were attracted to Bruno because he was a big, good-looking Italian.

He thought: *Bruno is as dumb as a rock. Maybe I can play with his ego until I figure out a solution. Then, I'll deal with Herr Bruno.*

Lucas planned to work on Thanksgiving because Americans celebrated it, and it was not a holiday Inga observed. She told him the Bavarians celebrate *Erntedankfest* which means Harvest Thanks Festival, and it took place in early October.

When Gino called and asked Lucas to work with him on a special event for the holiday, Lucas agreed. They would serve American civilians and whoever else wanted to come for Thanksgiving dinner. It would take place at the Keane Lodge in Garmisch. This was a convenient location for Lucas. Coming from Oberammergau, it was right off the main highway on Professor-Carl-Reiser-Strasse. There was plenty of parking, a big kitchen and extra counter-space to work on. However, the kitchen had only one stove and oven.

AFRC headquarters gave Gino permission to use kitchens at the International Bar and Grill, plus the Sheridan, the Green Arrow and the Von Steuben hotels. Chefs at those facilities would roast turkeys, make mashed potatoes and gravy, plus bake yams, stuffing and pies. They would use fresh cranberries, but frozen green beans and corn. Roasting 7 turkeys, each weighing 20 pounds, they could serve 125 people.

On Thanksgiving Day, The Event Team (Lucas, Gino, Eric, Bob Ostergaard, Scott and Faye Williams) had to drive around and pick up the cooked food from The Grill and the hotels.

The German chefs who prepared the food at 4 locations were all irritated—AFRC allowed these civilians to get in their way and impose on their kitchens. Although they did not hide their anger about having to participate, the chefs did a proper job preparing the food. Everything was hot, and ready to transport.

When all the food was delivered to Keane Lodge and made ready to serve, the Event Team checked out the dining room. Decorations looked great. Those were handled by ski patrol guys and their ladies. There were many, long folding tables, set with paper tablecloths, flowers and candles. They had 2 kegs of Augustiner beer, purchased wholesale, thanks to Gino, John Ferrell and Charles Henderson, the Manager of The Grill. Charles was a great guy, always friendly and polite, even to the people who he thought were "shady characters." Lucas wondered if he was categorized as one of those characters.

Dinner service went forward without any problems. After guests finished eating, and tables were cleared, Lucas came out of the kitchen with his dinner plate in hand, ready to sit and eat. He almost dropped his plate when he saw what was happening.

Dennis was prancing on top of a row of banquet tables which were placed end-to-end for the dinner. A self-declared homosexual and a waiter at Eibsee Hotel, Dennis was always happy and joking while he swished around the hotel dining room and waited tables.

Now, Dennis was only wearing a pink jock strap, except for the cast on his arm. He sang "Tiptoe Through the Tulips" as he danced across the tables with a long stream of toilet paper trailing and dragging behind him. One end of the paper was stuck in the crack of his exposed ass, and the other end was on fire.

People in the room were shocked, at first. But most of them had consumed enough beers or smoked enough hashish to appreciate this impromptu performance. Dennis' outlandish behavior seemed acceptable to many because he was likeable and outgoing. Everyone laughed and gave him a standing ovation as he pranced out of the room. He was still singing, and the toilet paper was still streaming from his rear when he strolled off and disappeared.

After standing there and watching in disbelief, Lucas considered the impact on dinner: *Well, at least the tables were cleared before Dennis did his little dance.*

Most everyone had gone, except the Event Team. While they were all cleaning, Gino told the story of Dennis, the Australian waiter.

"Dennis planned a long ride on a penny-farthing bicycle, going from England to Australia," he said. "During his trip, he was hit by a car on a curvy, mountain highway near Garmisch. The accident broke his arm. So, he is here, working as a waiter until he mends enough to continue his trip. The 'Flaming A' is the name of his dance."

Cleanup was now finished. Lucas, Gino, Eric, Bob Ostergaard, Scott and Faye got beers from a nearly empty keg. They sat for a few minutes, and all congratulated themselves on a successful Thanksgiving bash before saying goodnight and going separate ways.

As Lucas started to open the driver's door of his van, he heard a familiar voice, coming from the trees next to the driveway. He turned to see who it was, and Gabrielle appeared. She was dressed in black and seemed a little nervous, but Lucas smiled and gave her a big hug.

"It's nice to see you," said Gabrielle. "Andreas told me to find you and bring you back. He always talks about the dinner you prepared for us, the last time we saw you. We're staying at the same house."

Lucas asked if she was driving. She answered, "Yes. I'm in a VW van. It's parked down the street. Do you remember where the house is?"

"I do. Okay, I'll meet you there," he replied.

At the old house, Lucas parked around back. Gabrielle parked the RAF van next to his; both were out of view from the road. As Lucas walked with Gabrielle to the front door, he wondered if their van was stolen.

Lucas entered the house and heard a big cheer in the living room. It brought a smile to his face. He knew Andreas, Gudrun and Ulrike; but he did not know the two other members who were present. They were later introduced as Jan-Carl Raspe and Irmgard Möller.

Before anyone else spoke, Lucas said, "Hi everybody how goes the terrorist business?"

He sensed irritation when Gudrun spoke, "Lucas, we are not terrorists. We think of ourselves as Urban Guerrillas."

"I know. I was only joking," he replied. Everyone laughed and then asked questions, all speaking at once.

"Okay, please, one question at a time," said Lucas.

"Lucas, you have a military ID, don't you?" asked Andreas.

"Yes, I do," he replied. "I am working for the military again."

"Where do you work, Lucas?" asked Ulrike, looking excited.

"I am now the new chef for the NATO Officers Club at Hawkins Kaserne in Oberammergau," he replied.

"Hey, Andreas, I see you have a VW van now. Aren't you driving BMW cars anymore?" asked Lucas.

"Yah, we still drive the BMWs," he replied. "But, since there are so many VW vans in this area, we think it is less conspicuous to drive the van while we are here."

As he pulled his hash pipe out of his pack, Lucas asked, "Would anybody care to smoke some dope?"

He got kudos from the group, and a Paulaner beer from Gabrielle.

"How do you manage to avoid the law?" asked Lucas.

"If need be, there are eight million Germans and one American who will help us," said Ulrike. She smiled at Lucas, then said, "Also, the country was divided into Länder (states) after World War Two. They govern themselves, and there are no national police. We travel between the different states, knowing they share very little information from one state to another."

"Did your training in Jordan help you with regard to your rebellion against the German government?" Lucas asked.

"Hey, I supposed we would ask the questions," said Andreas. "But, since you asked, I would say we learned how to use Kalashnikov rifles, hand grenades and other explosives. We formed a relationship with Abu Hassan who is a well-known international terrorist. He is sympathetic about our cause, and he has been very helpful to us. In Jordan, however, I could not adjust to their desert lifestyle. I could not live the way they do, and I was glad to leave there.

"Since we returned, Ulrike is writing a manifesto, *The Concept of the Urban Guerrilla.* We are designing our logo. It will show a Kalashnikov rifle over a big red star and RAF in white letters over the rifle. We've also recruited a metal sculptor as our new weapons and bomb maker, and we expanded our Rote Armee Fraktion (Red Army Faction)."

When Lucas asked what they had planned, Andreas replied, "We have chosen the NATO base in Oberammergau, as one of our next targets. We hope you can get us information or maps of the base."

"I have heard nothing about RAF involvement in international events or actions outside Germany," said Lucas. "I think it will be a mistake to hit NATO at an American military base. Getting them after you will open a big can of worms."

"What?" Andreas asked.

"It will be a big mistake," said Lucas, "since you get sympathy from German people now, especially the younger adults. You even said the police aren't looking for you as hard as they could be in Germany."

"Yes, but it would be a big victory for our cause," said Andreas.

"I won't lie to you, Andreas," replied Lucas. "The NATO base is guarded like Fort Knox."

Seeing Andreas had a questioning look again, Lucas explained, "Fort Knox—it is a U.S. Army post where much gold is stored in America. Besides those issues, Andreas, I live and work at the base now. The last time we spoke, you promised you wouldn't attack Americans in Bavaria. I trusted you to include American military bases, plus AFRC facilities and hotels in Bavaria."

Andreas thought about it for a moment, then said, "Lucas, could you and Gabrielle go for a walk while I discuss this with the others?"

Lucas and Gabrielle put on coats, hats and gloves because it was a cool evening, and the forecast was for snow to fall. Gabrielle took Lucas out of the house which sits in a wooded area at the end of a long dirt road, close to the Loisach River. As they walked, Gabrielle made small talk and gave Lucas information about the house where the group was staying.

"The caretaker of the house is Victoria Von Düsseldorf Anderson who is Sonya's mother and sister to Frau Drexler," she said. "The Last Chance restaurant is owned by Victoria and Frau Drexler."

"I sure hope they do not bomb the NATO School at the base where I work!" exclaimed Lucas.

"Andreas is hard to figure out sometimes," she replied.

"It would be a big mistake," he said. "NATO would be relentless in bringing them to justice and maybe you too, Gabrielle."

Lucas thought: *Andreas seems to be a fun-loving guy. However, his expressions become harsh when he is discussing politics or the RAF. He gets serious, selfish and sometimes angry, trying to prove his point.*

"Andreas is determined," said Gabrielle. "He will carry this crusade to the finish. My brother Horst told me Andreas' father joined the Nazis, landed in a Soviet POW camp in nineteen forty-five, and never returned home. Andreas' mother convinced him that his father was weak and afraid which was why his father joined the Nazis. She insisted Andreas was different because he was never afraid, and she told him he must always finish everything to a logical conclusion.

"Ulrike is unique and complex. After she helped Andreas escape from prison, via the library in West Berlin, she had to go underground. On the same day Ulrike disappeared, her twin girls disappeared. She arranged for her girls to go to Jordan. They were shuttled from Berlin to France, and then to Sicily where the plan fell apart. The newspapers published a story about strangers who found the girls in Sicily.

"Their father sent his former employee, Stefan Aust, to pick up the girls in Sicily and return them to their father who has them now. The girls knew Stefan, so they were willing to go with him. Although he no longer worked for the *Konkret* magazine, he was a colleague of Ulrike, and he replaced her as an editor. He also knew members of the RAF, including my brother Horst.

"Ulrike realized the girls were in a better place with their father, but she had mixed emotions, and she felt betrayed. A short while later, the RAF leaders threatened to kill Stefan Aust."

This sent a chill down Lucas' back, and he said, "You sure don't want to cross these guys."

"Recently," said Gabrielle, "Ulrike wanted to see her daughters, but the others talked her out of it. I think she realized she could not be a terrorist and a mother at the same time. Ulrike is well-known as the publicist and spokesperson for the RAF; however, she is critical of herself, and she seems insecure."

"Let's walk back to the house and see what they have decided," said Lucas. He felt anxious.

Back in the warm living room, Andreas told Lucas, "I like you too much to put you on the spot and make you take sides. We have decided to choose another target, not because we fear retaliation from NATO, but because many of us also love Bavaria, and most important because you are our friend, Lucas. Next time we come back, please take time to cook for us, okay?"

Passing the hash pipe to Andreas, he said, "Yes, I will. Thank you, Andreas. I appreciate your decision. Also, thank you again for your help in the Bruno matter. As far as I know, he has been behaving himself. He tends bar now at the officers' club where I work, and I can keep an eye on him. He is dating a female bartender. She hasn't come to work with any bruises yet, but I'm watching him."

"We were happy to teach him some manners," replied Andreas.

Lucas turned to the group, including a frustrated Gabrielle, and said, "As much as I would enjoy staying to party with you, I've got a long day ahead of me at work tomorrow."

He gave everybody a hug and promised to cook a great meal for them when they return to Garmisch. Gabrielle followed him out to his van.

"I'm very disappointed you can't spend the night, Lucas," she said. "Next time I see you, I won't let you get away."

"Okay. You have a deal. Auf wiedersehen," he replied.

They kissed goodnight, and Lucas drove away.

Reflecting on the visit, he thought: *It is their charisma which makes them so dangerous; and it must influence the German sympathizers who seem to overlook the group's bombings and killings.*

CHAPTER 20

Berchtesgaden

Back in Oberammergau, it was late when Lucas arrived at the barracks. He awoke from a short night's sleep when he heard a trumpet playing reveille at 6 a.m. for a flag ceremony which seemed to be right outside his window. Lucas went downstairs to the men's locker room, took a shower and got dressed.

Before going to work, he took a few minutes to call Inga. Lucas was eager to see her later, and he planned to tell her about his relationship with leaders of the RAF and how it came about. He did not want to deceive her, and he felt sure she would understand.

When Inga answered the phone, she told him military police reported they found a bomb in a car at his base in Oberammergau, this morning. Luckily, the bomb was not activated and did not explode.

The news shocked Lucas, and he was speechless.

"Lucas, are you there? Is something wrong?" she asked.

Hearing about the bomb confirmed his decision to tell Inga everything about his interactions with the RAF.

"Inga, it is a long, complicated story," he said. "Will you let me bring dinner tonight? We can talk then."

"I will be waiting and not only for your story," she replied.

Off he went. Lucas was the first to arrive at the officer's club, and he set up his *mis en place* (French: things put in place).

While he worked, his thoughts turned to events of the last few days in Garmisch: *The Thanksgiving Dinner was great, and I had fun working with Gino, Eric and the rest of the volunteers. We successfully served a nice holiday meal to well-over one hundred hungry, young people who are all waiting for heavy snow, so they can go to work. The never-to-be-forgotten "Flaming A" dance, performed by Dennis, was both shocking and entertaining. My meeting with Gabrielle and RAF leaders was a challenge. I think I talked Andreas out of bombing the NATO base, and I believe this morning's incident was just a warning.*

It felt good to be at work, drinking Augustiner beer and cooking. Lucas enjoyed the fun-loving and hard-working Bavarians. Kurt told him the employees do not have to bring their own beer. AFRC hotels have beer machines, and a half-liter bottle of beer only costs 70 pfennigs at any military facilities. This was important to Bavarian employees. Drinking beer was a way of life here, and most of the locals get beer delivered to their homes instead of milk.

Throughout the officers' club, people were talking about the car and the bomb. Everyone believed the RAF was responsible. Lucas tried his best to look surprised by the news. He wanted to blend with the people who worked at the club, and they had just heard about it.

At the end of his shift, after a busy dinner service, Lucas fixed 2 Veal Cordon Bleu dinners with pommes frites and sautéed root vegetables. He wrapped those to take with him. On his way out, he noticed the bar was jumping with officers who were excited as they talked about the close call which was most likely a terrorist attack. Lucas wanted to hang around and hear what they were saying, but he had to get over to Inga's house.

Inga came to the door wearing a G-string and nothing else—so much for just dinner and a talk. Lucas took a quick shower, shaved and walked into the bedroom, wearing only his tennis shorts. His eyes fell on a real image of beauty. Inga was lying on her back with her muscular, fantastic-looking legs crossed, reading the November issue of *Stern Magazine* with Raquel Welch on the cover. When she saw Lucas, she tossed the magazine aside and jumped off the bed to greet him with a bare-bosom hug and a great big kiss. It was—game on!

Later, lying nude in bed and looking at the wood-beam ceiling, Inga said, "I guess you know I missed you, Lucas."

"I missed you too, Inga," he replied. "I've been rather busy. I'll tell you about it, but first let's discuss what the car bomb means to me."

"Car bomb! You?" she exclaimed, looking shocked.

"No. I had nothing to do with the bomb," he replied. "Matter of fact, I believe I stopped it from being detonated. I guess I'd better start at the beginning: George and I stopped to help Andreas Baader and Ulrike Meinhof after their BMW skidded off the highway near Mittersee Lake in Austria. We were on our way to Gomagoi where George and I met you and Sabine. After Andreas put his gun away, we gave them a ride to Landeck, and they joined their friends. Later, we ran into them in Venice, Italy, just after they had robbed a bank."

"You two really get around, don't you?" Inga interrupted.

"Yeah, I guess we do," he replied. "In Venice, George and I talked with them, we learned they like to party, and we let them hide in our van overnight. They joined their friends the next day. About four weeks ago, some of the leaders came to Garmisch and rented a house. I went there for a dinner party, and I cooked the meal."

He brought his story current, "Last week, they came back to Garmisch, and I met with them again. They told me they had plans to bomb someplace near the NATO Kaserne. I told them it was not a good idea for several reasons which I won't go into. Anyway, we talked, and then they promised me they wouldn't attack any Bavarian military facilities. Since they did not detonate the car bomb this morning, I believe they only intended to make a statement to the military. The RAF demonstrated their capability of planting a bomb wherever they choose if they want to."

Inga had a look of wonderment as she asked, "Mein Gott, Lucas, what have you gotten yourself into?" Hesitating, she added, "Although, I also might have helped them to keep them from being captured. Their story sounds romantic when you read about events like Ulrike Meinhof helping Andreas Baader escape from prison."

"I have enjoyed seeing them in a quiet social setting," he said. "But I can't forget their responsibility in the deaths of innocent people. It scares me, and I will try to stay away from them. Also, I'm not ready to tell Eric and Sabine about this yet."

"Well, thank you for telling me," she replied. "Now, we had better eat dinner and get some sleep. Tomorrow is another workday."

The next month was routine. Lucas enjoyed his job which seemed to be more fun than work. His coworkers were always happy and joking. Everyone drank beer at work, pretty much all day long. When the kitchen was prepared and work was slow, Lucas went to the bar.

The club manager, the sous chef and the twin bartenders all played bar games: foosball, darts and pool. It was an international club. Helmut and Lucas were the best foosball players. When there were no customers in the bar, they often had very competitive and sometimes loud games. Lucas was by far the best pool and darts player.

When Bruno challenged Lucas in foosball, Lucas humiliated him. So, they tried pool. They had both played a lot of pool in Long Beach although they did not know each other there; and Bruno was still not aware of Lucas' Long Beach connection.

Bruno held his own in 8-Ball Pool. Each of them won a game, and they played one more. It was even until Lucas got hot and ran the last 6 balls. Then, he could tell Bruno was irritated. They played darts, another night, and it was the same story. Playing with Bruno, Lucas always won.

Lucas forced himself to be friendly toward Bruno because he wanted to gain Bruno's confidence. He hoped Bruno would incriminate himself. If it did not work, Lucas was devising a new plan to deal with Bruno. For now, he would keep it to himself. He did not even tell Inga about his plan although he had already told her about incidents with Bruno which occurred in Long Beach and Ibiza. Finding Bruno was the original reason he asked George to join him and come to Europe. However, Lucas wanted to stay in Bavaria now, even after he deals with Bruno.

Within a few days, there was a lot of snow. On his breaks, Lucas and Inga skied a few afternoons at the Kolbensattel, close to her house.

After New Year's Day, Lucas and Inga took a trip to St. Johann, Austria. Eric went with them, and they all looked forward to skiing there. On their way, they stopped in Seefeld and picked up Sabine.

Since Eric and Sabine had not met, Lucas wondered how sleeping arrangements would work out on this trip. One thing was certain: Sabine was a ski instructor, and Eric would get free ski lessons if nothing else. Inga had made reservations for a stay at the Hotel Post in St Johann. Expecting a 2 1/2-hour drive, the snow slowed them down. Alongside the road, snow was over 2 meters high in some places. It was like going through an open tunnel. Lucas was a careful driver. He went slow and often pulled over to let faster traffic pass by.

They drank Paulaner beers, listened to music, laughed and joked. Sabine told funny stories about some of her private ski lessons. One story involved a wealthy, young cattleman from Texas.

"He was wearing a brand-new pair of blue Levis to ski in wet snow," said Sabine. "He fell a lot, and I had to help him get back on his skis many times. On one slope, he lost his balance, fell back and sat on the end of his skis, then slid about 50 feet down the hill. He left a trail of blue snow, colored by the wet Levis, and other skiers were laughing. It was comical to watch and hard for me to stay composed. The guy had a funny name, something like Regal Rock."

"That would be Regan Stone," said Eric, chuckling. "He's a recent law school grad who passed the Texas Bar Exam. Now, Regan works as a busboy at the Hausberg Restaurant in Garmisch. His family owns one of the largest cattle ranches in West Texas, near Corpus Christi."

"We have to razz him about the blue snow," said Lucas. "It will drive him crazy wondering how we found out about it."

"Please don't tell him I told you," said Sabine.

As the drive continued, Sabine entertained them with stories of Adolph Hitler and her grandfather, young Hitler's personal doctor.

To begin her story, Sabine Bloch said, "My grandfather was a Jew. He was a medical doctor in Linz, Austria, where I grew up. Hitler's mother was his patient, and he took special care of her. When she was dying and in a lot of pain, he never charged her for house visits. I did not know my grandfather, but my grandmother told me these stories so many times, I memorized most of the dates, names of events and names of people. If you get bored, please let me know, and I will stop."

"No, are you kidding? We've got to hear it now!" shouted Lucas.

She continued, "Doctor Bloch, my grandfather, studied medicine in Prague, the capital city of the Czech Republic. He served as a military doctor in the Austrian Army. In eighteen eighty-nine, he went to Linz and finished his military service. Two years later and still in Linz, he started a private medical practice. The Hitler family became his patients there. Since he treated Frau Hitler until the end, he got to know the family well, and he passed the information on to my grandmother. She told me about Hitler's father, Alois, who was quite a ladies' man and squired several children out of wedlock. Later, he legitimized those children. Alois fathered Adolph with his last wife, Klara."

"Why don't we get comfortable?" Eric interrupted. Then, he grabbed 4 Paulaner beers, passed them around to the others, and said, "Please continue Sabine, my dear."

"Hitler's father was a bully," Sabine said. "He tried to push Adolph into a government career, but Adolph wanted a career in art. When his father got frustrated, he would beat Adolph and his older brother, Alois (junior). He also beat his wife, Klara.

"When the young Alois had enough, he left home and worked as a waiter in London. After a few years, he opened his own restaurant in Berlin. He never kept in touch with his half-brother, Adolph.

"When the elder Alois died, Adolph was thirteen years old. Adolph and his mother sold the farm which his father had purchased before his death. Klara wanted to make a better life for her and her young son, Adolph. They moved into a three-room apartment which Frau Hitler kept immaculate, but they lived a simple lifestyle. All their activities were things they could do without cost, such as hiking in the mountains, swimming in the Danube, and attending free band concerts.

"Adolph excelled in primary school where his leadership skills were impressive; but he struggled in secondary school and dropped out. His mother encouraged him to follow his desire and become an artist. He wanted to go to the art academy in Vienna, so his mother offered to help him pay his tuition. Adolph refused his mother's offer and gave his small inheritance to his sisters.

"On his first trip to Vienna, Adolph was denied admission to both the Vienna Academy of Art and the School of Architecture.

"When Adolph Hitler's mother died, he told my grandfather, 'Doctor Block, I shall be forever grateful for all you've done on behalf of our family.' My grandmother, Lilli, told me Hitler exchanged letters with my grandfather during the rest of Hitler's life, and they had a special fondness for each other.

"Right after his mother died, Hitler went to Vienna again. He was nineteen years old, working as a hod carrier, shoveling snow and living in a men's shelter. Hoping to find a career in art, Hitler painted with oils and watercolors for five years. He sold many pieces to supplement his income, but he never got into the art academy. Since he did not finish secondary school, he was not eligible for architectural school.

"In nineteen thirty-eight, the Nazis closed my grandfather's medical practice. After my grandfather wrote a letter to Hitler, he received special protection by the Gestapo. In nineteen forty, Nazis allowed the Bloch family's immigration to the United States. Grandfather lived out the rest of his life there and died five years later. Ten years after his death, my grandmother returned to Linz."

After a 3-hour drive, Lucas pulled the van into the restaurant parking lot at Hotel Post. They had each consumed 3 Paulaner beers and shared a bowl of hashish, between Seefeld and St. Johann. Everyone scurried out of the van to find a restroom.

It was time to pass out 4 hotel keys. There were no complaints as Lucas handed 2 keys for Room 35 to Eric and Sabine. Although they met today for the first time, Lucas figured they could at least share a room. What they do when they get there is up to them.

Settled in their rooms, everyone showered and dressed for a night out. The group had planned to find a local disco after dinner. They got together in Lucas and Inga's room to smoke a bowl of hashish, drink another Paulaner beer and decide where to go.

Inga and Sabine had been here before and claimed the hotel's food was as good as any in town, so they had dinner downstairs.

Sabine asked for a quiet table if there was one. The hostess advised them an arm-wrestling contest was taking place in the bar which was packed, and the noise level was high.

In the dining room, everything was made of a dark wood, including the paneled walls, tables and chairs. Portraits of former Austrian royalty decorated the walls. A large crystal chandelier hung in the center of the room, flanked by smaller versions. A plum-red carpet covered a corridor in the center of the room. It separated rows of dining tables, placed along both sides of the long room. At the far end of the room, a big fireplace was faced with blue and white tiles. Each table was set with blue napkins, rolled around the silverware, a single candle centered on the table, plus white china soup bowls and saucers in place for each guest. The hostess sat them at the last vacant table. All the waiters were bustling as they served food, beer, wine and schnapps. An accordion player wandered through the room and serenaded guests with lively Tyrolean music. People were laughing, clapping and singing.

Since they all had the munchies, they ordered dinner right away. Lucas and Inga ordered the Seezungenfilet (filet mignon steak, stuffed with crabmeat, served with spaetzle and vegetable). Sabine went for the Zwiebel Steak (sirloin steak, smothered in roasted onions). Eric, the big eater, ordered the Schlemmer Teller (a gourmet plate of filet mignon, pork medallion, and boneless chicken in onion, mushroom and bacon sauce, served with spaetzle).

During a leisure dinner, Sabine continued her story, "Hitler and his mother had a special, strong bond between them. When Hitler's mother died, my grandfather claimed, 'Hitler was the saddest man he had ever seen. His mother had adored him.' He also said, '*Sie würde sich im Grabe herumdrehen, wenn sie wüsste, was aus iihm geworden ist*' (She would turn in her grave if she knew what became of him). Linz is the third largest city in Austria. My grandfather was the only Jew who ever got special protection by the Gestapo in Linz. He lived there until he took his family to the United States. Hitler's gratitude to my grandfather extended far beyond the time of his mother's death. Much later, when Nazi officers held a meeting in Berchtesgaden, Hitler told the group Doctor Bloch was an *Edeljude* (a noble Jew) and if all Jews were like him, there would be no Jewish question."

"How did Hitler, a young homeless man who lived in a Vienna shelter, become so powerful?" asked Lucas.

"A lot of people ask me about it," she replied. "World War One ended, and Germany was poverty stricken because of war debts. The country had no international trade, and its people were demoralized. Hitler got involved in politics and united the people of this crippled country. Hitler had his engineers invent and build autobahns (freeways). The German economy boomed because of his rearmament and military buildup. He gave the country a mission and something to focus on. He gave people back their self-confidence."

"Okay, I've talked enough about the Nazis for now," she added. "What are we going to do after dinner?"

"If you don't mind," Eric said, "I'm interested in arm wrestling, and I've practiced the sport. Maybe we could go to the bar, have a drink and check it out. It looks lively in there."

"Before we get up, let's order beers here," said Lucas. "We would have to wait in there, even if we could get to the bar."

They got another round of beers at their table. After Lucas paid the check, they went in the bar and got as close to the action as possible.

An arm-wrestling table was placed in the middle of the dance floor, surrounded by guest tables on 3 sides and barstools along the 4th side. Across from the bar, a Tyrolean band played music on an elevated stage, adding to the noise of people in the space.

Lucas' German was coming along, but Eric was better at speaking it, so he learned what was happening. Over the noise and music, Eric yelled, "This is the final match in the arm-wrestling contest, and the winner will be the local champion."

After the match, Eric talked to the winner, a big local guy who had a barrel chest and arms like tree trunks. He and Eric got into trash-talk. Although he had just finished a match, the champion challenged Eric to a match, right then and there.

While Eric and the champ prepared, doing whatever arm wrestlers do to get ready for a match, Lucas talked to the Bavarian and Tyrolean ladies in his group. He could hold his own in arm wrestling, so he knew about the sport, and he explained the strategy to them.

"One popular move is The Hook, an inside move which requires great arm strength, and you keep your arm close to your body," said Lucas. "Another move is The Top Roll, a leverage move, in which you apply hand pressure toward your opponent's fingertips, so his hand opens. The third move is The Press Strength, a move which comes from strength in the triceps, shoulders and chest, but it can be beaten by The Top Roll, using quick movement and a strong back pressure."

The big Tyrolean had a massive chest, however Lucas figured Eric had a chance if he could perform a good Top Roll. Lucas knew Eric had powerful arms, but he did not expect Eric to slam this big guy's hand against the table as hard as he did.

The Tyrolean's hand must be broken, thought Lucas.

Seeing fierce anger in the guy's eyes, an alarm went off in Lucas' mind. He pushed his way over, stood behind the Tyrolean and watched the guy approach Eric. Swearing under his breath, the Tyrolean had a beet-red face, and he raised his right fist.

As Lucas fell to his knees, right behind the big arm wrestler, Eric got the message. Eric ducked under the punch and pushed the Tyrolean who fell backward over Lucas and hit his head on the dance floor. The Tyrolean was stunned. Eric fell forward, sat on top of him and pulled the guy's arms up, pinning his arms straight back over his head.

To help keep the big guy down, Lucas sat on his legs. Then, he looked over at Inga and said, "Please order a round of Jägermeister for us and one for our new friend here."

The scene was so comical, everyone laughed, even the Tyrolean; and the band played music again.

Lucas and Eric helped the guy up. Inga brought the Jägermeister and someone toasted, "To the Meister im Schwergewicht Klassifizierung (The Heavyweight Champion)." Everyone then said, "Prost."

The big Tyrolean arm wrestler joined with them, and Lucas handed him a beer. A moment later, the Tyrolean and Eric patted each other on the back, laughing as much as their egos would allow.

Interpreting an announcement, Eric said, "The dance floor will be cleared, and a local band will get ready to play popular music."

"We can come back to drink and dance the night away. Why don't we go upstairs and smoke hashish while they clear the dance floor?" suggested Lucas.

Notwithstanding good intentions, after they smoked hashish, drank more beer and had shots of Jägermeister, everyone wanted to get some sleep because they were skiing the next day.

In the morning, the hotel served coffee and semmeln (rolls). Lucas convinced them to add boiled eggs, speck (smoked bacon) and Bavarian ham which made a nice continental breakfast.

Inga and Sabine suggested they drive for 10-minutes to Oberndorf, ride the Bauernpenzing gondola to the top of Bauernalm, and then ski through the trees to some other lifts.

When they arrived, Sabine said, "The runs are not so challenging here. I think this will be a good place to ski for the first day since Eric is a new skier. I love this terrain with all the beautiful trees, and a few of the runs are nice and long."

They were the only people on the gondola, so they smoked hashish as they rode to the top.

Since it was snowing, visibility was limited, and the light was flat. Lucas loved being on the mountain: it was quiet and peaceful, watching the snow fall softly to the ground and moving along the trails through the trees. Austrians laid out the runs well and had efficient ski-lift lines.

The group skied all morning together, then stopped for lunch and had the usual goulash soup, brotchen and beer.

Skiing behind Sabine challenged Lucas, and he felt his skiing was now at a peak. For a beginner, Eric was amazing on skis, except for a few falls, and those did not stop him. He was quick to learn, and he kept up with the rest of the group.

They had checked out of Hotel Post before they drove to Oberndorf. When everyone finished skiing, they jumped in the van for a 1-hour drive to Berchtesgaden.

One of Lucas' favorite subjects was the history of Berchtesgaden during Hitler's time. He had spent a lot of time with Helmut, the manager of NATO Officers Club, who knew the history of this area. While sitting in the bar and drinking Augustiner beer, Lucas listened to Helmut tell many stories about Bavaria, Hitler and the Nazis.

While Eric drove, Lucas and Inga sat on the bed, facing the front of the van, and they kept everyone supplied with Paulaner beer.

Sharing bits of information, Lucas said, "Helmut told me a lot about the Berchtesgadener Hof, the hotel where we will stay tonight. It was named Grand Hotel Auguste Victoria in nineteen thirty-six when the Nazis bought the hotel to host visiting royalty and other important guests. Hitler had it remodeled and renamed it, Berchtesgadener Hof. Many heads of state and royals stayed there, like the Duke and Duchess of Windsor, British Prime Minister Neville Chamberlain and Benito Mussolini, plus high-ranking Nazis, such as Josef Goebbels, Heinrich Himmler and the famous Erwin Rommel.

"Hitler's mistress, Eva Braun, lived in the hotel when she first came to Berchtesgaden. Later, Hitler moved her into the Berghof, his home in the mountains at the top of a winding road on Obersalzberg.

"Martin Bormann designed and supervised construction of a Nazi complex on Obersalzberg in nineteen thirty-five. However, Hitler was involved in designing the Berghof (which means Mountain Farm). Bormann's house overlooked Hitler's Berghof, and Göring's house was even higher on the mountain.

"Next door to the Berghof, the Hotel zum Türken owners got ousted, and the SS took over the hotel to use as their headquarters. They tore down many houses to make room for Nazi barracks.

"The Platterhof Hotel was also taken by the Nazis. It served them in various functions. First, it provided stately housing and a place for Nazi parties. Later, they used it for hospital convalescence until it suffered severe damage at the end of the war. In nineteen fifty-two, the American military rebuilt the Platterhof, and it became an AFRC facility. They renamed it the General Walker Hotel."

Sabine was somewhat familiar with history and current events in the Berchtesgaden Alps. She said, "This week, there is a World Cup race at Mount Jenner. Since I usually go to Salzburg, I haven't been in this area much, but I know some of the history. My grandmother used to talk about the village. She told me Hitler came to Berchtesgaden in the early nineteen twenties, and he used money from his book, *Mein Kampf,* to buy his house in Obersalzberg."

Arriving at the hotel, Eric parked the van behind the building. As they walked around to the front, they passed a stairway to the swimming pool and deck which were closed for the winter.

Lucas walked across the street to see the entire front of the hotel and his surroundings. The large size of the building surprised him.

The front entrance steps led to big double doors. Above the doors, BERCHTESGADENER HOF was painted in bold letters on the stucco. Two small columns supported an awning above the steps. To the right of the entrance, extending out about 10 feet from the main building, was a stairway going downstairs where there appeared to be a bar or pub. On upper floors, each room had windowed-doors which opened out to a narrow balcony, enclosed by a wrought-iron railing. Each balcony allowed enough room for two people to stand.

As he studied the front of the hotel, Lucas could imagine: *Hitler would have stood on one of those balconies, waiving to a huge crowd of followers below him.*

An American desk clerk greeted them in the lobby of the hotel. They got 2 rooms on the 3rd floor. Lucas went alone to find the employees' beer machine. Looking for an employees' entrance, he went outside to the left of the building and saw a cement pathway leading to a door. Sure enough, inside the door was shiny beer-vending machine. For 70 pfennigs apiece he could get 4 half-liter bottles of Wieninger beer which he assumed was from a brewery in the area.

Before he could put a coin in, he heard, "Gruss Gott."

Lucas turned and saw a tall, somewhat handsome man who was standing next to him. The man wore a chef's coat, a starched chef's hat and black pants. Lucas replied, "Gruss Gott."

"Are you American, Australian or English?" asked the chef.

"I'm American, and I am the new chef at NATO Officers Club in Oberammergau," he replied. "I just arrived here with three friends who will be very happy to learn I found the employees' beer machine. It's our first time in Berchtesgaden."

"My name is Gerhardt Grassl, and I am a sous chef at this hotel."

"My name is Lucas Gary." They shook hands.

"Buy me a beer and one for yourself, then come with me to meet the Executive Chef, Anton Held," said Gerhardt.

Lucas got 2 beers from the machine, handed 1 to Gerhardt, and then followed him to the kitchen.

After descending a short stairway and walking into the kitchen area, Lucas could see the long line of cooks and chefs. At the far side of the kitchen, they were passing plates from the broiler station, toward the end of the line where Lucas was standing. He watched the process as they passed plates: After the broiler station, came the deep fry station, then the sauté and gemuse (vegetables) stations. Next, was the garnish and saucier station. The Chef de Partie sat at the end of the line. He had a microphone which he used to call out the orders, and he inspected every plate before a waiter or waitress picked it up.

"If it isn't perfect, he sends it back," Gerhardt told Lucas.

There were 2 large gas burning stoves and salamanders above the chefs and cooks. Deep fryers and steam kettles were along the same line. All the other equipment was behind them.

There was a corridor in the center of the kitchen. Off to the left, Lucas saw a walk-in freezer and a walk-in refrigerator. To the right of those walk-ins, two old ladies stood and tossed something into the water in a tiled-pool which was waist high and six-foot-square.

"What are those ladies doing?" asked Lucas.

Gerhardt pointed toward the ladies, indicating Lucas should observe. A cook walked over to the pool of water and stepped in front of the ladies. With a white towel in one hand, he grabbed a long pole which was attached to a wire net. He scooped the net into the water and came up with a squirming, twelve-inch trout. Using the towel to hold the trout, he banged its head against the tile. Then, he wiped the blood off the tile and carried the trout back to the production line. Lucas watched the two old ladies. They looked sad as they went back to work, wiping the tile.

Then, Gerhardt answered, "They were feeding the trout."

Walking in front of the line of cooks and chefs, Gerhardt led Lucas to the chefs' office at the end of the kitchen corridor. Lucas saw 2 men, each wearing a chef's coat and black pants, sitting at a folding table, drinking beers. They were talking to a tall gentleman who stood next to the table, wearing a gray suit with a blue and white tie, also drinking a beer.

Gerhardt spoke in German, explaining Lucas is new to their country and still learning their language. The men agreed: Lucas would be more comfortable if they all spoke in English.

When Gerhardt introduced him, Lucas shook hands with the Hotel Manager, Herr Vogt, who was standing. Next, he shook hands with the Head Chef, Anton Held, who told Lucas he had worked there since the Nazis owned the hotel when it was in its prime. Last, he met the Executive Sous Chef, Herr Drummer, who looked as if he could be a little mean. Both chefs looked a little tipsy.

After Gerhardt excused himself, Lucas told the others about his two restaurants in Long Beach, and his new job at NATO Officers Club in Oberammergau. He also told them he was here for a few days with another American man, a Bavarian lady and a Tyrolean lady.

Speaking good English, Herr Vogt said, "I have to go now, but it is nice to meet you, Lucas. Please enjoy your stay here. Maybe we can have a beer while you are here, and I can meet your friends."

"It's a pleasure meeting you, Herr Vogt, and we would love to join you for a drink sometime," he replied.

Herr Held surprised Lucas, by asking if he had an ID card to buy liquor and cigarettes.

"Yes, I do," he replied. "But I don't smoke, and the only hard liquor I drink is Jägermeister." Lucas knew the low-cost of items purchased at a military base, made liquor and cigarettes a valuable commodity.

"Could you buy us some whiskey, vodka and Winston cigarettes?" asked Herr Held. "We'll pay double your cost."

"I don't want to make any profit, but I would enjoy a tour of the hotel, including my friends if possible," replied Lucas.

Herr Drummer said to Herr Held, "Anton, let's take Lucas and his friends to the Wieninger Brewery."

"Good idea, Klaus." Turning to Lucas, Anton said, "It would be our pleasure to show you around the hotel. We also want to take you to the local brewery for a tour. We will have a nice lunch there and sample the beer. Are you available tomorrow?"

"I'll ask my friends and let you know right away," he replied. "Now, I'd better get back to my friends. I only came downstairs to get 4 beers, and they don't know where I am. Tomorrow, I'll go to the Class Six Store and buy your liquor and cigarettes."

"Please buy us as much as you can, and then we will pay you," said Herr Held. "Also, let us know about lunch tomorrow. Thank you very much, Lucas. We enjoyed meeting you."

Returning to the beer machine, Lucas bought 4 Wieninger beers. Back in his hotel room, he had to explain his whereabouts since he was absent a long time. Eric, Sabine and Inga were waiting together.

"Lucas, please tell us where you were," said Inga.

"Okay, I was at the employees' beer machine when I met this German chef, Gerhardt, and we talked," he explained. "I told him I was a chef and where I worked. Then, he insisted I meet the head chefs and see the kitchen. I requested a tour of the hotel for all of us. Since you will see the kitchen tomorrow, I won't try to describe it now."

"We weren't too concerned about you, but we were waiting for the beer," said Eric. "What type of beer did you bring, Wieninger?"

"Yeah, let's light the pipe and try this local beer," replied Lucas. "I want to tell you what I learned about the chefs."

After a hit on the pipe, he said, "The Head Chef, Anton Held, is stocky, five foot ten, and fifty-five to sixty years old. He has a kind face, thinning hair, and he speaks excellent English. The Executive Sous Chef, Herr Drummer, has a more serious look to him. He has dark brown/blackish hair, a thin face and thin lips. Herr Held asked if I would buy them liquor and cigarettes from the Class Six Store at Strub Kaserne which is nearby. The chefs were drinking beer and invited us to the Wieninger Brewery in

Teisendorf. It is a forty-minute drive from here, and they will escort us. We will get a private tour and eat a nice lunch there. Of course, we will also sample their beer."

His friends gave an enthusiastic, "Let's go."

Lucas used the phone in the room, called to the kitchen and asked for Herr Held. When he answered, Lucas said, "Gruss Gott. Herr Held, this is Lucas Gary. We would love to go to the brewery tomorrow, and we will bring your liquor and cigarettes with us. What time do you want us to be ready, and where shall we meet you?"

"Twelve thirty; in the kitchen. Bis später (until later)," said Held before he hung up the phone.

Lucas said to the others, "Okay, we are all set for tomorrow. We don't have to meet them until twelve thirty." Then, he added, "Maybe Herr Vogt can give us a tour of the hotel after breakfast."

"Who is Herr Vogt?" asked Sabine.

"The Hotel Manager," he replied. "Herr Vogt and Herr Held worked here when Hitler, Nazi officials and many celebrities came to stay at this hotel. Apparently, it was like the Beverly Hills Hotel—Bavarian version. Now, let's decide what we will do tonight."

"I found some literature in our room," said Inga. "Tonight, there is a Bavarian show in the Weinstube (Pub) which is below the lobby. I also went looking for you, Lucas, and asked the desk clerk where they have venison. I know you enjoy it. He told me the Wildbraten (Roast Venison) is wunderbar (marvelous) at the Goldener Bar."

"Shall we go there for dinner?" asked Lucas. "Then, we can come back here for the Bavarian show."

"Let's walk to the restaurant," suggested Inga. "The desk clerk claimed it's a twenty-minute walk, and we had no exercise today."

Everyone agreed. Then, Eric and Sabine went back to their room.

Inga flashed a come-get-me smile at Lucas. "Want to shower with me?" she asked.

Pulling off his pants, he said, "You don't have to ask me twice."

An hour later, both were trying to catch their breath.

"Wow!" exclaimed Inga. "There should be a law against the way you make me feel, Lucas. It's like going to another planet for a while."

"I know what you mean, Mein Schatz," he replied. "I get lost exploring your fabulous body."

Sabine called to ask if Inga and Lucas were ready.

They were still naked on the bed. Inga answered the phone and lied, "Yes. We'll meet you at the bar in fifteen minutes. Bye!"

Downstairs, they each had one Wieninger beer in the bar. It was a bitter cold night when they walked outside.

"Okay, wait," said Inga. "Let's go back upstairs, put on warmer clothes, smoke another bowl and have a shot of Jägermeister before we tackle this cold. I know we could drive, but the desk clerk warned me there is no place to park at the Goldener Bar, and we need the exercise."

They tackled the elements, 30 minutes later, dressed in their warmest gear. Since it snowed the day before, this clear night was cold and crisp. It was a beautiful evening, except for the freezing temperature.

Sabine knew enough about the area to tell them about some points of interest as they walked.

"The high peak, covered in snow, is the Watzmann, the third highest mountain in Germany," she said. "It is over twenty-seven hundred meters (8,858 feet) high, with a twenty-acre glacier which is expanding. The glacier had reduced in size and even split before the turn of the century. During the last five years, it has grown at a slow pace. The lights you see are coming from houses on the hills of Obersalzberg. Oh, let's take a short detour to see the Hauptbahnhof (main railway station). In nineteen forty, Hitler had it built to entertain his visitors and celebrities. By design, the building is massive, like you see all over Germany in Third Reich government buildings which were designed by Hitler's chief architect, Albert Speer. The Hauptbahnhof even has a special reception area which was reserved for Hitler and his guests."

They walked up Hanielstrasse, veered right and walked along a tree-lined path behind some homes. The path made a couple sharp turns and led them to a stairway which went up to a covered wooden bridge. Above the bridge, 1937 was carved into the wood. It was the year construction began on the train station. Crossing the bridge took them over the railroad tracks to the rear of the train station.

Sabine told them Berchtesgaden is now classified as a market town rather than a village or city. The advantage is a market town has the right to hold markets.

The first thing Lucas noticed was the amazing size of the station; it was 3 stories. There were 2 impressive frescos: On the east wall, the 1st fresco featured a large brass clock. On the west wall, the 2nd fresco depicted a winter mountain theme with skiers dressed in colorful Bavarian attire and horses pulling sleighs.

"Thanks to Hitler and Speer, Berchtesgaden is the smallest town in Germany with a Hauptbahnhof," said Sabine. "I came here once with a group of ski instructors, and we got a tour of the station. Now, I will pass it on to you." She pointed to her left as she stood in the center of the main public area which had massive columns and high windows. "Follow me and we'll start in Hitler's personal reception area."

Hitler's reception room had a huge marble fireplace and stone walls. Above the fireplace, a large painting depicted Bavarian people, women in dirndls and men in lederhosen. The ceiling was beautiful, constructed with carved-wooden beams and large cross-beams. It was supported on one side by massive columns which were spaced the length of the room along a mezzanine, located halfway to the ceiling. The interior height of this room was 3 stories from floor to ceiling. A rich, woven carpet had a flower pattern. Large round tables and plush cushioned chairs were placed around the room. The exterior doors had once served as Hitler's private entrance to the reception area.

They went back outside, and Sabine led them around to the front. Looking at the length of the station to their right, they saw a big circular tower, the same height as the station, and attached at one corner. The main post office was at the other end of the station.

"Now, let's go back across the bridge because it will take us toward the Goldener Bar," said Sabine.

When they got to the post office, Sabine pointed to an outline of residual markings where the Reich Eagle used to hang over the entrance. They crossed the covered bridge, and she noted the date again, 1937 carved in the wood. Sabine said, "There are still a few signs of the Nazi regime, but nothing too obvious, except for the architecture."

They walked on Maximilianstrasse to Weihnachtsschützenplatz 5 and reached a large, beige building on the corner. A tarp-covered patio was now empty for the winter. Sabine said the patio was very busy when the weather was nice. Over the entrance, a rectangular sign displayed script lettering, GOLDENER BAR, and protruded outward toward the street. A sculpted figure of a golden bear stood on top of the sign. Behind the bear, a mural on the wall above the entrance depicted rock formation, a waterfall, and mountains in the distance.

Inside the restaurant, a young Bavarian lady greeted them with a smile. She was dirndl-clad and had ample cleavage showing which caught Lucas' eye. She led them past the Stammtisch and seated them at a polished wooden table with matching chairs.

"I remember trying to sit at a Stammtisch when I first got to Bavaria," said Lucas. "I was in Garmisch at The Last Chance. Wow, did I get yelled at! It scared the hell out of me."

"I think we'll be drinking Wieninger beer," said Eric, as he pointed to beer steins, placed on the table across from them. Unique, cream-colored steins bore a green coat of arms, in which a golden bear stood on four legs under an arch and above the lettering for *Goldener Bar*. Below the coat of arms, *Wieninger Beer* was scripted in large green letters. Most of the local clientele were drinking from these steins.

After they ordered Wieninger beers, Inga asked, "Do you know the origin of the word *Stammtisch*?"

Lucas and Eric shook their heads.

"Stammtisch comes from two German words, *stamm* and *tisch,* meaning regular and table." Inga explained. "When you put them together, you see how they call it the 'Regular's Table'. Locals are territorial about who sits there."

Throughout dinner, a Bavarian trio played lively music. Waitresses and waiters danced around the room and between the tables. On this Saturday night, the restaurant was filled with locals.

Lucas had Rehmedaillon (venison tenderloin, scented with juniper in red currant sauce) with spaetzle and roasted Brussels sprouts.

Inga had Konigsberger Schnitzel (pork cutlet, smothered in a white wine, lemon, caper and cream sauce) and Gekochte Kartoffelknödel (dumplings made from cooked potatoes) with sautéed cabbage.

Sabine ordered Alpine Schnitzel, topped with sautéed mushrooms and Swiss cheese, plus spaetzle and Rotkohl (red cabbage).

Always the big eater, Eric ordered a Dreimal Schnitzel Platter (triple schnitzel platter), Rotkohl and semmelknödel (a German dumpling).

With their dinner, they each had 2 beers and a shot of Jägermeister. Nobody had room for dessert. After dinner, they bundled up and stepped out into the icy cold. Returning to the hotel, they made the 20-minute walk in 17 minutes, all wanting to be in a warm place.

At the Berchtesgadener Hof, they all peeked into the Weinstube. Through the outside entrance which was down a short stairway from the sidewalk, they saw a big crowded room and many people dancing. The music was loud, but the food smelled good.

"This looks like fun. Let's go to our rooms, shed some of these clothes, smoke hashish and have a beer," suggested Lucas.

"I think I'll sit on the heater," Inga joked.

When they came back downstairs, they went into the noisy Weinstube and made their way to the bar. Lucas noticed it was full of GIs, all getting drunk, and there were not enough young women to go around.

Lucas and Inga danced to 2 lively songs. On the way back to the bar, he saw Chef Held and Herr Vogt at the other end of the bar. With beers in hand, Inga was busy talking to Sabine, and Eric was talking to a ski patrol guy next to him. Lucas excused himself and told Inga he would go see the Chef and the Hotel Manager for a few minutes.

When Lucas joined Chef Held and Herr Vogt, they smiled, shook his hand, gave him a shot of schnapps and said, "Prost."

While talking to them, Lucas noticed a guy, wearing a Bavarian hat, was leaning over Inga's shoulder. His back was turned, but it looked like he was trying to kiss her, and she was trying to push him away.

"Excuse me, I'll be back," Lucas said to Held and Vogt.

He pushed his way back over to Inga, and the guy was about to grab Inga's ass. Before he could touch her, Lucas grabbed his right arm and bent it backward with such force, people around him heard the bone snap, even over the loud music and noise. The guy went down to his knees and screamed with pain.

Lucas let go of the guy's arm, but seeing the guy's face shocked him. It was the CID super sleuth, Officer Robinson.

When Robinson recognized Lucas, he yelled, "You attacked me, Gary. I'll have you arrested."

Within seconds, Herr Vogt had arrived. He said to Robinson, "I am the Hotel Manager, and if anyone is getting arrested, it is you, sir."

Herr Vogt turned and asked, "Lucas, do you know this man?"

"Yes, I had the misfortune of meeting him," he replied. "CID Officer Robinson and I had an issue in Garmisch."

"I don't care who he is!" Herr Vogt exclaimed. "He can't come into this hotel and molest the ladies."

Looking at Robinson, Herr Vogt said, "I suggest you leave now, go to the hospital and have someone attend to your arm."

Robinson's friends helped him stand and walked him out the door. Robinson was screaming at Lucas, "You'll be sorry for this, Gary!"

Inga looked at Lucas, put her arms around him, gave him a big kiss, and said, "Oh, Lucas. Du bist Mein Held."

"No, Herr Held is over by the bar," he replied.

"*Mein Held* means 'My Hero' in German," she said. They laughed and called it a night.

Upstairs, when they got settled in their room, Inga showed "her hero" appreciation for defending her honor and more.

After they made love, Lucas thought about this special lady: *Inga has such an amazing body. She is not too soft and not too muscular. Her breasts are large, and she has sensitive nipples which respond to my touch. I get so tuned in to this gorgeous woman's body and her delicate areas, nothing else exists in those moments, except for the intensity of her responses to me, always to be rewarded.*

The next morning, Lucas and Eric went to the Class Six Store at Strub Kaserne. They used all their ration cards, buying whiskey, vodka and cigarettes. They delivered those goods to Herr Held and Herr Drummer at the chefs' office in the hotel kitchen.

Next, they each went to their rooms and got their ladies. Together, they all went downstairs to meet Herr Vogt in the hotel restaurant. Expecting an old-fashioned American breakfast, prepared by a German or Turkish cook, Lucas realized these hotel cooks needed lessons on how to make a proper omelette.

Herr Vogt looked like he might have had a rough night. To get their day started, everyone drank Wieninger beers.

Their hotel tour began in the main lobby at the base of a central stairway which led to the upper floors. Herr Vogt pointed out original marble cladding which framed the massive stairway opening. Remnant from days of the Third Reich, the same marble cladding is also seen on large pillars which support the open stairwell at the landing above.

Herr Vogt led them into the parlor and said, "Let me give you some background about this hotel. In eighteen ninety-eight, the hotel was built and named the Grand Hotel Auguste Victoria. It catered to wealthy and famous people for almost four decades. Then, it was purchased by the Nationalsozialistische Deutsche Arbeiterpartei (NSDAP) in nineteen thirty-six. In English, it is The National Socialist German Workers' Party, otherwise known as the Nazi Party. When the Nazis remodeled the hotel, they changed the name to Berchtesgadener Hof. It was a place for the rich, the famous and Nazi senior leaders to come and play. During busy summers, the terrace was always crowded and lively. Eva Braun lived here before she went to live with Hitler at Obersalzberg. In this very parlor, under the command of Field Marshall Albert Kesselring, German forces were surrendered to the U.S. Army in nineteen forty-five."

Looking around the parlor, Lucas took it all in: *Inset wall panels and a coffered ceiling, created with wood panels and beams, are all beautifully crafted in a golden-color wood, reaching the width of the room. Two large crystal chandeliers hang from the ceiling. The carpet and upholstered armchairs have a mixture of complimentary patterns in various colors of lavender, light blue, gold, burgundy and brown. The room has a festive and plush feel to it. A wide section of the outside wall is glass-paned doors which open to a large sun terrace and a fabulous view of the Alps.*

Next, they went into the dining room where Lucas noticed the same wall paneling and coffered ceiling as he had seen in the parlor; however, this large space was visually divided. He studied the room: *Although it is one big area, the floor space in this room is disrupted by large square pillars, cased in wood panels which meet the ceiling and attach to huge cross-beams, all in the same golden-color wood. Throughout the dining room, dark-wood tables are covered in white tablecloths, and dark-wood dining chairs have flower-patterned cushions. The carpet has a delicate design which seems to soften the boldness of so much wood. Small, gold shapes of gray-blue and darker blue colors, are woven into the thick carpet; and the pattern in the carpet creates the illusion of diagonal lines across the floor.*

"Looking out the parlor doors," said Herr Vogt, "below the terrace, you see our swimming pool which is a big attraction in the summer. Some ski patrol fellows serve as lifeguards. The pool offers a place to hang out for young ladies who are local, in addition to our hotel guests. We also have clay tennis courts on the other side of the hotel."

This bit of information interested Lucas very much. He had only played on clay once and would love to try it again.

Lucas wondered: *Will I still be around here, next summer?*

"Behind the hotel are the parking garages and maintenance housing," said Herr Vogt. "Beneath the maintenance building is a complex of Luftschutzraum (air-raid shelters). In the basement, you would see original ventilation equipment which was installed in nineteen forty. Next to it, the hotel furnace room has the original steam-heating apparatus. It was also installed in nineteen forty."

Following Herr Vogt, they walked down some stairs and into the main kitchen area. Lucas greeted Gerhardt who smiled and waved, and all the cooks stopped to check out Inga and Sabine.

As Herr Vogt led them back to the chefs' office, Lucas told his group about the trout pond and the old ladies who were feeding the fish.

In the chefs' office, Herr Drummer and Herr Held were drinking Wieninger beer. When Herr Drummer handed beers to everyone, they all raised their glasses and said, "Prost."

Another man came in, and Herr Vogt introduced him as Herr Schuster, the Assistant Hotel Manager, whose wife and daughter ran the gift shop, located near the lobby. While everyone chatted, Herr Drummer excused himself and went into the kitchen area.

Drummer returned with a tray of Sauvignon Steak hors d'oeuvres. He described them as a toasted slice of baguette, topped with a few grilled onions and a thin slice of filet mignon. Over it, he spooned a warm sauce, made of bell pepper, pimiento, finely diced salami, brandy and Sauvignon Blanc wine, plus a strong cheddar cheese, to coat the top of the meat.

Herr Drummer served each of them a Sauvignon Steak/Baguette with a napkin underneath to catch juicy drippings. Everyone in the room moaned with pleasure after the first bite. Herr Vogt told them this is Chef Held's signature hors d'oeuvre and his original sauce.

After 2 beers apiece and the Sauvignon Steak hors d'oeuvres, Herr Vogt said, "I want to show you something which I'm sure will interest everyone. Lucas, you will appreciate it, as a chef and restaurant owner. So, let's go to the hotel steward's storeroom."

Going behind the dish-and-pot-washing station, they went into a large storeroom. Heavy metal shelving held silver champagne buckets and trays of silverware. A whole wall was dedicated to table linens and napkins. Another row of shelves held fine china and dinnerware. Lucas wished they had more time. He knew he could spend hours going through all this stuff. Looking closer, he could see swastikas engraved on many items, and there were thousands of items in this room.

"We don't have time to see the employee quarters on the top floor," said Herr Vogt. "Most of our resident employees are young apprentices. It's like a zoo with loud music up there where German guys and gals drink beer and have fun. They are all hard-working young people. We do also have older employees who live here."

Herr Vogt concluded the hotel tour, saying, "I know you must get ready to leave for your brewery tour. But I hope you come back to see more of the hotel. My suggestion would be to return in late spring after the pool and tennis courts are open, or in the summer."

Everyone thanked Herr Vogt for the tour, told him they enjoyed their stay and promised they would return.

They hurried to their rooms, got their stuff packed, checked out, loaded everything into the van, and walked back inside the hotel. Of course, when they got to the kitchen, Herr Drummer and Herr Held insisted everyone have a beer before they all went to the brewery.

Instead of using 1 vehicle, Eric and Sabine rode with Herr Held in his BMW, and Lucas took Inga and Drummer in his van. Lucas tried to keep up with the BMW for a while, but he quit chasing it when Herr Drummer said he knew the way to the brewery.

Inga got out her swan-shaped, wood-carved hash pipe and filled it. Then, she asked Herr Drummer if he wanted to smoke hashish.

"Since I'm not driving, I guess I'll try some instead of smoking a cigarette, he replied."

"Believe me, Herr Drummer, this hashish is nothing like smoking a cigarette," said Lucas.

Inga passed the hash pipe around. After his turn on the pipe, Herr Drummer was silent for a few minutes. Then, he was curious, and he inquired how often they smoke hashish.

"We smoke hashish whenever the opportunity arises and conditions are suitable. In other words—all the time," Lucas replied.

"Why do you smoke so much hashish?" asked Herr Drummer.

Inga answered this time, "Because, Herr Drummer, music sounds better, sex feels better, food tastes better and life is better."

Herr Drummer shook his head, trying to fathom what Inga said.

When they arrived at the Brewery, Eric looked pale and shaken, as he and Lucas walked with Sabine. They were behind the others and just out of hearing range.

"Herr Held drives his BMW as if he's racing at Le Mans," said Eric. "He scared the crap out of me. However, Sabine didn't seem to mind at all. Did you Sabine?"

"I drive the same way. What can I say?" she replied.

The hostess in the lobby was a Bavarian beauty, wearing a dirndl. She had a great smile and made them feel welcome. Her blouse was cut so low, Lucas expected her tits to pop out. He did not catch her name, but she looked like a Heidi.

Everyone seemed to know Herr Held and Herr Drummer. One of the company's vice-presidents introduced himself as Herr Wieninger, and he conducted their private tour. Lucas felt special, and he noticed the extra respect which Herr Held received.

To begin, Herr Wieninger told how his name and the name of the brewery originated, "Philipp Vienna Inger, my great, great grandfather, was head of the Inger family. On February twenty-six, eighteen thirteen, the family came here from Schönau which is in the Bavarian Forest. The name Vienna Inger was combined to Wieninger. It is our adopted family name now, but we will always be the Ingers from Vienna."

He explained the steps of the brewing process and led them to the brew house which he called *The Heart of the Brewery*. As he showed them the main fermentation in open vats, and they descended into deep cellars to see the maturation process, Herr Wieninger kept talking, "The original brewery was first mentioned in legal documents which were dated in sixteen sixty-six.

"It was destroyed by fire in eighteen sixty-five. After the fire, the family built the Max Christian Wieninger Brewery to be a larger and more modern brewery, than what it had been before. The family added another brewery, *The Fischerbräu in Bad Reichenhall,* in eighteen seventy-five.

"From eighteen eighty-five to nineteen ten, Max Joseph Wieninger, Christian's son, bought twenty restaurants. Most of those restaurants are still owned by the brewery.

"In the disastrous international financial crises, between the first and second world wars, Hermann Wieninger, his brother Ernst Ludwig and the brewery staff managed to salvage the brewery.

"In nineteen forty-five, Max Ruprecht Wieninger modernized the entire operation, changing from wood and metal crates to new modern plastic crates and using crown cap bottles.

“The brewery became a fully automatic bottling plant in nineteen sixty-three. With the purchase and use rights of two mountain streams, he secured their own special brewing water for the brewery.

“This past year, Max Christian Wieninger implemented changes at the brewery, based on market requirements. Ahead of his time, he put the customer at the heart of his business policy. With increasing sales, he made a name for himself and for his brand of Wieninger beer.

“For years, technical development continued in our craft. Under his leadership, special emphasis was given to greening and preserving the environment of the brewery and the surrounding areas.

“Following the fundamental principles of Wieninger beer, we only use quality raw materials. Fine aroma hops come from the best growing areas, and Bavarian malt is tailored to each type of beer. Our greatest asset is the clear, pure, mountain spring water from the foot of the Teisenberg. It guarantees the specific purity and wholesomeness of Wieninger beer.

“We do not copy beers which have their home in other countries and regions of the world. Rather, we brew beers which have traceable roots in our Bavarian brewery culture. Being a private brewery, MC Wieninger is characterized by a unique connection between man and nature. Here, Wieninger beer is an element of enjoyment and socializing, and thus an indispensable part of peoples’ everyday lives.”

Beer certainly is an important part of a German’s life, and mine also, come to think of it, thought Lucas.

Herr Wieninger explained, “Bavarian brewery culture means we use local malts and hops, fermented with lager yeast from our own pure breeding brew, according to the Bavarian Purity Law. We do not add extra ingredients, like sugar or spices. We use traditional methods: open fermentation and aging in barrels or bottles.”

He ended the tour. “Thank you for the privilege of showing you our humble, Bavarian brewery. Now you can go drink beer and have a nice lunch in the brewery dining room. If you would please follow Heidi, she will show you the way, although I’m sure Herr Held and Herr Drummer know the way. Auf Wiedersehen.”

On the way to the dining room, Herr Drummer asked Lucas, Inga, Eric and Sabine what they thought about the tour.

“This place is hospital clean,” said Lucas.

“I loved the dirndls and lederhosen,” said Inga. (The workers all wore black and forest green lederhosen, or dirndls, plus striped knee-length socks to match.)

“I liked the hostess,” said Eric.

The rest of the group started chuckling.

Sabine poked Eric in the ribs with her elbow and said, "I liked the brewmaster." Now, everyone was laughing.

Seated in heavy wooden chairs at a heavy wooden table, they all had half-liters of Wieninger beer in the brewery's own beer glasses, each displaying the Wieninger name and logo. Next, they were served Leberknödel suppe (liver dumpling in a clear beef broth), and servers kept fresh glasses of beer coming steady. For the main course, they watched several servers bring out large platters of food and set them on the table for a family-style lunch.

Lucas surveyed the colorful food items. He spotted the Kartoffelpuffer (German potato pancakes), Spargel (white asparagus) with hollandaise sauce, Bratwurst and Weisswurst. A female server told them the tray of meat medallions were Wildschweinmedallons (wild boar medallions), surrounded with Fresh Herb Spaetzle. Another big, colorful platter held a layered item, Roasted Vegetable Strudel.

During lunch, the group listened as Herr Held and Herr Drummer told stories about the history of Bavaria.

"Napoleon's army looted Salzburg, but spared Berchtesgaden because a Prince-Provost was an old school chum of the commanding French General," said Herr Held. "Around eighteen ten, the palace became popular with the Bavarian royal family, the House of Wittelsbach. They often visited the Königssee and maintained a royal hunting residence at the property of the former Augustine Monastery (still used today by Franz, Duke of Bavaria).

"When King Ludwig the Third was forced to abdicate in nineteen eighteen, he fled to Berchtesgaden. His son, Prince Rupprecht, lived at the Royal Palace of Berchtesgaden, right in the center of town, until nineteen thirty-three.

"Then, Hitler and his Nazi entourage arrived. When Hitler became Chancellor, the Prince fled to Switzerland. He returned after the war and lived in the palace until nineteen fifty-three.

"For centuries, the local salt mines have contributed most of the wealth in this area, and those are still in operation.

"There is so much to see in Berchtesgaden, I hope all of you can come back soon. Lucas, I hope you will consider coming to work at 'The Hof' for the summer. It is a beautiful time of year here. I know you haven't had the opportunity to see much on this trip, but I'll mention a few things which you might enjoy seeing.

"The Kehlsteinhaus, more commonly known as the Eagle's Nest, was originally designed by Martin Bormann to be a birthday gift for Adolph Hitler's fiftieth birthday, on behalf of the NSDAP (Nazi Party). Located high above Berchtesgaden at the top of Kehlstein Mountain, the Eagle's

Nest rests on the summit where it has a sweeping view of the Alps, looking out over Germany and Austria from a one thousand twenty-eight meters (6,000 ft.) elevation. It was Hitler's private fortress, designed for living and entertaining on a big scale. However, he seldom visited the Eagle's Nest. In fact, when Hitler did visit it, he did not spend much time there because he hated heights and did not care much for elevators.

"Now, open to the public, tours take people to see the Eagle's Nest. It is beautifully constructed with thick, exterior walls of granite stone. The interior offers walls of wood paneling and high beamed ceilings, a large conference room, a conference-size dining room, a lovely garden terrace, a sun porch, a tea room, and a massive red-marble fireplace which was a gift to Hitler from Mussolini.

"At the end of World War Two, allied bombing did not damage the Eagle's Nest, thanks to intervention by Governor Jacob who was then in office. It was amazing the Eagle's Nest survived because most of the Nazi Party leaders' homes were bombed and destroyed in Obersalzberg. A few other buildings were also spared, including the Kampfhäusl, a small cabin which was used as a guesthouse. After Hitler's release from prison, the Pension Moritz Hotel offered the cabin to Hitler, and he wrote part of *Mein Kampf* while he stayed there.

"Some people refer to the Kehlsteinhaus as the 'Tea House' which Hitler walked to. However, he could not have walked to Kehlsteinhaus (Eagle's Nest). As tourists discover, you can only get there on a special bus from Obersalzberg. It takes you through a huge door at the entrance of a tunnel which is one hundred thirty meters (427 ft.) long, going into the mountain. An elevator then lifts you one hundred twenty meters (394 ft.) to the Kehlsteinhaus at the top.

"On his daily walks, Hitler visited the Mooslahnerkopf Tea House. It is near the Berghof (Hitler's home) on the Obersalzberg (mountain). Both structures were destroyed after the war. Bormann had planted a tree at the bottom of the driveway for Hitler to stand in the shade and watch crowds of his fans walk by. Although the tree got cut down, the stump is still there, and it grew into bushes.

"Hitler and a lot of Hitler's political friends came over and stayed at Hotel Deutsches Haus. Paula Hitler, Adolph Hitler's sister, lived in the Berchtesgaden area until she died in nineteen sixty. She used to walk with Hitler in the park near the hotel.

"Don't miss the Luftlmalerei (Bavarian frescoes) in the Altstadt (Old Town). There is an interesting story about the facade on the Hirschenhaus which was built in fifteen ninety-four. Looking at the fresco from a distance, it appears to be a typical Bavarian scene. If you look closer though, you see the townspeople in the scene have monkey faces. If you believe the story, the family who commissioned the mural did not pay the painter, so he painted over the faces of family members and gave them monkey faces for revenge."

Herr Drummer cleared his throat which caught Herr Held's attention, and then Drummer pointed to his watch.

"Now, we must return to the hotel," said Herr Held. "We thank you for coming and hope to see you again soon. Auf Wiedersehen."

During the storytelling, servers kept their beer glasses full. Fortunately, it was only a forty-minute drive from Teisendorf to Lake Chiemsee.

Lucas, Inga, Eric and Sabine gave their compliments to the staff and said, "Danke schoen und auf weidersehen," (thank you and goodbye) to everyone at the brewery.

They climbed into the van and headed for Rasthaus am Chiemsee, a hotel built by Hitler which served as R&R accommodations for his Nazi officers and politicians. The hotel now belongs to AFRC, and it is open to anyone who has a military ID.

Rasthaus am Chiemsee also houses some infamous party animals who are lucky to be stationed there, the U.S. Military Ski Patrol, known by locals as the Chiemsee Raiders.

CHAPTER 21

First Visit to Chiemsee

It was late afternoon when they pulled in the lot and parked the van at the Rasthaus am Chiemsee (Rest House on Lake Chiemsee), otherwise known as Lake Chiemsee Hotel.

They consumed several more beers than usual at the brewery, and none of them were feeling any pain. Climbing out of the van, everyone was laughing and joking around until they saw CID Officer Robinson. He had a sling and a cast on his right arm, plus 2 MPs at his side.

Robinson approached them and said, “Okay Gary, we are going to search your van for contraband. Please step aside.”

“Officer Robinson, we are all civilians,” Lucas objected.

“Oh, but you are on military property,” he replied.

Robinson opened all the doors on the van, then got inside and went through cupboards. While searching the food cabinet, he found a chunk of hashish in a metal saffron container.

“Lucas Gary, I am placing you under arrest for possession of hashish,” said Robinson. Then, a female MPs put Lucas in handcuffs, and they all walked into the lobby of the hotel.

“Robinson, if you value your job, I think you should make a phone call to Colonel Moyers, the AFRC Commander, and tell him what you are about to do,” said Lucas.

“I don’t have to call anyone. You’re going to jail!” he replied.

“Okay, I’ll call him myself,” said Lucas. “I believe, I’m entitled to a phone call. It’s your ass, Robinson.”

“Okay, let’s see how much pull you have, Gary,” he replied.

Annoyed and arrogant, Robinson walked to the front desk, grabbed the phone and called headquarters. When a desk sergeant transferred the call to Colonel Moyers, Robinson told him about hashish in Lucas Gary’s van; although he stood with the phone to his ear, others could hear Colonel Moyer’s loud voice, but not what he said. The short call ended.

Robinson spoke quietly to the female MP. She took the cuffs off Lucas, then reached in her jacket.

Without further conversation, the MP handed Lucas his saffron container with the hashish still inside it.

Robinson said, "Colonel Moyers told me to give this back to you and tell you he will come to the officers' club. He wants to see you about doing his birthday party in April. You got off this time, Gary. But you better be careful. You've been walking a thin line, ever since you got here."

When Robinson and the 2 MPs left, the front desk clerk introduced himself as Joe. "Since it is midweek, and winter is our slow season. You can have rooms on the second floor, overlooking the lake. What happened with the MPs and CID?" he asked Lucas.

"Oh, the CID and I have a little war going on," said Lucas. "So far, it seems my side is winning."

After everyone cleaned up and changed clothes, they gathered in Lucas and Inga's room and passed around the hash pipe.

"I'm sure glad the guy didn't take the hashish," said Sabine.

"It would not have been so bad—I have some hidden away which they did not find," replied Lucas.

They all finished their Wieninger beers and Eric said, "Let's go to the bar and see what is happening."

As they walked downstairs, they talked about their impressions of this hotel. The rooms were what they would expect in a hotel which was left over from the Nazi era. Now, it's an American military hotel in a fairy-tale setting. Yet, the paintings which hung on walls throughout the hotel had apparently been left there by the Nazis. Along one wall in the hallway on the main floor, glass-front cabinets held assorted souvenir items which were engraved with swastikas, including silver champagne buckets, silver goblets, fine china and crystal glassware.

The bar was noisy and crowded with American ski patrol guys, dressed in casual clothes, and gals who may be their girlfriends. They all seemed to be in their early twenties. Around here, Lucas was the old man at 30 years old; Eric was 26, Inga 24 and Sabine 25.

They each got a half-liter draft of Wieninger beer. All the bar stools were occupied. So, they sat at a table and got comfortable.

A stout, black gentleman appeared, wearing a yellow sports-shirt with gray slacks. He introduced himself as Bob Clarkson, the Hotel Manager, and asked, "Which one of you is Lucas Gary?"

"That would be me," said Lucas, as he stood.

Clarkson smiled, then he shook Lucas' hand and said, "CID Officer Robinson asked me about our room reservation list and gave me the name of the person he was looking for. When I checked the list, I told him your name was on it. I hope I didn't get you in any trouble. By the way, please call me Bob."

"Thank you, Bob," said Lucas. "No problem. Officer Robinson is always trying to catch me at something. So far, I seem to be winning the battle, thanks to Colonel Moyers."

"You are friends with Colonel Moyers?" asked Bob. "He is the nicest commander we could ever have. How do you know him, Lucas?"

"I am the Chef of the NATO Officers Club at Hawkins Kaserne in Oberammergau," he replied. "The colonel is a regular customer of ours. These are my friends: This lovely lady, Inga, owns a woodcarving shop in Oberammergau. We met in Gomagoi, Italy, where we skied together. Next, is her friend, Sabine, a ski instructor in Seefeld, Austria. She was in Gomagoi with Inga. This gentleman is Eric, my good friend. Eric was a baseball pitcher for the national championship team at the University of Minnesota, and he became the arm-wrestling champion of St. Johann, Austria, three nights ago."

Bob chuckled and said, "Wow, what a talented group of people. If any of you ever need a job, please apply here first. We need energetic people like you on our staff."

"Lucas, do you want to meet our chef?" asked Bob.

"Yes, I do," he replied.

Looking at the others, Bob said, "My apologies, but it's not a good time to take all of you into the kitchen because they are preparing to serve dinner. If you like, I will take you all on a tour of the hotel tomorrow."

"I would love to hear about the history of this hotel. I have driven past here many times, but I never stopped until today," said Sabine.

Lucas and Bob Clarkson walked down the hall and through a swinging, windowed door, to enter another hallway. Between the kitchen and the dining room, this long, wide hallway was well-trafficked by employees from all departments. Most of all, Lucas noticed the pretty, young ladies who wore green maid's uniforms.

Bob turned and went through double swinging doors into the kitchen. Lucas followed and stopped for a few seconds, as he surveyed the room to see the layout. It was a large kitchen, sectioned by work tables, with a big flat-top stove in the center of the space.

Pointing at what appeared to be the fronts of 2 radio speakers, side by side and built into the wall on their right, Bob told Lucas these were the intercoms to Hitler's private rooms.

"See here?" said Bob, as he pointed to engraved writing at the bottom of each speaker: *Fuehrerzimmer Eins* and *Fuehrerzimmer Zwei*.

Next, Bob introduced Lucas to a handsome man who had dark brown hair, piercing blue eyes and a nice smile. He wore a white chef's coat, monogrammed with the name Chef Bucherl.

"Please, call me Herbert," said the chef, as he shook Lucas' hand.

They chatted about the kitchen and Lucas looked at the menu. Then, he met the head sous chef who was a rugged-looking, 5'9" Bavarian native, named Fritz. He did not speak English too well, but he seemed to be a happy guy. Lucas noticed a few Wieninger beer bottles around the kitchen. An old, skinny man with white hair poured his beer into a coffee cup and put it under the counter where he was cutting vegetables. Chef Bucherl introduced the old man as Herr Schmechtig and said he had been there since the hotel first opened.

When Lucas told Chef Bucherl where he was working, Herbert said, "If you ever think of coming to work here, we sure could use you. It gets very busy in the summer."

Lucas thanked him and said, "I will certainly consider the offer."

Extra-wide, wood shutters in the wall were latched open to expose window openings with no glass between the hallway and the kitchen. Employees who trafficked the hallway were now visible to kitchen staff; and some young maids walked by in the hallway.

Suddenly, Lucas heard Herr Schmechtig yell out, "Hallo baby, ein bisschen lieben maybe—neunundsechzig?" (Translation: Hello baby, a little loving maybe—sixty-nine?)

Then, Herr Schmechtig laughed out loud which made everyone else laugh, around the kitchen.

"He hollers the same line to all young ladies who walk by the kitchen, and the ladies call him a dirty old man," said Bob. "He does it all day long, and he doesn't get much work done; but he is considered part of this place." Bob shook his head and added, "Herr Schmechtig lives in the Park Hotel, across the autobahn, where some other employees are housed. Besides teasing the ladies, he plays pranks with our fabulous pastry chef, Heinz Ostler. When Heinz goes to the bathroom, Schmechtig will go into the bakery and hide the spatula or something else from Heinz. When Schmechtig goes to the bathroom, Heinz will come in the kitchen, grab the old man's coffee cup and pour his beer down the drain."

After chuckling about Schmechtig and Heinz' antics, Lucas and Chef Bucherl exchanged a few pleasantries. Then, Lucas and Bob Clarkson walked back out into the hallway. As Bob turned right toward his office, he said, "I'll see you later or tomorrow. I've got paperwork to do before I close my office tonight."

"Thank you for the tour, Bob," said Lucas.

When Lucas got back to the bar, the crowd had thinned out. "Where did everybody go?" he asked.

Inga, Sabine and Eric were all sitting at the bar and chatting with the bartender. His name was Gunther, according to his nametag.

"Those ski patrol guys always have a few beers here after work. Then, they sometimes buy a case of beer and go down to the hotel game room," replied Gunther.

Hearing about a game room got Lucas' attention. He said to Gunther, "Hi. I'm Lucas Gary, the chef at NATO Officers Club in Oberammergau. My boss and good friend, Helmut, asked me to say hello to you."

Gunther smiled. "Danke schoen," he said. "Helmut and I had many beers together in this bar when Hitler stayed at this hotel."

"You worked here when Hitler was here?" asked Eric.

"Yah. Hitler told me I was his favorite bartender. However, he rarely drank any alcohol," Gunther replied.

"Gunther, what sort of games do they have downstairs in the game room?" asked Lucas.

"They play table tennis, darts and foosball," he replied. "They also have a pool table."

"Sounds like my kind of place. Could we go down there and look at the room?" asked Lucas.

"I think it's okay. If not, they will let you know," Gunther replied. "You should tell them who you are and where you work."

Their group walked down the stairs and into a basement room which was well-organized. All the games could be played at the same time. There were 8 people in the room: 6 guys and 2 young ladies. A lively game of mixed-doubles foosball was going on with 4 people. There were 2 guys playing darts. The other 2 guys were playing pool.

A half-empty case of Wieninger beer sat on a wooden bench next to 1 wall. Pool cues hung on another wall near the pool table. Foosball and table tennis were on the opposite side of room. In the back of the room, the dartboard was mounted next to a wooden case which held different types and weights of darts. The scoreboard hung on the wall which was closest to the thrower.

Catching one of the dart throwers' attention, Lucas said, "Gunther told us we could come and look at the game room."

The guy had a natural grin. He put out his hand and said, "All guests and employees are welcome. My name is Chip. I run the tennis courts here in the summer, and I am on ski patrol in the winter. This gentleman is John, and he takes care of the sailboats."

Lucas introduced Chip and John to Inga, Eric and Sabine. "Eric and I are AFRC employees. Eric is a bartender at the Von Steuben Hotel in Garmisch. I am the chef at the NATO Officers Club in Oberammergau. Inga has a woodcarving shop in Oberammergau; and Sabine is a ski instructor in Seefeld, Austria."

"I love Seefeld and the nice long runs," said Chip.

"I was fortunate to grow up in these mountains, and I can't imagine a more beautiful place on earth," replied Sabine.

"You are all welcome to play any game," said John. "If you want to, you can also challenge any table or game."

"Thank you, John," said Inga. "But we should eat dinner while the restaurant is still open. How is the food here?"

"The food is excellent," replied Chip. "Herr Bucherl is an award-winning chef. He competed at the Food Olympics in Frankfurt."

"It sounds good," said Lucas. "I guess we should get to the dining room. We'll see you around. It was nice to meet you."

He wanted to stay and play games; however, it had been a long day, everyone was hungry, and Inga was looking sexier by the minute.

After they were seated in the huge dining room, a young hostess with a British accent came to the table and asked Lucas if he was Mr. Gary. When Lucas acknowledged who he was, she led them to a different table. It was by a window and away from the stage where a Bavarian trio was playing lively and loud polka music.

From his seat at this table, Lucas surveyed his surroundings: *Most of the large paintings on the walls depict people in colorful Bavarian clothes, all engaged in local activities of fishing, farming, playing music and dancing in the street.*

This main dining room is a long rectangular area which is divided in the center by marble pillars. Chandelier lights hang from large, wooden beams which run the length of the room. I estimate about fifty smaller cross-beams which create a lattice effect on the ceiling. The dining room is only half-full. I can hear an American military family who sound excited as they share their skiing experiences of the day. This is one of the things I love about skiing—it puts everyone in a happy and friendly mood. On a nice day, I love to sit and drink a beer while I scan the crowds. It is wonderful to feel the energy and happiness radiate throughout the surroundings of a ski lodge.

I see at least forty tables set for dinner with white linen tablecloths and napkins. The lighting seems surreal in this room. Five-foot paintings hang on sections of the wall, between the windows. The top of each painting is the same height as the top of the wall, and each painting has a spotlight shining on it. Since the lighting is only from chandeliers and spotlights, it creates shadowed areas in sections of the room.

After they all studied the menu, it was time to order. Inga got Cordon Bleu (veal steak with ham and Swiss cheese, hand-breaded and served in burgundy sauce). Lucas had Zigeuner Schnitzel (succulent, hand-breaded pork, served over zesty mushroom, onion, pepper, tomato and bacon sauce). Sabine chose Karlsbadener Sahnegoulasch (a tender veal stew with mushrooms, onions, tomatoes and fresh cream). Eric, the big eater, had New York Steak au Poivre Verte (filet steak, flamed in green peppercorn, cognac and cream sauce).

Everyone agreed, the food was excellent. The group was excited about touring this hotel the next day. They wanted to learn the history of this place created by Hitler. For now, it had been an eventful day, and they were worn out. So, they skipped the usual shots of Jägermeister. Lucas paid the check, and they adjourned to their respective rooms.

As soon as the door closed, Lucas and Inga were in each other's arms, slowly undressing and caressing. In the shower, they washed, fondled and kissed each other. In bed, their lovemaking progressed from slow exploration to intense, mind-blowing ecstasy.

They each took pleasure from the other's body, and both gave back every ounce of love which they felt for their partner. Wrapped in each other arms, they drifted off and slept like babies.

The next day, Bob Clarkson joined them in the hotel dining room for a late breakfast. A young lady came with Bob. She wore a white uniform and carried a clipboard.

For a few moments, Lucas was stunned by her beautiful face which was framed by glossy, shoulder-length, black hair. He tried not to stare at her, but her appearance was striking. She looked strong, maybe large boned, definitely large breasted, and she had muscular legs which were shapely. Bob introduced her as Shelley, the Head Housekeeper.

"Gruss Gott," she said, as she greeted everyone. "No, I am not German. I am from Santa Monica, California, and I am having the time of my life. When I worked as a maid, the last head housekeeper quit, and Bob was kind enough to give me the job."

"It was the best hire I ever made," said Bob. "Is anyone, besides me, ready for a beer?"

When they all had a glass of Wieninger beer in their hand, Bob made a toast to Hitler, "Thank you, Hitler. You built one hell of a hotel!"

After breakfast, Bob excused himself to go do his work, and he turned the tour over to Shelley. Lucas thought she was eyeing him. Then, she goosed him when they rose from their chairs. Or, perhaps it was just a hard pat on his butt.

When no one was looking, Lucas said to Shelley, out of the side of his mouth, "I hope you didn't hurt your hand."

She laughed, and then spoke to the group, "After such a big breakfast and a few beers, we should walk outside. Does everyone have a coat?"

"Maybe we should all put on more clothes and smoke some hashish. Is it okay with you, Shelley?" asked Inga.

"Sure," she replied. "If you want to, we can grab more beers from the employees' beer machine."

In his and Inga's room, Lucas tried to not stare at Shelley again. They exchanged stories about California beaches where they both had lived before coming to Germany. Everyone had Wieninger beers and a shot of Jägermeister while they shared 2 bowls of hashish.

Lucas could see Inga was uneasy about the attention he was giving to Shelley. So, he suggested they begin the hotel tour. They were all bundled up as they went through the main lobby, got outside and started walking. Shelley led them past a miniature golf course, covered in snow, and then past a house which she called the Farm House. She said most of the ski patrol guys lived there, and she likened it to a fraternity house.

Further on, set back from the path and near the autobahn, they saw The Ranch House, a 2-story building, nestled in a group of trees. Shelley said it housed key employees: The hotel accountant lived in 1 of 2 upstairs bedrooms. Zeyla, an American hippie from San Francisco, also lived upstairs, and she was a kitchen employee. Mike, a desk clerk, lived downstairs with his wife. The Ranch House was close to the lake.

Across the way, there was a small marina and a boat dock with a boathouse attached. Shelley told them it was a private boat dock which American military personnel and their families use when they sail to the island for a tour of Schloss Herrenchiemsee (the palace).

Looking out toward the water, she said, "You can see the island today, and I'm sure you have heard of King Ludwig's castles."

Still trying to avoid staring at Shelley, Lucas said, "Eric and I took a tour of Neuschwanstein Castle where we learned a little about King Ludwig. Inga and Sabine were raised in Bavaria, so they have learned about the King since they were children."

"I have seen all the castles, except Chiemsee," said Inga.

"I haven't seen Chiemsee either, but I want to come back and take a tour in the summer," said Sabine.

"The design of Herrenchiemsee Palace symbolizes the affection and respect which Ludwig felt for Louis the Fourteenth of France. He was known as The Sun King," said Shelley. "The look of the palace and views of the parkland and fountains resemble the Palace of Versailles. Herrenchiemsee is a must see for those interested in King Ludwig. If you come in the spring or summer, we can take a sailboat out to the island. I heard Hitler only visited the castle once, but I've seen photographs of him on a boat which took people to and from the island. In fact, Gunther, our favorite bartender, has a photograph of himself with Hitler, standing next to each other on our lakeside boardwalk.

"It would have been a great day to ski, but I have to work— if you can call it work. Let's use the underpass and walk to the other side of the autobahn. You will see the Park Hotel and a movie theater. Also, my office and apartment are there, so we'll have another beer."

Compared to the other employee's rooms which they saw in this building, Shelley's space was an executive suite. Since her apartment was on the end of the building, she had a view of the mountains and access to the hotel balcony. In nice weather, many of the employees would barbecue on the balcony.

Pointing to the rafters above the balcony, a small bird stuck its head out of a nest to look at them. "Longtime German employees told me the birds have been nesting there for many years," said Shelley. "The young birds learn to fly from the balcony banister."

"Does anyone want a beer?" she asked.

Everyone said, "Yes."

Lucas pulled out his hash pipe, and he asked if it was okay to light it. Shelley said, "Are you kidding? You do not want to know what goes on behind some of these doors. All the maids have horror stories about things they find when they enter guest rooms in this hotel."

Shelley's living room was comfortable, although it had standard, military-issue furniture. Lucas felt very relaxed. He thought about his future in Bavaria. Unless Robinson intervenes and ruins everything, Lucas had exciting opportunities to choose from.

Back outside, they walked over to the movie theater, and Shelley said, "Use of this theater is like a family gathering for the employees. They all share popcorn and drink beer. During the movie, people shout out jokes until someone tells them to shut up."

Before crossing under the autobahn and returning to the lakeside hotel, she pointed out a gas station, some shops and a garage.

Approaching the hotel, Lucas looked at the hotel's facade which faced the street. Under the peak of the roof, a huge clock hung above 3 stories of large windows. Sculpted mermaids flanked the clock, each with an arm extended to it, as they appeared to hold the clock in place.

"When did this hotel open?" asked Lucas.

"The rasthaus opened in nineteen thirty-eight," replied Shelley. "During the war, this complex served as a hospital. After the war, the U.S. Army took it over, and they called it the Lake Hotel. Between the Lake Hotel and the Park Hotel, there are one hundred and seventy-nine rooms." Passing a loading dock, she said, "This dock is for kitchen deliveries, and the chefs do their ice carving out here. The bin holds leftover scraps of food which the dishwashers separate from paper and other inedible garbage. A local farmer comes by in a horse-drawn cart, and he takes the food to feed his animals. At Christmas time, the farmer is always generous with gifts for the kitchen staff. Let's continue out to the lake. Be careful, the path may be icy and slippery."

Arriving at the other end of the hotel which faces the water, she said, "The small round room on the corner is the *Führerzimmer*, Hitler's special dining area with a view of the lake."

Shelley pointed to a bronze statue of a woman's body, sitting on a rock wall at the terrace near the water, "A famous Berlin artist, Fritz Klimsch, created the statue and named it *Die Schauende* (The Looker). However, since it has bare breasts, Americans gave it a nickname, and we call it the Chiemsee Mermaid."

Back at the hotel, they saw Hitler's original dedication plaque on a wall: A large slab of marble, cut in a decorative shape with a beveled edge, engraved with a twin-tailed mermaid (the R•A•B Chiemsee Logo) above old-style German lettering. Near it, a 2nd plaque was installed by the American military to translate the original. It was a small, plain stone with square corners, engraved in old-style English lettering:

> ***Translation.***
> *The Resthouse on Lake Chiemsee was designed by order of Adolph Hitler under supervision of the General Inspector for German Roads, Dr. Todt. Interior and exterior by Prof. Norhauer. Construction was in the hands of the Supreme Construction Office of the Reichsautobahnen in Munich. Construction was commenced on 3 July 1937 and the Resthouse was opened 1 September 1938.*

They walked through the lobby and entered a long, rectangular room with a bank of windows which offered a wonderful view of the lake and Herrenchiemsee Island. A purple-colored carpet created a center isle which ran the length of the room. Comfortable lounge chairs were placed in groups on top of throw rugs, over hardwood flooring. Tables and cushioned armchairs were placed along the windows. Outside, below the windows, a wooden walkway separated the hotel from the water, and it extended beyond the hotel to the boat docks.

There was a brick fireplace at the far end of the room. On a wooden mantle above the fireplace, there were 5 large silver plates. As Lucas got close to inspect the silver plates, he noticed an engraved design and a small swastika on each plate.

"This is the *Aufenthaltsraum* (lounge room)," said Shelley. "It's a nice place to read a book, visit with others or play a game of chess. We have several functions in this room. Hitler's round dining room is on the other side of those doorways." She was pointing to the doors, one on each side of the fireplace.

The lounge walls were bare, except for 2 large landscape paintings and lantern-style lamps, mounted on the longest, windowless wall. Wooden benches and tables offered additional seating along the same wall. The room's main lighting was 4 sets of chandelier lamps.

"Lucas, I guess you've already seen the kitchen and met our great chef," said Shelley.

"Let's see if the chef is around, so my friends can meet him," Lucas suggested. "He seems to be a very nice fellow."

All the wood shutters were open, between the kitchen and the hallway which leads to the dining room and the manager's office. Looking into the kitchen from the hallway, they saw the chef. He was standing by the stove and talking to Fritz, the head sous chef.

When Chef Bucherl first saw the ladies, he did a double take. Then, he saw Lucas and motioned for them all to come into the kitchen.

Lucas introduced Inga, Sabine and Eric to Chef Bucherl and Fritz. The chef was eyeing the ladies and directing his voice toward them.

I bet this guy is a ladies' man, thought Lucas. *He wears a wedding ring; but I imagine he has a few girlfriends stashed around Bavaria.*

Bucherl took them into the bakery and introduced them to the pastry chef, Heinz Ostler. He is a chubby guy about 5'9" and maybe 60 years old. He also checked out the ladies, as he handed everyone an impressive slice of a Schwartzwalder Kirschtorte (Black Forest Cake). While eating cake, Shelley told the group about many things to see in the Chiemsee area. Ready to move on, they all thanked Chef Bucherl for the kitchen tour, and they thanked Herr Ostler for the delicious cake.

"Let's head to the bar, and I'll show you the game room downstairs," said Shelley.

"Oh, we saw the game room yesterday. We met two nice guys, named Chip and John," replied Lucas.

As they all walked toward the bar, Shelley said, "Chip and John are both on the ski patrol. Chip is also the hotel's tennis pro. John oversees all the sailboats and the dock areas which you saw when we were touring the Ranch House."

The bar was as crowded as it was the night before. Ski patrol guys and everyone else seemed excited, and they all were talking at once.

Shelley asked the bartender, Gunther, what happened.

He replied, "The Casa Carioca burned down last night in Garmisch, and officials think it was arson. They don't know who did it and have no suspects yet. At least, none of the terrorist groups have come forward to claim responsibility."

Hearing the news, Lucas felt concerned: *I wonder if Andreas Baader is back in Garmisch with his Celebrity Terrorist friends.*

Lucas turned to Inga and said, "I'm going to the front desk. I want to call Helmut and find out if he knows anything. Do you want to wait here or come with me?"

"You go ahead. I will stay and talk to Shelley while you make your call," replied Inga.

Lucas looked over at Shelley who was standing behind Inga, and she blew him a kiss.

"I'll be back soon," he said to Inga.

Talking to Helmut at the officers' club in Oberammergau, Lucas knew, by the sound of his voice, Helmut was alarmed.

"A lot of things are happening around Garmisch right now. I think you should come back as soon as you can," Helmut told Lucas.

Lucas didn't hesitate to say, "Helmut, we'll be there in 3 hours."

"Danke schoen, Lucas," he replied. "The Casa Carioca was reduced to embers. There was a problem with Bruno, and he is being transferred back to Garmisch. I want to ask Eric if he will come here and work. In fact, would you ask him? You can tell me when you get here. Or, if you can bring Eric with you, it would be even better."

Back in the bar, Lucas told the others about his conversation with Helmut and his promise to be at the officers' club in 3 hours.

"We can make it in less time," Sabine suggested.

"I'm sure we would if you or Inga drove," replied Lucas. "But Eric and I will drive. We have an hour to say goodbye, get our stuff together and check out of the hotel."

Everyone promised to return as they said goodbye to Bob Clarkson, Gunther, Shelley and the desk clerk, Joe.

After piling their bags and themselves into the VW van. Sabine passed the hash pipe, and Eric opened Wieninger beers for all.

Lucas pulled onto the autobahn, heading toward Oberammergau.

CHAPTER 22

The Hub: Around Garmisch

About halfway to Oberammergau, Lucas stopped to fill the tank with gas. Inga went next door to purchase a German newspaper, *Die Welt* (*The World*). Before they left the hotel lobby, Lucas had picked up the latest *Stars and Stripes* and the *International Herald Tribune.*

Now, they had sources of information about what is going on in the world, outside the fairy-tale land they lived in. Eric offered to drive the rest of the way, so Lucas took a break.

Lucas read to the others, *"The International Herald Tribune was founded in France in eighteen eighty-seven, and it's the newspaper of choice for the international community and for American expatriates."*

A moment later, he asked, "Do we classify as expatriates?"

"Maybe, since we now live outside the U.S. I still love the United States, but not always the people who govern it," replied Eric.

Lucas read aloud again, *"Munich is busy with preparations for the Olympic Games which take place in the fall, and construction is now in full swing."*

"I think I will stay away from Munich, as much as I can, until after the Olympics and the Oktoberfest have finished," said Inga. "Munich will be crazy busy with those two events about a month apart. I would rather watch the Olympics on TV, anyway."

Commenting on what he read, Lucas said, "Big news from New York is the construction on the World Trade Center is coming along."

He read to the others, *"The twin towers will be the tallest buildings in the world. The height of the north tower will be four hundred seventeen meters (1,368 feet), six feet taller than the second tower."*

Scanning the paper, Lucas said, "I guess you all heard the Beatles broke up. The last album they released was *Let It Be* which came out one month after they broke up. Here is an article about proposed changes for the Isle of Wight Festival which takes place in August, off the south coast of England. It's no wonder, listen to their list."

He read from the article, *"Some members of Parliament want to limit the number of people who can attend events on the island because they had such large crowds at the last Isle of Wight Festival. Performers included Jimi Hendrix, The Who, The Doors, Chicago, Richie Havens, John Sebastian, Joan Baez, Ten Years After, Emerson, Lake & Palmer, The Moody Blues and Jethro Tull."*

Lucas added, "Wow! This is only some of the artists who performed."

"It was a short while after the festival, when Jimi Hendrix died of a drug overdose in London," said Sabine.

"I think he could do more things with an electric guitar, than anyone else ever did," replied Lucas.

"Yeah, I agree. Hendrix seemed to combine blues with the hard metal sound," said Eric.

Reading to the others, the next article made Lucas almost choke on the words, *"In Berlin, the Baader-Meinhof Gang robbed three banks. Their loot totaled over two hundred thousand marks."*

Lucas turned to the back page of the newspaper and saw a timeline of the latest Baader-Meinhof acts of terror. He read the section aloud, *"In Kaiserslautern, three members of the RAF raided a branch of the Bavarian Mortgage and Exchange Bank. A police officer walked in on the raid, and they shot him. The officer died at the scene. In Kassel, the RAF raided two banks, netting one hundred fifteen thousand Deutschmarks. In keeping with their routine of driving a fast car which is easy to break into and hot wire, they drove away in a BMW Two Thousand which they had stolen in Frankfurt."*

"People link their group with BMW automobiles, and some joke about BMW standing for Baader-Meinhof Wagen," said Eric.

"The Palestine Liberation Organization hijacked four jets, flying to New York from Brussels, Frankfurt and Zurich," said Sabine.

"Where are these people coming from?" asked Inga. "Terrorism seems to be spreading everywhere."

"There was also an incident in Quebec, Canada, where they had to impose martial law," said Eric. "During a shoot-out, officials killed the leader of a group called Front de liberation du Quebec. Heaven help us if these terrorist groups ever unite; they would become organized and armed on a massive scale."

"Yeah, and don't forget some of the RAF leaders trained with the PLO in Jordan," said Lucas.

Lucas considered telling Eric and Sabine about his relationship with the Baader/Meinhof/Ensslin group. For now, he realized it was not a good idea. *Perhaps another time,* he thought. *I hope I don't see Andreas Baader again. It would only add more to my story.*

Inga pointed to a story in *Die Welt,* the German newspaper, and said, "There's an article here about the upcoming, early season BARC 200 Formula Two Race. It will take place in Thruxton, England."

She read to the others, *"Renamed, the race is now called 'The Jochen Rindt Memorial Trophy' in honor of the Formula One driver. In nineteen seventy, Jochen Rindt crashed and died in a Lotus race car while qualifying for the Italian Grand Prix. He became a World Driving Champion, the first to earn the honor posthumously. After Rindt's tragic death, Lotus made many changes to their designs. This year, they put a sports car on the market, the Lotus Elan Sprint."*

"It's cute in the photo, but it looks very small," added Inga.

"Do any of you enjoy formula one racing?" asked Lucas.

"I always go to the Austrian Grand Prix," said Sabine. "You should go in August. It's a lot of fun. Everyone camps out and parties late."

"Okay, count me in," replied Eric.

They were all laughing as the van pulled into Inga's icy driveway. "I'm sorry, but Eric and I have to drop you ladies off now. Helmut said he needs us there tonight," said Lucas. "Why don't you two come to the club for dinner? Or, if you prefer, we can go out and eat somewhere else."

"Dinner at the club sounds great," said Inga.

After Lucas and Eric kissed the ladies goodbye, Lucas climbed in the passenger seat, and Eric drove them to the officers' club. They pulled in front and knew it would be a busy night, based on all the cars in the parking lot. The bar was packed full. Briefly, they conferred with Helmut who was trying to keep up with the crowd. Lucas headed to the kitchen, and Eric stayed in the bar. Lucas put on his chef's coat, black pants, a white apron and chef's hat, then went to work.

About 9:30 p.m., the bar was clearing out, and most everyone had finished their dinner. Lucas cleaned his work station and took off his apron and chef's hat before he walked into the bar.

To his pleasant surprise, Colonel Moyers was standing at the bar and talking to Helmut and Eric. Margo was tending bar with Eric. There were several officers and a few civilian employees playing pool and foosball. Eric handed Lucas a draft Augustiner beer, and Lucas shook hands with Colonel Moyers.

"So, Lucas, I assume Robinson will stop harassing you and your lady," said Colonel Myers.

"Thank you for your help with that, Colonel," he replied. "It was a very embarrassing situation."

"Lucas, if we arrested everyone who possessed a small amount of hashish, we wouldn't have many employees left," said the colonel.

“Well, I am grateful to be free and back at work,” said Lucas. “I heard your birthday party will be at Keane Lodge.”

Colonel Moyers said, “I would appreciate it very much if you would cook the food for a small group of people, maybe forty or so. Talk to Craig Miller at Keane Lodge and let him know what you need in the way of supplies. The two of you can decide on the menu.”

“When is your birthday, Colonel?” asked Lucas.

“April third. Don’t ask what year it was!” he replied.

Helmut heard the conversation, and they all agreed: Lucas would do the dinner, and he could take time off from the club for the event. Then, something caught Colonel Moyers’ eye. Wondering what distracted the colonel, Lucas turned around.

The Bavarian beauties looked like they stepped right off the cover of a ski magazine, wearing their parkas and form-fitting pants. Lucas gave Inga a kiss; and Eric did likewise to Sabine when she walked over and greeted him at the sidebar.

Lucas introduced the ladies to Colonel Moyers. Inga knew everyone else, and she introduced them all to her good friend, Sabine.

Eric said to the ladies, “I know this is a dumb question, but what do you want to drink?”

“I think I’ll have a glass of Augustiner beer, please,” replied Inga.

“The same for me, Eric,” said Sabine.

“I have dinner prepared and ready to serve,” said Lucas.

Turning toward Colonel Moyers and Helmut, Lucas asked, “Will you gentlemen join us for dinner? I prepared plenty of food.”

“You know, I have had nothing to eat since lunch, and I would love to join you,” said the colonel.

Helmut also wanted to join them, so he set a table for 6. Lucas and Inga went into the kitchen to plate up the food.

Lucas had prepared one of his signature dishes. For dinner, he served Pork Sirloin Medallions with a balsamic glaze, potato croquettes, fresh asparagus and julienne carrots. For dessert, they had fresh turnovers, made with *pate sucree,* filled with mixed berries and apples, topped with vanilla ice cream. Everyone had a shot of Jägermeister after dessert.

During dinner, Colonel Moyers talked about the destruction of Casa Carioca which occurred last night. He said the arson is considered an act of terror, and officials suspect the Baader-Meinhof Gang.

This made Lucas cringe, and he asked the colonel, “Have you had any indication of RAF activity in Bavaria?”

“Since the defused-car-bomb incident here, in the Hawkins Kaserne parking lot, there’s been no other activity in Bavaria,” said the colonel.

"However, their group has been very active elsewhere in Germany and other areas of Europe.

"We will increase our security this week while Secretary of Defense Laird is visiting and staying in Garmisch. Casa Carioca was the most famous nightclub of the USAREUR (U.S. Army Europe), and it's a real shame we lost it. General George Patton's Third Army Engineers built Casa Carioca next to the Olympic Ice Stadium in August of nineteen forty-six. It was used by troops who visited the base which was known as the Third Army Rest Center."

"I heard about a nightclub near the Olympic Ice Stadium, but I missed seeing it. What was it about?" asked Lucas.

Colonel Moyers replied, "The performers were all German until nineteen fifty when they hired Terry Rudolph, a Hungarian who was raised in America. She produced the ice shows for eight years before returning to the U.S. She taught the basic techniques of ballet to develop thirty-five skaters who performed on a thirty-by-forty-foot sheet of ice. A two-level, curtained staging area stood at one end. On the upper level, a seventeen-piece orchestra played music during the ice show. They also played for dancing when the ice was covered by a dance floor. The roof was retractable. When it opened on warm nights and the stars were shining, the atmosphere was spectacular. Some of the world's best ice skaters performed at Casa Carioca."

After eating, Lucas excused himself and went into the kitchen to clean up. When he returned, only Eric, Inga and Sabine were still at the table. Margo was finishing her work behind the bar.

Eric and Sabine took Lucas' van to Garmisch for the night. They would return in the morning.

Inga drove Lucas to her house, using her car. They brushed their teeth and fell into each other's arms as they collapsed on the bed. With the thick comforter over them, both drifted off to sleep. Inga's phone rang about 45 minutes later. She answered the call and listened to Eric who told her he needed to talk to Lucas.

When Inga handed the phone to Lucas, Eric said, "Lucas, we are at The Grill. A young German lady asked Gino if he could get a hold of you, and he directed her to me. Her name is Gabrielle. She wants to see you, and her friends want to meet you. Olivia and Ashleigh are also here, and they are with a guy named Topo who says he is a friend of yours."

Lucas thought: *I cannot believe this. If I go to The Grill, I will run into three women who I have slept with, maybe four women if Sonya is there. And, Germany's most-wanted criminals might be in town to see me. Holy Shit! Now, I have to tell Eric and Sabine the whole story about me knowing the RAF people.*

He came back to bed and told Inga the RAF members were in town and someone asked Eric to contact him. Lucas left out his relationship with Gabrielle. He also did not mention Olivia, Ashleigh and Topo because he figured she would get to know them soon enough.

"I have to go talk to the RAF group. Perhaps, I can save lives if they will listen to what I say again," Lucas told Inga.

"Why is Eric working at the officers' club here, and not at his job in Garmisch?" she asked him.

"Because Bruno was dating Margo, and he roughed her up which is typical," replied Lucas. "It's the way he operates. She came to work with her face all bruised, and she said he had beaten her. So, Helmut asked headquarters to make the switch. Helmut appreciates Eric and his friendly manner of serving customers. I am the most pleased of all. It was hard for me, being nice to a jerk who beats and murders women. And, he got away with it far too long. I've been waiting for the right situation to deal with Bruno. Now, however, I may have to think of something creative, a plan of my own."

Inga drove Lucas in her car. She made the 25-minute drive in 22 minutes and parked at The Grill. They greeted the bouncer, Jordan Lewis, and walked through the doorway. As they entered the bar, they heard Rod Stewart singing "Maggie May." The band was on a break, and a DJ was playing the music.

Looking around the crowded bar and dance floor, Lucas spotted Eric and Sabine at a table, sitting with Topo, Olivia, Ashleigh and Regan Stone. He knew Ashleigh was dating Regan. Lucas gave Topo a big, warm hug, but he felt awkward when he hugged Olivia and Ashleigh. Lucas was keenly aware of all the great times he had with these ladies, along with his best friend George, when they traveled from Tarifa, Spain, to Cervenia, then on to Munich. Except for George, they are all here now, finding their own way in this mountain paradise.

Lucas introduced everyone to Inga. After looking out the corner of his eye at Sabine, he asked Regan, "How's your skiing going?"

"I am getting better every day," he answered. "It's really great to see Sabine here. She gave me my first ski lesson when I was in Seefeld."

Lucas had to restrain himself—he wanted to laugh out loud, as he visualized Regan, on his butt in the wet snow with a blue streak trailing behind him, color left by his brand-new blue jeans.

Lucas and Inga went to get beers at the bar. They were interrupted, by CID Officer Robinson who stepped in front of Lucas.

"Hey, Gary!" said Robinson. "You sure get around. Watch yourself, because if you screw up again, I'll be waiting; and you won't be able to run to Colonel Moyers, next time."

Without saying a word, Lucas stepped around Robinson. He and Inga went to the bar, ordered 2 Augustiner beers and said hello to Gino. Beers in hand, they ignored Robinson and went back to their table.

When Lucas got seated, Eric said "Look over at the table by the pillar on the far side of the dance floor."

Lucas looked at the table, and he let out a groan when he saw Bruno with his arm around Sonya.

He thought: *Will she ever learn? Will she get beaten to death or become missing, like two other ladies who dated Bruno?*

Lucas excused himself from the table and motioned for Eric to join him. Walking into the hallway, Lucas poked his head in an open door near the dishwashing station, and he saw Bob Ostergaard washing glasses.

Bob looked drunk, and he was washing one glass at a time. When he washed one, he put it in the glass rack and said, "One for the company." When he grabbed the next one, he threw it on the cement floor where glass shattered and pieces flew all over, saying, "And, one for me!" Then, he laughed out loud, all by himself.

A waitress brought in a pitcher of beer, still half-full. She stepped over the broken glass and placed the pitcher with the dirty dishes.

Bob picked it up, put it in the refrigerator, looked over at Lucas and said, slurring his words, "I like my shlag beer cold!"

Lucas laughed, as he stepped back and guided Eric away from the open door, but they stayed in the hallway.

After watching the whole thing from the doorway, Eric said, "This is interesting; Bob has a degree in Marine Biology from the University of Maryland, but here he is washing glasses at The Grill, and he seems to enjoy it."

"Around here, I have met many people who are well-educated and talented; but they all want to screw around for a while before their life gets too serious," replied Lucas.

"Bob is different," said Eric. "He and his GI partner, Steve, have the rebuilt VW van business. All Bob talks about is making money."

"They had better watch themselves," said Lucas. "CID Robinson, who has fallen in love with me, said he was out to get Ostergaard and Dobson. Robinson seems sure they are breaking the law, registering those vehicles with the military and receiving green plates; and he wants to find out how they are getting away with it.

"Robinson also said he suspects Bob of selling liquor and cigarettes to local Germans. I told him I knew of no one who did so, and he said I was stupid—precisely what I wanted him to think."

"Eric, do you remember your exact conversation with Gabrielle?" asked Lucas.

"First, she asked how you were," he replied. "Then, she told me how she met you in Formentera where you had a great time together, and you both went to Ibiza. She said a few of her friends are with her. They are all staying at the same place, and she wants to see you."

"It's true. We had a great time together," said Lucas. "Gabrielle's friend was the lady who disappeared while Bruno was dating her in Formentera. Later, we saw Bruno get on the boat in Formentera, going to Ibiza, and next on the boat from Ibiza to Valencia. There was never any sign of Gabrielle's friend, Kirstin. I think he beat her to death which is what he did to my fiancée Jodie, back in Long Beach."

"I need to talk to you about the RAF, Eric," Lucas added.

Eric looked surprised, but he listened patiently. Lucas told Eric about his relationship with members of the Baader-Meinhof Gang, how they first met and subsequent visits. Lucas also gave Eric permission to discuss this with Sabine as needed.

"I know Andreas Baader and Ulrike Meinhof are well-known as the leaders of the RAF," said Lucas. "However, I believe the real leader is Gudrun Ensslin. They all like to party and have fun, the same as we do, but their strong beliefs and willingness to act on them is very scary. I wonder if they were around when the Casa Carioca burned down. Since they are now in Garmisch, I need to go see them and find out what is happening with them."

Eric still looked a little bewildered when he mouthed the words, *"Baader-Meinhof Gang?"*

Heading toward the bar, Lucas peaked in at Bob Ostergaard again. He was still at it: While drinking from a glass of beer which he held in his left hand, he washed a dirty beer glass and placed it in the glass tray, or he added it to the growing pile of broken glass on the floor.

When they returned to their table, Inga and Sabine were sitting and watching the dancers. The others were dancing. The band was playing some great rock 'n' roll. The noise of the crowd around the dance floor, was almost as loud as the music.

Lucas spoke into Inga's ear, "I need to visit the RAF people and find out what is going on. I suspect they were involved in burning down the Casa Carioca. I have to find out what they want and whether I can discourage them from taking further actions in Bavaria."

Inga agreed: Lucas should go. Until he returned, she would hang out with Eric and Sabine in their room at the Green Arrow Hotel. Inga reached in her bag and handed him her car keys. Lucas gave her a kiss, and he waved goodbye to Eric and Sabine.

Lucas drove to the house on Griesener Straße and turned into the narrow driveway, going through a clump of trees. He parked beside a VW van which looked brand-new and was probably stolen.

Fear overcame Lucas as he approached the heavy, wooden door. He did not want to use the knocker without identifying himself; and he sure did not want to get shot. While banging the brass door knocker, he was yelling, quite loud, "Hello, it's Lucas Gary!"

After waiting 30 seconds, the door opened, and he saw Gabrielle. She looked out from behind the door and made sure there was nobody with him. Satisfied, she opened it wide enough for Lucas to squeeze through. Then, she grabbed him, hugged him and gave him a big kiss. He was not sure if she was glad to see him or frisking him, maybe both.

Andreas came around a corner on the left from the dining room into the entranceway, holding an automatic rifle at his side. Another guy who Lucas did not know came from the kitchen on the right, also with an automatic rifle at his side.

After he shook Lucas' hand and gave him a friendly hug, Andreas said, "Hello, my friend. I hope you can spend the night, and maybe tomorrow you will cook dinner for us again. Now, let's go sit by the fire, smoke hashish, drink beer and have some schnapps while we talk."

Andreas introduced Lucas to the other guy, named Manfred, who claimed he saw combat in Frankfurt. He and another member escaped from a shoot-out with one of the "pigs," and no one got shot.

They took seats around the fireplace, and Andreas said to Lucas, "I don't know if you have seen the news about Gabrielle's brother, Horst. He is locked up in Berlin, along with two other valuable members of our faction. We plan to kidnap your Secretary of Defense Laird and exchange him to get our three members out of Moabit Prison."

Andreas knew Lucas would object, but he kept on talking, "Lucas, I know I promised not to bomb anything around here; but no one will get hurt, and we will get back three members of our group."

Looking for Andreas' reaction, Lucas said, "Since the Casa Carioca burned down, military security has been increased in this area. Also, given the secret service who come with the Secretary of Defense, I think it would be suicidal to try and kidnap him."

"We are not afraid and will fight to the end," said Andreas. "I can give you examples, recent displays of courage by loyal members of our organization. Ulrike, please read to Lucas about our recent encounters with the 'pigs' which you have written in your journal."

"We feel encouraged by the support we get from ordinary citizens like you," said Ulrike, lifting a thick, leather-bound book off a side table.

This is scary, thought Lucas.

"The respected Allensbach Institute took a poll in Germany. They discovered one in five Germans, under the age of thirty, have some sympathy for members of our Red Army Faction," said Ulrike. "The poll asked this question: 'Assuming someone from the RAF asked you to shelter them for a night, would you take him or her in for one night?' Five percent of the polled Germans said, 'Yes, they would harbor an RAF member.' Nine percent said, 'They would consider it.' This means: eight-and-a-half-million Germans, out of sixty million, expressed willingness to house or consider housing a member of our group."

"Ulrike, please excuse me a minute," said Lucas. "I want to bring in the case of Wieninger beer which I brought for you."

As Lucas got up, he saw Andreas nod to Gabrielle, and she got up.

I guess they don't trust me too much, thought Lucas.

Gabrielle told Lucas she needed some fresh air, and she followed him outside. Without further conversation, Lucas grabbed the case of beer he had placed in the trunk of Inga's car.

Returning to the house, they handed Wieninger beers to everyone. Lucas took a hit on the hash pipe which Gabrielle passed to him, and he passed it on.

"Here is a perfect example of how stupid the 'pigs' are," said Ulrike. Then, she read aloud from the journal, *"Two Berlin radicals, Thomas Weissbecker and Georg von Rauch were in a Berlin courtroom, charged with beating a journalist from the Springer Press. The court convicted Von Rauch and acquitted Weissbecker. When the judge announced their sentences, spectators caused an upset and confusion in the court room. In appearance, the two men look similar. During the confusion, von Rauch and Weissbecker switched places, and von Rauch walked out of court a free man. When enough time had passed for von Rauch to escape, Weissbecker announced he was the person acquitted, and he demanded release. Shocked and embarrassed, the judge forced court personnel to release him."*

"This is only one example of 'pigs' being stupid," said Manfred.

"Ulrike is almost finished with the RAF manifesto, *The Concept of the Urban Guerrilla,* and it will be published soon," said Andreas. "The cover will have a big Kalashnikov Rifle (Russian AK-47) in the center. The letters *RAF* are printed in white over the top of the rifle. We all fell in love with it during training with the PLO when we were in Jordan."

Andreas raised his rifle. The rest of them cheered, raised their glasses and shouted, "Prost."

"We like the poll results," said Ulrike. "With proper motivation, we believe those sympathetic Germans will band together and revolt against the fascist state which they have now."

"I think the 'pigs' know if they approach us again, as they did to Astrid and me, we are willing and able to go against them and shoot it out, the same way we did in Frankfurt," said Manfred.

"We will look at options to kidnap Secretary Laird," said Andreas. "If we find the security too tough, as you say it is, we will find another way to free our people. The only reason we are telling you this, Lucas, is so you can keep yourself and those you love away from Secretary Laird while he is in Garmisch. If we do go ahead with our plan, there might be a shoot-out."

"I really hope you reconsider," replied Lucas. "Otherwise, I believe it could end for you here; and thinking this make me very sad."

Gudrun said, "Thank you, Lucas. We know the authorities outnumber us, so we must choose our actions with careful thought. We believe this is a great opportunity to gain support and more notoriety, but nothing is decided yet. Right now, the day is new, so let's party."

Lucas realized it was well into the morning. He knew Inga was waiting for him at the Green Arrow Hotel. By coincidence, it was the hotel where Secretary Laird would stay when he came here for 1 night. Laird would be in a private cabana, a small 2-bedroom house which is separate from the hotel and sheltered in a grove of trees.

Lucas said goodbye to Andreas, Ulrike, Gudrun and Manfred; he kissed and hugged a disappointed Gabrielle. Then, he took off.

He drove to the Green Arrow Hotel in Garmisch. Before parking, he drove around the hotel grounds to see the area around the VIP cabana where Secretary Laird would be staying. Then, he parked Inga's car next to his van.

When he knocked on the door at Eric and Sabine's hotel room, a groggy Eric opened the door and told him everyone was asleep.

"Sorry to be so late," said Lucas. "I'll crawl in the van and sleep for a couple hours. You still need the van to take Sabine home. Right?"

"Yes," replied Eric.

"Okay. Inga can take me to work," said Lucas.

Inga, Eric and Sabine were dressed and waiting for Lucas when he got to the room. They went to the hotel restaurant for breakfast and listened as Lucas shared the events of his RAF meeting.

"They greeted me at the door with Kalashnikov rifles, hugs and some of their political propaganda," said Lucas. "Ulrike Meinhof showed me a manifesto which she is writing for the RAF. It is called *The Concept of the Urban Guerrilla* and will be released soon.

"Ulrike told me about a poll which was conducted by some institute. The basic conclusion was eight-and-a-half-million young adult Germans support the RAF's cause, and all those people would help or consider helping RAF members to escape capture. In fact, one of the men at the house claimed a citizen helped two members escape from a shoot-out with police in Frankfurt, recently.

"Andreas told me they are here to kidnap Melvin Laird, the American Secretary of Defense, when he comes this week to visit. They plan to offer him in exchange for the release of three RAF members who are in prison. I told them it's a bad idea, given the tight security they would face; and I do not think they will go through with their plan."

"Where will Laird be staying? Do you know?" asked Eric.

"Yes. Secretary Laird will stay at the Green Arrow Hotel in their Luxury Cabana," replied Lucas. "It is often used for high-ranking military officers, government officials and traveling dignitaries."

Wanting to change the subject, Lucas said, "Speaking of the cabana, a few guys from The Grill went there last year. John, Bob and Gino told me they watched the heavyweight fight between Muhammad Ali and Joe Frazier, sitting in the Cabana last March. They said it was great to watch the fight on a nice a big TV, but the fight was at three a.m. The head housekeeper, an English lady named Maggie, is Ostergaard's girlfriend. She gave him the key, and the guys promised to clean the Cabana after the game. I imagine it was a lot of fun."

Inga looked at Sabine and said, "I do not think I would get out of bed in the middle of the night to watch two black guys beat the crap out of each other."

Based on her remark, Lucas assumed Inga does not like boxing.

Then, Sabine said, "Me too, I would decline that."

"What are you going to do about the RAF, Lucas?" asked Eric.

There was a long moment of silence before he said, "I do not know what to do. I have to think about it."

CHAPTER 23

Linderhof Castle

Inga was driving Lucas to NATO Officers Club. She would drop him off, and then she would go back to her house. Inga was not sure if she would open her shop today or not. It had been a long night. She was exhausted, and she knew Lucas must be too.

"Lucas, I feel bad about you working all day. Will you be able to get a nap, between lunch and dinner?" she asked.

"Yes, it's a good thing I have a room in the barracks," he replied. "I will sleep awhile and grab a shower before I set up dinner service.

He added, "I am in a dilemma about what, if anything, I should do with information about the RAF. I don't want to be the person who brings down Andreas, Ulrike and Gudrun because I like them so much. Well, there it is—problem solved. Let the security people handle it."

"Couldn't you make an anonymous phone call?" she asked.

"I think it's better to stay out of the way," he replied, "and I hope Secretary Laird does not come to Oberammergau.

"Hey, this is getting too serious! How about some music? Oh, damn, I forgot to talk to Topo about buying more hashish."

"Who is your very handsome friend, and where do you know those people from?" asked Inga.

"Topo waited on George and me at a French restaurant in Nice," said Lucas. "He is from Argentina, and he is a great guy."

"He has a great smile," she said. "Where did you meet the two ladies who were with Topo and Regan?"

"We met them on the ferry," said Lucas, "going from Tarifa, Spain, to Tangier, Morocco. I also ran into David Burns, a guy who played basketball with me in high school. Those two ladies were with David and his girlfriend, so we hung out with them for a while." Not wanting to give more details about the ladies, Lucas turned on some music which they enjoyed the rest of the way.

Inga dropped Lucas off at the officers' club. As soon as he got inside, he opened a beer because he did not get much sleep, and his head was feeling a little dull. He stayed in the kitchen until the lunch rush was over, then he went into the bar. Eric had just arrived at work with Lucas' van. He had driven Sabine home to Seefeld.

Helmut was in his office most of the morning. Lucas approached him and asked, "Could you tell me what happened between Margo and Bruno? I have a personal interest which I want to tell you about."

"Well, Margo came in to work one day with bruises on her neck and arms, red marks on her face and signs of a black eye," he replied. "When I asked her what happened, she called Bruno an asshole and said she never wanted to see him again. She told me if he continued to work here, she would not stay and work here. I knew we might also lose her sister since they stick together. So, when Bruno came into work, I stopped him at the door, took him to the office and told him he was being transferred back to the Von Steuben Hotel in Garmisch. Then, I asked him to clean out his locker before he left; and I told him to report for work at the hotel, the next day at three p.m."

Lucas thought he owed Helmut and Margo an explanation about his interest in the incident. He felt bad for Margo and guilty for not warning her about Bruno's violent temper and wild jealousy. He and Helmut went out to see Margo and Eric in the bar. It was otherwise empty.

"I've kept quiet long enough about Bruno," said Lucas.

In brief details, he told them about Bruno beating women, how he may have beaten Lucas' fiancée to death, and the disappearance of another woman he dated. Eric had heard it before. Margo had not—she was horrified to realize she slept with such a person, but glad he was gone.

Secretary of Defense Laird's visit went forward without incident. Lucas knew the security was tight. He assumed Andreas decided the risk was too high, and he was not ready to die.

Lucas thought: *I hope RAF members don't come back to Bavaria. Now, it is more dangerous for me to visit with them, and CID Robinson is always snooping around. I would hate to find myself in the middle of a shoot-out while I hung out with Celebrity Terrorists.*

Working at the officers' club and enjoying life with Inga at her house in the big meadow was a very happy time for Lucas. Her house was walking distance to the Wanklift T-bar. When they got off the T-bar, they skied over to the Kolbensattel double chairlift which took them to the top for a nice downhill run, ending in her backyard.

One afternoon, while riding the chairlift, Inga asked him, "Lucas, do you think this could be your permanent home?"

Her question surprised Lucas, and he said, "Oberammergau has all the things I love—mountains, lakes, streams, skiing, good hashish, great food, fabulous beer and, best of all, Inga, you are here."

Looking at her, he saw her beautiful face and her smile as she said, "Thank you, Lucas, but you still didn't answer my question."

There is one word I hesitate to include, and it is the word permanent, thought Lucas.

In reply to Inga's question, he said, "Right now, I wouldn't want to be anywhere else or with anyone else; and this is the absolute truth."

On one of Lucas' days off, they went to Linderhof Castle, and Inga conducted a private tour for Lucas Gary, her very own special tourist. They were lucky it was a sunny day, but it was still cold. A lot of snow was piled along the side of the roads, and it covered all the tree branches. As they drove from her house, Inga talked about the castle.

"My great uncle, Carl von Effner was a great-grandson of the famous architect Joseph Effner who was the son of Carl Effner, the Bavarian Oberhof gardener," she said. "Carl von Effner's education was financed by King Ludwig the Second's father, Maximilian, for whom he worked as a gardener until he was appointed head of all Bavarian courtyard gardens. It was Carl von Effner who designed the magnificent gardens which we will see at Linderhof Castle. He was educated in Vienna, Ghent, Paris, England, and at Sanssouci Palace."

Noticing a puzzled look on Lucas' face, Inga said, "Sanssouci is the summer palace of Frederick the Great, King of Prussia. With eighteenth-century decor and unique, terraced vineyards, the Germans say it rivals Versailles. It's in Potsdam, southwest of Berlin."

She continued the story about her great uncle, "Carl von Effner also designed the gardens of Herrenchiemsee. King Ludwig honored him with a title, the Royal Director of Court Gardens, and later raised him to the nobility (von) for his work at the gardens of Linderhof Castle. King Ludwig planned it as a small retreat, similar to the palace of King Louis the Fourteenth.

"You will see this formal garden layout is in the shape of a crucifix, and the castle is at the center of the cross. Linderhof is the smallest of the three palaces which were built for King Ludwig the Second, and it is the only one which he lived to see completed."

They parked the van in the near-empty parking lot. Since it was winter, Inga reminded Lucas they would not see colorful gardens, and they would have to come back in the summer to enjoy the flowers in full bloom. Inside the van, they sat across from each other, shared a bowl of hashish and each had a Paulaner beer.

Looking out at the trees around the parking area, she said, "As you can see, Linderhof is secluded in this narrow canyon, surrounded by forests and hills. This area is Graswang Valley, and the nearest town is Ettal."

Pointing at a path which disappeared into the trees, she said, "You can't see the castle from here. It's about a ten-minute walk, along the winding path." As they walked, Inga told Lucas why Ludwig built this retreat in a such a secluded area. "Ludwig was a recluse, and he could escape to his fantasy world here, away from his duties of ruling Bavaria."

Then, she explained how King Ludwig selected this site. "This castle is where Ludwig stayed often and spent the most time. It was built on the original site of a royal hunter's cottage. Ludwig's father, Maximilian the Second, had built it for his hunting. Rather than destroy it, King Ludwig moved the hunter's cottage because of his personal connection to the building. It now sits two hundred yards to the west."

Holding gloved hands, they walked along the winding path under snow-covered trees. After climbing some slippery stairs to the front of the castle, they arrived at the main entrance. Lucas stood still for a moment. He looked around and said, "Right away, I noticed both the castle and the surrounding landscape are very symmetrical."

"The grounds are a mixture of different garden styles," she replied. "The most prominent styles are Baroque and Rococo. The Baroque is from Italian origin, and the Rococo is from French origin."

Looking down the stairs and in front of the castle, they saw a large tree-lined pond, covered in ice and snow. Inga said, "In the center of the pond is a fountain where you see the gilded statues. The fountain shoots water in the air, ninety-eight feet high.

"Behind the pond are three levels of garden terraces. At the top, you see an open structure; it's a round temple which houses a sculpture of Venus, surrounded by tall columns, under a big dome crown. Ludwig planned to build a theater there, but then decided he only wanted one large building on the estate, thus they built the Venus Temple. You can see a three-hundred-year-old Linden tree next to the temple. At one of the garden arches, there is a bust of Queen Marie Antoinette of France. King Ludwig wanted a replica of the Palace of Versailles and its gardens because he became enchanted by The Sun King, Louis the Fourteenth. However, Ludwig realized this piece of land was too small, so he bought Herrenchiemsee Island for his Versailles replica. But Versailles is a whole other story. Let's go into the Palace Vestibule to start the tour, and I'll tell you a little about Ludwig and The Sun King."

When they walked into the vestibule, Lucas was impressed by the splendor of the room.

Inga began the indoor tour, "Bavarian royalty is displayed in the statues, other figures and the facade supports around the grounds and throughout the castle. Ludwig dedicated his vestibule to King Louis the Fourteenth of France, and Louis' statue sits in the center of the room. It's a copy, smaller than the original which was destroyed during the French Revolution. There is another copy at the Louvre in Paris."

Pointing to the ceiling, she said, "Overhead, you see the sculpted depiction of the Sun King Icon, a golden spray of rays which covers most of the ceiling. In the center, two naked cherubs (putti) seem to be floating. They each hold one end of a ribbon between them; and written on the ribbon, you see the motto of the Bourbon dynasty, 'Nec pluribus impar' (not unequal to many). The reddish-marble columns around this vestibule create a temple atmosphere.

"In Ludwig's imaginary world, this castle's interior was his homage to King Louis the Fourteenth."

"From what little I have learned, King Ludwig and King Louis were very different," said Lucas. "Louis embraced all the challenges of governing, whereas Ludwig shunned the responsibility."

"You are correct," she replied. "Louis the Fourteenth acquired several nicknames which distinguished him as the most powerful man alive which he may have been for his time. People called him Louis the Great, The Grand Monarch and The Sun King.

"In the Palace of Versailles, they designed a layout for the daily routine of *le Roi-Soleil* (the Sun King) which followed the course of the sun. He thought he was like the sun since everything seemed to revolve around him. Louis was an absolute monarch. He was King of France for seventy-two years. When he was asked about the State, his reply was *'L'État, c'est moi'* (I am the State).

"According to rumors, Louis the Fourteenth took only three baths during his lifetime. In those days, people believed a good layer of dirt would protect you from disease, but water would spread disease. Most people didn't bathe more than once a year. However, wealthy people changed their clothes often, and women doused their bodies with heavy perfumes or fragrant powders to mask the odor."

"I think it's called a French Bath," said Lucas.

Inga smiled and continued, "Those rumors about Louis may be untrue. Some people claimed he was fussy about cleanliness. In his Palace at Versailles, he used a big Turkish bath often and changed his underwear three times a day. Whichever way he did it, he did something right because he lived to be seventy-seven years old, longer than any other French monarch in history."

Inga led him into the Tapestry Chambers. "There are two Tapestry Chambers which serve no specific function," said Inga. Lucas admired the tapestries on the walls, woven with scenes of ladies lounging in the forest. He also noticed some heavenly scenes, painted on rough canvas to imitate real tapestries.

Entering the glittering Hall of Mirrors, Inga said, "King Ludwig used this as a living room, of sorts. He would sit and read in the niche." She was referring to a small room, off to the right, where purple drapes were tied-back at the entrance. "Sometimes he would read all night because he preferred sleeping during the daytime. These mirrors created an unbelievable lighting effect for him, reflecting the light of candles which were in the chandeliers. The parallel placement of the mirrors gives the illusion of a never-ending corridor. This carpet is made of ostrich plumes, and the candelabra in the alcove is made of ivory."

While following Inga into the Speisezimmer (Dining Room), Lucas studied the room: *This is very different from any dining room I have ever seen. The only things which might associate with dining are carvings in the wall panel. The carvings depict farming, hunting and fishing which would all put food on the table.*

"This dining table is part of a mechanized system called *Tischlein deck dich* (Table be set, or table cover yourself), said Inga. The table disappears through the floor, into the kitchen below. Servants would set the table, load it with food and send it back up to the dining room, so King Ludwig did not have to see his servants. This room is one of only four rooms which had a functional purpose in the castle."

Gazing at details in design, Lucas studied the room: *The candelabra chandelier is amazing. It hangs over the dining room table which is centered over an ornate purple and gold carpet. The marble table top is supported by an ornate, gilded base. This entire room is embellished with gold, including wall panels, the fireplace, mirrors, table, chairs, doorways and the domed ceiling.*

Inga said, "One of his cooks wrote about Ludwig in his memoirs. He claimed the King was always alone at the table, but he required enough food for three or four people, so he wouldn't feel alone; and he spoke out loud as if dining with Louis the Fourteenth, or Louis the Fifteenth, or their friends, Madame Pompadour and Madame Maintenon."

"Yeah, no wonder they said he was nuts," replied Lucas.

"Since King Ludwig was so preoccupied with building his castles, he neglected his royal duties," she said. "He became more withdrawn and obsessed with his dramatic building projects. The King used his own money and borrowed family money for construction costs. He also took out loans and owed over fourteen million marks when he died.

"King Ludwig's political advisors plotted against him; but there was no legal way to remove him from office, except by illness. While the King was not properly diagnosed as being nuts, four government-sanctioned psychiatrists declared he was insane without examination. Two days later, the King was arrested at Neuschwanstein Castle which was still being built. From there, he was taken away and imprisoned at Berg Castle, a manor house at Lake Starnberg in Bavaria, about seventy kilometers from here. This all happened in June of eighteen eighty-six."

"I heard he committed suicide," he said. "Is it true?"

"Nobody seems to know for sure how he died," she replied. "On June thirteenth, eighteen eighty-six, three days after he was declared insane, the castle staff found King Ludwig dead. The King's body was floating in Lake Starnberg next to the body of Dr. Gudden, his psychiatrist. One theory is they struggled, and Ludwig killed the doctor; afterward, Ludwig committed suicide, or he drowned in the lake, accidentally. People who oppose this theory say the King was a very good swimmer, he was not a violent person, and he would never have killed himself."

"What about his obsession with Richard Wagner?" Lucas asked.

"His obsession began at a young age," she replied. "Ludwig was captivated by Wagner's operas and German mythology which the music was based upon. As King, one of his first actions was to summon Wagner to his court. In many respects, Wagner and Ludwig enjoyed a creative and productive relationship. To honor Wagner's work, Ludwig organized huge musical festivals and built large concert halls in Munich and Bayreuth. People say Wagner would never have achieved such fame as he has today, without King Ludwig. Their partnership worked for Ludwig too. Wagner inspired Ludwig's creativity which he used in planning his castles and theater projects.

"Ludwig's interest in Wagner became so passionate, he lost himself in the fantasy world of Wagner's works. Ludwig even dressed like some of the operatic characters. He would sleep during the daytime and only venture out at night. In opposition to King Louis who was called The Sun King, Ludwig became known as The Night King."

From the dining room, they entered the Rosa Kabinett (Rose Closet), and Inga said, "The layout of the East Wing is identical to the West Wing. This room served as a dressing room for the King. As you can see, all the fabrics and chairs are pink. In those oval frames, the portraits are members of the court at Versailles. There are four closets which are identical in shape, but each are different in decoration. All the closets served as anti-chambers to larger connecting rooms."

As they entered the magnificent Schlafzimmer (Bedroom), she said, "The bedroom was an important part of ceremonial life for Louis the Fourteenth, an absolute monarch. Each day, King Louis would give his first audience and last audience while he was in his bedchamber. It was not a practice of Ludwig's since he was reclusive and slept in the daytime. The position of this bedroom faces in the opposite direction from Louis' bedroom in Versailles, further validating King Ludwig's nickname as The

Night King. However, in proportion and relative to the size of their castles, both kings had very large bedrooms."

As seen in other rooms, gold embellishments were everywhere in Ludwig's Bedroom. The colors of royal blue, white and gold dominated this room, and there was another magnificent chandelier with over 100 candles. At the rear of the room, a huge bed with ornately carved and gilded framework rose above a special platform. The sleeping area was surrounded by a gilded balustrade. Close to the ceiling, a large canopy hung above the bed. Fabric of the canopy was royal blue velvet, as were the bed coverings, pillows and footstool. The same velvet flowed down the wall from the canopy to the floor behind an ornate, gold headboard. All the framework for the canopy and other bedroom structures were embellished in gold-leaf. Above the headboard, hand-painted angels seemed to float on a royal blue velvet backdrop.

"The bedchamber and the carved balustrade around it make this room so majestic. It looks like a shrine," said Lucas.

Next to the bedroom, Inga led him into the west closet, known as the Lila Kabinett (Lilac Closet). The colors in this closet blended with a purple tint in the adjacent bedroom.

Next, they walked into the Audience Chamber, and Inga said, "King Ludwig never used this room to hold an audience. He considered this his private domain; therefore, he did not conduct governing business in here, as it would invade his privacy. Instead, he used this chamber as a study where he could dream and plan his new building projects."

Inga completed the tour when she said, "The last two rooms are copies of another closet and the other tapestry room. Right now, I am starving for some strange reason."

"Let's go have dinner at the International Bar and Grill," said Lucas. "I'm hungry for a good steak au poivre."

"We have to come back this summer," she said, "to finish the tour of these wonderful gardens, designed by my great uncle Carl. However, we should get going now. I have a plan for us after dinner."

With a mischievous smile, she stood on her toes and gave Lucas a nice, soft kiss. She grabbed his gloved hand, and off they went.

They walked back to the van, climbed in and grabbed 2 Paulaner beers from the cabinet. Next, they headed for Garmisch.

CHAPTER 24

Seefeld: Exploration

Lucas and Inga walked into the dining room at the International Bar and Grill. They spotted Gino and Sonya at a table with 4 chairs.

Gino saw them, walked over to Lucas and gave him a hug. He invited them to join him and Sonya.

When Lucas got close enough to see Sonya's face, he felt nauseated. She was wearing sunglasses, but they did not hide 2 black eyes and a very swollen lip. Lucas did not have to ask what happened. He clutched his fist as he sat next to Sonya.

Lucas looked her in the eye and said, "Okay, Sonya, have you had enough? Will you please help me deal with Bruno? I have a plan, but I will need your help."

"Oh, yeah? What is your plan? What can you do?" she asked.

"I tried to warn you about Bruno," he replied. "He is suspected of beating two women to death, due to his anger and outrageous jealousy. Sonya, you don't want to be his next victim."

"Okay. I'll help you," said Sonya. "I hate the asshole for what he has called me and for beating me, too many times. Let's get this guy. Why can't we go to the police about the murders?"

"We have no evidence, so the police won't even listen," said Lucas. He was steaming with anger, and he was mad at himself for not taking care of Bruno before this happened.

"Tell me your plan," she said.

"I'll tell you later. For now, let's order dinner," he replied.

Gino and Lucas had the New York Steak with green peppercorn sauce, baked potato and green beans, sautéd in garlic. Inga tried the Roast Duckling with orange sauce, rice pilaf and the green beans. Sonya wanted the Leberknoedelsuppe (liver dumpling soup) because her sore mouth made it hard to chew food.

After dinner, most of the people Lucas knew were in the bar and disco. They were all looking for a place to sit. Eric and Lucas found a table and some chairs in a back room. When those were arranged, their friends sat facing the dance floor in a big semi-circle. While the band was on break, a DJ played music. People on the dance floor rocked out to a song by Santana, "Black Magic Woman." Inga and Faye tried to talk, but it was a difficult task since the music was loud.

Lucas tapped Sonya's shoulder and asked her to join him outside where they could discuss his plan for Bruno's downfall. They went by a line of young partiers at the door where bouncer Jordan Lewis checked their IDs. Moving along the walkway and past the restaurant, Lucas thought about his first arrival in Garmisch. It seemed like ages ago. He recalled making love with Sonya and remembered how great it was; although, it was only for those few days.

Now, however, Lucas was certain, he was falling in love with Inga. He thought about staying in Bavaria and settling down with her.

As Sonya and Lucas walked along the path on St. Martin Strasse, snow began to fall.

"Lucas, I'll never forget our short time together, here in Garmisch," said Sonya. "I thought we might have had something special between us, but you left rather abruptly."

"Yes, and I want to explain my actions to you," he replied. "The real reason I came to Europe was to find Bruno. In California, he and I lived in the same city, and Bruno was an ex-boyfriend of my fiancée. Her name was Jodie, and someone found her beaten to death. Bruno was the main suspect, but he skipped town before the police could charge him. Then, I learned Bruno went to Garmisch.

"By the time I got here, he had gone to Ibiza. My friend George wanted to go to Ibiza, anyway, so we headed there. We saw Gino in Valencia, and the three of us went to Ibiza together.

"Next, we all went to Formentera for some fun and to search for Bruno. I met a young German lady, whose friend was hanging out somewhere on the island with Bruno. I never saw her friend; she became a missing person. A few days later, our group saw Bruno board a ferry, going from Formentera to Ibiza. Later, we saw him board another ferry, going from Ibiza to Valencia. No one could find the young German lady who he was dating on Formentera. She was never seen again."

"I wish you would have told me," said Sonya.

"The way things turned out, I also wish I had told you, but I didn't know you would end up with him," he replied. "I didn't tell anyone about Bruno. You know how his temper is, Sonya. I believe he murdered those two women, and there may be others. Plus, who knows how many women he has beaten up?"

Lucas had Sonya's attention now. He told her his plan and explained why he needed her help. Although it involved her being with Bruno for one last time, Sonya agreed to help him. Lucas told her he would give her a date when it was time for a trial run.

They walked back into the bar and Lucas noticed their friends were shouting to each other, sitting in a big half-circle and raising their beer glasses for a "Prost." A band was on stage now, playing its own version of "Joy to the World," a song by Three Dog Night.

Before he could sit, Inga asked, "Lucas, can we dance?"

Lucas bowed and waved her toward the dance floor. While dancing, his thoughts kept going back to the semi-circle of friends who are now so special to him.

He thought: *I am with a unique group of people. I met a lot of them skiing in Cervenia and Zermatt where we also enjoyed being extras in the movie Snow Job.*

There is my new best friend, Eric, a tall, muscular, blonde-haired Swedish guy from Minnesota. He has a great smile and reminds me of Robert Wagner.

Sitting next to Eric is Judann. She was dating Steve Dobson who is partnered with Bob Ostergaard in the "Shifty Sales" rebuilt VW van business. It may be on the edge of illegal because CID Robinson is always trying to bust Bob and Steve for something.

Sitting next to Bob is Maggie, his girlfriend from England. She is talking to Faye Williams and her husband, Scott.

I remember smoking hashish and going out to dinner with Faye and Scott in Ibiza. Scott was a little slow with his wallet when it was time to pay the check. They look and act like what they are, two real hippies from U.C. Berkeley who always talk against the Vietnam War; Faye and Scott are anti-establishment. Andreas and Ulrike might profile them as great recruits in the RAF, except Fay and Scott are not violent.

Then, there is Gino who became my good friend. He seems to know everybody. He is a streetwise person who knows about the world and fits-in anywhere, as if he belongs in any country. Gino is also a superb skier, a true perfectionist, multi-talented, and he has a great sense of humor. Gino is sitting next to Ashleigh, an Australian lady who dated Regan Stone, the Cattleman/Attorney who came from Corpus Christi, Texas, and goes by the great name of Tex.

Next to Ashleigh is her friend Olivia from Australia, a great surfer, a former travel companion of mine and a fantastic bed partner. Olivia is a hell of a lot of fun. I will always cherish our trip from Morocco to the Matterhorn, and then to the Oktoberfest. Wow, I'm feeling nostalgic about our time together. However, I could not pick a better partner for Olivia than Topo who is now with her. He is a handsome Argentinean drug dealer/waiter with a great smile. When we traveled to the French Riviera,

Topo waited on us in a delightful French country restaurant on a hill overlooking Nice and the Mediterranean Sea. I remember having dinner when Topo whispered, "Do you get high?" Since then, Topo has become my designated hashish dealer.

Lucas spotted Bruno who was sitting on the far side of the horseshoe bar. Bruno seemed to be glaring at Sonya with an angry scowl.

Bruno must have seen me take Sonya outside and walk back in together, thought Lucas. *If he realizes I know about his involvement with the murders, people who are close to me may be in danger. I had better put my plan into action as soon as I can get it together.*

Inga and Lucas danced to 2 more songs. Then, they visited with the people in their group, as much as they could. Over the loud music, they were all yelling back and forth to each other.

After saying goodbye to their friends in the bar, Lucas and Inga took Topo outside to the van. Lucas bought some hashish, packed a pipe and passed it around while they each had a Paulaner beer. Topo told them about his new life in Garmisch and all the great people he had met. His business, selling hashish, had never been better.

"Before I met Olivia, I never knew Australian women were so much fun," said Topo. "We have a great apartment near The Grill, and I've been playing basketball at the gym. I hear you play the game well, Lucas. Why don't you come over and play with us some evening? Regan, Eric and John play most nights, plus the big Italian guy, named Bruno, who is pushy and aggressive. He gets mad a lot."

Lucas cringed when he heard the name of the woman beating creep, but he did not want to discuss Bruno. "I've been playing at the gym in Hawkins Kaserne with guys from the NATO School, and they also play an aggressive game," he replied.

When it was time to leave, Inga and Lucas gave Topo a big hug. They watched him walk back into The Grill, and then they drove to Inga's house in Oberammergau.

Lucas worked the next afternoon at the club. The kitchen crew was efficient, and everything was prepared early; they were ready for dinner service. Lucas went into the bar for a beer with his favorite coworkers, Eric and Helmut, the bartender and manager.

Eric handed Lucas a draft Augustiner beer, flashed his great smile and said, "We were with a great group of people at The Grill last night. Those Australian ladies are crazy fun."

"Yeah, they sure are fun to be around," replied Lucas.

Helmut was following their conversation, and he said, "We had an Australian bartender once, but he was a little too crazy for the job, so we had to let him go." Then, Helmut heard his office phone ringing. He excused himself and went to answer it.

"Eric, did you see Sonya's face, last night?" Lucas asked, quietly.

"No, I was paying attention to our friends, and it was dark where we were sitting," he replied.

"Bruno beat her again, and it looked very bad. I think it is time to get moving with my plan," said Lucas.

"Whatever you need me to do, Lucas, I'm in all the way," said Eric. "The asshole deserves to suffer a little."

"Thank you, Eric," said Lucas. "I haven't worked out the details yet, but I know we need Sonya to get Bruno on the mountain. Also, we still need to find a suitable spot for it to take place. I did not intend to get other people involved. This is my personal deal because of what he did to my fiancée, Jodie. At least, her death was my original reason for tracking him down. Now, I've seen what he is really like, and I have no hesitation—my plan will go forward. Bruno does not seem to have any remorse for his horrific actions and harming women. He appears to live his life as a normal person, but he is a horrible beast."

Helmut came back and joined them, saying, "I think we should have a bar games tournament for employees. We can invite a few of our best customers to come, such as Inga and Sabine."

"It sounds like a lot of fun," replied Lucas. "Next week, we're all going skiing in Seefeld. We'll be available for a tournament when we return. I'm also committed to do Colonel Moyer's birthday party in April."

"Lucas, I know you are in demand, and I hope you are not wasting your talents here in our humble officers' club," said Helmut.

"Helmut, I love it here," he replied. "If I have a kitchen to work in, a good beer to drink and friends around, I've got it all. Now, I'd better get back to the kitchen. Thanks for the beer and conversation."

Driving on the highway to Seefeld, Lucas took Inga and Eric through the small towns of Oberau and Farchant, then stopped in Garmisch and picked up Sonya at The Last Chance. Sonya tossed her skis and boots on the floor with the other gear and sat next to the window. Her black eyes and bruises were almost healed, and she seemed upbeat.

Inga and Sonya competed against each other in school sports, but they did not get to know each other and never became friends. Sonya was raised in Garmisch-Partenkirchen and Inga was raised in Oberammergau. On this trip, Lucas and Eric did most of the talking.

"Okay, I plan to find a place where I can help Mr. Bruno disappear forever," Lucas said to everyone.

Inga and Sonya both gasped in shock. Eric had already heard the plan, and he remained quiet.

“Lucas, you can’t be serious—it would be murder!” exclaimed Inga.

“I know, Mein Schatz,” he replied. “But this man has murdered at least two women, and he’s beaten many. Bruno is a coward. I want to do this, not only as payback for my fiancée, but to make sure he can’t beat anyone else to death. I’ve labored over this in my mind, hundreds of times. This seems like the best solution. If he disappears, authorities will think he is on the run which makes sense because he is a murder suspect.”

“I want to see him hurt and broken, lying deep in a canyon where he will freeze to death, slowly, and think about why,” said Eric.

“Well, I also hope we can have a good time skiing here,” said Lucas. “Sabine will ski with us and show us around Seefeld. She and I already talked about my plan, and she knows a good spot. So, please open beers for everybody, and let’s get this party started.”

Inga selected an album by Chicago. For the rest of the 40-minute drive, they listened to music, each to their own thoughts.

When they arrived in Seefeld, Lucas noticed the area was very similar to the location of Inga’s house with ski lifts on the hill.

Sabine had made reservations for Lucas and Inga. They would stay at the Gasthof Batzenhäusl on Klosterstrasse. It was an authentic Tyrolean gasthof with superb Tyrolean food, live music and dancing. Lucas would cover the cost of a single room for Sonya. Eric and Sabine would stay at her house which was in a wooded area near 2 small ski lifts, the Geigenbuhel Lift and the Forderband Lift.

Lucas and Inga checked into the German-style inn and got cleaned up. When the others arrived at their room, they passed the hash pipe around and drank Stiegl beer which comes from a local brewery on the outskirts of Salzburg.

Lucas thought: *Am I really here to plot a murder? No, it is more like the extermination of a rodent.*

Acting as a tour guide, Sabine led them to the gasthof bar. Sitting at a round, wooden table, they ordered 5 Klosterbräu beers plus 5 shots of Jägermeister and settled in for an evening of Tyrolean night life.

Talking about the family who owns the Gasthof Batzenhäusl, Sabine said, “In nineteen sixty-seven, the Kaltschmid family bought this inn, and they bought a dance bar, known as the Tenne. A year later, they added a restaurant to Tenne, named Restaurant Klause. This year, they completed an expansion of Tenne, in which they built the longest bar in Austria. As owners, the Kaltschmid family makes you feel welcome in their inn and bar. When Fritz Kaltschmid returned from his schooling as a chef and waiter in nineteen sixty-two, he took over management of the gasthof, and he was only nineteen years old.

"Two hundred meters down the strasse, there is a hotel which was originally a monastery. Now, it's Hotel Klosterbräu, the place where they brew this fine beer. We should walk there after dinner."

Lucas' mind wandered back to special restaurants he had visited: *The most memorable restaurant was at the Post Hotel in Wallgau, dining with Inga, Sabine and George. Inga paid the check. Two other great places were the Goldener Bar in Berchtesgaden, and La Luna Restaurant in Valencia. Thinking of George, I realize how much I miss my old friend. I must write him a letter, soon.*

After everyone consumed 3 beers and 2 shots of Jägermeister, they made their way to the dining room. They ordered more Klosterbräu beers and set their sights on the menu.

Lucas looked around the room. It had light-colored wood panels. Pink-printed drapes hung in the windows and the tables were all dressed in pink and white tablecloths. The room was lit by dome-shaped lamps which hung above the tables.

Sabine ordered for Eric and herself: Bayerische Schlachtplatte (a Bavarian plate for 2 people with sauerkraut, red cabbage, 2 smoked pork loin, 2 nürnberger, 1 polish, 1 bratwurst, 1 smoked pork chop, dumpling and fried potatoes). She knows Eric can put away the food.

Sonya ordered Forelle Müllerin (trout sauté with a brown-butter-lemon sauce, served with rice and vegetables).

Inga chose Linguini mit Schnitzelstreifen (linguini with pork loin strips in apricot-cognac-cream sauce, plus a salad).

Lucas had Schweinshaxe (knuckle of pork with bread dumpling and red cabbage).

They all had another Klosterbräu beer and a shot of Jägermeister. After Lucas paid the check, they adjourned to Lucas and Inga's room for a bowl of hashish. Everyone wanted to go to Hotel Klosterbräu and enjoy the local night life. It was only a 5-minute walk, but it was cold outside. They did not put on thermal underwear since they would be dancing; thermals would be too warm, and they would get sweaty. So, they walked fast and made it in 3 minutes. Several horse-drawn wagons formed a line in front of the Hotel Klosterbräu, waiting for passengers. All the trees were void of leaves, and fluffy snow covered the branches. The lights were quite a sight at night, including yellow lights on the peak of Harmelekopf and lights coming down the ski trail from the Hochanger Lift to the village. They all stood and looked at the mountain peak.

"Just think, we'll be up there tomorrow," said Lucas.

"Yeah, looking for a cliff," said Sonya.

"I think I know the perfect place," replied Sabine.

“Okay, great, but do we have to be so serious about it?” asked Eric. “Let’s have fun while we’re here. I mean, it’s only Bruno.”

They were trying not to laugh as they entered the Hotel Klosterbräu and walked into the lobby which had a small piano bar. The first thing Lucas noticed were many stone archways, creating separate sitting areas in a very large room. Above the massive stone archways, the ceiling had multiple dome-shaped sections. Cobblestones covered each section of the ceiling. Huge columns appeared to be solid granite which supported the archways. There was a small bar with padded stools which would seat 8 people; but Lucas knew it would be a little tame for their group.

Sabine led them to Kanne, the busy nightclub where many famous entertainers have performed on stage. They sat at a corner table in a semi-private cove of a jazzy room. Multi-colored strobe lights lit the bar and dance area. A large disco ball hung over the crowed dance floor, and the band was playing great rock ‘n’ roll music.

After they drank half of their Klosterbräu beers, Lucas and Inga wanted to dance. When they got back to the table, a fresh Klosterbräu beer and a shot of Jägermeister were waiting for each of them.

Lucas looked over at Eric who smiled, then raised his glass of beer and said, “Prost, mein freunden.”

“It’s interesting to learn Klosterbräu beer is brewed in what used to be a monastery,” said Inga.

“The monastery was built in the fifteen hundreds,” replied Sabine. “Five generations of the Seyrling family have run this hotel for over one hundred and fifty years. They maintain a cozy, friendly atmosphere and provide first class service. While they restored the property, they kept most of the historic features and original charm.”

When they finished their drinks, Sabine said, “I want to show you the rest of this fine hotel, including the five-century-old wine cellar. There is also a Bräukeller and Grill where we can have another beer.”

Going downstairs and into the wine cellar, Lucas noticed the jagged, golden-colored-rock ceiling in the cellar was in keeping with the archway layout in the reception and piano bar areas upstairs.

On the left side of the wine cellar, Lucas saw 12 brick compartments which were 4 feet high and 4 feet deep, shaped like fireplaces and filled with bottles of red wine. Bottles were stacked and lying on their sides. In each compartment, the bottle configuration was unique.

The cellar had only 1 window, an opening which was 2 feet square and covered by an ancient-looking copper grate. Left of the entrance, a copper lamp hung from the ceiling, holding a single candle.

Throughout the cellar, they saw many free-standing candelabras and wall lamps made of wrought-iron as well as decorative racks of various styles filled with wine bottles. Blonde wood furniture was scattered around the room, and wooden benches were placed along 1 wall.

The floor, walls and ceiling were covered in cobblestone. In the middle of the main cellar, multiple archways were joined at their base, forming one massive stone pillar. Curving all the way around the pillar, a wide, stone platform displayed crates of wine. Some crates were open, exposing wine bottles nestled in straw.

There were 3 cellar rooms, and each room had its own uniqueness. Sabine led them through an open doorway and into a room with more stone archways, except these archways were much shorter than those in the main wine cellar. On the right wall were more fireplace-shaped brick compartments. These had crates of wine in them, guarded by locked wrought-iron gates. On the left beneath a low stone archway, there was a long, wooden table and benches with purple and white throw pillows. Birdcage lamps hung from the ceiling. This room looked like a plain old cellar. It had exposed drain pipes, wine barrels with lamps on them, and hanging pots and pans. Again, there was only 1 window. It was covered by a wrought-iron grate, facing a brick wall.

Another room had wine barrels full of unused bottle corks. In an arched alcove, 2 tables were set and ready for dining, both with gold-colored tablecloths and napkins, wine glasses and silverware. At each table there were 2 high-back, upholstered chairs for seating.

Eric spoke up, "Sabine, this cellar tour has been great; but we are all beer drinkers. Did you say something about a Bräukeller?"

Sabine led them down a dark, red-carpeted stairway to another room with a multi-arched ceiling. It was more modern and decorated in the same style as most Bräukellers, using heavy, blonde-colored wood tables and chairs. The room was crowded with Austrians.

On the stage, the entertainers were 3 generations of the same family, all wearing lederhosen. The oldest was the Opa (Grandfather) who played a string bass. The Vater (father) played an accordion, and the young man (Sohn) played guitar. The Tyrolean music was lively. Several couples danced, men in lederhosen and women in dirndls.

People seated at tables and those standing around were all talking, laughing and enjoying the hospitality of the hosts. It was an evening of beer, schnapps and Tyrolean food.

Looking around the room, Lucas thought: *I love ski resort areas because people are always having fun and laughing a lot.*

While seated at a table for 4 people, they squeezed their group of 5 around it. Everyone ordered the usual Klosterbräu beers plus shots of Jägermeister, and they joined in the fun.

It was snowing outside by the time they were ready to leave Hotel Klosterbräu. So, everyone hurried during the walk along Klosterstrasse. Upon arrival at Gasthof Batzenhäusl, they separated and went to get warm in their respective rooms.

Lucas and Inga were enjoying this night together in Seefeld, and they were both feeling it. They smoked a bowl of hashish while they were kissing and undressing each other. In the shower, they took turns washing and rinsing, especially the fun parts of their bodies.

At 9 a.m. the next morning, everyone wished they had skipped the last beer and the shot of Jägermeister at the Bräukeller.

After eating breakfast at the gasthof, they got ready to go. Outside, they could see the Standseilbahn (railway) on the face of the mountain. It would carry them up to Seefelder Joch Station where they would start their day of skiing. Now, everyone's enthusiasm increased.

Walking to the van, Lucas was glad to see fresh snow, clear blue skies and sunshine. Being here with 3 beautiful women and Eric, his new best friend, Lucas knew this would be a special day.

Everyone felt great, even Sonya whose bruises had healed from the last beating Bruno gave her. Sabine had already gotten passes for the group. They put on their ski boots, grabbed their skis, got on the standup train and rode to the *Rosshütte*. Next, they took the Seefelder Jochbahn (cable car) to the peak.

Getting off the lift and skiing a short distance, Sabine led them to the far side of a groomed slope which ran along a steep embankment. They stood at the top of a narrow canyon and peered into the silent space below. It was covered with snow and studded with the tops of trees which indicated how deep this ravine might be.

Next to them, a cluster of trees grew at the edge of the cliff above the ravine. Sabine pointed to a place in those trees which was hidden from the view of skiers and anyone on the cable car.

Lucas said to his 4 fellow-conspirators, "This could go one of two ways for Bruno. He will have a soft landing in the snow, or a hard landing into trees and rocks. Either way, I do not believe he can climb out of there, even if he survives the fall."

Inga was still concerned, and she spoke up, "Lucas, I wish you would reconsider and let the police take care of Bruno. If anyone finds out about this, you could be convicted. If you had to spend the rest of your life in prison, I would be unhappy because I love you so much!"

"I'll consider a talk with police," replied Lucas. "If they do nothing, I will follow through with this plan while we still have snow."

After he studied the area, Lucas said, "Thank you, Sabine. I think this will be a perfect spot for Mr. Bruno to disappear."

They all skied for 2 hours and stopped for lunch at the *Rosshütte* Mountain Restaurant. Everyone had the traditional, Austrian skier's lunch: lots of beer, goulash soup and brotchen.

After lunch, they went over to the Hochangerbahn, skied downhill to the Reitheralmbahn, and rode it up to the Harmelekapfbahn. From there, they skied some nice steep runs with no traffic.

After skiing and getting back to Lucas' van, they smoked a bowl of hashish, and each had a Klosterbräu beer.

Saying goodbye to Sabine, everyone thanked her for showing them around the village and getting their lift tickets. She promised to come and visit them in Garmisch and Oberammergau, very soon.

Settled behind the wheel and ready for the 40-minute drive back to Garmisch, Lucas said to everyone, "I really enjoyed seeing Seefeld. It is a winter playground for skiers of all ages. Although, it might be too mild for very experienced skiers."

CHAPTER 25

AFRC: Bar Games

On the drive back from Seefeld to Oberammergau, the group talked about how Sonya would lure Bruno to the cliff sight. They discussed the actual execution of what Lucas called the "Bruno Event" and how they would coordinate the timing.

When they arrived in Oberammergau, Lucas dropped Eric off at the club and Inga off at her house. He and Sonya headed to Garmisch.

Lucas planned to discuss the RAF with Sonya, in private. He knew her mother provided a house to them when they were in Garmisch. Whether she rented it or she was a sympathizer, Lucas did not care. He wanted to know if Sonya and her mother were involved with RAF activity, or not. This was his opportunity to find out, and he asked, "Sonya, does your mother have a house which she rents out?"

"Yes, she does. Are you interested in renting a house?" she asked.

"No, I'm interested in knowing if she understands who she is renting to," he replied.

Sonya looked surprised and said, "Lucas, let's not play games. You must have learned the leaders of the RAF stay there sometimes. How did you find out about it?"

"It's a long story," he said. "The condensed version is I met them a while ago when I was in Austria. Then, I ran into them again in Venice. Here in Bavaria, I visited them at your mother's house and cooked dinner for them. I do not consider myself a sympathizer of their cause, and I certainly do not condone the bombing and killing of innocent people, or any other people. But I found them interesting and always had a good time with them. I try to understand the reasons for their actions and realize they are becoming a folk legend in Germany and central Europe. However, I believe they will soon come to a bad end. I don't want to be around when it happens, and I hope you and your mother don't get caught in the crossfire. If you would please let me know when they are coming to Garmisch, I can make plans to be out of town while they are here."

"I promise, I will let you know if we hear anything from them," said Sonya. "Mother and I are not interested in their cause or crusade, no matter what you want to call it. Although, like a lot of Germans, we enjoy the way they make the police look stupid. We recognize them as folk heroes because they provide the common citizens of Germany an opportunity to snub our noses at people who govern us."

After dropping Sonya off at The Last Chance, Lucas returned to daily life in Oberammergau, and every day seemed new and exciting. Beauty surrounded him, whether he was in Oberammergau, Garmisch, Seefeld or Berchtesgaden.

With no anchor to tie him down, Lucas felt happy and free; although, his feelings for Inga were unlike any prior experience in his 31 years. Freedom was important to him for as long as he could remember, and now it seemed more important than ever.

Realizing he felt free while being with Inga, Lucas thought of selling his restaurants in Long Beach and staying here. Yet, he knew only time would tell about such a big decision.

When he faced major changes and important matters, Lucas always believed the right decision would be obvious. That is, if he had the patience to wait for the answer to become obvious.

Lucas loved his job. Working with Helmut was fantastic, and they seemed to enjoy each other's company. Both loved to joke around while playing different bar games, and they had some fierce competition with other employees.

Lucas, Helmut, Eric, Kurt and even the twins, Margo and Karin, were all becoming skilled at various bar games. They spent most of their afternoons and late evenings, playing games and drinking Augustiner beer in the bar.

Helmut wanted to hold an AFRC Bar Games Tournament and invite the best 2 players from several AFRC facilities. They would include Garmisch, Berchtesgaden, Chiemsee and Oberammergau. When he told everyone of his plan, Helmut suggested they hold it there at the NATO Officers Club.

"Helmut, do you need permission from the commander or anyone before you announce this tournament?" asked Eric.

"Hell no, this is the military," he replied. "They don't care what we do, providing we don't interfere with their operations or cause legal trouble."

The next 2 weeks went fast. The club was very busy since it was the height of ski season, and they had great snow conditions. Lucas, Helmut and Eric worked on the details and format for the tournament. They scheduled it to take place on a Sunday night because the bar usually cleared out early.

The AFRC Bar Games Tournament was set for March 12, 1972. There would be 3 sporting events: Foosball, 8-Ball Pool and 501 Darts. They considered Table Tennis, but they did not have enough space. Each team (or player for singles) plays all teams (or players) once. Champions are determined by most wins; if a tie occurs, they have a playoff. We will have doubles and singles' championships. Inga made 2 hand-carved wooden trophies. The club paid for the trophies and all the refreshments, using NATO petty cash.

Participants will be: Chip and John from Chiemsee, John Ferrell and Topo from Garmisch, Helmut and Lucas from Oberammergau, plus Gerhardt Grassl and Herr Drummer from Berchtesgaden. Eric will be the referee, scorekeeper, bartender and bouncer.

Eric told contestants the tournament rules and sequence of players. Lucas and Helmut's 1st event is foosball, their best game in bar sports.

Helmut talked about different names the game had acquired in various countries, over the years. "In Turkey, Foosball is called *Langirt.* France calls it *Bebe Pied* (baby's foot). Switzerland calls it *Kicker.* Hungary calls it *Csocso* (soccer). It is *Table Football* in the United Kingdom; *Futbolin* in Spain; and *Fussbal* in Germany."

Helmut continued with how Foosball started, "In the early nineteen sixties, a man named Lawrence Patterson was in the U.S. Military and stationed in West Germany. He knew table football was popular, and he had a table made to his specifications, by a manufacturer in Bavaria. He took his table back to the U.S. and trademarked the name *Foosball* without a uniform set of rules. However, other countries claim to have invented the game, including Germany, France and England."

Before the tournament started, Lucas and Topo went to Lucas' van and smoked hashish. "This is from a Sativa strain of marijuana which boosts your energy and concentration," said Topo.

"Perfect," replied Lucas.

Having read about each of the tournament games, their origins, rules and equipment, Lucas thought Topo would be interested in hearing how foosball came to different countries.

Lucas said, "Topo, I read about the controversy regarding who first invented foosball, and I know it is catching on in the United States, Europe and South America. Some people claim it came from Europe as a parlor game during the late eighteen hundreds.

"In another claim, Lucien Rosengart, a French engineer, invented foosball to keep his grandchildren entertained during the cold winters. Rosengart was an amateur inventor who had several patents, including the automobile seat belt and a rocket which exploded in the air.

“As the game became more popular, the French created miniature figures, attached them to poles, and stuck the poles through holes in the sides of the table. The table men had red, white and blue uniforms, and the French thought their superior inventiveness would certainly impress the rest of the world.

“The Spanish claim the real creator was Alexandre de Finesterre who invented the game while he was a patient in a Spanish Basque hospital. In the early thirties, Alexandre was recovering from injuries which occurred in a bombing during the Spanish Civil War. He asked a local carpenter to build a table which he designed, using the concept of table tennis. In nineteen thirty-seven, he got a patent on the table. However, he lost his paperwork in a storm while he was crossing the Pyrenees. Alexandre had also written a novel. The manuscript got damaged by rain during the same trip. So, he lost his manuscript and his foosball patent papers.

“Many years later, Alexandre de Finesterre was in Guatemala. In nineteen fifty-three, he built a mahogany foosball table and played often with Ernesto Che Guevara. Apparently, Che never beat him, but Alexandre never beat Che’s first wife, Hilda Gadea.

“In an interesting side story, Alexandre de Finesterre was flown back to Spain against his will in nineteen fifty-four, the result of a coup in Guatemala. He made a dummy bomb, wrapping a bar of soap in foil, and convinced the flight crew he was a Spanish refugee. They took him to Panama. Thus, he became one of the first airplane hijackers.

“An Englishman, Harold Searles Thornton, was an avid soccer fan. He worked on an idea for table soccer, using a big match box and laying wooden matches across it. He patented his table in nineteen twenty-two. His uncle saw the table and took the idea back to his home in the United States. Within a year, he got a U.S. patent on it.

“Eric, Helmut and I talked about all this, over a few beers one night, here at the bar. Eric told us about his friend in Missoula, Montana, one of the places Eric lived before he came to Europe. The man’s name is E. Lee Peppard, and he has been working on a new design for a foosball table, scheduled to start production sometime next year. His design includes a major change—he will make his tables using solid rods instead of the hollow ones which German manufacturers make. Peppard owns the Eight-Ball Billiards Tavern in Missoula, and he plans to use his tables in organized tournaments which will promote them.

“At the NATO Officers Club, we play on a German-made table. Germans use a soft wood for tables and foosmen, giving a player more control of the ball. Americans use a harder material for tables, such as mahogany wood, and they use hard plastic for foosmen. On American-made tables, the game is much faster and more of a power game instead of a finesse game which the French like to play. The French tables have a sticky linoleum surface and a cork ball for more controlled play. They put the emphasis on passing the ball and setting up shots, such as you do in real football. Italians surface their tables with sandblasted glass for faster play. They also make some with plastic laminate which slows the game, but it is easier to handle the ball.

"Most tables are four feet long and two feet wide. In the U.S., two teams have foosmen in set positions. Both teams have eleven foosmen. There are 3 attackers in front of five midfielders, and behind them are three strikers (two defensemen and one goalie). Each team has four rows, playing in one direction. The foosmen are made of wood, plastic, metal, or carbon fiber. The balls are made of marble, metal, cork, or plastic."

"You have done a lot of research on the game, Lucas; and it's all very interesting," said Topo.

Lucas and Topo returned to the bar. Eric surprised them when he said they would play against each other. Lucas and Helmut were partners. Topo and John Ferrell were teamed against them.

Helmut and Lucas knew nothing about their opponents' foosball skills, but they got off to a good start. When Helmut passed the ball back to Lucas' first defense line, Lucas drilled shots past all four lines of the opponent's defense: He went through them with the first shot straight in. The next 2 shots hit to either side of the table and ricocheted into the goal, passing right behind Topo's goalie.

This was like playing a warm-up game for Lucas and Helmut, and they won, 11 to 3. They both had put in hours of practice on this same table, so they had a definite home-field advantage.

Helmut had taught Lucas different shots, including a method of passing the ball side to side which he called a *tic tac shot*. Lucas' favorite shot was called a *snake shot*, and he had mastered it recently. For this shot, he would begin a spin (it is illegal to spin the player in a 360-degree circle), but he would use his wrist against the rubber handle and catch the handle with his hand before the spin completed a full circle. This was such a powerful shot, there was no defense for it. Then, there was a *total eclipse shot* which came from the back defense. He rolled the ball, using the foot of a foosman, and shot when he saw an opening. In a close game, he used this shot to kill his opponents' morale.

After foosball, Lucas would rotate to the dart board for singles play against Gerhardt who came from Berchtesgadener Hof. During a ski trip with Eric, Inga and Sabine in January, Lucas had stayed there and Gerhardt had introduced Lucas to his fellow chefs at the hotel.

All players in the tournament had competitive personalities and wanted to win. Yet, Lucas felt confident and thought he would do well.

Eric changed the music and played a Led Zeppelin song, "Stairway to Heaven." Gerhardt and Lucas each grabbed an Augustiner draft beer while they waited for Ferrell and Herr Drummer to finish their game.

Lucas sat at the bar and told Eric what he had learned about darts. He did not know if Eric was interested, but Eric appeared to be listening while he watched the activity and kept everyone's glass filled.

"Eric, do you know what dartboards are made of?" asked Lucas.

"I think they are made with camel hair," he replied.

"I've always thought the same thing," said Lucas. "But I learned the sisal plant, also known as a century plant, is used to make dartboards. It's a grass-type hemp, grown in Africa and China. I did research and found nothing to confirm camel hair was ever used for dartboards. Anyway, darts probably originated from spear-chucking Neanderthals. Some say it started in England during medieval times when archers sized down their arrows and used the bottom of wine barrels as targets. After World War Two, darts became popular in the U.S. when our soldiers returned from England and brought the game back with them. However, I also read the pilgrims brought darts on the Mayflower ship, coming to the United States two centuries earlier."

Eric nodded, as if he heard the whole story, but Lucas knew he was busy tending bar. Lucas and Gerhardt went outside behind the building to smoke hashish while they waited. They asked Eric to call them when John Ferrell and Herr Drummer finished their game of 501 Darts.

Gerhardt was tall and thin, about 6'3" and 180 lbs. He had dark blonde hair, neatly trimmed and shoulder length. Gerhardt looked like Lucas imagined an Aryan Nazi Storm Trooper might look. However, Gerhardt was a teddy bear with an easy smile.

Their conversation got awkward when Gerhardt told Lucas about his night life in Berchtesgaden, or across the border in Salzburg. He talked about a sex orgy which he enjoys sometimes, and he asked if Lucas would be interested when he returned for a visit in Berchtesgaden.

"Thank you for the kind invitation, Gerhardt," he replied. "But I am a one-woman-at-a-time guy, and group sex never interested me. However, I understand people have different tastes. When I come to visit, maybe we could go out to party and drink, instead."

"Oh good, Lucas. I would enjoy going out with you. I know some nice young women who love to party," said Gerhardt.

"Well, I am committed to my relationship with Inga. I think you met her during our visit at the start of the New Year," he replied.

"I do remember her, she is a very beautiful woman, and I don't blame you a bit," said Gerhardt. "She is from Bavaria, right?"

“Yes,” he replied. “Inga was born and raised in Oberammergau, and she has a woodcarving shop there.”

Glad to change the subject, Lucas said, “Oh, here comes Eric. It must be time for us to play.” Holding out the pipe to Eric, he said, “Hey! This is Topo’s finest hashish. Want a hit?”

“No thanks, I’ll stick to beer,” he said. “Someone has to keep score.”

Walking back in the bar, Lucas thought about Gerhardt: *What is it with Germans, orgies, porn and infidelity? Am I simply naïve?*

Then, he recalled a department store full of prostitutes in Frankfurt. *It seems so long ago when George and I arrived. I wonder if George will come back here. It would be fun to see him again.*

Before Lucas and Gerhardt played darts, Eric turned the music down and announced, “We use regulation measurements: the board height being 5 feet 8 inches (1.72 meters) from the floor to the center of the bullseye, and the throwing distance being 7 feet 9 1/4 inches (2.37 meters) from front of the dartboard to the throwing line. Each player gets three dart throws, per turn. Each player throws a dart, and the closest dart to the bullseye goes first. The next closest goes second, and so on.

“You have to *Double In* to begin the game, meaning only the outer double ring and the inner bull will allow scoring to begin. Scoring a *double bullseye* is 50 points, a *Single Bull* is worth 25 points, and each number on the board can score as a single, double or triple. The highest score on the board is a triple 20 for 60 points. A perfect game is called a *Nine-darter* and there are multiple ways you can accomplish it. One method is to get two 180 maximum scores (6 straight triple 20’s), plus finish with triple 20, triple 19 and double 12.

“In the game of 501 Darts, you will not only need a double to start, you will also need a double to finish the game. All players start with *501* points and try to reach zero. When a player scores more than he needs to reach zero, he *Busts* on the turn, and his score returns to the total he had at the start of the turn.”

It was time to play. Gerhardt never had a chance in this match since Lucas started off with a double 20, then threw a triple 20 and a single 20 for 381. Gerhardt threw 3 single 20’s. Lucas threw 1 more triple 20 and 2 single 20’s for a total of 281. Gerhardt threw a double 20 and 2 single 20’s for 361 points. Lucas had another triple 20, a single 20 and an errant 20 for 200. Since Gerhardt had warmed up, he threw a triple 20 and 2 single 20’s for a total of 261.

Lucas paused to finish half a glass of Augustiner beer and set his strategy. Then, he threw exactly what he intended to throw. 1 triple 20 and 2 singles again for 100 to make. Gerhardt hit 3 single 20’s for 201. Lucas missed the triple, but all 3 darts hit 20’s for 60 points. So, all he needed was a double 20 to finish. Gerhardt was still trailing after he threw another 60 for a total of 141.

Lucas missed his first shot at a double 20, hitting just outside the outer wire. He hit the next one just inside the left wire for the win.

Knowing he only played 17 darts, Lucas wondered: *Was this luck or skill?* Then, he realized: *There is no luck in this game. It takes skill. To go out in seventeen darts is not bad since nine darts is a perfect game.*

Next up, Lucas and Helmut would play 8-Ball Pool against Gerhardt and Herr Drummer. Lucas appreciated the competitive spirit of these guys, and they all seemed to have a good time.

Looking around the room, Lucas thought of the people: *What a great group this is. They are all drinking beer and Jägermeister, playing and having fun. No one seems to care about the time. It is two a.m., and we have a long way to go before we declare a tournament champion.*

Lucas had spent many a night and early morning shooting pool with his Long Beach buddy, George, and some other beach people who he used to hang out with. George was a great pool player, and Lucas had learned a lot from him. Lucas even beat him from time to time.

He and Helmut would need all of Lucas' skills, playing against Chip and John who played as though they spent plenty of time in bars and pool halls. Lucas knew they had access to a pool table, and they played on a regular basis in the game room at the Chiemsee Hotel.

Lucas became street wise by necessity; although crime and drugs were not prevalent in the 1950s. Since the late 1960s and now in the early 1970s, crime and drugs seem to be everywhere. For the most part, Lucas had been on his own since he was 12 years old. He was the youngest of seven children. When his mom went into the hospital for a hysterectomy, his dad left which led to a move across town and a change of schools. Lucas made friends with a guy named Al Cropsie who only had 1 arm and was 5 years older than Lucas. Al taught him how to shoot pool, drive a car, play 3rd base and got him interested in girls. At age 16, Lucas made a fake ID for himself and went to bars. He learned all the bar games: pool, darts, table tennis, pinball and shuffleboard. Foosball was not popular until the mid-sixties.

Now age 31, Lucas could hold his own in bar games. He was also good at baseball, fast-pitch softball, basketball, flag football and tennis. While he had only skied for 3 years, he showed great improvement since he skied in Europe with Gino, Inga and Sabine, his expert friends.

Eric went over rules of the game which he read from his rule book, *"Eight-ball is played with a cue stick for each player and sixteen balls. A cue ball and fifteen object balls, consisting of seven striped balls, seven solid-colored balls and the black eight-ball. After the balls are scattered by a break shot, players are assigned to either the group of solid balls or the stripes, based on the first ball being pocketed legally from one group. The ultimate object of the game is to pocket the eight-ball in a called pocket. It can only be done after all the player's assigned balls have been cleared off the table legally."*

After a sip of beer, he continued reading, *"To start the game, the object balls are placed in a triangular rack. The base of the rack is parallel to the end rail (the short end of the pool table) and positioned so the apex ball of the rack is on the foot spot. Ideally, the balls in the rack are placed in contact with one another. This is accomplished by pressing the balls together from the back of the rack toward the apex ball. The order of the racked balls should be random, with the following exceptions: the eight-ball must be placed in the center of the rack, a striped ball must be placed in one back corner, and a solid ball in the other back corner. The cue ball is placed inside the kitchen anywhere the breaker desires. The kitchen is the square area marked by the first and third diamonds on the end rail and the side rail. The cue ball cannot hit any balls on or before the kitchen line after a scratch.*

"The first shooter is chosen by a lag, a win or loss of previous game, or a coin flip. He or she uses a cue stick to break the object ball rack apart. If the shooter who breaks fails to make a legal break, defined as at least four balls hitting cushions or an object ball being pocketed, the opponent can call for a re-rack and become the breaker, or he can elect to play from the current position of the balls.

"According to World Standardized Rules: If the eight-ball goes in a pocket on the break without fouling, the breaker may ask for a re-rack and break again, or have the eight-ball spotted and continue to shoot with the cue ball in hand behind the head string, leaving other balls as they lie. If the breaker scratches or pockets the cue ball, the incoming player may call for a re-rack and break, or have the eight-ball spotted and shoot with the cue ball in hand behind the head string, leaving other balls as they lie.

"Once all a player's or team's group of object balls are pocketed, they may attempt to sink the eight-ball. To win, a player must first designate which pocket he plans to sink the eight-ball into, then shoot the eight-ball in the called pocket. If the eight-ball falls into any pocket other than the one designated, or if it is knocked off the table, this results in loss of game, except if the eight-ball goes into a pocket on the break without fouling.

"After the break is completed, a shooter loses the game if any of the following things occur:

- *Pockets the eight-ball on same stroke as the last of his balls.*
- *Jumps the eight-ball off the table at any time.*
- *The eight-ball in a pocket other than the one designated.*

- *Pockets the eight-ball when it is not the legal object ball."*

When Gerhardt and Herr Drummer won the 8-Ball game against Lucas and Helmut, Lucas said, "Congratulations to the winners. Now, if you will excuse us, the chefs will go to the kitchen and bring out some tapas."

Lucas, Herr Drummer and Gerhardt (the chefs) put the final touches on colorful platters of tapas. At the early morning hour of 3:30 a.m., they set each platter along the bar, plus plates, napkins and silverware. The 9 feeling-no-pain bar athletes were hungry and ready to eat.

Explaining what each tapa was, Lucas said, "Starting on this end, we have fried calamari and miniature Reuben sandwiches." Pointing to the next oval platter, he said, "These are squares of eggplant and zucchini, stuffed with wild mushroom duxelles."

"What is duxelles?" asked John Reilly.

"Duxelles is a minced preparation of mushrooms," replied Lucas, "combined with finely diced onions, shallots and herbs. The mixture is sautéed in butter to a dry, pasty consistency. Using domestic or wild mushrooms is a matter of taste. I sometimes add cream to tone down the strong flavor of wild mushrooms. One of its many uses, duxelles makes a good coating on Beef Wellington."

Lucas stopped in front of the next item and described a platter of Sauvignon Steak Hors d'oeuvres which Herr Held had sent over from Berchtesgadener Hof. When Lucas, Inga, Eric and Sabine were visiting there, they sampled it, and Lucas loved the medium-rare, thin slices of beef tenderloin, topped with a delightful cheddar cheese, roasted red pepper and brandy sauce, all served on a toasted slice of baguette.

Music came on, and Lucas had to speak loudly, over "American Woman," a song by The Guess Who, a Canadian rock group.

"The tortilla chips, guacamole and salsa were made in-house," he said. "These are breast of chicken pinwheels with pesto and creamed cheese.

"Last, we have my own recipe for pizza with roasted plum tomatoes, goat cheese, Kalamata olives and caramelized sweet onions. I worked on this pizza crust for several years. Now, I finally perfected it—right here at the NATO Officers Club in Oberammergau." Everyone watched Lucas pick up a slice of pizza, eat a small bite and offer his opinion.

"It's a little chewy, crispy on the bottom, and light in texture with air pockets scattered throughout the crust," he said.

The room erupted with cheers and the beer-drinking, indoor athletes dug into the delicious array, an Oberammergau version of tapas, presented by Lucas, Herr Drummer and Gerhardt.

At 4:30 a.m., the beer and bullshit still flowed and games continued. So far, Chip and John Riley were undefeated in doubles semi-finals. Next, they play foosball against Gerhardt and Herr Drummer in the doubles' championship round for the doubles' trophy.

Also, there were now only four contestants in the singles' semi-finals. By each of their actions, Lucas could tell they all hated to lose as much as he did. This is war! It does not matter if your opponent is a girlfriend, a best friend or your mother; winning is everything. Lucas will have to square off against 1 of his new friends, John Ferrell, in a game of 501 Darts. John is a competitor, like Lucas and the rest of this group. The other semi-final will be Chip against Gerhardt at the foosball table; it should be a lively match.

The 2 winning singles will then move to a final game of 8-Ball Pool, the singles' championship round.

Lucas caught Topo's eye, pointed toward the kitchen and mimicked smoking. Both went out back to smoke Topo's fine hashish. Lucas and Topo had become good friends since their first meeting in Nice.

"How is Olivia?" asked Lucas.

"You know Olivia. She is a blast," he replied. "I love Australian women. I've never had so much fun, as I've had since coming to Garmisch and living among these great people. No matter where you came from, this AFRC group seems to be one big family. Lucas, I hope you have no hard feelings about me and Olivia. I know how close you were when you were traveling in Morocco and Cervenia."

"Topo, I think the world of you and Olivia," said Lucas. "I'm glad you got together. Now, I see both of you more often. I've been living with Inga for a while, and it is getting serious between us. Maybe it's time for us to make a commitment to a lasting relationship."

"It is so amazing here," he replied. "Bavaria seems to be home base for travelers like you and me, coming from different places in the world. I've met people from Australia, the U.S., Canada, South Africa, England, Ireland, Scotland and most of the other European nations."

"Where exactly are you from, Topo?" asked Lucas.

"You know I'm from Argentina, right?" he replied.

"Yeah, but we never talked about your youth there, or your travels from there to here," said Lucas.

"I was very fortunate to grow up in the best ski area in Argentina, a village called San Martin de los Andes which is close to the Chilean border," he replied. "The area gets a lot of snow and periodic storms, otherwise the weather is sunny and beautiful. The Andes Mountains serve to protect the village. I received a good education, and I earned a degree in economics at the Universidad de Buenos Aires. I traveled to Europe right after graduation. In Argentina, there is a lot of political unrest which has gone on quite a while, between the communist left and the Peronist right government. I've lost track of the political jockeying there, and I have no plans to go back, anytime soon."

Looking at their surroundings of forest and mountains, right before daybreak, Topo added, "Anyway, how could I leave this?"

Lucas laughed before he replied, "I've met quite a few recent college grads who are working here and traveling. Another great thing about Garmisch is its central location in Europe. You can drive to a completely different culture in a matter of hours."

Since he was curious, Lucas asked, "Topo, I've been learning a lot about World War Two and the Nazis, but I know little about what happened at the end. For instance, which Nazi higher-ups escaped to South America? Do you know anything about it?"

"Oh, I did a lot of skiing with my family, and we vacationed in Bariloche, Patagonia," he replied. "In my youth, I became friendly with the locals and heard many stories about Nazis who escaped capture and came to South America.

"Much later, I became acquainted with Erich Priebke, a former SS Hauptsturmführer. It is rumored he took part in the massacre of three hundred and thirty-five people at the Ardeatine Caves in Rome; the massacre was in retaliation for an attack led by the Resistance against the Nazis. Priebke arrived in Argentina with a Vatican passport. I heard a story about a pro-Nazi bishop in Rome who arranged for Nazis to be smuggled out of Italy. The Pope approved it, and the Catholic Church helped create an escape route to South America. Priebke and many other Nazi higher-ups have settled there."

"What is Bariloche like, and where is it, Topo?" asked Lucas.

"Bariloche became a German Alpine colony," he replied. "Many of the transplanted Bavarians say being there feels like they never left the Alps. Erich Priebke and other Nazis seem to have the protection of a group, or multiple groups, such as the Vatican, the Mossad (Israeli Intelligence Agency), or even the American CIA."

"Why would the American CIA help them?" asked Lucas.

"I heard the CIA got involved in exchange for access to Nazi war technology," he replied. "Also, there were stories about Adolph Hitler and his wife Eva Braun who faked their suicides, escaped to Spain, and made it to Argentina. Supposedly, they lived in the Bariloche area, each with a new identity and change of appearance."

Topo paused for a moment, then said, "German styles of Bavaria are copied in Bariloche. I fell in love with their ski resort and the German food in their restaurants. So, I came to see the real Bavaria for myself, and I am not disappointed at all."

"I know what you mean," said Lucas. "I also can't see leaving here. Has anyone ever claimed they actually saw Hitler in Argentina?"

"I have not talked to anyone who saw Hitler or his wife. But I read about Joseph Stalin who claimed Hitler escaped to South America in nineteen forty-five," he replied. "In Bariloche, Erich Priebke owns a hotel, and he also has a delicatessen which specializes in sausage and other German menu items. He uses his real name and does not seem concerned about who knows of his past. He has been the director of the German school in Bariloche for several years. I heard they have a private party to celebrate Hitler's birthday on April twentieth every year; but I've never talked to anyone who went to it."

"April twenty. I think the date has some connection to marijuana." said Lucas. "I don't know what it is, or I can't remember."

"One of my business associates told me a story about guys who are known as Waldos in San Rafael, California," he replied. "They got named for hanging out and smoking pot at a wall near their high school. The Waldos searched for an abandoned marijuana crop in the hills around San Rafael. Every afternoon at four twenty, they met at a statue of Louis Pasteur on school grounds. They went to the wall, smoked pot, and then went looking for the abandoned crop which they never found. Since then, *Four Twenty* is a code word for marijuana use."

"What sports did you play growing up?" asked Lucas.

"My first sport, besides learning how to ride a horse, was football which Americans call soccer," he replied. "Later, I played basketball, tennis and volleyball. I also did a lot of sailing."

"What is Argentina's national sport?" asked Lucas.

"You won't believe this," he said. "A game called *Pato* (duck) is played on horseback, using a ball like a soccer ball, but it is encased in a round, wooden framework with two handles. While riding a horse at a fast clip, any player can grab a handle and try to wrestle the ball from the player who has the ball. It is a dangerous and sometimes brutal sport."

"What is the object of the game and what does 'Pato' have to do with it?" asked Lucas.

"The game combines the skills of basketball and polo," he replied. "The object of the game is for a rider with the ball to put it in the opponents' net. The net is attached to a three-foot-diameter ring and mounted on a pole which is over seven feet high. When the sport first began, they used a live duck instead of a ball. Can you imagine a tug-of-war on horseback—with a live duck?"

After a good, hard laugh, Lucas asked, "Did you have role models or heroes when you were growing up?"

"There were a few good football players, and we had Che Guevara. Do you know much about Ernesto Che Guevara?" he asked.

"I only know he was involved in the Cuban revolution," said Lucas.

"Okay, let me tell you a little about the most popular Argentinean of them all, in my book." Topo began his story, "Che studied at the University of Buenos Aires, the same school I went to. On campus, students talked about him as if he were a God. Che Guevara was from a well-to-do family, and he was raised in Rosario which is a large city, three hundred kilometers northwest of Buenos Aires. He became many things during the short time he lived. He was a doctor of medicine, an author, a revolutionary leader and a common soldier, willing to fight and even die for the poor people.

"In nineteen fifty, while he was a student at the university, he took off on a bicycle with a small motor attached, and he traveled around Northern Argentina. On this trip, he discovered his compassion for the huge number of poor and underprivileged people, not only in Argentina, but all-over Latin America. When he returned, Che and a classmate got inspired to see other countries. They bought used motorcycles, traveled around South America and became troubled by living conditions of the poor people. During this long, hard trip, he outlined his dream of seeing Latin America become united without borders and have a Marxist-style government. Following the trip, Che went back to the university and earned his degree as a Doctor of Medicine.

"Later, Che met Raúl and Fidel Castro in Mexico City, and he joined their cause—to overthrow Batista in Cuba. Che was impressive, so Castro promoted him to Second-in-Command. Che was instrumental in their success after two years of guerrilla warfare. While in Cuba, he also served in other capacities, including his work as the National Bank President.

"In nineteen sixty-five, Che left Cuba, traveled to other countries and promoted his revolutionary ideas. While he was in Bolivia, he was captured by Bolivian forces who were backed by the CIA. As a result of the capture, Che was executed. Although some people believed he fought for a good cause, others viewed him as a ruthless rebel who used excessive violence in his campaigns."

Topo concluded his story, saying, "In my opinion, Che Guevara was one of the most influential people of this century."

The story of Che sounds like a story of the RAF, thought Lucas, *given revolutionary ideals proclaimed by Andreas, Ulrike and Gudrun.*

Taking his last puff on the pipe and passing it to Topo, Lucas said, "We had better get back inside. I want another beer, and it might be time for my dart game against John Ferrell. Thanks, Topo. I want to hear more about Patagonia and your trip to Garmisch, sometime."

Walking back inside, Lucas thought of John Ferrell, his next opponent: *John calls himself Ferrelli. Working as an employee in Garmisch, he is an exception because he does not drink beer at work. Most everyone else does. Although, when John Ferrell drinks, he drinks a lot, and he does not let his friends pay for drinks while he is drinking. He is a scholarly person with a Mathematics Degree from Boston University. John can read and write the Russian language, something he learned while he was in the U.S. Army, stationed at a base in Vicenza, Italy. He also gained the name Ferrelli and his knowledge of the Italian language in Vicenza.*

As Topo and Lucas got back to the bar, Eric said, "You missed a great foosball game. Chip and John Riley won the doubles' trophy."

"Well, I'm not surprised since they spend a lot of time in the game room at Lake Chiemsee Hotel," replied Lucas. "I imagine Gerhardt and Herr Drummer gave them a good run."

Getting back to the tournament, it was early morning. Everyone had consumed a lot of beer, but they were still going strong. Lucas and John began their semi-final game of 501 Darts, exchanging trash talk. Then, they wished each other luck. John appeared to be sober until he threw darts like he was drunk. Lucas won easily, although it took over 30 darts to *Double Out* with a double 4. At the foosball table, Chip defeated Gerhardt, 15-13 and 11-9, in their semi-final game.

The final singles match was Lucas and Chip, playing 8-Ball Pool for one of Inga's hand-carved wooden trophies. The first player to win 2 games would be the Singles Tournament Champion at the First Annual AFRC Bar Games Tournament.

Lucas squared off against Chip, and trash talk began the minute they got to the table, but it was in good humor, and they all had a laugh. Lucas broke first and sank the 1-ball solid, but he left a tight pack. Then, he tried a combination, but he missed sinking the 7-ball in the corner pocket. Chip then missed his solid, and Lucas missed a long corner shot. Chip knocked in the 9 and 15 and missed the 11 again. They both missed their next shots, and then both took long pulls on their beers. Lucas made the 2-ball in the corner. Chip made a nice double bank shot on the 13-ball and made a long corner 12-ball. Lucas made the 3-ball in the corner, railed the 7-ball into the corner pocket, and set up his last 3 balls at the opposite end from where he left the cue ball. Lucas made a difficult try on a corner bank which left Chip with no shot, and Chip hit the wrong ball. Lucas made a long corner 4-ball. Both missed their next shots, jockeying for position. Lucas made the 5-ball for an easy shot in the corner pocket, and he made a great lag on the 6-ball to the far corner which dribbled into the pocket. After Lucas missed a shot, Chip missed again. Lucas put Chip out of his misery as he banked the 8-ball off the end rail, and everyone watched it run back to the corner pocket for the win.

Chip broke to start the 2nd game, and he barely missed making the 1-ball. Lucas made the 1-ball and broke the cluster, but he missed on the 3-ball. Chip broke a cluster of four balls and almost scratched. After a Lucas miss, Chip made a nice double bank on the 9 and another good shot on the 14 in the side pocket. Lucas then made the 2-ball in the corner, but he missed on another corner shot. Chip double-banked both the 10 and the 12. Lucas missed another easy bank shot. Chip double-banked the 11 in the corner. Lucas missed his shot again and shook his head as he watched Chip scratch the cue ball in the side pocket. Lucas took advantage, and he made the 3-ball in the corner, but he missed the next shot with a double kiss off the 4-ball. Chip missed his bank for the side pocket. Lucas ran the 4-ball down the rail, into the corner pocket, and the 5-ball into the same pocket. Ending it, Chip ran the last 3 balls and won the second game.

Lucas went to the bathroom and stepped outside for a quick hit on his hash pipe. When he returned, he grabbed another beer from Eric.

The other guys stopped playing, or whatever they were doing. They grabbed another beer from the bar and gathered around the pool table.

Chip and Lucas chalked their cues; and they each said, "Prost." After a swig of their beer, the final game was on.

Lucas broke. He made the 1 and the 5, but missed the 2-ball to the side pocket. Chip sank the 13-ball in the side pocket and the 9-ball in the corner; then, he kissed the 11-ball into the side pocket, but he missed the 14. Lucas missed the 7 to the corner, but the 6-ball went in the other corner. Now, they each had made three balls. Lucas made an easy corner shot on the 4-ball, but he just missed a corner shot on the 3. Lucas led four balls to Chip's three. Chip tried a difficult combination shot on the 10 and the 14 without success. After both players tried and missed tricky shots, Lucas made a long shot on the 3-ball which rattled into the corner hole. Lucas had no remaining shot at all, so he nudged the 2-ball into position. Chip made the 12-ball in the corner pocket and the 10-ball went next; then, he made the 15-ball in the side, followed by the 14 in the corner pocket. All Chip had to do was make the 8-ball in the corner for the win. Everyone gasped when the ball rattled out of the hole. Lucas sank both the 2-ball and the 7-ball, then kissed the 8 into the corner pocket for the win.

As the Singles Tournament Champion, Lucas picked up his hand-carved trophy. Everyone groaned instead of cheering. Lucas shrugged and said, "That was tough luck, Chip. But I don't make the rules."

Chip flashed a big smile and said, "Congratulations, Lucas. I will get even with you this summer on the tennis courts at Chiemsee. Or, maybe we will play in Berchtesgaden."

"Okay, Chip, you're on," he replied.

After Chip and Lucas shook hands, Chip said to Lucas, "I'm sure we will meet again."

"I'll be looking forward to it," he replied. "I'm so glad you came to play with us."

"I'm also glad I came," said Chip. "This was a lot of fun. We should schedule a summer tournament to take place at Lake Chiemsee Hotel in the downstairs game room."

"A Chiemsee tournament sounds great," said Lucas. "I hope to play tennis there. When I came to visit, the courts were covered in snow."

"We have a fun tennis program in the summer," said Chip.

"You have some tough military duty," he replied. "Winter ski patrol and summer tennis by the lake."

"I know, but somebody's got to do it," said Chip. "John Reilly also has it rough, teaching people how to sail and managing the sailboat dock in the summer. If you would come and take over the kitchen, we would have everything covered. With our friend Shelley as the head housekeeper, Gunther as the head bartender and Clarkson as the hotel manager, the hotel would be like Club Med for all the employees and ski patrol."

At 6:30 a.m., Eric, Lucas and Helmut jumped in and cleaned the bar. Herr Drummer made fast work of cleaning the kitchen because Kurt and Herr Becker would soon arrive to prepare for breakfast service.

Hearing a loud knock on the kitchen door, Helmut opened it.

There stood CID Officer Robinson. He said, "I want to speak with Lucas Gary if he is here."

"Please come in," said Helmut. "It's cold outside. He is in the bar."

As Helmut pointed toward the bar, Robinson said, "I know where it is. I've been here many times, thank you."

Lucas was at the bar with a few guys. Other guys were scattered around the room. Everyone felt tired, but they were still drinking beer, joking and laughing. When Lucas saw Robinson entering the bar from the kitchen, he let all the air out of his lungs at once. Whenever he sees Robinson, it means trouble.

There are only a few people I dislike, and this guy is right down there with Bruno, thought Lucas.

As Robinson came toward him, Lucas stood and excused himself from Eric and the guys at the bar.

Lucas started walking. When he reached Robinson, he slowed a little, but he kept moving toward the kitchen as he said, "If you are here to talk with me, please follow me."

CHAPTER 26

Garmisch: Transitions

Robinson followed Lucas through the kitchen at NATO Officers Club. Not caring what Robinson wanted at this hour, Lucas was tired, so he wanted to get this over with, and he was walking fast.

Lucas stopped, just inside the back door, and checked the bathrooms to make sure they were alone.

"Okay, what can I do for you?" asked Lucas.

"Yesterday I had a talk with Bruno Castignoli," he replied. "After you came to work here, Bruno worked here for a short time. So, I know you are acquainted with him."

"I first met Bruno while playing basketball at the gym in Garmisch," said Lucas.

"I'm looking into the backgrounds of some civilian employees who work for AFRC," said Robinson, "and people around military facilities who have any questionable events in their history. I found out you and Castignoli are both from Long Beach, California."

Robinson waited before speaking again. He seemed to be waiting for an answer. When Lucas did not respond, he continued, "I also learned you were both acquainted with a murder victim in Long Beach. The young lady was beaten to death, and her body was found floating in a canal there, over a year ago."

"What does all of this have to do with me?" asked Lucas.

"The young lady was engaged to a Lucas Gary," he replied.

He added, "Bruno Castignoli is a former boyfriend of the deceased. He is also the main person of interest in her murder… Both of you ending up here in Bavaria sure seems to be an odd coincidence."

"I didn't know Bruno in Long Beach," said Lucas. "Like I told you, the first time I met him was at the gym in Garmisch. Jordan Lewis, the bouncer at The Grill, is also from Long Beach, and we only met last year in Garmisch."

"Bruno said the same thing when I told him about the police report from Long Beach," said Robinson.

Perceiving this as a warning sign, Lucas said, "I don't know what you are trying to accomplish, but I don't want to be involved. You are speaking about a part of my life which is behind me, and I intend to leave it there. Is there anything else you want to talk about?"

"Yes. Try to stay out of trouble, Gary," he replied. "And remember, I'll be keeping an eye on both of you guys."

"Have a great day, Robinson," said Lucas, opening the back door and showing Robinson the way out from the kitchen.

Lucas walked back inside. Eric was the only person left in the bar. He was washing the last of the glasses when he looked at Lucas.

"The rest of the guys headed over to the barracks. They all need to get some sleep before driving back to their homes," said Eric.

Lucas' mind was somewhere else. "I've got to talk to you, Eric," he said. "Would you pour us each a beer? Robinson told me something, and it is really bothering me."

Eric put the last clean glass on the shelf under the bar, and filled two half-liter glasses with Augustiner beer, both with perfect, creamy heads. Then, he came around from behind the bar, and he sat sideways on a bar stool, facing Lucas.

"Guten morgen, Herr Lucas," Eric said as he raised his glass.

"Guten morgen, Herr Eric. Prost," replied Lucas.

After a long drink of his beer, Lucas said, "Robinson told Bruno I came from Long Beach and was engaged to Jodie. She was found dead in a canal, beaten to death, and I think Bruno did it. I have been very careful to not let Bruno know who I am or learn I've been tracking him. Now, Robinson has been snooping around where he doesn't belong. If Bruno realizes I am after him for killing Jodie, he may try to get at me in any way he can. So, I am concerned."

"Wow, are you kidding me?" asked Eric, looking shocked.

"No," replied Lucas. "Robinson confirmed Bruno is the main suspect since he is an old boyfriend of Jodie's, and he has a history of abuse. He also said Bruno has ties to the mafia."

Lucas stopped for a moment, took a deep breath and said, "I need to call Inga, warn her we may be in danger, and tell her I will be right over. Then, I'll try to figure out what to do about Mr. Bruno."

Eric handed Lucas the phone from under the bar, and Lucas dialed Inga's number. There was no answer which alarmed Lucas. Inga should be awake, and she should hear the phone ring, even from the shower, because her phone rings very loud.

"I have to get over there and check on her," said Lucas.

"I'll follow you for backup," said Eric.

Lucas made it to Inga's house in record time. Eric was right on his tail all the way, driving a light-brown van which Bob Ostergaard sold to him, recently. Inga's car was in the carport. Both Lucas and Eric hurried to the front door which was unlocked. Lucas pushed it open and passed through the entrance hall, shouting, "Inga, Mein Schatz, I won your beautiful wood-carved trophy so…"

Lucas stopped abruptly as he stood at Inga's bedroom door and saw the nightstand overturned. He opened the door wider. The bedroom scene was so shocking, Lucas thought it was not real, and he felt as if things were happening in slow motion. Eric came and stood behind Lucas. Neither one could move. They were frozen with disbelief at the horrific sight. Inga was on the floor with her head in a pool of drying blood.

Eric grabbed Lucas by the arms, pulled him back into the living room and sat him in a chair. Next, Eric called the German police.

The police arrived and questioned Lucas and Eric. They both told the police everybody who knew Inga loved her; she was a very kind person. Neither of them said anything about who might have done this. The police got their contact information, and then they let Lucas grab a few of his personal things from the house.

Lucas and Eric drove their respective vans with care, making their way to Garmisch where they could find a place to stay and get some much overdue sleep. They arrived at the Sheridan Hotel, asked for a room with twin beds, got checked in and slept for a solid 8 hours.

They awoke and got dressed, then used the phone in the room.

Lucas called Sonya at The Last Chance. He told her what happened to Inga and said he needed to talk to her as soon as she could get to the Sheridan. Lucas did not want to go out in public until he resolved his situation with Bruno. Sonya promised she would be there in an hour, and she would bring dinner from The Last Chance kitchen.

Eric called Sabine and broke the news about Inga, her best friend. He told her they suspect Bruno killed her, trying to get at Lucas. They thought Bruno got frustrated because Lucas did not come home all night—he was in the tournament at the officers' club.

Sabine got hysterical, and she wanted to come to Garmisch. Lucas got on the phone and calmed her down. He told her not to come now because he was putting the plan together, and they would be in Seefeld to execute it, very soon.

An hour later, Sonya knocked on the door of their room. When Eric opened it, she walked in and set down a box of packaged dinners, plus 6 half-liter bottles of Spaten beer. When she turned around, she fell into Lucas' arms. They hugged and both let loose, crying like babies. Next, Eric began to cry.

Realizing what they were doing, they all started laughing at the same time as they were crying.

Raising their beers, they all gave a tearful toast, "To Inga." Then, Lucas lit his hash pipe and passed it to Sonya.

"If I ever had any misgivings about what we plan to do to Bruno, they are all gone now," said Lucas. "I only wish we could do something more painful. If everything works out as we expect, our plan is a good one. Hopefully, the police will realize Bruno murdered Inga and assume he disappeared. I believe we have found the best method to dispose of such a piece of garbage."

"Are you still in for this?" asked Lucas, looking at Sonya.

"Yes, more than ever," she replied. "I want to see him beg and suffer for what he has done."

"Do you know how you will get him to Seefeld?" asked Lucas.

"I will tell him it is important for me to talk with him; and I'll say I want to go skiing with him again," she replied.

While Eric was in the bathroom, Sonya spoke to Lucas, "The RAF people are coming, any day now, and Andreas asked me to get in touch with you. They want you to stay with them. Gabrielle will also be here. They know you are going through a terrible time."

"A visit with them might work out for me," said Lucas. "I have to tell Gabrielle about Bruno; we think he killed her friend in Formentera. I can only hope the house doesn't get raided while we are there. Right now, I care little about anything else; and I will not be satisfied until I know Bruno is taken care of."

"I'll set it up, Lucas, as soon as I can," she promised.

Eric came back and joined them. "I'm sorry, but I'm ready to dig into the food Sonya brought for us," he said.

Sonya opened a plate of Sauerbraten (marinated beef in a rich, tart and spicy sauce), a plate of Jäger Schnitzel (pork cutlet smothered in a cream sauce, made with white wine, onions and mushrooms), and Weisswurst (a white sausage), plus red cabbage and buttered spaetzle.

Lucas had no appetite, given his difficult, emotional state. Yet, he tasted everything and told Sonya how delicious it was. Before she left, she promised to meet him at the house in the woods by 10 a.m.

The next morning, Lucas and Eric gathered their stuff together and checked out of the Sheridan. Eric called Sabine and headed to Seefeld, wanting to give her support for losing Inga, her closest friend. Lucas drove over to the house on Griesener Straße.

Sonya was unlocking the front door when Lucas arrived at 10 a.m. He always made it a point to be prompt for any appointment. Since he did not like to be kept waiting, Lucas arrived early, most of the time, as a courtesy to others. Sonya greeted him with a hug.

Today, this familiar house was so quiet it felt eerie.

"Do you know any history of this house?" Lucas asked Sonya.

"Yes. I do, in fact," she replied. "You should get settled in your room. It is upstairs, the last room on the right. Then, we can have a beer, and I'll tell you about the house."

Lucas went to the van, got his stuff and took it to the room. He put things away and went back downstairs. Sonya had started a fire in the blue-and-white-tile fireplace, and she had moved 2 comfortable chairs over in front of the fire. She handed him a glass of Spaten beer.

As they sat, Sonya said, "It's beginning to snow outside."

"I hope we have a snowy day for our Seefeld trip," said Lucas.

When he pulled out his hash pipe, Lucas lit it and passed it to Sonya. After taking a hit and passing it back to him, she asked, "Why do you smoke dope, Lucas?"

"I enjoy it because it makes everything better, including music, food, sex, skiing, creativity and concentration," he replied. "I was hyperactive in my youth. I still have excess energy, but pot helps me keep it under control, and it makes me feel how I want to feel."

"Why do you like to smoke marijuana?" he asked.

"I began smoking pot when I was on the ski team at school because most of the team did," she replied. "And I loved the feeling I got when we smoked it together. As a group, it became hilarious. Also, I agree with you about food, music and sex."

"To sum it up," said Lucas, "Smoking marijuana or hashish enhances the pleasures of life. I do not use it to escape bad things, but rather to enhance good things. It also seems to expand my mind."

"You know, Sonya, I haven't met too many people, under the age of thirty, who don't smoke pot," he added.

"Come to think of it, I haven't either," she said. "My mother has tried it, but she doesn't have time for it since she is running the restaurant. Now, you asked about this house. Most of the outside is original, except for some repairs and paint…"

The phone rang which interrupted her.

Sonya went into the kitchen, answered the call, then returned and said, "It was Gabrielle. She said they will arrive in about an hour. I will stay and wait with you until they get here and everyone gets settled. Before you arrived, I stocked the refrigerator with food. If you need something else, Gabrielle can go to the store since the police are not really looking for her now. She said the group would love for you to cook, but if you don't feel up to it, they would understand."

"I will be happy to cook a nice meal for them," replied Lucas. "If I don't stay busy, I'll go crazy."

He lit the hash pipe again as Sonya brought 2 more Spaten beers from the kitchen. After they both took a hit on the pipe, she told Lucas about the house while she gave him a tour. They went from room to room, drinking their beers as they strolled.

"Richard Strauss was a Bavarian music composer and conductor, known worldwide for his music, operas and tone poems," said Sonya. "He wrote his first music when he was six years old, and he wrote his first opera at age nineteen. He was born in Munich, but spent most of his adult life at his home in Garmisch—this home. His mother was from a wealthy family, the Pschorr Brewery family of Munich, to be exact.

"Richard Strauss paid for this house with money he made from three of his operas, *Salome, Elektra* and *Der Rosenkavalier.* He hired a well-known German architect, Emanuel von Seidl, who designed the house, using Strauss' specifications. The builders created this place for him to compose his music, entertain his guests and enjoy being with his family. He had one son, Franz, who married a Jewish lady, Alice, which proved to be a problem during the Nazi regime. The Gestapo abducted Alice and her husband, twice. Since Richard Strauss had been appointed President of the Nazi Music Bureau, he used his position and gained their release. However, after they returned to Garmisch, Franz and Alice had to spend the rest of the war under house arrest. Unfortunately, Alice's mother remained in the Theresienstadt concentration camp, and Strauss could not secure her release. He wrote several letters to the SS command, but he never received a reply."

They walked into a long hallway and past the dining room which was on their left. Behind the stairway on their right, there was a salon or sitting room. Next, they came to Strauss' library and study where he composed. They walked through the study, then to the left and into a short passageway which led them to the dining room. From there Sonya pointed out the adjoining *Erker* (cove) where Strauss drank afternoon tea and played Skat, a card game he enjoyed playing with his friends. Sometimes, he would take a nap in there.

"Richard Strauss' son Franz had two sons, Richard and Christian," said Sonya. "My mother and Christian are friends, but he doesn't come around much. So, my mother is the custodian of the house when he is away. Being an opportunist, my mother collects rent from the RAF when they want to use the house. She has been the caretaker here since nineteen forty-four. She brings in cleaners when the house is used, and she oversees gardeners in the summer months."

"Tell me about Strauss' mother and the brewery," said Lucas.

"I'm not sure if it was the first brewery in Munich," she replied. "It began around fourteen seventeen. Joseph Pschorr, the owner of Pschorr Brewery, married Therese Hacker. Her father owned Hacker Brewery which was also located in Munich. Joseph Pschorr bought the Hacker Brewery from Therese's father. After Joseph died, his son George oversaw the whole business. When George passed it on, each of his two sons took control of a brewery. One son operated Pschorr, and the other son operated Hacker.

"The Pschorr Beer story has an interesting side story which relates to Crown Prince Ludwig. For his wedding celebration in the early eighteen hundreds, Ludwig commissioned the brewmaster of Pschorr Brewery to develop a special beer for the event which took place in Munich. It became an annual celebration, known as Oktoberfest. Now, the Hacker-Pschorr Brewery is one of only six breweries with privileges to serve beer at the Munich Oktoberfest."

"Wait, I think I can name the other five," said Lucas. "I've tried them all. Augustiner Bräu which we serve in the AFRC bars and restaurants, Hofbräuhaus, Spaten, Löwenbräu—aaaaand Paulaner."

"Spoken like a true Bavarian, Lucas," said Sonya.

"Do you know what's been going on with the RAF?" he asked.

"Oh, there have been bank robberies, a few bombings and some shoot-outs with the police in Northern Germany," she replied. "I'm sure they will fill you in when they get here. Also, Ulrike made a movie, but it is banned in theaters and on television. So, she is angry."

Changing the subject, Sonya said, "Grab your parka and gloves, Lucas. I want to show you around outside. The others will be here soon. Then, I will go find Bruno and convince him to go skiing in Seefeld."

Outside, snowflakes were floating to the frozen ground and forming piles. They walked away from the front of the house to view the whole scene of this property which rests in a grove of big alder trees.

Lucas stood still and studied his view of the grounds and the unique design of the house: *The steep tile roof, now covered in snow, has a pointed-dome section above the study at a back corner of the house. From the study, Strauss had a panoramic view of the Zugspitze and surrounding forests. There is a large-leaf lime tree and a weeping-willow tree, one to the right and one left of the house. Tall, trimmed hedges line the winding, narrow driveway. The front of the house is well-hidden, and there is only one way to get in.*

Before Sonya could say anymore, a brand-new, VW van came into view, and they watched it park at the side of the house where the white van could not be seen from the street. When the van stopped, Gudrun opened the front passenger door, and Manfred climbed out of the driver side. Then, the sliding side door opened, revealing Gabrielle, Ulrike and Andreas. They all got out to say hello.

Lucas and Sonya received hugs; and the RAF members gave Lucas their condolences. Once inside, Gabrielle took Lucas into the kitchen. They wanted to check the food supplies and talk about what has been happening in their lives. Sonya left to go find Bruno. The rest of the group scattered to get settled in their respective rooms.

"I'm so sorry for your loss, Lucas," said Gabrielle.

"Thank you, Gabrielle," he replied. "I think I'm still in shock over it. Why is the RAF in Bavaria? Not on business, I hope."

"I wanted to see you, Lucas, and they all needed a break," she replied. "We couldn't be in a more beautiful place. If you need me for anything, I'm here for you."

He handed Gabrielle a Spaten beer and his hashish pipe. He lit the pipe for her, and she took a deep hit.

"Do you have any idea, who murdered Inga?" she asked.

"Yes. I need to talk to you about it," he replied. "I am positive it was Bruno Castignoli, and I believe he also murdered your friend when you were in Formentera."

"He's the guy Andreas and Horst gave a physical warning to about his abuse of women," she said.

"Yeah, but I plan to take care of Mr. Bruno with the help of a few friends," he replied. "I will tell you the plan, Gabrielle, so please let me know what you think about it."

"Lucas, I don't care how this guy dies," she said. "I want him to suffer for what he did to my friend, Kirsten."

"Several of us looked at a spot on a mountain which is so steep and so isolated, no one will find his body for years, maybe never," he replied. "To lure Bruno up there, Sonya is asking him to go skiing with her, and she will let us know if he agrees. Then, we will make sure he goes off the cliff with his skis on, and he will know our reasons for doing so."

"Lucas, I want to go along with you," said Gabrielle, "to see his face and to tell him why I want him to die in such a painful way,"

"You should not be there, in case something goes wrong," replied Lucas. "We were careful with our planning, but it's still a risk."

"Look who I hang out with!" she said. "Everything we do is a risk! Without a doubt, I want to be there and watch him beg."

"Gabrielle, you should not tell anyone of our Bruno plan. For our security, only the people who will be there will know about it. If one of us is guilty, we are all guilty. Do you agree?"

"*Bestimmt* (certainly). Now, let's check the refrigerator for food and plan our menu," she replied.

Seeing Gabrielle was good for Lucas. He was glad she was here. They always had fun, and it began in Spain. They met on a beach in Formentera and made crazy love every night, then went to Ibiza and played—until Gabrielle had to go home without her friend.

Thinking of Spain, he said, "We should cook something Spanish."

The refrigerator was full of exciting foods which even Lucas did not expect to see. Since he knows Sonya and her mother run a successful restaurant, he figured they buy meat, dairy, fruits and vegetables from the local farmers whose products are always excellent.

Lucas wrote in his pocket notebook while he spoke aloud, and Gabrielle brought the items out, one by one. He said, "A whole rabbit, a whole chicken, a half-dozen bratwurst sausages, two racks of spare ribs and about two pounds of ground lamb. There are several artichokes, carrots, red bell peppers and two large eggplant. Now, let's check the freezer... Okay, it appears we have everything we need. They must buy some of this stuff at the commissary since Sonya's father is an officer in the American Air Force. However, he lives in Frankfurt, and I guess he is gone most of the time."

With her thoughts on Spain, Gabrielle said, "Lucas, I remember the delicious tapas we had in Formentera and Ibiza. I know this is a sad time for you, and you may feel overwhelmed; but I am glad to be here and spend this time with you."

"Thank you, Gabrielle," he replied. "Our time together in Spain will always be special to me. The fact is, I need to keep busy now. I feel responsible for Inga's death, and I am trying not to dwell on it. I believe Bruno wanted to get at me, and when I was not available, he decided to take it out on her."

"Lucas, he has murdered three women which we know of," she said. "We have to get rid of this *drecksack* (scumbag), so we can all put it behind us. I am here for you, any way you want me."

Lucas smiled, and then he said, "Keeping with the Spanish theme, this is our menu: We'll have *Sangria* for a beverage. With the ground lamb, we can make *Albondigas cordero* (lamb meatballs in light spices). Using the rabbit, we'll make *Conejo de blanco* (a slow braised rabbit in white wine, garlic & fresh thyme). We must have *Paella*, the national dish of Spain, made with chicken, shrimp and sausage."

"Do we have any saffron here?" she asked.

"Yes. I always carry a container of saffron, although it is the most expensive spice in the world," he replied. "Did you know it takes around ten thousand flower stigmas to make one ounce of saffron threads, and the dark red ones are the strongest fragrance? Historians believe saffron was first used in the Orient. Today, it's used worldwide in different ways.

"In India, saffron is used for rice, sweet dishes, ice cream, some medicinal purposes and religious rituals. In Saudi Arabia, it is used in coffee along with cardamom. Italy and Switzerland put saffron in Risotto. France puts it in Bouillabaisse. Spain puts it in Paella. Sweden puts it in saffron bread."

Before he could finish the menu, Andreas came into the kitchen and asked, "Lucas, do you have any good hashish like you brought the last time you were here?" Lucas went over to the coat rack in the hallway, took his hash pipe and lighter out of his parka, lit the pipe and handed it to Andreas. He took a hit, then passed it around.

Gabrielle opened 3 Spaten beers. They each lifted a beer and said, "Prost," as they clicked the bottles together.

"It is very nice of you to let me stay here while I try to reorganize my life," said Lucas.

"After all you've done to help us, are you kidding? I understand you are cooking dinner for us this evening," Andreas replied.

"It will be my pleasure," said Lucas. "Gabrielle and I were just going over the menu. Where is the rest of the group?"

"They are all taking naps," he replied. "We will talk at dinner and drink Jägermeister while we all share our stories." Then, he left.

The phone rang and Gabrielle answered it. She held out the phone and said to Lucas, "It's Sonya. She wants to talk to you."

Sonya's voice was excited as she told Lucas, "I found Bruno at the Garmischer Hof on Bahnhofstrasse. He seemed quiet and agitated when he first saw me, but I told him it was important. When I said we could talk on the chairlift without interruptions, and nobody would overhear us, I'm sure it got him thinking. Anyway, he agreed to go skiing tomorrow. We will get a late start since he is not an early riser. So, you have time to get everyone together, and I think you should be there by eleven a.m. For me, it is a good time to shoot for."

With Sonya still on the phone, Lucas was quiet for a moment. Then, he said, "I will call Sabine and Eric at her house in Seefeld. Gabrielle insists on going along, so there will be five of us. Can you come for dinner tonight? We are having a Spanish Tapas menu."

"I would never pass up a chance to eat one of your meals, Lucas," said Sonya. "I hoped you would invite me."

"We will eat about eight thirty," he said. "Thank you, Sonya,"

"You are welcome, and I'll see you this evening," she replied.

When he got off the phone, Lucas told Gabrielle, "Bruno agreed to go skiing with Sonya tomorrow."

Next, he phoned Sabine and said, "You and Eric should plan for the 'Bruno Event' to take place at eleven a.m. tomorrow."

“We will be there. I’m glad it is tomorrow,” she replied. “The sooner we can do this and put it behind us, the better.”

Lucas and Sabine agreed on where to meet and ended the call.

He told Gabrielle the plan. They would leave early in the morning, drive to Seefeld and meet Eric and Sabine at the entrance to the main parking lot for the Seefelder Jochbahn.

Gabrielle simply said, “Gut, prima” (good, excellent).

“Well, tonight will be a short night’s sleep, but it’s for a worthy cause,” he said. “Tomorrow, we have to dump despicable trash off a cliff. Please remember, we can’t ever tell anyone, outside our group of five, about what we do tomorrow.”

“I promise, Lucas,” she said. “And I will try to never even think about Bruno after tomorrow.”

“Okay, Gabrielle,” he replied. “Now, let’s have another Spaten beer and get on with dinner.”

Next, he explained the menu to her, “We’ll use the salmon filet to make *Empanadas*, little pastry pies filled with salmon and leeks. They originated in Portugal, but are very popular in Argentina. I think *Braised Oxtails* are underrated since they make the richest red wine sauce I’ve ever tasted, and it has such a unique flavor. We can bake the eggplant in a spicy tomato sauce for a Spanish dish called *Berenjena con salsa de tomate*. To prepare it, we slice the eggplant and bread each slice in flour, egg and parmesan bread crumbs. Then, we brown the slices in cooking oil, drain them well, layer the browned eggplant in a pan, and add the tomato sauce. We will bake it with a layer of unsweetened custard on top, as you would do for *Moussaka*, the Greek dish. For dessert, let’s make a traditional Spanish dessert, *Almond torta de Santiago* (almond torte and vanilla ice cream).”

Creating a fine meal with an energetic menu, Lucas focused on dinner preparation, and he tried to keep a light mood in the kitchen. This is what he wanted to do, today. He did not want to think of outside events which he would face later.

Tonight, an evening with the Celebrity Terrorists would keep his mind busy. Gabrielle, hashish, Spaten beer and a little Jägermeister would take care of any other anxiety. By Lucas’ own choice, these were all tools for coping and for healing.

The dinner impressed each of the famous RAF leaders who had all vacationed in Spain. They loved the food and appreciated all the effort required for preparation of such a special meal.

Everyone at this table had their own problems and challenges in the world outside this old Bavarian house which contained so much history. They were a strange combination of personalities, sitting together and enjoying a magnificent meal with Sangria, a lot of hashish and a feeling of comradery between them. When she first arrived, Sonya felt stressed. It was understandable. Earlier, she had to sweet-talk Bruno and convince him to go skiing in Seefeld, the next day.

Manfred built a great fire, and they all lounged around the family room by the fireplace. When Lucas lit his hash pipe, he passed it to Gabrielle, and she passed it around.

Manfred declined a hit on the pipe and said, "I never understood what all the fuss is about, regarding marijuana. I tried it once and did not feel a thing. From what I have read about research on marijuana, it may cause euphoric illusions, feelings of separation from your body and from reality, even hallucinations or paranoia."

Lucas looked straight into Manfred's eyes and said, "Well, Manfred, I've been smoking pot or hashish for the last five years, and I can only speak for myself. I must confess, a few of those findings are my reasons to smoke it, and I think it makes life better. It helps me stay focused, expands my mind, increases my creativity and enhances my sex life. I also think music sounds better and food tastes better. It's nice to be high now, enjoying the pleasures of life."

After a short pause, Lucas continued, "We should learn from every single event in our lives, as we experience them. I believe the perfect experience in life is living in the moment while enjoying the positives and discarding any negatives."

Looking at Sonya, Lucas detected a smile, and he felt encouraged.

Ulrike spoke up, "What you have stated may be true. However, it seems impossible when the fascist 'pigs' are in control, and they prefer we accept only what they want to give us. We are fighting to free ourselves and live our lives without being suppressed. A lot of revolutionists gave their lives for a cause. In the end, it may happen to us, but we have started something. We hope it will continue to grow until the 'pigs' have to surrender, and a new form of government will emerge for the people, due to our efforts."

RAF members stood, raised their glasses, and all said, "Prost."

Lucas thought: *Right now, I would not be surprised to hear someone say, "Heil Hitler."*

Ulrike had the floor, and she was determined to emphasize her point. "Most people do not realize what a fascist government can mean to them. Fascists always have their symbols and slogans, and they have complete control over the military, religion and mass media."

Looking at Andreas, Ulrike went on, "Male domination and the fact that women possess fewer rights are only a small part of the problem. Many people are obsessed with national security and the control of civil liberties, including homophobic fascists. Fraudulent elections are held as valid, and voters are being suppressed. The government and big business are in bed together, both equally corrupt and supportive of each other. They think intellectuals and artists are an inferior subculture who should be treated with disdain by the fascist government."

Andreas spoke, directly to Lucas and Sonya, "As you can see, Ulrike is a little edgy this evening, since they banned her movie, *Bambule,* because of her association with us and the RAF."

"What is your movie about, Ulrike?" asked Lucas.

"The title, *Bambule,* is a slang word for riot; and the movie is about horrible brutalization of reformatory girls in Breitenau, Germany," she replied. "For instance, the girls were required to work in agriculture and industry for twelve hours a day. If the girls did anything the authorities disliked, punishments were severe, including starvation diets which caused sickness and even some deaths. The authorities had complete control about how long they could keep these young people. The girls could only send out one letter a month. Authorities opened those letters and censored them, any way they wanted to, or they chose to not even send the letters. The basic story is about three young girls in a Berlin reformatory. Irene is one girl who escapes, but realizes she cannot survive in the outside world and returns to the reformatory. Another girl, Monika, also escapes, but she gets caught and transferred to another home which is run by nuns. The third girl, Evelyn, provokes her roommates, and they start a riot, one night.

"This was my first attempt to write a movie, and I felt proud of the result, except I did not agree with the director. For the movie to appear realistic, I wanted the reformatory girls to act as themselves. Itzenplitz, the director, objected to my idea, so we had to use actresses. Now, the 'pigs' have banned my movie and refuse to show it on TV, or anywhere else, because of my part in Andreas' escape from prison. Young people are being abused and mistreated. They are singled out because they are poor, uneducated, vagabonds, beggars, prostitutes, street musicians, or even nonconformists. All of this inspired me to write the movie. Now, the public may never see it."

As Ulrike was talking, Lucas studied the faces and postures of people in the room. The RAF members looked worn out, and they seemed unsettled. On the other hand, Gabrielle was upbeat and optimistic.

He turned to Gudrun and asked, "So, Gudrun, how is your quest for reform going?"

"We have more favorable support from the German people," said Gudrun. "Our strategic strikes against the 'pigs' emphasize the purpose of our mission. Today, we received good news: Regis Debray, our friend and a supporter of our cause, was released after serving four years of a thirty-year sentence in Bolivia. Have we ever told you about our connection with Regis Debray?"

"Excuse me, Gudrun," said Lucas. "Isn't he the French scholar who was with Che Guevara in Bolivia before Che's execution in nineteen sixty-seven? I have a friend who came from Argentina. He told me about Che Guevara, and I remember the name, Regis Debray."

"I never met Regis Debray. However, after we left Frankfurt in a hurry, we stayed at his house in Paris," she replied.

"Why did you have to leave in a hurry?" asked Sonya.

"The court had sentenced Andreas, Horst, Thorwald and me to serve three years in prison for arson," replied Gudrun. "We were out while our case was on appeal. When we lost the appeal, the court ordered us back to prison. Horst turned himself in, but we went to Paris instead. One of our French sympathizers told us Regis knew about our movement, and if we needed to go underground, his house was open to us in Paris. While we stayed there, we made other plans, and then went to Italy."

"What ever happened to Debray?" asked Lucas.

"I read Che's revolutionaries were no match for the American CIA, and the CIA backed the Bolivian Army," said Ulrike. "When Debray and another man got separated from the revolutionists, the Bolivian Army found them and put them in prison. There was a rumor about Debray or his companion exchanging Che's location with authorities in return for a lesser sentence. Apparently, it did not happen. Debray and his companion, Ciro Bustos, were sentenced to thirty years in prison. But they were freed, last December."

"My understanding is the French President Charles de Gaulle, novelist André Malraux, and philosopher Jean-Paul Sartre were all influential in the early release of Regis Debray," said Gudrun.

"How did Debray get involved with Che?" asked Lucas.

"Regis Debray was a professor of philosophy at the University of Havana, and he became associated with Che Guevara in Cuba," said Gudrun. "Then, Debray went to Bolivia and joined a small group of revolutionists who were led by Che in the mid-sixties. Debray wrote a book, *Revolution in the Revolution?* In his book, he assessed guerrilla warfare in Latin America. Andreas, Ulrike and I have all read it, and we learned much from it, along with Che's own manual.

"We followed and admired Che for his many accomplishments. He was a man looking to start a revolution and overthrow a government. When Che and Castro succeeded in Cuba, Che became National Bank President and Instructional Director for Cuba's armed forces.

"Che Guevara traveled the world as a diplomat, on behalf of Cuban socialism. Being an excellent writer, he published a manual on guerrilla warfare. He also wrote a great memoir about his youthful motorcycle journey when he traveled around South America, witnessing poverty, hunger and disease. He left Cuba in nineteen sixty-five with plans to form a guerrilla army. Che first went to the Congo where his plan was rejected. Next, he went to Bolivia where he led a guerrilla force for about a year. Finally, he was stopped by Bolivian military (backed by the American-CIA) and executed without a trial or any hearing.

"At the time, no one was more feared by the CIA, than Che Guevara. He had international fame, and his followers idolized him because they knew he could lead a rebellion against the capitalist exploitation of South America. Therefore, authorities executed him quickly. They did not want him to be a martyr and become a champion of the people. Klaus Barbie is a person associated with the capture of Che Guevara. Barbie is a former Nazi SS Captain who the CIA protected and used. He was instrumental in Che's capture and execution. Now, Barbie is a drug lord in Bolivia; and it is public knowledge."

Looking at the Celebrity Terrorists, Lucas asked, "Do you ever get tired of hiding out and looking over your shoulder?"

"We are completely dedicated to our cause," said Gudrun, "and our legacy is for those who carry on the crusade to bring down the fascist 'pigs.' There is no turning back now. We have always believed if we attack the state with bombings and push them hard enough, they will respond by exposing their hidden fascist elements; the German people will recognize this and join us in attacking the state which will create an all-out revolution. Already, a quarter of the young people in Germany are willing to help us."

"To answer your question, Lucas," said Andreas, "about whether we get tired of hiding from the 'pigs' and evading capture, I say no. But, please note my use of the word *I* instead of *we*. I cannot feel what others feel about what we do. I only know it excites and energizes me, more than any other thing I have ever experienced. Watching the movie *Bonnie and Clyde*, I identified with the characters, and we've been compared to them in the news. *The Battle of Algiers* is another movie I enjoyed. It is about the Algerian struggle for independence. I also admire Che Guevara and have a poster of him, hanging on my bedroom wall."

"Andreas, did you say you went to Italy after you stayed at Regis Debray's home in Paris?" asked Lucas. "Was it the same trip when we ran into each other near Gomagoi?"

"Yes. And you saved us from freezing to death when we ran off the road," he replied. "Whatever happened to the guy you were with?"

"George returned to 'The States.' However, I heard he might be coming back to Garmisch," replied Lucas.

"Well, I hope we are still around to see your friend George again," he said. Lucas saw a deep sadness in Andreas' eyes which he had not seen before. At this point, he did not know what to say to Andreas.

So, Lucas asked Ulrike about the RAF manifesto. She answered, "I have finished it, and we changed our logo. The cover now shows a big, five-point red star under a Heckler and Koch MP5 assault rifle; *RAF* is typed in bold white letters across the center of the rifle. The manifesto tells how we will have a socialist revolution in Germany, and it explains how current society and government have strong hidden ties with a lot of fascist elements."

Ulrike declared her perspective, "It's appalling to realize former Nazis now dominate the West German government and many industries there. Nazis were never held accountable for crimes they committed during the last war. The current government denies our citizens of civil liberties which their freedom should guarantee, and this should not be allowed. A person's civil liberties should not be abridged by law, nor by judicial interpretation. My examples of those liberties are freedom from torture, freedom of press, religion and speech, the right to privacy, the right to own property, the right to defend ourselves, the right to a fair trial and the right to life. These should all be international freedoms and rights. This is what the RAF is fighting for, and it is the reason we made many sacrifices. Gudrun and I even gave up our children for the cause."

Lucas studied Ulrike's face. At different times when he had been with Ulrike, she revealed many faces—one was tired; one was sad; one was hardness; one was deep in thought; and one was spiteful. Her dark brown hair was still at shoulder length, except for her signature bangs. Her face seemed rounder than when he first met her, and she seemed more unkempt, as did the other members of the group.

They all seemed to be on edge and smoked a lot of cigarettes. Lucas could never figure out what cigarettes were about. If you are going to smoke, he figured it should be pot or hashish, something to get you high. Otherwise, why do it?

"Since we are going skiing tomorrow, I need sleep," said Sonya.

Lucas filled his pipe with hashish, lit it and took a drag. Then, he passed it on to the rest of the group before he retired.

Insisting she and Lucas share a room together, Gabrielle said she wanted to cuddle with him in bed. Even if she couldn't have all of him, she knew their closeness would be comforting.

After Lucas got into the shower and adjusted the water temperature, Gabrielle pulled back the curtain. Stark naked and looking very sexy, she stepped into the shower. They took turns washing strategic spots, and Lucas even managed a laugh or two.

However, when they crawled into bed, Lucas could not bring himself to have sex. It was not a good time for him. The only thing he could do was apologize to Gabrielle.

"It's okay, Lucas. I understand," she said. "Can we be close and hold each other for a while?"

Lucas wrapped his arms around her, and they snuggled. It was not long before both fell asleep; and they remained in the embrace until the alarm went off at 8 a.m.

The house was quiet when they woke up. Lucas and Gabrielle put on their ski gear and hustled off. Stopping at the PX snack bar to eat, they each had over-easy eggs with ham, hash browns and wheat toast.

It was time to head for Seefeld where they would meet Eric and Sabine. Together, they would all go find the spot on the mountain which they now referred to as *The Garbage Dump*.

CHAPTER 27

Seefeld: Dead Ends

When Lucas and Gabrielle returned to his van, they climbed in the back. Knowing they both felt nervous, Lucas got his hash pipe out, filled the bowl with some of Topo's finest hashish, lit it and passed it to Gabrielle. He grabbed 2 Spaten beers from the cabinet behind the driver's seat, opened them and passed 1 to Gabrielle. Next, Lucas got into the driver's seat. He took a big pull on his beer while Gabrielle jumped in the front and sat alongside him.

As they started the 40-minute drive to Seefeld, Lucas thought: *These German and Austrian women like beer as much as I do.*

"Gabrielle, what is it like for you to be around Andreas, all the time?" asked Lucas.

"Well, I'm not around him all the time," she replied. "Before my brother Horst went to prison in Berlin, he told me a lot about Andreas. Talking to Gudrun, Horst had learned about Andreas' youth. He was the son of a talented historian who had gone off to fight in Russia and never returned. According to Gudrun, Andreas confessed to being a mama's boy, and he did not do well in school. His grandmother told him he was weak; but his mother always supported him, and she wanted him to be a journalist. Andreas wanted to give art school a try."

"What type of art?" he asked.

"I think he took pottery, but he discovered it did not really interest him," she replied.

Gabrielle took a drink of her beer, and then she continued the story, "In Munich, Andreas was popular with young ladies who were attracted to his dark skin, black hair, long eyelashes and blue eyes. But he became a young hoodlum, got tossed out of school and landed in jail. When Andreas got out of jail, he tried to work, but he lost one job after another. He lived on income from various sources: working as a male model, robbing men in gay bars and restaurants, and selling stolen cars and motorcycles. At some point, Andreas had an illegitimate daughter who he abandoned. Despite his history, he is an intelligent guy.

"He met Gudrun Ensslin right after a policeman murdered Benno Ohnesorg. It happened in Berlin during a student demonstration against a visit by the Shah of Iran. When the demonstrators became threatening, police beat them with batons, and one policeman shot Ohnesorg in the back of the head. Following the incident, there were controversial stories about a coverup, and some details were missing from the autopsy report. Ohnesorg became a martyr for the student demonstrators.

"When Gudrun met Andreas, she learned he had worked as an intern for a conservative newspaper, the *Bild-Zeitung*. Ironically, the newspaper became a mortal enemy of the RAF. Axel Springer, the founder/editor of the paper, is now a definite target of theirs.

"Gudrun was the daughter of a pastor. As a young adult, she became a nuclear protestor, went from boyfriend to boyfriend, appeared in a porn movie, got married and gave birth to her son, Felix.

"During a later demonstration, Gudrun saw Andreas speaking to a crowd and calling for violence against the German States. She became attracted to him because they were both fanatical about protesting and revolution. Gudrun thought it was a match made in heaven when they fell in love, and they are still together, fighting for their cause. She left her marriage and her child to be with Andreas.

"Andreas and Gudrun joined the Studentenbund (Socialist German Student Union); however, the group proved to be too passive for them. Andreas enjoys reading books written by Frederick Nietzsche or Jean-Paul Sartre. He loved the movie *Bonnie and Clyde* and has a poster of the movie. Both he and Gudrun identify with those two bank robbers. Fast forward to their current leadership in the RAF: Andreas occupies his time with planning and execution of missions in their war against the German States. He lets Gudrun and Ulrike deal with the politics.

"From what I've seen and heard, Andreas is always itching for action. He is a man on a mission with no self-control, and he does not repress his thoughts, feelings or actions. Whenever violence erupts, he acts like a callous psychopath."

"Do you know about what happened in Jordan during their terrorist training?" asked Lucas.

"RAF members claim accomplishment since they all learned how to shoot AK-47s," replied Gabrielle. "My brother Horst was there, and he felt it was a waste of time. Horst told me most of the group did not apply themselves to the strict regimen in Jordan. Andreas was probably the most rebellious. He refused to change his stylish pants and even wore them while crawling on the dirt.

"The RAF women became a problem too. They would sun bathe nude on the roofs of buildings, and it agitated the strict Muslim PLO fighters.

The camp commandant was also not pleased, and he told the women, 'This is not the tourist's beach in Beirut.'

"After two months, the Palestinians got tired of being disrespected and put them all on a plane which took them out of Jordan. From there, the RAF members went back to Berlin, according to Horst."

"What happened to Ulrike's children while they traveled to Jordan? I heard they were going to be re-schooled?" he asked.

"I don't know how the twins' transportation got off track," she replied. "The papers reported the girls were found in Sicily; and they were taken in by some hippie family who lived at the foot of Mt Etna."

"I think you know Ulrike was editor-in-chief at *Konkret* for seven years. The magazine was founded by Klaus Röhl, her ex-husband and father of the girls. After Ulrike left, Stefan Aust became the editor.

"Horst told me about Peter Homann who was in Jordan with the RAF group for a short while. Although he had personal ties to Ulrike, Homann disassociated from the RAF, left Jordan and hooked up with Stefan Aust. They planned to rescue the girls. I guess Homann saw how other children were being 'schooled' in the Jordan PLO camp. Anyway, Aust went to Sicily alone. He got the girls and took them to their father who was in Italy. Now, Homann and Aust are on the RAF shit list and hit list."

Gabrielle paused for another sip of beer. "I know there are times when Ulrike wishes she could see her daughters, but Andreas and Gudrun have some control over her. They manage to get her back on their track. Gudrun invariably finds a new project to keep Ulrike busy, such as the manifesto which she just completed. Ulrike is the general spokesperson of the group; however, Andreas and Gudrun are the true leaders."

"Gabrielle, what is your role in the RAF?" he asked.

"I am Horst's sister, and I only travel with them when they come to Garmisch," she replied. "Most of time, I stay at home in Hanover, and I work part time as an air traffic controller."

"Ulrike seems to be such a talented writer. What do you know about her life, growing up?" he asked.

"Well, her father passed away when she was five years old," she replied. "Her mother returned to school to finish her education; and she began a romantic relationship with Renate Riemeck, a female student. Riemeck moved in with Ulrike's mother and helped raise Ulrike. The two young women became elementary school teachers and joined the Social Democratic Party of Germany. A few years later, Ulrike's mother passed away, and Riemeck became Ulrike's foster mother.

"In the late fifties, Riemeck became a local celebrity when she wrote a petition which West German teachers and professors signed. In the petition, they asked trade unions to threaten a strike if West Germany became armed with nuclear weapons. Renate Riemeck was opposed to any remilitarization after World War Two.

"Ulrike idolized her foster mother, and Ulrike's political beliefs became the same as Riemeck's. Later, Ulrike wrote an article about how Riemeck lost her professorship, *Geschichten von Herrn Schütz* (Tales of Herr Schütz). She claimed: in the entire history of the Federal Republic, this was the first time a professor was asked to resign because of his or her ideological beliefs."

"Were there any men in Ulrike's younger life?" he asked.

"Gudrun told me Ulrike had a pretty unhappy childhood which is understandable," she replied. "Ulrike lost her father at a young age, and then she was exposed to the leftist beliefs of her mother and Renate Riemeck. I'm not aware of real romance in her early life. After her mother died, Riemeck continued having lesbian relationships. Ulrike had a relationship with a girl named Marie. They met in secret because her foster mother didn't approve. Ulrike broke it off after a year.

"In the early sixties, she married Klaus Röhl who was a communist. She wrote political articles for his magazine, and they had the twins. The following year, Ulrike had brain surgery for removal of a tumor. Although the tumor was benign, they inserted a metal plate in her head. Several people told Horst about changes they observed in Ulrike. She seemed to be a different person after the surgery."

"What do you mean, different? How old was she?" asked Lucas.

"Ulrike was twenty-six," she replied. "Her friends noticed the changes when she stopped showing much emotion. She also seemed depressed and always looked untidy. But she continued to live with her family and write for *Konkret* magazine until the twins were about six years old. Then, Ulrike divorced Röhl and moved to Berlin where she began to hang out with radical people. Before long, she was living with Andreas. When Andreas was caught and put in prison, Ulrike helped him escape, and they went underground.

"Horst told me a story of how brain surgery might have affected Ulrike—it occurred at the PLO training facility in Jordan. When they instructed her how to prime a Russian grenade, she pulled the pin, but didn't throw the grenade. Some fast-thinking terrorist grabbed it from her and threw it away, so it was a safe distance from them when it exploded. Horst told me another story about Ulrike using LSD; she had a horrible panic attack, and she never fully recovered from it."

"Do you know why Ulrike got a divorce?" he asked.

"Not all the details, but there was some talk about Röhl molesting both of his daughters," she replied.

"We know the RAF members all smoke pot, and they've talked about LSD. Do you know if they still take acid?" he asked.

"As I said, I'm not around them much," she replied. "My brother told me stories about their drug experiences. He said when he first met Gudrun, she was smoking a lot of pot."

"Well then, she can't be all bad," he said.

They both laughed.

Gabrielle said, "Andreas and his friends took LSD and amphetamines, then they would fantasize about revolutionary ideas. According to Horst, Andreas and his friends served time in prison for setting a department store fire in Frankfurt. Upon their release in nineteen sixty-eight, they celebrated by injecting themselves with liquefied opium."

"Oh, I heard nothing about opium. Gudrun talked about Regis Debray and going to Paris. Where did they go next?" he asked.

"After they left Paris, they went to Italy and stayed with some leftist, underground people," she said. "When they returned to Germany, they met and bonded with Ulrike Meinhof. She had a romantic interest in Andreas for a while. Horst had none of those details, but he said casual sex was popular within the student and radical organizations. I think you know the rest of the story."

"I guess, after they connected with Ulrike, they were all over the place," he said. "George and I met Andreas and Ulrike in the south part of Austria when they ran off the icy road and crashed their BMW. We gave them a ride to meet other members of their group. Another time, we spotted them at a café in Venice during a tornado. They had just robbed a bank, and we let them hide in our van for the night. The next morning, they joined some friends and escaped by boat. I first met Gudrun at the house in Garmisch when you introduced me."

Snow began to fall as they pulled into the parking lot at Seefeld Bergbahnen Rosshütte. Looking for Eric, Lucas drove slowly. He saw parking cones which Eric set out to hold a space next to his VW van. When they heard Lucas' engine, Eric and Sabine got out, removed the cones and watched Lucas park in the vacant space.

Sabine and Eric gave Lucas a clinging hug. Then, Lucas introduced Gabrielle. He briefly told them the story of Gabrielle's friend, Kirstin, how she disappeared after spending a week with Bruno, and no one had heard from her since.

"Gabrielle came here to participate in Bruno's day of reckoning. Now, he will have to face five of us," said Lucas.

The slopes would not open until 8:30 a.m., and they were there early. So, everyone climbed into Lucas' van to stay warm and have a beer. Sabine brought *wild boar pâté* plus brotchen and mustard. The pâté was made by a friend of hers. Lucas raised the dinette table, Sabine set the food out with some napkins, and they all enjoyed the snack.

"This is the best pâté I have ever eaten," said Lucas. "It makes me want to eat more. Please, put it away, or I will eat it all."

They laughed at Lucas. Then, Sabine said, "Well, let's go ski some turns in the snow before we meet Sonya and Bruno."

Sabine brought extra skis, poles and gear for Gabrielle to use. Since she had not planned on skiing, her ski gear was at home in Hanover. Everyone put on ski boots with a lot of moaning and groaning.

"Sometimes, it seems like torture to get into my ski boots and get them adjusted," said Lucas. They all agreed with him.

Grabbing their skis and poles, they headed to the Standseilbahn (standing train). It would take them up to the Jochbahn gondola.

Everyone was quiet, riding the train. Maybe they were groggy from the night before; but they certainly were deep in their own thoughts, considering what they were about to do.

As Lucas looked out at a picket fence which bordered the train tracks, he thought of his intentions: *Snow is coming down harder, and visibility is not great. Conditions are perfect for what we will do. I feel rather numb. It may be the lack of sleep and too much alcohol, but I'm not usually affected this way. Nothing will quash my determination to avenge the deaths of Jodie and Inga, two of the finest women I have ever known. I have no reservations about disposing of Bruno. He will never be able to abuse another woman. Later this morning when this is over, I will try to move on with my life, and I may get out of Garmisch for a while. I want to be away from Robinson, his endless questioning and his snooping into my private life. I might head to Chiemsee or Berchtesgaden for the spring and summer. However, I still must do Colonel Moyer's birthday party which will take place next month.*

When they got off the Standseilbahn, everyone grabbed their skis and poles from an outside rack on the train, and they walked over to the gondola. The 4 of them got in, and Lucas pulled his hash pipe out of his parka. The gondola started moving across the gorge which would soon be Bruno's new home.

Lucas lit the pipe, passed it around and said, "When I'm riding a gondola or a chairlift with only my friends, this is my tradition."

Sabine pointed to a clump of bushy trees below the gondola, and she said, "The place where we will confront Bruno is completely hidden and out of view from any lifts. We have all seen the place, except for you, Gabrielle. It's not a ski run, but rather a trail through the trees which is only known by locals. I honestly think it's the perfect spot, and I really want this to be over with."

"We do too, Sabine," said Lucas. Everyone nodded.

At the top of the lift, they jumped out, grabbed their skis and poles, stepped into their bindings, adjusted their goggles and followed Sabine down the mountain.

After two long runs, they stopped near the restaurant.

"I think we have time for a beer, before we head back up to meet Sonya," said Sabine.

Snow was falling heavily, and visibility got poorer by the minute. They sat at a table, and each had a half-liter glass of Gasser lager.

"This poor visibility makes skiing difficult, but it suits our purpose today," said Sabine.

"Sonya must have seen the weather report," said Lucas, "because this is exactly what she and I talked about."

As Lucas looked at the others, he could not detect any nervousness or fear in their expressions. He only saw very determined people, ready to carry out the task at hand.

Sabine was the last to finish her beer. Then, she stood and said, "Auf den Berg" (top of the mountain).

Riding the gondola to the *Rosshütte* Summit, Lucas passed the hash pipe around again. Trying to keep their minds off the task ahead, he told everyone the story of how he and George chased down 2 bank robbers at the Matterhorn, driving snowmobiles which they did not get to race in the movie, and both carrying policemen as passengers.

"Oh yeah, I was there," said Eric. "We were extras in a movie called *Snow Job*, starring Jean-Claude Killy and Rozzano Brazzi. It's about a guy who robs the village bank and escapes, riding up the mountain on top of the cable car, and then skiing off into the sunset."

"Before the movie crew arrived to film the fake bank robbery, two guys actually robbed the bank," said Lucas. "My friend George and I were on the mountain, last in line to drag race snowmobiles in the movie. An Alpini policeman ran toward me, jumped on the back of my snowmobile and yelled something in Italian. I told him to speak English, and he yelled, 'Bank robbers, hurry, follow the snowmobile!' He was pointing at two guys, riding down the slope toward Zermatt. George followed us with another policeman on his snowmobile. We were not going as fast as the bank robbers because we had been skiing this slope. We knew about a pile of big rocks and the sharp turn required to avoid hitting the rocks. The bank robbers didn't see the danger until it was too late. They crashed, head first into the rocks."

"What happened to the bank robbers?" asked Sabine.

"Both had crushed skulls and didn't make it," replied Lucas.

Getting got off the gondola, they could barely see ten feet ahead, and Sabine said, "I think this should be our last run today!" The others managed a chuckle, and they followed her.

Being careful, the group skied toward the thick clump of fir trees which were on the right side of the trail. Sabine slowed down as they approached the trees. Then, she disappeared. The others followed her, slowly making their way through the trees and stopping when they reached Sabine. She had turned around.

Sabine said, "Okay, stay right behind me. We're approaching the cliff." Following Sabine to a small clearing in the trees, they could see the path ended at the cliff, but they could not see any further. Sabine said, "We can wait behind those trees," pointing to her left.

"Sonya told me she would time their arrival and be here right after eleven, or as close as she can," said Lucas. "Now, we had better be quiet. We don't want Bruno to know we are here until he is near the edge of the cliff. Then, we can confront him with complete surprise."

The group stood in silence as they waited.

Lucas thought about the past 6 months: *Bruno's actions changed my life. I often wondered how my life would have been if Jodie and I had married, and Bruno had not beaten her to death. Now, I also wonder what my future with Inga would have been like in Oberammergau. I will never know because those two tragedies were caused by Bruno, a narcissist maniac who does not deserve to live. Yet, I do see positives, even with the pain. I have new friends, and I am in one of the most beautiful places on earth. If I had not followed Bruno here, I might not have seen Bavaria; nor would I have gone to Ibiza and Formentera where Bruno murdered Gabrielle's friend, Kirsten.*

Lucas sensed tension when his group heard skis, breaking the silence of the moment. Next, they heard Bruno's New Jersey and Italian accent. He said, "Sonya, this is far enough. No one will see us here."

Sonya skied close to the edge of the cliff which Bruno was not aware of. He followed and stopped next to Sonya. She reached into her parka and pulled out a pipe, then acted like she was looking for a lighter. This was her signal to the group. She was getting ready for them to appear. Sonya dug into her pocket as she slowly turned around on her skis. This maneuvered Bruno and put his back to the cliff.

"I know I put my lighter in my parka, somewhere. But I can't seem to find it. Do you have a lighter on you, Bruno?" asked Sonya.

Bruno laid his poles down while he looked through his pockets. Then, Sonya said, "Oh, here it is."

Before he could reply, Bruno heard the rattling of tree limbs and the sound of skis, sliding through the snow. As he looked behind Sonya, he saw 4 skiers, two women and two men, coming through the trees toward him, and they were getting closer.

"Don't light the pipe now, Sonya," said Bruno. "There are skiers coming this way."

Sonya moved over as Lucas and the others got in front of Bruno.

Now, everyone faced Bruno. Sonya and Eric stood on Lucas' left. Sabine and Gabrielle stood on Lucas' right. The edge of the cliff was right behind Bruno.

Lucas saw the shock on Bruno's face when he realized who stood in front of him. Bruno was face to face with the man whose girlfriend he had beaten to death.

"What are you guys doing here?" asked Bruno.

"Hi Bruno," said Lucas. "We're here to talk to you about three dead women who all had a connection with you. Standing here in our group, every person knew at least one of those women."

Bruno wanted to move, away from the group in front of him, but the semi-circle of 5 people was not budging.

"I don't know what you are talking about," Bruno gasped.

As he tried to move forward, 5 sets of ski poles stopped Bruno. Their sharp points were aimed straight at his chest and neck.

"You can't do this to me. Let me go, or I'll have you all arrested!" yelled Bruno.

"You are no position to call the police," said Eric. "Besides, we all agree, it would be best for you to disappear."

"Each of us want you to know how your actions have affected us as individuals and as a group," said Lucas. "I will speak first. Bruno, you are the reason I am standing here in front of you. You beat my fiancée Jodie to death during a fit of jealous rage in Long Beach; then, you took her body to Naples and threw her in a canal."

Now, everyone saw the look of fear on Bruno's face. He was in shock, being so exposed and realizing the group knew about him. Before this moment, he thought he had gotten away clean.

Lucas continued, "I followed you to Europe, and now this young lady will tell you about her friend, Kirsten, in Formentera."

"I don't know what you are talking about," Bruno repeated.

Lucas looked at Gabrielle and gestured for her to speak.

"I was with Kirsten," said Gabrielle. "In fact, I was with her when she had the misfortune to meet you. Since you are so full of yourself, you probably don't remember me at all. Kirsten was my best friend. You took her away from me, and I will never see her again. Today, I want to make sure you vanish. When you're gone, I never have to see her murderer again, either."

Sonya spoke next, "You know how you treated me, Bruno, and you cannot deny it, because I'm still alive and standing here. I came to watch you disappear from our lives, forever."

"What about you, Eric?" asked Bruno. "We played basketball at the gym and on the same team. I thought you were my friend."

"Bruno, my man, I see none of your friends here, assuming you have any friends," replied Eric. "The world will be a better place without you in it. Also, I must say, I never liked you very much, and I will not miss you at all."

"What are you going to do?" asked Bruno, his voice trembling.

A look of terror crossed Bruno's face. He realized his back was at the cliff and he had no idea how far down it went, due to falling snow and poor visibility.

"You can't do this—you will be murderers!" he exclaimed.

"No. You are the only murderer here, you asshole," said Sabine. "You beat my best friend until she was a bloody mess. I hope you suffer more, way more than Inga. She was innocent. You're a monster!"

"I have no feelings of guilt about disposing of you, Bruno," said Lucas. "You murdered two people who I loved very much, and I will sleep better, knowing you can't abuse any more women. Now, let's see you turn around and ski off this cliff like a man. Otherwise, you can die like a coward who beats women to death, as we help you go over the edge."

Bruno flailed his arms, trying to knock the 10 ski poles off his chest. He felt his body being pushed backward, and he knew he was sliding toward the edge. He looked at his arms and turned white when he realized he could not use his poles to stop from being pushed off this cliff and into a ravine which appeared to have no bottom. He had laid his poles down when he looked for his lighter.

Noticing this, Lucas reached over, pulled Bruno's ski poles out of the snow and said, "Here, Bruno, are you looking for these?"

Lucas tossed Bruno's poles over the cliff. He repositioned himself with the sharp tips of his own poles against Bruno's chest, and Lucas pushed hard. The others did the same thing, and they all moved forward, pushing Bruno backward with their ski poles.

There was nothing more Bruno could do, except slide off the cliff and disappear over the side.

Bruno fell into the snowy fog, screaming, "Nooooooooooooo."

Suddenly, it was quiet. The group waited to hear any sign of life. There was no sound from below the cliff.

Everyone turned around and followed Sabine out of the trees. They got onto the ski slope and skied through fresh powder. The snow was really dumping now, and visibility was horrible, as they skied all the way to the parking lot and took off their skis.

Gathered in Lucas' van, Eric, Sabine and Sonya were on the cushioned bench at the table in back. In the driver's seat, Lucas turned around and faced his friends. Gabrielle did the same. Lucas lit his hash pipe while Eric passed out Spaten beers. They sat quietly, took hits on the hash pipe and long pulls on their beers.

The group knew they were now bonded together in a very special way; and they could never speak of this deed, outside their group.

They were all good, fun-loving people. Today, however, they dealt with evil and felt justified in their vengeance. This was retribution for the murders of 3 young women who did nothing to deserve their fate.

After several minutes, Sonya broke the silence, "I talked with my mother about Bruno. She categorized him as an unprincipled narcissist with antisocial behavior."

"That about sums it up, Sonya," said Lucas. "Now, unless anyone has something they want to add, I think we should all close the book on Mr. Bruno Castignoli."

The others agreed with Lucas. Everyone wanted to forget about Bruno, as soon as they all could do so.

"Lucas, have you had a chance to think about what you want to do next?" asked Eric.

"My friend, you ask a great question," he replied. "I weighed some of my options and have several ideas. But I can't stray too far, right now. In a few weeks, I must handle Colonel Moyer's birthday party in Garmisch. After the party, I feel like I must get away from Garmisch for a while. I also want to avoid any further questioning by Robinson and the German police. I might go back to Chiemsee and talk to Herr Bucherl about working there for the spring and summer. Come winter, maybe I'll go do some skiing in Salzburg and Berchtesgaden. How about you Eric, what are you planning to do now?"

Eric showed his great smile and looked at Sabine before he replied, "You know, Lucas, I really enjoy skiing and have come to appreciate Austria and Germany."

Raising his bottle, Eric added, "I love the beer and the women!"

Everyone cheered and said, "Prost."

As they said goodbye, each of them hugged and kissed.

Eric and Sabine were going back to her house, and then Eric was heading back to work at the officers' club.

Sonya had come in her German Ford Transit van, and she would give Gabrielle a ride back to Garmisch.

Lucas would stop at the NATO Officers Club in Oberammergau to talk with Helmut in person. Wanting to take the next 2 weeks off, Lucas knew he needed this time to relax and consider his options. For the coming spring and summer, the idea of transferring to Rasthaus am Chiemsee was most appealing.

When Lucas walked into the officers' club, Helmut was standing at the end of the bar, Margo was behind the bar, serving a group of people, and two GIs were playing a game of pool.

It was a complete surprise when Lucas recognized who was sitting at the bar with their backs turned toward the door—his old, Long Beach buddy, George Bennett, and those 2 fun-loving, Canadian ladies, Judy and Deanna.

CHAPTER 28

Lake Chiemsee

Lucas could hardly believe it. There sat George with Judy and Deanna. George and Lucas had met these ladies while traveling in Italy which was soon after they first arrived in Europe.

Helmut saw Lucas come in, and he said, "Hello, Lucas. Here are some friends of yours."

George, Judy and Deanna turned and got off their bar stools. George hugged Lucas first. Deanna gave him a short hug, and then Judy hugged him as if she wanted to squash him.

Lucas was stunned to see these people here in Bavaria. He thought, *I'm so glad George is back. The last time I saw these ladies was in Barcelona, Spain. George and I met them at the campground in Savona, Italy, where we hooked up as couples and partied a few days. From there, we all traveled together, driving through the French Riviera, staying overnight in Nice, and ending in Barcelona. Then, the ladies headed home on a flight to Banff, Canada.*

Margo set a half-liter glass of Augustiner of beer on the bar in front of Lucas. She said, "Hi stranger, it's nice to see you back. Or, I guess I should ask, are you back?"

"Thank you for the beer, Margo," replied Lucas. "At the moment, I'm not sure what, why or where I am. Although, I am very happy to see all of your smiling faces."

Judy put her arm around Lucas' neck, and it seemed like she would not let go unless he kissed her. He thought about giving her a kiss, but it would have to wait until later.

"When did you all get to Bavaria?" he asked.

"We all met in Frankfurt. From there, we took the train and arrived in Garmisch this morning," replied George. "I called Gino, and he gave us a ride here to see you. Gino told us about Inga. I'm so sorry, Lucas. Gino said the police have no suspects, no one had a motive to murder her, and it didn't appear to be a robbery."

"It is a mystery for all of us," he replied.

He wanted to tell his old buddy about the "Bruno Event." But Lucas knew he could never discuss it, except with the "Seefeld Five."

Looking at Lucas, Helmut said, "I have paperwork to do, but I want you to know your job is open here. Also, I understand you must decide if you want to return and work at the club."

"Thank you, Helmut," said Lucas. "I've had a great time working here with you and the other fantastic, crazy Bavarians. I plan to think about my options, and I want to enjoy visiting these old friends of mine. I may go over to Chiemsee for a few days, then to Berchtesgaden and maybe to Salzburg. I'll be back, sometime next week, with plenty of time to prepare for Colonel Moyer's birthday party."

Helmut gave Lucas a hug, and then he went to his office.

Turning to George, Judy and Deanna, Lucas asked, "Do you have a plan or a place to stay?"

"No. We were in a hurry to come and see you," replied Judy.

Lucas smiled. "Well, I can call the Lake Chiemsee Hotel and ask if we can get rooms there. Does Chiemsee sound good to you?"

"How far is it?" asked George.

"It's about one hundred and twenty-five kilometers. The drive takes an hour and a half," replied Lucas.

Both ladies were nodding.

Lucas drained his beer glass and said, "I'll go call the hotel."

While Lucas made his phone call, George, Judy and Deanna finished their beers. When he returned, Lucas said, "Okay, let's get going. I guess those three large backpacks are yours, by the entrance. I like the way you travel. What about skis?"

"We all decided we need new skis and boots, and we want to look for some good deals," Deanna replied.

Lucas gave Margo a kiss on the cheek, a hug and a nice tip.

Then, he led the way to his van, thinking: *This whole day was surreal. Now, it is playing out as if it is scripted. While I am facing a major decision, George and the two Canadian ladies appear at the same time. This may be the perfect distraction, and I welcome it. So, if I can pull it off, I will go with the flow. At least, I will do my best.*

When he opened the side door of the van, his friends tossed in their backpacks and made themselves comfortable. Lucas climbed in the back with them, closed the door, loaded the hash pipe, handed it to Judy and lit it for her.

"Some things never change," said George, and he chuckled.

"You're right!" replied Lucas. He opened each of them a Spaten beer and said, "Now, please tell me what you've all been doing since we were together in Barcelona."

"I worked on getting back to be with you in Europe," said Judy.

"Thank you, Judy," he replied. "It's great to see you too. I take it you broke up with your boyfriend."

"He told me it broke his heart, and I hated to hurt him. But I would never forgive myself if I did not make this trip," she replied.

"George and I have kept in touch," said Deanna. "I went to Long Beach for a visit with him; and he came to Banff where we had a great time skiing and partying."

"I've taken a whole year off from my teaching job in Long Beach," said George. "This time, I will learn more about Europe and see other places here. I have missed you a lot, Lucas. You look great, but I'm sure you might need more sleep, or a little R&R."

Raising his beer bottle, Lucas replied, "Well, then let's get started with the R&R."

Lucas got into the driver's seat, and Judy got into the passenger seat. When they stopped for gas, they bought a case of Hacker-Pschorr beer, some bread, cheese and Lieberkase (baked loaf of ground corned beef, pork and bacon).

"We're off to Lake Chiemsee, and I think you'll love it," Lucas said, as he started the van.

"Have you had any more contact with the German terrorists, Lucas?" asked Judy.

"Oh. Do you mean the RAF? From what I've heard, they are still doing their thing, being fugitives and all," replied Lucas. He did not want to discuss his personal knowledge of the RAF.

"What is it they actually do?" asked Deanna.

"They rob banks, blow up cars and buildings, and have shoot-outs with the police," he replied. "They gather support in Germany, and they want to overthrow current government leaders. Andreas Baader, Ulrike Meinhof and Gudrun Ensslin escape capture because they get help from the German people who sympathize with their cause and view them as modern-day heroes."

Changing the subject, Lucas said to Judy, "I realize you just got here, but do you have any immediate plans?"

"I hoped you would give Deanna and me guidance about finding work and getting settled here," she replied.

Lucas realized: *I may not be ready for it, but hanging out with George and these fun ladies will be good for me.*

"After giving it great thought, Judy, I would love to be your personal guide in Bavaria, starting at the Rasthaus am Chiemsee," said Lucas. "However, before we go, could we have a couple more of those Hacker-Pschorr beers, George?"

"Did you ever see the handsome waiter again, the one who sold you hashish when we were in Nice?" asked Deanna.

"Yes. You are smoking some of Topo's finest," said Lucas. "He is alive and well in Garmisch. Topo has an Australian girlfriend now. You'll see him soon, and you'll meet great people who come here from all over the world. The AFRC community is like a big family with one common goal—to have the most fun a person can have."

They all raised their beer bottles and said, "Prost."

On the stereo, John Denver was singing "Take me Home." Lucas turned down the music, and he continued talking, "I suggest we only stay one night at Chiemsee Hotel. We can come back this summer, take a boat to the island and see one of King Ludwig's castles. Although the king never finished it, people say the Herrenchiemsee Palace is spectacular."

Speaking of King Ludwig got Lucas thinking about Inga and their tour of Linderhof Castle. He had to fight off the tears before he could continue talking. Then, he forgot what he was going to say.

On the drive to Chiemsee, they listened to music and chatted about old times together. When Lucas turned into the snow-filled parking lot at Lake Chiemsee Hotel, he recalled what happened the last time he pulled into this lot—CID Officer Robinson searched his van for drugs, found his stash and arrested him.

He thought: *My friends will laugh when I tell the story of my arrest.*

They walked through the lobby to the front desk. Joe, the head desk clerk, remembered Lucas because of the episode with CID Robinson. Joe had made their reservation and prepared for their arrival.

Joe spoke first and said, "I am so sorry for your loss, Lucas. I hope we can make your visit pleasurable. If there is anything you need, please tell me what I can do, or see whoever is working this desk. I believe you know your way around the hotel. I have advised Bob Clarkson, Chef Bucherl and Shelley Carpenter about your stay here. They all look forward to seeing you and meeting your friends."

Lucas introduced his friends to Joe, the desk clerk.

"It's nice to meet you all. I hope you have a great time," said Joe.

"Thanks for your hospitality, Joe. We'll see you later," said Lucas.

Joe is smart, thought Lucas. *He did not give us the same rooms which Eric, Sabine, Inga and I used when we came here in January.*

Everyone brought in what they needed and got their stuff settled in their rooms. By then, it was time to go for dinner.

As he did before, Bob Clarkson made sure Lucas had a window table, away from the musician's stage, so they could enjoy dinner conversation. The band had an accordion player, a bass violin player and a guitarist. They played lively Bavarian music.

Lucas was glad to be here, in this fantastic dining room, gazing at the original frescos and paintings on the walls, chandelier lights, marble pillars and wooden beams. There were numerous military families and couples who were talking quietly or eating their meals.

There were a few tables of young military men, out for a good time. They sounded cheerful, but also loud and obnoxious. Lucas did his best to ignore the distraction as he talked with his good friend George and the charming, fun-loving Canadian ladies.

First, they all ordered Wieninger draft beer. Then, each couple put their heads together and studied the menu.

Judy put her hand on Lucas' leg, and she looked at him with those big blue eyes. "I am so happy to see you and be here with you, Lucas. Bavaria is as beautiful as advertised. It will be interesting to learn about local history, the customs and the language. Most of all, I want to spend quality time with you, but only if you want to."

"Thank you, Judy, I will be happy to share what I've learned about Bavaria and its great history," he replied. "It's also good to see you. Now, let's order your first Bavarian dinner."

Lucas ordered Zigeuner Schnitzel (hand breaded pork over a zesty mushroom, onion, pepper, tomato and bacon sauce) since he enjoyed it when he ate here before. Judy chose Veal Cordon Bleu (veal steak with ham and Swiss cheese, hand breaded and served in burgundy sauce). Deanna wanted to try Wienerschnitzel (breaded veal cutlet, served with lemon), plus boiled gold potatoes and red cabbage. George went for the Steak au Poivre Verte (filet steak, flamed in a green peppercorn, cognac and cream sauce).

After everyone ordered, Lucas realized he and Judy were having exactly what he and Inga had ordered for dinner, his last time here.

"What do you know about the location of this hotel?" Judy asked Lucas while they waited for their dinners.

"The autobahn we drove on was one of the first built for Hitler's autobahn system," he replied. "Autobahns are local freeways, except the autobahns don't seem to have speed limits. Hitler loved going to his home in Obersalzberg which is above Berchtesgaden, coming from Munich. These villages are beautiful, fairy-tale places which you will see soon. Anyway, Hitler traveled this route, so he wanted everything to be first class along this autobahn. The engineers wanted to build the hotel closer to the mountains for better support of this massive hotel complex on more solid ground. Of course, Hitler got his way, and the hotel got built next to the lake where they had to set deep pilings in soft soil. The construction was first class and all top grade, using the best concrete, quarried stone, beautiful woodwork and fine metalwork. This hotel operates twenty-four hours a day, and it was built to last."

"When was it opened?" she asked.

"The hotel opened as an autobahn rest stop in nineteen thirty-eight," he replied, "the same year as the Annexation of Austria by Germany. However, it only operated as a hotel for two years after it first opened. During the war, they used it as a hospital. After the war, the Americans took control of this hotel, along with several other Bavarian hotels and military facilities. Since then, American armed forces have used and enjoyed these recreation areas. Not to mention, many ski patrol and civilian employees who are privileged to work at American hotels and facilities in Bavaria, as I am now, and you will be soon."

Lucas told them about the great people he had met since he arrived in Garmisch, the fun they all have, and how everyone enjoys hanging out at the International Bar and Grill. George agreed with Lucas because he was here last year. He met a lot of these people, including Gino, Eric, Regan Stone, Sonya and John Ferrell.

They called it an early night after George pointed out he was tired from traveling, and Lucas and Judy needed time to reacquainted. Judy looked at Lucas, and she smiled. After Lucas signed the check and left a hefty tip, they all went upstairs to their respective rooms.

When the door to their room closed, Judy turned and threw her arms around Lucas. She gave him a kiss which he would not forget for a while. They both got undressed, and Lucas led Judy to the shower where they became reacquainted with each other.

As they dried off, Lucas wondered: *I want to be with Judy, but I am not sure I can focus, and I do not want to disappoint her. Well, I guess it is time to take my own advice and "go with the flow."*

Any doubt he had about his ability to participate was quickly put to rest. As Judy slid her head down his chest and past his stomach, she said, "I've dreamt about sucking your cock for a long time."

Case closed, thought Lucas.

The next morning, bright sunshine greeted the sleepy foursome who were sitting in the dining room. It looked like steam was coming off the lake. After the waiter poured coffees, they all ordered steak and eggs for breakfast. Glancing at his coffee, Lucas called the waiter back.

"I'm sorry, but coffee will not work for me this morning," he said. "Would you please bring me a glass of Wieninger beer?"

The waiter was Bavarian, and he did not bat an eye. "Will it be only one beer?" he asked, as he looked around the table.

"Better make it two," said George.

"Three," said Judy.

"You can make it four," said Deanna.

Everyone laughed, including the waiter who left and came back promptly, carrying 4 Wieninger beers on his tray.

"Welcome to Bavaria and the breakfast of champions," said Lucas, as he raised his glass. When the food arrived, Lucas explained they were about to have an American breakfast, cooked by a lady from Turkey and a German sous chef. His remark made the group chuckle.

After breakfast, George, Deanna and Judy took Lucas' van to go shopping for ski gear in Rosenheim, a thirty-minute drive.

Lucas stayed behind to visit with people he knew: Bob Clarkson who managed the hotel. Chef Bucherl in the kitchen. Gunther, the bartender. Chip, the tennis pro who played bar games. He might even see Shelley, the head housekeeper who came from Santa Monica.

At Bob Clarkson's office, he tapped on the open door. Seeing Lucas, Bob stood, walked around his desk, shook Lucas' hand and said, "I'm so sorry for your loss, Lucas. She was such a beautiful young lady; this is a true tragedy."

"Thank you for the kind words, Bob," said Lucas. "So many horrible and senseless things are happening in the world. There are far too many bombings, terrorist attacks and airplane hijackings, not to mention the Vietnam War."

"Yeah. It is better not to mention Vietnam around here," he replied. "The war is a real embarrassment."

"Have there been any new bomb threats at the military facilities in Bavaria?" asked Lucas.

"I haven't heard of any recent threats," he replied. "But we now have three military police officers who stay here all the time."

"By the way," he added, "Robinson and some other officers came around, two days ago. He asked about you and showed me a photo of a man who had an Italian name. Anyway, I told them I hadn't seen you or the other man."

"Well, I'm trying to move on with my life which is hard enough," said Lucas. "I'd rather not have to deal with any nonsense or questions from Robinson right now."

Lucas thought: *Maybe I shouldn't have come here. There are too many memories since I was here with Inga*. Then, he realized: *I think of Inga, no matter where I go. It will take time, but I will get through this. Bavaria is exactly where I want to be.*

"Bob, I know you are busy, but I would like submit an application to work here this summer if there is an opening," said Lucas.

"For you, Lucas, we have an opening, and you don't need to bother with an application," he replied. "Chef Bucherl and I discussed it, already.

You will be our new Head Sous Chef, and I will submit the official request for your transfer."

"Thank you, Bob," he replied. "I look forward to the summer here. Now, I'm going to see Gunther in the bar. I'll visit with him until my friends get back from Rosenheim. They all want to ski tomorrow, and we plan to leave this afternoon."

"Do you know where you will be skiing?" asked Bob.

Not wanting anyone to know where they are headed, he said, "We haven't discussed it yet. Where do you ski around here?"

"My family and I are all beginners," replied Bob. "We often go to Berchtesgaden and ski at Skytop. It is part of AFRC, and many of our ski patrol hang out there."

Lucas knew he did not want to ski in places he had been with Inga, Eric and Sabine during his last trip here. So, he might suggest Salzburg which has many ski resorts, all within 200 kilometers. None of them had been there. He had also heard Zell am See is a beautiful place, and it was only an hour and a half drive from Lake Chiemsee.

Gunther was opening the bar. He greeted Lucas with a smile, and he gave his condolences. Gunther remembered Lucas' girlfriend, the local woodcarver and a native of Oberammergau. His friend Helmut had told him she was beaten to death by an unknown assailant.

"Thank you," he replied. "I'll have a draft Wieninger beer."

He felt comfortable with this friendly bartender, and Lucas was the only other person in the bar.

When Gunther asked Lucas if he came alone to Chiemsee, he replied, "I'm visiting with some friends who are from the U.S. and Canada, but they went to buy ski gear in Rosenheim."

Seeing an opportunity to learn more about the history of this area, he asked, "Hey Gunther, do you remember Sabine, the other lady? She was here with my tall, Swedish friend, Eric."

"I remember them well, a very handsome couple, and they were fun to talk to," replied Gunther.

"She is a ski instructor in Seefeld," said Lucas. "Her grandfather was the Hitler family doctor. Sabine told me some great stories about Hitler's youth and his rise to power. Did you know Hitler, personally?"

"I don't know if anyone really knew Hitler, but he always called me his favorite bartender," replied Gunther. "It was odd because he rarely drank alcohol, and we never had a personal conversation. What Hitler did best was make speeches and give orders. I know a few stories of his youth in Austria. Also, Martin Bormann lived in Berchtesgaden. He stopped here every time he motored by, with or without his Fuehrer. In the afternoons, Bormann would sit on a bar stool, get drunk and tell me stories. I could have been shot—just for hearing his stories. Did you know Hitler was born in Braunau am Inn, a town on the German and Austrian border? It's about one hundred kilometers northeast of here. His father, Alois, worked as a customs officer, and his mother was from a poor family. Ironically, his great grandmother was a Jewish maid.

"Lucas, if Sabine's grandfather was the Hitler family doctor, she must have told you about his youth in Braunau."

"Yeah, she told me about his youth, up to the time when his mother passed away, and he moved to Vienna," he replied.

"Then, you know Hitler didn't finish school," said Gunther. "He did well as an underclassman, but he dropped out at age fifteen. Competition overwhelmed him in higher grades, and he lost interest in school. After his mother died, he went to Vienna. He applied at the Vienna Academy of Art and the School of Architecture, but they turned him down. He worked odd jobs and took an interest in politics.

"During World War One, he joined the German Army. Hitler became a corporal, but he suffered a shrapnel injury. Next, he got injured by mustard gas, right before Germany surrendered in nineteen eighteen. After the war, Hitler had a period of depression. Then, he started going to meetings of the German Workers Party, first as a government spy, later as an interested member."

"Hitler, a government spy? What did he do?" he asked.

"When the war ended, Hitler was in the military, working as a corporal for Army intelligence," replied Gunther. "They ordered him to spy on the German Workers Party. While he did so, Hitler learned about the party's support of German nationalism, anti-Semitism and worker's rights. He became interested in the party, but he got annoyed with the party's leadership. To support the party, Hitler made speeches and got the crowds worked up. While his speeches aroused the crowds, the membership grew in numbers. Hitler became the new leader and renamed the party, the National Socialist German Workers Party (aka Nazi Party).

"In nineteen twenty-three, Hitler devised a plan for something they called the Beer Hall Putsch (revolt). He announced this plan during his rally at a beer hall called the *Bürgerbräukeller.* The next morning, about two thousand men of Hitler's Nazi Party marched to the center of Munich, and they tried to overthrow the local government. His coup d'état failed, resulting in the deaths of sixteen Nazis and four policemen.

"Two days later, Hitler was arrested. After a month-long trial, he was convicted of treason and sentenced to five years in prison. He used his time in prison wisely and began to write *Mein Kampf* with the help of Rudolf Hess. Hitler's autobiography, his political ideas and his plans for Germany's future were in the book, and it became two volumes. Hitler's original title was rather lengthy, *Viereinhalb Jahre des Kampfes gegen Lüge, Dummheit und Feigheit*. In English, the title means: Four and a Half Years of Struggle against Lies, Stupidity and Cowardice. His publisher talked him into using the shorter title, *Mein Kampf* (My Struggle).

"The judge who presided over Hitler's trial became sympathetic to Hitler's ideals. Therefore, he served only nine months in minimum security which the Bavarians call *Festungshaft* (Fortress confinement). Hitler received much public support and recognition from the trial. Although Hitler had concerns about being deported back to Austria, he seized the opportunity and spread his ideas. The sympathetic judge let him stay in Germany, based on his patriotic ideals and doctrines of wanting a better Germany and a better way of life for all citizens.

"An interesting outcome of the Beer Hall Putsch was Herman Göring got wounded and received morphine for the pain. He became addicted to the drug, and he carried the addiction with him for the rest of his life. Göring was a decorated fighter pilot during World War One, and he was awarded the prestigious *Pour le Mérite*, also known as the *Blue Max*, one of the highest awards given for extraordinary personal achievement, either military or civilian.

"Göring became a very powerful political figure in Nazi Germany, as Hitler's second-in-command. He founded the Gestapo, but he later gave Heinrich Himmler authority to oversee them. Göring was also appointed commander of the Luftwaffe (German air forces). He managed the successful economic recovery in Germany, and the arms build-up for World War Two. Hitler picked Göring as his successor, in addition to Göring being second-in-command of all government departments.

"By nineteen forty-two, Göring's good standing with Hitler was greatly reduced since the Luftwaffe failed to fulfill its commitments, and the German war effort was stumbling on all fronts. Göring then withdrew from playing a large role in the military and political scene. He focused on acquiring property and artwork, most of which was confiscated from Jewish victims of the Holocaust.

"In nineteen forty-five, Göring heard of Hitler's intentions to commit suicide. He sent a message to Hitler, asking for permission to take over as head of the Reich. Hitler claimed it was an act of treason. He expelled Göring from the party, stripped him of all authority and ordered his arrest. When the war was over, Göring was convicted of war crimes during the Nuremberg trials. He was sentenced to death by hanging, but he beat them to the punch. The night before his execution, Göring committed suicide by swallowing cyanide."

Lucas felt a hand on his shoulder. Turning his head, he saw a smiling Herbert Bucherl, the Executive Chef of the Rasthaus am Chiemsee.

Chef Bucherl gave Lucas his condolences as they shook hands. Then, he took a long swig of beer which Gunther had handed him.

"Lucas, I understand you are doing Colonel Moyer's birthday party in Garmisch, and it will happen soon," said Bucherl.

"Yes. I promised Colonel Moyer I would take care of the food," he replied. "My friend Eric is taking care of the bar, along with Gino and John Ferrell. It's nice to see you, Chef Bucherl, would you care to be involved with the party?"

"I would love to assist you in any way I can, and please call me Herbert," the chef replied.

"It would be great, but I think you should take charge of the food and allow me to assist you," said Lucas.

"Well, let's tackle this job together," Herbert suggested, "and we'll have a great time doing it."

"Thank you, Herbert. I know we'll have a good time," said Lucas.

Catching movement, out of the corner of his eye, Lucas also felt her presence. He stood, stepped around his bar stool and feasted his eyes on the beautiful face of Shelley Carpenter, Head Housekeeper of the Rasthaus am Chiemsee.

Shelley's fantastic smile faded as she gave Lucas a hug and said, "I am so sorry for your loss. Inga was a lovely person. When you came here before, you mentioned the possibility of transferring to Chiemsee for the summer. Will you be staying now in Oberammergau, Lucas?"

Before Lucas could answer, Herbert said, "We all look forward to having you on our kitchen staff, as the Head Sous Chef."

"I have done a lot of soul-searching, the past few days," said Lucas. "Being here now, I know I will enjoy my summer at Chiemsee."

"I have to get back to work now," said Herbert. "We will talk about everything later. How long are you staying for this visit, Lucas?"

"My friends just arrived from 'The States' and from Canada," he replied. "They want to ski in Austria, so we are leaving this afternoon. In a few days, I will get in touch with you, and we can begin planning for Colonel Moyer's party."

Herbert agreed, shook Lucas' hand, finished his beer and went back to the kitchen.

Shelley grabbed Lucas' hand, saying, "Lucas, why don't we go for a walk? I'll show you some living quarters for your move here."

They walked through the main lounge area which was nearly empty. This time of day, everyone was out skiing or sightseeing.

"Isn't this jumping the gun a little, Shelley?" he asked.

"It's all I could think of to get you alone," she replied.

Lucas looked her in the eye, and he smiled. He felt stunned as he walked with Shelley. They went out the front entrance and down the stairs. He thought: *The way she looked at me as she said, "... to get you alone," was hot enough to melt a snowball.*

Going toward what Lucas remembered to be the Ranch House or the Farm House, one or the other, Shelley said, "I won't show you the Farm House where most of the ski patrol live. We all call it the Animal House. You do not want to live there. You would never get to sleep."

Shelley took Lucas' gloved hand and squeezed it a little.

Lucas studied her appearance: *There is something irresistible about this lady. She has beautiful white teeth and very inviting lips. Her straight hair is black and shoulder-length. Bangs cover half of her forehead, and she has the most perfect nose I have ever seen.*

Shelley showed Lucas the Ranch House. On the ground floor, there was a 1-bedroom apartment, but everyone who lived in this building had to share the kitchen. The upstairs had 3 small bedrooms, and 1 bathroom which was shared. Then, Shelley said she had a better deal for him, and they headed for the front door.

Grabbing Lucas' hand again, she led him under the autobahn and over to the Park Hotel. First, they got two beers from an employees' beer machine. Then, they walked upstairs to the second floor and went into Shelley's corner apartment.

"Lucas, do you have any hashish with you?" asked Shelley. "I feel like getting high."

"As a matter of fact, I do," he replied. Lucas pulled out his hash pipe and filled it with some fine hashish, courtesy of his friend Topo.

I should try and talk Topo into coming with me to Chiemsee for the summer, thought Lucas.

He handed the pipe to Shelley. She took two hits and handed it back to Lucas. He took two hits and set the pipe down.

Shelly opened 2 Wieninger beers, handed 1 to Lucas, raised her beer bottle and said, "Here's to a great summer by the lake."

Before Lucas could respond, Shelley was in his arms, kissing him passionately. Then, she took a step back and said, "Lucas, I've been hoping we would get to know each other better. How would you feel about living with me in this apartment when you move here?"

Feeling astonished, Lucas looked at Shelley. "I don't know what to say, except I am flattered and glad you feel this way," he replied. "As we walked over here, I thought there is something very special about you, something I have to pursue."

The next moment, they were kissing and undressing each other. If Lucas had drawn a curvy woman's body to suit him, it would be Shelley's.

Other people might say she was a little overweight. However, in Lucas' eyes, here was a goddess. Ample and perfect-shaped breasts, strong skier's legs and a beautiful face. He could not take his eyes off Shelley.

Their lovemaking was wild and passionate. Although Lucas was 31 and Shelley was 23, they acted like love-starved teenagers. Lucas did not want to stop. This felt so good, and it was something they both wanted. After they satisfied each other, Lucas knew this lady had him hooked, and he would be back for more.

They got dressed, kissed again and stepped outside. Lucas wished they could go back in and start all over.

"Okay. Shelley, my dear, when I come to live here, I will choose this apartment, but only if you come with it."

Shelley smiled, then she led Lucas back to Lake Chiemsee Hotel, and they walked into the bar. Judy, George and Deanna were seated at the bar, talking to Gunther.

Judy came over, put her arm around Lucas, gave him a kiss on the cheek and said, "We were looking for you."

"Oh, Judy, this is Shelley, the head housekeeper here," said Lucas. "She was showing me around." The two ladies eyed each other, and they exchanged polite greetings.

After meeting George and Deanna, Shelley said, "I had better get back to work now. It was nice meeting all of you."

Looking him in the eye, Shelley said, "I hope you enjoyed the tour, Lucas, and I hope to see you later." Then, she walked away.

Lucas asked Gunther for a glass of beer. He turned to the other three and asked, "Did you all get new skis and gear?"

"I bought Rossignol skis and a pair of Lange boots," said George.

"I got beautiful Blizzard skis and Solomon boots," said Deanna.

"I can't wait to try out my new Volkl skis, and I also got a pair of Lange boots," said Judy.

"What do you think about leaving now and heading south to Zell am See?" Lucas asked. "I've heard it is beautiful and a great place to ski. The drive will take us an hour and a half, and we can check in at a hotel this afternoon. It will give us time to relax, look around and have a nice dinner tonight. We can get an early start and go skiing tomorrow."

George and Deanna were nodding.

"Skiing sounds good. Where will we stay?" asked Judy.

"Let's go to the front desk," said Lucas, "and see if Joe knows of a nice hotel for us to visit."

CHAPTER 29

Zell am See

George agreed to drive because Lucas had already consumed a few beers, plus a shot of Jägermeister and a few hits on the hash pipe. He felt spacey, and perhaps it was right where he wanted to be. The surprise get-together with Shelley left him with little energy. Now, he wanted to kick back and enjoy being with his friends for a while.

The group went to the bar, purchased 2 cases of Wieninger beer, and all said goodbye to Gunther.

Ready to leave Chiemsee and head for Zell am See, everyone piled into the van and got situated. With George driving and Deanna riding shotgun, Lucas and Judy got in the back. All the ski gear was stored behind the leather seat which faced the front of the van. George had the music turned down low, so they could talk while he played a Three Dog Night song, "Joy to the World."

Directing her question to Lucas, Deanna said, "I am curious about the Baader-Meinhof Gang. I've read a little about them, and they seem to have a following of sympathizers in Germany and other countries. What do you think they will achieve?"

"I don't know their deep, dark secrets, but based on conversations I have had with a person who knows RAF members, these homegrown terrorists are a product of the left-wing anti-establishment," he replied. "Their group originated in the sixties and became a subculture of people who indulged in casual sex, rock 'n' roll music, plus all kinds of illegal drugs. They all love to party, and they do get messed up.

"I heard stories about Ulrike Meinhof. She had a very bad trip on acid, years ago, and later had a tumor removed from her brain. She had a short fling with Andreas Baader. Yet, he and Gudrun are still together. Ulrike wrote a movie, but it has never has been shown to the public because of her association with the RAF. Ulrike almost blew herself up with a hand grenade while being instructed by members of the PLO (Palestine Liberation Organization) at a terrorist training camp in Jordan.

"Apparently, the members are crude and sometimes klutzy. They may be so hopelessly inept, they will never accomplish anything, except calamity. When we stayed in Nice, we all witnessed an example of such ineptness when those two RAF guys crashed their BMW on the sidewalk, right in front of us."

"I don't want to be around those people," said Judy. "They sound out of control, and I hope you have seen the last of them, Lucas."

"I think any leftist fanatics who have communist beliefs are blind to what is going on behind the Berlin wall and in other communist countries," said Lucas. "There is no true equality—and I doubt there ever will be. East German citizens will never see new Volkswagens, vacations in Spain, or the homes which their parents built in West Germany, using leftover rubble after World War Two. For the most part, East Germany is a police state."

"I will never forget the wreck in Nice and the dead RAF guy," said Deanna. "We were lucky they didn't hit us. Do you know if the members still drive BMWs?"

"The last time my friend saw any of them, they were driving a new VW van," replied Lucas.

Wanting to change the subject, Judy said, "Lucas, I would love to come back in the summer, visit the island and see the castle at Lake Chiemsee. I understand King Ludwig built several castles, including the Disneyland Castle which we see so many photos of. Have you seen any of these castles during your time in Bavaria?"

"Yes," he replied. "I was fortunate to have private tours of both the Neuschwanstein Castle and the Linderhof Palace. I look forward to a tour of the Herrenchiemsee Palace in the summer."

Sharing what he heard about King Ludwig the Second, Lucas said, "A native of Bavaria told me Ludwig's Palace on Herrenchiemsee was fashioned after the Palace of Versailles. It has a spectacular Hall of Mirrors. In the Vestibule, a sculpted ceiling pays tribute to 'The Sun King' above a statue of King Louis the Fourteenth.

"During my castle tours, I learned a lot. Ludwig was never interested in government duties as the King of Bavaria. He spent most of his time as a recluse; building the castles kept him busy. King Ludwig was known as *Märchenkönig*, meaning the Fairy Tale King. He had two main interests: King Louis the Fourteenth of France and his friend, Richard Wagner.

"King Ludwig was a true romantic and a strong supporter of Richard Wagner. To design his castles and incorporate many of Wagner's opera themes into the building plans, Ludwig hired theater set designers instead of architects. He loved Wagner's operas.

"Ludwig lived in his own self-absorbed world. Ministers of State became frustrated by Ludwig's lack of attention to civic duties, his costly life of luxury and the frivolity of his self-indulgence. In the end, the Ministers of State accused him of being insane, and he was arrested at his Neuschwanstein Castle.

"Within a few days, Ludwig was taken to another castle at Lake Starnberg. The following evening, he took a walk on the grounds and disappeared. After a searching for hours, they found his body, floating in the lake. He had drowned, along with the psychiatrist who had certified him as insane. Officials ruled his death a suicide, but it was disputed. His cause of death is still unknown."

"Lucas, how old was King Ludwig when he died?" asked Judy.

"King Ludwig the Second was only forty years old at the time of his death," he replied.

"Did he ever get married or have a lady friend?" she asked.

"Good question," he replied. "King Ludwig was engaged once. He planned to marry a cousin who also loved Richard Wagner's operas, but Ludwig broke it off. He had close male friends, and people said he struggled to suppress his homosexual desires."

"Okay, I've talked enough," he added. "I want to hear from all of you. Tell me what's been going on in your parts of the world."

"All right, but let's have another Wieninger beer," said George. "This may be the best beer I've ever tasted."

Remembering his visit to the Wieninger Brewery with Eric, Inga and Sabine, Lucas was prompted to tell the others about it. "I was lucky enough to have a tour and lunch at the Wieninger Brewery. It's between Lake Chiemsee and Salzburg. Since then, I drink Wieninger beer—whenever I can find it. Lake Chiemsee Hotel and the AFRC hotels in Berchtesgaden stock it in the employees' beer machines."

Everyone got a fresh Wieninger beer as George tried to think of events or details which might interest Lucas.

"Let's start with sports," said George. "In their first Super Bowl, the Dallas Cowboys won Super Bowl Six, beating the Miami Dolphins twenty-four to three. The Cowboy's Quarterback, Roger Staubach, was named Super Bowl Six MVP; it made Staubach the first player ever to receive both the Heisman Trophy and a Super Bowl MVP. Nebraska beat Alabama in Miami's Orange Bowl. In the Rose Bowl, the Stanford Indians beat the Ohio State Buckeyes, twenty-seven to seventeen; and Stanford's MVP was their quarterback, Jim Plunkett."

"Did you know Sandy Koufax, Yogi Berra and Early Wynn were all inducted into the MLB Hall of Fame?" George asked Lucas.

Realizing he felt as if he had been on another planet for the past few weeks, or longer, Lucas shook his head and said, "No."

"Also, Bob Douglas is the first black player to be inducted into the National Basketball Association's Hall of Fame," said George.

"Speaking of basketball, what is going on in California, closer to home?" asked Lucas.

"The UCLA Basketball Team won their sixth straight National Championship, coached by the legendary John Wooden," said George. "The Lakers started this year with three wins which gave them thirty-three straight wins and set a record for the longest winning streak of any team in American professional sports. Unfortunately, the Bucks beat them in their next game."

"So, ladies, what's the big news in your part of the world?" Lucas asked Judy and Deanna.

"Let me think," Deanna replied. Then, she took a few sips of beer. "Canada adopted multiculturalism as an official policy which means all citizens will be treated as equals, regardless of race, language or religious beliefs. Being one of the first countries to adopt such a policy, Canada goes a step further than other countries, including the United States, by encouraging all citizens to take an active part in government affairs, whether they are political or social." After another sip of beer, she added, "Also, our Montreal Canadiens won the last Stanley Cup."

"You're right," said George. "They beat the Chicago Black Hawks, and I read the engravers made a mistake on the trophy cup."

"Yes, the coach's first name was missing," she replied. "The officials corrected it on the replica cup."

"This is not recent, but Canada has had its share of terrorist news," said Judy. "It happened about a year ago when our trade commissioner, James Cross, was kidnapped and held for two months by a group called Front de libération du Québec (FLQ). Their ransom demands included the release of twenty political prisoners, a half million dollars in gold and a public broadcast of the FLQ Manifesto on radio and television. As it turned out, the FLQ settled for free passage to Cuba.

"Within days, another kidnapping occurred, and it didn't end so well. A group of FLQ members kidnapped the Minister of Labour, Pierre Laporte; they took him from his front yard. The FLQ called him the 'Minister of Unemployment and Assimilation.' Seven days after the kidnapping, Quebec officials found his body in the trunk of a car. The media referred to it as *The October Crisis*. Trudeau, the Canadian Prime Minister, called in the Army to keep the peace and to protect our beautiful capitol city of Ottawa."

"It seems to me, terrorism is becoming the next big threat to world peace," said Lucas.

"We also have it in the United States," said George. "Last year, a group known as Weather Underground set off a bomb in the restroom of the U.S. Capitol Building. Personally, I hope we don't run into members of the Baader-Meinhof group again. I don't want to be around when shootings or bombings happen."

Lucas did not want to respond to George's last comment. He realized telling them about all his visits with the RAF in Garmisch would scare his friends. So, he changed the subject.

"I made hotel reservations for us to stay in Zell am See," said Lucas. "The hotel is right on a ski slope where we can ski in and ski out."

"Why did you want us to go to Zell am See, Lucas?" asked Judy.

"George and I skied glaciers while we traveled in Europe, and I read about the Kitzsteinhorn Glacier near Zell am See," Lucas replied. "It sounds beautiful, and I've heard the locals are very friendly."

"I remember when we met you, you told us you had skied at an Austrian glacier. What other glaciers have you skied?" asked Judy.

"Let's see…" said George, "we skied at Stelvio Pass near Gomagoi. Then, we skied both sides of the Matterhorn in Cervenia and Zermatt, and we were extras in the unforgettable movie."

"What movie?" Judy asked.

"The movie would be another whole story," replied Lucas. "We also skied a glacier on the Zugspitze near Garmisch."

"I've had fun skiing in Germany, Austria and Switzerland," said George. "All the ski resorts have been great. Now, we will ski at—what is the name of this next one?"

"The Kitzsteinhorn Glacier," Lucas answered. "It is above Kaprun which is a ski town near Zell am See. I've heard Kaprun has better skiing than Zell am See, but Hotel Berner is close to the lake and it looks like a great place to stay. If conditions are favorable, we can stay for several days, ski both areas and experience their famous nightlife."

They had reached Lake Zell, and Lucas knew they must be near the hotel. He pulled out a travel book, handed it to Judy and said, "Please see if you can find a map of Zell am See. I think we are getting close."

Judy found an area map and asked, "What street are we on?"

George pulled over and stopped at the next corner. The street sign read *Loferer Bundesstraße*. Judy studied the map and said, "Continue on this street which becomes Brucker Bundesstraße, then turn right onto Mozartstraße." After they made the turn, she said, "Now, curve left onto Nikolaus-Gassner-Promenade and make the next right turn. Hotel Berner will be on the right."

"Each new town is more enchanting than the last one," said Judy.

"This is fantastic," said George. "Our hotel is so close to everything; we won't even have to move the van."

Both rooms had a balcony, overlooking the town and the lake from the 3rd floor. The view in these upper Austrian Alps was amazing.

As they carried their belongings upstairs, Lucas evaluated his feelings: *This is as nice as any romantic place I've stayed at, except I don't know how romantic I will feel. I miss Inga, and then Shelley came along which made my life more confusing. Now, I am with this gorgeous Canadian lady. I hope I can stay in the moment.*

In the hotel room, they got settled and opened 2 Wieninger beers. Lucas got his hash pipe, filled it with crumbled hashish and shared it with Judy. Then, they opened the sliding door and stepped out onto the snow-covered balcony. Lucas put his arm around Judy, and she put her arm around him. They stood in silence, a little breathless, as they took in the beauty of the moment and let the frosty wind cool their faces.

Judy broke the silence, saying, "Lucas, I know my coming back now must be the worst timing in the world, but I want you to know why I am here. Since I enjoyed our time together in France and Spain, I had to come back and see you. I want to find out if our relationship can be more than what we shared during our short time there."

Lucas looked out across the lights of the town below and across the lake to Kaprun. Then, he turned, looked into Judy's blue eyes and said, "I think some things are simply meant to happen. So, perhaps this is supposed to be our time together."

Looking in his eyes, Judy said, "Well, I say we make the most of our time together."

It felt as if they bonded, in that moment, and Lucas thought: *I must be the luckiest guy in the world.* Hugging and kissing, they got close to the point of no return.

Lucas gently pulled back and said, "Judy, I'd rather not rush. I want to enjoy every precious moment with you after our evening out."

Judy agreed with him. So, they went to the bar and ordered 4 half-liter glasses of Stiegl beer. Their beers arrived with perfect foam heads, right before George and Deanna walked in.

They all moved to a table which was away from the little stage. The band was playing oompah music and waitresses were dancing around the bar. To hear each other, they had to speak up over the music and the other people who were clapping, laughing and talking.

"When we were at the club, Helmut said you won the first annual bar games trophy," George said to Lucas. "I would want to play in next year's tournament. It sounds like lots of fun."

"You know, George, I felt lucky when I won the tournament," Lucas replied. "Those guys are great players, and it took a lot of luck for me to win. But, it's hard to talk about, or even think about, because I wonder what might be different if I had been with Inga at her house instead of playing games at the club. Anyway, with all your skills in sports, I'm sure you will be in next year's tournament if you are still here."

"Do they allow women to compete?" asked Deanna.

"We had no women competing in the last tournament," replied Lucas. "I'm sorry we didn't because the two lady bartenders, twin sisters at the officers' club, can compete with anybody and not be ashamed."

"Why don't we have an early dinner, get a decent night's sleep and ski all day tomorrow?" Lucas suggested, as they finished their beers.

"I agree with you," said Judy. "Trying on all those ski boots and clothes left me exhausted."

A buxom waitress, wearing a dirndl, led them to a large table by the window which gave them a great view of Lake Zell. Across the lake, a band of lights brightened the ski slope to the top of the Schmittenhöhe, and other lights outlined the edge of the lake. Beyond the far side of the lake, they could also see lights sparkling in the famous ski town of Kaprun and on the slope below the Kitzsteinhorn Glacier. With this view, they had a spectacular setting for a romantic dinner.

The same waitress returned and seated an older Bavarian couple at their table. Lucas found it difficult not to stare at the waitress' ample bosom, poking out of her low-cut, dirndl blouse.

The older couple settled themselves at the table and greeted them with, "Gruss Gott."

When Lucas, Judy, George and Deanna gave the same greeting to the couple, the gentleman asked in English, "Are you Americans?"

"Wow, I guess there is no hiding it!" said George.

They all had a chuckle. George's use of German was limited as was Judy and Deanna's. Lucas had developed a decent understanding of the language because Inga had spoken it with him. But everyone continued to speak English this evening.

The native Bavarian couple introduced themselves as Franz and Brigitte. They were born in Zell am See and got married at age eighteen. Both studied English, and they hoped to visit America someday.

Lucas thought: *These Austrian people are so friendly, happy, fun-loving and a pleasure to be around.*

The menu was written in German, and Lucas was pleased to discover he could read most of it. Lucas translated the menu for his friends with a little good-natured help from Franz and Brigitte.

Franz and Brigitte ordered Grillwurstel mit Pommes Frites (grilled sausages with French fries).

Lucas chose Hirschbraten im Pfandl serviert mit Pilzsauce, Späetzle und Apfelscheibe mit Preiselbeeren (roast venison saddle in mushroom sauce, plus spaetzle and sliced apples with lingonberries).

Judy chose Lachsforelle vom Grill mit Zitronenbutter, Gemusegrostl und Sauerrahmdip (grilled filet of salmon-trout, plus fried potato slices and vegetables, served with sour cream dip).

George decided on Beiriedschnitte mit gebratenen Kartoffelscheiben und Grillgemuse (tenderloin of beef, served with fried potato slices and grilled vegetables).

Deanna ordered Wiener Schnitzel vom Schwein mit Kartoffein und Preiselbeeren (breaded and pan-fried escalope of pork, served with potatoes and cranberries).

Lucas was getting into the spirit of the evening. He enjoyed watching the oompah band and the people who were all drinking beer, singing, clapping and swaying to the music.

The waiters and waitresses danced around the dining room, smiling and laughing while they were serving the guests. Lucas ordered shots of Jägermeister and another round of beers for everyone at his table. Brigitte said she would tell them a story about Easy Company and their stay in Zell am See during the summer of 1945. She and Franz got there right after Germany's surrender which ended World War II.

Brigitte began the story, "It was a summer which I never will forget. When the Easy Company of American soldiers came into town, there were wounded German soldiers were everywhere, sheltered in all the hotels and extra rooms. The Americans were *schmutzig* (dirty). They appeared to be the losers of the war, wearing soiled, wrinkled uniforms, unshaven and unorganized compared with the defeated German army which was organized, polished, and… How do you say? Oh, I think you use the word *spiffy*. There were around twenty-five thousand Germans, but only six hundred American soldiers came here to process them. I worked as a translator for a Captain Speirs."

"Franz, were you in the military during the war?" asked Lucas.

"Yes, I was a translator for English-speaking prisoners in a POW camp," he replied. "Brigitte and I had studied English in school, so we served as translators for both English and German. At the end of the war, I worked my way back to Salzburg, and then home to Zell am See where I reunited with my Brigitte. We volunteered our services to the Americans. I worked for Captain Winters at headquarters in Kaprun. So, between the two of us, Brigitte and I were very much involved with the Easy Company, and we knew what they did while they were here. It was between June and August of nineteen forty-five."

After a drink of beer, Brigitte continued her story, "Americans had to process each German soldier, and they discovered many Nazis had changed to regular army uniforms in hope of not being arrested. One famous Nazi escaped to Argentina, but the Israelis located and executed him by hanging in nineteen sixty. There were stories about other Nazis who made it to South America. Some people claimed Adolph Hitler and his wife were still alive and living in Argentina."

"How did the Austrians treat American soldiers?" asked Judy.

"The Austrians and Germans treated them well, and they had good relationships with Americans," replied Brigitte. "Austrians took care of preparing meals, doing laundry, house cleaning and construction work. Officials paid them in food, cigarettes and money. At first, the American soldiers had little to do, except drink, carouse and chase women. Captain Speirs issued an order for 'No Public Drunkenness'. The men got drunk anyway, and they could not drive well on our winding, mountain roads.

"There were many accidents with fatalities and serious injuries, caused by drunken soldiers. Most of the mountain passes were closed by snow, so the accidents were close to town. It made me feel sad. These soldiers had dashed into enemy fire, fought in the bloodiest battles and survived, only to die in a drunken accident."

"Still, there were fun times," said Franz. "Captain Winters created a sports area with a running track, tennis courts and a baseball diamond. Some men saw this as an opportunity to train for future competitions back home. Soldiers were getting anxious to get home after the war, even with so many activities to do here. A lot of men toured the Alps, but most of them drank and chased women. It was ideal here for healthy, American soldiers because young, local women were pretty, fair-skinned, well-scrubbed and willing. Soldiers discovered an endless supply of liquor in Nazi hoards which were also filled with confiscated artwork, sculptures, money, gold and silver."

"I will never forget the American holiday," Brigitte said, "on the Fourth of July in nineteen forty-five. It was a large celebration, but it rained on the fourth and the fifth of July, so they held it on the sixth of July. They had food, liquor, music, dancing and many sports. There were gliders in the sky, and men jumped out with parachutes."

"Oh, don't forget the officers' party which took place a week before at headquarters in Hotel Zell," said Franz. "One night, there was a big fight between a general and another officer. The general rode back from Kaprun to Berchtesgaden in Hitler's Mercedes which they had confiscated from Hitler's house in Obersalzberg. A disgruntled soldier had siphoned most of the gas out of the Mercedes. So, the general ran out of gas. He was halfway to Berchtesgaden, and he was not happy about it. However, the general did not hold a grudge. He let the soldiers go forward with a Fourth of July party, anyway.

"In one of the saddest events here, an American soldier was drunk by the side of the road, and he shot two German soldiers who didn't speak English. The drunken soldier thought they were resisting capture. When Easy Company soldiers came across the mess, the drunk shot one of those soldiers in the head, then he fled the scene. They found the drunken soldier later, trying to rape an Austrian girl. Officials arrested him and turned him in. He showed signs of a very serious beating. Captain Speirs wondered why they had not killed him for shooting one of their own soldiers."

The group finished dinner, and nobody wanted dessert, but they all had another shot of Jägermeister before saying their goodbyes.

Speaking to Franz and Brigitte, Lucas said, "Vielen Dank für die wunderbare geschichten." (Thank you for the wonderful stories).

Then, he paid the check. Everyone thanked Lucas, and they all headed to their rooms.

Although he was tired, Lucas was too high to feel it. He and Judy smoked another bowl of hashish and took a long, fun shower together. Moving to the bed and making love in slow and deliberate motions was spectacular. Lucas focused on unselfish desires, brought his partner to a place of ecstasy, and he hit the finish line soaring. Before long, Judy was asleep and naked on top of the comforter. Lying next to her, Lucas' reflected on his day until he drifted off to sleep.

In the morning, they made love again, took a shower, got dressed and went downstairs, both ready to ski.

Everyone had agreed to meet in the dining room for breakfast at 9 a.m. George and Deanna got there early and held a table by the window. When the others arrived, they all had coffee and dove into a tray full of sliced Westphalia ham, schinkenspeck (smoked bacon), sliced sausages and croissants with marmalade.

Lucas said, "There should be a law against how good I feel this morning. When I saw the sun shining on a layer of fresh snow..." he looked at Judy with a grin, "... I perked up, shall we say."

George said, "Maybe 'not say' would be better!" Everyone laughed.

Following breakfast, they went through the torture of putting on ski boots. This was most difficult for George and the ladies since they each had new boots.

After checking to see if they had everything, the group was ready for a new adventure. Carrying skis and poles, they all headed out to explore Zell am See. It was a new and unfamiliar place for them to play. Right outside the hotel, they snapped into their bindings and took off, skiing on a snow-covered path, through some trees, onto a groomed slope and down to the City Express gondola. This took them to a quad chairlift, the Hirschkogel Express. When they all got off the chairlift, they skied a short distance, and then road in the Areitbahn gondola which took them to Schmittenhöhe Peak.

Before they started the downhill run together, Lucas asked the ladies, "Hey, will you ladies from Banff take it easy on me?"

"Maybe we should ask you to go easy," replied Judy. "This the first time we are skiing in Europe, and we both have new skis and boots."

"Okay then, you show us the way," said Lucas.

From the peak, they had a choice. They could have traversed across the peak to some challenging runs, but they chose a long intermediate run to the neighboring town of Schuttdorf. It was a great warm-up run.

At the bottom, they rode a different gondola from Schuttdorf to the Schmittenhöhe Peak, and they enjoyed another bowl of Topo's finest hashish. They were all feeling good. Lucas loved the privacy 4-passenger gondolas offered. It allowed them to smoke hashish on the way to the top. The camaraderie of passing the pipe around was an act of bonding and of showing trust within this group.

After a long ride, they stopped to enjoy breathtaking views from the peak. Standing on top of the mountain, the bright sun was almost blinding, even with sunglasses. Below, they could see Zell am See, Lake Zell, the small town of Kaprun and far beyond.

This is the moment I look forward to the most, thought Lucas. *It's fantastic to be at the top, right before I start down the mountain. It is a solitary experience—nothing but me on these skis, ready to point them downhill and go.*

Since it was Friday, the weekend crowds were not on the slopes yet. Deanna led the way down the slope, Judy was right behind her, and the guys were close behind Judy. This time, the ladies were setting a brisk pace on a long, intermediate slope, but Lucas and George kept up.

On the gondola, riding back to the top, they studied the trail map and agreed to go over the summit in search of more challenging runs on the back side of Schmittenhöhe. When they arrived at the top of Zell am See's home mountain, they had to stop and take it all in again. The panoramic view was magnificent.

"I'll bet we've all seen sights similar to this when we have skied at other resort areas," said Lucas. "I remember great views of Lake Tahoe from the ski areas around the lake, including Squaw Valley, Alpine Meadows, Northstar, Homewood and others. By comparison, every new place in Bavaria appears more magical than the last one."

"I've heard about the skiing in Austria," said Judy. "But I did not visualize anything as spectacular as I have seen today. This is better than I could imagine. I am so happy to be here with you, Lucas."

They all had fun skiing and took a few of the black runs, then stopped for lunch.

There was a small ski hut at the top of a T-bar on the south side of Schmittenhöhe Peak. The owner, Bruno Mayr, his wife, Ingrid, plus two young Bavarian ladies were running the place, and it was busy. Although the ski hut was small, it had a large patio with tables and benches. It was cold, yet also a nice sun-shiny day.

Sitting outside, they had half-liter glasses of Stiegl beer, goulash soup and brotchen. It was Lucas' recommendation, a typical Bavarian and Tyrolean skiers' lunch.

They tried to ski all over the mountain and had a great time, letting it all out when the slopes allowed them to do so. Late in the afternoon, sitting in the gondola, Lucas got his hash pipe out of his parka, lit it and passed it around.

"Lucas, is hashish difficult to buy here?" asked Deanna.

"I have no trouble finding hashish," he replied. "Topo, the friendly waiter who we all met in Nice, lives in Garmisch now; and I always buy from him."

"I have always smoked pot when I'm skiing or at a party, but I know lots of people who smoke it all day long," said Judy. "If I did, it would make me sleepy."

"Aha, I've learned a lot about marijuana and hashish," said Lucas, "from Topo and David, a guy George and I met on the way to Morocco. It turned out, I knew David in Fresno, California. We played basketball on the same high school team. He told me the effect you feel depends on the strain you smoke. We are smoking hashish which comes from a female marijuana plant. Male plants have very little THC, the magic ingredient which gets you high. From female plants, you have a choice of strains. The Indica strain makes you want to hit the couch. Indica plants are kept separated from other plants, and they grow low to the ground. The other strain is called Sativa. It gives you energy and creativity along with happy, sometimes euphoric, feelings."

"This must be Sativa since I don't feel sleepy, but I can identify with the euphoric feelings," Judy said, looking at Lucas.

Lucas grinned and replied, "I say Sativa is a fun, 'head high' which affects cerebral function and produces an energetic feeling. Indica is more of a 'body high' which is relaxing and a deeper, heavier feeling. I find the Sativa expands my mind and enhances my sexual experience, plus food taste better and music sounds better.

"We are fortunate since Topo gets his Sativa hashish from Colombia or Mexico. Thailand also grows Sativa. Afghanistan and Pakistan are the primary sources of Indica. David told me Sativa plants can grow as tall as twenty feet, much taller than the Indica plants. Sativa leaves are thinner and a lighter color; the buds are elongated; the plants grow closer together and take longer to mature. Indica buds are short and fat; the plants do not grow taller than about eight feet; and the leaves are broader and a darker green."

"Did you hear from David Burns again, Lucas?" asked George.

"No," he replied, "and since I have not spoken to his two Australian friends in a while, I've heard nothing about him. They are working in Garmisch now, and one of them is with Topo."

Of course, George had to ask, "Which one?"

"I don't recall, right now," he replied. "I think I saw them together in The Grill, one night."

Since Judy and Deanna were present, Lucas did not want to pursue the subject of past escapades when he and George traveled with Olivia and Ashleigh, so he turned and looked out the window.

As the cable car approached the top of Schmittenhöhe, George said, "Let's make this our last run. I want to go relax at the hotel."

They got off the gondola, grabbed their skis and poles, then headed down the mountain and skied all the way to the hotel. Everyone looked forward to an evening of fun in Zell am See, Austria.

At the hotel, they all smoked hashish. Then, everyone put on their swimsuits and hotel robes, grabbed a bottle of Wieninger beer and headed downstairs to the spa area.

Outside, they found a large, rectangular-shaped Jacuzzi, surrounded by piles of snow as high as their knees. A cloud of warm steam rose above the hot water. Everyone hung their robes on hooks and got in, each with their beer in hand.

There was only 1 other person in the Jacuzzi, a mature Austrian lady who had a nice figure for a woman her age (maybe 50 years old). She was drinking a bottle of Stiegl beer. As soon as the 4 Americans got settled and comfortable, the Austrian lady introduced herself.

She spoke in perfect English, "Hello, my name is Nora Klammer. By listening to you speak, I would say you are Americans. What part of 'The States' are you from?"

"These ladies are from Banff, Canada," replied Lucas, gesturing to Judy and to Deanna. "My friend George and I came from Long Beach, California. Now, we all live in Garmisch, Germany, where we will all soon work for the Armed Forces Recreation Center. We're in Zell am See for two days of skiing. Are you here on vacation, Nora?"

"No, I was born in Mooswald," she replied, "a farming community, one hundred and seventy kilometers south, where I grew up and went to school. I moved here when I was twenty years old."

"What do you do for a living or profession?" George asked Nora.

"I have been the head housekeeper for the Porsche family since I moved here," she replied.

"I read something about the Porsche family's roots in this area," said Lucas. "Nora, you must tell us how life is for you, being around such famous and talented people."

"I know as much about the Porsche family, as anyone," she replied. "I can give you the short version, but it will still be a long story."

"Then, I should get a lot more beer and bring it to the Jacuzzi, or we can go upstairs and hear about the Porsche family," said Lucas.

Nobody was ready to leave the Jacuzzi, so Lucas left and came back with a whole case of Wieninger beer. He was shaking from the cold. Wasting no time, Lucas set down the beer, got into the Jacuzzi and warmed himself in the hot, swirling water.

"Oh, my goodness, Lucas. How far did you go to get the case of beer?" asked Nora.

"Just out to the van," he replied.

"What type of van do you have?" she asked.

"It's a pop-top VW, a nineteen seventy-one version," he replied.

"Oh, it must be rather cozy with the four of you," she said.

Looking at his 3 friends, Lucas smiled. Then, he said, "Just right."

When everyone had a fresh beer, Lucas reached into his robe pocket, pulled out his hash pipe, lit it, took a hit and passed it to Nora. The others were watching to see her reaction. Everyone relaxed when Nora took a big hit and passed it to Deanna.

"I've spent every winter skiing since I was a young girl," said Nora. "So, I have been exposed to marijuana and hashish, and I like it very much, danke schoen. Also, thank you for the beer."

"Nora, why is it you are here in the hotel Jacuzzi? Do you live here?" asked Judy.

"No," she replied. "My boyfriend is the hotel manager. He lets me use the facilities, and I enjoy the Jacuzzi. Now, if you are ready, let me tell you about the Porsche family."

"Yes, please," said Lucas while the others nodded. They all wanted to hear her story.

"I live in the big house at the Porsche family estate which they call Schuttgut," said Nora. "The only job I have ever had is with the Ferry Porsche family. Ferry is a nickname for Ferdinand Anton Ernst Porsche who is the oldest son of Ferdinand Porsche.

"The elder Ferdinand Porsche was the founder and brains behind the Porsche Empire. He was eleven years old when the automobile was invented, and he had the ability to invent things at a young age. Since he was interested in electricity, he put doorbells and electric lighting in his family home at age sixteen. Ferdinand Porsche grew up in Mattersdorf, Austria, southeast of here near the Yugoslavian and Italian borders. Back then, it was a part of Bohemia.

"In the year nineteen hundred, when he was twenty-five years old, he put together the first all-wheel-drive car, plus a car powered by both petrol and electricity. Then, he began to race his automobiles; but, not only for the sport and the thrill of speed. He raced to test and improve his automobiles while he designed them.

"In nineteen hundred and six, Ferdinand (Senior) married Aloisia Kaes, and they had a daughter, Louise. Ferdinand Anton Ernst Porsche, my longtime employer, was born in nineteen hundred and nine. On the day of his birth, his father was racing one of his cars in Semmering. He found out about his son's birth by telegram. The younger Ferdinand was born in Wiener Neustadt, a city in Austria. His name came from his father Ferdinand, his grandfather Anton and his uncle Ernst."

"Where did the nickname Ferry come from?" asked Lucas.

"Having the name Ferdinand, the family might have called him Ferdie for obvious reasons," replied Nora. "His mother thought Ferdie was too common, so someone suggested Ferry, and it stuck."

"Nowadays," said George, "his nickname might be a problem in places like San Francisco."

"Why would it be a problem, George?" she asked.

"It sounds exactly the same as a common slang name which refers to homosexual men," he replied.

"Oh my, I hope Ferry never hears about it," she said. "He might want to be called Ferdie after all."

Nora suddenly jumped out of the steaming water and walked over to the snowbank which surrounded the Jacuzzi on 3 sides. She jumped in the snow, landed on her butt, and rolled around in it. Then, rinsed herself under the outdoor shower, and got back into the Jacuzzi.

"We used to do the same thing at home in Banff. People think of it as a national sport in Finland," said Judy.

"What does it do for your body?" asked Lucas.

"The change in temperature stimulates your respiratory system and your blood circulation," replied Nora.

Both Canadian ladies repeated the same ritual, and they got back into the Jacuzzi.

"Okay guys, your turn," said Deanna.

The guys were too macho to decline the challenge. When they got up, George whispered something to Lucas. Doing forward flips, they landed on their butts, and then screamed from the icy cold shock.

Back in the Jacuzzi, George said, "I'm getting hungry. Could we go to dinner soon?"

"Yes. It's time to eat," said Lucas. "Nora, would you care to dine with us this evening at the Grand Hotel? Your boyfriend is welcome to come along with you."

"I would love to have dinner with you," she replied. "My boyfriend has to work this evening, so now I won't have to dine alone."

"Great, you can finish your story about the Porsche family while we have dinner," said George.

Everyone went to their respective rooms. Lucas and Judy showered again and bundled up.

Ready for a fifteen-minute walk, they all went to the Esplanade and walked along Lake Zell to a small peninsula which held the famous and majestic, five-storied Grand Hotel of Zell am See.

They strolled along the tree-lined esplanade, past empty boat slips, and went through a snow-covered garden patio which had many old statues, fountains and trees. Everything was dusted with snow. The area was so beautiful, it looked like it belonged in a storybook.

The old statues and fountains reminded Lucas of Inga: *This takes me back to touring Linderhof Castle with Inga and the splendor surrounding both spectacular structures. She was a beautiful woman.* He felt a sadness which was always with him, concerning her premature death.

Meeting Nora in the main lobby of the Grand Hotel, Lucas said, "This hotel is very impressive. What can you tell us about it?"

"Back in nineteen forty-five, right after the World War Two ended, the American military took over this hotel, and they operated it for ten years," she replied, as they all walked through the main lobby

"Last evening, a nice local couple told us a story about the Easy Company while we had dinner at Hotel Berner," said Lucas.

"Okay, then you will understand when I tell you about my wild experience as a youth, spending time with my girlfriends and the heavy-drinking, partying men of the Easy Company," said Nora.

They continued walking through the bottom floor, toward the rear entrance, back outside, and across a short walkway to a much smaller and older building.

"This was the original hotel building," said Nora, "named Hotel Elizabeth when it first opened in eighteen seventy-nine. The Grand Hotel was built alongside in eighteen ninety-four. While the Americans have occupied the hotel, it has had problems, including a fire which did a lot of damage. In nineteen sixty-six, they had severe thunderstorms, and the bottom area became flooded. If you look closely, you can see the hotel is still due for some renovations. In nineteen sixty-eight, the Spa and Sports Center opened in Zell am See. It was a real boon to local tourism as you see it today."

The original hotel building was approaching one hundred years old. Seeing classic marble floors and pillars, Lucas thought the lobby was impressive, despite its age. Colorful afghan rugs were laying in open areas of the tan-colored marble floor and in several seating areas, all under a brown and gold, coffered ceiling. Between the lobby entrance and the lounge areas, a beautiful curved staircase looked like it was suspended in the air as it led upstairs.

To the left of the entrance, they saw a small stairway going downstairs, but there was a chain across it and a sign, written in German, *Wegen reparaturarbeiten geschlossen* (closed for repairs).

"What is downstairs, over there?" Deanna asked Nora.

"It was a well-used Bierstube which got flooded during the nineteen sixty-eight storms. Repair work is slow down there," she replied.

Pointing to the large, curved staircase, Nora said, "The bar area is upstairs, and it is very nice. If you all want to, we can go there for a drink after dinner." They continued walking through the lounge and past the hotel's reception desk.

Arriving at the restaurant, they were greeted by the hostess, a young Austrian lady. A colorful dirndl showed off her shapely figure and large bosom. Like most young, Norwegian ladies who Lucas saw when he was in Spain and Ibiza, the hostess had blonde hair and unblemished skin. Lucas imagined Nora looked the same way as a young lady.

The hostess introduced herself as Annika, and she led them to a window table. With a view across Lake Zell, they could see the glacier looming behind the town of Kaprun.

"Will you ski Kaprun while you're here?" Nora asked the group.

"We might go there tomorrow," said Lucas. "It would be great if you and your boyfriend joined us and showed us around the mountain."

"I would love to ski with you tomorrow, and I'll ask Stefan if he wants to go with us," she replied.

In the dining room, a spectacular Austrian Buffet was displayed on tables which followed the curve of the stairway. The room was very large, but the buffet tables and several elaborate partitions sectioned the dining room into smaller areas. Dining tables and chairs were scattered around the room, near the stairway railing and on the other side of the opening. From their table, they could hear Bavarian music, coming from the other end of the room. They were served Stiegl beers in flute-shaped glasses, each with a perfect, foamy head.

Lucas was excited to see a classical Austrian Buffet. "Do they have a buffet every night?" he asked Nora.

"No. The buffet is only one night a week," she replied. "As you can see, it is a lot of work. We can each choose to eat from the buffet or order from the menu." After a day of skiing, they were all hungry, and everyone decided on the sumptuous buffet which looked wonderful.

The dining room was getting full, so they joined the buffet line before it got too long. Standing in line, they could see the small stage where a trio was playing a lively Bavarian tune. There was 1 lady, dressed in a dirndl and playing the accordion, plus 2 men who were playing tuba and guitar. Both men wore lederhosen and Alpine hats with a feather.

As they approached the buffet table and food, Lucas stood there and admired the display. This scene was grandiose. What stood out most was a spit-roasted, suckling pig at the meat carving station. The pig, head and all, was a shiny bronze color. It had crispy skin and a large red apple stuck in its mouth.

Draped in multiple levels of brown and gold linens, the semi-circular arrangement of buffet tables offered a variety of local Austrian dishes. They loaded their plates with several of the many choices: Meats included pork schnitzel, rotisserie chicken, Weisswurst, bratwurst, venison and wild boar, plus goulash stew, beef roulade and bread dumpling with bacon. Fish items were fresh trout, either spit-roasted or poached, freshwater crayfish, and mussels in white wine, shallots, parsley and cream. Chafing dishes held braised red cabbage and potato latkes with apple puree. On large platters, fresh fruit, sliced deli meats and local cheeses added color to the display.

A swan ice sculpture towered above the table in the center of the buffet, illuminated by aqua-blue light and surrounded by an impressive selection of local desserts. Lucas recognized Linzertorte, dobos cake, apple strudel and a cream cheese strudel. There was also a shiny, dark chocolate Sachertorte, plum cake, several fruit tartes and little dishes of Salzburger Nockerl which Nora defined as individual, sweet soufflés, served with raspberry sauce and sprinkled with confectioner's sugar.

Back at their table, they got settled with a healthy selection of foods on overflowing plates.

Pausing between bites, Nora continued her story of the Porsche family, "When Ferry was born, his father worked for Austro-Daimler Automobile Company. He liked to design smaller automobiles, but Daimler preferred the larger Mercedes automobile. After he supervised construction of the Mercedes, his father left the company. Within a few years, he designed an air-cooled aircraft engine with four cylinders, said to be the original model for later development of the Volkswagen engine.

"As an adult, Ferry claimed he was born attached to the automobile. On one Christmas Eve, when Ferry was ten years old, he received a gift which surprised him. It was a miniature coach pulled by a goat, and he didn't know what to say. The family chuckled at him when his father produced his real gift, a miniature car with a two-cylinder engine which his father had designed. So, Ferry learned to drive at age ten. When he was sixteen, he got a driver's license, and he drove a real race car, an Austro-Daimler Sascha which his father had designed.

"Ferdinand (Senior) left Daimler to start his own company in the early nineteen thirties. He got involved with Adolph Hitler's project, the so-called *People's Car*, also named the KdF-Wagen, in nineteen thirty-four. Ferry and his father designed the Volkswagen automobile the same year, and they worked together from that point on. Hitler recruited Porsche (Ferdinand Senior) and his son to design a heavy tank which they built and named The Tiger. Their tank proved to be inferior on the battlefield compared with the Panzer tanks. Later in the war, Nazis used Porsche's Tiger chassis, mounted with eighty-eight-millimeter anti-tank guns which proved very effective in destroying enemy tanks."

"Where did the Porsche family live during the war?" asked Lucas.

"Well, let me backtrack," said Nora, "to a short time before World War Two, so I can tell you about some things the two Porsches did. In nineteen thirty-two, Russia invited Porsche (Senior) to visit automobile, airplane and tractor factories. They offered him a job as Chief Vehicle Designer for the Soviet Union, but he turned it down. Ferry believed it was the language barrier, more than anything else, which kept his father from taking the Soviet job.

"In nineteen thirty-four, Porsche received the contract to design the Volkswagen. In the German Automobile Industry, other companies were not too enthusiastic about competition with the *People's Car*, and the Porsches had limited funds for production of the Volkswagen. They built the first models by hand at a private garage in Stuttgart, Germany. The next thirty cars were made at the Daimler-Benz factory under the Porsche team's supervision. The Porsche driving team, including both Ferdinand Porsches, tested the cars.

"By nineteen thirty-seven, Porsche designs were in high demand, so they built a small factory in Stuttgart. They produced the Volkswagen, as we know it today, and developed air-cooled engines, airplane engines, wind-driven electric generators, military transport units and tanks. During nineteen thirty-seven, the two Porsche men went to the United States and learned about American manufacturing techniques.

"When they returned to Germany, they used the knowledge acquired in the U.S. to open the Volkswagen plant in Wolfsburg. Since Ferdinand Senior's time was consumed by the Volkswagen plant, he appointed Ferry as Deputy in Command for the entire Porsche business."

"How was their relationship with Hitler?" asked George.

"Ferdinand Porsche was Adolph Hitler's favorite engineer," replied Nora. "Hitler gave both Porsches money to build racing cars and the Volkswagen 'Bug.' Nazis also got the Porsches to design tanks, ships and aircraft engines for their military. Ferdinand (Senior) was not much interested in politics. His passion was in automobiles, designing and building things. During the war, the Porsche business did very well in manufacturing military vehicles. Thousands of Russians served as their employees, but they were Russian prisoners of war, sent by the Nazis who used them as slave labor. The Porsches are not proud of this fact."

"Nora, what did the KdF stand for?" asked George.

"KdF stood for *Kraft-durch-Freude* which means: strength through joy," she replied. "Nazis forced workers to join a union. They called it the German Labor Front, and Nazis collected ten percent of their union dues to fund the Volkswagen auto project. Both Ferry and his father said there was no way they could refuse Hitler and the Nazis, so they went along with it all. A few years later, Ferry moved his family from Stuttgart to Zell am See to avoid the bombing."

"How many children does Ferry have?" asked Deanna.

"Ferdinand is the oldest, then Gerhard, Hans-Peter and Wolfgang. They are all about three years apart," replied Nora.

She continued, "After settling his family in Zell am See, Ferry moved the Porsche Design Departments to two locations in Austria: the first in Gmund/Carinthia, and the other in Zell am Zee near the family farm. Ferry remained in Stuttgart. His father stayed in Wolfsburg, working as the General Manager of the Volkswagen factory, with a Nazi Party officer always looking over his shoulder.

"After the war, French authorities accused Porsche (Senior) and his son-in-law of war crimes, and both went to prison. However, Ferry said the French really wanted Porsche to work in their automobile industry and develop a car, like the Volkswagen."

"Why was Ferry's father arrested and not him; wasn't he involved with the company along with his father?" asked Lucas.

"Ferry always denied moral responsibility and political affiliation with the Nazi regime," replied Nora, "However, Heinrich Himmler, the SS Chief, had appointed Ferry as an honorary SS Officer. Like everything else the Nazis did, Ferry claimed he could not refuse them. Based on affiliation with the SS, Ferry spent six months in a French prison.

“According to Ferry, there was only one reason for his release from prison. The French wanted him to earn money and pay them a ransom for his father’s release. After the family paid one million francs, the French authorities released Porsche (Senior). He had served twenty-two months in prison. The French dropped all charges against him, but never returned the money.

“The Porsche Company had to start over after the war because the new government canceled their contract. Ferry decided to change location. He closed the factory and opened a new one in Gmund, Austria, three-hundred-and-fifty-kilometers northeast of here.

“Then, Ferry received a contract to build an Italian race car. He designed the Cisitalia Three Sixty with a mid-engine layout and four-wheel drive. Upon inspection of the completed race car, Porsche (Senior) told Ferry and other employees he would have built it the same way, down to the last bolt.

“In nineteen forty-eight, the Porsche Three Fifty-Six prototype won its first-class victory at Innsbruck. Over fifty of these Three Fifty-Six Porsches were built manually in Gmund, between nineteen forty-eight and nineteen fifty, the same year a Porsche automobile got sold in the United States for the first time.

“In nineteen fifty-one, Ferdinand (Senior) died at age seventy-five. He was buried at the family estate, or ‘Schuttgut’ as the locals call it. Later in the same year, production of the Porsche Three Fifty-Six exceeded five hundred vehicles. So, now you know how the Porsche Sports Car came to be. I’m sure you all know of their success in the automobile industry.

“One more thing about the elder Ferdinand, and then I’ll give him a rest. To my knowledge, no one has ever publicly confirmed or denied it, but Ferdinand (Senior) helped a prominent Jew escape from Germany during the war. Ferry told me about the Jew his father hid from Nazis. It was his business partner and financial backer, Adolph Rosenberger. As Hitler took over Germany, Rosenberger’s contributions to develop the German Auto Industry did not matter to the Nazis. They put him in Karlsruhe prison. Ferdinand (Senior) was able to obtain his release, but Rosenberger had to leave the country. He fled to France and became the Porsche representative there during the war. In the late nineteen thirties, he went to California, got involved in the auto racing industry and became a race car driver. According to Ferry, the Porsche Automobile Company might not exist today without Rosenberger’s contributions. He passed away two years ago.”

“I would love to have a nineteen sixty-six Porsche Targa with the removable roof panel and reinforced roll bar,” said George. “Not long ago,

I sold a nineteen sixty-five Triumph TR Four. Did you know it was the first automobile to combine a roll bar and a removable top?"

"Yes," said Lucas. "I remember the time you borrowed my tricked-out VW 'Bug' because it had a stereo and four speakers. I guess, it was to impress your date with sound. Anyway, I drove your Triumph TR Four to Manhattan Beach from my house in Long Beach. I drove back at three a.m. on a Saturday morning. With no one else in sight on the 405 Freeway, I had your Triumph going one hundred and thirty miles an hour which felt like the wheels were not touching the pavement. Did I ever tell you my story about driving your sports car, George?"

"No, you hadn't," he replied, "and I wish you still hadn't." The rest of the group chuckled.

"Didn't James Dean die in California, driving a Porsche race car?" asked Judy.

"Yes, in nineteen fifty-five," said George. "James Dean was close to completing the movie *Giant*, and he bought a silver Porsche 550 Spyder. It proved to be a successful racing automobile, especially in Europe. Dean had a clause in his movie contract which did not allow him to race cars until the movie was finished. But he bought the car while he was making the movie, and he entered it in a competition race which was scheduled to take place on October first in Salinas, California.

"September thirtieth, James Dean was driving the Spyder on the road to Salinas. *Little Bastard* was painted on the hood of the car. The nickname came from someone at the movie studio. On his drive north, near Paso Robles, a young driver pulled in front of Dean's speeding car. James Dean, possibly blinded by the sun, died with a broken neck. The other driver and Dean's passenger survived the crash."

Everyone finished their dinners, Lucas paid the check, and they all climbed the curved staircase to the bar. They were lucky enough to find a table where they ordered more beer and Jägermeister.

A young Austrian rock band was playing their version of Beatles' songs. So, Lucas and Judy went to dance on the crowded dance floor. The others stayed seated at the table and talked. After finishing their drinks, they all walked outside and around the main hotel to the esplanade. Fresh snow started falling.

"Perfect," said Nora. "Tomorrow, we get fresh powder to ski on."

On their way back to the Berner Hotel, Nora pointed out buildings and businesses as they passed by. Everyone said goodnight and agreed to meet in the morning at the Kitzsteinhorn cable car in Kaprun.

After the huge dinner, Lucas and Judy felt too full to jump around in bed. They undressed and Judy grabbed Lucas' hand. She led him into the shower where they took turns washing and exploring each other's bodies.

There was not much jumping around, but there was plenty of moaning and groaning before they fell asleep. Wrapped in each other's arms, both slept soundly until their wake-up call rang.

Lucas, Judy, George and Deanna all had the breakfast buffet which the hotel provided to guests, including delicious coffee.

The buffet had traditional Austrian rolls: the *Kornspitz* (made with wheat and rye flours, along with wheat bran, soy, flax seeds, malt, fennel, caraway, coriander, anise and yeast), *Schwarzbrot* (black bread made with rye and wheat flours), plus the *Semmel* (Bavarian roll) which had a crusty outside and a fluffy, light interior, served with butter and marmalade. There were also platters of sliced ham, cheeses, hard-boiled eggs, smoked trout and fresh melons.

It had snowed during the night, and a light snow was falling when they walked outside. The skies were gray, and the weather was cold. The fresh, powdered snow would be great to ski on, but visibility would be bad in this light. They brushed snow off the van and climbed inside. Waiting for the engine to get warm, Lucas took a hit on his hash pipe and passed it around while George handed out Wieninger beers. As Lucas began the drive, George was sitting in the front, and the ladies were in the rear, talking. Lucas put in a Buffalo Springfield tape and turned the music down, so they everyone could talk.

"I've been wondering about Bruno. What happened to him, Lucas?" asked George. "Did you ever have a showdown with him, about Jodie and the other lady who disappeared in Formentera?"

"Well, the day you left on the train, Gino told me Bruno was dating Sonya," he replied. "Gino thought he was beating her because she had several visible signs. Then, Bruno got transferred to the officers' club where I worked in Oberammergau. He dated one of our lady bartenders, and he roughed her up bad. So, our manager sent Bruno back to the Von Steuben Hotel in Garmisch, and he brought Eric to work at the club. Bruno and Sonya continued to see each other for a while, but I heard they argued a lot. I don't recall seeing him for the last few weeks, not at The Grill or any other popular spots."

"Maybe he is off on another trip, somewhere," said George.

"Yeah, and I hope he doesn't come back," said Lucas. "I'm tired of seeing him around. When I do, it upsets me."

"Lucas, we came all the way to Europe, so you could find the guy who killed your fiancée. Remember?" asked George. "If you knew where he was, wouldn't you want to settle things with him?"

"George, look around you," he replied. "Why would I want to leave this magical paradise and go searching for a scumbag? He will get what he deserves. One of these days, he will beat the wrong woman. I'm tired of worrying about Bruno. For me, the chapter is closed."

Wondering if George had any reaction to his last comment, Lucas glanced at him, out of the corner of his eye. George was busy, looking straight ahead at the slippery, snow-covered road.

"Remember the time we spun out in Austria and almost crashed this van?" George asked Lucas.

"Yes. Why do you think I'm being so careful and driving slowly? I know very well how you can lose it on icy roads," he replied.

Lucas drove in to the Kitzsteinhorn cable car lot and parked the van. They all put on ski boots, grabbed skis and poles, and then met Nora and her boyfriend, Stefan Liechter. His weather-beaten skin made him look rugged, but he was handsome, fit and tall, maybe 6'4".

In the cable car, their group stood and formed a half-circle in the front-left corner, facing the mountain.

Nora gave them information about the ski area, "This cable car system was completed in nineteen sixty-five, and it climbs to over three thousand meters (10,000 feet) above sea level. These cars each have a capacity of thirty-five people. The cable tower is one-hundred-and-thirteen-meters tall (371 feet). It's the highest cable car tower in the world."

"Can you ski here all year?" asked Deanna.

"No. We ski around ten months a year," she replied.

"What type of lifts do they have on the glacier?" asked George.

"The answer is T-bars, also known as drag-lifts," said Nora. "The first one was installed in nineteen sixty-seven, using a complex technology to accomplish it. The glacier moves in a downward flow. It's very slow, but always moving which makes fixed construction impossible. Throughout Europe, they use the same technology of T-bars in glacier lifts. This past week, our local government decided to build a funicular railway for transportation to the glacier."

"A funicular railway?" asked George.

"The basic idea is two tram cars carry passengers up and down the mountain, using a single cable to counterbalance the cars," she replied. "An electric motor at the top of the track powers the cable. It keeps the cable moving and provides enough power to compensate for the weight of passengers and skis. When they build a funicular railway at this location, it will have one long set of tracks, plus a short double-set of tracks in the middle. The double-set will allow the two tram cars to pass each other."

"George and I rode a cog-train to the Zugspitze Glacier. It's also called a rack railway," said Lucas. "The cog wheels underneath mesh with the rack rail. Powered by electricity, it starts at the bahnhof (railroad station) in Garmisch, goes past Lake Eibsee and up to the glacier. Besides the Zugspitze, we skied at two other glaciers, but we had to ride on three trams getting to those."

When the cable car stopped, they left skis and poles leaning against the building, and Nora led them to the observation platform. This was one of the most spectacular views Lucas had ever seen.

It was cloudy until they arrived at the top. Now, Lucas could see the clouds below him, drifting across the mountain peaks, as he gazed at the view. *I'm on top of the world, and I can see forever.*

Since they were the only people on the deck, Lucas pulled out his hash pipe and lighter, shielded them from the wind, took two good hits and passed it to Judy. She did the same and passed it on.

When George offered the pipe to Stefan, he said, "No thank you. I do not know why people smoke hashish. It smells terrible."

Lucas remembered what Inga told Herr Drummer when they drove to the Wieninger Brewery: *He had asked Inga why we smoked so much hashish. She told him, "Because, Herr Drummer, sex is better, music is better and food tastes better. In other words, life is better." However, Drummer did not seem to get it.*

"I can't speak for others, but I can tell you why I smoke it," Lucas said to Stefan. "Hashish helps me focus and stay in the moment, it reduces anxiety, it expands creativity, it's a functional high and instant mood-changer, always for the good, making everything I do more fun and meaningful. The best part is fabulous sex when my partner and I are high, and I feel exactly the way I want to feel in all respects."

Instead of saying something to Lucas, Stefan shook his head and mumbled, "Unbelievable," as he headed out and grabbed his skis along with everybody else. Nora and Stefan led the way on a groomed slope. The snow was perfect for skiing, but the light was flat, so it was hard to see the bumps. The next slope was wide-open, and they followed the two Austrians down a long, eight-minute run. With few places to rest and being close to ten thousand feet in altitude, they were all out of breath.

George suggested they stop and have a beer when they got near the Weinhutte, but Stefan said, "Let's take a few more runs, first. I'll show you a different way down." So, they took 2 more runs.

When Stefan led them to the restaurant for lunch and beers, they all felt relieved. Lucas got his goulash soup, brotchen and Stiegl beer, then he joined the others and sat at a wooden table, between Judy and Stefan. Located near the highest tram station, the Krefelder Hut was very busy, and it offered another great view.

"So, Lucas, how do you like skiing on the glacier?" asked Stefan.

"The snow is great today," he replied. "This is the same as every other glacier I've skied. The slopes are wide open, not too challenging, and there are very few obstacles, such as trees and rocks."

Stefan spoke with a thick Bavarian accent, but compared to other Austrians who Lucas had met, he sounded different. So, Lucas asked Stefan where he grew up.

"I was born and raised in Walbrzych, Poland, a coal mining town near the Czech border," he replied. "My father was a foreman at one of the mines. I refused to work in the mines and ran away from home when I was thirteen. I did not go back until after the war."

"What did you do when you ran away?" asked Lucas.

"I made my way to Vienna and got a job in a restaurant," he said. "I liked the fast pace, got interested in cooking and worked as a waiter. During the war, I got drafted into the Austrian Army, and I suffered through both the German and the Russian occupations. It was a long battle between the two armies before the Russians chased the Germans back toward the west. For me, the worst part was seeing those fine buildings destroyed and laying in ruins. The people had no water, electricity or gas. Looting and assault were common because there was no police force. At first, the Soviets behaved well, and then their group moved on. The next bunch of Soviet troops began a wave of violence, looting and raping. It was as bad as you can imagine. The Russians held me as a prisoner of war for a while. When they released me, I got out of Vienna, headed to Salzburg and started working in a hotel. After several years, I had saved enough money to attend the Hotel Training College which is in Bad Reichenhall near Berchtesgaden. I have worked in several of the large hotels in Bavaria. I came here five years ago, and I don't think I will ever leave this area."

George went to the counter with Deanna, and they came back to the table with fresh Stiegl beers for the whole group. It was snowing heavy outside, and no one was in any hurry to get back out there. Since Lucas wanted to learn more about local history, he was glad to stay inside.

Stefan continued telling Lucas his story about his home area in Poland. "During the war, Adolph Hitler built a secret underground system below the many mountains and meadows around Walbrzych. This very large project was used by the Nazis as military headquarters, and all the tunnel openings were well-camouflaged. Have any of you ever heard of the Amber Room?"

Nobody responded. So, Stefan continued, "The Amber Room was a gift from Germany to Peter the Great of Russia. He had admired the room which was on display during his visit to Berlin. At one time, people called it The Eighth Wonder of the World. The walls had been decorated in panels of amber, sculpted over gold-leafed mirrors. As the story goes, Nazis looted a train which carried about three hundred tons of gold. The train left Breslau in East Germany and headed toward Walbrzych in the spring of nineteen forty-five. But it disappeared, and no one has found it yet. The Amber Room panels disappeared about the same time, and people think it was on the same train.

"My brother, Dominik, was a miner who spent his whole adult life searching for the train. He is no longer alive, but my nephew, Miroslaw, carries on his father's search, and it consumes him too. Dominik knew about the underground complex which the Nazis constructed. He had heard about the train from miners who claimed they saw German soldiers push the train into one of the tunnels in nineteen forty-five."

"Wow! We could go to Poland and join in the hunt!" said Lucas.

A local rock band began to play, and several people went to dance in front of the stage at the far end of the lodge. As many skiers came in from the cold, the building got full.

"It's really dumping out there," Deanna said, looking outside.

"Okay, I'll get more beer and some Jägermeister if someone would be kind enough to help me," said George.

Deanna volunteered and went with George to the counter.

"I guess we're done skiing," said Nora. "I think we will have a lot of fun, right here."

They all stayed and had a good time, surrounded by Austrians and Germans who were celebrating life, drinking and dancing.

I can see why Stefan said he won't ever leave here, thought Lucas. *Crime is almost nonexistent. Zell am See and Kaprun are beautiful, and the friendliness of these people is unlike any place I have ever been.*

It was now late afternoon, so they made their way down the mountain. In the parking lot, Lucas, Judy, George and Deanna said their goodbyes to Nora and Stefan.

Wanting to be in Berchtesgaden for the evening, Lucas called "The Hof" and reserved 2 rooms. Next, he talked to Herr Held in the kitchen. Lucas advised him they were coming, and they would stop at the Class Six Store to buy liquor and cigarettes for him and Herr Drummer.

When they got on the road, it was still snowing hard, so they knew the drive might take longer than an hour and a half.

After such a fun day, they were all feeling great. Wanting to hear some music, Judy played the Buffalo Springfield tape.

Lucas looked forward to showing George, Judy and Deanna around Berchtesgaden and Obersalzberg. He felt sure they would appreciate the hotel accommodations and enjoy seeing the sites in an area packed with so much Nazi history. He also knew they would enjoy meeting the Hotel Manager, Herr Vogt, and the Chefs: Grassl, Held and Drummer.

Thinking of his last trip to Berchtesgaden with Inga, Eric and Sabine, Lucas knew he did not want to feel sad.

He thought: *Well, here we go on another adventure, and I plan to enjoy myself. This trip will be fun.*

George was leaning between the seats when Lucas asked him, "Would you open a Wieninger beer for me, please?"

CHAPTER 30

Return to Berchtesgaden

Lucas had to concentrate on the road because the snow was blowing directly toward them, and his visibility was not good. The snow plow must have come through, not too long ago, because the road was clear, and the strong wind kept snow off the road. Everyone was listening to the Buffalo Springfield song "Bluebird."

"Lucas, I remember when we saw Buffalo Springfield at The Long Beach Arena in nineteen sixty-eight. They played a twenty-minute version of this song," said George. "We did not know it at the time, but it was their last concert together. It was a shame they broke up. Palmer, their lead guitarist, had been in trouble for marijuana possession, numerous times. When he got deported back to Canada, the group started to break up. Later in the year, there was another drug bust with three other members of the group, including Eric Clapton. It was the last blow for their group."

"Eric Clapton is a great musician," replied Lucas. "However, he moves around to a lot of different groups, and he isn't the only one. I think many musicians feel their way around until they find the right combination; and when it is right—it's sensational! Look at The Rolling Stones, or Crosby, Stills, Nash and Young."

"The Stones are great too," said George. "Although, compared to when they started, they are different since they lost Brian Jones. He was the person who first put the group together. I read Jones chose each band member, handled all their bookings and selected the music they played. When Mick Jagger and Keith Richards became leaders of the group, Jones began to do a lot of drugs and lost it. He drowned in somebody's pool, a few weeks after they kicked him out of the band."

The wind was blowing hard now. As the van poked along on the road, they heard a "whoosh" noise.

"What was that?" asked Lucas.

"I think we lost the driver's windshield wiper," replied Judy.

With snow on his side of the window, Lucas could barely see the road. He pulled over and got out to inspect the damage. Looking back down the road, he thought about searching for the windshield wiper, but it could be anywhere. The snow banks were deep on both sides of the road. When he realized the wiper arm was also gone, he knew the wiper blade would not reattach, anyway.

Lucas got back in and Judy suggested a plan. With no other options available, they put Judy's plan in motion. It would get them to the next town or village for repairs. If it was not such a dangerous situation, it would seem hilarious to anyone who saw Judy. Her legs were across Lucas' lap, her upper body was sticking out the driver's side window, and she was scraping snow off the windshield, using a hand-held squeegee. She wore a bright-pink, knit cap, yellow-tinted goggles and a red scarf which was wrapped around her neck. Deanna was now in the front passenger seat, holding on to Judy's feet.

Within two kilometers (1.2 miles), they were at the German border. No Austrian border guards were on duty, but there were two young, German border guards who saw Judy hanging out the window. One guard stood in front of the van and held his hand up for them to stop. The other guard approached the drivers' side of the van.

Seeing such a comical sight at this remote border crossing in the middle of a blizzard, the guard was trying not to laugh when he shouted, "*Das reicht! Raus aus dem wagen!*" (All right. Get out of the van).

Lucas knew enough German to know what the border guard wanted. Judy climbed down out of the window, plopped her feet on the ground next to the border guard, smiled at him and said, "Hello, Officer."

"Do you speak English?" Lucas asked the guard.

The guard did not answer him, but he called to his partner, "Klaus, Englisch sprechen bitte."

Lucas looked back at George and whispered, "We don't want them to search the van, especially my backpack. So, hand me the bottle of Jim Beam. It's in the cabinet above the table." Lucas grabbed the whiskey from George, and then he stepped out of the van.

The border guard, Klaus, walked over and asked Lucas, "What is happening here? Why is this lady hanging out of the window?"

Lucas stood there, holding the bottle of Jim Beam in front of him, and he said to the guard, "I know it is cold here, and you must be working all night, so this is for you." Lucas was smiling as he handed the whiskey to the border guard.

Klaus smiled back and said, "Danke schön." He took the bottle and held it high for his fellow guard to see.

The fellow guard said, "Fein, aber was los ist?" (In English, it meant: Fine, but what is the matter?)

Lucas understood the guard who spoke German, so he went to the windshield and showed Klaus the mangled fitting where the windshield wiper broke off.

Now, Klaus was friendlier, and his English was good. He gave them directions to Gasthaus Motzenwirt, a hotel and restaurant in Melleck, only 2 kilometers (1.2 miles) from the border. Klaus told them the owner of the gasthaus, Herr Grassl, would get someone to fix their windshield wiper when they arrived.

Lucas and Judy got back in the van. He drove slowly as he pulled away from the border shack. Judy was hanging out the window and waving goodbye to the guards.

"I've never had to use the whiskey bribe before, but Bob Ostergaard told me it always worked for him. I'm sure glad we had a bottle," said Lucas, driving toward Melleck.

"I think the guards were in a hurry to get back inside and drink the whiskey," said George. "They didn't even check our passports."

"Remind me to buy another bottle of Jim Beam for the van at the Class Six Store in Berchtesgaden," said Lucas.

The van crawled along the winding, snow-covered road, across an icy bridge which took them over a river, then into Melleck, and they arrived at Gasthaus Motzenwirt. No one was happier to see the sign than Judy who leaped off Lucas' lap, out of the open window, and landed on her feet again. Wiping the snow off her hat and goggles, Judy yelled out, "Wow, it sure was fun!"

Everyone was laughing when they piled out of the van and headed for the Gasthaus Motzenwirt. The snow was ankle-deep when they walked through the parking lot.

Lucas studied the surroundings as he drove in. This gasthaus sat in a low, pastured valley next to a mountain, but close to the highway. The back wall of the building was only a few feet from the guard-railing. Tall fir trees lined the highway near the hotel. The driveway went around the front, past the 2-story hotel, then curved around the side of the building to a limited parking area. There were multiple buildings close to the base of the mountain. Various species of trees grew around the edges of the valley and over to the rocky face of the mountain.

They shook and brushed the snow off themselves and entered the warm space of a typical Alpine gasthaus. The first thing Lucas noticed was a large circular fireplace, painted white with layers of red brick around the base, and a six-foot-wide chimney, tapered to the wood ceiling. They sat near the fireplace at a rectangular table, dressed with a white and tan tablecloth and plum-colored napkins. Seating was a blue-cushioned bench against the wall, plus comfortable chairs on the other side of the table. The dining chairs and the bar stools at a small bar on the right side of their table also had blue cushions.

On both sides of the fireplace, white Ram's heads were stuffed and mounted on the wall. The dining room and bar were about half-full. The people looked local. An accordion player and a guitarist, both male, dressed in the traditional lederhosen and long stockings, were playing their instruments as they moved around the dining room.

The waitress wore a blue dirndl and a low-cut blouse, exposing her cleavage. Lucas smiled, as he thought: *I sure love those dirndls*.

"They have Wieninger beer. I like this place already," said George, when they were served half-liter glasses of Wieninger.

Lucas asked the waitress to see if Herr Grassl had a moment to speak with him. Within minutes, a tall, blonde-haired man, maybe in his 40s, came from the kitchen. He smiled at their group, and then he introduced himself as Josef Grassl, owner and chef of the gasthaus.

"Klaus called me from the border haus, and he told me about your *scheibenwischer,*" said Grassl, as he waived his hand in the air and mimicked a windshield wiper.

"Yes, the wind blew it off. Klaus told us you know someone who can fix it," said Lucas. Then, he introduced himself and his friends.

"I've already spoken to my cousin, Alois Grassl, and he is on his way here to fix it for you," Herr Grassl replied. "If you give me your car keys, I will have my helper meet him outside, and you can have your dinner, uninterrupted."

Lucas thanked Herr Grassl and handed over his keys.

"I met a chef, Gerhardt Grassl. He works at the Berchtesgadener Hof. Is he your relative?" asked Lucas.

"Gerhardt Grassl is my younger brother," said Herr Grassl. "He wants to open his own restaurant. For now, he is happy working at the Berchtesgadener Hof. He is still young, and he enjoys the night life, of which there is none close to here.

"Well, since you are a friend of Gerhardt's, I will fix you something special, and you can taste a few of our local dishes. We use only fresh, seasonal and local products. It is a slow night with the stormy weather, and I can join you for dinner if I may. I might be interrupted if a tour bus stops here for dinner, but I do not expect one tonight. It would be nice to hear your stories, and I will tell you a little about the Grassl family. Also, please call me Joseph."

With everyone in agreement, Joseph Grassl would join them.

"Why don't we start off with shots of Jägermeister?" asked Lucas.

"Please, let me introduce you to our own, family-produced, Enzian Schnapps to help you get warm from the cold," replied Joseph. "I heard one young lady was hanging out of an open window, wiping snow off the windshield as you were driving, so you all must be *einfrieren* (frozen). Your waitress, Regina, will bring the schnapps, and I will go prepare your dinner." Josef smiled, then left and spoke to Regina.

The lovely Regina brought them each a shot glass, filled with a clear liquid. She told them to be careful because it is a potent alcohol. When they raised their shot glasses and said, "Prost," Lucas noticed people in the dining room were watching them. They drained their shot glasses and swallowed the Enzian Schnapps, but no one said a word.

Lucas, Judy, George and Deanna were used to the sweetness of Jägermeister. They looked at each other with odd expressions.

"It wasn't at all what I was expecting," said George.

"I think the locals here knew what our reaction would be," said Lucas as he scanned the room.

His friends noticed all the smiling Austrian faces, looking at them. So, they raised their empty shot glasses and smiled back.

"Köstlich," Lucas said to the Austrians, meaning delicious. Then, he immediately reached for his beer, and his friends did the same.

"What are we going to tell Josef about the schnapps?" asked Judy.

"I don't know what we will say to Josef," said George. "But I think it tastes like bittersweet dirt. Although, something about it seems more complex than plain dirt."

"Now I know what Enzian tastes like," said Deanna.

"It does have an earthy, bitter taste and a somewhat offensive odor, but it's intriguing. I could get used to it," said Judy.

"I would say it has an earthy taste, similar to a truffle flavor, but it is a little bitter," said Lucas. "I wonder what the alcohol content is."

Josef Grassl came out of the kitchen, followed by a young cook and the waitress, Regina. Each of them carried a large platter of food. Josef introduced his assistant, Max, who is also his son. Then, he grabbed a chair from another table, and sat with their group. Max brought warm plates from the kitchen, and Regina brought utensils, plus 5 fresh glasses of Wieninger beer.

Josef stood and pointed to items as he described the food, displayed beautifully on platters.

"Here are venison medallions on steinpilz-rahm-nudeln (porcini mushroom noodles). These are grilled trout filets from Lake Hintersee, served with noodles and seasoned with chili garlic pepper and pine nuts. This last platter is our local pork roast, braised in a dark beer; the roast is surrounded by bread dumplings and Rotkohl (red cabbage). Now, everyone please help yourselves *famile stil* (family style)."

"What did you think about the Enzian schnapps?" asked Josef as everyone filled their plates.

"We all found it different from any other liqueurs," replied Lucas. "It tasted a little bitter with an earthy odor and a high level of alcohol. We were wondering what the alcohol content is?"

"The law requires Enzian Schnapps to have an alcohol content of at least thirty-seven and one-half percent, by volume," replied Josef.

"I think one shot will last a whole evening," said George.

"A wise decision," said Josef.

"What is Enzian?" asked George.

"Enzian is German for the word *Gentian*, a yellow or sometimes blue, trumpet-shaped mountain flower, from which we use the root to make Enzian Schnapps and other liqueurs," replied Josef. "Enzian Schnapps originated in the Alps, and our distillery is the oldest Enzianbrennerei in Germany. Built by our family in the early sixteen hundreds, it is in the mountains between Berchtesgaden and Salzburg. Enzian roots grow wild, but harvesting is strictly regulated. Our distillery has the sole right to dig here for the protected roots.

"Each district of Germany has their own version of schnapps. Different fruits are also used to make schnapps, such as apples, plums and pears. Cherries are used for Kirshwasser. Around the Berlin area, Doppelkorn (corn schnapps) is popular."

Raising his shot glass, Josef added, "This is a Stamperl, and it holds two centiliters."

"I've heard about certain kinds of schnapps having medicinal benefits. Is this true?" asked Lucas.

"Original Enzian Schnapps from the Grassl Distillery stimulates the appetite and aids digestion," replied Josef. "As an apéritif, some people like it over ice. After dinner, it is best served at room-temperature. Either way, it will warm you in this cold weather. In Northern Germany it is both common and popular to serve schnapps with a beer."

"Is everyone named Grassl a descendent of the seventeenth century distillery founder in Bavaria?" asked Lucas.

"Around Berchtesgaden, the Grassls are all related in some way. There are enough Grassls here to make their own city," said Josef.

"I've heard the Enzian name used for other things. Isn't there a train called The Blue Enzian here in Germany?" asked Deanna.

"In the early fifties, the Deutsche Bundesbahn named an express train The Blue Enzian. It ran from Northern Germany to Munich," said Josef. "Last year, they extended the service to Austria. Also, a German World War Two anti-aircraft missile was named The Enzian, but they did not put it into service during the war."

Regina had cleared the dinner dishes while Josef was talking. Next, she appeared with many sample-sized desserts, displayed on a large blue and white oval platter which prompted "Oohs" and "Ahhs." The assortment included small custard dishes with crème brûlée, warm slices of apple strudel, slivers of Linzertorte, and small Sachertorte petit fours. She also brought a bowl of homemade, vanilla bean ice cream. Everyone had a taste of each dessert. It was all delicious.

When they had finished eating, Josef said, "I think you all ordered Jägermeister when you came in, so…" A moment later, Regina brought five Stamperl (shot glasses) of Jägermeister.

Everyone laughed, and then they toasted Chef Joseph, Regina and Max (Josef's son and assistant).

Josef insisted on paying for their schnapps and Jägermeister. Lucas paid for the food, beers and the windshield wiper. Alois Grassl did the repair while they were eating, and Max returned the keys to Lucas. They all said goodbye and expressed appreciation for such great hospitality. Josef invited them to come back in the summer, and he suggested they bring Gerhardt Grassl since he rarely sees his brother.

The weather had calmed down, and the phantom auto repairman had cleaned the snow off the van. They all got seated, and Lucas warmed the engine while George passed the hash pipe around. Everyone was so full from dinner, they declined having more beer. As Lucas drove the van onto the main highway and headed toward Berchtesgaden, he realized a snowplow had come by. The road was clear, and it was salted. Lucas still drove with care and focused on the road while everyone listened to John Denver, singing "Take Me Home, Country Roads."

After such a busy day, they were all tired. Judy and Deanna relaxed and closed their eyes in the back of the van. Lucas and George listened to soft music in front.

"Tell me about the Berchtesgaden area, Lucas," said George.

"Oh. I forgot. You never went there during your last trip to Europe," he replied. "You know, I could tell you things I have heard, but I'm hoping we can get Chef Held to tell us about the local history. During the war, Chef Held was a young chef at the Berchtesgadener Hof, and he no doubt has a lot of stories to tell about Hitler, Eva Braun, Martin Bormann and all the main characters of the Third Reich. Hitler and his Nazi group basically took over Obersalzberg from nineteen thirty-five to nineteen forty-five. Hitler's home, the Berghof, was built there.

"I will say the drive down from the Berghof to Berchtesgadener Hof is about four kilometers of steep, winding road, one of the steepest roads in Germany, and it gets very slippery in the winter."

Since Lucas got no response from George, and the ladies were silent, he knew his passengers were all drifting off. For the rest of the drive, he occupied his mind, pondering his non-stop European experience, so far: *It began in Frankfurt where George and I got military IDs, as planned. We went to Garmisch and met some great people—Eric, Gino, John, Sonya and many others. We had a memorable trip to the southern part of Austria where we met Andreas Baader and Ulrike Meinhof. We continued to Venice, and then to the islands of Ibiza and Formentera where I met Gabrielle. Next, we went to Torremolinos and stayed in Los Boliches for the experience at The Alamo with Ty Hardin. On a ferry, we ran into David Burns and the two Aussie ladies, Olivia and Ashleigh. We traveled with them to Morocco, back to Spain and on to the Matterhorn where we all got to ski and be in the movie. I wound up in Bavaria, working at the NATO Officers Club and living with beautiful Inga. Our relationship was terrific until I lost her. CID Asshole Robinson, told Bruno who I was, and Bruno killed her. I am starting to feel much better, although I still think about Inga, quite often. Now, I ski a lot, and I feel free, even a bit irresponsible. Wow, it has been quite a ride since George and I left Long Beach, seven months ago.*

It was late at night when Lucas pulled into the parking lot behind the pool area at the Berchtesgadener Hof. He woke everybody, they grabbed their backpacks, and Lucas locked the van.

The lobby was quiet when they checked in. With their room keys in hand, everyone said goodnight.

Lucas and Judy went to their room, got undressed and fell into bed. They kissed, cuddled together, and fell asleep, right away. Both slept well until the phone rang at 9 a.m.

CHAPTER 31

Nazi History in Obersalzberg

Judy and Lucas took separate showers. They had to meet George and Deanna downstairs for breakfast; and they knew what would happen if they showered together.

In the hotel dining room, they had an American breakfast, cooked by a Turkish cook and a German sous chef. After breakfast, they planned to go shopping at the Class Six Store. The Hotel Manager, Herr Vogt, came into the dining room. Seeing Lucas, Vogt walked over, shook his hand and gave Lucas condolences for his loss of Inga.

"Thank you, Herr Vogt," he replied. "Allow me to introduce my friends who arrived in Bavaria last week." Pointing to George, he said "This is my longtime buddy, George, from Long Beach, California."

Herr Vogt reached out and shook George's hand.

Lucas continued, "These two pretty ladies, Judy and Deanna, are from Banff, Canada. They all want to get jobs with AFRC."

"Do you have plans for today?" asked Herr Vogt.

"We are going to shop at Strub Kaserne, and then we're going to Obersalzberg," replied Lucas.

"Do you have time for a beer?" asked Herr Vogt. "I need to tell you a few things, Lucas."

Everyone followed Herr Vogt to the lounge where they got seated at a table and received complimentary glasses of Wieninger beer.

A few moments later, Herr Vogt excused himself and Lucas from the group, and he led Lucas to his office, past the front desk and down the hall, both carrying their beers.

Herr Vogt sat behind his desk and tasted his beer. Then, he said, "Lucas, CID Officer Robinson has been inquiring about you and another American fellow, whose name I cannot remember, regarding your friend Inga's murder investigations. The German police have also been asking about you because they want to ask you more questions. Besides breaking his arm and embarrassing him in front of a crowd, Robinson seems to be after you."

"Yeah, he's becoming a pain in the ass," he replied. "I'm sure I will see him again in the near future."

"Robinson also said he wants to talk to the fellow who has a vehicle repair business," said Herr Vogt. "He claimed the man uses illegal registrations, or something similar."

"He was referring to Bob Ostergaard," said Lucas. "Bob buys old rusted-out vans from German farmers and rebuilds them. His renovations are basic. If needed, he installs new engines or transmissions. In general, he turns the vans into small campers, and he sells them to GIs who use them to travel around Europe. Bob seems to have a good business, and he sells as many vans as he can find and fix up."

"Well, please let him know he is being watched, and he should be careful," said Herr Vogt.

"Thank you again," replied Lucas. "I think I'd better get going, so we can get back here before dinner. We are headed over to the Class Six Store. Can I get anything for you, Herr Vogt?"

"No. If I want to drink hard liquor, I go see the bartender. Or, I go into the kitchen for a drink with Herr Held and Herr Drummer. Are you buying for them?" he asked.

"Yes. While we are here, I am hoping to learn some Berchtesgaden history from them," replied Lucas.

"Good. I'll see you this evening," said Herr Vogt.

Back in the dining room, Lucas joined his group. They had ordered another round and had a fresh beer waiting for him.

"What did he want to talk about, Lucas?" asked George.

"Right after you returned to California, an officer from the Criminal Investigation Division, took away my ID card," he replied. "His name is Robinson. Since we first met, he and I have had a few disagreements. He has been here, talking to Herr Vogt. Apparently, the police also want to question me again, regarding Inga's murder investigation."

"They don't suspect you, do they?" asked George.

"No, I was at the officers' club, playing bar games all night with several AFRC people," he replied. "By the time Eric and I got to her place and discovered her body, it was daybreak. Anyway, let's get our shopping done, and then we can head to Obersalzberg."

Lucas knew his way around this area because he had been here with Eric, Inga and Sabine, months ago. Driving about 5 minutes, Lucas took Judy, George and Deanna through the forest and past some houses. A left turn into the parking lot took them by a stone lion which guarded the entrance. In front of them, a massive, five-story turret rose above the end of the main building it was attached to. This scene fit with the theme of buildings, constructed by Hitler and his head architect/builder, Albert

Speer. The Nazis had named this Gebirgsjäger Kaserne. After the war, the Americans changed the name to Strub Kaserne.

Lucas and George walked into the Class Six Store. The ladies went to the PX and did other shopping. Using all his liquor and cigarette rations, Lucas bought as much as possible for the chefs at "The Hof."

The guys were gathering their purchases and ready to go find the ladies when they heard a man's voice, behind them, "Oh, there you are, Gary. I want to see you."

Lucas turned around and saw it was CID Officer Robinson.

"Oh no, here's trouble," he said to George.

Robinson walked over to Lucas at the check-out counter. "I hope you are not selling those goods to the Germans," said Robinson.

"How's the arm, Robinson?" asked Lucas.

Robinson ignored the question and asked, "Do you know the police are looking for you? They have more questions about Inga Mueller."

Lucas told Robinson he knew nothing because he had been out of the country for a while.

"It seems the guy from Long Beach, Bruno Castignoli, disappeared. You wouldn't know where he is, would you?" asked Robinson.

"Like I said, Robinson, I've been gone, so I'm out of touch with Garmisch people," he replied. "But, thanks for the information."

Lucas turned around, shaking his head, and he left Robinson standing alone. He and George grabbed their purchases and headed for the door.

Robinson yelled out to Lucas, "Oh, hey, when you see your friend, Bob Ostergaard, tell him to come in to the MP station in Garmisch. We have questions about his used van business. He is switching license plates and doing business without proper permits. He needs to get those from the military and the German authorities."

As they walked out of the store, George said, "Lucas, let me guess—he is not a close friend of yours."

"You are correct," he replied. "He is extremely annoying, and he loves to harass the civilian employees."

"What did you mean, asking how his arm is?" asked George.

"It was an incident at 'The Hof' where we are staying," he replied. "Inga and I were in the Bierstube downstairs. While I was at the bar, talking to Chef Held and Herr Vogt, I looked over at Inga. She was standing and talking to Sabine. Then, some guy put his arm around Inga and was trying to kiss her. I could see she wanted no part of it, so I went to confront the guy. His back was toward me, and he wore a Bavarian hat. As I got to them, he reached down to grab Inga's ass, and I reacted so violently I broke his arm. When I saw his face, I recognized it was

Robinson. Before he could respond with any action, Herr Vogt told him to leave and get his arm looked at.

"I think you should be careful around him, George. Now he knows you are my friend; he might put you on his watch list too."

The ladies were still in the PX, waiting for Lucas and his ID card, so they could pay for their purchases. When they all got back to the hotel, the ladies went to their rooms while Lucas and George delivered liquor and cigarettes to the chefs, Herr Held and Herr Drummer.

Going through the back employees' entrance, Lucas led the way to the kitchen. He almost ran into Herr Drummer who had a gray rabbit with a rope on its feet, hanging in the middle of the doorway. The chef was slicing open the rabbit's neck, and blood was gushing into a metal pail, resting on a chair below. Herr Drummer had a somewhat guilty expression when they surprised him. However, he recognized Lucas and smiled when he saw the bags they were carrying, full of liquor and cigarettes.

"Gruss Gott, Herr Gary," said the chef.

"Gruss Gott, Herr Drummer," replied Lucas. "This is my friend George, from California. He came with me to Bavaria last year, and he just returned, along with two lovely Canadian ladies who we met when we traveled in Italy. Is Chef Held in the kitchen?"

"Yes. Go on back to the kitchen," replied Herr Drummer. "I'll finish here, and then I'll join you for a beer."

As they walked past the rabbit, dripping blood into the pail, George whispered, "The chef seemed to enjoy slitting the rabbit's throat."

"He did have a sinister look," Lucas whispered back.

"It was a little creepy," said George.

Walking into the kitchen, Lucas waived to Gerhardt Grassl who was working on the service line. They went past the tiled-pool of trout, and Chef Held greeted them at the door of his large office.

"Gruss Gott, Herr Gary," said the chef. "I was so sorry to hear about your lovely friend, Inga. Her death is a horrible tragedy. Have they found the murderer yet?"

"Thank you, Herr Held," replied Lucas. "I do not know what the authorities found in their investigation. I can't imagine why anyone would harm Inga, and I miss her. Let me introduce you to my old friend, George. He's from Long Beach, California. George came back with two of our friends, beautiful Canadian ladies who we met in Italy last year. We are going to Obersalzberg this afternoon. I hoped you might tell us some history of the town and suggest places we should see."

After they exchanged greetings, Chef Held took a bag of liquor from George and put it on the table. He opened the refrigerator, put the liquor inside, and grabbed 3 bottles of Wieninger beer.

"Let's sit where we can drink our beer and talk," he said, handing a beer to both Lucas and George.

"What brings you to Berchtesgaden, Lucas? Are you going to come and work with us?" he asked.

"Thank you, Chef, but this trip is only for sightseeing and visiting with my friends," replied Lucas.

"If you are going to Obersalzberg, would you mind if I come along with you?" asked Chef Held. "I will act as your tour guide and bore you with stories. My Uncle, Heinrich Held, was Prime Minister of Bavaria from nineteen twenty-four to nineteen thirty-three, so I learned a lot from him. I can also tell you about some of my experiences with Adolph Hitler, Eva Braun, Martin Bormann and other important Nazis.

"We can have lunch at the General Walker Hotel which used to be the Platterhof Hotel. I am ready to go anytime, but I have to be back in time for dinner service."

"Okay," said Lucas. "We'll get the ladies and meet you out back in the parking lot. We're in the cream-colored VW with a pop-top camper, and we have plenty of beer onboard."

"I'll see you there," said Chef Held.

Lucas and George smiled, nodded, and drained their beers.

In the van while Lucas drove, Chef Held sat next to him in the passenger's seat. The others sat close behind them, so they could hear the chef as he shared his stories.

"Earlier, I told Lucas and George about my uncle, Heinrich Held, who was the Prime Minister of Bavaria," said Chef Held. "When the Nazis abolished the Bavarian government, my uncle had no choice, but to retire from politics; and he did not get his government pension from the Nazis. He fled to Lugano, Switzerland, where his son, my cousin, lives now. Nazis put his other son in the Dachau concentration camp. At the age of seventy, Uncle Heinrich died in nineteen thirty-eight."

"When did Hitler first come to Berchtesgaden?" asked George.

"I don't have an exact date," he replied. "Hitler vacationed here in Berchtesgaden and in Obersalzberg as early as nineteen twenty. He gathered many supporters for the Nazi Party in this area.

"Near the end of nineteen twenty-three, Hitler came to Obersalzberg and met with his mentor, Dietrich Eckart. At the time, Eckart was hiding from the police. Then, he got involved in promotion, fundraising and leadership of the Nazi Party.

"In November, Hitler led his fanatical Nazi group, including Eckart, in a march to overthrow the Bavarian government in Munich. Their attempt failed and Hitler got arrested. He later faced trial. Dietrich Eckart also got arrested, but they released him since he was ill. A month later, Eckart died of a heart attack.

"In April, nineteen twenty-four, the court sentenced Hitler to a five-year term for treason, but he only served nine months in Landsberg Prison. While Hitler was in prison, he worked on the first volume of his book, *Mein Kampf* (My Struggle), assisted by a fellow conspirator, Rudolf Hess. In December, Hitler was released from prison.

"When the New Year began in nineteen twenty-five, Hitler returned to Obersalzberg, using the name Hugo Wolf. He rented a small cabin on property owned by the Pension Moritz Hotel. He wrote the second volume of *Mein Kampf* while he stayed in the cabin. Hitler became well known here, as Herr Wolf, and he fell in love with this area.

"In nineteen twenty-eight, he rented the Haus Wachenfeld, a stylish vacation chalet next door to the Hotel zum Türken which I will talk more about later.

"In nineteen thirty-three, Hitler became Chancellor of Germany. He bought Haus Wachenfeld, using money from the sales of his book, and he planned to remodel it. By nineteen thirty-five, Hitler had expanded the chalet to an enormous size with a big terrace, a pine-paneled dining room, and a large hall which contained a red-marble fireplace. He had a big study, adjoining a telephone switchboard room and a movie projection room. A huge glass window, mechanized to open for fresh air, gave him a panoramic view of Berchtesgaden, the surrounding areas and the Austrian mountains. Hitler called his new home the Berghof. In English, it means mountain court."

Chef Held stopped talking when they pulled into the parking lot at the General Walker Hotel.

Lucas' attention was on the buildings: *The Nazis know how to make a so-called luxury hotel look like a bunch of barracks. This large group of buildings seem out of place, surrounded by picturesque mountains and Alpine chalets. More chalets dotted the landscape before Nazis confiscated and demolished them to build massive Nazi structures.*

Entering the hotel dining room, Lucas thought it looked familiar: *Like the dining room at Chiemsee, this room has a heavy-beamed ceiling and oversized paintings.*

A young waitress seated the group next to a window. This blonde Bavarian had a nice smile and great cleavage which was in full view as she bent forward and handed out the menus.

Chef Held glanced at his menu. Then, he stood and said, "Please allow me to order lunch for all of us. This hotel's chef and I are old friends, and I think he'll prepare something special for us."

On his way to the kitchen, Chef Held spoke to the waitress, and then he disappeared. Within a few minutes, she brought 5 half-liter glasses of Wieninger beer to the table.

"Herr Held wants to order a shot of schnapps for everyone here," the waitress said with a delightful Australian accent. "We have Enzian Schnapps. It comes from the local Enzianbrennerei Grassl Distillery."

"Oh, we are all familiar with Enzian schnapps," said Judy. "Do you have any Jägermeister?" They all laughed, including the waitress.

As the waitress brought the Jägermeister, Chef Held returned. When he saw the shot glasses, he asked, "Are you aware of the local distillery, owned by the Grassl family? Lucas, you know Gerhardt Grassl, one of our chefs at 'The Hof.' The Grassl family has property all over the Berchtesgaden-Salzburg area, and they are all related."

"Yesterday, we had dinner at Gasthaus Motzenwirt in Melleck," replied Lucas. "We all sampled Enzian Schnapps there."

Chef Held said, "Oh, I forgot. You Americans love your Jägermeister." He smiled and raised his shot glass; the others did the same, and they all said, "Prost."

"Chef Held, I'll bet this hotel has great history. Was it the Americans who acquired it as the Platterhof Hotel and renamed it the General Walker Hotel? asked Lucas.

"Yes. The hotel's original name was Pension Moritz until nineteen twenty-eight," he replied. "When it was sold, the name changed to The Platterhof which was a popular vacation hotel, but nothing like it is today. Since it was damaged during the war, the Americans had to rebuild it."

Deanna was looking out the window and up at the mountain. Then, she turned and said, "Chef Held…"

Chef Held interrupted her and said, "Please, all of you call me Anton, and I won't feel so old around you, younger people. I'm sorry, Deanna, what were you going to say?"

"What is the mountain peak called?" asked Deanna.

"Untersberg," he replied. "It divides Salzburg from Germany and Austria which includes Berchtesgaden. There are several legends about the Untersberg. Some locals claim Charlemagne is waiting inside the mountain and being cared for by *Untersberg Mandln.* I believe you would call them dwarfs. Every hundred years, based on this legend, he awakens and sends one of his dwarfs out to see if the ravens are still flying around the mountain. If they are not flying, Charlemagne will put on his armor and go out with his knights to fight the final battle between evil and good which will end the world."

A waiter and their waitress appeared, each carrying a platter of food. Also, a robust fellow, with a pink complexion and a big smile, carried a large platter of steaming food which he held in front of a substantial beer belly. He was wearing a chef's hat.

Anton introduced them to Chef Florian Grassl, Executive Chef of the General Walker Hotel. Then, he explained, "Chef Grassl is a cousin of Gerhardt Grassl who works as a chef at our Berchtesgadener Hof. Today, Chef Florian will join us for lunch."

Chef Florian (Grassl) stood and pointed to the dishes, prepared for their special luncheon, as he described each item in both German and English. "We have Kalbsbrust mit Brez'nfüllung (veal breast with sausage and pretzel stuffing). Butter Späetzle (homemade noodles in clarified butter). Rotkohl mit apfel (Bavarian red cabbage with apples). Then, Brotchen (German bread rolls) and Bayerische Crème (Bavarian Cream)."

Lucas was more than impressed when he saw the stuffed veal breast. Having prepared this dish himself, several times, he knew how much work was involved. Obviously, Anton had phoned ahead to give them time for preparation. The Bavarian Cream was also impressive. It was molded into a flat-topped, pyramid shape known as a charlotte mold and made with 3 flavors: dark chocolate, vanilla and coffee. The Bavarian Cream was in the center of the platter, surrounded by thin slices of Zwetschgenkuchen (German plum cake).

"Anton tells me you are all interested in our Bavarian history," said Chef Florian.

His three companions were nodding when Lucas replied, "Yes. We're eager to hear about local history and this fine hotel. Most Bavarian and Austrian people we've met, have told us their personal stories and stories of their area. It's fascinating."

While everyone ate, Chef Florian entertained them with more history of the hotel. "Well, the original structure was part of a farm purchased by a lady named Mauritia Mayer, but everybody called her Moritz. This was back in the late eighteen hundreds. She rebuilt it to use as a boarding house and named it Pension Moritz. It became a popular hotel with celebrities of the era, such as Johannes Brahms and an author named Richard Voss. She was friends with Richard Voss who wrote a novel, *Zwei Menschen* (Two People). Judith Platter was the name of his main character in the novel; however, his story pertained to his good friend, Moritz. She, Mauritia Mayer, passed away around the turn of the century. Her sister took over the hotel operation and ran it as a mountain Kurhaus (a health resort) until nineteen twenty. Bruno Büchner leased the hotel for eight years, and then he bought it in nineteen twenty-eight. Büchner's wife, having read *Zwei Menschen*, renamed it The Platterhof Hotel because she believed the character in the book, Judith Platter, had lived there and was an actual person."

"Is it true, the Nazis forced residents out of their homes, so the Nazis could move in and take over all of Obersalzberg?" asked Lucas.

"Yes, it did happen to most people," replied Chef Florian. "Many Nazi leaders acquired residences in areas around the Berghof. Also, security zones were established to shield Hitler from the public."

"How did Nazis force Büchner to sell the hotel?" asked George.

"At first, the Nazis made up bad publicity about Büchner's hotel, claiming his food was spoiled, he had a criminal record and he mistreated his family," said Chef Florian. "When their publicity did not work, the SS shut off the hotel's electricity and water, and they built a fence around it. Büchner consented to sell, but he only received half of what it was worth. In the end, he was forced to leave Obersalzberg.

"The Platterhof had served as a hotel for the common people of Germany until Nazis took over. They remodeled and made it a larger hotel, by adding several wings which surround the original hotel. Due to Martin Bormann's efforts, the area around the Berghof (Hitler's home) became secluded, and the Platterhof became a luxury hotel, only used for high-ranking Nazis and their celebrity guests.

"During the war in nineteen forty-three, Nazis used it as a military hospital. The hotel suffered considerable damage from bombings in nineteen forty-five. Afterward, it sat untouched for seven years until the U.S. Army rebuilt, remodeled and renamed it the General Walker Hotel. It became part of the Armed Forces Recreation Center (AFRC) which allowed Anton and me to keep our jobs."

Looking at Lucas, Chef Florian said, "Anton tells me you are the chef at the NATO Officers Club in Oberammergau, and he thinks you might move within AFRC. We can use a talented chef here."

"I'm sorry Florian, but he is already spoken for," said Anton.

Everyone chuckled, and Florian said, "I have to get back to the kitchen now. I hope to see you this summer, or maybe sooner."

Chef Anton Held announced he had taken care of the check. They all finished their beers, bundled up and headed outside. It was a cold, sunny afternoon in Obersalzberg.

Outside the front entrance, Anton said, "I'm glad it is such a clear day. We can climb the hill to the Hotel zum Türken next door. We'll pass by the ruins of Hitler's Berghof. British RAF bombs destroyed it in nineteen forty-five. Please be careful because the path is icy and slippery. Before we leave this hotel, I want to point out the two-story building with a parking garage on ground level. Hotel staff have accommodations on the upper floor, and they love to party. It's wild like a zoo. I hear the fourth floor at Berchtesgadener Hof has the same crazy activity."

"I've spent a few wild nights with employees at the Green Arrow Hotel in Garmisch," said Lucas.

Anton smiled at Lucas. Then, he pointed to another area and said, "At the other end of the main hotel building, you see an extension which was Terrassen Halle until the US Army renovated the hotel. Now, it is a restaurant, named the Skyline Room. During Hitler's time here, Albert Speer used Terrassen Halle, as his private studio."

"Didn't Albert Speer write a best-selling book, *Inside the Third Reich*, not too long ago?" asked George.

"Yes. It went on sale last year," replied Anton. "Albert Speer was Hitler's chief architect. They planned many buildings and cities together. After the former minister died in a plane crash, Speer also inherited a job as Minister of Armaments for the Nazis."

Walking through the woods, right above the main road, Anton pointed to a shrub-covered retaining wall, made of stone and extending to the mountain side. He said, "Only this wall remains of Hitler's Berghof, except for a few pieces of foundation which are under the snow."

"Didn't Speer and Hitler have a falling out, toward the end of the war?" asked Lucas.

"Yes. Several days before Hitler committed suicide, Albert Speer left Hamburg," replied Anton. "He survived the horrible bombing of the city, as he went to visit Hitler in the Berlin bunker. They disagreed on how the war was going. Speer told Hitler the war was lost. After they had a combative conversation, Speer left the bunker and returned to Hamburg. Hitler dropped Speer from Nazi government and replaced him with Speer's own aide."

They walked past a stone guardhouse and up a curved, snow-covered driveway to reach the entrance at Hotel zum Türken.

"Let's go inside, get out of the cold, and have a beer," said Anton.

He banged on a heavy, wooden door, using the fancy door knocker. It was made of solid brass, yet it was worn from use.

A large gentleman, wearing lederhosen, opened the door. When he saw Anton, he gave him a great smile and a warm handshake.

"Welcome to Hotel zum Türken, my name is Klaus," said the big Bavarian, speaking excellent English.

Anton introduced his group, and Klaus led them all into the dining room. Sitting at a round table near a fire pit, they were in a cove area which extended out to the snow-covered patio. Everyone admired the magnificent views of the meadow below, beyond into Austria, over to Salzburg, and the Unterberg peaks, overlooking Berchtesgaden. It was mid-afternoon, so hotel guests would be skiing or sightseeing, and the small dining room was nearly empty.

With the others seated around Anton, he sat in the middle of the padded bench which curved below the window. He said, "The Schuster family owns this hotel, and they treat me like family. I have known them since I was a young child."

A jolly bartender brought 5 bottles of Hofbräuhaus Berchtesgaden beer, made by a local brewery.

After saying, "Prost," and taking a drink of his beer, Anton said, "If you are a guest here, and there is no one available to serve you, you can help yourself to drinks and snacks, then add them to your bill. Here, the guests use the honor system, and it seems to work out well. They give each guest a key to the front door which is locked at all times."

"Why do they keep it locked, Anton?" asked George.

"If they did not maintain privacy, tourists would overrun the hotel and hound them every day," he replied.

"Lucas, have you met Herr Schuster, the Assistant Manager at the Berchtesgadener Hof?" asked Anton.

"I met him once in your hotel office, and you told me his wife and daughter have a gift shop in the hotel," he replied.

Anton nodded and said, "Oh, yes. I remember. Well, this hotel was the Türkenhäusl (Little Turk House) before it was sold in nineteen eleven to Karl Schuster who is our Herr Schuster's uncle. Karl Schuster converted it to a guesthouse and named it Hotel zum Türken. It became a popular place which hosted celebrities and royalty often, such as Bavarian Prince Regent Luitpold, Composer Johannes Brahms and the Crown Prince and Princess of Prussia.

"When Nazis took control of Obersalzberg in nineteen thirty-three, Karl Schuster tried to hold out, but he was forced to sell his hotel. Karl Schuster was very outspoken. He did not approve of Nazis forcing out landowners to build their Nazi compound. Herr Schuster even tried to exclude SS Officers from this lounge. He said he was tired of seeing so many SS Brownshirts and Nazis in Obersalzberg. Martin Bormann, a prominent Nazi official, forced Herr Schuster to sell Hotel zum Türken, by putting him in Dachau Prison for three weeks. The Nazis paid him only half of what the hotel was worth."

"What became of him? Did he leave Obersalzberg?" asked Judy.

"He moved his family to the city of Salzburg," replied Anton, "and he continued to speak out against the Nazis' takeovers of his beloved Hotel zum Türken and other local properties.

"The Nazis even removed roofs of homes while native Bavarians still occupied them. As Karl Schuster had done, many landowners tried to hold out, but they were also sent to Dachau Prison until they consented to sell.

Karl Schuster always blamed himself for the loss of the hotel. In nineteen thirty-four, he died of a heart attack. He was fifty-eight years old.

"Bormann used this hotel and buildings in this area as housing for the Reichssicherheitsdienst (RSD), Hitler's personal bodyguards and the SS Guard Detachment. There were cells in the basement above the bunker system, and who knows what went on down there."

"Oh, can we go into the bunkers?" asked Deanna.

"Do you want to see the bunker system?" asked Anton.

Everyone agreed, it would be exciting to visit the bunkers.

"We can go there. The entrance is at this hotel," said Anton.

"Why didn't they bomb this hotel when they bombed Hitler's house next door?" asked Judy.

"They did bomb this hotel, and it sustained a lot of damage," replied Anton. "During the war, Karl Schuster's widow and his daughter had moved to Salzburg. After the war, they overcame the bureaucratic obstacles to re-acquire Hotel zum Türken, and they completely restored it. Since the late nineteen forties, it has been one of the most popular hotels in this area. Schuster's widow passed away a few months ago. Her daughter, Ingrid, is now managing the hotel."

Lucas paid the bartender. Then, everyone put their coats on and followed Anton. He led them out the front door, turned right and went around to the side of the building near the parking lot.

"Tourists always pay a small entrance fee, but no one is here today. So, I will give you a guided tour," said Anton. "Please, stick with me because you can get lost down there."

They walked by paneled glass windows into a small office which had dim lighting, went through an arched doorway, down the stone steps of a spiral staircase and through another archway which was outlined with red brick. Now, they were in a cement tunnel, dimly lit by electric lights, spaced every 15 feet in the ceiling. On the left side was a wood-slat walkway, 6 inches below the concrete walkway. At ankle height, there were tying hitches, made of wood and attached 10-feet apart on the left wall. They walked in the tunnel until they came to a brick wall. The word ENDE was painted in red on the wall.

Turning around, they went back to the spiral staircase, turned left under the staircase, and walked to another stone stairway which went down to the next level. Using a wood handrail, attached to the left side of the stairwell, they arrived at the base of the stairs and saw a wall with 3 small windows and German writing below them.

"Those windows are machine gun placements, and the writing tells what type of placement it is," said Anton.

The corridor veered to the left, and then it made a sharp right to another stairwell which had a fancy, wood handrail, attached to the wall on the left. It was twelve steps down to another arched corridor, then through a short hallway to another steep stairway which had the same style handrail. At the bottom, they passed another machine gun stand, turned to the right, then made a sharp left and walked in another corridor to a room. A hole had been blown through the wall in the room, exposing steel cable and concrete supports. Looking closely, they could see more small windows for machine gun placements. They turned left again and saw what looked like a cell with a steel-barred gate which was closed.

"This was an emergency exit," said Anton.

They kept going left and turned into another arched corridor. At the end, they saw a doorway, sealed off with used brick.

"This was the doorway to Hitler's room," said Anton. "You can see there is one brick missing in the left upper corner. Eva Braun's room and Dr. Morell's room are also behind this doorway. Those rooms were all ruled unsafe, so they had to be sealed off."

"Did I count right? Did we go down four levels?" asked George.

"Yes, we did," said Anton. "These tunnels go for miles underneath Obersalzberg. Some tunnels interconnect while other tunnels pass above and below. Martin Bormann did not want his tunnel to connect with Goring's tunnel, so they bypassed one below the other. Scattered around the area, they even had small shelters for the personnel to use, in case they couldn't make it to the main shelters."

Concluding the tour, Anton said, "We've seen all there is to see here. I should get back to Berchtesgaden if you are ready to go."

"Oh yes, I'm ready to go up," said Deanna. "These tunnels are scary, even without bombs dropping overhead. Although, I wonder what type of accommodations Hitler and Eva had in their space."

"The bunkers for Hitler and his Nazi leaders had shower rooms, dining rooms, electric lighting and water systems," replied Anton. "It was all well-guarded; you saw some of the machine gun ports. During the Nazi takeover, Bormann oversaw all development for the entire bunker system and the augmentation of Obersalzberg."

On the way out, Lucas thought he heard water dripping and noticed how damp, chilly and creepy this place was.

"Anton, tell me us more about Martin Bormann," said Lucas.

"People called him the God of the Obersalzberg," Anton replied. "Bormann was Rudolf Hess' private secretary before he moved up to a higher rank than Hess had in the Nazi Party. When Bormann became Hitler's private secretary, most of Hitler's inner circle disliked him because of his protective position and relationship with Hitler."

"Was Rudolf Hess the guy who flew to England and tried to negotiate a treaty on his own?" asked Judy.

"You are correct, but he failed and spent the rest of the war in a British prison," replied Anton. "Hess was lucky to be in prison; Hitler gave orders for him to be shot if he returned to Germany.

"When Hess defected to England, Bormann took over Hess' duties. Hitler was occupied with the war and foreign affairs while Bormann ran the show and controlled who had access to Hitler."

"Whatever became of Hess?" asked George.

"During the Nuremberg trials, Hess was sentenced to a life term at Spandau Prison, along with Albert Speer and a few other Nazi officials," replied Anton. "Hess is still in Spandau, and he is the only inmate left in the prison. While Speer was in prison, he wrote two books about his Nazi experiences. He was released five years ago."

"I heard Bormann had the Eagles Nest built as a present for Hitler. What can you tell us about it?" asked Lucas.

"Yes. Bormann created the Kehlsteinhaus for Hitler. Americans named it Eagles Nest," replied Anton. "The whole Nazi complex at Obersalzberg was planned and created by Bormann. After he bought out or forced out most of the local landowners, he built barracks for the security troops, and he created an experimental farm with cattle, horses, pigs and bee hives. Barracks housed the SS guards who had to control big crowds of people, trying to catch a glimpse of Hitler. Bormann also managed the remodeling of Haus Wachenfeld which became Hitler's Berghof, plus Bormann's own house and Albert Speer's house. Hermann Goring did not want his house remodeled. It was above the others, and he preferred the style of the old country estate; it fit his outdoor personality."

As they walked back down the hill toward the van, they passed the ruined Berghof site. Anton told them how Eva and her sister lived a carefree life, protected from the public's eyes during the war.

Getting settled in the van, they positioned themselves as before. Lucas drove, Anton sat in the passenger seat, and the others huddled behind them to hear Anton speaking.

"Lucas, be very careful driving on this steep road. It gets very slippery on the way back to Berchtesgaden," said Anton. "After a night of drinking, a lot of GIs go off this road when they leave here. Several men lost their lives by driving too fast."

Pointing to the road, Anton said, "Up here, off to the right is the former location of Bormann's experimental farm. Later, the Americans built a golf course there. In the winter, they use it for skiing."

Driving at a safe speed, Lucas checked his rearview mirrors as usual. When he saw a VW "Bug" coming very fast behind them, he pulled over and stopped to let it go by. The "Bug" flew past them and did not bother to slow down.

Anton said, "I sure hope the driver makes it down this road."

"Me too," said Lucas as he started driving the van again.

A few moments later, Anton said, "Anyway, I wanted to finish telling you about Albert Speer…"

Rounding a blind curve, they saw the VW "Bug" had gone off the side of the road, backward into a snowbank.

Lucas drove past the spot where the "Bug" sat, pulled the van over and parked where it seemed safe. He got out and went around the van to open his sliding side door, being careful not to slip and fall into the snowbank. Reaching into a cabinet behind the passenger seat, Lucas grabbed his warning triangle with reflectors. He walked back 100 meters on the road, as required by German law, and set the warning triangle in the center of the road ahead of the blind curve.

After he returned to the van, Lucas and George made their way through knee-deep snow, going to the VW "Bug."

"It seems to me, we have done this before," said George. "I hope we do not find more terrorists, like those we picked up in Italy."

Inside the "Bug" were 2 guys, trying to push open the car doors, but snow held them closed. Lucas and George dug the snow away from the doors, using their hands, and the doors were finally opened. Lucas knew the guys were U.S. Ski Patrol because they wore familiar plumb-red sweaters with 2 white stripes around the chest, back and sleeves. At first, Lucas did not recognize the driver.

When the passenger climbed out, Lucas saw who it was and shouted, "Chip, are you hurt?"

"Oh, Lucas! No, but my car is," he replied. "John thought I was too drunk to drive. Now, we are stuck in a snow bank. Thanks, John."

Before John could say anything, Lucas said, "Hi John, this is my friend, George Bennett, from Long Beach, California."

Considering the situation, Lucas asked, "Chip, what do you want to do? I need to move my van before someone plows into it."

"Could we get a ride to B'gaden with you?" he asked. "I will have to call and get a tow truck to come and pull my car out."

Lucas agreed, and they all piled into the van. The ski patrol guys introduced themselves to the ladies. Anton said he had seen them around the hotel, but they had not met before. With the group settled, Lucas put on a John Denver tape and got the van going again. George passed Wieninger beers around to everyone. The new passengers were excited after their frightening skid off the road, and everyone in back seemed to be talking at once.

Chef Anton Held and Lucas kept quiet and enjoyed the music. They were listening to "Sunshine on my Shoulders."

Arriving at the hotel, they all agreed to freshen up, change clothes and meet in the lounge for drinks before dinner. Chef Held headed for the kitchen. Chip and John had to go call a tow truck. Lucas and Judy went to their room while George and Deanna went to theirs.

In the privacy of their room, Lucas watched Judy while they both got undressed, and he got aroused.

He said, "You are looking very sexy, young lady. I think you are in for trouble when we get back from dinner tonight."

Judy looked at him and said, "From here, it looks like you can't wait until after dinner." She slipped out of her panties, put her arms around his naked body and kissed him, passionately, until both pulled away.

"You are tempting me, but I don't want to rush," he said. "We had better get dressed before we reach the point of no return."

"Okay, but you also look tempting," she replied.

Dressed and ready to leave the room, she asked, "Lucas, do you know why all these chefs want you to come and work with them?"

"It might be because I'm an American, so I can buy them liquor and cigarettes," he replied.

"I don't think so," she said. "They must know how talented you are, or they have heard about you. I can't wait to see you in action."

"You will have an opportunity soon," he replied. "I will be doing Colonel Moyer's birthday party in three weeks. He is the Officer in Command of the AFRC in Garmisch."

"Oh, it sounds fun, Lucas. Can I come to the party?" she asked.

"Of course, you can come, Judy," he replied. "You can also work the event if you want to."

In "The Hof" lounge, Lucas, Judy, George, Deanna, Herr Vogt, Chef Anton Held and Gerhardt Grassl sat facing the fireplace.

"We are getting fresh snow. Are any of you interested in going skiing tomorrow?" asked Gerhardt, looking out the window.

"I would love to ski tomorrow," replied George. He turned to Lucas and asked, "What do you think, Lucas?"

"Whatever all of you decide, I'm ready for anything," he replied. Then, he asked Gerhardt, "Where do you go to ski around here?"

"Berchtesgaden isn't popular for downhill skiing. I usually ski at the Jenner," replied Gerhardt. "It is a local's mountain where everybody knows everybody, and we all have a good time. There are smaller ski areas around Berchtesgaden and Ramsau, but those are nothing compared to Austria where you have been skiing. If you want to, we can go to the Jenner tomorrow, and I will show you around."

“Thank you, Gerhardt. It sounds like fun,” said Lucas.

George, Judy and Deanna agreed.

“I wish you would all call me Grassl,” said Gerhardt, “as everyone does. Except, do not yell it out—you might get mobbed because there are so many Grassls in and around Berchtesgaden.”

Judy turned to Anton and asked, “What can you tell us about Hitler’s mistress, Eva Braun? Did you say she lived with Hitler at the Berghof?”

“Yes, she did,” he replied. “Eva and Hitler met at Heinrich Hoffman’s photography studio in Munich. At the time, Hitler was the head of the National Socialist German Workers Party (Nazi Party). He was forty and Eva was seventeen. Hoffman introduced Hitler as Herr Wolf. Since Hitler was interested in Eva, he visited Hoffman more often to see her. He brought her little gifts and took her on outings with members of his party. However, it would be a long while before they lived together at the Berghof. When Hitler met Eva, he was still grieving the loss of Geli Raubal, his reported mistress who was also his half-niece.”

“I thought Eva was Hitler’s only love,” Judy said to Anton.

“Well, Maria Reiter was said to be Hitler’s young lover when he was thirty-seven years old. She was only sixteen,” he replied. “They met at a shop where she worked in Obersalzberg. Her family owned the shop. After several dates, Hitler told Maria he wanted to marry her, but she had to wait until he accomplished his mission. Hitler then went to Munich and ignored her. While he was gone, she got very depressed, put a clothesline around her neck, tied it to a doorknob and let herself slide to the floor. Her brother-in-law found her unconscious, but she survived. Later, she married, divorced, remarried, and then became a widow. Frau Reiter is still alive today.”

Herr Vogt spoke up. Adding to the story, he said, “After Hitler and Mimi, or Mitzi as he called her, went their separate ways, Hitler sent for his half-sister, Angela Raubal. She came to be his housekeeper at Haus Wachenfeld in nineteen twenty-five; and she brought her daughter, Geli, who was Hitler’s half-niece. Geli was only seventeen years old, nineteen years younger than Hitler, and she called him Uncle Alf. In time, as Hitler became a more powerful leader of the Nazi Party, he became a lot more possessive of Geli.

“In nineteen twenty-eight, Hitler moved Geli into his house in Munich. Later, Hitler found out Geli and his chauffeur, Emil Maurice, had become lovers right under his nose. Hitler fired Maurice and forbid Geli to see her young friends. He had someone watch and accompany her wherever she went. However, Geli got into a relationship with a man in Linz, the Austrian town where she was born. She wanted to move there, marry the man, and then pursue a singing career. Geli and Hitler argued, and he forbid her to go to Vienna. She could neither take the voice lessons nor have a relationship with the man from Linz who was a Jew. The next day, Hitler was in Nuremberg at a meeting, and Geli was found dead at the house in Munich. She had been shot in the chest, and Hitler's pistol was beside her body. Geli was only twenty-three years old when she died in nineteen thirty-one."

Anton spoke again, "I've heard many stories of her death and how the body was found. In one story, Rudolf Hess broke down the door to her bedroom. In other stories: they had to call a locksmith, or the housekeeper's husband opened the door, using a screwdriver. The whole situation was muddled and confusing.

"Franz Gurtner, the Bavarian Minister of Justice, allowed Geli's body to be taken out of Germany and buried in Vienna. Gurtner was a Nazi sympathizer who later became a key figure in the Nazi Party.

"Hitler's doctor was the only person to examine her body before it was transported and buried. Sending the body to Austria eliminated any chance of someone exhuming the body for further examination."

Herr Vogt said, "Catholic funerals are forbidden by the church in cases of suicides. Apparently, a priest thought she was murdered because Geli was given a catholic funeral and burial in consecrated grounds. Later, the priest claimed he would not have allowed those services if Geli had committed suicide.

"If Hitler was responsible for her death, he certainly had a motive. Hitler had drawn many pornographic drawings which were explicit, and Geli was the subject. She also knew of his perverted sex habits. As we learned later, Hitler's enemies and people who threatened him were always silenced during his career as Chancellor."

"Why don't we have a round of schnapps?" asked Anton Held.

"Jägermeister for me!" said Judy.

"Have you tried Grassl family's Enzian Schnapps?" asked Grassl.

"Oh yeah, we tried it, but I'll have Jägermeister," said George.

"Schnapps is a matter of tastes, German versus North American," said Herr Vogt. "I guess it will be four Jägermeister and three Enzian."

"I'll get these," said Lucas. George stood and went with him to the bar. Lucas ordered the schnapps and Jägermeister, plus 7 glasses of beer. While they waited at the bar, they had a chance to talk.

"I know we came at a bad time, Lucas," said George. "We wanted to surprise you, and Judy seemed anxious to see you again."

"Judy's arrival surprised me because those last few days before she left Europe, she no longer seemed interested," he replied. "Do you know what changed her mind?"

"I think she felt guilty about her boyfriend in Banff," said George. "She said she broke up with him right after she got home. She looked forward to coming back here and getting together with you. Are you not happy to see Judy here?"

Before he responded to George, Lucas paid for the drinks. This gave him a minute to decide how he would answer the question.

"Judy is a great gal," he replied. "While we seem to share common interests, I'm living day to day. I try not to think about the past or the future. I only want to focus on here and now."

When Lucas and George returned to the table, Lucas mixed up the shot glasses on purpose, and everyone laughed. They all stood and raised a shot glass. Everyone said, "Prost," and they downed their Jägermeister or Enzian, depending on what they picked up.

"If you stick around long enough, you will eventually drink Enzian Schnapps," said Grassl.

"Grassl, what is the difference in ingredients?" asked Deanna.

He replied, "Jägermeister, meaning Hunt Master in English, is a German liqueur which is a complex blend of fifty-six herbs, fruits and spices. Serving Jägermeister icy cold minimizes the sharpness of its strong herbal flavor. Enzian Schnapps is distilled from the root of the yellow Gentian flower. It is best served at sixteen degrees Celsius (60 degrees Fahrenheit). Due to strict controls on harvesting Gentian from the wild, some distilleries use purple, brown or spotted Gentian flowers which they farm to make schnapps."

"What is the process for a flower root to become such a complex liqueur?" asked George.

Grassl explained, "Chopped roots get fermented in mountain-spring water and yeast for six weeks. After a double-firing process, the liqueur gets stored in wooden barrels and placed in tunnels under the center of Berchtesgaden. The classic Enzian Schnapps takes about three years, whereas their specialties require extended periods. For example, the Funtensee Enzian takes up to seven years; it is a long process. Enzian Schnapps is good for people with digestive problems. I can take you on a tour of Enzianbrennerei Grassl. It's the oldest Gentian distillery in Germany, started by the Grassl family in sixteen ninety-two."

They laughed when Judy asked "Do they serve Jägermeister?"

"Where did we leave off in the story of Hitler?" asked Lucas.

"I mentioned Hitler's enemies and people who threatened him were always silenced," replied Herr Vogt.

"The best example I can think of," said Anton, "relates to Franz Gurtner. He became Minister of Justice for the Nazi Party, and Hitler used his devotion to the right-wing party in a way which effectively legalized murder. Gurtner helped protect killers, the Nazis who were involved in the *Nacht der langen Messer* (Night of the Long Knives). It was called Operation Hummingbird by some people, and it was called Röhm-Putsch by the Germans.

"Earlier in nineteen twenty-four, when Hitler was imprisoned for the failed Munich Putsch, Gurtner arranged Hitler's early release from Landsberg Prison. Later, however, when Gurtner tried to go against illegal acts of the SS and Nazis, Hitler overruled him."

"What was the Night of the Long Knives," asked Deanna.

"It was one night of slaughter and elimination," said Anton. "Close to one hundred people got murdered and over a thousand got arrested because Hitler wanted to purge potential rivals and all the top political leaders of the SA. Gregor Strasser was among those killed; he was a rival leader of the liberal, left-wing Nazi Party. Some others who died were two anti-Nazi men who helped stop the famous Beer Hall Putsch, and Ernst Röhm, the leader of the Sturmabteilung (SA); they were the Nazis' paramilitary Brownshirts. This was how Hitler dealt with threats to his authority as leader of Germany and the Nazi Party."

"Why did people call it Operation Hummingbird?" asked Lucas.

"The word *Kolibri* means hummingbird," he replied. "It was a code word, used to initiate execution squads—the SS (Schutzstaffel) and the Gestapo (Geheime Staatspolizei) would then begin their operations."

"Anton, how do you know all these personal things about Hitler and the people in his close circle?" asked Judy.

"I have lived here most of my adult life," he replied. "Hitler's sister, Paula, lived in Berchtesgaden after the war. She was cared for by Nazi associates who somehow escaped prison. Paula seldom went out, but her stories got passed on in this small community."

"When did the relationship with Eva Braun begin?" asked Deanna, going back to the story of Eva Braun.

"After Geli Raubal's death, Hitler had a period of depression, and he devoted all of his energy toward politics," replied Anton. "When he recovered from depression, he pursued Eva Braun and invited her to his group events, but never as a couple in public. Hitler kept their relationship a secret, and the German people were not aware of it."

"What did Eva like to do?" asked Judy.

"Eva enjoyed photography, and she had other interests," said Anton. "She was a very active person. In the early years, I think Eva became frustrated with uncertainty regarding the type of relationship she had with Hitler, alias Herr Wolf."

"How did you say she met Hitler?" asked Deanna.

"She was an assistant to Hitler's photographer, Heinrich Hoffman, and Hitler often visited the photography shop in Munich," said Anton. "Seeing Eva as a young, energetic lady, he became interested and he took her for rides in his Mercedes. Sometimes, they went to the theater. From the start, she fell in love with Hitler, and she wanted his attention. Hitler was busy with his politics which did not interest her. She got so depressed over his lack of attention and long periods of absence, she shot herself in the chest, using Hitler's pistol."

"Herr Vogt, I think you said Hitler's other girlfriend shot herself in the chest. Am I correct?" asked George.

"Yes," he replied. "But, only Geli's attempt was fatal. Eva's was not life-threatening. After Eva's suicide attempt, Hitler paid more attention to her, and she stayed overnight at his home in Munich. Still, Hitler was so involved with building his massive structures and his leadership of Germany, he neglected Eva for many weeks at a time. She attempted suicide a second time by taking sleeping pills in nineteen thirty-five, and she survived again. Hitler responded by giving a Munich apartment to her and her younger sister, Gretl. A little later, he gave them a villa which was also in Munich.

"The following year, Eva became the mistress of the Berghof in Obersalzberg. She played hostess to Hitler's close companions and his entourage. However, when dignitaries and persons outside his personal circle stayed at the Berghof, Eva had to stay in her room which overlooked the front entrance. It must have been difficult for her. However, to her credit, she had her own agenda. In her spare time, she became a talented photographer, and she was the only person who Hitler allowed to take candid photos of him."

"Did she or Hitler ever stay in this hotel?" asked Judy.

"Eva Braun stayed here several times before she moved into the Berghof," said Herr Vogt. "Afterward, she stopped here with Bormann or Hermann Fegelein. Eva's sister Gretl married Hermann Fegelein at the Kehlsteinhaus (Eagles Nest). Eva arranged and planned the whole wedding as if it was her own. She doubted she would ever have one. Since being related to an SS Officer allowed Eva to travel with Hitler, Gretl's marriage was a blessing for Eva. Fegelein was a liaison officer on Hitler's staff. As his sister-in-law, Eva gained status and had an official reason to be present at some official events. Hermann Fegelein and Eva became close. Eva said if she had met Fegelein before she met Hitler, things might have turned out different.

"There were rumors of Fegelein cheating on Eva's sister and being intimate with Eva. However, Eva was devoted to Hitler, and I do not believe she would have risked their relationship."

Anton said, "Bormann came into our hotel with his entourage, and Fegelein always joined them for drinks. Eva was sometimes with them. She and Fegelein would dance and flirt. Everyone got drunk.

"Fegelein was a horseman and a real prankster, as was Heinrich Himmler, Fegelein's boss and mentor who treated him like a son. Fegelein carried one of his pranks too far, and a commanding officer committed suicide because of it. Fegelein faced trial and got sentenced to ten years in prison. Heinrich Himmler got Fegelein released, and he commended his antics. Himmler, a practical joker himself, took Fegelein under his wing and taught him methods of pranking.

"Fegelein also pursued a friendship with Hitler's constant companion and private secretary, Martin Bormann. They spent many nights in this lounge with fellow officers and wives, getting roaring drunk.

"Fegelein made it known: the only things he cared about were having a good time and his military career. Thanks to Heinrich Himmler, Fegelein rose very fast in the ranks. He earned medals for leadership in battle and commanding the SS Cavalry Brigade."

Herr Vogt said, "In nineteen forty-five, Fegelein was with Hitler, Eva and others in the Berlin bunker under the Chancellery, as the Russian army was closing in and bombarding the city. Fegelein pleaded with Eva Braun to flee Berlin, and he tried to convince the others. He seemed to be more interested in Eva than he was in his wife, Gretl. Fegelein stopped trying to convince everyone to leave, and he left alone.

"Hitler got upset when he discovered Fegelein was missing from the bunker, so he sent SS Officers outside to find him and bring him back. They found Fegelein drunk and in bed with one of his mistresses in Berlin. There are many versions of this story, but the Nazis believed he would escape to Sweden or Switzerland with a large amount of cash and jewelry. The SS returned him to Hitler's bunker, and a mock trial took place for his desertion. Fegelein was immediately shot and buried in the Chancellery garden.

"Two days later, when the Russian army took over Berlin, Hitler and Eva committed suicide in their bunker."

"What became of Fegelein's wife, Gretl?" asked Deanna.

"She got some of Eva's valuable jewelry, gave birth to a daughter and named her Eva Barbara Fegelein," replied Anton. "Later, Gretl remarried, and she now lives in Northern Germany. Her daughter lives somewhere in Bavaria."

"It sounds like Eva Braun lived a fairy-tale life while she was in Obersalzberg. What did she do with her time when Hitler was away for long periods?" asked Judy.

"I think Eva considered herself to be royalty," said Anton. "She took advantage of her relationship with Hitler, the most powerful man in Germany, and one of the most powerful men in the world. She would shop in Munich and treat herself to expensive jewelry, clothes and photography equipment, even a fur coat. Eva stayed active and enjoyed sun bathing, waterskiing, gymnastics and snow skiing. She loved to skinny dip at Lake Königssee and Lake Obersee. A bowling alley was built for her in the basement of the Berghof.

"While the rest of the country struggled during the war, Eva lived a life of luxury. Hitler disliked her smoking, skinny dipping and wearing makeup. Cosmetics got banned in latter stages of the war. Eva complained so much to Hitler, he terminated the ban to keep her happy, but he still halted further production of cosmetics."

Herr Vogt said, "Eva loved to play with her two Scottish Terriers, but avoided Hitler's German Shepard, named Blondi. In the end, they used the dogs to test the poison which Hitler and Eva planned to use for their own suicide. The poison worked for all three dogs."

"Is anyone else getting hungry?" asked George.

"It is getting late," said Anton. "I had better get to the kitchen and finish closing it up."

"Anton, thank you for a wonderful day," said Lucas.

"You are welcome. I enjoyed spending the afternoon with all of you," said Anton. "Please come back this summer when the pool and tennis courts are open."

Grassl offered a suggestion, "I know a place which is still serving and has great food—The Hobelbank. It's a ten-minute drive, and I know the owner and chef, Werner. This late in the evening, many of the ski patrol guys go there, so it will be loud and lively."

"Where is the check for our drinks?" Lucas asked.

"This tab is on AFRC for official business," replied Herr Vogt. He smiled as everyone said thank you, and the group left with Grassl.

Lucas, George, Deanna, Judy and Chef Grassl piled into the VW van. They took the short ride along Hanielstrasse, around a sharp curve to the right, onto Berchtesgadener Strasse which curved to the left and arrived at the Hobelbank. The parking lot was full, so they parked at the end of a row of cars, perpendicular to the street which goes toward Salzburg.

After he parked, Lucas asked George to hand him his backpack. He pulled out his hash pipe, lit it and passed it on. Then, he asked Grassl, "Do many of the local people smoke pot or hashish?"

"Oh, yah," replied Grassl. "I would say, one fourth of the Bavarian people, age thirty or younger, smoke hashish. If you ever need to buy some, I can get it for you."

Lucas was glad to hear this from Grassl since Topo seemed content to stay in Garmisch for now.

"Thank you," said Lucas. "I do have a regular supplier in Garmisch, but it is good to know where I can go in Berchtesgaden."

When he walked in the door at the Hobelbank, the scene reminded Lucas of Garmisch: *This is "The Last Chance" of Berchtesgaden with a bunch of tipsy, ski patrol guys and their following of young ladies. They are all looking for the same thing—a good time.*

Lucas and the others waited by the door while Grassl disappeared into what Lucas supposed was the kitchen. He noticed all the dining tables were workbenches.

Grassl came back with a smiling gentleman who he introduced as Werner, Owner and Chef of the Hobelbank. In German, a *hobelbank* is a workbench. With a receding hairline and a beer belly, Werner stood about 5'9" and wore glasses. He was around 30 years old, close to Lucas in age. Dressed in lederhosen, Werner led the way to a big table next to a large plate-glass window at the back of the restaurant. Then he left.

After the group got seated and ordered beers, Grassl said, "Since Werner opened this hotel and restaurant last year, it became a favorite, late-night spot for ski patrol and their AFRC friends. So, Werner has to tolerate some ridiculous stuff with the young partiers."

"What type of menu does he have?" asked Lucas.

"Because it is so late, Werner will prepare Pork Jaeger Schnitzel if it is okay with all of you," replied Grassl.

Everyone agreed, and Grassl said, "Let's all order schnapps, and then we can relax. The Hobelbank does not have the fastest service, but the food is wonderful."

They ordered 4 Jägermeisters, plus 1 shot of Grassl Enzian which comes from the nearby Grassl family distillery, just up the highway going toward Salzburg.

Lucas studied his surroundings: *This place is noisy. Everybody is talking loudly over the sound of Bavarian music, coming through big speakers which are mounted throughout the restaurant. There are various types of wall hangings, woodcarvings of different animals and lamps hanging from the dark, beamed ceiling. Our table is against a window with a split curtain. The wood benches are perpendicular to the window. Across the aisle from our table, an old wagon wheel is hanging from the beamed ceiling.*

Their waitress was busy, but she had a great smile and showed enough cleavage to catch Lucas' attention. She brought a large bowl of Potato Leek Soup with a basket of Brotchen, and she let them serve themselves.

Grassl left again and brought back 5 more bottles of Wieninger beer. This gave everyone another reason to say, “Prost.”

“You seem to have the run of this place, Grassl. Is the owner another relative of yours?” asked Lucas.

“Werner is like a brother,” said Grassl. “We attended the same hotel school, the Hotelfachschule in Tegernsee. It is a beautiful place, an hour and a half west of here, or a half-hour drive south of Munich. You should stop and see it when you have time.”

The waitress brought plates, each with a very large pork cutlet, covered with a creamy, caramel-color sauce, studded with chanterelle mushrooms and placed alongside a mound of buttery spaetzle.

As she set the last steaming plate in front of George, there was a loud tap on the window next to their table. Lucas reached over, pulled the curtain back, and immediately wished he hadn’t. What he saw was 6 bare butts, all pressed against the window and forming a pyramid. The whole room went quiet. After everyone realized what was happening, they all roared with laughter.

“Looks like a bunch of pressed ham to me,” said George.

“They must be freezing,” said Judy.

“I don’t believe what I just saw!” exclaimed Deanna.

Meanwhile, the mooners had pulled their pants up and walked in the front door. They received a round of applause from the AFRC people. The Bavarian guests in the room simply shook their heads in wonder. Lucas recognized Chip, John and Doug, but he did not know the other three guys who also worked in Chiemsee.

“Crazy American GIs,” said Grassl.

Lucas spoke aloud for all to hear the most obvious thing which came to his mind, “What a bunch of assholes.”

The room filled with another round of laughter.

Directing his voice across the room toward Chip, John and Doug, Lucas said, “Thanks a lot for choosing our window. Our dinner came as you knocked on the glass. I hope everyone still has an appetite.”

Despite the rude distraction, they dove into their Jaeger Schnitzel. During the meal, they observed ski patrol antics at a table of young ladies. The Chiemsee guys joined the ladies and passed around a Bierstiefel.

Lucas and George had seen the Bierstiefel Challenge before, but Judy and Deanna had not.

Grassl explained how it worked, “A group of people play a game to determine who pays for the next Bierstiefel. They pass the Bierstiefel around in a circle without setting it down. If a person does not finish drinking all the beer in the stiefel, and the person he passes to finishes the rest of the beer, the last person who passed it loses and has to pay for the next stiefel."

The Bierstiefel is a shaped like a large, glass boot. They all watched a young lady drink from the Bierstiefel, and when she got to the end of the boot, beer suddenly gushed out and soaked her face.

Grassl laughed hard, and the others started laughing too.

"You saw what happens if you don't know the trick of the Bierstiefel," said Grassl. "An air pocket forms in the toe. If you hold the stiefel straight and drink, you get soaked with beer when you get to the end. The trick is to drink with the toe pointed right or left. It prevents an air bubble forming, but I guess nobody told her about it."

After eating huge portions of meat and spaetzle, Judy cuddled close to Lucas and gave him a come-on look.

Lucas suggested the group needed rest before a full day of skiing at Jenner, the next day. On the way back to the hotel, George lit the hash pipe and passed it around. When they got to the hotel, Lucas parked the van, they all said goodnight and headed to their respective rooms.

In their room, Lucas and Judy smoked more hashish. Then, with an eager expression, he asked, "Do you want to shower together, or do you want some privacy?"

Judy pulled off her turtleneck sweater and said, "I don't want to keep anything private from you, Lucas."

Lucas did not hesitate. He followed her lead and marveled at her body. Judy was in great shape. Using every inch of the king-sized bed, they made love until they were both completely spent.

Lucas thought: *I don't know if it was the dope we smoked, or Judy's prowess in bed, or a combination, but wow!*

It seemed as if he had barely fallen asleep when the phone rang. It was the wake-up call which Lucas had requested. He and Judy got dressed, went to the dining room, and found Grassl sitting at a table by himself. George and Deanna came in right behind them. Everyone had a quick continental breakfast of croissants, jam and coffee. Although Lucas really wanted a beer, he abstained.

After a 20-minute drive on Jennerbahnstrasse, they unloaded ski gear and 5 of them climbed into a 4-person gondola. They would be at the top of the mountain in only 15 minutes. Keeping to his tradition, Lucas passed the hash pipe around during the 1st ride of the day. Everyone enjoyed seeing the magnificent views from the gondola.

"Didn't they film part of the movie around here when they made *The Sound of Music*?" Lucas asked Grassl.

"Yes. They filmed the opening scene in a high meadow on Mehlweg Mountain near Mehlweg-Marktschellenberg," he replied. "It's northeast of Berchtesgaden, a sixteen-minute drive. The closing scene was filmed on the Obersalzberg in the Bavarian Alps."

"I watched the movie six times and loved it," said Deanna. "My favorite parts were the opening scene with Julie Andrews singing 'The Hills Are Alive' and the ending when the family climbed the mountain, escaping to Switzerland. It won five Oscars at the Academy Awards."

Passing the hash pipe to George, Grassl asked, "Did all of you see *The Sound of Music*?" Everyone nodded.

"About seven years ago when it was filmed, we all learned the movie story and the real story of the Trapp family," said Grassl. "The basic story was followed in the movie, but with several changes to what occurred in real life. Maria came to the von Trapp family as a tutor for only one of his children who was recovering from rheumatic fever. In the movie, she came as a governess for all seven of his children. Also, her last name was Kutschera, not Ranier which the movie used.

"Maria wrote a book which was published in nineteen forty-nine, *The Story of the Trapp Family Singers.* Writing about her husband in the book, she claimed she did not marry Georg because she loved him. Rather, she married him because she loved his children so much. Together, they had three more children. For Maria, marriage was a big change from living with the nuns at the Nonnberg Abbey.

"The von Trapp's villa is in Salzburg-Aigen, a suburb of Salzburg and a very upscale neighborhood. The Porsche and Piech families also have homes in Salzburg-Aigen. After the von Trapp family had gone, Heinrich Himmler, the head of SS, took over Trapp Villa and used it as his summer quarters. While Himmler occupied the villa, Hitler stayed there several times and had his own room."

"What year did Maria join the family, Grassl?" asked Deanna.

"It was nineteen twenty-six when she arrived," he replied. "They got married the following year, not in nineteen thirty-eight which was the year of the *Anschluss Österreich* (Annexation of Austria)."

Everyone oohed and aahed as Lake Königssee came into view, surrounded by a lush forest.

"Did the Trapp family actually hike over the mountains, going to Switzerland?" asked Deanna.

"No, it was only in the movie for drama," said Grassl. "They walked out of their villa, went across the street and boarded the train, carrying all their suitcases and musical instruments. The train took them to Italy. One day after the family left, the Nazis closed all Austrian borders, so they fled at the right time. Later, another train took them to England. From there, the family got passage to America."

"What happened to Trapp Villa after the war?" asked George.

"The villa is three stories with twenty-two rooms and a basement," replied Grassl. "In nineteen forty-seven, the Trapp family still owned the villa. A group of missionaries bought the property, and it became a seminary which it still is today. The villa could not be used for the movie since the missionaries live such a secluded way of life.

"Other locations in Bavaria and sets in movie studios were used in the movie. The scenes of a lakeside terrace, gazebo and gardens represented the villa, but filming took place at Schloss Leopoldskron which is south of Salzburg and very near the real Trapp Villa. Their wedding scenes were filmed at Mondsee Abbey in Salzburg."

"Didn't the von Trapp family lose all of their money, and then they recovered?" asked Lucas.

"Yes. In nineteen thirty-five, they lost a fortune when an Austrian bank failed," replied Grassl. "To survive, they rented out the lower floors of the villa while they lived on the top floor. During this time, the von Trapp family first began to sing for money.

"Contrary to the movie character, Georg von Trapp was not the family's pushy music director. The von Trapp's priest was their music director for twenty years. The family earned money singing and became popular here for many years.

"Before they left Germany, they declined an invitation to perform for Hitler's birthday celebration in Berchtesgaden. While traveling, they stopped and performed in Italy before going to England for more of the same. Later, they booked a three-month tour of the U.S. and performed all around the country. They settled in Pennsylvania for a while, and then bought a farm in Stowe, Vermont. They loved its likeness to their Austrian homeland. Several years later, the farmhouse in Vermont became the Trapp Family Lodge."

"What else can you tell us? Are they all still alive?" asked Judy.

Grassl said, "Georg von Trapp was a kind, warm-hearted and gentle person. As for Maria, she was a caring and loving person, but she had brief outbursts of yelling, slamming and throwing things. For the most part, everyone said she was very nice.

"They had two more children before leaving Austria, and their third child was born before they went to the U.S. The last I heard, they are all living, except Georg and his daughter, Martina. Georg von Trapp passed away in nineteen forty-seven. A few years later, Martina died while giving birth to a stillborn daughter during a complicated Cesarean section. George is buried at the family lodge in Vermont, and Martina is buried next to him with her baby in her arms."

The gondola came to a midway station at 1,200 meters (3,937 ft.). It was the 1st of 2 stops. They stayed on, rode past a small reservoir and up to the Berg Station at 1,800 meters (5,905 ft.). After grabbing their skis and poles from the gondola's outside rack, they snapped into their bindings and followed Grassl on the steep slope.

Lucas was thinking, *Here I am again, feeling like I'm in over my head. Well, the conditions couldn't be better and the snow feels good. So, I will follow these four experts and let myself go.*

Skiing was never more exhilarating for Lucas. However, he had to work hard on the steep terrain. Since he did not ski yesterday, his legs were rested. Grassl kept everyone moving today, so Lucas did not have time to think about the steepness. They were all laughing at Grassl and his yodeling as he flew down the mountain. Everyone felt great, the morning went fast, and they skied to the middle station for lunch. After a few beers, some great goulash soup and brotchen, they were all ready to go again.

Riding in the gondola, they smoked another bowl of hashish as Grassl entertained them with bits of useless information. They enjoyed his sense of humor; it felt good to laugh, and everyone agreed: Grassl had great stories about the Berchtesgadener Hof.

"How were Chef Held and Herr Vogt able to stay out of the military during the war?" George asked Grassl.

"When Nazis bought the Grand Hotel Auguste Victoria in nineteen thirty-six, they remodeled and renamed it the Berchtesgadener Hof," said Grassl. "It hosted visiting royalty and many government officials: The Duke and Duchess of Windsor, the British Prime Minister Neville Chamberlain, and Nazi leaders, like Joseph Goebbels, Heinrich Himmler and Erwin Rommel.

"With such important people coming from all over Europe to stay there, the hotel needed skilled employees. With their talents, Chef Held and Herr Vogt were more useful working at the hotel than in combat.

"Eva Braun, Martin Bormann and Hermann Fegelein were regulars when Hitler was out of town. Martin Bormann's brother had lived in the hotel. So did Hitler's sister, Paula. She complied with Hitler's request and used the name of Paula Wolf.

"After the war, Field Marshal Albert Kesselring lived in the hotel until he was arrested in Italy. Authorities claimed he slaughtered three hundred and fifty innocent Italians during the war. He was sentenced to death, but he was pardoned and freed in nineteen fifty-two. Kesselring died in nineteen sixty."

Lucas spent the rest of the afternoon following Grassl on steep, black runs at speeds he was not used to. Lucas found it to be one of the most thrilling experiences he ever had on skis.

By the end of the day, they all were dragging, but they were keeping up with Grassl.

“I have never skied so fast in my life. This was an amazing day,” Lucas said to Grassl.

“You all did well,” he replied. “Don’t forget, I was raised on skis and on this mountain. At an early age, I learned to not fear speed. You point those skis downhill, and you go.

“Also, going with a better skier is a great way to improve. Learn from your mistakes and do it over until you get it right. When you are standing at the top of a run, stop a few minutes and enjoy the view. You will be inspired to return again and again.

“I do not know how others feel when they fly down the mountain, but when I do it, everything else in my mind is quiet. I stay focused on the scene in front of me and the exhilarating feeling it gives me.”

They all finished skiing, loaded their ski gear in the van, and drove back to “The Hof” where Grassl got dropped off. Before leaving the hotel, they thanked him and said goodbye until next time.

With everyone ready to travel in the van, they headed west toward Garmisch for another new adventure.

CHAPTER 32

Garmisch: The Birthday Party

George was behind the wheel. Deanna was in the passenger seat, choosing music. She picked out a tape of Joni Mitchell's new album, *Blue.* Lucas and Judy settled in the back, each with a bottle of Wieninger beer, and enjoyed the music, listening to "A Case of You."

"I wonder what type of jobs we can get in Garmisch," said Judy.

"You and Deanna can go by the personnel office tomorrow, and they will let you know what jobs are available," said Lucas.

"What are your plans, Lucas? Do you know what you want to do next?" asked Judy.

"I am going back to Oberammergau," he replied, "to work at the officers' club and work on the big birthday bash for Colonel Moyers. It will take place on the third of April. I also want to play basketball with my friends."

Speaking to everyone, Lucas said, "On our way to Garmisch, I need to stop in Chiemsee and talk to Chef Bucherl. He is supervising the food production for the party, and it's becoming a hot ticket around AFRC. Chef Bucherl won gold medals at the World Culinary Olympics in Frankfurt. He wants to do a classic buffet. Heinz Ostler, the pastry chef, will do the cake, some other desserts and maybe an ice carving."

"How far is it to Chiemsee?" George asked, over his shoulder.

"We're about twenty minutes away," replied Lucas. "Shall we have dinner at Chiemsee again? Maybe a Filet Mignon or New York Steak with a baked potato and salad? If you want to, I suggest we eat early, and then head on to Garmisch."

The others agreed with enthusiasm.

Lucas wondered how this would work out: *I know how affected I was by Shelley on my last trip to Chiemsee, and I really enjoyed being with her. I almost hope I won't see Shelley on this trip because it could get uncomfortable with Judy here.*

"Lucas, you seem to get special service anywhere you go. How did you become so well known in such a short time here?" asked Judy.

"Perhaps my basketball skills are now legendary," he replied.

George overheard Lucas and said, "Judy, you should have seen him in his prime, playing in the Long Beach AAU League."

"Wait a minute, George," said Lucas. "I believe I am just now reaching my peak in life."

"Oh, lucky me," said Judy. Then, she smiled at Lucas.

Her comment brought a chuckle from the others.

Deanna was ready to play a tape which she brought from Canada. She said, "For our trip, I chose *The Beatles Again* album before I left home. The featured song is 'Hey Jude.' It first sold as a single and remained the number one hit since its release in nineteen sixty-eight. It is one of the longest singles ever released, over seven minutes long, and they used a 40-piece orchestra in the recording. Did you know the song 'Hey Jude' was first named 'Hey Jules' by Paul McCartney?"

"Why did they change the name?" Judy asked Deanna.

"Paul claimed he wrote it for John Lennon's son Julian, to comfort him when John and his first wife, Cynthia, were separated," she replied. "He said he changed the name of the song because Julian was so young. There is controversy over who the song is about. It seems more like a love song between two adults; and Julian was only five years old.

"I read some terrible reports about John: He had an explosive temper and used to hit Cynthia. Also, she caught John and Ono having sex one night when she was not expected to come home."

"It is a great song, regardless of who the subject is," said George. "But those reports could explain some lyrics in the song.

"In an interview last year, John Lennon claimed the song referred to his relationship with Yoko Ono," said Deanna. "But McCartney denied it. John married Ono a year after the song's release. Anyway, here it is."

Deanna pushed in the tape and played "Hey Jude."

They all sang along with Paul's voice, had fun with the lyrics and finished the song in unison with a strong, "… nah nah nah… hey Jude."

"Well, it was fun," said Lucas. "Yet, the lyrics do not sound like something I would write to a child."

"Julian was also responsible for another Beatle's title," said Deanna. "He showed his dad a watercolor drawing of a girl and a bunch of stars around her. John asked him who was in the drawing. Julian told his dad, 'It's Lucy in the sky with diamonds,' which became the title of a song John wrote. Someone referred to the song, using the LSD abbreviation. But John Lennon insisted it was not a song about acid."

Everyone was laughing, as George slid into the driveway and parked at Lake Chiemsee Hotel. They were only 4 spaces from the entrance walkway, and they headed straight to the dining room.

It was still early, and the restaurant was quiet. Musicians were setting up, but not yet playing. For now, they could all talk in a normal voice and hear each other.

The waitress, a cute brunette with a giggly personality and a New England accent, introduced herself as Gayle. During dinner, she told them she loved working and living in Chiemsee because the people here and the ski patrol were the most fun people she had ever met.

Lucas and George both ordered Steak au Poivre Vert with Pommes Frites. Judy had Fresh Sautéed Trout with Pommes Frites, and Deanna got Sauerbraten with Kartoffelpuffer (potato pancakes).

Hungry from skiing all day and smoking hashish, they enjoyed a nice, quiet dinner. For dessert, they split 2 big wedges of Pastry Chef Ostler's, Schwartzwalder Kirschtorte (Black Forest Cake).

After dinner, they walked into an empty bar. The bartender, Gunther, greeted them, and they ordered Wieninger draft beers. Lucas excused himself for 10 minutes, and he went to see Chef Bucherl about the party. When Lucas returned, he asked, "Where is everyone tonight?"

"It's still early," said Gunther. "Some of the ski patrol are in the game room. You're all welcome to go down there."

Lucas had seen the game room when he was here with Inga, Eric and Sabine, but he had not yet played any bar games there.

Tonight, everyone wanted to see it. So, Lucas led them down a narrow, winding stairway and into a busy game room. The first person he saw was Chip, playing table tennis. When Chip saw Lucas, he stopped playing, walked over to them and shook Lucas' hand.

"Who is following who around?" asked Chip.

"Great show last night at Werner's restaurant, Chip," said Lucas.

Chip smiled. "Are you going to stick around tonight and let us get revenge for your victory at the AFRC tournament?" he asked.

"We hadn't planned to, but I wouldn't mind playing a little. How about the rest of you?" Lucas asked his friends.

"It looks like fun," said Judy.

Deanna said, "You guys better watch out. Judy and I have bar game experience too."

Lucas looked at George and said, "I know your answer." Then, he turned and said, "Okay. Chip, can we get a case of beer at the bar?"

"Yeah, let's take up a collection for it," replied Chip.

"I got this one," said Lucas, heading for the stairs.

When Lucas returned with the case of beer, his friends were waiting at the foosball table. Chip had gone back to table tennis.

Everyone cheered as Lucas set a case of Wieninger beer in half-liter bottles on the bench near the pool table. A bottle opener was attached to the wall next to the pool cue rack. They all grabbed a beer and stood in line, waiting to use the opener.

Lucas opened 3 beers and handed them to his 3 friends. Then, he saw Shelley which surprised him, and he almost dropped his bottle. She was playing darts with a ski patrol guy. Lucas had seen the guy here before, but did not know his name. Shelley did not seem to notice Lucas yet, or maybe she was ignoring him on purpose.

Lucas made himself concentrate on the foosball game. He and Judy dominated George and Deanna, and they won two games, easily; most of the points were made by Lucas' defensive plays. While they took a break and got more beer, Chip came over and said he would introduce them to the rest of the young people who were playing games, drinking beer and having fun.

Lucas thought: *This is different from Garmisch because the people who work in Chiemsee also live together at this hotel, like a family. In Garmisch, employees are scattered, living at AFRC hotels, a Bavarian gasthaus, or apartments where German economy rates are good. I wonder if Shelley's invitation is still open to live with her.*

Going around the room, Chip introduced them to the others: Shelley, Greg, Doug, Bill, John Reilly, Gayle, the cute brunette waitress, and her friend Larry. They also met Rosie, a talkative, perky Scottish girl, and a tall handsome guy named Brad. Everyone played bar games.

Shelley shook Lucas' hand, saying, "It's nice to see you again. I hope your ski trip went well." Then, she turned back to her dart game.

Chip challenged Lucas to a game of table tennis. Lucas had seen Chip's game in action, and he knew Chip was a great player. Lucas considered himself as a better-than-average player, and he was skilled at any games he played with a ball. The table tennis match between Lucas and Chip confirmed their competitive spirit; it got more intense every time they went against each other. It seemed as if they were evenly matched, no matter what game or sport it was. Lucas realized this was another good reason to make the move to Chiemsee for the spring and summer.

Before they left, Lucas and George were waiting outside the ladies' restroom while Judy and Deanna went in. Shelley came out first, patted Lucas on the butt, winked at him and said, "See you later, champ."

As the guys watched Shelley walk away, George inquired, "What is going on with her, Lucas?"

"She is always joking and playing around," he replied. "Shelley is the head housekeeper of the hotel. When I came here before, she gave us a full tour. We all smoked dope and drank beer at her apartment."

"I forgot how friendly everyone is in Bavaria," said George.

"It must be all the beer they drink," said Lucas.

Judy and Deanna joined the guys, and they all walked to the van.

It was late, but Lucas' adrenaline level was high, so he drove the van. Judy played "Stairway to Heaven" on a new Led Zeppelin cassette. She listened to the song 3 times until George got tired of hearing it, and he said, "Okay, I've had enough of the same song."

Before leaving the hotel, George grabbed two newspapers. He said, "Let me read you some news of the world."

It is a world I have become less familiar with, thought Lucas.

As George said, "Controversy over smoking appears to be heating up," Judy changed the music and turned down the sound.

George read aloud to the others, *"In a recent press release, the Tobacco Institute's President stated, 'The cigarette industry is vitally concerned in determining whether cigarette smoking causes human disease... and despite this effort, the answers to critical questions about smoking and health are still unknown.' A week earlier, the Senior V.P. of Philip Morris was quoted by the Wall Street Journal, as saying, 'If our product is harmful... we'll stop making it.' Philip Morris published a research report in early January, titled Motives and Incentives in Cigarette Smoking, in which one of their principal scientists stated, 'People smoke to obtain nicotine... Nicotine is the industry's product... No one has ever become a cigarette smoker by smoking cigarettes without nicotine.' Although, cigarette ads were banned on American television and radio last year, the Tobacco Industry still claims there are no scientific facts which prove smoking is harmful to a person's health."*

"I think smoking cigarettes and nicotine are more harmful than marijuana, and I think the laws should be reversed," said Lucas. "Pot should be legal and cigarettes should be banned. Besides being a health risk, cigarettes do nothing for me, except make me cough. Pot makes me feel good, and it works as a pick-me-up.

"However, I do use my military rations to buy cigarettes and sell them to the German chefs along with hard liquor. It has made me new friends here, and some have invited me to dinner. My use of the German language is not great yet. But I'm working on it."

"How about this?" asked George. He read, *"Liechtenstein attended the Winter Olympic Games in Sapporo, Japan. Although they took no medals home, they did well in Alpine Skiing. Liechtenstein gained extra notice in the news because it is the last European country where women are not allowed to vote."*

"Where is Liechtenstein?" asked Deanna.

"It's a ninety-minute drive, southwest of Garmisch," replied Lucas. "Switzerland borders Liechtenstein on the west, while Austria borders it on the east and the north. It is a mountainous area where they have lots of winter sports. It is the only doubly landlocked country in Europe which means: a landlocked country entirely surrounded by one or more other landlocked countries."

"How do you know so much about Liechtenstein?" asked Judy.

"I learned about places to ski when George and I drove to Gomagoi, Italy," replied Lucas. "I also read an article about Liechtenstein's involvement in World War Two. Or rather, its non-involvement by being neutral like its neighbor, Switzerland. At the end of the war, they gave refuge to five hundred Russian soldiers who had collaborated with the German Wehrmacht during the war. Some two hundred of them agreed to return to Russia. They got put on a train which was going to Vienna, but they disappeared without a trace and were never heard from again. A few non-collaborators turned up in South America, mysteriously."

George read more news aloud, *"The California Supreme Court is reviewing the state's death penalty statute. A ruling on the People vs. Anderson is expected next month. It could overturn a death penalty verdict as unconstitutional which would veto existing law for capital punishment; therefore, it would affect current prisoners on death row who are very dangerous, such as Charles Manson."*

"I followed the Manson murder trials," said Deanna. "His attorneys played the Beatles' album *Helter Skelter* during his trial last year. Manson contended the album was a calling for all the mayhem his group created. The jury did not believe it and recommended the death penalty. I read Manson's interpretations of the Beatle's *White Album,* and he thought the song 'Rocky Raccoon' was a calling for black men to revolt against whites. So, he and his followers tried to jump start the revolution by creating their own helter skelter."

"Yeah, those people are crazy or spaced out on acid," said Lucas.

"Have you guys ever tried acid?" asked Judy.

Both George and Lucas said, "No."

Then, Lucas said, "Back in Long Beach, a friend of ours told me I don't have the personality for an 'acid trip.' He told me he had taken it several times, but he suggested I leave it alone. Although I don't really know what he meant, I took his advice and never have tried it."

No thanks, thought Lucas. *I heard how Ulrike Meinhof's mind got messed up on acid, and she had a bad panic attack on one of her "trips." Also, Peter Green, the founder of Fleetwood Mac, went on an "LSD trip" and never came back from it.*

George read again, *"NASA launched the Pioneer Ten Spacecraft on March third. It is on track to be the first spacecraft to travel through the asteroid belt and the first to visit Jupiter. If all goes well, it will land on Jupiter in twenty-one months."*

"I'm surprised, you have not found sports news," said Lucas.

"Let me see," replied George. "Okay, here are the sports." He read, *"UCLA won its sixth consecutive national basketball title... LA Lakers broke the NBA record, winning sixty-nine of eighty-two games... And, the NBA named Kareem Abdul Jabbar, as their MVP."*

"Great!" said Lucas. "I hope some of those players from UCLA will play for the U.S. Olympic Team this summer."

"Now, here's something which will interest you, Lucas," said George. "I know you were reading *The Godfather* during my first trip to Europe when we traveled to Ibiza and Formentera." He read, *"The Godfather, directed by Francis Ford Coppola, is starring Marlon Brando and Al Pacino. The movie, based on the book, premiered in New York City on March fifteenth."*

"They have a movie theater at Chiemsee," said Lucas. "Maybe I'll see it there this summer. Is Brando in the lead role as Godfather?"

"Yes, and Pacino plays his son, Michael," replied George.

"Now, here's an interesting item with a photo," said George. He read, *"John Lennon and Yoko Ono stood in front of the Immigration and Naturalization Service offices in New York City with their attorney. Lennon overstayed his visa, and the Nixon Administration had him served with deportation papers."*

"It's no secret, Lennon and Ono oppose the Vietnam War. They ask fans to vote against Nixon at antiwar rallies," said Deanna.

"Last year, I read a South African broadcasting company lifted a five-year ban on the Beatles," said George. "The ban was in effect because John Lennon had said something like, 'The Beatles were more popular than Jesus.' His comment also wasn't very well-received in 'The States.' Some American radio stations banned their songs, there were anti-Beatles demonstrations, and the Beatles received death threats while they toured in America. The Vatican even denounced John Lennon, and many people were burning their records in public."

Now, they were close to Oberammergau. George was done reading, and everyone listened to music, thinking of what they would be doing next. Lucas would stay in Oberammergau and work for a few weeks. George dropped him off at Hawkins Barracks where Lucas still had a room. Then, George took the ladies to Garmisch. They would stay in a hotel, and the ladies would apply for jobs at AFRC Headquarters.

Lucas wanted to regroup and realized he needed some rest. After taking a shower in the locker room downstairs, he got a good night's sleep. He looked forward to having a set routine, and playing basketball at the barracks gym.

Back at work the next day, Lucas was glad to be around fun people who enjoyed working and playing together. When he was not at the officers' club, he usually went to the gym and played 3-on-3 basketball with military guys who also worked and lived at Hawkins Barracks. These GIs were enthusiastic about basketball, but none had Lucas' skills or shooting ability. They compensated by using over-aggressive plays and sometimes brute force. Lucas thought about playing in Garmisch because he was getting bruised when he played with the GIs. Then, he thought how much fun it would be if Robinson played basketball, and Lucas could rough him up a little on the court.

Time went by fast at the officers' club. Lucas would be in Garmisch for the next 4 days, working on Colonel Moyer's party at Keane Lodge. Planning to leave in the morning and go to Garmisch, Lucas closed the kitchen and headed toward the bar. As he passed the main entrance, he saw Shelley, of all people. Lucas was speechless. He stood there, looking at her beautiful face, and she was the first to talk.

"Hi Lucas. I thought I would surprise you," said Shelley. Lucas tried to gather his thoughts, as Shelley explained, "I rode with Chef Bucherl and Herr Ostler from Chiemsee to Garmisch. Then, I got a ride here with a GI and his wife who I met at the PX."

Impulsively, Lucas gave her a big hug, took her by the hand and said, "It's great to see you! Come and meet my coworkers."

Eric had already gone to The Grill in Garmisch. Karin was tending the busy bar this evening. Lucas introduced Shelley to Helmut and Kurt who were playing foosball, then he took Shelley to a booth, so they could sit and talk while they drank beer.

"Lucas, do you live in Oberammergau?" asked Shelley.

"I have a room in the barracks," he replied.

"Would you enjoy having a roommate tonight?" she asked.

"Well, women are not allowed in the men's section of barracks," he said. "We could try to sneak you in, but I only have a single bed."

"I don't think we'll need any more space," she replied.

They finished their beers, said goodnight to everyone and went out into the cold air. Light snow was falling as they passed the hash pipe back and forth. They walked along the path and went through the gate to the barracks grounds.

Lucas led Shelley to the women's locker room and asked her to wait there while he checked upstairs in the men's section. If the coast was clear, he would sneak her to his room.

This is ridiculous, he thought. *We should have gone to a hotel. Yet, the risk of being caught increases excitement for our coming event.*

It seemed unreal, but he got Shelley to his room without being seen. Lucas opened 2 Spaten beers which he kept stored for his stays there, and he handed a beer to Shelley.

There was little furniture in the room. On one wall, a mirror hung above a 4'x2' dresser. From a small window with curtains, a big clock on a building with an onion-shaped dome could be seen across the way. Below the window, there was a small desk and chair. The single bed had 2 sheets, 2 army blankets and 1 pillow. The room was heated, but it was still on the cool side. Lucas opened his sleeping bag to use as a comforter.

Lucas and Shelley did not need warming up. They were undressing each other, between passionate kisses and explorations with their hands. They managed to use the bed, the floor (with the sleeping bag spread out) and the desktop. When they ran out of energy, they fell asleep in the single bed, wrapped in each other's arms.

After what seemed like only minutes since they drifted off, Lucas and Shelley heard someone banging on the door of his room. A deep male voice yelled out, "Open up. We're searching all the rooms because some joker has stolen the flag."

Both Lucas and Shelley were completely naked. Lucas yelled back toward the door, "Okay, let me put some clothes on."

Turning to look at Shelley who was also hurrying to put clothes on, Lucas whispered, "Busted!"

When Lucas opened the door, Shelley was hiding behind it. Then, 2 MPs burst into the room. They were shocked when they saw Shelley. Directing his statement to Lucas, one MP said, "You can't have women in your room."

Shelley flashed them a nice smile and said, "Gruss Gott."

The other MP said, "This section of the barracks is only men. We have to report this, and the lady has to leave now."

There was nothing Lucas or Shelley could say, except, "Okay."

Now, they were outside. It was 4 a.m., the ground was frozen, and the temperature was about 0 degrees Celsius. George had taken Lucas' van to Garmisch. All they could do was start walking to the train station, then take the train to Garmisch. If they found a hotel room, they could stay there while Lucas worked on the party for the next 4 days.

It was a 30-minute walk from the officers' club to the Bahnhof. Lucas and Shelley were not in a hurry since the first train was at 5 a.m., and it was only a little past 4 a.m. They enjoyed being together so much, they did not feel the cold. Walking along Michael-Diemer-Strasse, they made a jog left and got on Am Kreuzweg, turned left onto Daisenbergerstrasse, turned right onto Dedlerstrasse, went to Sankt-Lukas-Strasse and passed the famous Wittelsbach Hotel. They continued walking on Dorfstrasse, then took Bahnhofstrasse across the bridge and over the Ammer River, turned right on Zur LOK and arrived at the Bahnhof.

As they arrived at the station entrance, Lucas thought: *Inga's house is behind the Bahnhof. I'm glad I am leaving here. For me, there are too many ghosts around this town now.*

Shelley cuddled with Lucas in the train station. They were laughing and kissing with great lust for each other, and even this uncomfortable situation was a fun adventure.

"Lucas, tell me what you know about the barracks." said Shelley.

"The original complex was built in the mid-thirties for a German Mountain Brigade, and Hötzendorf Kaserne was the original name," he replied. "When the Americans took it over, they named it Hawkins Barracks and decided it would be the U.S. Army School of Europe. In nineteen fifty-three, NATO opened the school and offered students many courses in military-related subjects.

"In nineteen forty-three, Messerschmitt Company used the complex for research and development of aircraft. Willy Messerschmitt, an aircraft designer and manufacturer, designed the top German fighter plane in the Second World War. In aircraft development and design, Willy was a talented man, like Ferdinand Porsche was in automobile development. The Nazis favored both men, and their factories used slave labor from concentration camps. After the war, they both faced trials and got put in prison for collaborating with the Nazis. Messerschmitt spent two years in prison. After his release, he resumed his position as head of the company; but restrictions did not allow the company to manufacture aircraft until nineteen fifty-five. When the aircraft industry got busy, Messerschmitt remained chairman of the company until he retired last year.

"Thirty-seven kilometers of tunnels were dug into Laber Mountain which is behind the NATO School where we got busted."

They started laughing about her getting caught in the men's barracks.

Shelley said, "I hope this means you are coming my way."

"I wouldn't miss it for the world," he replied.

They settled in 2 seats on the 3rd car of the train. The ride would take 1 hour-and-15 minutes, getting to Garmisch. The train went in the opposite direction for a while, and then it turned around. It passed through Unterammergau, a village of about a thousand people. The next stop was Saulgrub, also home to about a thousand people. Both villages are due north of Oberammergau.

The train went on to Murnau am Staffelsee which has a population of about ten thousand. Inga had told Lucas it was a prisoner of war camp for Polish officers. When Lucas told Shelley about it, she said, "The Nazis probably killed all the Polish enlisted men, and the only guys left were Polish officers."

"You may be right," said Lucas. "I think the Russians lost more lives than any other country involved in the war. I read they lost over twenty million. China also lost around twenty million.

"Anyway, Wernher von Braun was a Nazi SS Major. As a space engineer, he was the architect and the developer of the V-Two Rocket for Nazi Germany. After the war, he moved to 'The States' and developed the Saturn Five for the U.S."

"If he was an SS Major, why wasn't he tried for war crimes, along with the rest of the Nazi officers?" asked Shelley.

"Oh, the U.S. wanted the German scientists to work on developing their space program," he replied. "So, they overlooked the crimes of these Nazi scientists and engineers who used slave labor—prisoners from the concentration camps, working hard labor jobs. The U.S. took in about fifteen hundred German scientists after the war. Most of them changed their identities, and some are still working for NASA. Wernher von Braun was in his early thirties when he worked in Germany's rocket program at Peenemünde Army Research Center. It is considered the birthplace of rocket science. The first launch of a missile into space took place there in October nineteen forty-two. Peenemünde is on an island in the Baltic Sea, two-hundred-and-fifty kilometers (150 miles) north of Berlin. It's where they produced and tested the V-Two Rocket, named the Vergeltungswaffe Two (Vengeance Weapon 2)."

Finishing the story, he said, "After the allied bombings in nineteen forty-five, scientists faced the threat of being captured by the Soviets. All scientists were transported by train to Oberammergau. They were guarded by the SS who were told to shoot Germany's top scientists, rather than allow the Allies to capture them. Wernher von Braun and some other scientists had escaped the allied bombing. They made it to Austria, but had to surrender to the Americans. The American CIA also tried to keep the scientists' war crimes a secret for fear of endangering the U.S. Space Program which von Braun and others were such an important part of."

The train pulled into the Garmisch-Partenkirchen station. Lucas and Shelley grabbed their backpacks, headed for the Bayerischer Hof Hotel and got a room for the next 4 days. Lucas had stayed at this hotel once. He knew they would have to walk down the hall to take a shower which never seemed to have enough water hot. All the AFRC hotels were full this week, so they felt lucky to get a room.

When they were not working on Colonel Moyer's birthday party, Lucas and Shelley had such fervor and mutual desire for each other, they were all over each other, either in Lucas' van or in their hotel room. They were compatible, and their chemistry together was undeniable.

Lucas and Shelley talked about skiing. She learned to ski in California at Big Bear, Mammoth Mountain and Lake Tahoe resorts. He had skied at all those locations. After Colonel Moyer's birthday party, they would take a day and ski together, somewhere in Bavaria.

Shelley seems to be the whole package, thought Lucas. *She is full of energy, always in a fun mood and always ready for sex. My lust for her seems endless. I do not know where this is going, but I am determined to find out and enjoy the trip.*

At Keane Lodge, Chef Bucherl and Lucas worked together in the newly remodeled kitchen, along with cooks from the Green Arrow, the Von Steuben, the Sheridan and the General Patton hotels.

The guest list had expanded from an original estimate of 40 or 50 to the current estimate of 250 people. With a new kitchen layout, Keane Lodge offered a 12-burner Wolf stove, a big salamander (broiler), 2 deep fryers, adequate refrigeration and larger work tables. It had plenty of space for numerous cooks to work in the kitchen.

Gino proved to be an excellent organizer and motivator, almost to the point of irritation, but he was a likeable person to be around.

Although Chef Bucherl was a little anxious, he was the most detailed chef Lucas had ever worked with. Since he considered it a privilege to work with one of the best chefs in Germany, Lucas kept things on the lighter side with a casual demeanor and sense of humor.

Lucas thought: *Things always seem to work out for the best, and the pieces of "my life puzzle" all fall into just the right places. When I get to Chiemsee, I will work with Bucherl in a one hundred and seventy-nine room hotel built by Hitler. At no cost, I will share living quarters with the talented and beautiful Shelley Carpenter. I can eat like a king in the kitchen, and be with good people who love to play games, party and have fun. Resorts nearby offer great skiing. The hotel has a movie theater, plus sailing and tennis. At the employees' beer machine, a half-liter bottle costs only seventy pfennigs (20 cents) for the best beer in the world. I love the way Bavarians live. Since I can sell my liquor and cigarette rations to German employees, my paychecks can go straight into savings.*

The night before Colonel Moyer's big bash, Lucas, Chef Bucherl, Heinz Ostler, Shelley, Eric, Gino and several cooks from AFRC hotels worked until 4 a.m. Everyone felt confident and ready for the party before they all took a break. They would be back at it in a later this morning.

Military people were coming to this party from all over Germany and Europe as well as "The States."

Shelley and Lucas bounced out of bed, both naked and aroused. They showered and started the day with passionate lovemaking.

On the road, they stopped at the store, bought 2 cases of Spaten beer and some brotchen, then headed for Keane Lodge. As Lucas drove, Shelley studied the buffet menu which Lucas and Chef Bucherl had prepared. It was an "International Buffet" which included American and German dishes, plus enough variety to be interesting. Lucas asked Shelley to read the menu out load, so he could hear it.

Shelley read, *"Carving Station: Various roasts or grilled meats, carved to order, including Prime Rib, Roast Turkey, and Roast Leg of Venison with Sauce Grand Veneur and Lingenberries.*

"Bavarian Station: Pork Schnitzel with a selection of sauces and garnishes, such as Jäger Schnitzel (pork cutlets with a brown mushroom sauce), Paprika Schnitzel (pork cutlets, breaded and fried with a creamy paprika gravy), or Zigeuner Schnitzel (pork cutlets, breaded and fried with a spicy tomato, bell pepper gravy). Rindsgulasch mit Nudeln (beef goulash over egg noodles) and Rouladen (sliced beef rolls, stuffed with onions, German double-smoked bacon, mustard and gherkins—all roasted and served with gravy). Side dishes include red cabbage, spaetzle and potato pancakes.

"American Station: BBQ Ribs, Meat Loaf and Fried Chicken. Side dishes include ranch beans, coleslaw and potato salad.

"Mexico: Chicken Enchilada Casserole and Carnitas (pork butt, seasoned with herbs, cooked slow, crisped on the outside, and then pulled apart), served on a tortilla with onion, salsa, guacamole and re-fried beans. Side dish is Mexican Caesar Salad.

"Italian Station: Eggplant Parmigiana and Pizza. Side dishes include various pastas, marinara and pesto sauces, plus garlic bread.

"Country Style French: Beef Bourguignon and Cassoulet.

"Chinese Station: Mu Shu Pork with crepes and plum sauce, Shrimp with Broccoli, Steamed Rice and Mandarin Fried Rice."

Shelley was near the end of the menu, but Lucas interrupted her. "Do you know where Caesar Salad was invented?"

"No, I don't. Was it in Italy?" she asked.

"You are close," he replied. "An Italian chef, Caesar Cardini, invented the salad, but he was in Tijuana, Mexico. He had immigrated to the U.S. Later, to avoid prohibition and gain access to wines, he moved to Mexico. On the Fourth of July in nineteen twenty-four, his kitchen food supplies were low, so he had to get creative with what he had. He used lots of garlic, with coddled eggs, croutons, romaine lettuce, anchovies, parmesan cheese, olive oil, vinegar and coarse black pepper. For effect, he displayed all items on a tray and took it to the dining room where he tossed the salad items together and served at tableside."

"What an interesting story," she said.

Then, she read the last two menu items:

"North Africa: Cous Cous and assorted Kabobs.

"Spain: Paella and Albondigas (meatballs in garlic-tomato sauce), Spain's national dishes."

"Wow, Lucas this is a lot of work. Are we going to be ready by eight o'clock tonight?" she asked.

"Yes. Everything is prepped," he replied. "We have lots of help to put it all together. Chef Bucherl is the most organized chef I've ever seen, and the pastry chef, Heinz Ostler, is fantastic. We will be ready tonight. Please, hand me a beer, and let's get this party started."

The whole day went by without a glitch. Chef Bucherl and Lucas supervised the cooks who worked diligently. They all drank beer and had a good time. With everything running smooth, Lucas and Chef Bucherl stepped outside the kitchen door at the rear of the building.

"You seem to have endless energy, and you go non-stop. Do you ever get tired, Lucas?" asked Chef Bucherl before he lit a cigarette.

"If I feel tired, which is seldom, I smoke some dope," he replied. "When I go back to work, I feel more energized and able to concentrate better. Have you ever tried it, Herbert?"

"No. I haven't, but when we go back to Chiemsee, I'll try it," said Chef Bucherl. "Then, we can go out drinking. I'll take you to fun bars which I sometimes go to without my wife."

"Uh oh, sounds like dangerous fun," said Lucas.

Heinz Ostler, the pastry chef, outdid himself with a fantastic display of classical desserts, including Apple Strudel, Black Forest Torte, Individual Fruit Tarts, German Chocolate Mousse Torte, Tiramisu, Vacherin Cloud, Pear Tarte Tatin, Cream Puff Swans filled with pastry cream, Cannoli, Chocolate Mousse Cake, Carrot Cake and New York Cheesecake with a variety of sauces, toppings and fresh berries. Ostler had good help since he brought Deiter to work the party with him. Deiter is the pastry chef at the officers' club in Oberammergau.

Eric, Gino and John had the bar stocked with 2 kegs of beer, a large assortment of local bottled-beers, and plenty of hard liquor for the 250 expected party goers.

Lucas was at the carving station, ready to greet people before 8 p.m. The guests were forming lines at various food stations around the large dining room.

A local band played Bavarian music. They would play rock 'n' roll for dancing after dinner.

Colonel Moyers was first in line with his family and friends at Lucas' station. The colonel heaped praise on Lucas, Chef Bucherl, Heinz Ostler and everyone involved in creating his birthday party.

I love to work the carving station because I'm good at it, thought Lucas. *This gives me the opportunity to greet each person at the party, or at least the meat eaters. Also, I get to chat a little with each of my special friends as they come through the line.*

Then, Lucas spotted CID Robinson. He was there with some of his MP friends. When he and his friends came to Lucas' station, Robinson said to Lucas, "I guess we won't see Bruno Castignoli at this party. You haven't seen him or heard anything, have you Gary?"

Lucas shook his head and asked, "What meat do you want me to carve for you, Robinson?"

Ignoring the question, Robinson said, "You know, the Bavarian Police notified Interpol to be on the lookout for Castignoli. They want to question him for your girlfriend's murder."

One of the MPs poked Robinson and said, "Hey, he wants to know what meat you want."

"Okay, I'll have venison and roast turkey," said Robinson.

After they were served, Robinson and the MPs left Lucas' station without further conversation.

When Sabine Bloch came through his line, Lucas felt a little sad; he missed Inga. Yet, he was glad Sabine and Eric were still together.

A short while later, as Lucas finished carving meat for a guest, he saw 2 young ladies approaching. Sonya had come to the party, and Gabrielle was with her. Gabrielle's presence surprised him.

Lucas thought: *Gabrielle travels sometimes with the RAF leaders. She and I met in Formentera, and now she is here from Hanover. I can still see us all on the mountain in Seefeld; Sonya, Gabrielle, Sabine and Eric waited with me, and we took care of Bruno in a snow storm.*

"Hi, Lucas. It's nice to see you," said Gabrielle. "My cousin Sonya brought me to this wonderful party and great food. Maybe we can talk when you are finished."

Still thinking about Gabrielle, Lucas said, "I'll come find you when things slow down." He watched the ladies walk away with slices of turkey and venison piled on their plates. They headed toward other food stations to get various items before finding their table.

George came through the line with a busty and sexy young lady, named Judann. Lucas had seen her at The Grill and hotels in Garmisch. He kind of remembered her from the Cervenia trip. Whether Judann heard him or not, Lucas had to ask George the question.

"What became of those Canadian ladies, George?" he asked.

George looked like he did not want to answer, right then. However, he said, "They got waitress jobs at the Berchtesgadener Hof. Your personal introduction to the manager there didn't hurt them."

Lucas said, "Well, they are great gals. I'm certain we will be seeing them around."

Big Bob Ostergaard, the civilian with a degree in Marine Biology, had quit working nights as a glass washer at The Grill. Now, he spent all his time running his used VW van business. Bob loved to eat. So, when he got there, Lucas carved good-sized portions of each meat and put them on a plate, separate from the overflowing plate of food which was already in Bob's hand.

"It's nice to see you, Bob. Has CID Robinson been harassing you and Steve about your van business?" asked Lucas.

"You know, he really annoys me," Bob replied. "I laughed my ass off when I heard you broke his arm, a few months ago. He hassled me so much about registration violations, I had to go to city hall and get a dealer's license from the Germans. Now, I don't have to use green military plates when I sell the refurbished vans. However, we still use them because my partner Steve is in the Army. I hope CID Robinson gets transferred or something."

"Yeah, I do too, Bob," replied Lucas.

There was a break in the carving line, and most of the guests were seated. Everyone enjoyed the food, music and beer.

Dennis and Lewis came to the microphone. Dennis acted like his queer self, and Lewis did his fag-waiter routine with a German accent. Guests who watched them were amused and laughing at the act.

Lucas' attention shifted to a guy heading his way, followed by 2 young Grill Queens (single young ladies who go The Grill, a lot). He thought the man looked familiar, and Lucas noticed his "movie star" appearance. His thick black hair seemed too long for the military. He had a nice black mustache, a la Clark Gable, and a great tan. He also appeared to have a perfect athletic build.

The man looked at Lucas and said, "Hi, I'm Mike Harker. You look familiar. Where do I know you from?"

"I'm Lucas Gary, and I think I have seen you at the gym in Garmisch, playing basketball."

"No, it was somewhere else, before Garmisch," he said.

"For the past ten years, I lived in Long Beach, California, but I grew up in Fresno," said Lucas.

"Hey, I'm from Torrance, and I used to go waterskiing at the Long Beach Marine Stadium," he replied.

"That's it!" said Lucas. "My friend George and I had a ski boat there. I remember you, but you didn't have a mustache then. You rode a bike and towed your ski on a small trailer. We pulled you, and you skied behind our boat. George is also here tonight."

"Yeah, I remember now," said Harker. "You let me ski for free. Most of the people made me pay a dollar for every ride."

"We passed you a few times, along the road," said Lucas. "It is a long bike ride, going from Torrance to Long Beach Marina."

"It was twenty miles, but well worth it." He suggested, "Hey, Lucas, let's get together with your friend, later tonight."

Lucas put a big slice of medium-rare prime rib onto Harker's full plate and said, "Sounds good. When I'm done with carving, I'll get George and come find you. We can all talk about old times in Southern California and learn what brings each of us to Bavaria."

"Thank you, Lucas. I'll talk to you later," he replied.

Next, the 2 Australian ladies came with plates in hand to Lucas' station. Lucas and George had met them on the ferry to Tangiers

"Do you know him?" asked Olivia, as she watched Mike Harker walk away. "He may be the cutest guy in Garmisch."

"Even cuter than Topo?" asked Lucas. Olivia shrugged.

"I think it's a draw since they are both hunks," replied Ashleigh.

Lucas carved them each some turkey and a small slice of prime rib. Then, he said, "I'll see you later."

Watching the ladies walk back to their table, Lucas thought: *Olivia and Ashleigh are so much fun. If I ever see David Burns again, I must thank him for introducing me and George to them. Spending time with those ladies added another chapter to our travel experiences.*

Scott Williams came back for seconds, asking for prime rib, turkey and venison. His plate was packed when he came through the line earlier. Lucas could not believe this skinny hippie from Berkeley ate so much. Then, he remembered: while they were in Formentera, Scott smoked more hashish than he did.

As Lucas carved the roasts, Scott said, "Hey Lucas, I found a job, managing the food program at the American School; and Faye works as a maid at the Sheridan. If you find time next week, maybe you could come by and give me tips on organizing the school kitchen."

"I think I'll be out of town next week, but if I'm around, I'll sure drop by," he replied.

Another cook took over at the carving station to serve latecomers or people who wanted more meat. Going to the kitchen, Lucas met Topo and asked him, "Do you have time to smoke a little hashish?"

"I always have time to smoke dope with you, Lucas," said Topo. "I will meet you in the kitchen after I check on my tables and ask Dennis to watch them."

In the kitchen, Lucas congratulated all the cooks on a job well done. Then, he told them to take a break and eat something.

When Topo came into the kitchen with Olivia and Ashleigh, Lucas smiled and gave them each a Spaten beer. They followed him out the back door and stood on a snow-covered porch. Lucas lit his pipe and handed it to Ashleigh who passed it on, and they all took hits.

"Lucas, you and the chefs outdid yourselves on dinner," said Olivia. "I've never seen such a beautiful display of different ethnic foods, and everything tasted great. But you didn't have Australian food!"

Lucas laughed. "I never tried Australian food. Also, I have not seen any Australian restaurants in my travels—not in Europe or in the U.S. Maybe you and your Aussie friends can cook some of your most famous dishes for me," he said. They all laughed.

"We have Vegemite and Lamington!" said Ashleigh.

"What exactly are Vegemite and Lamington?" asked Lucas.

"Vegemite is a spread, made with brewer's yeast extract, vegetables and spices," said Ashleigh. "Lamington is the National Cake of Australia, a square cut of delicious sponge cake, iced with chocolate and dehydrated coconut. It's named after Lord Lamington who was the Governor of Queensland around the turn of the century. There are several stories about the original recipe. My favorite is: Lord Lamington's French chef had short notice to prepare a meal for guests. He sliced a day-old génoise (French sponge cake), dipped the wedges in melted chocolate and coated them with dehydrated coconut."

Olivia said, "I'm sure you've heard the expression, 'Throw another shrimp on the barbie.' Australia's king prawns are some of the best in the world. Our hamburgers are also great, but our burgers come with a thick slice of beetroot. We have a delicious fish, known as Barramundi, an Asian sea bass which has a mild flavor and a white, flaky flesh. The word *barramundi* comes from the Aboriginal language and means a large-scale river fish. It is popular in countries around the Western Pacific Region. We also have meat pies and assorted wild game, such as kangaroo, emu and crocodile."

"Don't forget Chiko Rolls and Barbecued Snags," said Ashleigh.

"What are those things?" asked Lucas.

Topo said, "I know one of those—Snags are sausages. Every country seems to have their own type of sausage. In my country, Argentina, the popular sausage is chorizo, and most of the South American countries have the same. What is America's favorite sausage, Lucas?"

"I guess it would have to be our country sausage," he replied. "It is a breakfast sausage seasoned with sage, although Americans eat all kinds of sausages. Bratwurst and knockwurst are popular. We also eat Polish sausage, kielbasa, chorizo and a lot of frankfurters."

"So, what is a Chiko Roll?" Lucas asked Ashleigh.

"Our Chiko Roll is an offspring of the Chinese Spring Roll," she replied. "We fill ours with a mixture of cabbage, barley, carrot, green beans, beef tallow, wheat cereal and onion. We roll the mixture into a tube shape and wrap it in a thick pastry of egg and flour. Then, we deep-fry it in vegetable oil, and we eat it without utensils. Chiko Rolls are extremely popular all over Australia and New Zealand."

"In England, they serve Bangers and Mashed Potatoes," said Olivia. "Their sausages are called Bangers because they explode on the grill and make a loud 'bang' sound." The group chuckled at her story.

They finished their conversation and went back inside. Lucas walked over to the bar where Eric was talking to Sonya and Gabrielle.

Eric said something to Gabrielle, and she turned around which put her and Lucas face to face.

In fear of being overheard, Lucas did not speak this, but he thought: *I hope the RAF isn't planning anything. The military doubled their security for this event, due to the recent attacks which took place at military bases in Northern Germany.*

After warm hugs, he and the ladies stepped away from the bar.

"What brings you to Garmisch, Gabrielle?" asked Lucas

"I came to visit Sonya who invited me to this party," she replied. "Lucas, you are so talented. I've never seen such a wonderful buffet. Everyone is friendly, and we're having a great time. After you finish here, we hope you will come by the house for a drink."

Lucas had a quizzical expression which Sonya noticed, and she said, "Oh, yes. Please stop by. We heard you are going to work at Chiemsee, and we want to give you a proper sendoff."

"If it's not too late, I'll stop by after I finish here," he replied.

"Please come, Lucas. We'll be up late tonight," said Gabrielle.

Eric was at the bar, waiving to Lucas. After he excused himself from the ladies, Lucas walked back to the bar, and Eric handed him a glass of Augustiner beer.

"You guys sure put out a fine spread tonight," Eric said to Lucas. "Everyone is talking about the fabulous food."

"Thank you, Eric," he replied. "Everybody did a fantastic job this week, and it was a lot of fun. I appreciate you being here to help with the colonel's party."

Next, he spotted George who was across the room, standing with Mike Harker and an American photographer, Walt Nielson. Lucas headed over to join their conversation.

Lucas recognized Nielson. He owns a custom-built VW van which Bob Ostergaard made for him. Besides the cabinets, a bed and a folding table, like Bob installs in most vans, the special design included some rather unusual requests. Nielson asked Bob to cut off the top of the van and weld a metal fishing boat on top, upside down. It gave him standing room inside the van. Then, the front console was removed, and a regular toilet was installed between the bucket seats. A 3-inch rubber hose, attached and rigged through the van's floor, allows Nielson to dispose of human waste in any discrete spot; he simply places the end of the hose on the ground and lets it drain away from the van.

Lucas noticed Harker held onto a bottle of water while everyone else was drinking beer.

He asked, "Mike, I remember when you competed in the Catalina Ski Race. Did you ever do it again?"

"Yeah," replied Harker. "The first time I competed, I was ten years old, and it was a big deal for me to finish nineteenth. When I was fifteen and doing well in school, my father gave me money and a bus ticket to Clear Lake in Northern California. I had a great summer there, waterskiing. I stayed with a friend of the family and worked my tail off, cleaning boat bottoms. At sixteen, my dad suggested I could be a ski instructor for the sons and daughters of movie stars and producers; but I had to convince the hiring office I was eighteen. I used a phony ID, got the job, started working in Central California and had another great summer, waterskiing at Huntington Lake and Shaver Lake. I skied in Catalina competitions for a few years. After I had finished fifth, third and second place, I finally won the Grand National Catalina Ski Championship in August of nineteen sixty-six."

"Mike, didn't you get into competitive rowing?" asked George.

"Yes, rowing is a great exercise; it helped train me for waterskiing," he replied. "As a freshman at age seventeen, I joined the Orange Coast College rowing team. We surprised the higher-rated UCLA team, rowing in the Newport Beach Regatta. Then, I met Christie, a gal whose family had a house on Lido Island in Newport Beach, and I started sailing. It was a lot of fun. My first experience sailing was on their fourteen-foot Lido Sailboat. I also raced Hobie Sixteen Catamarans."

"I've been to Lido Island and the three man-made islands which form Balboa Island," said Lucas. "Residential properties on those islands are extremely expensive. We went there from Long Beach for the Easter holiday parties. Young people got wild, there were lots of police around, and college students got arrested for drunk and disorderly conduct."

"Mike went to Florida, the next year," said Walt. "He waterskied in shows at Cypress Gardens, and tried parasailing behind a ski boat."

"Well, I thought parasailing was fun," said Harker. "When I learned about the Rogallo Wing Hang Glider, it looked more exciting, so I studied it. When I returned to Southern California, I built my first hang glider out of bamboo tubes, plastic sheeting and duct tape."

"Did you ever fly it?" asked George.

"Yes," he replied. "I flew it, a short distance, jumping off the sand dunes at Dockweiler Beach near the end of the LAX runway.

"Then, I got drafted and went for basic training at Fort Ord near Monterey. In nineteen sixty-eight, the Vietnam War was in full swing. Since I did well on exams, they put me into an engineering division and sent me to Germany instead of Asia. My job was Boat Driver for the Five Hundred Twenty-Second Floating Bridge Company in Germany. Our company called my boat California Dreamin' Number Nine.

"Later, I volunteered for the Black-Berets, a group trained to blow up bridges and things behind the lines, but I never had to do it."

"What brought you here, to work in Garmisch?" asked Lucas.

"I did my job well and earned some R & R time which I spent here in Garmisch-Partenkirchen," he replied. "To be more specific, I spent it at Lake Eibsee. I paid one dollar to waterski around the lake, twice, going forty miles an hour, and I skied barefoot. The colonel in charge of the Armed Forces Recreation Center happened to be there with his two daughters, and they invited me to lunch.

"To make a long story short, I never returned to the engineering company. AFRC assigned me to drive ski boats at Lake Eibsee. For the rest of the summer, I wore a new uniform: red swim trunks and a white T-shirt with a lifeguard symbol on it. When the snow fell in October, I applied and passed a test to become a ski instructor for the winter which is what I'm doing now."

"Mike, tell them about our discussion, the possibility of hang gliding off the Zugspitze," said Walt.

"Right now, it's still in the talking stage," he said. "The idea is for me to glide off the mountain, going from Germany into Austria, and Walt will film it. This would be only one segment in a series of similar stunts, or it might be a series of firsts in several extreme sports—all performed by one person, yours truly."

"What sports or activities do you have planned?" asked George.

"Both snow skiing and waterskiing, motorcycling, hang gliding and maybe sailing," replied Harker.

He added, “Since I am here, I also want to travel around Europe when I get out of the military.”

“Well, I’d better get back to work and clean things up,” said Lucas. “It’s been great talking to you guys. I’m heading to Chiemsee for the summer. Why don’t you guys come over and sail on the lake there?” Both Harker and Nielson said they would for sure.

George and Lucas headed for the kitchen. As they were walking, Lucas said, “Mike Harker sure has an ambitious agenda.”

“Yeah. I hope he survives it all,” said George. “Before you got there, they also talked about hang gliding off of Mount Fuji in Japan.”

Lucas wanted to finish cleaning before he decided whether to go visit Sonya and Gabrielle. He figured Andreas, Ulrike and Gudrun would be there. Oher members may also be there. He might go, so he can find out what the RAF is currently planning.

It was 3 a.m. when the group finished cleaning. They had everything put away, and everyone was tired. Before going separate ways, they all congratulated each other.

Still not sure if he wanted to go visit the RAF gang, or not, Lucas realized he was more afraid not to go.

He thought: *If Andreas and his group are planning an attack around Garmisch, or anywhere in Bavaria, I want to know about it. At least, I can try to talk them out of it.*

Back at their hotel, Lucas asked Shelley if she would get a ride to Chiemsee with Chef Bucherl and Herr Ostler, later in the morning. He would drive over and join her in the afternoon.

Lucas had a short time to decide about visiting the RAF. Meanwhile, both he and Shelley needed to rest.

CHAPTER 33

RAF: The Final Visit

Lucas slept until noon at the Bayerischer Hof. He awoke when the maid knocked on the door. Shelley left earlier, riding with Chef Bucherl and Herr Ostler to Chiemsee. Lucas took a quick shower, got dressed, checked out and headed to George's hotel, across from The Grill.

George was getting dressed when Lucas knocked on the door of his room. He opened the door, and Lucas saw Judann's ample, naked butt as she scurried into the bathroom.

"Hi, George. I'm sorry if this is bad timing," said Lucas.

"No, but we want breakfast. Care to join us?" he asked.

Whispering, Lucas said, "Thank you, but no. I came to see if you want to join me and go visit Andreas and Ulrike. They are in town, and Gabrielle asked me to stop by the house where they are staying."

"Is it safe? Or, will we get tangled in something which we don't want to be involved in?" he asked.

"I think about safety when I go to see them, and nothing has happened yet," replied Lucas. "Each time, I tell myself it will be the last visit, but I want to find out if they are planning anything around here."

"Okay, I will go with you," said George. "But, let's go to the PX and eat before we head over there. All right?"

Lucas agreed and went ahead to the PX. He found Eric, Regan and Bob Ostergaard there, and they all looked hung over. As usual, Bob was drinking coffee and reading business sections of the *Stars and Stripes* and the *International Herald*. Eric and Regan were drinking beer.

Lucas ordered a Denver Omelette. Then, he sipped on a beer while he listened to the guys' stories about last night's birthday party.

When George got there, he ordered toast, grabbed a beer and joined the rest of the group.

"Hey, George. You and Judann looked pretty cozy last night," said Bob. "You should know my partner, Steve, has his eye on her. Are you guys a couple or just friends?"

"Bob, please tell Steve I'll keep him posted on my status with Judann," he replied. The whole group laughed.

"Do you know Mike Harker?" Lucas asked Eric, Regan and Bob.

"I do," replied Eric. "He gave me free ski lessons, and we've played basketball at the gym. Sometimes, we hang out together at Eibsee or The Grill. He will get out of the military this summer; and he has a job waiting for him to teach waterskiing at a Club Med near Athens, Greece. At the end of the summer, I plan to head there myself."

Eric had Lucas' attention—going to Greece sounded magical.

Since Lucas was going to Chiemsee for the summer, he dismissed his thoughts about taking a trip to Greece for now.

"When I talked with Mike last night, I realized George and I met him before. We pulled him with our boat while he waterskied at the Long Beach Marine Stadium. Did he tell you about his plan to hang glide off the Zugspitze, going down into Austria?" asked Lucas.

"Yeah, Mike Harker sets high goals for himself," replied Eric.

On their way to the house on Griesener Straße, Lucas asked George, "How did you hook up with Judann?"

"I was in The Grill, and she came on to me," he replied. "She is an aggressive lady and very sexy. Judann said she and Shelley became good friends when Shelley was living in Garmisch."

"Uh oh, I don't know if their friendship is a good thing or a bad thing. I guess we have to wait and see," said Lucas.

"Since you were busy, I did not tell you last night, but I got a job as coach and math teacher at the American School," said George. "Now, I have to find a place to live in Garmisch."

"Great, George. Congratulations!" said Lucas. "I think you will like living in Bavaria, and I hope it all works out for you. Maybe you can come visit me this summer. I'll be living with Shelley while I work at Lake Chiemsee Hotel."

"Lucky you," he replied.

"Yes. We both met aggressive, sexy young ladies," said Lucas.

He pulled off Griesener Straße and followed the driveway to the side of the house where he parked next to another VW camper van. Lucas grabbed a case of Spaten beer while George grabbed a bottle of Jägermeister. Approaching the front door, they saw it open a little, and Gabrielle's smiling face appeared from behind the door. Lucas planted a kiss on her cheek as she opened the door all the way.

They took off their parkas which Gabrielle hung up, and she led them into the living room. Andreas and Gudrun were sitting by the fireplace, and both were reading newspapers.

Andreas looked up and smiled. Then, he stood, shook Lucas' hand and gave him a hug. He recognized George and said, "I remember you; we met in Italy last year."

"Right," said George. "I went back to 'The States' after we met you. My return to Garmisch was very recent."

"Is Ulrike with you?" asked Lucas.

"Yes, she is upstairs," replied Gudrun. "She will be happy to see you. Are you able to stay for dinner?"

"No, not today," said Lucas. "This afternoon, I must be in Chiemsee to start my new job as Hotel Sous Chef for the summer."

Maybe I shouldn't have told them where I am going to work, thought Lucas. *But, if they know I am there, it might influence their decision not to bomb the place.*

"Lucas, if you can't stay for dinner, will you help me prepare a late lunch for everyone?" asked Gabrielle. "Andreas, Ulrike, Gudrun and Manfred are here. I don't believe you have met Astrid yet."

Gabrielle motioned for Lucas to follow her, and they walked toward the kitchen. She said, "Sonya will be in and out because she is running errands for us."

In the kitchen, Lucas said, "Tell me what's been going on and what's new. Is the RAF planning anything in this area, such as an attack on AFRC or NATO while they are here?"

"No, we are here to catch our breath and try to relax," said Gabrielle. "This Urban Guerrilla business is exhausting, trying to keep ahead of the police. Did you know my brother Horst will be on trial next week for bank robbery and for helping Andreas escape prison?"

"I'm sorry to hear about Horst," he replied. "I know nothing about any recent activities of RAF members. What's been happening?"

"They are using this time to acquire financing and recruit some more members," she said, "while they arm themselves for a big push, leading up to the Summer Olympics."

"Oh no!" he said with concern. "Gabrielle, are they planning to do something at the Olympics?"

"I never know what they plan to do," she replied. "After this trip, I plan to stick around home in Hanover, because it is getting stranger and more dangerous to be around this group."

"How is RAF recruiting going?" he asked.

"They have now joined with another group, the Socialists Patients Collective (SPK). Ulrike can fill you in on the other things which have happened since we last saw you," she replied.

Lucas and Gabrielle put out a nice spread of food, using items in the refrigerator which Sonya had stocked with a generous selection.

They prepared several full platters: Smoked salmon with horseradish cream. Liver pate and whole grain crackers. Miniature, Bavarian-style Reuben sandwiches, made with Westphalia ham, sauerkraut and Tilsiter cheese, grilled on pumpernickel bread. German potato salad, made with onions, slices of cooked sausages and radishes, all tossed in white wine vinaigrette with spicy mustard.

Lucas and Gabrielle set all the food, plates and utensils on the dining room table. Everyone could grab a plate, serve themselves and gather in the living room near a cozy fire. Outside, the sun was shining. But it was a cool day.

For dessert, Sonya had purchased apple strudel from a local bakery, and they would serve it with vanilla ice cream.

When everyone had filled their plates and settled in the living room, Lucas noticed they all seemed to be in a pleasant, happy mood.

Andreas was telling the story of how he and Ulrike met Lucas and George. He planned to steal their VW van, but Lucas convinced them it would be safer to travel together as a foursome. It made sense, and he agreed because the police were looking for him and Ulrike.

"Yeah, and we took you to Landeck where you met your friends," said Lucas. "Andreas, do you remember what you said when I asked what you did for a living?"

Andreas replied, "It was Ulrike who said, 'We rob banks.' "

Everyone roared with laughter. Ulrike added, "You guys also gave us a place to hide after we robbed the bank in Venice."

"It would have been a shame if we shot you when we first met," said Andreas. "We would have missed out on all the great meals you have prepared for us."

"I wish I could have seen the buffet you created last night," said Gudrun. "Gabrielle told us all about it, and it sounded wonderful. We miss social activities; it is one of our difficulties. Being wanted by the police, we must remain underground to pursue our cause."

Lucas pulled out his hash pipe, loaded it with some of Topo's finest hashish, lit it and passed it to Astrid. She took a hit and passed it on.

As Gudrun took a hit on the hash pipe and gathered her thoughts, Lucas studied her. Gudrun's black hair and general appearance looked neglected. He thought Gudrun looked very German. She had long, straight hair, long fingers, a long chin and a long nose. Her blue eyes looked sad, and she wore dark eye makeup which made her look gaunt.

When Gabrielle brought shots of Jägermeister and bottles of beer for everyone, they all raised their shot glasses and shouted, "Prost."

"How did your Urban Guerrilla tactics get started?" asked George. "I don't recall hearing how it all came about."

"For me, it began June second, nineteen sixty-seven, when the Shah of Iran came to the West Berlin Opera House," replied Gudrun. "There were thousands of us protesting the Shah's brutal treatment of his people, his alliance with the U.S. and their involvement in Vietnam."

"I wanted to attend the protest," said Ulrike. "However, I was moving into a new home and shopping for furniture in Hamburg."

"I was in jail for stealing a motorcycle," said Andreas.

"The demonstration was peaceful, except for paint-filled balloons and rotten tomatoes which got thrown," said Gudrun. "The protestors wore paper masks of the Shah which were printed and distributed by Rainer Langhans and Holger Meins. They belonged to a group called Kommune One. As the crowd broke up, the police became aggressive, and some East German 'pig' shot a poor kid, Benno Ohnesorg, in the back of the head. Benno was only twenty-six, my age at the time, and he was married with a child on the way. The man who shot him was a Stasi (East German State Security). A short while later, Andreas and I met at another event. We hit it off and have been more-or-less together since."

Gudrun looked at Andreas, and he managed a scarce smile.

Lucas noticed all the RAF members looked weary, and he realized being on the run must be exhausting them.

Andreas seemed to be elsewhere in thought, and his expression was more of a smirk, than a smile. His black hair was one length, except a little longer in back, and combed forward over the top half of his forehead. He had long sideburns, growing below his ears, and it looked like he was growing a new mustache.

Gudrun was the brightest and the true leader of the RAF.

Being a talented journalist, Ulrike was the group's spokesperson. Ulrike had shoulder-length, straight black hair and bangs covering her forehead. She wore no makeup and looked very thin, like she might be ill. She seemed to be nervous as she was rubbing her fingers together. Lucas noticed she was making little paper balls with her napkin.

"Ulrike, when did you meet Andreas and Gudrun?" asked Lucas.

"I heard Gudrun speaking to a crowd of protestors and admired what she said," replied Ulrike. "Then, I found out about the department store bombing in Frankfurt, for which she and others got arrested. It was in April of nineteen sixty-eight. The Urban Guerrilla Movement began in Germany, during the same year. Elsewhere in the world, these same things were happening. For instance, in Poland it was anti-Semitism. In France it was about the economy; five thousand students battled with the police who threw gas grenades and attacked the barricade which the protesters had set up."

Looking at Lucas and George, Gudrun said, "I believe people in your country have been rioting over racism. It was most evident when Martin Luther King got killed. In Ireland, it's been about segregation. In Germany, it's about civil rights, political rights and the Vietnam War. Mexico City had a massacre of protestors, before the summer Olympics took place there."

"And, during the medal ceremony at the Olympics in Mexico City," said George, "the American sprinters, John Carlos and Tommy Smith, raised their gloved-fists in the air to signify a Black Panther salute. It was a protest of something about black power or human rights."

"Black Panthers began as a revolutionary group of black males who challenged police brutality," said Gudrun, "and armed themselves in Oakland, California. It led to many shootouts with police in Oakland and Los Angeles. Between nineteen sixty-eight and nineteen sixty-nine, the size of their group grew in numbers from a national revolutionary movement to an international movement, including women in key positions. Their members carried and studied Mao Tse-tung's *Little Red Book*. Our RAF members are very familiar with the book, and our group emerged in much the same way; women hold leadership roles. Both groups, the Black Panthers and the RAF, are staunch opponents of American imperialism and the Vietnam War."

"Gudrun, you seem to know a lot about events in 'The States.' Have you traveled in the U.S.?" asked George.

"I attended high school for one year in Pennsylvania," she replied. "It was nineteen fifty-nine, and I was eighteen. Even then, I was interested in politics. When the Black Panthers first began, women were expected to stay back and let the men handle operations. This was never the case for the RAF. Now, half of the Black Panthers' members are black females, and many have leadership roles."

"So, how did the RAF come about?" asked George.

"I know the Sozialistische Deutsche Studentenbund (SDS) had great influence on me," said Ulrike. "Those students opposed the Vietnam War and Germany's political involvement in it as well as the use of nuclear weapons. They also had strong objections to the former Nazis holding influential positions in German government."

"In nineteen sixty-seven, the Kommune One began in West Berlin, led by Dieter Kunzelmann and Rudi Dutschke," said Gudrun. "It was the first political commune in Germany, created to replace the so-called *nuclear family* (traditional family structure) which consisted of a husband, a wife and children. Fritz Teufel and Rainer Langhans became the group's poster boys. They set a trend of long hair, beaded necklaces, army jackets and Mao suits. The same year, Kunzelmann, Langhans, Teufel and several others were arrested for planning an attack against U.S. Vice President Humphrey when he came to visit Berlin. Officials released them when they learned it was a satirical demonstration, throwing flour, pudding or yogurt. The three men were evicted from their house and eventually went to live in the Berlin-Moabit district where they continued satirical attacks. They climbed to the top of Kaiser-Wilhelm-Gedächtniskirche and threw hundreds of *Little Red Book (s)* to the ground below.

"Fritz Teufel spent six months in nearby Moabit prison, charged with treason for planning attacks against the government. There were many student demonstrations for his release. I remember one of the slogans, *Fahren Sie den Teufel aus Moabit!* In English, it means: Drive the Devil out of Moabit! (in German, Teufel means Devil)."

Since George heard Gudrun refer to the *Little Red Book* again, he asked about its importance. She replied, "Black Panthers carried the *Little Red Book* during their revolutionary movement in the U.S. The real title of the book is *Quotations from Chairman Mao Tse-tung.* In nineteen sixty-seven, the book got translated and approved for distribution throughout the world. It went to one hundred and seventeen countries. We all carry a copy of our own."

"I was writing for the *Kronket,*" said Ulrike. "Kommune One was compared to San Francisco's Haight Ashbury District. It was a time when everything seemed linked together with everything else: politics, Vietnam, rock 'n' roll, hashish and sex. I remember stories about Uschi Obermayer, the model who lived at the Amon Düül Kommune, a music commune in a suburb of Munich. She met Rainer Langhans at a music concert, and he fell in love with her at first sight. She moved to Berlin and shared a bedroom with Langhans in Kommune One. It had a revolving door of artists and musicians. The commune also catered to new-left and libertarian political activists. Their life at Kommune One was all about drugs, sex and political discussions, lasting hour after hour. They slept on mattresses on the floor, and all available money was shared. The bathrooms had no doors, and phone calls were played over loudspeakers for everyone to hear. Any mail coming to the house was also shared with everyone."

Andreas said, "Langhans and Obermayer's pictures were in all the newspapers. Many celebrities visited Kommune One, including Jimi Hendrix. Uschi was the number one rock groupie in Germany. There was a photo of Uschi and Jimi Hendrix, hugging and kissing, as they walked out of the Kempinski Hotel where Hendrix stayed in West Berlin."

"When Kommune One folded in nineteen sixty-nine, Langhans and Obermayer started the Highfisch-Kommune in Munich," said Ulrike.

"What does the name Highfisch stand for?" asked George.

Ulrike kept talking, "I understand the new commune was luxurious, compared to Berlin. They rented a very large house in Schwabing which is one of the nicest districts in Munich. The house had seventeen rooms and offered them many, comfortable amenities."

Gabrielle answered George's question, "The word *highfisch* means shark. However, I also heard it means stoned fish."

"That sounds more like it," said Lucas. He chuckled.

"It was a higher class than the Berlin commune," said Gabrielle. "But, the agenda in Munich was still sex, drugs, constant parties and lots of rock 'n' roll. I heard Uschi Obermayer met Peter Green of Fleetwood Mac at the Munich airport. She invited him to the Highfisch-Kommune where people served him drinks laced with LSD. Green had such a bad and intense trip, he never really recovered from it. Now, he is a schizophrenic, living a mental institution."

"I read an article about Peter Green," said George. "He was a talented songwriter and blues rock guitarist who started out in London and played with several groups until nineteen sixty-six. He filled in for Eric Clapton, and played with John Mahal's rock band, the Bluesbreakers. Later, when Clapton left the group for good, Green got the job full time. After performing with the band for about a year, Green left the Bluesbreakers and started a group with Mick Fleetwood on drums and Jeremy Spencer on guitar. In nineteen sixty-seven, John McVie, the bass player for the Bluesbreakers, joined the Fleetwood Mac group. Peter Green wrote many hit songs, including 'Black Magic Woman' and 'Albatross.' I had read about him experimenting with LSD, but I did not know the drug messed him up so bad."

"Uschi and Rainer thought they could soften him up, but lacing his drink with LSD was not the way to do it," said Gudrun. "They wanted Peter Green to arrange for The Rolling Stones and Jimi Hendrix to perform at a Woodstock-type festival in Bavaria. Green got so paranoid at the Highfisch-Kommune, he wouldn't leave for three days. He only agreed to leave the commune when some of the Fleetwood Mac group went to get him, including Mick Fleetwood."

"How many members are in your RAF now?" asked Lucas.

"We have thirty core members," Ulrike answered. "But, depending on our needs, we can draw from some other leftist groups.

"One group is the June Two Movement, named for the date Benno Ohnesorg got shot and killed at the Berlin Opera House. As Gudrun said earlier, the Berlin demonstration was about the Shah of Iran's treatment of Iran's citizens. It turned deadly when police attacked the demonstrators. The guy who shot Benno was a fucking idiot, an East German Stassi who didn't know what he was doing. When it happened, young people learned they need to fight back when they get attacked by fascist 'pigs.' Now, they want to retaliate."

Andreas wandered into the kitchen to make a phone call. He came back from the kitchen, very excited, and said, "Margit Gaier-Czenki, Rolf Heissler, Karl-Heinz Kühn and Roland Otto pulled off a bank robbery in Frankfurt. They took out fifty thousand deutsche marks. Karl-Heinz and Roland were caught, but Rolf and Margit got away with the money. The press dubbed Margit as The Bank Lady."

Ulrike explained, "Margit lived at the Highfisch-Kommune and played drums at the Amon Düül Kommune in Munich. Now, the press makes a big deal about her because she is a lady bank robber."

"So far, fifty thousand deutschemarks, plus the other three banks makes about five hundred and eighty thousand dollars for this year, and it's only April," said Gudrun.

"Since the big push is coming, we'll be more active," said Andreas. "We'll bring the fascist assholes to their knees." He grabbed his crotch and said, "While they're on their knees, they can suck this."

Lucas forced a laugh while everyone else roared with laughter.

Wow! Andreas gets worked up, thought Lucas. *I imagine listening to one of Hitler's rants would sound like this.*

"We all must be on our toes," said Gudrun. "The fucking 'pigs' have now created a special section of the Bundeskriminalamt (BKA)."

Looking at Lucas and George, Gudrun explained, "It is the new Federal Criminal Police Office. They will oversee anti-terrorism efforts for the government. I would say it's like your FBI. Horst Herold, a former criminal prosecutor, will head the BKA, and they will target us. Until now, all the individual states have handled their own criminal investigations, and they haven't shared information with other states. The BKA hopes to acquire full authority on a national scale. For us, they will only be another Nazi enemy to avoid."

"Well, now the 'pigs' have two more of our members," said Andreas. "A few months ago, we almost lost Astrid and Manfred."

Andreas looked at Lucas and George. Then, he turned to Astrid and said, "Tell them about your close call."

"I'll never forget, it scared the shit out of me," she said. "We were walking on the street, and two undercover 'pigs' tried to arrest us. When we took off running, they shot at us, but did not hit either one of us. Some stranger was getting into his car, and he motioned to us. We got in and he took off. We get help from all kinds of people, and many Germans are sympathetic to our cause. The *Springer Press* stated it was a shoot-out. However, Manfred never fired his gun, and I was unarmed, so I think the 'pigs' were trying to kill us."

"Astrid, what got you involved with the RAF?" asked George.

"I wasn't aware of the demonstrations and student protests until I learned my brother Thorwald got arrested along with Andreas and Gudrun for those department store fires in Frankfurt," she replied. "I had to find out what was going on, so I drove from Kassel to Frankfurt in my VW 'Bug.' I went often to visit my brother at the prison which is where I became acquainted with Andreas and Gudrun.

"When they got released from prison, their cases were pending an appeal and review. I got interested in photography. Andreas and Gudrun worked at a youth home, but Andreas spent much of his time teaching the young kids how to steal motorcycles. After being free for five months, the Federal Court ordered them all back to prison. Horst turned himself in, but Andreas, Gudrun and my brother Thorwald went to Paris and stayed at Regis Debray's house. Regis was serving time in a Bolivian prison for helping Che Guevara in his attempt to overthrow the government. Che got killed during the attempt."

"How old were you then, Astrid?" asked Lucas.

"I was only twenty when I met these RAF members," she replied. "I joined the RAF group in Paris. Then, we went to Strasbourg. My brother Thorwald left the group and went to England. Later, Thorwald returned to Berlin and turned himself in. He is still in prison there."

Astrid added, "My passion is cars. I like driving them, working on them and even stealing them." Some people chuckled.

"Did you also go to Jordan?" Lucas asked Astrid.

"Yah, after we got Andreas out of prison," she replied.

"How did Andreas get caught, anyway?" asked George.

"Andreas and I went to purchase guns, and we got stopped by the police," said Astrid. "The police discovered Andreas' ID card was a forgery, and they arrested him, but they let me go. When we helped him escape, I was driving the getaway car. Soon after, we all went to Jordan for guerrilla training."

"Please, tell me how your escape went down. I never heard the story of how you pulled it off," said George.

Ulrike replied, "Gudrun had a plan: I had to convince prison officials Andreas and I were writing a book together, and we needed to use the library outside the prison to do our research. Klaus Wagenbach Publishing verified the book plans, and prison officials agreed."

"The plan was for Ulrike to wait in the reading room," said Gudrun, "which would be closed to other people."

After she took a sip of beer, Gudrun continued, "The car from the prison pulled in front of the Dahlem Institute for Social Research. Andreas was handcuffed when two prison guards took him in through the front door. Inside, his handcuffs were removed, and a male librarian took him to the reading room where Ulrike was waiting. Then, Irene Goergens and Ingrid Schubert, young ladies, dressed in colorful clothes, knocked on the front door of the library. It was locked. The librarian let the gals in and told them to wait in the front hallway. When I rang the doorbell, Irene and Ingrid tripped the electric lock and let me in with a friend of Andreas' right behind me. We wore masks and carried loaded guns. I had two more guns in my bag, and I gave those to Irene and Ingrid. The old librarian came into the hall, saw the guns and started to run away. Andreas' idiot friend shot the librarian in the back. All four of us rushed into the reading room and fired warning shots toward the prison guards. Then, we all jumped out of the window and escaped. Everything went as planned, except for the librarian getting shot."

"Who was the masked guy with you, Gudrun?" asked Lucas.

"Yeah, Andreas, who was that masked man?" asked Gudrun.

Andreas smiled, turned to Lucas and said, "I told our members not to ask me about him because I promised never to reveal who he was."

"I'm truly sorry I asked," said Lucas.

Everyone laughed and dropped the subject, except for Ulrike.

"Yeah, Gudrun's plan worked fine," said Ulrike. "But, the 'pigs' pulled my movie because I was now a fugitive. It was scheduled to be shown on TV, four days after the prison break."

"What is the movie about, Ulrike?" asked George.

"It's about young gals living in a Borstal School," she replied, "where they try to revolt against horrible living conditions. The revolt fails, resulting in even worse conditions."

When she saw George's questioning face, Ulrike added, "In case you don't know, a Borstal School is reformatory. It's a detention center."

"Thank you for clearing it up," said Lucas.

"What is the name of your movie, Ulrike? And, why did you make the movie?" asked George.

"The name of the movie is *Bambule.* The word means 'riot' in German prison slang," she replied. "I wanted to encourage reform by getting the public's attention on the terrible conditions in the Borstal system."

While everyone was sitting near the fire, Gabrielle started gathering dirty dishes. Lucas wanted to talk to her alone. He grabbed a few dishes and followed her to the kitchen. They made several trips, back and forth. When all the dishes and leftover food were in the kitchen, they put things away, then both stood at the sink to wash and dry the dishes.

"Gabrielle, is Ulrike all right?" asked Lucas. "She seems distracted and out of sorts."

"I think she misses the political discussions which used to happen on a constant basis within the group," she replied.

"Are you saying they don't have political discussions with Ulrike anymore?" he asked.

"They avoid Ulrike because she over-analyzes every situation, and she is obsessive about it," she replied. "However, Ulrike is the person who finds apartments or other housing for the members. So, she has discussions with sympathizers who provide those places to stay."

After she paused for a moment, Gabrielle said, "I've been thinking, while you were all talking, Lucas. What I've noticed about spending time around this group is I really enjoy visiting with you and Sonya. I need to get away from this place. They even came to my apartment in Hanover and stayed overnight. This underground living is boring, and it scares the crap out of me to be around all these guns and bombs, never knowing when the next shoot-out will happen. Lucas, could I come with you to Chiemsee and maybe get a job there?"

Lucas looked into Gabrielle's eyes, and he could see she was scared. He said, "Gabrielle, I will be happy to take you to Chiemsee. You know I have a new girlfriend there, and I plan to live with her. Shelley is the head housekeeper. Until you get settled in your own room, I'm sure we can find you a room to share."

"I met Shelley at the party last night. She is beautiful and a very nice person," she replied.

"Okay. Get your stuff together and tell them you're leaving," he said. "We'll drop George off at wherever he is staying. Then, we'll head to our new home, the Rasthaus am Chiemsee."

When Lucas went back into the living room, he was carrying beers for everyone. He lit his hash pipe, took a hit and passed it to Andreas who looked as if he needed nothing more. Andreas took a big hit and passed it on to Gudrun.

Astrid was talking when he came in, and Lucas only heard the end of her comments, "… I could not live the way those guys do."

"What guys Astrid?" asked Lucas.

"The Hash Rebels," she replied.

Before Lucas could ask, Gudrun said, "It is a group, headed by Bommi Baumann who was a member of Kommune One. Last June, he and Fritz Teufel formed a new group and named it Movement Two. We tried to combine the groups, but they wanted to stay independent."

"I'm glad they didn't join our group," said Astrid. "I lived in a house with few women at Kommune One. We were exploited and required to be fair game for the men of the group who passed the women around at their will. I won't live in such a degrading situation again, and I'm sure I speak for other women in our faction when I say we have equal rights."

"What sort of name is Bommi?" asked Lucas.

Ulrike answered, "He would tell you it means plum-flavored spirit. People who know him would say his nickname reflects his skill for making bombs. The Hash Rebels have a motto: *Terror without measure is measurelessly fun.*"

George looked surprised, and Ulrike explained the motto, "The Hash Rebels pledge there is nothing they won't do to prove their point. They believe they must resort to violence because social change will not be achieved by peaceful means.

"The RAF agrees with the need to return violence against violence. But you will never see us fire the first shot, or shoot to kill. We only act in self-defense, and we certainly don't take pleasure in it, as they do."

"Our organizations have coordinated some of our actions against the fucking 'pigs.' We cooperate with each other," said Andreas.

Gudrun shared a phrase she often tells RAF followers, "Violence is the only way to answer violence. This is the Auschwitz generation, and there's no arguing with them!"

Gabrielle entered the living room, carrying her backpack and a small suitcase. She told the group she was going to Lake Chiemsee with Lucas. Her plan was to relax, spend some time there and see Ludwig's castle on the island.

Everyone hugged and said goodbye. The RAF members gave their good wishes to Lucas, George and Gabrielle.

"Oh, I almost forgot," said Lucas.

He pulled 2 cartons of Marlboro cigarettes and a bottle of Jack Daniels out of his backpack. Their faces lit up at the sight of his gifts.

On the way out, Lucas could not help but notice the 2 assault rifles, sticking out of a large, heavy umbrella holder at the main entrance. He had seen one of those rifles pictured on the cover of the RAF manifesto under the title, *The Concept of the Urban Guerrilla*. Lucas was glad to be leaving these Celebrity Terrorists.

As Lucas drove away from the house on Griesener Straße, George and Gabrielle sat in the back, listening to soft music. The van was quiet, except for the music, leaving each with their own thoughts.

Lucas thought: *I hope this is my last visit with the RAF. It is time to focus on positive things and have fun. I think Chiemsee will be the perfect place for me to do it.*

When they arrived at The Grill, George asked, "Why don't you come in for a beer and say hello to John, Gino and whoever is here?"

Lucas looked at Gabrielle who nodded, and they all went inside. Now late afternoon, only a handful of people were in the bar. Unfortunately, one of them was Robinson, CID asshole.

Lucas sat on the 2nd stool, Gabrielle sat on his right and George on her right. Gino was tending bar. John Ferrell was on the other side of the horseshoe-shaped bar, eating a hamburger, reading a newspaper and drinking coffee. Everyone else appeared to be drinking beer. Lucas remembered John did not drink while he worked, but he made up for lost time when he was off.

CID Robinson was talking to Jordan, the bouncer, until he saw Lucas come in. Then, he stopped talking and walked over to the bar. Robinson stood next to Lucas and said, "You sure get around, Gary. You know the German Police still want to talk to you about Bruno Castignoli and the Inga Mueller murder."

Lucas stared at Robinson and refrained from speaking. A moment later, Robinson walked away, going toward the restaurant.

"Who was he?" asked Gabrielle. "The guy didn't even say hello."

"He is the head of the Criminal Investigation Division for military police. Due to an unfortunate encounter in Berchtesgaden, he seems to think of me as his mortal enemy. It's a long story, replied Lucas."

As a band was getting set on the stage, Eric and Sabine walked in. After giving them all a hug, Sabine said, "Lucas, I hear you're leaving us and going to work in Chiemsee for the summer."

"Yes," he replied. "I look forward to working with Chef Bucherl, playing tennis and volleyball, sailing, bike riding and lots of bar sports, depending on my free time. In German kitchens, the chefs work six days a week, split shifts: nine to two and five to closing. In California, I worked those hours in the restaurant business. I know I will have long days, but they go by so fast when I am doing the things I love to do—cooking and drinking beer."

Lucas was being serious, but everyone laughed.

"We will all miss your smiling face around here," said Eric.

"Well, you will have to come to Chiemsee," said Lucas. "Gabrielle is going with me. She also wants to get a job there for the summer. In fact, we better get going while I'm still able to drive."

When Lucas and Gabrielle got outside and headed for the van, they saw a German police car with 2 officers sitting inside. The police officers saw Lucas, got out of their car and walked over to him.

The tallest officer said, "Gruss Gott," and then he asked, "Are you Lucas Gary?"

"Yes, I am. What can I do for you?" he asked.

The shorter, heavier officer said, "We are investigating the murder of Inga Mueller and still trying to locate a person of interest. Could you give us any information about Bruno Castignoli—for instance, do you know where he might have gone?"

"Like I told the investigators in Oberammergau, I don't know him very well," he replied. "I worked with Bruno for a short time at NATO Officers Club, and I played basketball with him once or twice at the gym. We were not friends and never talked much."

The tall officer said, "I understand you and Herr Castignoli are from the same city in California? Did you know each other there?"

"No. I had never seen him before I came to Europe, and I haven't seen him here for quite a while," he replied.

The short officer said, "Well, if you learn anything about him, please call me at this number." As he handed Lucas a business card, he said, "Auf Wiederschaun." Then, both officers went back to their car.

Lucas and Gabrielle got in the van and went to the Bayerischer Hof on Partnachstrasse. Lucas wanted to buy hashish from Topo, and he had called Topo from The Grill, so Topo was waiting outside the hotel. When Lucas pulled up, Topo climbed into the back of the van and pulled the sliding door shut.

Lucas parked under a fascinating, sycamore-maple tree by the river. He turned off the engine and said, "Topo, this is Gabrielle. She is from Hanover, and we met in Formentera."

"I know Gabrielle," said Topo. "We met and talked at the party last night. Hello, Gabrielle."

Turning to Lucas, Topo said, "We talked mostly about you. I hear you are leaving us and going to Chiemsee."

"We're on our way now," he replied. "You should come with us."

"Don't tempt me," said Topo. "I will consider it since I love to sail, and I understand the hotel has sailboats which employees can use."

"Besides sailing, there is plenty to do at Lake Chiemsee Hotel," said Lucas. "They have clay tennis courts, a big game room downstairs below the bar, and a movie theater with American movies. I also play to build a sand volleyball court."

"So, do you suppose I could get a job as a waiter?" asked Topo.

"I'll let you know when there is an opening," he replied. "And I will arrange your interview with the manager, Bob Clarkson. Meanwhile, grab a beer out of the cabinet there. What type of hashish do you have for us today, my friend?"

"This hashish is very hard to get," said Topo. "It comes from a Sativa plant called Oaxacan Highland Sativa. Smoking this, you will get as good a cerebral high as you'll ever experience."

“Well, let’s get on with it,” said Lucas as he pulled his pipe out.

They were passing the pipe around when Topo said, “In Afghanistan, it is a custom to eat a melon while smoking hashish. They say melon will increase the high and decrease any negative effects.”

Lucas replied, “I’ve not had negative effects from marijuana or hashish, except my first experience. I got paranoid, walked around the block and imagined the police were coming to get me. Then, I went home, crawled in bed, pulled the covers over my head and missed going to a good jazz concert at the Lighthouse in Hermosa Beach.”

Topo and Gabrielle cracked up when they heard Lucas’ story.

“Oh yeah,” said Topo. “You will discover everything you say and hear sounds hilarious when you smoke this.”

All 3 were laughing. Then, Gabrielle said, “I see what you mean!”

Each had two beers and hits of hashish while they continued talking. They all laughed again—and again.

After paying for the hashish and waving goodbye to Topo, Lucas and Gabrielle headed northeast toward Oberammergau.

This new journey seemed to be full of hope and promise, and they each planned to go full speed ahead with as much energy as possible.

Lucas and Gabrielle were brought together by special circumstances, and they were bound together by the secrets they shared.

CHAPTER 34

Summer in Chiemsee

Finally, Lucas and Gabrielle were on the road. If the traffic was light, the drive to Chiemsee would take an hour and a half.

Gabrielle played a cassette tape of a new Rolling Stones album called *Sticky Fingers*. While listening to the music, they sang along with Mick Jagger to "Wild Horses" and "Brown Sugar."

"I think the Rolling Stones have the best rock 'n' roll band I've ever heard," said Lucas.

"I love the Stones. Did you ever hear about Uschi Obermayer's sex romp with Mick Jagger and Keith Richards?" asked Gabrielle.

"No. Was she with both men at the same time?" he asked.

"I don't know," she replied. "I guess anything is possible since 'free love' is practiced worldwide."

Lucas lost all perception of time after smoking Topo's finest hashish. He had driven northeast and gone past Oberammergau. Now, he was looking for Sindelsdorf, Germany. Then, he would turn and head east. From there, Lucas figured they would have about an hour to go.

Still processing his thoughts after visiting with the RAF members, Lucas said, "Manfred does not talk much, does he?"

"His English is not too good," she replied. "Also, he still misses his girlfriend, Petra Schelm, who was shot by German police, last July, after she and Werner Hoppe ran through a roadblock in Hamburg. Hoppe tried to get away, but a police helicopter followed and caught him. Petra ran in a different direction. When she got trapped and tried to shoot it out with the police, she was killed. Manfred is twenty-six. Petra was only twenty when she died. He was a member of Kommune One, and they both had gone to Jordan for guerrilla training."

"When George and I met Ulrike and Andreas in Austria and saw them in Italy, they were traveling together, but they didn't appear to be lovers. Later, when I met Gudrun, she and Andreas were together in a romantic relationship. I guess my question is: Besides her ex-husband, does Ulrike have or has she had a boyfriend?" he asked.

She replied, "Ulrike's father was a museum curator who passed away at age forty. Ulrike's mother received a grant after her husband's death. She returned to school and studied art history. Last month, when you and I talked, I told you the story about Renate Riemeck, a fellow student who had a lesbian relationship with Ulrike's mother for a few years until her mother died; then Renate had relationships with other women while she cared for Ulrike; and Ulrike had a relationship with a girl named Maria. So, her formative teen years were influenced by lesbian relationships, at least at home. By age seventeen, Ulrike was attending an academic school. She was a bright student, well-liked by other students and teachers, but I never heard of any boyfriends during her school years. On the wilder side, she would smoke dope and go out dancing with her friends until early in the morning."

"Do you know what Ulrike studied in college?" he asked.

"She attended the University of Munster to study psychology and education," she replied. "Ulrike became a spokesperson for a socialist committee which protested nuclear armament, and she wrote articles which opposed nuclear weapons. Ulrike met her future husband, Klaus Röhl, at a press conference. She went with him to East Berlin where they met members of the banned Communist Party. Around nineteen sixty, Ulrike went to work for his magazine, *Kronket*. She wrote articles which supported peace over violence, involving political disputes."

"What was her marriage to Klaus Röhl like?" he asked.

"It's a long story," she said. "They married in nineteen sixty-one. At *Konkret,* they worked together, Klaus as Publisher, and Ulrike as Editor-in-Chief. In nineteen sixty-two, Ulrike got pregnant and had severe headaches. The doctors wanted to operate on her brain, but she waited until the pregnancy was over. She had brain surgery when the twins were seven months old and went right back to work. During her seven-year marriage, Ulrike found out Klaus had cheated on her and been with many women. When she divorced him, she got custody of the girls. Ulrike said she became caught between two ways of living. On one side, the establishment respected her work as a writer. On the other side, she had trouble in the relationship with her husband, and she was uncomfortable in the role she had to play. She felt it was not her true self, and she needed to be part of a group or a movement with a real cause."

Lucas thought: *I have a side of myself which is separate from my work, my family and some of my friends. In the early sixties. I was a chef's apprentice in Long Beach. I did a lot of things with my white friends, such as waterskiing, snow skiing, fast-pitch softball, dining out, or attending Dodger and Laker games. When I played basketball, I went to gyms where most of the players were black. We became friends, and they accepted me because of my basketball skills. I was elected captain of a team, on which I was the only white guy. Although I tried to bring all my friends together socially, it never worked out. Things were just different back then.*

Gabrielle said, "Ulrike became somewhat of a celebrity after she wrote an article about Franz Josef Strauss, a Bavarian politician. She, suggested he was a Nazi. He sued her in a well-publicized court case which she won, and she became a champion of human rights, so to speak.

"My brother Horst thinks Ulrike has no self-confidence. She latches onto a stronger person for support, and she blends in with her surroundings like a chameleon. About nineteen sixty-eight, Ulrike started to change. Formerly a passive activist, she became more radical and leaned toward violence. In an article I have read, Ulrike wrote two now-famous lines: First, *'If one throws a stone, it's a crime, but if a thousand stones are thrown, that's political.'* Second, *'If you set fire to a car it's a crime, but if a hundred cars are set on fire, that's political.'* I think she meant an event based on political purpose is a political action and morally justified; therefore, it would not be a crime in usual terms."

"She had quite a turnaround from where she began her writing career and promoted peace," said Lucas.

"Yes," said Gabrielle. "She emphasized her new aggressive attitude and her position with another statement: *'It is a protest, if I say this or that does not suit me. It is resistance if I ensure that what does not suit me no longer occurs.'* Ulrike planned to take over the *Konkret* offices, by force if necessary, but her ex-husband heard of the plan and abandoned the offices beforehand, so nothing became of the takeover. Next, Ulrike moved to Berlin where she met my brother Horst, Andreas and Gudrun. Horst was an attorney who represented many of the leftist youth, including Andreas, Gudrun and himself."

"What does Horst say about Andreas' escape?" he asked.

"Horst, Andreas, Ulrike, Gudrun, Irene Goergens, Ingrid Schubert and Astrid would all tell you the same thing: the moment Andreas escaped from prison custody, the RAF was founded," she replied. "Well, all but Horst and the mysterious masked man. Horst can't say since he's in prison, and the masked man disappeared. The library escape was a dramatic event in the way it happened. Ulrike was supposed to pretend she was an innocent bystander and stay seated at the table where she was working with Andreas. When shots got fired, she went out the window and became a fugitive with the rest of them."

"I heard the twin girls were found at Mount Etna in Sicily, but I never got the whole story. What happened to them?" he asked.

"Ulrike had already planned to smuggle the twins from Europe to a Palestinian orphanage camp, out of their father's reach," she replied. "So, her children disappeared the day of the escape. Before long, their father, Klaus, had Interpol looking for the girls. While Ulrike went to the Palestinian terrorist camp in Jordan, the girls stayed with friends for a few days in Berlin. Two women drove them south and snuck them into France. They made it to Italy, and they followed a deserted road across the border. When they got to Sicily, the women left the twins with someone named Hanna, and the women went back to Germany. The girls played on the beach, studied school books and played games. Then, Hanna went back to Germany, and the girls stayed with four German hippies, living in huts on the beach at the foot of Mount Etna. When Klaus learned where the girls were, he sent Stephan Aust to get them and return them to him. Aust had worked for Klaus as a journalist at *Konkret* magazine. In fact, he worked alongside Ulrike Meinhof for three years, and he also knew my brother Horst."

"Do you know what happened to Aust?" he asked.

"He does political shows on TV, and he is writing for magazines and newspapers," she replied. "There was a rumor about Aust receiving a death threat from the RAF, but nothing ever came of it. I don't know much more about him."

"Gabrielle, it must have been hard for Ulrike to leave her children. Do you think she ever regrets her decision?" he asked.

"She seems hesitant or uncomfortable to talk about them, Lucas," she replied. "I know she misses them, but she realizes she cannot be both a mother and a terrorist. Ulrike chose to fight for justice in the world, and it demands personal sacrifices. Sometimes, she shrinks away from Andreas because he abuses the surrounding women. He enjoys calling them 'muschi' (cunt) and other terrible names. In many ways, she has simply adapted to the life of an Urban Guerrilla."

"I hear Ulrike and other RAF members use the term *Urban Guerrilla*. What does it mean to them?" he asked.

"It's about planning attacks and coordinating their safe movement," she replied. "But they're struggling. Ulrike knows how to steal a car, and she carries a pistol all the time. However, some things have proven difficult for her. Once, she broke the wheel off a car she was stealing. Another time, she left most of the money inside the bank which they had robbed. She has put the wrong addresses on some important documents. When they were training in Jordan, she forgot to throw a grenade after she had pulled the pin. A Muslim instructor saved her life when he grabbed it and threw it a safe distance away. On our last trip, driving to the house in Garmisch, Ulrike and Andreas argued the whole time. Ulrike claimed the group is disorganized and not planning properly before executing their actions. Andreas claimed mistakes made in the past were all due to human error, not poor planning. I don't know if their relationship will last much longer. The group's social enjoyment is gone. No one seems happy, and everyone does their own thing."

"I'm glad you left today, Gabrielle," he said. "It seems the police are getting serious about stopping the RAF now. The government has a new branch of law enforcement, aimed at terrorism."

She replied, "When the police spoke to us at The Grill, I got scared, Lucas. I even thought they might arrest us for associating with terrorists. I guess it was a little paranoid on my part. But then, the officer mentioned Bruno which pushed another button."

"I try not to think about all the negative stuff, unless I have to," he said. "I want to live day to day and enjoy myself. Right now, this is fun for me to spend time with you and talk while we drive."

"It's fun for me too. We've been through a lot together, and I enjoyed each time I've been with you…" She smiled, then added, "… especially our time in Ibiza and Formentera."

"Thank you, Gabrielle," he said. "For me, our time together and our friendship will always be special. Now, let's have another beer and turn up the music. This summer, we are going to party!"

"I want to say one more thing about Andreas which may interest you," she said. "You know he loves to drive cars. I would say, he is obsessive about cars since he has stolen very expensive sports cars for himself and other RAF members. However, Andreas never got a driver's license."

"I guess traffic violations don't matter much if you are one of the most-wanted criminals in the world," he replied. "Come to think of it, Hitler never got a driver's license, either."

Driving through Frasdorf, Germany, they listened to music and admired the scenery of a typical, magical Bavarian town. Lucas figured they would reach Chiemsee in about 10 minutes.

The winding highway through the hills was peaceful until they came around a somewhat blind turn. There were about twelve cars stopped on the highway, all parked at different angles. At first, Lucas thought it was a wreck, but he could not tell for sure.

He pulled to the side of the highway, turned off the engine and said, "Look, Gabrielle! They're playing music in the street—The guys have an accordion, a guitar and a saxophone, and a lady has a tambourine."

"Those other people are dancing, and they're in costumes," she replied. "Come on, Lucas. Let's go dance with them." Lucas followed Gabrielle's lead, as she got out of the van. They both walked toward the music and the dancers. Many other people were doing the same.

"Okay, now maybe we can find out why we're stopped," he said. "At least, it will be entertaining."

The Bavarians love to party and dance, but this was extreme, even for Gabrielle. Everyone was drinking beer and laughing. Lucas and Gabrielle heard some cattle were blocking the highway ahead of them.

Cars were forming a line on one side of the highway. A police car came over from the far side which was clear of traffic. The officer parked his squad car, got out and walked along the road. He told people to get back in their cars and be ready to go when the cattle get moving.

When the officer walked by Lucas' van, he saw the green military license plate, and he waited nearby for the driver to show up.

Lucas and Gabrielle returned to the passenger's side of his van, so he could unlock the door for her.

When the officer came over to the van, he seemed cheerful and said, "Gruss Gott."

Lucas and Gabrielle felt cautious, but they returned the greeting.

The officer asked in English, "You are American military?"

"We're civilians, going to Lake Chiemsee Hotel where we will be working for AFRC this summer," replied Lucas.

"I noticed your military plate. Police are looking for an American, Bruno Castignoli. He worked as a bartender for the AFRC in Garmisch last year," said the officer.

He added, "I am asking because German police want to question him about a murder which occurred in Oberammergau."

"I know who he is, but I don't know where he is, and I haven't seen him for quite a while," said Lucas.

"When was the last time you saw him?" asked the officer.

"It was several months ago at the gymnasium in Garmisch, playing basketball," he replied.

"Well, thank you. I think I'll stop by the gym and ask around," said the officer. "Do you know what time they usually play, or what would be the best time to go there?"

"They play in the evening," he replied, "around seven p.m."

"Thank you. Now, it looks like the road is clearing, except for the *kuhscheisse,*" said the officer who then smiled.

Seeing the blank look on Lucas' face, Gabrielle interpreted what the officer was talking about. She said, "Cow shit." And they all laughed.

When the officer said, "Auf wiedersehen," Lucas and Gabrielle bid him farewell and climbed into the van.

Walking away to direct traffic, the officer tried not to step in the piles of kuhscheisse. When it was their turn to go, Lucas tried to avoid the big piles, and all the other drivers did the same. The traffic moved slow, but they got back on the winding highway.

Gabrielle handed Lucas another beer and opened one for herself. "Lucas, it is so scary when we talk to the police," she said. "I don't feel like a criminal, but I have things which I must hide from them."

"You know, Gabrielle, I don't dwell on the past," he replied. "I do what I need to do in the moment. Then, I let it go without questioning if it is right or wrong, legal or not. When I talk to police, I try to be brief and simple with my answers to their questions."

Arriving at Lake Chiemsee Hotel, Lucas slowed down and turned into the parking lot. It was so full, he had to park at the far end of the lot.

"Thank you for bringing me here, Lucas. I hope I can get a job soon. I also want to put the RAF and Bruno behind me," said Gabrielle.

"You're welcome," he replied. "Get ready for a new adventure!"

As they entered the lobby, going toward the front desk, Shelley walked in from the lounge which overlooked the lake.

She greeted them and said, "Your timing is great!"

"It wasn't easy, but we made it. Have you two met?" asked Lucas.

"Yah, we met at the colonel's birthday party," replied Gabrielle. Then, she spoke to Shelley, "I asked Lucas to bring me here, hoping to work for the summer and perhaps longer. I need a bed for the night, or maybe I can sleep in Lucas' van."

"There are plenty of jobs here," replied Shelley. "We just started hiring for the summer rush. We get very busy, but we have a lot of fun. Also, you won't have to sleep in the van."

After Shelley kissed Lucas on the cheek, she grabbed his hand and Gabrielle's hand, led them out the front door and said, "Let's take your van to the Park Hotel. It's cold out, and it's a long walk over there."

Lucas drove under the autobahn, past the gas station and parked the van at the Park Hotel. Shelley went into her office and grabbed a key from the keyboard on the wall behind her desk. Then, she led them upstairs to the 2nd floor and down the hall to Room 22.

Shelley opened the door to the room, handed Gabrielle the key and said, "I will call the front desk and ask them to get you some dinner. If you tell them you are a new employee and a friend of Lucas and mine, they will also show around and introduce you to people."

Anxious to leave, Shelley grabbed Lucas' hand and said, "Lucas and I are having a quiet evening in. So, have fun Gabrielle, and welcome to the Rasthaus am Chiemsee. We'll see you tomorrow."

Shelley led Lucas to her apartment at the east end of the building. As soon as Lucas closed the door, he turned and looked into Shelley's beautiful blue eyes. Lucas found it hard to contain himself. Then, he noticed she had set the dining table with a candle in the center.

"I see a nice dinner for two is planned," he said.

“Dinner comes later,” she replied. “You should go back to the van and get what you need for the summer. You are all mine now—no more love on the run.”

“It started kind of crazy, but it sure has been fun,” he said.

“I would not have had it any other way,” she replied. Pressing her perfect breasts against him, she gave him a great, lengthy kiss.

Lucas returned to the apartment with his bags and miscellaneous items. He opened 2 Wieninger beers and filled the hash pipe with a new batch of hashish from Topo. He almost dropped the pipe when Shelley came out of the bedroom. She was wearing the shortest miniskirt and the skimpiest, sexiest bra. Her long black hair fell straight to the sides of her shoulders with bangs across her forehead.

“Your towels are the white ones. Don’t camp in there. I’ve got plans for you tonight,” she said.

“You look absolutely wonderful!” Pulling off his sweater as he headed to the shower, he said, “I won’t be long.”

Lucas loved what Shelley had planned. After several hours of lustful lovemaking, it was around midnight when they sat and ate. They had Hungarian Goulash and noodles which came from the main hotel kitchen, plus Sachertorte, a dessert made by the Pastry Chef, Heinz Ostler.

They finally closed their eyes, and both slept until noon. For brunch, Lucas made home fried potatoes, Denver omelettes and crepes. After they took another nap, they showered together, and then played again on her king-size bed, making love and laughing.

“How did you manage to get a king-size bed?” he asked.

“Hey, I’m the Head Housekeeper of this hotel,” she replied. “I get first choice on furniture and whatever household supplies I need for this apartment. By the way, you should know I expect to eat very well, now, since I’m living with a chef.”

“After last night, my dear, I’m putty in your hands,” he said, “Your bed is a lot more fun than my single bed at Hawkins Barracks.”

Shelley flashed a beautiful smile, and then said, “It was embarrassing to get caught in your room there. But, walking to the train station was fun, even in the freezing cold. It has been fascinating, getting to know you, Lucas. Do you always live your life in the fast lane?”

“Timing is everything,” he replied. “In my profession, it’s a basic principle. Auguste Escoffier, a famous French chef, was quoted as saying, ‘The essence of culinary art is time—we ask your kind indulgence.’ ”

“I have heard the name, Escoffier,” said Shelley. “But I know nothing about him.”

Lucas explained, “In Long Beach, I did a four-year apprenticeship at a great restaurant where the Executive Chef preached Escoffier’s basics of cooking and restaurant organization, known as Brigade de Cuisine (kitchen brigade system). It refers to the structured responsibilities of a kitchen staff. Auguste Escoffier created a system in which a kitchen is set up to serve a large group of people in a short period, so all the cooks and chefs are utilized to their maximum efficiency. At the turn of this century, Escoffier was at his peak. He became known as the *King of Chefs and Chef of Kings*, a title which he received from news media. I also studied his book, *Le Guide Culinaire*. It was the first cookbook I ever bought, and I have it in my van.

"Of all the places I've seen in Europe, the Post Hotel in Wallgau, Austria, was best example of brigade-style food service. They served one of the greatest meals I have ever had. I peeked into their kitchen which was the most immaculate and orderly kitchen I've ever seen. The Berchtesgadener Hof has a similar type of kitchen setup, except it is on a smaller scale."

"It's very interesting," she said, "you and I were only thirty miles apart in California, but we had to come six thousand miles to meet in Europe. Now, we are here, living together as lovers in this fairyland. It's the same with George, your best friend, and Judann, my best friend; he came from California, and now they're together in Europe."

"Yes. And it appears George will stay in Garmisch because of his job," he replied. "I'm sure they will come visit us during the summer. George will want to play volleyball here when the new sand court is built."

"I'm so excited about summer," she said. "I can't wait to sail with you to Herrenchiemsee and give you a personal tour of the palace."

"I can't remember ever being on a sailboat," he said. "I've been on ski boats and fishing boats, plus big ocean ferries when George and I went to Ibiza and Morocco, but I've never been sailing."

"I'll teach you how to sail," she said. "Now, Lucas, since you start work tomorrow, why don't we go to a gasthaus tonight and have dinner in Bernau? I know right where to go; although, I've never been there. It's only a ten-minute drive from here."

"Okay," he replied. "I look forward to working tomorrow, but I'm hungry now. Let's go eat."

Lucas drove on Rasthausstrasse, going toward Munich. Following the curve of the road, he went over the autobahn and turned right onto Chiemseestrasse, drove another quarter of a mile and parked behind a large patio area at the gasthaus. The patio furniture had been put away, and the patio was closed. It looked like a fun place to sit under the shade of big chestnut trees when the weather gets nice.

Winter would soon be over, but patches of snow could still be seen on the sloped roof and on the ground. It was just before sunset. The skies were clear, and the evening felt cool.

Shelley held Lucas' hand, as they walked to the front of the 3-story gasthaus. Lucas was most impressed by an exterior wall on the 3rd floor, set back under the eaves of the peaked roof: The entire wall was covered in dark wood and carved in elaborate and decorative designs; multiple doors opened out to a balcony; and bright yellow lights were strung along a wrought-iron railing. The dark wood made an attractive contrast to the creamy-white stucco exterior of the lower floors. The entrance had an arched doorway, a large wooden door, and menus in a glass case. Scripted lettering on a coral-painted ribbon displayed the name over the entrance, GASTHOF ZUM ALTER WIRT. On both sides of the name, murals depicted traditional farm scenes of people riding horses and wagons pulling horses. Above the name, a painting of a mother and child on a pink background was framed and inset on the stucco. Other inset paintings on coral or blue backgrounds decorated the octagon-shaped rooms which protruded from the 2nd floor corners of the building. Lower floors had carved frameworks on the windows, all painted coral; but the framework designs were different on each floor. Behind the gasthaus, a church steeple towered above everything.

Inside, the entrance hall turned right and served as a waiting area. It had 1 table, an antique dresser and benches along the wall. The hostess led them through a series of dining rooms. Furniture, cabinets and paneling were all made of light-colored wood. The tables were dressed in linens: white tablecloths and sky-blue napkins. Seated in a room which had very large windows and a great view, they could see the sun going down behind surrounding hills.

As they sat, facing each other, Lucas thought: *Shelley has the same hair style and shiny black hair as Ulrike. However, Shelley's hair is much neater; she always looks fresh; her enthusiasm is overflowing; and smiling comes easy to her. By comparison, Ulrike has a very hard look, and she rarely smiles. Also, Shelley is much prettier, and she does not carry a Heckler and Koch assault rifle.*

"Lucas, you were telling me about Auguste Escoffier, the famous French Chef. I want to hear more about him," said Shelley.

"Okay, but let's order first. What looks good to you?" he asked.

"I want Schwäbisches Zwiebelfilet mit Späetzle und Gemuse (pork medallions, topped with creamy onion sauce, served with Späetzle and vegetable of the day) and a Wieninger beer," she replied.

"I love the combination of bread dumpling and pork shank," he said. "So, I will have the Knusperige Schweinshaxe mit Semmelknoedel,

Sauerkraut und Rotkohl (Bavarian-style pork shank in a crème sauce called Rahmsauce, served with sauerkraut, bread dumpling and apple-flavored red cabbage). I will also have a Wieninger beer."

This place was lively with the Bavarian music piped-in and upbeat. Above each table, 2 bright lamps hung from the ceiling on gold chains. The light-colored wood, cream-colored interior, and the lighting gave the space a bright atmosphere. The waiter was a tall, cheerful man with a red face, wearing lederhosen and a Bavarian hat with a feather. He took their order and returned with their beers.

Shelley raised her glass and said, "Here's to friends, lovers and loved ones. May we all have enough time together!"

Lucas smiled, raised his glass and said, "Give me a woman who loves beer, and I will conquer the world." This made Shelley laugh.

She said, "Cook me dinner, and I'll be happy. Now, please tell me more about Chef Escoffier."

"Before Escoffier's time, there were very few restaurants. Travelers dined in taverns and inns," he said. "Women could not dine in public, only in private rooms or apartments. What we consider restaurants first appeared in France toward the end of the eighteenth century.

"Georges Auguste Escoffier was born in Southern France in eighteen forty-six. When he was a teenager, he spent six years as an apprentice at his uncle's restaurant. He was a small guy, and he wore elevated shoes to keep his head a safe distance above the flames on the stoves."

"Do those tall, white hats with pleats have anything to do with fire?" she asked.

"Yes, they do," he replied. "If the hat catches fire, you can pull it off; but if your hair catches fire, forget it. The tall, white hat is called a toque. Back in the eighteenth century, kitchen hats were different shapes and sizes. The taller your hat, the more important your position was on the kitchen staff.

"At nineteen, Escoffier went to Paris and cooked at Le Petit Moulin where he worked for several years. At the start of the Franco-Prussian War in eighteen seventy, he was appointed Chef de Cuisine for the French Army. Army meals needed to be preserved well, so he devised techniques to can vegetables and meats.

"After being discharged from the army, he went back to work as Head Chef of Le Petit Moulin in Paris, until eighteen seventy-eight. Escoffier hated conditions in restaurant kitchens of the time. The heat was always uncomfortable, and workers drank beer or alcohol, a dangerous situation when working with sharp knives and cleavers. Escoffier disliked the rule which restricted women from eating in public. He became one of first restaurateurs who allowed women to dine in public places. Working at Le

Petit Moulin, he reorganized the food service departments. Escoffier did not smoke, drink, yell or swear in the kitchen; and he expected the same work ethics from all his staff. His kitchens were clean, he was meticulous and his work was organized. He divided the kitchen into five departments which worked simultaneously and assembled each order as the Announcier called them out. Before Escoffier came on the scene, the Aboyeur, meaning the barker, was the person calling orders. He thought the title of Announcier was more sophisticated."

"What were the five departments of his kitchen?" asked Shelley.

"The five basic stations include the Saucier, the Rotisseur, the Garde Manger, the Entremettier and the Patissier," he replied. "The Executive Chef was in charge, the Executive Sous Chef was second-in-command, and they managed all operations."

"I guess the Saucier is the chef who make sauces," she said.

"Right on, my dear," said Lucas. "A Saucier handles sauces, plus soups, stocks and garnishes, although Escoffier wasn't too keen on heavy garnishing. The Rotisseur does roasts, broiled and fried dishes. The Garde Manger (French for 'keeper of the food') refers to the pantry chef, so he takes care of all the cold food and kitchen supplies. The Entremettier does egg dishes, vegetable dishes, pastas, other starches and some soups. The Patissier oversees baking and pastry.

"After leaving Paris, Escoffier went to Lucerne, Switzerland, where he joined Cesar Ritz, the Hotel Manager at the Grand National Hotel. Escoffier became Executive Chef of the summer resort hotel, and they acquired a following of famous people and European aristocracy. In the winter, Escoffier and Ritz went to Monte Carlo, and Escoffier became Directeur de Cuisine, of the Grand Hotel. Three years later, Escoffier, Ritz and Louis Echenard, the Maître d'hôtel, plus a well-trained kitchen brigade and wait staff moved to London. Ritz became Hotel Manager of the Savoy Hotel and made Escoffier the Executive Chef."

"What does a Maître d'hôtel do?" she asked.

"He manages the front of the house, takes reservations, greets the people, supervises the wait staff and assigns tables to them," he said. "The Maître d'hôtel also ensures each guests' satisfaction in the overall dining experience, including all room and buffet services. Sometimes, he does tableside food preparations, such as boning fish, carving meat or poultry, flambéing certain dishes and tossing salads."

A young lady, wearing a dirndl, cleared their table. Lucas paid the check and continued talking as they went to the van, "Escoffier named many of his dishes after famous people, events and places. Peach Melba was named and created for an Australian Opera Singer, Nellie Melba. She starred in Richard Wagner's *Lohengrin* at the London Opera."

"I've heard of Peach Melba. What exactly is it?" she asked.

"My mentor, Chef Robert Johnson, described the original dish as sliced peaches over vanilla ice cream, topped with sweetened raspberry puree and spun sugar," he replied. "It is served in a silver bowl which gets placed on top of a beautiful, swan-shaped ice sculpture. The bowl is cradled in an area which is carved out of the swan's back."

"Wow! Lucas, will you make it for me?" she asked.

"I would, but I think it's too simple for you," he replied. "If I put your name on it, I must create something more elaborate."

Lucas went on with the story, "Sarah Bernhardt, the stage actress, would stay at the Savoy for long periods of time. She and Escoffier became close. He often made scramble eggs and served them to her with Moet Champagne. He created Poularde La Tosca for her when she performed the title role in a play by Puccini. He also named other dishes in her honor, such as Fraises a la Sarah Bernhardt which is strawberries topped with pineapple pulp, sweetened strawberry puree, whipped cream and spun sugar."

"What's Poularde La Tosca?" she asked. "It sounds intriguing."

"It is a whole chicken, stuffed with truffled rice pilaf, then roasted and served with braised fennel," he replied.

"Oh. For me, stuffed chicken does not sound exotic," she said.

"In their time, I guess it was," he said. "Escoffier also named a soup for Sarah. It is a consommé, thickened with tapioca and garnished with quenelles which are small, oval-shaped meat or fish dumplings, along with truffles and poached bone marrow."

"I think I'll stick to chicken noodle, thank you," she replied.

Lucas laughed, as they approached the van. Then, Shelley stopped before he could open the passenger door. When she turned, put her arms around his neck and kissed him, her passion made his toes curl up.

He opened the door and asked, "What was that for?"

"Just for being you, and it was only a preview," she replied.

On the drive home, they passed the hash pipe back and forth while Lucas finished his story about Escoffier, "The Savoy of London became the first modern luxury hotel in Europe. Escoffier and Ritz worked at the Savoy until they were fired. Both were accused of taking kickback money from food purveyors and *cooking the books* (skimming money which belonged to the hotel).

"In eighteen eighty-nine, Ritz opened a brand-new hotel in Paris, the Ritz Hotel at Fifteen Place Vendome in the First Arrondissement. Escoffier was there to open the hotel and oversee the food program. It was one of the first hotels to provide each room with a bathroom en suite, a telephone and electricity in Europe. Ten years later, Escoffier and Ritz opened The Carlton in London. Escoffier had a kitchen brigade of sixty people, and they could serve five hundred people at breakfast, lunch or dinner. Cesar Ritz had a nervous breakdown at the turn of the century, and their famous team broke up.

"Escoffier's work continued and his organized kitchen methods became essential on luxury liners, like the Titanic and the SS Imperator. His menus inspired the last menu served in the first-class dining room of the Titanic before it sank in nineteen twelve. Also, his own kitchen brigade was on board the Titanic when it sank. Later, Escoffier was on board the SS Imperator, and he met Kaiser Wilhelm the Second who told him, 'I am the Emperor of Germany, but you are the Emperor of Chefs.' Kaiser Wilhelm was the oldest grandson of Queen Victoria who was Queen of Great Britain and Ireland.

"During his career, Escoffier gained credit for many things. He was quoted as saying, 'A cook is a man with a can opener. A chef is an artist.' Besides kitchen organization, his contributions for processing canned foods became well known. For Queen Victoria's Golden Jubilee in eighteen eighty-seven, he introduced the flaming dessert, Cherries Jubilee. Auguste Escoffier made the chef's profession respectable and transformed the pleasure of eating while dining.

"He worked at the Carlton for twenty years. In a story I read, one of his young apprentices was Ho Chi Minh, and Escoffier trained him to become a pastry chef, although there is no real evidence the story is true. If it occurred, it would have been many years before Ho Chi Minh became Prime Minister of Communist Vietnam.

"Escoffier wrote at least four books about cooking. If you read them, you recognize his *triad* which was truffles, foie gras and caviar. He used those three items most, and they may be the most expensive ingredients in the world. In nineteen twenty, he was awarded the French Legion d'Honneur. Escoffier died in nineteen thirty-five—only two weeks after his wife had died. He was eighty-eight years old."

They arrived back at the Park Hotel, and he added, "Now, my dear, you know the whole Escoffier story."

"Thank you, Lucas. It was fascinating," she replied. "I think it's time for the Shelley and Lucas story."

Opening the van door, he said, "Yes, my favorite bedtime story."

The next morning was all business. They did not risk taking a shower together because they shared a mutual, uncontrollable, sexual attraction, and they could never get enough of each other. Part of their daily routine was walking to work. It gave them a chance to discuss things and enjoy the extra time together. They always held hands as they walked.

It did not take long for Lucas to settle into his new job as Head Sous Chef. Working together with Chef Bucherl, they prepared for Colonel Moyer's birthday party which gave them a smooth beginning. On his way into work, Lucas made a habit of stopping at the employees' beer machine to buy three beers. He kept a beer for himself, and he gave a beer to Herr Schmechtig, the old (maybe 75) Bavarian who worked the pantry and made soups. To hide his drinking, Herr Schmechtig kept a coffee cup under his work-counter, filled with Wieninger beer, although everyone drank beer at work. Lucas also gave a beer to Fritz, the other sous chef. Fritz was a well put together man who used to be a boxer, but he did not speak much English. He was about five foot nine and had red hair. Since he drank for so many years, his face was also red. While Lucas worked with Herr Schmechtig, Chef Bucherl and Fritz, they helped him learn how to speak German.

For the next several weeks, Lucas and Shelley were busy, working in their respective jobs. Shelley had to hire new maids, train them and get the hotel in tip-top shape for the summer rush. Lucas ran the kitchen because Chef Bucherl was always busy, doing paperwork, ordering, writing menus and attending staff meetings.

The menu, geared for American military personnel, offered steaks, burgers, fried chicken and apple pie. Chef Bucherl added Bavarian and French specials which made work anything but boring.

Lucas knew they must always be prepared for large groups. Surprise tour buses stopped there at all hours of the day and evening. The work atmosphere was busy. Sometimes, it was intense and over-the-top busy which required extreme concentration.

When his kitchen was running at maximum efficiency, there was no better feeling of accomplishment. It felt like being "in the zone", the same as in sports. If his team was in-sync, it was a total team effort.

Gabrielle used her language skills and fun personality, working as a waitress. Being attractive and sexy was also an asset.

The hotel manager, Bob Clarkson, was a delight for Lucas to work with. He was a true professional at his job, yet a little laid-back which suited Lucas. So, their relationship was more of a friendship, based on mutual respect, rather than employer and employee.

After working for 30 days, Clarkson called Lucas into his office for a chat, and he asked, "Lucas, I need a strong head waiter and some good waiters or waitresses. Do know anyone who might want to come here and work for the summer?"

"As a matter of fact, yes," he replied. "I met a guy who worked at a top restaurant in Nice. Now, he works at the Von Steuben Hotel in Garmisch. Last time we spoke, I suggested he come work here, and he was interested.

Do you want me to call him? I will also ask him to speak with people he knows and see who else might be interested."

"Yes, good! How are things in the kitchen?" asked Clarkson.

"Our crew functions very well as a team," he replied. "Chef Bucherl is great to work with. Everybody works hard, and they get the job done. Chef Bucherl is a student of Escoffier, so he maintains a professional level, effectively, with a staff of diverse personalities. They all seem to enjoy each other's company, except for Herr Schmechtig and Herr Ostler who seem to dislike each other."

"Toward the end of summer, I want to have a pig roast for the hotel employees and ski patrol. It's something to think about," said Clarkson. "Oh, and I spoke to Chip this morning. He told me about your suggestion to build a sand volleyball court. Where do you think would be the best place to put it?"

"We could put it down by the boathouse, but I would put it closer to the hotel because I would play on afternoon breaks," he replied.

"Okay, let's look for a spot, maybe near the tennis courts," said Clarkson. "Lucas, it's great to have you aboard. I guess you know it will be busy and crazy here. It will also be a fun summer. If you need anything or have a problem, come and see me."

"Thanks, Bob. I love it here already, and I'm looking forward to this summer," he replied.

"Also, I'm glad you and Shelley got together," said Clarkson. "She is an enthusiastic lady and a wonder at her job."

"Well, I agree with you," said Lucas. "After all, she is a California gal. Like my friend George who came with me to Europe—Shelley is ready for anything, anytime and always with a smile. I feel very lucky to be here. Thank you for inviting me."

Shelley and Lucas worked long hours. They got creative to find time for each other and maintain the magnetic attraction and passion they had together. Lucas would go looking for Shelley, and sometimes he found her in a guest room, filling in for a maid. When this happened, they could not control themselves. They messed up the bed in the room, and Shelley had to make it over again with clean bedding.

Lucas scheduled his breaks to occur between 2 p.m. and 5 p.m., but he often worked until 2:30 and got back to work at 4:30. Some days, he went to the hotel game room for indoor sports. If he could find someone to play with, he would also drink a few beers.

One day, Shelley was alone in the movie theater when Lucas tracked her down. They kissed and fondled each other which led to making love on the floor behind the stage curtain. Rolling around on the floor was not the most comfortable situation, but it was spontaneous, and they thought it was very exciting.

Afterward, she said, "Act one was great. Act two takes place tonight. Why don't you bring home something nice for dinner?"

"What about a rib eye steak, potato croquettes, and white asparagus with Sauce Maltaise?" he asked.

"I love living with a chef. What is Sauce Maltaise?" she asked.

"It is a hollandaise sauce, made with the zest and juice of a blood orange," he replied. "It goes great with asparagus."

During an afternoon break, Lucas headed over to the boathouse to see John. Instead, he ran into Gabrielle who now lived in the Ranch House, and they started talking.

"I am glad to see you, Lucas," she said. "I have some news about the RAF. Do you have time to hear the story now?"

"Oh yeah, Gabrielle, I want to hear about them," he replied. "I was wandering toward the boathouse to talk with John. Let's walk over to my van and grab a beer. You can tell me while we walk."

Since his van was in the lot at the Park Hotel, they walked back past Lake Chiemsee Hotel and under the autobahn.

As they walked, she said, "Lucas, do you remember when they told us they would be active soon? Well, now we're in May, and they have begun the push which they talked about. Four days ago, Andreas, Gudrun and some others placed three pipe bombs at the entrance to the I.G. Farben Building which includes the U.S. Army Headquarters in Frankfurt. I heard one of the pipe bombs killed an American Army Colonel, and they did over a million Deutschmarks in damage. The RAF is claiming it was revenge for the murder of Petra Schelm who got killed during a shootout with police after she ran through a roadblock."

"When did they set the pipe bombs?" he asked.

"It was May eleventh, and there's more," she replied. "On the twelfth, some other RAF members placed pipe bombs which exploded at the Augsburg Police Station and injured five policemen. The RAF claimed it was retaliation for Augsburg police shooting and killing Tommy Weissbecker, a member who reached for his ID when the police thought he was pulling a gun. The same day, Andreas, Gudrun and Holger placed a car bomb in the parking lot of the Bundeskriminalamt (Federal Criminal Police Office) in Munich. It destroyed sixty cars."

"What about Astrid Proll? Is she still with them?" he asked.

"No," she replied. "Last week, Astrid was pumping gas at a station in Hamburg. The attendant recognized her from a wanted poster, and he called the police. She is now in jail."

As Gabrielle finished giving him the news, she and Lucas were sitting on the floor of the van. The sliding door was open, and they were drinking bottles of Wieninger beer. Then, Shelley showed up.

She asked, "What are you two doing?" "Can I have a beer?"

Lucas reached into the cabinet behind the driver's seat, grabbed a beer for Shelley, opened it and handed it to her. Next, he stood, took Shelley's hand and motioned for her to sit next to Gabrielle.

He felt concerned since Shelley had a look of wonderment. Lucas said, "Gabrielle was telling me about some mutual acquaintances."

Shelley got seated, and he said to her, "I don't remember if I mentioned this to you. I met a few members of the Red Army Faction—the press calls them the Baader-Meinhof Gang. It is a long story, Shelley. If you want to hear it, I will tell you after work tonight."

Shelley looked shocked and said, "Oh Lucas, I hope you are not going to be put in jail."

"No. I haven't robbed any banks or done anything bad," he replied. "They are only a social acquaintance. I'll tell you about it tonight."

"Why can't you tell me now? I have time, and you are on your break. Right?" asked Shelley.

Gabrielle got up, finished her beer and said, "Thank you for the beer. I've got to go. But, if I hear more, I'll let you know. See you later."

Lucas sat next to Shelley, gave her a kiss on the cheek, grabbed her hand and said, "Shelley, you have nothing to worry about. George and I met these people in the southern part of Austria when they were stuck on the side of the road. For some reason which I can't explain, we made a friendly connection, maybe because we all like to party. They are an interesting group of people who believe their actions are justified and claim they will die for their cause."

"Lucas, I've read about them," she said. "They have killed innocent people, robbed banks, bombed buildings and stolen cars."

"My relationship with them is purely social," he replied.

"What about Gabrielle's relationship with them?" she asked.

"Her situation is a bit more complicated," he said. "I promise to give you all the details tonight."

A moment later, he pulled Shelley further into the van, and he looked outside as he closed the sliding door. There were no other people in the vicinity of the van. Lucas put his arms around Shelley and kissed her. Physical attraction between them was powerful. They undressed each other and became lost in the experience; neither of them noticed the van was rocking.

While both were lying there, staring at the roof of the van and catching their breath, he said, "Shelley, when we are together, it's as if I am out of control. I must have you, and I cannot stop myself. It seems like we are magnetic, and it's even more exciting now."

"I know the feeling because I have the same reaction to you," she said. "Lucas, you are my guy. From the first moment we met, I knew I had to be with you."

"Well, you've got me—hook, line and sinker," he replied.

As they went back to work, both were tingling and feeling great after their romp in the van.

At home in the evening, Lucas and Shelley had a nice dinner, did the dishes, then showered and made love again. Later, they continued their conversation about the RAF. Lucas was honest with Shelley, but he kept his comments brief and simple which was his usual manner, especially on controversial subjects. She agreed: the RAF was not a topic they would want to discuss with other people in general. When they finished talking, Shelley was at ease and comfortable with Lucas' explanation. Curled in each other's arms, they drifted off to sleep.

Lucas and Herbert Bucherl had fun working together in the kitchen. They shared a passion for food, and both went about their craft in a very careful, detailed way.

One night, Bucherl invited Lucas out for drinks. Lucas insisted on driving. After he rode with Helmut once in Oberammergau, he swore he would never ride with another Bavarian driver. Lucas thought they were all speed crazy. Also, Lucas planned to get Herbert "high" for the first time. Bucherl suggested they go to a place near a castle which was only thirteen kilometers (8 miles) from the hotel.

On the ride over, Bucherl told Lucas about the Schloßwirtschaft Wildenwart, "In eighteen sixty-two, King Francis the First purchased Schloss Wildenwart from a mining company. He and his wife used the castle for summer vacations. When he died, King Francis left the Schloss to his niece, Maria Theresia, sometimes called Mary Theresa, who later used the title Queen Mary of Bavaria. She married Prince Ludwig of Bavaria who later declared himself King of Bavaria (King Ludwig the Third) and replaced crazy King Otto who was the younger brother of Ludwig the Second. As you may know, King Ludwig the Second was 'the King of castle and palace building' in Bavaria."

"I count three Ludwigs. Am I right?" asked Lucas.

"Yes," replied Herbert. "Ludwig the First was the King of Bavaria for twenty years. He married Princess Therese of Saxe-Hildburghausen on a field in front of the city gates. All Munich citizens were invited to attend the wedding, and there was a horse race. Since then, a big celebration is held every year, except for some temporary interruptions: In the early twenties, a cholera epidemic and a financial crisis prevented the event;

also, there were no celebrations during either of the world wars. It has been over one hundred and sixty years since the first celebration took place. What started as a local event became known as *Oktoberfest,* and now it takes place all over the world. If you have been there, you saw what it grew into."

"My friend George and I went there last year with some of our buddies," said Lucas. "We all had a good time and enjoyed the party atmosphere. Everyone thought the beer tasted great, but it had a higher alcohol content than regular beer."

"I think it is two percent stronger than usual beer," said Herbert.

They parked in a spot, behind the restaurant which was in front of the castle. Lucas pulled his hash pipe from his backpack, held it out and asked, "Herbert, are you ready to smoke a little hashish?"

"I said I would try it. Okay, let's do it," he answered. They passed the pipe back and forth twice. Then, Herbert took too big a hit and had a coughing spell.

"I think one more hit, and we will be good to go," said Lucas. "Please finish telling me about the Ludwigs. We can also drink a beer before we go inside." Lucas reached into the cabinet behind the driver's seat, pulled out 2 Wieninger beers and gave one to Herbert.

"Danke schoen," said Herbert.

Clinking beers, both said, "Prost."

Herbert continued talking about Oktoberfest and the Ludwigs, "In nineteen sixty, horse racing ended for the Oktoberfest. Instead, before the festival begins every year, they have parades with local participants who are the workers and officials of the festival. King Ludwig the First loved fine art and had a large collection. He was a member of The Order of Saint Hubertus. He also had several mistresses during his reign, including the Irish actress and dancer, Lola Montez."

"I've heard the name, but I know nothing about her," said Lucas.

"Lola Montez got around," said Herbert. "She spent time in Paris and had many affairs with prominent men: Franz Liszt, the composer; Alexandre Dumas, the writer; Frédéric Chopin, another composer; and George Sand, the author who was a French woman, so it was a lesbian affair. Then, Lola Montez moved to Munich. She met Ludwig the First and became his mistress. He made her a countess, over many objections which were voiced by the Bavarian population."

Herbert took a drink from his beer, then continued the story, "Many believe Lola was the reason Ludwig gave up his throne. He was popular with Bavarian people, but they resented the favoritism he gave her. When the king resigned, Lola Montez moved to London and got married. When her husband drowned, she went to California and got married again. Her second marriage failed. A doctor testified against her in court, and he was murdered. Later, she moved to Australia where she received a bad review and attacked the theater critic with a whip. The same year, she sailed to San Francisco, and her manager fell overboard. People around her seemed to die or disappear."

"Whatever became of her?" asked Lucas.

"She died of syphilis at age thirty-nine," he replied.

"Wow, she had a fast life," said Lucas. "When Ludwig the First stepped away from his throne, who took his place?"

"His oldest son, Maximilian II, became king. He was also the father of Ludwig the Second," he replied.

"How about Ludwig the Third and Maria Theresia?" Lucas asked.

"They purchased Leutstetten, a farming estate south of Munich, and a raised most of their children there," he replied. "Ludwig and Maria Theresia had thirteen children and a happy marriage. When he was crowned as King Ludwig the Third, they lived at Wittelsbacher Palais. Five years later, the king abdicated his throne, and they came to live in Wildenwart Castle which her uncle, King Francis the First, had willed to her. Ludwig and Maria Theresia remained here until they died."

"Are you ready to go inside? How do you feel?" asked Lucas.

Herbert gave Lucas a big smile and said, "Wunderbar, gehen wir (wonderful, let's go)."

They had parked near a large wrought-iron gate. After walking to the gate entrance, they found it closed and locked.

Herbert chuckled, and then he laughed for no reason, except he was "high." He said, "I don't know why this is so funny, but it is."

"I guess we can't go in to see Wildenwart Castle. Does someone live there?" Lucas asked Herbert who was grinning.

"I heard Bavarian Princess Helmtrud lives here," he replied. "She is Ludwig the Third's youngest daughter."

Looking through the gate, Lucas noticed the castle had been built on a hilltop. The road was a bridge, leading to the front of the castle. Stone parapets, about 3 feet high, lined both sides of the bridge. Under the bridge, lavish gardens covered the grounds at a level far below the castle. Trees grew from the gardens and showed their tops above the bridge. It was like a moat, filled with beautiful landscape instead of water.

Lucas shifted attention to the restaurant, located right outside the castle gate. It had a steep, sloped roof with 3 attic windows and 2 onion-shaped domes. The building was 4 stories high, and the windows all had dark wood shutters. He thought it must have been something else before it was a restaurant. The outside had Bavarian-style adornments, but it looked like a barracks building.

"This was estate offices for the House of Wittelsbach, thus the name Schlosswirtschaft (a business on palace grounds)," said Herbert.

Standing in the doorway of the bar, Lucas took it all in and thought: *I hear music, coming from a quartet at the back of the bar, and I can see the small stage. The dance floor is crowded with people in front of the stage, and the tables around the dance floor look full. There are no unoccupied tables or chairs. Most of the people dancing are in Bavarian dress. The women are in colorful dirndls with white, low-cut blouses. The men are sporting lederhosen and Bavarian hats, each with a plume of feathers. I am always amazed to see how much the Bavarians love music, dance, laughter, singing and beer. They seem to have endless energy, and they radiate happiness.*

Herbert flagged down a waitress and ordered 2 beers. They stood next to a waiter's station at the end of the bar, waiting for people to leave their seats. It was a long bar with plenty of stools in front, but all the stools were occupied. Lucas noticed there were more women at the bar than men. It was noisy, and everyone spoke loudly.

"What kind of fur is on the tall man's hat, over there?" asked Lucas.

"The hat is a *Tirolerhüte*, and the fur is *gamsbart,* a tuft of chamois hair," replied Herbert. "The chamois is said to be a cross between a goat and an antelope. In the old days, the more tufts of chamois hair on a hat, the wealthier the wearer claimed to be. Nowadays, they use chamois hair imitations, and it is meaningless."

"What's with all the ladies here?" asked Lucas.

"This bar is a local pick-up-place," he replied.

"Herbert, you mentioned the Bavarian Order of Saint Hubertus. Is it also the International Order of Saint Hubertus?" asked Lucas.

"Wait," said Herbert. "Let's grab those open stools, over there."

After they claimed the only 2 stools available, he said, "Let's get a shot of Jägermeister. I want to show you something."

When the bartender poured shots, Herbert asked him to leave the bottle because he wanted to show something to his friend.

Lucas and Herbert were raising their shot glasses of Jägermeister, when a female voice, coming from behind them, said, "Prost."

When the men turned around and said, "Prost," they saw 2 lovely Bavarian ladies who were about 30 years old. They had beautiful skin and great smiles. The tallest lady was maybe 5'10". She had blonde hair in a long ponytail, tied with a flowery scarf. Her mid-thigh dress matched the scarf, and a white belt cinched her waist, emphasizing her hour-glass figure. White boots rose to the top of her calves.

"Gruss Gott, Petra," said Herbert.

"Hallo Herbert, wie gehts dir?" asked Petra.

“Mir geht’s gut, danke,” he replied.

Then, Herbert spoke in English, “This is my friend Lucas who came from California. He is living here at Chiemsee, and he is a chef.”

“Welcome to Bavaria, Lucas,” said Petra. “This is my friend Inga.”

Surprised to hear the name, Lucas managed to say, “Hello Inga.”

“We have a table in the corner next to the bandstand,” said Petra. “If you want to join us, please come over.”

Then, the ladies turned and walked away. Lucas watched Inga as the ladies walked back to their table. Inga wore skin-tight pants which flared from her knees to the tops of her high-heeled shoes. She was also tall, maybe 5'9". Blonde hair, a little darker than Petra’s, draped over Inga’s shoulders and flowed onto her back. Lucas couldn’t help but stare as she swayed her hips and curvy-butt, going across the room.

“Well, Lucas, would you enjoy a little female companionship this evening?” asked Herbert who was also staring at the ladies.

“It sounds tempting, but I have a great lady waiting for me at home,” he replied. “I’m a one-woman-at-a-time guy, so I have no desire for another woman. I hope I’m not cramping your style, Herbert.”

“I used to pick up women, but I love my wife. So, I too have decided to not fool around anymore,” he replied.

Lucas laughed, then asked. “What does your wife do Herbert?”

“My wife is a doctor in the U.S. Army. She’s stationed in Augsburg,” he said. “We met two years ago when she came to our hotel and attended a medical conference.

“Okay. Now, let me continue with my story of the Bavarian Order of Hubertus. The name of the ‘order’ commemorates a battle victory and honors Saint Hubertus or Hubert, the patron saint of hunters and knights. As a young man, Hubert skipped church to do what he loved the most—go hunting. He was stalking a large deer when it turned toward him, and he saw a shining cross between the antlers of the deer. Then, he heard a voice, telling him he must repent. A short time later, Hubert lost his wife. He abandoned his lifestyle and became a priest. Early in the eighth century, he became a bishop. Later, Hubert was sanctified as the patron saint of archers, forest workers, furriers, trappers and hunters (professions of huntsmen). He is also a patron saint of mathematicians, machinists, precision instrument makers, smelters and others.”

Herbert grabbed the Jägermeister bottle, showed the label to Lucas and said, “On the label, you can see the stag and a shining crucifix between the antlers. This is the Jägermeister logo. The word *Jägermeister* means hunting master, and the creator’s name was Mast. He was from the town of Wolfenbüttel which became the first local chapter of the Nazi Party outside of Bavaria. Mast joined the Nazi Party to keep his position in city government. Soon, the town named Hitler as an honorary citizen.

"Mast struggled with finances while he perfected his herbal liqueur and designed the bottle. In nineteen thirty-four, he got a patent for his liqueur and named it Jägermeister because he was a hunter. Then, Mast founded the distillery in Wolfenbüttel. By then, Herman Goring had already created a hierarchy of elite Nazi hunters, and he became the Reich's Head Gamekeeper, appointed to make new hunting laws. His name became synonymous with Mast's Jägermeister, and some people called it Goring Schnapps. Curt Mast passed away about a year and a half ago."

"Where was this town? Wolf something?" asked Lucas.

"Wolfenbüttel. It is southeast of Hanover, and it was a recreational hunting area," he replied. "The Nazis also had a stronghold there."

He tipped the bottle of Jägermeister, so Lucas could see the logo better. Then, Herbert pointed to the green border around the label, and said, "See this writing: *Das ist des Jägers Ehrenschild das er beschützt und hegt sein Wild weidmännisch jagt wie sich's gehört den Schöpfer im Geschöpfe ehrt.* This means: It is the hunter's honor that he protects and preserves his game, hunts sportsmanlike and honors the Creator in His creatures.

"There are actually two patron saints of hunters, Saint Hubertus and Saint Eustace. It is said both had the same vision of the cross between the antlers and became Christians because of it, but at different times. I am not sure which inspired the logo. They had very different lives.

"Hubert was a noble and the head of a household. After his vision happened, Hubert became a man of the cloth. He rose to bishop and then to sainthood.

"Eustace was a Roman General. The name of *Eustace* means good fortune. However, he had anything but good fortune. After Eustace saw the vision and got baptized, he and his family became religious, then things went bad for him. He lost his riches and all his servants died of the plague. Eustace took his family on a voyage, and the ship's captain kidnapped his wife. Next, his two sons were killed, by a wolf and a lion. He didn't lose his faith, but when he refused to make a pagan sacrifice, they roasted him to death inside a bronze statue of an ox."

Lucas made a sour face and said, "Phew."

Herbert put the bottle back on the bar and said, "The music sure sounds good tonight."

"It's the hash, Herbert," said Lucas. "It makes things better, like music, food and sex. Now, tell me, how is Jägermeister made?"

He replied, "Jägermeister is made with fifty-six herbs, fruits, roots and spices, such as citrus peel, licorice, anise, poppy seeds, saffron, ginger, juniper berries and ginseng. The ingredients are ground, steeped in water and alcohol for a few days, then filtered and stored in oak barrels for a year. It is filtered again and mixed with sugar, caramel and alcohol, resulting in thirty-five percent alcohol and seventy proof."

"I imagine it sneaks up on you like tequila does," said Lucas.

"I've never tried tequila," he replied. "But I know from my experience how Jägermeister can affect you."

"I have a friend, Regan Stone, who works in Garmisch," said Lucas. "He is a lawyer who owns a large Texas ranch and is now working as a busboy at the Hausberg Restaurant. One snowy day last winter, Regan and I sat in the lodge and drank beer all afternoon. He told me all about the International Order of Hubertus, Texas style. He became a member after he graduated from college, and they hunt birds: dove, quail, duck and maybe eagles."

"Eagles?" he asked.

"Regan told me he knew a few rich guys who hunted eagles, shooting from an airplane," replied Lucas.

"Is it not illegal in the U.S.?" he asked.

"I'm sure it is," replied Lucas. "I don't think Regan hunted eagles. But I wonder about his rich friends, members of the Texas 'order.' Do you think the Texas 'order' is the same organization as your Bavarian Order of Hubertus?"

"I have heard of it," said Herbert. "I think their roots came from the same vision, and the international group grew out of the 'order' here in Bavaria. Although, the original group allowed women to be members, the international group has only men."

"Regan told me the International Order of Hubertus got started in the U.S. at the Bohemian Club in Northern California. Have you ever heard of the Bohemian Club?" asked Lucas.

"I read something about the group," he replied. "Isn't it a secret club of wealthy men who camp together in the woods?"

"You're right," said Lucas. "The Bohemian Club is a fraternity of wealthy men who enjoy hunting and partying. The members are or were highly successful businessmen, politicians, artists and military leaders, like current U.S. President Richard Nixon, plus former U.S. Presidents Dwight D. Eisenhower and Theodore Roosevelt.

"In a famous speech, President John F. Kennedy declared opposition when he spoke about secrecy as '… repugnant in a free and open society' and claimed people are '… inherently and historically opposed to secret societies, to secret oaths and to secret proceedings.' "

"It is scary to think small groups of wealthy, powerful white men can band together and unofficially control the world," he replied.

"I believe these groups have secret initiations," said Lucas. "Regan told me the Texas members of the International Order of Hubertus wear green robes, bearing an emblem of a special cross at meetings. When I asked him about what went on during the meetings, he told me he was sworn not to disclose club secrets."

"Have you heard of The Thule Society?" asked Herbert.

"I don't think so. What is it about?" asked Lucas.

"It was formed from two smaller, secret organizations in Munich," he replied. "The original intention was to return power to Germany after losing World War One. Under the cover of a German history study group, the Deutsche Arbeiterpartei (German Workers' Party) was formed. When Hitler and the Nazi Party gained power, Hitler used influential members of the Thule Society and their financing to aid him in his quest to control everything. People who wished to join the Thule Society had to sign a declaration, stating they had no Jewish or colored blood, including all family and ancestors. Many of the Nazi elite were members of the Thule Society, such as Dietrich Eckart, Rudolf Hess and Alfred Rosenberg. When Hitler felt it had too much power, he put an end to the society. The Nazis laid claim to the Thule Society's swastika emblem, their 'Sieg Heil' form of greeting, and their propaganda newspaper."

"What about the Bavarian Order of Hubertus? Did they survive the Nazis?" asked Lucas.

"Well, as I understood it, Herman Goring executed the Grand Master of the 'order' because they refused to give him membership," he replied. "Then, Hitler banned the 'order.'

"After the war, it was renamed International Order of Saint Hubertus. The same organization your friend is a member of."

Herbert stopped talking while he took a long drink from his beer.

"So, the members of these secret organizations seem to have money and power. If you think they try to control our lives, what areas of our lives would they try to influence?" asked Lucas.

"It may have started with the Catholic Church and the Freemasons," he replied. "They fought over the same money and power which you are talking about. I believe all these secret societies have their own individual agendas and purposes. However, the members of these societies also have resources and the ability to influence the general economy, along with politics, religion and education."

Lucas looked at Herbert, and he thought: *Herbert rarely talks, but tonight he won't shut up.*

While Lucas listened, drank beer and watched the dancers, Herbert talked, "You know, Lucas, I hate to spring this on you tonight, but I have to tell you—I am leaving my job to open a restaurant in Rosenheim."

"Huh? Herbert, what did you say?" asked Lucas.

"My friend, you are the new Head Chef at Rasthaus am Chiemsee," he replied. "My brother is a pastry chef, and we will be opening a restaurant in Rosenheim. It has a population of about fifty thousand, and it's a twenty-minute drive from here. Lucas, this means you and I will both be in the restaurant business. By the way, how are your restaurants doing in Long Beach?"

"My restaurants are doing well, thank you," Lucas replied. "I am lucky to have such good employees, but I may decide to sell the restaurants. I am not ready to go back and live in California. Now, with this new responsibility here, I feel needed in Bavaria."

The 2 local ladies who stopped to talk earlier, had now found other guys to join them. They were all on the dance floor, close to where Lucas and Herbert were sitting and watching. Petra looked at Herbert and stuck out her tongue. Lucas laughed out loud.

Herbert finished his beer, set his glass on the bar and said, "I guess it's time for us to leave. What do you think?"

"I think we should go to the van, smoke hashish, and then go home to our ladies," said Lucas. "Are you ready to go, Herbert?"

"Yes, I agree," he replied. "And if hashish makes sex better, I'm all for it. I can only hope my wife is."

CHAPTER 35

Hintertux Glacier

After dropping off a very "high" Herbert Bucherl in Prien, Lucas drove back to Chiemsee. Shelley was sound asleep when he got home. He showered, crawled into bed and slept like a log.

Lucas woke early, just as Shelley was coming out of the shower, sexy nude. She bent over to kiss Lucas who was still lying in bed. He pulled her next to him, and they had an unbelievable lovemaking experience which happens when intimate partners are fresh and energetic.

They got dressed and walked to the hotel, both ready to start work. On the way, Lucas surprised Shelley when he said, "Herbert is opening a restaurant in Rosenheim with his brother. I will take his job as head chef at Chiemsee. He told me about it last night. I guess Bob will discuss it with me today. Have you heard anything about this?"

"No," she replied. "If they kept it from you, they would keep it from me too. Wouldn't they?"

Arriving at the hotel, Lucas climbed the steps from the loading dock to the back entrance of the kitchen. A note on the kitchen door told him to go to Bob Clarkson's office, and his door was open.

When Bob saw Lucas, he came from behind his desk, shook Lucas' hand and said, "Congratulations Lucas, you are the new Head Chef of Chiemsee Hotel. I thought it would be nice if Herbert gave you the news. Since you are familiar with the kitchen and staff, Herbert will not be back to work. He and his brother are getting started with their new restaurant in Rosenheim. Headquarters is sending us two cooks who can begin work next week. One is an American who has military cooking experience. He completed his tour of duty and traveled around Europe for the past few months. I trust you approve of these changes."

"Yes. While our German staff is efficient and fun to work with, it will be nice to have an American cook in the kitchen," he replied.

"Our staff respects you because you are so professional," said Bob. "Lucas, I want to tell you how glad I am to have you running this kitchen. I believe you are the first American chef to work in an AFRC hotel.

German chefs are talented, knowledgeable and efficient; however, they are sometimes arrogant and abusive with the staff."

"I believe in the Escoffier method of kitchen conduct," he said.

"Okay. How do you describe it?" asked Bob.

"Escoffier never smoked, swore or yelled in the kitchen, and he expected the same work ethics from all of his staff," he replied. "The only difference here is the kitchen staff can enjoy drinking their beer. Escoffier did not allow alcohol in the kitchen; But restriction of alcohol would not work in Bavaria or Germany."

With his added responsibilities as the head chef, the days flew by. Since Lucas and Shelley did not have much leisure time together, he thought they needed to get away for a few days.

Lucas wanted to surprise Shelley. So, he went searching for her after lunch service was over. He found her on the second floor above the kitchen, filling in for a sick maid. The door to the guest room was open, and Shelley had her back turned. She was bending over the bed which allowed Lucas to admire her well-toned legs.

"Do you want to go skiing for the next two days?" asked Lucas.

Shelley turned and asked, "Where can we go and still find snow?"

He replied, "There are two glaciers which have skiing three hundred and sixty-five days a year: The Matterhorn at Zermatt/Cervenia, and the Hintertux Glacier which is a lot closer. I talked to Gunther in the bar, and he said Hintertux is a two-hour drive, depending upon the weather. You know, we have not skied together yet. Let's go have fun. This hotel won't fall apart without us."

Shelley put her arms around Lucas, gave him a passionate kiss and said, "You sure look handsome in your chef's coat and black pants."

She closed the door to the room, locked it, came back to him and unbuttoned his coat. There was no hesitation—they made love with passion and extreme pleasure on the queen size bed with fresh sheets. Afterward, Lucas offered to help remake it. But Shelley sent him back to work, and she stayed to finish the guest room.

As he went downstairs, Lucas met Gabrielle coming up the stairs, followed by Topo, his Argentinean buddy. It was a delightful surprise for Lucas to see his friend in Chiemsee.

Lucas broke out a happy grin, Topo did the same, and they hugged. "Are you planning to stay here for the summer?" asked Lucas.

"It's so great here, I may stay past summer if I can," replied Topo.

"Have you got a room yet?" asked Lucas.

"I've been here one day, and things are happening quick," he replied. "Gabrielle told me about her room at the Ranch House. Also, a desk clerk and his wife are going to Morocco, so the apartment downstairs will be vacant. It has a kitchen and a bathroom with a shower. Gabrielle and I want to share it, so we're going to see Shelley about it."

Lucas smiled. "I thought I was a fast mover," he said. "Topo, this is amazing. And it is a great apartment. What will they do with Gretchen, their little Yorkie?"

"They will leave her with us," replied Gabrielle. "She is a smart dog and very obedient."

Walking back to the kitchen, Lucas appreciated the timing of Topo and Gabrielle's visit: *I am sure glad they did not come while Shelley and I were making love in the hotel room.*

The following morning, Lucas and Shelley walked to work together. They met with Gabrielle when they passed the miniature golf course which is in the courtyard to the left of the hotel's entrance.

"I have news of our Garmisch friends," said Gabrielle.

Lucas suggested they go get coffee at the waiter's station and move to his office. Walking through the kitchen, they all said good morning to Herr Schmechtig and to Fritz, the sous chef. Schmechtig was old, but he loved the young ladies. After they got seated in Lucas' office, Herr Ostler, the pastry chef, brought in 3 pecan Danish which were right out of the oven and smelled heavenly. They all thanked Herr Ostler, and he left. Lucas shut the office door and sat at his desk.

"Gabrielle, you can talk to both of us," he said. "I already told Shelley about it." Turning to her, he asked, "Okay, Shelley?"

"Sure, as long as I am not involved with terrorists," she replied.

"Oh, but they are Celebrity Terrorists," he said.

Then, he turned to Gabrielle and asked, "Now, what have our Urban Guerrilla friends been doing?"

"It is not good news, Lucas," she replied. "The RAF increased their activity as they said they would do. Today's newspaper has some information about their attacks against the US military last week. Do you want me to read it for you?"

Lucas looked at Shelley. She nodded. "Okay, let's hear it," he said.

Gabrielle read, *"More news on the May eleventh bombing of the I.G. Farben Building: Andreas Baader, Gudrun Ensslin, Holger Meins and Jan-Carl Raspe exploded three pipe bombs at the entrance to U.S. Army Headquarters. Shrapnel from one bomb killed a U.S. Army Officer. This was the first American military person to be killed by the Red Army Faction (RAF). The headquarters building sustained over one million Deutschmarks in damages."*

"Shelley and I are going skiing for two days," he replied. "I hope this place is still here when we get back."

"Not funny, Lucas!" exclaimed Shelley.

Gabrielle continued reading, *"May twelfth: At the Augsburg Police Department, Angela Luther and Irmgard Moller exploded two pipe bombs which injured five policemen. Later in the day, Baader, Ensslin and Meins left a car bomb in the parking lot of the Bundeskriminalamt in Munich, destroying sixty cars. The Baader-Meinhof Gang claimed these attacks were in retaliation against police who murdered RAF member Thomas Weisbecker last March. RAF members believe the Munich Kripo and the Augsburg Police had no intention of taking Weisbecker alive, and the police shot him in cold blood."*

"The RAF seems to be getting more serious," he said.

"Well, they told us they had big plans," said Gabrielle. She read more news, *"Three days after the Munich and Augsburg bombings, Baader, Raspe and Meins placed a car bomb in Judge Wolfang Buddenberg's car because the judge signed most of the Baader-Meinhof arrest warrants. The Judge's wife was driving his car, and she suffered severe wounds from the blast. RAF members claimed responsibility in the name of Manfred Grashof who was transferred from the prison hospital to a regular cell. Manfred protested the transfer and claimed he was too ill to leave the hospital, thus came the RAF retaliation."*

"Wait a minute! We saw Manfred six weeks ago in Garmisch. How did he get to a prison hospital?" he asked Gabrielle.

"Oh, I thought I told you," she replied. "Soon after we saw him in Garmisch, Manfred was with Wolfgang Grundmann in an apartment in Hamburg. They used the place to produce fake papers and identities. When police raided the apartment, Wolfgang surrendered, but Manfred shot and killed a policeman. During the shoot-out, Manfred got hit. His wounds were bad, so they put him in a prison hospital."

"They sure have been busy. Is there more?" he asked.

"Yes, but I have to get to work," she replied. "Keep the newspaper, and you can read the rest yourself."

Lucas put the newspaper in his desk, and they all went to do their jobs. The next few days and through the busy weekend, CID Robinson hung around the hotel with 2 MPs as extra security, due to the recent RAF bombings and shooting. Lucas did his best to avoid contact with Robinson. However, he was always mindful of the Bruno incident. Now, since the snow was melting, Bruno's body might be found.

On a Thursday morning at 6 a.m., Lucas and Shelley piled all their ski gear, a case of Wieninger beer, the ham-and-cheese croissant sandwiches which he had made, and other food into the van. They had picked up coffee to go from the kitchen, and some warm pecan rolls, made by Herr Ostler in the bakery. Now, they were headed toward Hintertux, Austria, to ski for 2 days. Lucas and Shelley were excited since this was their first trip together. They both had been working hard and needed a little break. It would also be their first time to ski together.

On their way out, Shelley grabbed a copy of the *Stars and Stripes* at the front desk. She read some of the latest RAF news as Lucas got on the autobahn and started the 2-hour drive. Summarizing it for him, she said, "There were more Baader-Meinhof attacks last month on the nineteenth, bombings at the Springer Building in Hamburg."

"What happened? Did anyone get hurt?" he asked.

Shelley read aloud, *"Ulrike Meinhof, Siegfried Hausner, Klause Jünschke and Ilse Stachowiak planted six bombs at the Springer Press offices in Hamburg. Three of the bombs failed to explode, but the other three injured seventeen people. It was in retaliation for anti-leftist propaganda put out by the RAF's enemy, the Springer Press, who declined to publish a retraction. In a written statement to the press on May twentieth, the RAF claimed they made two calls to the Springer Press office and one call to the police before the explosions, warning them to evacuate the office building, but their warnings were ignored; therefore, innocent workers were injured."*

"It sounds like they have moved their operations north. Were there any more attacks last week?" he asked.

Looking back at the newspaper, she read, *"On May twenty-fourth, Irmgard Moller and Angela Luther drove two cars, bearing American license plates, to Campbell Barracks in Heidelberg. The cars were loaded with fifty-pound bombs and were left in a parking area used by the soldiers and their families. As it was later discovered, the license plates on both cars had been stolen, but were not yet reported."*

Shelley stopped speaking as she studied the details.

Then, she said, "Oh Lucas, this is terrible—it says, *'The bombs went off about six o'clock when Clyde Bonner, a U.S. Army Captain, and his friend Ronald Woodward were blown to bits; their body parts were scattered around the parking lot. A wall next to the base clubhouse collapsed and knocked over a coke machine which fell on another American soldier, Charles Peck; and he died. The RAF took credit for this bombing in the name of Fifteen July Commando for last year's killing of Petra Schelm.'* Did you ever meet her, Lucas?"

"No, she died before I came to Europe," he replied. "Petra Schelm, was in a shoot-out with police, and they killed her. She was Manfred's girlfriend. I first met Manfred Grashof in January of this year."

"Why are they attacking the American military?" she asked.

He replied, "They say it is because the Americans are bombing in Vietnam, and the U.S. supports the current German government which is controlled by ex-Nazis."

Shelley said, "It lists recent attacks in the newspaper," and read, *"The May eleven attack in Frankfurt was called the Petra Schelm Commando. May twelve was the Thomas Weissbecker Commando. The May sixteen attack was the Manfred Grashof Commando."*

"What do these Commando names mean?" she asked.

He replied, "Those are RAF units, honoring the dates of death or the names of the dead RAF members, except for Manfred who is still alive in prison. He is the guy who got shot when he killed a policeman, and they transferred him out of the hospital, still wounded and ill."

"Lucas, how do they keep from getting caught?" she asked.

After thinking about this for a moment, he replied "They get a lot of help from ordinary people like you and me. However, they have become deadly, and I will not associate with them anymore. I do not think it will end well for them; and it makes me a bit sad since they are interesting people. It was an unusual experience to spend time with them, and I'm glad I lived through it. Now, it's time to move on."

Driving through Frasdorf, Lucas remembered his dinner with Chef Bucherl at Wildenwart Restaurant when they got "high" together.

He asked Shelley, "Have you been to the Wildenwart Castle, or do you know anything about it?"

"No. I know nothing about it," she replied.

He said, "The castle is about seven kilometers south of here. Herbert told me King Ludwig the Third lived there for a while with his wife, Maria Theresia of Austria. She inherited the castle from her uncle, King Francis the First. During Ludwig's reign, Maria Theresia was known as Queen Mary of Bavaria. After he gave up his throne, she and Ludwig lived out their lives in Wildenwart Castle."

"I've learned a lot about King Ludwig the Second, and I sometimes conduct tours of Herrenchiemsee Palace," said Shelley. "This summer, when we sail over to Herreninsel Island, I will give you my tour."

"The bartender shared several stories with me. Have you ever talked to Gunther about local history?" he asked.

"Yeah, he knows a lot of interesting facts about Hitler," she replied. "I was sitting at the bar with several people, and he told us surprising things about Hitler and the Nazis. I think it's extraordinary to hear Gunther, a native Bavarian, talk about serving Hitler in person at the bar."

"Yeah, a lot of Germans don't want to talk about Hitler or World War Two. What sort of stories did he tell you?" he asked.

"He shared stories about Hitler's love life," she replied. "Hitler went to prison for the Beer Hall Putsch incident. After he got out, he met Maria Reiter at a shop where she worked in Obersalzberg. Her family owned the shop. Hitler called her Mimi or Mitzi, but whether they had a love affair, or if Hitler even had a sex life, is only speculation. Some things I have heard about Hitler and his sex life, I wouldn't even repeat. But, let's assume he could have a normal sex life.

"I heard she was young. Did Gunther say how old Hitler and Maria Reiter were at the time of their romance?" he asked.

"Yes. She was only sixteen, and Hitler was in his late thirties," she replied. "Maria must have been in love with him. When he ignored her for several months, and then he broke off with her, she tried to hang herself. Her brother-in-law found her and saved her life. Later, she got married twice. Her second marriage was to Georg Kubisch, an SS member who had served under Joseph Goebbels. Hitler stayed in touch with Maria Reiter; they had sex between her marriages, and he sent her flowers after Kubisch died.

"Hitler's next relationship was with Geli Raubal, seventeen years old and his half-niece, the daughter of his half-sister, Angela. They came to live with him at Haus Wachenfeld next to the Platterhof Hotel in Obersalzberg. Angela came to be his housekeeper. Geli had a six-year relationship with her 'Uncle Alf' (Hitler). He was possessive about her and perverted in his sexual needs. Meanwhile, Geli got into a relationship with Emil Maurice, Hitler's chauffeur, who was also a top member of the SS (Schutzstaffel). When Hitler found out they were having an affair, Hitler fired him as a personal chauffeur, but he let Maurice keep his position as a Senior Officer in the SS.

"As Gunther told this story, everyone at the bar listened quietly. He said Hitler was gaining power as head of the Nazi Party, and Geli moved into his Munich apartment, but Hitler was gone most of the time. Geli had an affair with a Jewish music instructor from Linz. She wanted to go to Vienna and marry him, but Hitler refused to let her go. Then, Hitler traveled to Nuremberg on business. He received news of Geli's death, and he returned to Munich. There were several versions of how people discovered her body."

Lucas said, "I heard some people think she got murdered, by one of Hitler's close associates."

She replied, "Gunther told two versions: Rudolph Hess claimed he found her body when he broke down the locked door, accompanied by Heinrich Hoffman, the housekeeper and her husband, George Winter. However, Winter claimed he forced the door open with a screwdriver, went in with his wife and two ladies, and they found Geli lying face down with a bullet hole in her chest and a pistol lying on the couch.

"What I find most interesting is the absence of any investigation or autopsy. Her body was taken to Vienna and buried at a Catholic Church which does not allow church burials for cases of suicide. The Priest who conducted the funeral service was a longtime acquaintance of Hitler's, and people thought he knew something about Geli's death which caused him to believe it was not a suicide."

At 7:58 a.m., Lucas pulled into the lot at the base of the gondola lift. It would open in 1 hour and take them to the Hintertux Glacier. So, they ate the croissant sandwiches, made with sliced Black Forest ham and Muenster cheese, and drank Wieninger beers. While eating, they sat and listened to a cassette tape of a new album, *Jackson Browne.* It had 2 great songs, "Doctor My Eyes" and "Rock Me on the Water."

"I read an article about Jackson Browne who is now traveling and performing with Linda Ronstadt and Joni Mitchell in the U.S. He spent his youth in Germany as a military brat," said Lucas.

"Oh, Lucas, there is a gal at Chiemsee, a maid named Karen Tyler, who plays guitar and sings Joni Mitchell songs. There also is a guy, named Jeff, who sometimes plays with her and sings James Taylor. The next time she is playing, we will go. Okay?" she asked.

"It sounds good," he replied. "I can't wait. Where do they play?"

"They have played in the game room and in the lounge," she replied. "In nice weather, they played on the deck of our building where we live. They're so popular now, we may have to use the theater."

It was time to close the van, grab their skis and head for the gondola. There were few people in line for the lift, and they timed it well, so they were alone in a 4-passenger gondola. Lucas lit the hash pipe as they rode up the mountain on this first lift, his own personal tradition.

It would take 3 cable cars to get to the top. This reminded Lucas of the glaciers in Cervenia and Gomagoi which were also above tree-line. He felt great, going to the top of the world. He looked forward to skiing with Shelley since the guys on ski patrol had told him she skied like they do. If so, Lucas was in for a challenging day. They both relaxed, leaned back and enjoyed the Alpine scenery around them.

"Shelley, do you know if anyone determined whether Geli Raubal's death was a suicide or murder?" he asked.

"I don't know the answer, but Gunther told us there was no suicide note," she replied. "They found a note torn in pieces and left on the floor of Geli's room, but it was a note from Eva Braun to Hitler. Eva wrote it to thank him for taking her to the theater and to say she looked forward to seeing him again. If Geli committed suicide, maybe Eva's note was her reason. Gunther said Geli's best friend was Heinrich Hoffman's daughter, Henriette Hoffmann."

"Heinrich Hoffman was a photographer. Right?" he asked.

"Yes," she replied. "He was Hitler's private photographer who took over two million photos of Hitler. Eva Braun worked for Hoffman, and she became an amateur photographer. She took many candid photos and movies of Hitler at the Berghof."

"Well, Geli must have known Eva Braun then," he said.

She nodded and continued, "There are stories, reasons Hitler may have had her killed, such as Nazi leaders wanting to get rid of her since she knew too much about Hitler and his perverted sex habits. Also, there were many pornographic drawings which Hitler had drawn of Geli. If those had gotten out to the public, it would have harmed his image."

After riding 3 cable cars, they were at the top of the Sommerberg Lift, standing still on their skis for a few minutes to take in the breathtaking scene before them. They could have gone right or left when they started skiing, but Shelley veered right and went between mountain peaks. Lucas followed Shelley, skiing through a shallow mogul field and onto a wide-open, groomed slope. From there, they rode a T-bar to the top of the glacier which was over 3,200 meters (10,500 feet).

Shelley was gliding down the mountain with little effort.

How lucky I am, thought Lucas, *to have found such a delightful and talented young woman as Shelley.*

They enjoyed ideal snow conditions and made several runs, using the Olperer T-bar lift. Then, they took another T-bar on the western side of the mountain and were spellbound by another spectacular view from the top. To the west, they could see over Brenner Pass toward Innsbruck and all the way to Seefeld, Garmisch-Partenkirchen and the Zugspitze. It was a clear, beautiful day.

Shelley and Lucas skied a long downhill run, then rode 2 cable cars to the Tuxer Fernerhaus, surrounded by a wooden deck where they joined sun-worshipping skiers, all drinking beer, eating, laughing and having a great time.

They found places to sit at a table, next to an Austrian couple who appeared to be in their fifties and looked fit. Speaking excellent English, the Austrians introduced themselves as Otto and Bertha from Salzburg. Both were friendly and said they loved to ski. They asked where Lucas and Shelley were from and how they were enjoying Hintertux.

"We're from Chiemsee, and we are having fun," said Shelley.

"Otto, where do you most enjoy skiing in Austria?" asked Lucas.

"There are over one hundred ski areas in Tyrol, but I like Kitzbuhel best of all," he replied. "Have you two skied much in Austria?"

"I have been to St. Johann in Tyrol, Zell am See and Kaprun, Seefeld and here," said Lucas. "I've also been to Gomagoi which I think is in Italy, but didn't it used to be Austrian?"

"Yes," replied Otto. "We skied there and learned the area's history. They fought many battles in those mountains. Gomagoi was part of the

Austrian Empire of the Habsburgs, mostly German-speaking people. Italy had eyes on the area, and many Italians settled there. During the First World War, Erwin Rommel was a German First Lieutenant who made a name for himself, using brilliant leadership as he won battles on the Italian front, including Gomagoi which is considered a part of South Tyrol. Farmers and mountain people in the Austrian Mountain Troops fought brilliantly for a few years, but they had to withdraw. In nineteen eighteen, South Tyrol became part of Italy, and it still is, although it is close to the Austrian and Swiss borders. Twenty years later during World War Two, Erwin Rommel became a Nazi Field Marshall. He deployed troops in surprising and lightning-fast strikes which earned him the prestigious *Blue Max* decoration."

"Will you see the Ice Caves while you are here?" asked Bertha.

"We haven't heard about them. Have you been?" asked Shelley.

"Oh, yes," she replied. "You must ski to the entrance from the top of the lift at Gefrorene Wand, also called the Panorama Terrace. For a small fee, they offer a mini-tour of 30 minutes, or you can take a grand-tour of sixty minutes.

"A yearly event we go to is the Austrian Grand Prix auto race at the Österreichring in Zeltweg," said Otto. "You would enjoy it."

"How far would it be from Lake Chiemsee?" asked Lucas.

"It is about three hundred kilometers, a three-hour drive southeast of Salzburg, near the Yugoslavian border," replied Otto.

Lucas looked at Shelley and said, "We could make two days of it and sleep in the van." Turning to the couple, he asked, "When is it?"

"It's on the thirteenth of August this year," replied Bertha.

"Do you want to take a run with us after lunch?" asked Otto.

"Yes. It sounds…" Lucas stopped talking and his mouth fell open, as he stared across the room toward the exit which led outside to the lifts. Then, he finished his sentence, "… like a lot of fun."

As he was getting up, still looking toward the exit, Shelley asked, "What's the matter, Lucas? You look as if you've seen a ghost."

"Oh, it's nothing," he replied. "I thought I saw somebody I knew, but I don't think it was him. Anyway, I must go to the restroom, and then let's go skiing."

After seeing someone who looked like Bruno, Lucas knew it was improbable, but he felt shaky. He wanted to forget about it, but he would be on the lookout this afternoon for a big guy with black hair, a dark complexion and a red ski parka.

They got settled into a 4-passenger cable car with Otto and Bertha. Lucas pulled out his hash pipe and asked, "Would you care to smoke some of the finest hashish on earth?"

“We both tried smoking hashish, only once, and we felt no different,” replied Otto. “Some of our friends smoke it, and they enjoy it.”

Shelley said, “Oh, you will feel this, and it will feel good.”

Otto and Bertha nodded to each other. Otto said, “Okay, we’ll try it again. Tell me, what are we supposed to feel? I’ve heard people say it makes them paranoid, and I don’t want to be paranoid.”

Passing the pipe around, Lucas said, “I would describe it as more aware and careful, not paranoid. Maybe we should only have two hits. I don’t want you to get paranoid; but, if you feel odd, remember we are all together and having fun.”

Lucas and Shelley had a delightful time, skiing with Otto and Bertha. As he suspected, they were expert skiers, so it was another challenging day for him. Still, he enjoyed skiing while trying to keep up with the others on the slopes. They stopped twice to get more beer, and they kept to the upper slopes where the snow was best. For the last run of the day, they skied from the top T-bar below the peak of Olperer at 3,476 meters (11,404 feet) to the Tuxer Fernerhaus at 2,660 meters (8,727 feet) where they had met earlier.

They stopped and had another beer before skiing all the way down to the Sommerberg Gondola at 2,100 meters (6,890 feet). Then they skied a challenging, red run which went under the gondola and wound around some rocks. With the gondola above, they stopped behind a huge boulder and shared the hash pipe again, out of sight.

The further they skied, the snow got browner and more bare patches appeared. At the bottom where the snow was slushy, they had to ski through some puddles of water. It was time to take off their skis and walk the rest of the way to the parking lot.

They agreed to meet later for dinner at Hotel Hintertuxerhof. The Austrians were staying there, and Bertha said the food was excellent. Otto and Bertha would leave the next day to go and ski Zugspitze.

Back in their room at the Hotel Alpenhof, all Shelley had to do was look at Lucas in a certain way, and they got into bed. Following a delightful lovemaking session, they showered, got dressed for dinner and sat on the deck of their 3rd floor room, gazing at the panoramic view of the Hintertux Glacier and surrounding mountain peaks.

“It’s hard to imagine, being in a fairy-tale place such as this. I mean, look at this view,” he said. “We are skiing on June first, and when we drive through Tyrol, we see one quaint village after another, only a few miles apart, each with at least one ski lift. I really love Austria.”

“Me too,” she said. “I have to pinch myself sometimes when I look at surroundings like this. You know Lucas, I have seen little of Europe yet.

I told you about my ski trip to Klosters, Switzerland. Then, I went to London and right back to Garmisch. Now, I'm in Chiemsee."

"Let's see, George and I traveled to Italy, France and Spain. Eric told me he was going to Greece after the summer; and Mike Harker… you met Mike Harker, didn't you?" he asked her.

"If you mean the handsome hunk who all women stare at, yes, I know who he is," she replied.

"Mike is headed for Athens, Greece, to work as a waterski instructor at a Club Med. The idea of going to Greece sounds tempting, although it would mean driving through Yugoslavia, a communist country along the Adriatic Sea. Would you consider a trip to Greece?" he asked.

"Is this an invitation?" she asked.

Lucas hesitated for a second, then he said, "Yes, I guess it is."

"Well, we still have a big summer ahead of us at Chiemsee. Did you see the special events schedule?" she asked.

"I did," he replied. "The next event is a genuine Hawaiian luau in two weeks. Native Hawaiian people will put it on with the help of our staff and the ski patrol. They will dig a pit and cook a whole pig underground, Hawaiian-style. Also, we will have traditional Hawaiian music, plus sword and fire dancers."

"Going to the Austrian Grand Prix should be a lot of fun," she said. "Maybe we can get a group of people from the hotel to go."

"I know this summer will go by fast, and I want to enjoy each day as it comes," he said.

"I think you're right, Lucas," she replied. "Sometimes I get so involved in planning for the future, I forget to enjoy the present. So, let's go have fun tonight. It is a beautiful evening with a bright crescent moon and the stars are shining."

They walked and held hands, going to Hotel Hintertuxerhof, only 15 minutes away. The hotel sat at the base of the Sommerberg Cable Car. It was a 3-story building. Most rooms had a private deck and planter boxes of colorful flowers on the railings. One side of the hotel overlooked the village of Tux; the other side had a view of the mountain. Approaching the front entrance, they saw Otto and Bertha waiving and motioning for them to come to their room on the 3rd floor.

The door of the room was open. Lucas knocked, and Otto yelled out, "We're on the deck, and we've got the beer out here." When everyone had a beer in hand, Otto raised his bottle of Zillertal Pils and said it came from a local brewery. Lucas and Shelley agreed, it tasted delightful.

Otto looked at Bertha and said, "Skiing today was a lot of fun. I don't know if it was the dope or the *kameradschaft*."

Seeing blank expressions on Lucas and Shelley's faces, Bertha said, "I think he means camaraderie."

When Lucas pulled out his hash pipe, handed it to Bertha and lit it for her, Otto asked, "How long have you been smoking hashish?"

Shelley replied, "I have smoked it a few times at parties, but now I only smoke it with Lucas. I enjoy it in certain situations."

"What situations?" Bertha asked.

Shelley looked embarrassed, and she turned to Lucas for help.

Lucas caught her look and said, "Smoking hashish or marijuana makes things better. Music sounds better and food tastes better. It keeps me mellow and helps me stay focused to experience life as it happens. I believe it also expands my mind and increases my creativity. Not to mention, the munchies which everyone seems to get."

"We both felt strange at times today, but we had fun," said Otto.

"The impact on your brain depends on what type of marijuana you smoke or eat, such as making brownies with it," said Lucas. "I've found each new batch of pot is a somewhat different experience. For me, the clincher is the sexual experience when I smoke dope."

When he saw the eye contact and grins between Otto and Bertha, he said, "Let's face it. Marijuana affects the brain, and the brain is the most important sex organ in your body."

They all laughed and headed downstairs to dinner. Walking through the lobby, they saw a crowd gathered at the far end of the room.

"Let's go see what is going on," said Bertha. They could barely hear the news on a television in front of the crowd, and they were not close enough to see it. Otto spoke to a man wearing lederhosen and a Bavarian hat. They talked in German, too fast for Lucas to understand, but he heard the name Baader, and he waited for Otto to relay the news.

Otto turned to Lucas and said, "One leader of the Baader-Meinhof Gang was captured."

Lucas felt anxious. "Do you know which one?" he asked.

"It was Andreas Baader," said Otto. "After a shoot-out with police, they shot him in the leg and carried him away."

Not wanting to show any real interest, but feeling sadness, Lucas said, "I guess police will also be getting the other members soon."

They arrived at the restaurant and found the hostess who had a well-scrubbed, healthy look which is common in young, Austrian women. Once seated, they ordered Zillertal Pils beers and studied the menu.

Lucas loved to eat game, so he chose the Hirschpfeffersteak mit Pfifferlingen dazu Kroketten und Broccoli (deer pepper steak with chanterelles, potato croquettes and broccoli).

Shelley chose Rehfiletspitzen in Pilzsauce mit Schupfnudeln und Rotkohl (venison with mushroom sauce, noodles and red cabbage).

Otto and Bertha wanted Fleischfondue - Chinoise mit verschiedenen Saucen (meat - cooked at the table, served with 5 sauces: Béarnaise, Madeira, Gorgonzola, creamed horseradish and garlic butter).

"Since you got here yesterday, I would guess you have only seen the glacier," said Otto. "Some popular things here are the natural mineral springs and the Spannagel Cave, the largest tourist cave in central Austria. The cave is ten kilometers long with stalactites and crystals, banded marbles, frozen waterfalls and an underground lake beneath the glacier where we skied. Everyone tours with a guide, and people must be fit to climb ladders and make their way around the cave."

"This hotel has been around since nineteen fifty-eight," said Bertha. "It was called the Auenhof until the Kofler family took it over. They renamed it the Hintertuxerhof in nineteen sixty-eight. The kitchen takes great pride in using local products, grown and produced here."

"Is there is a disco or bar with music and dancing?" asked Lucas.

"Yes. We can go to the Hohenhaus which is a short walk from here," replied Bertha. "It's a fun place and usually crowded, but this is Tuesday night, so I think we will get in."

"I ate so much, dancing sounds like a good way to work it off. Let's go," said Shelley.

Lucas and Otto split the check, and they all walked outside into a beautiful, cool evening. They passed Lucas' hash pipe back and forth and laughed during their walk to the Hohenhaus, attracting stares from a few people along the way. It was one of those unforgettable evenings. They drank Zillertal Pils beers and shots of Jägermeister. Hearing each other was difficult since they had to shout over the music, so they danced, drank and laughed the night away. Around 1 o'clock in the morning, they had enough and walked back to the Hintertuxerhof.

While saying goodbye, Lucas said he and Shelley might have a quiet day ahead of them, and Otto said, "Gemütlichkeit."

"I've heard the word before. What does it mean?" asked Shelley.

Otto replied, "It has no translation to English, but I think the word *cozy* is close. In a group with good camaraderie and coziness, the Danes use the word *hygge* which has a more communal meaning."

They all agreed to meet on the 12th of August at 4 p.m. in front of the entrance to the pit area at the Austrian Grand Prix auto race. Then, everyone hugged and said, "Auf Wiedersehen."

Lucas and Shelley went back to their room at the Alpenhof. While they were undressing each other and kissing, Shelley paused and asked, "What do you think about Andreas Baader being captured?"

"It was bound to happen," he replied. "I'm surprised Andreas is still alive." He added, "Anyway," as he undid the clasp on her bra, "I have other things on my mind now."

She unzipped his jeans and said, "Come to think of it, me too!"

Lying in bed during the aftermath, they both felt satisfied, relaxed and extremely close. Looking out the window at the moonlit glacier, Lucas thought: *Lovemaking with Shelley keeps getting more intense. I cannot get enough of this lady.*

In the morning, they had an Austrian breakfast of Wiener Frühstück (coffee or tea, a bread roll or croissant with butter honey or jam, plus sliced ham and Emmentaler cheese) while they sat on the small deck and enjoyed the great view of the Olperer, a Tyrolean mountain peak.

After breakfast, they went skiing on the glacier and had so much fun, they did not even stop for lunch. Lucas followed Shelley on the slopes and they skied until 2:30 p.m. When they returned to the van, each had a beer and ate brotchen with Black Forest ham and Muenster cheese. Then, they packed their ski gear away and headed back to Chiemsee.

While Lucas drove, Shelley read the *International Herald* from the hotel. He asked, "What does it say about Baader and the gang?"

She replied, "It happened in Frankfurt," and read aloud, "*Police were staking out a garage at the end of a side street. After they looked in a window and saw boxes of explosives, but no people inside, they took away the explosives, left the empty boxes and placed a listening device inside the garage. Expecting a shoot-out, police asked city workers to stack sandbags at key places outside the building. A little before six a.m., a plum-colored Porsche Targa pulled in front of the garage, and Andreas Baader, Jan-Carl Raspe and Holger Meins got out. Jan-Carl Raspe spotted some men on roofs and on the street. He pulled out his gun and started shooting. An officer tackled him before he shot anyone. They captured Raspe, but Meins and Baader made it inside the garage.*"

"This sounds like a movie," said Lucas.

"As you said, they are known as Celebrity Terrorists since they dress like celebrities and drive BMWs or Porsches," she replied.

Shelley continued reading to Lucas from the newspaper article, "*A television camera crew arrived to broadcast the event. After waiting for about three hours, police drilled a hole through the garage wall and dropped tear gas canisters inside, but most of the gas floated upstairs into a loft apartment. A sniper shot Baader in the leg. Meins gave himself up. The police stripped him down to his thong-style underwear, handcuffed him and marched him over to a squad car.*"

"How did they find out about this garage?" he asked.

“The article claims it was based on a tip,” she replied. “They had been watching the building for two weeks and became suspicious about expensive sports cars which were parked in the area.”

“I’m sure glad the police didn’t raid the house in Garmisch while I was visiting them,” he said.

Shelley paused for a moment, then said, “Lucas, I hope they don’t come anywhere near Lake Chiemsee Hotel.”

“Me too. In my opinion, CID Officer Robinson and his MPs would not be a match for the Celebrity Terrorists,” he said.

She continued reading, *“The police all wore body armor, and over one hundred law enforcement were on the scene. Using an armored vehicle, they entered and stormed the garage. Baader was screaming as police drug him out and yanked him by the collar of his leather jacket which exposed his back to the ground. Police found hand grenades and a bomb in the trunk of the Porsche.”*

“There is a picture of him on the sidewalk, lying on his back with his sunglasses on. I know you said RAF members dressed well. However, he looks like a punk in this photo,” she said.

“Andreas loves expensive sports cars, and he always wore a leather jacket and sunglasses, the same as you see in the photograph,” he replied. “He may look like a punk, but he can be kind and generous. Andreas has a criminal mind, and I’ve been told he is sometimes a total asshole. His personality seems to be all over the place.

“You read about police finding hand grenades and a bomb in the trunk of the purple Porsche Targa. It makes me wonder what action the RAF was planning in Frankfurt. I imagine they would have attacked one of the U.S. military facilities. George and I worked in Frankfurt for four days, soon after we arrived in Europe.”

“Is it true? Members of the Baader-Meinhof Gang trained with Muslim terrorists to learn how to shoot automatic weapons, blow up things and kill people? How could you be friends with them, Lucas?” she asked.

“I can’t say I was friends with them; and when I met them, I don’t believe they had killed anyone yet,” he replied. “They only robbed banks, stole some cars, bombed empty buildings, and became public celebrities, a status which they enjoyed for a few years.

“Their trip to Jordan was not very successful. They sunbathed nude, and the men slept with the women. So, they had to leave because they would not obey camp rules. While they were there, I doubt they learned much about being Urban Guerrillas which they often call themselves.

“The RAF lost public support when they killed those soldiers last month. Whether by bombing or shooting, killing innocent people marked the first stage of failure for them.”

"Lucas, what is your opinion of the three leaders? When you were there, did they smoke, drink or do a lot of drugs?" she asked.

"Ulrike and Gudrun are well-educated, but Andreas didn't finish high school. They all smoke cigarettes," he replied.

"It was a party atmosphere when I was around them. We smoked dope, drank beer and schnapps, or Jägermeister, ate a lot of good food, traded stories and laughed a lot. Visiting them was like an ordinary get-together of normal people, except for the Kalashnikov rifle and a German-made Heckler and Koch assault rifle, stored next to the front door in an umbrella holder. The Heckler and Koch is on the RAF logo.

"Ulrike is a chain smoker who always appeared to be nervous. Before joining the group, she was a respected journalist. She left her husband and twin girls because she wanted to support the RAF.

"Andreas is a thrill seeker. He is intelligent, but he channeled it in a criminal and often violent way. His exciting lifestyle made him a folk hero in Germany, and he certainly attracted the ladies because he was tall, dark and handsome. He started out stealing cars, and he bragged about not having a driver's license, but he always drove a fast, classy car or motorcycle. Andreas abandoned one child for the terrorist life.

"What can you tell me about Gudrun?" she asked.

"Gudrun is the real brains and leader," he replied. "She graduated from a Pennsylvania high school in the U.S. which she attended one year as an exchange student. After she met Andreas in Europe, she abandoned her family, including a child. I found Gudrun to be the most interesting. She started out as a nuclear protestor and became one of the most notorious terrorists in history.

"The press claims they are all delusional, due to drugs they have taken. But with or without drugs, I think they must be delusional to take on the U.S. Military, as a protest of the Vietnam War or any cause of the day. German law enforcement is taking this very serious now. They had over a hundred officers at the capture and shoot-out in Frankfurt."

Shelley suggested they listen to some music, and Lucas agreed. A short while later, they arrived at Lake Chiemsee Hotel.

As Lucas pulled the van into the parking lot, Shelley said, "Let's find Gabrielle tomorrow, and see what she has to say about the RAF."

CHAPTER 36

A Real Hawaiian Luau

The next week flew by since Lucas, Shelley and the hotel staff were busy getting ready for a big Hawaiian Luau. The ski patrol dug a pit, gathered rocks and got chicken wire to wrap-up the pig. Everything was ready to bury and cook the pig. Lucas was busy ordering supplies which twenty Hawaiian cooks, coming from U.S. Military bases all over Europe, would use to prepare the food. A big Hawaiian guy, Eddie, worked all week and drank beer with Lucas while he organized the event. The Hawaiian cooks were all large guys with big appetites, and they loved the German beer. Most other people were locals who worked for the event; they always drank plenty of German beer.

It was Thursday, the 8th of June 1972. Lucas sat in his office, doing paperwork. Gabrielle came in very excited and gave him RAF news, "Lucas, police arrested Gudrun in a Hamburg clothing boutique."

"How did it happen?" he asked. "I figured she would hide out after Andreas' arrest last week."

"I guess she got careless. The store clerk noticed a pistol in her jacket pocket and called the police," she replied.

"Gudrun must be going crazy, being locked up," he said. "Do you know where she is?"

"Not yet," she said. "It seems as if it was just the other day when we were all sitting and talking around the fireplace in Garmisch."

"Do you think this might be the end of the RAF? Or, will remaining members carry on?" he asked.

"There are some with strong beliefs in the cause, but whether they will carry on remains to be seen," she replied. "I know they have weapons which come from East Germany and also from Jordan."

"Well, Gabrielle, all we can do is go back to work," he said.

During the week, many hotel guests came for the luau. Lucas invited his Garmisch friends, and several of them arrived Friday. They planned to stay overnight for the feast on Saturday. Lucas purposely invited Eric, Sabine and Sonya, 3 of the 5 involved in the Seefeld-Bruno encounter;

Gabrielle, the 4th, was already here, living with Topo at Chiemsee. Gino, John Ferrell, Bob Ostergaard, Regan Stone, George Bennett and Judann (Shelley's friend) all came from Garmisch. The Canadian ladies, Judy and Deanna, surprised Lucas when they came with Gerhardt Grassl, the sous chef from Berchtesgadener Hof.

Lucas was glad the Australian ladies, Olivia and Ashleigh, did not come to this event because their presence might have been uncomfortable for him, George, Eric and Topo. Those ladies get around. They are both fun and gorgeous, so it is no wonder they are popular. They still work as waitresses in Garmisch.

The pit for the pig-oven was dug in a remote area beyond the tennis courts, located on the west end of the grounds at the lakeshore's edge. Since over half of the hotel guests were there for the luau, the restaurant would not be as busy as usual on the night of the luau. Lucas would be able to relax and enjoy more time with his friends who he had not seen since he came to work at Chiemsee.

While everyone was still coherent, Lucas got the "Seefeld Five" group together for a walk. They went down by the lake where they could talk without other people around.

Lucas, Gabrielle, Eric, Sabine and Sonya stopped at the shoreline near the Chiemsee Mermaid statue which sat on a short rock wall.

"I had hoped we would never have to speak of this subject again," said Lucas. "Something happened when Shelley and I were skiing in Hintertux two weeks ago. While we had lunch in the lodge, I saw a guy who looked like Bruno, but I could not get a close look at him. Then, he went out the far door, and I didn't see him again."

"Even if Bruno survived the fall, he would not have the nerve to hang around because we know he committed murder," said Eric.

"I never thought Bruno was daring or smart, but should we go there and try to find out what happened to him?" asked Sonya.

"I've been back to the cliff and looked over the edge. He could not have survived the fall unless he landed on a deep pile of soft snow which is very doubtful. I do not think we should attempt a climb to the bottom of the ravine," replied Sabine.

"If he survived, don't you think he would try to get revenge on us?" asked Gabrielle.

"Bruno was a monster. He never thought about what he was doing, but he reacted to everything. If he was only injured in the fall, nothing would surprise me," replied Sonya. "He would have plenty of time to reflect and plan his revenge while lying at the bottom of the ravine."

"I say he is gone, and we should forget about him," said Eric.

It took a moment before everyone nodded in agreement.

They could hear Hawaiian music, coming from the dining room. Lucas pulled out his pipe and said, "Okay, enough business. Let's smoke this hashish. Then, we can get back to the luau and have fun."

As they walked toward the music, Gabrielle asked, "Did you say they are cooking the pig in the ground? How is it done?"

Lucas had watched the big Hawaiian guys prepare the pit and bury the pig in the ground to cook for eight hours. He explained the process to his friends, "The Hawaiians call the method *Kalua Pig*. The pit is called an *Imu* (underground pit oven). They dug a pit seven feet by five feet and three feet deep. In the center of the pit, they built a wood fire around a hollow-metal post which is three inches by six feet, then put coals on top of the burning wood. When the coals were red hot, they added big rocks on top to get them hot. Eddie, the head chef of the luau, told me they prefer lava rock. It holds heat for a long time with little chance of exploding. Since lava rock was not available, we had to use river rocks. I suggest you stay a safe distance from the Imu. If the river rocks do explode, we don't want anyone hurt."

"How big is the pig they buried?" asked Sonya.

"They actually cooked two pigs, each weighing about one hundred twenty-five pounds," replied Lucas. "We got them from a local farmer who is a friend of Fritz, our sous chef."

"How many will those feed, Lucas?" asked Eric.

"About two hundred fifty people," he replied. "But, if they all had your appetite, Eric, it would be about one hundred fifty. While the rocks got hot, they prepared the pig which Hawaiians call *Poaa*. The pig was seasoned with rock salt and wrapped with chicken wire. Then, hot rocks got spread out on the floor of the Imu. It's the bed for the Poaa."

"How long does it take to heat the rocks?" Sonya asked.

"It took about two hours," he replied. "They covered the rocks with pieces of banana wood and placed banana leaves on top."

"Why do they use banana leaves?" asked Gabrielle.

Lucas explained, "Eddie said it gives the Poaa a special smoky flavor. After placing the banana leaves, they put hot rocks inside the pig and wrapped the pig in chicken wire. They set the pig on top of the hotbed in the Imu, then covered it with more banana leaves and water-soaked burlap sacks. Next, they covered the whole Imu with a canvas tarp, and they covered the tarp with dirt until no smoke escaped from the pit. They wet the dirt on top to seal it and to find any smoke coming out. They repaired any leaks with more dirt, then they sprayed it with water again. Eight hours later, they uncover it. Then, they prepare it for the large buffet table which is the dining room. In about ten minutes, we can watch them pull the Poaa out of the pit. If anyone is crazy enough to order from the menu tonight, they can go to the bar and be served."

He led his friends over behind the tennis courts, and they joined about 50 other people who had gathered around the pit where the Poaa was cooked. Hawaiian guys had finished removing the dirt. They were now removing the tarp and the burlap sacks. Next, they pulled off the banana leaves, lifted each Poaa out of the Imu and placed them onto large trays which sat on picnic tables. The crispy Poaa skin was a beautiful bronze color. Hawaiian workers pulled meat from the bones and transferred it to hotel pans. From there, still steaming, the meat went to buffet tables in the main dining room.

After waiting in a line of people, guests entered the dining room where Asian ladies, wearing Hawaiian dresses, greeted them and placed a flower lei around the neck of each guest.

Lucas scanned the whole scene as he stood at the entrance: *Right here in the Bavarian Alps, we have a real Hawaiian Luau with tropical drinks, hula dancers and Hawaiian music. The Hawaiian band is on a stage at the far end of the dining room and away from the lake. Everyone has on colorful shirts, and many are enjoying tropical drinks. Of course, others are drinking beer.*

The bar had 3 bartenders, including Lucas' good friend Eric who could use the extra cash for his trip to Greece.

Topo was now Head Waiter of Lake Chiemsee Hotel. He arranged a special table for Lucas and Shelley's group to dine in the round corner room which had been the Führerzimmer (Hitler's special dining area). Since the Hawaiians took care of hosting and serving the guests, Topo could sit with Lucas and their friends from Garmisch and Berchtesgaden. There were seventeen people around the table, and they had the room to themselves with windows looking out on the lake.

Lucas got seated with Shelley on his right. She is from Santa Monica. Seated next to her is Sabine from Seefeld, Austria. Then, Gino who came from Miami and everywhere. On Gino's right was Bob Ostergaard from Wisconsin. Next to him were Judy and Deanna from Banff, Canada. Then, Gerhardt Grassl from Berchtesgaden. Continuing around the table: Regan Stone owns a cattle ranch near Corpus Christi, Texas. John Ferrell grew up in Boston. Sonya is from Garmisch. She sat next to George from Long Beach, who was with Judann, his current lady from Kentucky. Dennis, an Australian who is famous for his "Flaming A" dance, sat with Jordan Lewis, the bouncer at The Grill who came from Long Beach. Lucas' Argentinean friend and hashish dealer, Topo, sat with Gabrielle, his current lady from Hanover, Germany. All were travelers who came to Bavaria to have fun and work for AFRC.

There were four ladies in this group with whom Lucas had been intimate. Shelley and Gabrielle were comfortable around each other, but Lucas did not want the others to feel uncomfortable, and he did not want the four ladies sitting together. So, Topo separated Judy from Sonya when he seated them at the table, and both were away from Lucas.

Lucas took time to reflect on his relationships with these people: *Seated next to Gabrielle is my good friend Topo. He is a super guy, friendly, intelligent, well-educated in Argentina, a good athlete and he always has the best hashish for sale. Topo can do anything he wants to do in his life, and the ladies sure love him. Gabrielle is a lovely German lady. When we met in Formentera; it seems we were bound together by circumstances. Bruno murdered her friend after he had murdered my fiancée. We had a special, intimate time together in Formentera and Ibiza. Then, we were drawn together again, during our associations with the Baader-Meinhof group. And now, we both work and live at the same hotel. I am glad Gabrielle is living with Topo; she seems very happy. We are comfortable in our friendship and have no sexual tension between us.*

Judann is with my best friend George. She is like a sister to Shelley. Judann is smart, sexy and loves to party. I think she will marry a guy with money. George loved being a high school coach and math teacher in California. He is a superb athlete, his favorite sport is volleyball, and he is always ready for anything, day or night. We always have fun together, and we traveled through Europe last year. It's great he came back to Bavaria. However, I think he will return to coaching in California, and he will marry a lucky, athletic woman.

Shelley was talking to Sabine on her right. Gabrielle and Topo were talking on Lucas' left. So, Lucas continued thinking about his friends: *John Ferrell is a bartender at The Grill in Garmisch. He was stationed in Italy when he took a "European Out" and left the U.S. military. Intelligent and well-educated, he also has deceptive athletic ability. Everyone likes John and appreciates his generosity; he always pays the tab when you drink with him. Next to John is Regan Stone who is easy to talk to, fun-loving and an excellent basketball player. He passed the Texas bar exam before coming to Europe, and he will no doubt go back to Corpus Christi, manage his cattle ranch and practice law. Regan also aspires to sail around the world.*

Looking at Shelley, his beautiful lover and roommate, he thought: *I remember the first time I saw her in Cervenia, but I don't remember talking to her then. She was with the group of people from Garmisch; George and I were with Olivia and Ashleigh, the two Australian ladies; and we were all involved with the "Snow Job" movie. However, I sure remember meeting her here at Chiemsee when she patted me on the butt.*

Now, I enjoy teasing her, so I claim she goosed me. To summarize my relationship with Shelley, I would say we have fun together, no matter what we do, and our lust for each other seems to increase daily. I laugh when I think about all the different places where we have made love, including my barracks room in Oberammergau, the van, the theater stage and Shelley's office at the Park Hotel. At Lake Chiemsee Hotel, we have used several of the hotel's guest rooms and even the kitchen after everyone had gone home. I have never felt such urgency in the moment as I do with Shelley, and she always seems to match my eagerness. Because we are so busy with our respective jobs, we both want to take advantage of time together, wherever or whenever we find the time available.

I feel a strong kinship with Sabine since she has become Eric's girlfriend. We've all been through so much together. In the short time they have known each other, Sabine became very special to Eric. It's too bad Eric is tending bar for the luau tonight. Yet, Sabine is in here among friends. I had hoped Eric would come to work at Chiemsee, but he wants to stay at NATO Officers Club in Oberammergau because it is close to Seefeld where Sabine lives.

Bob Ostergaard has a marine biology degree, but he is much more interested in making money and selling used vans. His "Shifty Sales" business is going well; he may become a millionaire soon. I miss talking with Bob. We often ate breakfast together at the PX in Garmisch. He is a very interesting man.

The Canadian ladies, Judy and Deanna, met George and me at an Italian campground on the Ligurian Sea. Later, they surprised me when they returned to Bavaria with George, and we all went on another road trip together. They both got jobs as waitresses for a short time in Munich. Now, they work at the Berchtesgadener Hof where Gerhardt Grassl works as a sous chef in Berchtesgaden. It seems natural for Gerhardt to be here with two women since he claims to enjoy orgy sex. He even asked me to go with him to an orgy once. Group sex does not turn me on, but I wonder about Judy and Deanna.

There is Gino who always blends in, regardless of the situation he gets involved in. Gino is a somewhat short man with a big heart. He is a well-traveled, street-smart guy who can pass for many nationalities with no trouble. Gino worked in the porn film industry before he came to Europe. I think he will return to Los Angeles and work in the movie business as a director. He would do well with action movies. Gino is the most organized person I have ever met.

Dennis is from Australia, working as a waiter in Garmisch while his broken arm heals. In the process of riding a penny-farthing bicycle from London, England, to Sidney, Australia, he got hit by a car on a local mountain highway. Dennis is a self-described, "flaming fag" and he does a table dance to prove it. I hope he does not pull his stunt tonight, like he did last year at Thanksgiving Dinner in Garmisch.

Jordan Lewis is sitting next to Dennis, and they have become friends which seems odd. Lewis lives with his girlfriend who came with him from Long Beach, California. I met her at The Grill in Garmisch where Jordan is the bouncer. He knows how to handle any situation.

Waiting in the buffet line, Lucas stood next to Bob Ostergaard, and he asked Bob how his used VW van business was going.

"We are always on the search for old rusted-out vans," said Bob.

"Where are you looking for them?" asked Lucas.

"We find them on farms," he replied. "We've covered most of the Garmisch area, so we will look around here tomorrow. If you see an old van for sale, let me know, and we'll come get it."

"Are you still restoring them as you did before?" asked Lucas.

"Yeah. We sand the rust, fill the holes, slap on some paint and add a few cabinets, plus a folding bed," he said. "If needed, we change the engine or transmission with salvaged parts. New GIs love them. So do others who want to travel in Europe, and we make a good profit."

"Well, it sounds like you still enjoy the business," said Lucas.

"You know, Lucas, the best part is we get to see a lot of countryside, plus we meet some of the nicest, most generous, fun-loving people in the world," he replied. "We had a common bond before we even met because we all love to drink beer."

Since the buffet was placed along the inner wall of the dining room, guests had fabulous view of the lake from every table. Real Hawaiians worked alongside hotel staff in the dining room. All the servers dressed in bold patterns of Hawaiian-style clothing. Each adorned with a flower lei, men wore a colorful shirt, and ladies wore a muumuu.

Next to food items, labels displayed interesting names: *Maui-style Mahi-Mahi* (a 'strong-tasting' fish), *Island-style Chicken* (chicken, marinated in lime juice, honey, soy sauce, olive oil, garlic and cumin), *Lomi Lomi Salmon* (salmon, tomatoes and onions), *Big Island Sweet Potatoes* (sliced and served warm), *Huli Huli Pork Ribs* basted with pineapple *Haupia* (coconut pudding) and *Kalua Poaa* (roasted pig).

When Lucas saw *Spam with Sautéed Cabbage*, he could not believe his eyes, and he had to ask the server, "Why Spam?"

"Spam is popular in Hawaii," the server replied. "We have a dish called Spam Musubi which is teriyaki-flavored Spam, wrapped with seaweed and served on a bed of rice."

"What is Spam made of?" asked Lucas.

"It's made with pork shoulder meat, ham, starch and preservatives," said the server. "Spam requires no refrigeration and has a long shelf life. During World War Two, it became popular and in high-demand around the Pacific Islands. In Hawaii, we also have Hot-and-Spicy Spam, Honey Spam and Spam with Bacon."

Lucas' group went through the buffet line and returned to their table. Everyone was busy spreading macadamia nut butter on fresh-baked taro rolls, served warm in a starched white napkin.

Judy, a Canadian, asked no one in particular, "What is the purple stuff in this little bowl?"

Lucas knew poi came from the taro plant, but he looked to George who had taken many trips to Hawaii for volleyball tournaments and had attended many island luaus.

George explained, "Poi is mashed taro root which has been baked or steamed. The taro for this poi was roasted in the Imu with the pig, sweet potatoes and carrots. In Samoa, their version of poi is a creamy pudding, made from bananas, papaya or mangoes. In Hawaii, poi at the table is a sacred part of daily life. What I can't understand is their love for Spam. Where did they get the name for it, anyway?"

John Ferrell answered, "I served four years in the Army, have eaten my share of Spam and asked the same question myself. The makers of Spam say only a few company executives know the origin of the name. I have heard Spam could be an abbreviation for Spiced Ham, Shoulder of Pork Ham, Special Processed American Meat, or even Special Processed Army Meat."

"This is my first trip to Chiemsee," John added. "I'm impressed by the colossal-dining room. What was it like during Hitler's time?"

Looking at Shelley, Lucas said, "Shelley can answer your question since she is the resident tour guide. She knows everything about Lake Chiemsee Hotel and the Palace on Herrenchiemsee."

"The hotel is much the same now as when the Nazis operated it," she replied. "It was built to serve as a rest house for the autobahn between Munich and Salzburg, and Hitler wanted it right next to the lake. The soil was soft here, whereas the soil close to the mountains was firm. So, it was a lengthy process to even lay the foundation.

"The hotel opened in nineteen thirty-eight and operated for two years. Then, it served as a hospital until the Americans took over in nineteen forty-five. The Americans did not make many changes. They left the dedication plaque on the wall at the main entrance, and the magnificent large frescos and paintings which you see around the hotel and in the rooms. The oil paintings, here in the dining hall, were painted by an artist from Garmisch, named Bickel. He was a fresco painter who painted houses, taverns and storefronts. He painted about the everyday life of a Bavarian village. If you look at the paintings in the dining hall and around the hotel, you will see his scenes of a farmer from Eggstatt, a skier from Lofer, a hunter from Grabenstatt, a milkmaid from Frasdorf and rafters from Schechen."

Using his falsetto voice, Dennis said, "With so much wood and marble, this massive room is incredible."

"The ceiling joists are solid spruce, and the floors are oak or walnut," said Shelley. "Those three columns are local Ruhpolding marble. If you visit the Kehlsteinhaus (Eagles Nest) in Obersalzberg, you will see the elevator waiting room. It has a circular ceiling which is also made of Ruhpolding marble, and it's amazing."

"How many people can this hotel accommodate?" asked Dennis.

"For opening day in nineteen thirty-eight," she replied, "the hotel had many distinguished foreigners, about eight thousand total guests, eighteen hundred vehicles, and they served five thousand cups of coffee. However, the exact date of their opening is uncertain.

"The Lake Hotel has eighty-three rooms, one hundred sixty-six beds, a restaurant, a bar, several meeting rooms and the dining room which will seat three hundred and fifty people. Across the autobahn, the Park Hotel has seventy-three guest rooms with one hundred and forty-six beds. The other structures include an office building, a gas station, workshops, garages, a boathouse, a movie theater, laundry facilities and housing for over one hundred and fifty employees."

"What is the significance of the mermaid statue on the terrace wall, outside?" asked Grassl.

"Ah. Your question is the one most asked by our guests," said Shelley. "We Americans call it the Chiemsee Mermaid. The statue was created by Fritz Klimsch, a famous German sculptor, and it was originally named *Die Schauende* (The Looker).

"Many of the Nazi elite used to stop here, as did Hitler, going back and forth from Munich to Berchtesgaden and Obersalzberg. Our head bartender, Gunther, worked here as a young man, and he has many stories about the things he saw and heard during Hitler's days."

Sitting in the dining room where Hitler had entertained his personal entourage, Lucas said, "There are two intercom speakers in the kitchen. They are labeled *Führerzimmer Eins* and *Führerzimmer Zwei*. One is for this room. The other was probably for Hitler's hotel suite."

After dinner, the group went to the dining room and found seating on benches, situated right inside the entrance door. They all watched the end of the Hawaiian Show which was Polynesian Dancers, followed by the Fire and Knife Dancers. Next, came audience participation which seemed like a mistake when Dennis (the famous "Flaming A" dancer), Jordan Lewis (the bouncer from The Grill), and beer-fueled ski patrol were all trying to learn the hula dance.

"I'm glad they won't be doing fire and knife dances," said Lucas.

"Yeah, Dennis loves fire," replied George.

Lucas and Shelley said goodnight to the group, early. The next day would be busy for both: The Head Housekeeper and the Head Chef.

Before falling asleep, Lucas thought: *I wanted a job here, but I did not plan to work this hard.* Then, he realized: *Yeah, but I love it!*

It was June 15th, and a week had passed since Gudrun Ensslin was captured by the police. During their afternoon break, Lucas and Shelley ate lunch on the terrace by the beautiful lake and enjoyed a warm, sunny day. The islands served as a great background while they watched the sailboats glide through the water. Gabrielle and Topo came around the corner, and they each had 2 Wieninger beers in their hands.

"May we join you?" asked Gabrielle. "I want to tell you some news about the RAF."

"Please. It's good to see you away from work," said Lucas. "Thank you for the beer. Now, tell us your news about the RAF."

"Ulrike was captured today along with Gerhard Muller in Hanover, my home town," she replied.

"How was she captured? Was there a shooting?" asked Lucas.

"No shooting, but my mother got the story first-hand from her friend's husband, Fritz Rodewald," she replied. "He is a teacher who became suspicious of Gerhard and Ulrike being terrorists."

"How did this teacher know those two?" asked Shelley.

"They knew Herr Rodewald offered shelter to U.S. Military deserters because of his views against the Vietnam War," she replied. "Ulrike and Gerhard came to his door and asked if they could stay overnight. He agreed, but then he became concerned and called the police. When the police came, they waited outside until they saw Ulrike and Gerhard enter the apartment building. Then, police waited until Gerhard came out to use the pay phone. The police approached him, and he pulled a gun, but they restrained and arrested him."

"Was Ulrike armed, or did she try to resist arrest?" asked Lucas.

"My mother's friend said the police weren't sure, at first, if it was her or not," she replied. "I guess she had lost weight and looked ill. Frau Rodewald claimed Ulrike was screaming, hysterically, as the police took her away. They found several guns and grenades in her room which she must have transported on a streetcar. Apparently, police had doctors anesthetize Ulrike, so they could take an x-ray of her head. She had a silver clamp in her head, placed during brain surgery ten years ago. The x-ray gave them a positive identification."

"Having spent time with them, it makes me sad," said Lucas. "These young people are all educated, except for Andreas. They got lured into thinking violence was the correct method of revolution."

Gabrielle said, "I think Ulrike became depressed and irrational after the Springer Press bombings in Hamburg. She and other RAF members had planted six bombs in those offices. Only three exploded, but it was enough to injure seventeen innocent people. On May thirty-first, Ulrike wrote an article which was a plea to end the bombing in Vietnam and remove all troops from Indochina. She claimed there had been more bombings in Laos than in all of World War Two. Yet, she also called for militants in Germany to target American establishments."

"I read a disturbing article about a young member who phoned her mother, crying because she wanted to return home and quit the RAF," said Topo. "It was the last time anyone heard from her alive."

"It was Ingeborg Barz who wanted to quit the group," said Gabrielle. "When she mysteriously disappeared, it bothered me too."

"Now, that really scares me," said Lucas. "I don't think the U.S. should be involved in the Vietnam War, but all people are entitled to change their minds and support, or not support, any organizations."

"I am afraid!" said Gabrielle. "My mother is friends with the teacher who gave them a place to sleep. My brother is in prison for bank robbery. And, I helped them at the house in Garmisch. What happens if the authorities learn about my association with the RAF?"

"Police will interview people, but they won't arrest everyone who knew them," Lucas replied. "RAF members were bound to get caught. One hundred fifty thousand officials were searching for them."

To change the subject, Lucas asked Topo to play tennis before they went back to work. Topo agreed to get his racket and meet Lucas at the court. Gabrielle and Topo left, heading back toward the hotel. Shelley and Lucas stayed to enjoy a few more quiet moments before they also walked away from the sunny, lakeside terrace.

Lucas kept himself in great physical shape and did not want to lose it. He and Shelley could eat anything from the kitchen, so a healthy diet was no problem, but they needed exercise since they drank lots of beer.

Thinking bicycles would be fun, Lucas bought an orange Peugeot twelve-speed road bike, and Shelley got a yellow one. One day, they rode around Lake Chiemsee on special bike paths and stopped for beers at every bar they came to. When they turned a four-hour trip into six hours, they realized this old habit (drinking beer) might never change.

During afternoon breaks, Lucas and Shelley often played volleyball with other employees at the sand court which Lucas, Chip, John and ski patrol guys had built. It was surrounded by a grassy area. A few oak trees and a large willow tree gave shade around the court. On nice days, there were always civilian employees and ski patrol playing volleyball, drinking beer and having fun.

When possible, Lucas played tennis with Topo or John Reilly. One day, Topo and Lucas played doubles against Chip and John. It began as a fun game, then Lucas and Topo won, 2 sets to 1. Lucas knew if he played singles against Chip in the future, Chip would remember this loss.

Lucas missed playing basketball with Eric, George, John Ferrell and Regan Stone at the gym in Garmisch. Yet, there is so much to do here at Chiemsee. Most people are ready to party any night of the week.

Often, after work, a few employees and ski patrol get a case of beer from the bar and take it to the game room in the basement. Chip told Lucas about the *luftschutzraum* (air-raid shelter) which is also in the basement. When Chip took him in there, Lucas saw poems and murals on the walls of the shelter, depicting local activity.

The young employees and ski patrol who work and live at Chiemsee are a diversified, close-knit group of athletic, fun-loving people. Some are talented, some are ambitious, but all are having a good time.

The manager, Bob Clarkson, encourages employee activities and barbecues. For these events, Lucas provides most of the food from the kitchen. So far, the list included a whole pig, leg of venison, leg of lamb, hamburgers, hot dogs and steaks.

There are several talented musicians in the group of employees. A young lady, Karen Tyler, originally from Portland, Oregon, came to Chiemsee from Big Sur, California. She plays guitar and sings Joni Mitchell songs. Sometimes, Jeff, a young guitar player, accompanies her. He plays and sings James Taylor songs.

Karen had attended the 1969 Big Sur Celebration, held at the Esalen Institute, and she claimed the event inspired her. It took place a month after the huge music festival at Woodstock. Planners who coordinated the Big Sur event limited ticket sales which only allowed attendance of a few thousand people. Most of the spectators were hippies from California. The musicians included Joni Mitchell and Joan Baez, plus Crosby, Stills, Nash and Young.

This was life in the fast lane, and the days flew by. Lucas and Shelley worked 6 days a week, but always spent their day off together. They would ride their new bikes, play volleyball or tennis, sit and relax by the lake, or read books on the balcony of their apartment. Sometimes, they grilled a chicken on their small hibachi. Other times they went out for dinner to a local Bavarian restaurant.

Together, Lucas and Shelley had fun. Their relationship got more exciting as time passed, and they always found time for passionate lovemaking. One evening during dinner, they talked about things they could do nearby, or within a few hours' drive, and made plans.

On August 12, they will take 3 days off and go to the Austrian Grand Prix. Otto and Bertha are coming from Salzburg and will meet them there. They hope some friends and a few hotel employees will join them and make it a big party. The trip is only 3 weeks away.

On their next day off, they plan to use one of the hotel sailboats. They will sail to Herrenchiemsee, and Shelley will give Lucas a private tour of King Ludwig's unfinished palace on the island.

Although he looked forward to sailing with Shelley and seeing the palace, this plan made Lucas think sadly of Inga and the day she gave him a private tour of Linderhof Castle. It was a reminder; he was still healing from the loss of Inga.

Over all, Lucas firmly believed he was right where he should be.

CHAPTER 37

Herrenchiemsee Palace

Monday was a day off together. Lucas and Shelley stopped by work to check on things. Lucas turned in his grocery orders, and then he fixed 2 box lunches with slices of peppered-beef tenderloin, roasted tomato, Muenster cheese, caramelized onions and roasted red pepper tapenade on Herr Ostler's croissants from the hotel bakery, plus Wieninger beers. It was mid-morning, so they had most of the day to enjoy.

They walked over to the boat dock, and both greeted John Reilly with a combined, "Gruss Gott, John."

"Hello. Are you going sailing today?" he asked.

"We would like to," replied Shelley. "Do you have a sailboat we can use for the whole day?"

"For you two? Yes, of course I do," he replied.

Lucas reached into his backpack, pulled out a Wieninger beer and handed it to John. "Then, have a beer and let's get started."

Shelley was an experienced sailor. Since Lucas never sailed before, she selected a Sailstar 17 Daysailer II, named Candy. She thought it would be the simplest boat for Lucas to learn about sailing. They got in and stored all their gear in a cubby area at the bow of the boat. This left the cockpit clear for them to move around.

Before casting off, Lucas and Shelley put on PFDs (personal floating devices). Next, Shelley explained some sailing terminology and parts of the boat—how to tell the wind direction by checking the wind vane at the top of the mast; how to trim the sail and manage it for best performance; and how to respect the boom, so they do not get knocked in the head.

She described how to steer the boat, "Relative to the wind, we will use different methods. First—we *tack* the boat, sailing into the wind at an angle and turning the bow (front of the boat) through the eye of the wind to one side then the other. Tacking moves the boom and the sail to the opposite side and moves the boat forward on a zig-zag course. Second—we *run* straight downwind with the stern (back of the boat) facing the eye of the wind while the boom and sail stay out to one side. Third—we *reach* downwind and *jibe* (turn) to one side then the other, with the wind at various angles behind the stern. Jibing moves the boom and sail across the boat at great force, as it turns the stern through the eye of the wind, and it allows you to move the boat on a zig-zag course.

"How long will it take from here to the island?" he asked.

"It is about four kilometers to the south side of the island, plus three to the dock on the north point of the island. With this wind, we can make about four knots. It will take us an hour before we dock, so please open a beer for me," she replied.

It was a glorious, sunny day for their adventure on the lake, sailing to Herreninsel Island and touring the Palace of Herrenchiemsee.

While sailing toward the island, Shelley said, "Lucas, I see you brought the *Stars and Stripes* newspaper with you. Is there any news about the Baader-Meinhof Gang?"

"It has information about the three RAF leaders and other members." He read to Shelley, *"Brigitte Mohnhaupt was arrested on June ninth in Berlin, along with Bernhard Braun, a member of the group called the June Two Movement, named for the killing of Benno Ohnesorg. Acting on a tip, police raided the home of Scottish businessman, Iain Macleod, on June twenty-fifth in Stuttgart. When Macleod became hysterical, they shot and killed him, but they were not able to link him with the RAF."*

"This is terrible," he said. "The police must feel spooked, due to the bombings in May. Here is another disturbing article."

"After being caught by police, a new member of the RAF has agreed to provide information about other RAF members."

He added, "When the other members hear this, the new member's life won't be worth much."

"Are all the leaders in the same prison?" she asked.

Lucas looked through the paper, found the prison information and said, "Okay, here it is." He read, *"Andreas Baader is in Schwalmstadt Prison, located between Frankfurt and Hanover. Gudrun Ensslin is at a prison in Essen, north of Düsseldorf and close to the border of Netherlands. Ulrike Meinhof was put in isolation, known as the dead section of Ossendorf Prison. Jan-Carl Raspe and Astrid Proll are in the same prison as Meinhof, but in a separate section. Other members are scattered around: Holger Meins is in Wittlich. Irmgard Möller is in Rastatt. Gerhard Müller is in Hamburg."*

"Do you think they are in different locations because authorities fear other gang members will try to help them escape?" she asked.

"Yes. I think it's a logical conclusion," he replied.

Looking out over the water, he said, "You know, Shelley, this is very relaxing, and the panoramic view is spectacular. I can see why King

Ludwig the Second and Hitler liked it here. I also see why Hitler built the hotel next to this beautiful lake, along the autobahn which took him to his mountain hideaway in Obersalzberg. They both built colossal buildings which survived the war for us to enjoy. It's great!"

"I agree," she said. "Now, let me give you some background about the island, King Ludwig and his palace. Herreninsel Island is where Ludwig built a complex of royal buildings, known as Herrenchiemsee. The palace was his personal sanctuary, a place where he could live his fantasy life in a self-created utopia without anyone around to bother him."

"Building this palace may have been the last straw for the government officials, and it brought his downfall," said Lucas.

Shelley nodded and continued, "In eighteen seventy-one, Wilhelm the First of Prussia, Ludwig's uncle, became the first German Emperor. At the time, the unification of all German states included Prussia and Bavaria. Ludwig dropped out of politics and built more castles because he was no longer active as King of Bavaria. He became so involved in design and construction of the castles, all the architecture, interior decorating and furnishings required his approval. He later admitted he was much too young to be King at eighteen. I think he must have felt unwanted."

Lucas handed Shelley another beer, opened one for himself and asked, "Tell me about Ludwig's childhood. Did he have friends?"

"From what I have read, he had a happy childhood," she replied. "However, Ludwig and his younger brother, Otto, had parents who did not get along with each other, and they didn't take care of their children. During most of his childhood, Ludwig was left to his own world of fantasy at Hohenschwangau Castle near Füssen. King Maximillian the Second, Ludwig's father, reconstructed it from an older, smaller castle. If you've been to Neuschwanstein Castle, then you know the two castles traded names. Originally, the Hohenschwangau Castle was built near the village to replace the Schwanstein Castle at the sight of his family's summer home. Years later, Ludwig built a new castle on the hill above the village and named it New Hohenschwangau Castle. Then, he changed the name to Neuschwanstein Castle. The name changes confuse most tourists."

"Why did Ludwig rename it Neuschwanstein?" he asked.

"The word means New Swan Stone. It was a tribute to Wagner's opera *Lohengrin*," she replied. "Wagner never visited the castle before he died. But Ludwig honored him and decorated many castle rooms in themes of Wagner's operas. Ludwig only spent eleven nights in Neuschwanstein Castle, but those were very happy times for him. I mean, he lived in a fairy-tale castle at one of the most beautiful places in the world.

"As a prince, Ludwig met a Bavarian military officer, named Paul, who became his best friend. They spent time together in Berchtesgaden, but mostly they were in Hohenschwangau, or at Lake Starnberg which is the same lake where Ludwig died. When Ludwig was King, he made Paul his personal aide-de-camp. They rode horses together, read poetry and shared their love of Wagner's operas. Paul was Ludwig's closest friend and confidant. He received the title of Prince Paul from his family of German nobility—The House of Thurn und Taxis. Ludwig called him Faithful Friedrich. Letters between Ludwig and Paul suggested they had a sexual relationship. There were also stories, or rumors, of Ludwig being in homosexual relationships with other young men, including soldiers, construction workers and stable boys."

"How about Ludwig's relationship with Wagner?" he asked.

"When Ludwig was fifteen years old, he saw two of Wagner operas, *Lohengrin* and *Tannhauser.* He became obsessed with Richard Wagner and his works," she replied. "Ludwig's three passions were music, art and architecture. The King built public concert halls and sponsored large music festivals, all to pay tribute to Wagner and his music. Ludwig also built stages in his castles for private performances. He thought he would use his castles as theaters for Wagner's musical dramas. Wagner encouraged and inspired Ludwig's creativity, used in his fantasy world. Ludwig became so obsessed with the operas, he would dress like a character from one of Wagner's operas and go out at night.

"Lucas, you told me you took a tour of Linderhof, so I won't linger on it, but he designed Linderhof to be a secluded retreat. Linderhof was the only castle which Ludwig completed. Hidden in the forest outside of Oberammergau, it was built for one person to live in. The castle only has ten rooms, and four of those rooms were used by servants. Ludwig always dined alone at his special table, but the servants said he talked to fantasy guests like Louis the Fifteenth and Marie Antoinette. In fact, he used her Petit Trianon at Versailles as his model for the Linderhof Castle."

"What was the Petit Trianon?" he asked.

Shelley said, "It was a château on the grounds of the Palace of Versailles, built by King Louis the Fifteenth for his mistress who died before it was completed. Later, it was given to nineteen-year-old Marie Antoinette by her husband, King Louis the Sixteenth. She used it for her personal enjoyment. No one outside her inner circle of friends ever came there; interaction between guests and servants was discouraged. It had a mechanical table, like the ones at Herrenchiemsee Palace and Linderhof Palace. The table would be lowered into the kitchen below the dining room, filled with platters of food, and then raised to the dining room for an intimate dinner, a feast or whatever they did. No servants were allowed in the room when it was occupied."

"Whatever they did was not well-liked by the hungry people on the streets of France," said Lucas.

"Yeah, it didn't work out well for Marie Antoinette," she replied.

"Didn't Wagner have a lot of financial problems and wasn't he exiled from Bavaria?" he asked.

"Yes, but they also inspired each other," she replied. "Ludwig encouraged Wagner and offered financial assistance to help Wagner create his romantic operas. Wagner got exiled twice, not only from Bavaria, but from all of Germany. After he was involved in a failed political revolution in Dresden, Germany, Wagner fled to Switzerland. Governing officials did not allow him back into Germany until Ludwig became Bavarian King. He persuaded Wagner to move to Munich. One year later, Ludwig banished Wagner because of his outlandish lifestyle. Wagner had an affair with conductor Hans van Bulow's wife who was the illegitimate daughter of composer Franz Liszt."

"Boy, this story is getting messy," he said.

Shelley laughed, and then continued, "Wagner had to leave Munich, due to many scandals floating around and based on his political beliefs. Ludwig thought about giving up the throne and leaving with him, but Wagner talked Ludwig out of it. Wagner would have nothing to gain and no financial help if Ludwig was not the ruling King. In the end, Ludwig bought Wagner a villa in Tribschen, Switzerland. He also provided him with an income, so Wagner was comfortable."

"If Ludwig had stepped down, who would be King?" he asked.

"He considered turning the throne over to Otto, his younger brother, who could provide an heir to the throne," she replied. "As it turned out, Otto was crazier than Ludwig, or he appeared to be nutty sooner. Ludwig wrote about his brother; he claimed Otto made weird faces, barked like a dog and did not take off his boots for eight weeks. Whew!"

Suddenly, the boat shifted and Shelley declared, "Okay, we'll dock the boat right over there. We can go to the garden and have our lunch in front of the palace. While we eat, I will try to finish my story about Ludwig, Wagner and Prince Paul."

"Oh yeah, whatever happened to Prince Paul?" he asked.

"I'll tell you during lunch," she replied. "Now, hold on to the line and prepare to step off the boat. Be careful and keep your balance."

At the dock, they secured the boat, grabbed their backpacks and walked along a tree-lined path.

Shelley wore a short blue-and-white dirndl with a low-cut white blouse. Her dark, brunette hair framed her lovely face.

This lady is so sexy, I lust for her constantly, thought Lucas. *I can hardly wait to be back in our apartment this afternoon.*

Being guided by Shelley's firm hand, Lucas walked with her to an intersection of wide promenades, lined with cone-shaped bushes. Since it was the middle of summer, most of the wooden benches were occupied. The tourist season would reach its peak in August. They found an empty bench and sat, facing the palace.

Enjoying a grand view, they ate the gourmet lunch which Lucas had prepared, and Shelley continued her story. "Wagner chased women, he was a gambler and an outspoken political radical. He was also thirty years older than Ludwig. Although Ludwig preferred younger men, Wagner's music was likely the main factor of Ludwig's devotion to the composer. Since he had Ludwig's financial backing, Wagner was able to construct *Festspielhaus,* an opera house dedicated to performance of his operas in Bayreuth. A festival is still held there every year."

"What became of Prince Paul?" he asked.

"When Wagner lived at his villa in Switzerland, Paul became the messenger, between Ludwig and Wagner," she replied. "Paul and Ludwig even stayed at the villa together, using false names. At some point, they had a falling out, Ludwig transferred Paul, and the friendship ended."

"Were there ever any women in Ludwig's life?" he asked.

"He and his cousin, Duchess Elisabeth, were close friends," she said. "They enjoyed the outdoors together and gave poems to each other. Elizabeth's family called her Sissi, but Ludwig called her Dove. She called him Eagle. They spent much time together on Rose Island at Lake Starnberg, between Garmisch and Munich. Elizabeth was eight years older than Ludwig. She married Emperor Franz Joseph of Austria and became Empress Elizabeth at age sixteen. Later, Ludwig was expected to crank out an heir, and he was engaged once to Elizabeth's younger sister, Sophie. Then, he broke it off. Ludwig and Elizabeth remained close friends until his death."

"So, why didn't Ludwig marry *what's-her-name*?" he asked.

"Her name was Duchess Sophie Charlotte," she replied. "Her father had arranged the marriage. They shared a passion for Wagner's music, but Ludwig thought she would not be happy with him. After several postponements, Ludwig broke off the engagement. Much later, love letters surfaced which Sophie wrote to her pre-wedding photographer during her engagement to Ludwig."

"Wagner wrote a marathon opera, correct?" he asked.

"Yes, the opera called *Der Ring des Nibelungen (The Ring Cycle)* is a series of four parts," she replied. "The opening performance was at the first Bayreuth festival. The opera lasted sixteen hours over the course of four nights. It took Wagner twenty-six years to write the lyrics and music. Contributions came from wealthy donors, including King Ludwig the

Second who kept the festival operating through a rough beginning. Now, with a few exceptions and changes, the same play goes on every year at the Bayreuth Festspielhaus."

"Did the festival continue during World War Two?" he asked.

"Yes," she said. "But, during the war it was turned over to the Nazi Party, and Hitler approved many changes to original Wagner sets.

"In the nineteen twenties, Hitler had met Winifred Wagner, and they became friends, due to mutual admiration of Wagner's works. Hitler attended many of Wagner's operas at the festival. Winifred had married Richard Wagner's son, Siegfried, who she met at the Bayreuth Festival. He was eighteen years older than her, and they had four children. Hitler often visited Winifred's home, and her children called him Uncle Wolf. After the failed putsch in Munich, she supported Hitler with amenities, including paper for his book, *Mein Kampf,* while he was in prison. Her husband, Siegfried, was rumored to be a homosexual who did not care what she did. When Siegfried died in nineteen thirty, she kept the festival going. She could have married Hitler. He proposed to her twice, but she turned him down, perhaps because they had opposite views about Jews. They remained close and exchanged letters. Hitler continued to visit her, and she supported Nazis to the end, but never admitted it to the Allies. She referred to Hitler as USA, an acronym for *Unser Seliger Adolf,* meaning Our Blessed Adolf."

"What became of Winifred after the war?" he asked.

Shelley replied, "For her involvement with the Nazi Party, the Allies banned Winifred from working with the festival. Her sons eventually got to manage it. Meanwhile, she remained friends with wives of Nazi officers and assisted ultra-conservative political events, often serving as hostess. Winifred never denounced Hitler. She said he was a kind and gentle person, not like the person he was accused of being. Winifred claimed she never saw his dark side, and he was great with her children. The thing which sealed their friendship was Richard Wagner's music. Winifred now lives in the family villa, named by Wagner. On the front of the villa, there is a plaque, engraved with Wagner's motto: *Hier wo mein Wähnen Frieden fand–Wahnfried–sei dieses Haus von mir benannt* (Here where my delusions have found peace, let this place be named Wahnfried). The name combines the word *wahn* which stands for delusion or madness, plus the word *fried* which stands for peace or freedom. Richard Wagner and his wife, Cosima, are buried in a garden gravesite at The Villa Wahnfried in Bayreuth."

"How do you know all this Bavarian History?" he asked.

"When I was a junior at a high school in Santa Monica, I read about the castles and stories behind them. The history here is the reason I came.

I talk to locals and get different versions of the same story. Then, I try to determine the true story," she replied.

Next, Shelley asked, "Are you ready for your private castle tour?"

"I'm all yours," said Lucas.

They were standing on a wide center walkway, named The Avenue. It extended from the palace with gravel paths running through manicured lawns and sculpted gardens on both sides, all the way back to the open area where they sat and had lunch. From there, it was grass downhill to the canal which ran west and connected to the lake. On the outer edges of the grounds, parallel to The Avenue, rows of lime trees and other trees lined the gravel paths. Behind those were six-foot hedges.

Shelley kept talking as they walked to a large, round pond and fountain, centered in The Avenue. A sculptured grass area, all framed by a low stone border, surrounded the fountain pond.

"This is the Latona Fountain," she said. "You can see the Titan Goddess with Apollo and Diana, her children. According to the fable, she turned the Lycian peasants into frogs after they refused to give her water. You can see frogs at her feet, and there are turtles and alligators on the bottom tier."

The fountain went on, and Lucas said, "Wow! It's spectacular!

Water spouted from the mouths of the frogs toward the statue of Latona with her two children in the center of the pond. Turtles and alligators on the bottom were spraying water away from the center.

"How often is the fountain set off?" he asked.

"Every thirty minutes," she replied.

They continued walking toward the palace, then stopped and looked back to where they began. Besides being grand and beautiful, Lucas noticed how symmetrical these gardens and landscape were.

Turning around and walking toward the palace, he said, "This place looks huge. How many rooms are there?"

"The original plans designated seventy rooms," she replied. "Only twenty rooms were completed."

Shelley led him to the left of The Avenue, and she stopped at another pond. "This is the Fama Fountain with the winged Fama astride a horse, blowing a horn to celebrate a victory over envy, falsehood and hatred. This sculpted work includes mythical figures, climbing on a pyramid of rocks toward the Fama at the top. Water sprays straight up, coming from the winged Fama's horn and from various frogs which are out in the pond, on six piles of rocks which circle the main sculpture."

They walked to a 3rd fountain on the opposite side of The Avenue, and she said, "This is the Fortuna Fountain. The sculpted lady on top is the goddess of good fortune. Look at the cherubs. There are six of those, riding on dolphins in the pond."

Following Shelley up seven steps to the entrance of the palace, he said, "The size of the whole thing is overwhelming."

"Wait until you see the inside!" she exclaimed.

At the top step, Lucas turned around and looked back at the palace grounds. Coming to the entrance, they passed people who were sitting on the steps. Looking out, he saw people sitting under white umbrellas and others wandering around in the garden. A few people were trying to see over the trimmed hedges which were six-feet-high, serving as walls and partitions for different areas of the landscape. As he viewed The Avenue from this position, he could see past the ponds with fountains spraying full-blast, flanked by identical sculptured lawns. Rows of colorful flowers and rose bushes extended out to a wide, tree-lined area of grass which spread toward the canal.

Lucas watched as a colorful, horse-drawn carriage arrived. It seated about a dozen people who all seemed happy to be here.

Standing behind him, Shelley grabbed his hand and said, "See how the palace is hidden by all the big trees? This reflects Ludwig's pursuit of solitude. He didn't want to see the outside world."

"I wonder how they could build all of this here, given it this sits on an island," he said.

"Oh, it was a huge operation to clear the forest land, then level the hills and valleys," she said. "They constructed huts, barracks, dining facilities and various workshops for the workers. Using a steam-powered saw and a steam train, they moved the large amounts of building materials around the grounds. For example, over one million bricks were shipped to this island, based on a construction estimate."

Anxious to take Lucas in the palace, she said, "Let's go inside now. We'll see more of the gardens later."

He followed her through one of the three front entrance ways, into the great Hall of Mirrors.

"We might as well start here," she said. "It's the most impressive room in the palace, and it has a fantastic view of the gardens. This surpasses the original Hall of Mirrors at the Palace of Versailles. The seventeen arched windows are wider than the windows at Versailles, so this space is larger. This hall is ninety-eight meters long, whereas the Versailles' Hall of Mirrors is ninety-two meters long. There are thirty-five chandeliers and forty-four candelabrums, using over two thousand candles which take forty servants about thirty minutes to light. Fresco paintings on the domed ceiling depict battles of the French Military. Those are copies of frescos in Versailles. Busts of Roman emperors are on display in each of the three front halls."

"The parquet floor alone is impressive, but this room is overblown," said Lucas. "It's too much. Being this extravagant, it's beautiful and ugly at the same time."

Shelley nodded and said, "We will go into the State Bedchamber, also called the Parade Bedroom. This room is a shrine to King Louis the Fourteenth. At Versailles, King Louis used the State Bedchamber for his first and last audiences of the day. Ludwig made this room larger and more elaborate. On the walls, velvet tapestries are embroidered with gold thread. Over thirty women spent seven years, completing those tapestries, and their work began long before construction of the palace. The painting over the bed is Apollo, riding the chariot of the sun. This was the first room finished in the palace, but it was never used. It served only as a shrine to Louis the Fourteenth."

Lucas studied the bedchamber: *A gigantic bed dominates this room. The carved bed frame sits below an extravagant bed canopy, made of pinnacles and panels which are gilded in gold. The fabrics, upholstery and tapestries are taupe color, all embroidered in gold. Various shades of blue sky create backgrounds in the ceiling fresco and smaller frescos at the top of the walls around the room. As in most other rooms, the chandelier is huge. This room reminds me of the King's Bedroom at Neuschwanstein Castle. I think was a Neo-Gothic style.*

They stepped outside and stood on a checkerboard floor in a giant courtyard, surrounded on 3 sides by the palace. The open end faced east, toward the lake. This was once the main entrance to the palace.

Shelley took Lucas by the hand and walked back inside through a different door. She said, "This is the State Staircase. It's a replica of the one at Versailles which was destroyed in the mid-seventeen hundreds. Since this was the first room you would enter, coming into the palace from the courtyard, the checkerboard floor continues in here. You can see this room has a glass ceiling with iron frames. Those marble panels are copies of the ones at Versailles, but the ceiling is not."

Lucas stood at the foot of the stairs and looked around with his mouth open. Other tourists did the same. Everyone was in awe of all the glittering gold, carvings, statues and large paintings with gilded frames. Two large chandeliers hung from the iron framework on the ceiling.

"There are fifty chandeliers in the palace," she said.

"A little over done, I'd say. Do you know who those marble statues represent, around the room?" he asked.

"Roman gods and goddesses," said Shelley as she pointed to each one, "There is Apollo, then Diana, Minerva, Ceres and Flora."

“Smart ass—cute ass, too,” he replied.

Shelley laughed, then said, “Okay, let’s go upstairs to the Bodyguard Room.” They followed a Japanese tour group into the room which was decorated in colors of a pale blue and gold.

Lucas first looked at the ceiling and said, “Wow! What is this?”

“This is a fresco of Mars, the God of War, looking over one of his conquests,” she replied. She pointed out another magnificent chandelier and a big fireplace, above which a very large landscape painting hung on the wall. There was no furniture in the room. Hatchet-shaped spears stood in tall holders which were placed along the entire span of the longest wall. “Those spears are called *halberds*.”

They moved on to the first ante-chamber, named the Parade Room. This room had another spectacular chandelier, a ceiling fresco, a big fireplace and paintings. There was also a large ornate cabinet which served as storage for musical instruments. It had decorative panels, all adorned with beautiful, intricate carvings and gilded in gold.

Next was a second anti-chamber, much like the last parade room. After pointing out the fresco on the ceiling, Shelley said, “Lucas, look at those oval windows and lavish decoration on the frieze around the top of the walls. Above the doors, those paintings are of Louis the Fourteenth and his family. This impressive bronze statue is King Louis on horseback.”

She led him back through the State Bedchamber and said, “We have already been in this room, but it is worth seeing twice.” They walked on through, but they had to step around a family of five people who were speaking French and taking photos.

They went into what Shelley called the conference hall. It was known as the Council Chamber. Lucas’ eyes went to a huge portrait of Louis the Fourteenth, hanging behind a large table and a high-back arm chair where the King would conduct business. The table was draped with blue tapestry, embroidered in gold thread. Giant candelabras stood over ten-feet tall on each side of the portrait. All the furnishings were carved with elaborate details. Hints of blue, Ludwig’s favorite color, appeared here and there. This room also had a fresco on the ceiling. A large, gilded chandelier, full of glittering crystals and candles, hung in the center of the room. Around the room, white panels covered the walls and the frieze, displaying various gilded carvings.

“The clock in this room is the largest clock in this palace, and it was actually made for Louis the Fourteenth,” said Shelley. “Each room in the palace has at least one clock. Now, Lucas, I will take you to see Ludwig’s personal bedroom. He slept there even though it was only for nine days.”

They stood inside the doorway of Ludwig’s bedroom, looking at white walls which were covered in gold trims, gilded carvings and ornate decorations. In a very large alcove behind a gold balustrade, an extravagant bed canopy was shaped like a crown and gilded in gold. Royal blue velvet drapery hung from the canopy to the floor on both sides of the bed. The velvet was embroidered in gold thread. In this room, the domed ceiling was white. Carved and gilded figures adorned the base of the ceiling, and a crystal chandelier hung from the center.

"Shelley, what style of decorating is in this room?" he asked.

"This is French Rococo," she said. "Linderhof Castle has this theme. Neuschwanstein Castle has a mixture of styles, including Romanesque, Baroque Revival and Victorian Gothic."

As they were entering the Blue Salon, she said, "Oh, I forgot to tell you about the two secret doors behind the King's bed."

"Secret doors, huh," he replied. "I wonder what those were for."

Shelley chuckled. Then, she continued, "The fireplace mantle is made of Meissen porcelain. The chandelier was supposed to be made of ivory, but it is plaster. The mirrors make the area look larger than it is."

The mirrors were in an alcove where an ornate divan was installed, offering a place to rest. All the mirrors were covered in gilded, sculpted gold carvings and framework. It made Lucas feel a little dizzy.

Wandering into the next room, he said, "Look at the desk!"

"The Writing Room is dedicated to Louis the Fifteenth," she said. "His portrait is on the wall behind the beautiful desk. This desk is a reproduction of one in the study of Louis the Fifteenth at Versailles. It is the most valuable piece of furniture in Herrenchiemsee Palace. Look at the woodwork with unusual patterns on the marquetry floor."

"Did you say marquetry floor? I know what a parquet floor is. What is the difference?" he asked.

"Parquetry is made of blocks or strips of wood which form a geometric design, often containing various types of wood for contrast in the design. Marquetry is a craft of application, adding a veneer design to a smooth surface. It may have other materials in addition to wood," she replied.

Leading him by the hand, she said, "Now let's go see the dining room and the kitchen. Those rooms will finish our tour."

When they entered the King's Dining Room, Lucas stared at the huge chandelier. He said, "I know I've said this about every room we've been in, but this room is too extravagant. I mean, look at the chandelier. I bet there is a story behind it."

Moving to the center of the room, she said, "It's the most expensive chandelier in this palace and the largest Meissen porcelain chandelier in the world. The work is so intricate, especially those little flowers of different colors and those tiny birds."

Below the chandelier, a porcelain vase full of fresh flowers sat in the center of the dining table which was covered with a decorative, mulberry-colored tapestry, embroidered in gold thread. Two beautiful dining chairs had gilded frames which were ornately carved. The chair cushions, upholstered in tapestry, matched the table cover.

"This table works the same as one at Linderhof Palace," she said. "It was ideal for Ludwig's personality, being a shy reclusive. Although he enjoyed riding or walking in the countryside where he spoke to the farmers and workers, he didn't want to see servants during his meals. So, Ludwig had this built with an apparatus which lowered the table into the kitchen. The staff set the table with all the food and beverages, then sent it back to the King's Dining Room for Ludwig to enjoy his solitude. We will see the mechanism when we go into the kitchen. The table is called a *Tischlein deck dich*, meaning table set yourself, or wheels on meals, or something like it."

"Why is this dining room oval shaped?" he asked.

"It is fashioned after the famous Hotel de Soubise in Paris," she said. "Those busts are of prominent ladies of the court: Countess du Barry, Marquise de Pompadour, and the Duchesse de Lavallière who was a mistress of King Louis the Sixteenth. Behavior in those days was similar the current hippie movement, everyone sleeping with everyone."

"For sure, but it's without this luxury in today's world," he replied.

"Hotel de Soubise is now a French history museum," she added.

They walked next door to the Small Gallery, a very small version of the larger Hall of Mirrors. She said, "This gallery connects the King's private staircase to his private apartments which we have seen."

Shelley walked to an open doorway and motioned for Lucas to come over and look. From the doorway, she described the King's bathroom, "The self-flushing toilet is something which the Palace of Versailles did not have. This palace has running water and a central heating system which heats this elaborate swimming-pool-sized bathtub."

"I wonder if Ludwig ever got to use the tub," he said.

"Ludwig was a good swimmer, but at the end of his life, he was fat. So, maybe he needed a large, round pool-tub," she replied.

There were murals in this bathroom. On the ceiling mural, men appeared to be working in the clouds. The murals on the wall depicted women, bathing and playing in the water under the clouds. The room was bright with sunshine, coming in through big arched windows.

Downstairs, they entered the large kitchen area, and Lucas said, "Okay, here it is. I could live with this."

Lucas studied the room: *This kitchen is much smaller than the one at Neuschwanstein Castle, but it is similar in design and basic layout. It has the huge marble pillars which support a vaulted ceiling, consisting of numerous arched sections. It also has a big rotisserie with a spit, a large stove and ovens, plenty of prep space, granite counters and lots of copper cookware. Here, the big difference is the mechanism which lifted and lowered the table, moving it to and from the King's Dining Room, one floor above. The device appears to be modern, not what I expected to see from the nineteenth century.*

"At the far end of the kitchen, you see a large, round table and matching chairs," she said. "Those wooden pieces were all carved by hand for the staff and special guests to use."

"The elevator device which raises the table looks out of place," said Lucas. "It seems too modern for Ludwig's time period."

"Yes. I agree," she said. "Ludwig the Second was the first to use electricity in Bavaria. Steam engines generated electricity for modern venting and heating in each building. Over four thousand people did construction at this palace before they ran out of money."

Finally, they went back upstairs, found their way to the Hall of Mirrors, and went outside into the sunshine and beauty of the garden. Holding hands, Lucas led Shelley to a bench under a tree. They were secluded and away from the view of others. He pulled out his hash pipe, and they took a few minutes to relax before walking back to the dock. They still must sail over to the mainland.

"Thank you for the private tour, Shelley. I feel honored to walk with you, the sexiest and most beautiful tour guide," said Lucas.

"Thank you," she replied. "Most of the tour guides are age sixty or older, and they have done tours here since the park opened."

"What can you tell me about Ludwig's death?" he asked. "I have heard stories, but each one was somewhat of a mystery."

Shelley grabbed Lucas' hand and said, "Let's start back to the boat, and I'll tell you what I've heard or read about it."

As they began their stroll along the tree-lined path, going toward the boat dock, she talked about Ludwig's death. "King Ludwig the Second died at Lake Starnberg on June thirteenth in eighteen eighty-six. There are several versions of what happened at the lake. Five days earlier, Bavarian Ministers had Ludwig declared insane and incompetent to rule. Then, they titled his uncle to replace him. On June twelfth, Ludwig was taken to Castle Berg where he was held under strict supervision. With bars on the windows of his room and no door handles, he was a virtual prisoner at Castle Berg. The next day, June thirteenth, Ludwig went for a walk, accompanied by two aides and Dr. Gudden, a psychiatrist. Around six p.m., Dr. Gudden told the aides to return to the castle, following Ludwig's request. The doctor claimed he and Ludwig would be fine by themselves.

When Ludwig and the doctor did not return by eight p.m., a search began for them."

"Shelley, wasn't the psychiatrist one of the doctors who had declared Ludwig insane?" he asked.

"Yes," she replied. "He and three other doctors, but none of them had examined the King in person. They declared written documentation was enough evidence to prove his mental condition.

"Now, here is what I find mind-boggling about what happened at Lake Starnberg: When Ludwig and the doctor did not return by eight p.m., the entire castle staff searched for two hours, looking everywhere for them. Both were found dead, and their bodies were floating in waist-deep water. The doctor's body showed signs of being beaten and strangled, but a report said he drowned. The report also said Ludwig drowned while committing suicide, but the report conflicted itself. When the official report was released, it claimed Ludwig had no water in his lungs, yet the doctor did have water in his lungs. Based on such evidence, I would think of different scenarios for what happened."

"I can imagine Ludwig was pissed at the doctor for what he did. He could have beaten the doctor, choked him and drowned him, but it seems out of character for a shy, homosexual dreamer," said Lucas.

"There were witnesses," she replied. "They became known after the King's death. However, the Bavarian Ministers and other officials forced the witnesses to swear an oath with their hands on a crucifix and a bible, never to tell anyone what they saw."

"So, nobody came forward and told what happened?" he asked.

"One witness was Ludwig's personal fisherman," she replied. "He did not come forward while he was alive, but he left notes. In those notes, he claimed to be hiding in the woods, waiting to go get the King and take him out on the lake to meet some followers who would help him escape in a larger boat. According to the fisherman, the King got shot as he stepped into the fisherman's boat, but the autopsy reported no scars or wounds on the King's body. There is another story which gives the gunshot theory more detail. In the home of a local countess while having an afternoon tea, the countess showed her guests a coat which she claimed the King was wearing when he died. There were two bullet holes in the back of the coat."

"Why did she have possession of the King's coat?" he asked.

"The countess had worked as an accountant for his family—The House of Wittelsbach," she replied.

"There was also a story about a painting of Ludwig's dead body, made within hours of his death," she said. "In the painting, blood flowed from the King's mouth which could not happen if he had drowned."

Lucas speculated, "Maybe the doctor tried to stop the escape, they fought, and the doctor drowned. But, what about the King?"

"As the fisherman described it, Ludwig fought off the doctor, and he got shot by someone else," she replied. "Since none of the witnesses ever came forward, and only the fisherman's notes were left behind, the so-called experts say it will never be known how King Ludwig died unless his body is exhumed and examined by modern methods. So far, the Wittelsbach clan will not allow it."

"Did they have a funeral and bury him in Bavaria?" he asked.

"There was an elaborate funeral," she replied. "His body laid in state at the royal chapel of Berg Palace in Munich. They dressed the King in formal attire of the Order of Saint Hubert since he was the Grand Master of Bavaria. His remains are entombed in the crypt of St Michaels Church in Munich—except for his heart. It was placed in a silver urn on display in a chapel next to the hearts of his father and grandfather. The chapel is in the town of Altötting, a one-hour drive north of here.

"Now, I must tell you the heart story of Louis the Fourteenth. Grave robbers stole the Sun King's heart, and it was eventually sold to the Dean of Westminster. When the dean died, the heart was inherited by his son who wound up eating it. Pretty gruesome, huh?"

"It's disgusting," said Lucas.

When they got back to Candy, the sailboat, they got settled in. Lucas opened two Wieninger beers and handed one to Shelley.

Sitting side by side, Lucas looked at her, admiring how sexy she looked in her dirndl, and said, "We've not made love in a boat yet."

She said, "I've not been with you in a boat before."

"You know, Shelley, it's very secluded here with all the bushes and trees around us," he said.

Shelley looked at him and said, "You're kidding, right?"

Lucas moved to the front of the cockpit where he laid out his seat cushion and said, "Why don't you come find out if I'm kidding?"

She shrugged, tilted her head and smiled. Then, she handed him her seat cushion and their PFDs for cushions, and she took off her dirndl.

After rocking the boat with some passionate lovemaking, they both dozed off for about an hour.

When Shelly woke up, she was alarmed. Poking at Lucas, she said, "We have to get going! Look at those dark clouds on the horizon. Sometimes, there are bad thunder storms here in the afternoons. I hope we can make it back before the storm arrives. Let's move it!"

CHAPTER 38
After the Storm

Lucas was not much help with sailing the boat, but Shelley did not need help—until the storm caught up with them, and they got tossed around. Suddenly, a powerboat appeared to assist them. John Reilly drove the rescue boat close enough for Chip to toss them a line. Lucas caught it and tied it to the front of the sailboat. Shelley released the mainsail, lowered it and secured the boom.

John yelled to them, "We knew the storm was coming, so we thought we had better come find you."

"How embarrassing!" Shelley hollered.

John yelled back, "We won't tell anybody."

It was a rough ride with thunder and lightning above them while the sailboat was being towed. So, Lucas and Shelley sat low on the floor of the cockpit, holding on to the boat and each other.

When the boats got back to the mainland, Shelley exclaimed, "Lucas, look! John said they wouldn't tell anyone; but it looks like the entire hotel staff plus ski patrol are standing on shore, watching us!"

With both boats secured at the dock, Lucas, Shelley, Chip and John went across the street to the Ranch House. Topo and Gabrielle lived in the 1st floor apartment, and they were passing out Wieninger beers. Everyone was now in their front yard, greeting Lucas and Shelley with cheers, plus some catcalls for not getting back before the storm hit.

Topo handed them each a beer and said, "Here, have a Wieninger. We get it delivered to our door once a week, and it's cheap too."

"Thanks for the beer, Topo. I guess the party is on," said Chip.

Then, Chip turned to face Lucas and Shelley. He said, "Lucas, I think we are even now."

"Thanks for the rescue. I am new to sailing," replied Lucas.

"What does Chip mean, '… we are even now'?" asked Shelley.

"Lucas rescued John and me near Berchtesgaden after we ran off the road, coming from the Rossfeld," explained Chip. "Anyway, I am glad we could help. It was Bob Clarkson's idea. He said we couldn't afford to lose both our head housekeeper and our head chef in the middle of the summer, right before the Olympics start in Munich."

Chip and John went over by the dock to talk with some females.

Gabrielle had RAF news. Topo said, "Let's go inside. I don't want to be associated with terrorists. Drug dealers… okay, terrorists… no!"

Laughing, they went in the apartment. Sitting at the kitchen table, Topo crumbled some hashish and loaded a glass bong. He said, "This is great Sativa hashish. It's called Colombian Black."

Topo handed the bong to Lucas and lit it for him.

"Hey, how about some music?" asked Gabrielle.

"We have a brand-new album, by David Bowie, *The Rise and Fall of Ziggy Stardust and the Spiders from Mars*," said Topo.

"What is his album about?" asked Lucas.

"I don't know," replied Topo. "But, it's a funny title for an album."

Gabrielle pushed in a tape and said, "Instead of David Bowie's music, I'm playing my current favorite cassette, *Sticky Fingers,* by the Rolling Stones. Everyone passed around the bong while Gabrielle handed out beers and poured shots of Jägermeister."

"If it's a cassette, we don't get to see the record cover with a guy in tight jeans," said Shelley. "People think it is Mick Jagger's crotch."

"I read about *Sticky Fingers.* Andy Warhol designed the cover, but he won't say who the model was," said Topo. "Whoever it was, when you unzip the jeans on the cover, you will see his underwear."

"I love two of the songs on this album: 'Wild Horses' and 'Brown Sugar.' I hope their next album is this good," said Gabrielle.

"The store clerk told us the Rolling Stones are in France, working on a new album at Keith Richard's villa which is close to Nice. The stories coming out of there are not so flattering," said Topo. "Keith Richard is shooting heroin while people and drugs are flowing in and out of the villa. So, work on the album is going very slow."

"Topo, what did you call this hashish?" asked Shelley.

"Colombian Black Sativa," he replied. "It is excellent, but different from the common Afghanistan Indica."

"Okay, you've lost me," she said.

"All right," said Topo. "I'll give you a quick course in cannabis, sometimes called pot, weed, grass, ganga, dope, herb, reefer, Mary Jane or just plain bud. There are two types of marijuana which produce the 'high' from smoking or ingesting it. Sativa cannabis is grown in tropical climates, mostly in countries near the equator: Colombia, Mexico, Thailand and Southeast Asia. Indica cannabis is grown in Turkey, Morocco, along the foot of the Himalayas and in the Hindu Kush mountain range which runs through Afghanistan and Pakistan."

"What's the difference in marijuana and hashish?" she asked.

"Marijuana is a dried mixture of flowers, leaves and small stems of cannabis, whereas hashish is a paste made from the resin of female flowers," he replied. "Male plants are only used to provide pollen for female plants to make seeds, and then male plants are separated from female plants. The little hairs, growing at the tops of female flowers, are called trichomes, the most potent part of the plant."

"How do you know all of this stuff, Topo?" she asked.

"This is my business, so I do my homework," he replied.

Then, he explained, "Having smoked pot since I was eight years old, I became familiar with the stages of marijuana and hashish production. As an adult, I traveled to pot farms and processing plants in Morocco and all-over South America, looking to find the best products."

"In California, everybody smokes marijuana, but here in Europe, most people smoke hashish. Do you know why?" she asked.

"I only deal in hashish because I sometimes cross a border. It is much easier to conceal," said Topo. "Hashish can be up to four times as strong as marijuana, so you don't have to smoke or consume as much. A kilo (1,000 grams) of weed can turn out ten grams of hashish."

"How do they separate little hairs from the plant?" asked Lucas.

"You ask a good question," said Topo. "In Morocco and other North African countries, hashish is made by pounding mature buds, then sifting the crushed buds through a series of sieves to make a powder. The powder gets heated until the resins melt. The resins are cooled, compressed into blocks and sealed."

"Do they harvest a certain time of the year?" asked Lucas.

"They harvest around September and October," he replied. "Then, they dry the buds and wait for cool weather when it is easier to separate the trichomes (hairs) from the flowers. In Morocco, they also smoke hashish mixed with tobacco which is called *Kif.* Moroccan women never smoke hashish by itself."

Shelley took a long hit on the bong and passed it on. As the bong went around again, she blew out the smoke and said, "Wimps."

Topo laughed, and he continued, "In India, people make hashish by rubbing the resinous tops of the plant, using the hands or a leather apron, until the resins stick together. They scrape the resins off the skin or leather, roll it into lumps of various sizes and compress it into blocks. In a place called Tosh Village at the base of the Himalayas, the locals are famous for Tosh Ball Hashish, made by rubbing the trichomes in their hands until it forms a ball."

"Whew, good stuff, Topo. Can I buy an ounce?" asked Lucas.

"Yes, you can," he replied. "Remind me before you leave tonight. When I first got this batch of hashish, I took two hits and went to work. Then, it took three beers to settle me down before I could wait on any tables." They all cracked up—laughing and giggling for what must have been 5 minutes. It was a continuous sound of humor.

Still laughing, Lucas wiped tears from his eyes, composed himself and said, "Topo, get out the darts. I can't sit still any longer."

Topo liked to use heavy darts, made of brass and real feathers. Lucas liked plastic darts with steel tips which came with most dartboards. People always laughed at Lucas until he out-scored them. Topo's fancy brass darts had red turkey feathers, and Lucas' cheap darts had orange-colored plastic shafts and flights.

They threw one dart each to see who goes first for a game of cricket. Topo edged out Lucas, by hitting closer to the bullseye. Then, Topo got one 20, Lucas got one 20, and Topo got another 20. Next, Lucas got one 20 and one double 20 which made 20 points. While Topo closed his 20's with a triple, Lucas watched Shelley and Gabrielle rummage in the refrigerator for something to eat. Not paying attention to Topo's last throw, Lucas threw a double 20, plus one 20.

Before he could write it on the chalkboard, he heard Topo say, "Nice darts Lucas, but I already closed twenties."

Lucas chuckled. Turning to Topo, he said, "This sure is good dope!"

Next, Topo tossed one 18 and added another 18.

Lucas stopped playing to drink his beer and check out the food which the ladies had placed on the dining room table. He asked, "Hey, do I see poached trout?"

"I caught those trout this morning at the river in Bernau, a fifteen-minute walk from here," replied Topo.

"Those are good size. Do you need a license to fish here?" asked Lucas.

"After I caught four trout, I heard someone chopping wood nearby. Then, I wondered what the penalty might be for poaching," replied Topo. "I headed home, looking over my shoulder, in case some farmer had a shotgun. When I asked Gunther, the bartender, if he knew who owns the land, he said most of the land along the river is private and owned by farmers. I don't think I will go back there."

"What other delights do you have for us to eat?" asked Lucas.

Gabrielle replied, "We have smoked salmon, Schwarzbrot (German black bread), and in this *dampfkochtopf* (pressure cooker), we have Carbonada Criolla. It's an Argentinean beef stew, made with onions, peppers, stewed tomatoes, sweet potatoes, white potatoes, winter squash, dried apricots and beef. I made cornbread which goes great with the stew. However, we have nothing sweet for dessert."

Lucas threw two 18's and said, "Dessert? We may have to raid the hotel kitchen tonight."

Next, Topo tossed two 19's and stopped to take a drink of beer.

"Okay, Topo," said Shelley. "You mentioned Black Colombian hashish and Afghanistan… something. What is the difference?"

Lucas watched Topo step away from the black tape on the floor which marked the throwing line. He thought: *This will be a long dart game*. Then, he lit the bong and passed it around.

"Sativa plants are tall, loosely branched with long, narrow leaves. Most of the plants are grown outdoors, and some reach heights of twenty feet," said Topo. "Indica plants are short, densely branched with wider leaves. Besides the difference in physical appearance, the effects of Indica and Sativa are different for each user."

"What do you mean by different effects?" asked Shelley.

"Hashish made from Sativa gives you a light, mental effect—it's known to be a creative and energetic herb, whereas Indica will give you a heavier, more 'stoned' effect," he replied.

"Okay, pot and hashish both give you the munchies and enhance sexual experience," she said. "What else are they good for?"

"Sativa cannabis gives you a cerebral and stimulating high," he replied. "It's thought provoking, energizing and euphoric with feelings of well-being and happiness. It also promotes creativity, increases your focus, and boosts your imagination as well as your sex life. Remember, marijuana and hashish affect your brain which is the most important sex organ in your body."

Looking at Lucas, Shelley said, "Where have I heard that before?"

"Speaking only for myself, I think smoking hashish or marijuana makes everything better," said Lucas. "Music sounds better, food tastes better, and it helps me stay focused to experience life as it happens. I believe it expands my mind, increases my creativity, keeps me mellow, and my concentration is better. Sativa seems to give me a lift and more energy even if it only masks the fatigue. What I know for sure is I have liked pot since my first hit."

"You both describe it as if it's a wonder drug. Maybe I should buy an ounce for myself," said Shelley.

"No need," Lucas replied. He turned to Topo, "I'll buy two ounces if you have it. I might want to make hash brownies and take those to the Austrian Grand Prix. We hope you and Gabrielle will join us on the trip. We leave on August twelfth. Anyone else who can get off for three days is also welcome to come along."

"Putting it in food should be a safe way to take dope across the border," said Topo. "The guards will think it's a cake."

"I only hope they don't ask for a piece," said Lucas.

Everyone laughed, as Topo and Lucas turned back to their dart game, playing cricket.

Lucas got a triple 18 for a total of 56 points. They each threw a 19, then Topo threw two 19's for 38 points. Lucas came back with two more 18's, giving him a total of 92 points and the lead.

"This Sativa hashish is great, Topo. What do you tell people who worry about getting paranoid?" asked Shelley.

"Lucas, you have been smoking pot for what? Five years? What is your overall experience with it?" asked Topo.

Remembering he answered this question before, he said, "I don't think of it as paranoia, I think it as being more careful. For myself, I try to stick with Sativa because I'm an active person, and I consider sleep a waste of time, anyway. If I had to describe my overall experience with marijuana and hashish, I would say it ranges between ecstasy and panic."

Everyone laughed again.

Topo said, "I love the whole experience of pot, and I enjoy turning other people on to it. It makes me money, and it allows me to share one of my great pleasures in life. When I smoke dope, it opens my mind. Also, there is no evidence of any deaths, directly related to marijuana use. If you stop using, there are no symptoms of withdrawal.

"Some people feel better when they smoke it. I'm one of those people, and I think Lucas is too. Sometimes, when I first smoked pot, I got paranoid. Now, I remember it is a temporary feeling and let it pass, so I can enjoy the experience."

Looking at Topo, Lucas said, "I believe it's your turn."

Topo tossed one 19 and one 16 for a total of 57 points. Lucas threw another 18 for 110 points, and Topo got two 16's. Lucas got one 18 for 128 points, and one 16. They each got one 16, making the score 128 for Lucas and 73 for Topo.

Lucas grabbed 2 more beers and handed 1 to Topo. Then, he asked, "Gabrielle, do you have any news about the RAF?"

"As of June fifteenth, the day Ulrike Meinhof got captured, all leaders of the RAF are in the custody of law enforcement," she replied. "I have a feeling they were intentional in bringing it to an end, based on their aggressive actions in May. My mother sent me a copy of the *Hanover Zeitung* newspaper which has a long article about the RAF. It shows a detailed timeline of their exploits, up to the dates when their leaders got captured. It also mentions my brother Horst."

"How did their *revolution* get started? And what did they hope to accomplish, bombing buildings and robbing banks?" asked Shelley.

Lucas answered her question, "In the late sixties, they linked with German college students and sympathizers to follow the most radical principles of a protest movement. RAF members believe the West German Government is full of fascists who came from the Nazi period. They also condemn the United States as an imperialist power."

"I agree with Lucas. Their original goal was to set off a militant revolution and force a government response," said Gabrielle. "As Shelley mentioned, they were robbing banks, stealing vehicles and blowing things up. At first, they only used guns when they were attacked or fired upon. As time passed, they became more aggressive, and I think May was the turning point.

"According to the *Zeitung* article, between May eleventh and May twenty-fourth, the RAF set off at least ten bombs in different areas of Germany; seventeen U.S. military personnel got killed, and several got wounded. It also listed five West German police officers and at least twenty civilians who got injured."

"They got everybody's attention," said Lucas. "But I think most of the sympathy and support which they had received from the younger German population ended when the RAF attacked the U.S. Military and killed innocent people in Germany. I'd bet the U.S. put pressure on the German government to stop the attacks."

"I think the police were getting nervous before May," said Gabrielle, "and it affected their behavior. Last October for example, a Hamburg police officer got killed during a shoot-out with Gerhard Muller and Irmgard Moller. Another incident happened in Tubingen, a scenic university town where one third of the residents are students; police shot and killed Richard Epple, a seventeen-year-old student who was trying to drive away from police because he did not have a driver's license. The police shot him with a machine gun."

"Yeah. A few weeks ago, I read the police busted into a Scottish businessman's apartment in Stuttgart. When he became frightened and started screaming, police shot and killed him, thinking he was an RAF member," said Lucas.

"I also read about the man in Stuttgart, and there was no evidence of him being involved with terrorists," said Gabrielle. "However, I can understand the police being spooked and their need to be careful when they make a traffic stop. Right after the first of last year, Andreas got pulled over in Cologne, driving a BMW Two Thousand. The cop did not know who he had stopped, but he knew the RAF's reputation for stealing BMWs. The cop aimed his gun at Andreas when he asked for vehicle registration. Andreas reached in the glove box, pulled a gun, fired one shot and escaped. No one got injured which was fortunate."

"Speaking of Andreas, he looked cool in the photo, still wearing his sunglasses after they pulled him from the building," said Lucas. "I always thought the three leaders had charisma together. Before it got out of control in May, they appeared to be reckless outlaws, and the public romanticized them for some reason. Ulrike could have had her own following, through her journalism, but she did not seem to be a leader."

Topo picked up his darts and tossed two 16's for 105 to Lucas' 128. However, Lucas threw a triple 18 for 182 to 105. Topo came back with two 16's for 137 to 182. Lucas got 1 more 18 for a 200 to 137 advantage. Topo closed out 18's, and Lucas closed out 16's. Then, they stopped to get more beer. Next, Topo got one 15 and Lucas pitched three 17's.

Gabrielle said, "The newspaper article offered details about all the Red Army Faction attacks which included multiple bombings, bank robberies and some kidnappings."

"I wonder if they had planned anything to disrupt the Olympics next month in Munich," said Topo.

"Are you going to see any of the Olympics events?" asked Lucas.

"I don't know what Olympic event I would want to see. But I would like to go to the Oktoberfest this year," said Gabrielle.

"Well, before those events begin, we can look forward to seeing the Austrian Grand Prix," said Lucas.

The partiers outside were getting louder all the time. Hearing the noise, Shelley asked, "Where is Gretchen?"

"She's outside, having a ball, playing and showing off," said Topo. "Gretchen is the smartest dog I've ever been around. When she wants to join us in bed, she stands on her hind legs at the side of the bed until one of us invites her up."

"Yorkies are the cutest dogs of all," said Shelley, "and Gretchen is about as loveable as Lucas."

Everyone said, "Awwwww." Then, they all laughed.

"Shelley and I will see what's going on outside," said Gabrielle.

"Okay, we'll be out as soon as I take care of Lucas, here," Topo replied. Lucas watched Topo throw one 17. Then, Lucas got one 15, and Topo tossed a triple 15, plus one more 15 for 30 points. It was 167 to 200. Lucas came right back with two 17's for a 234 to 167 edge. Topo fired a 15 to make the score 182 to 234. Then Lucas threw a 17 and had a 251 to 182 upper hand. Topo pitched in two 15's for a total of 212 to 251. Lucas came back with a 17 for 268 to 212.

With the ladies outside now, Lucas and Topo were really focused on their game. Topo only threw one 17 and Lucas tossed two 17's for a 302 to 212 margin. Topo came through with a triple 15 for 257 points, but Lucas came back with 2 more 17's for 336. Topo closed out 17's on his first throw, but he missed two bullseye attempts. Lucas then closed out 15's and threw a double 19, closing those. The only thing left to throw was 3 bulls for the win. Topo made one bull. Then, Lucas tossed one bull. Topo missed his next three tries, and Lucas finished the game with two bulls for a 336 to 257 win.

They shook hands, shared a bong of Colombian Black, grabbed some Wieninger beers and headed out to join the party. A smaller crowd was still rollicking outside. Several people had gone to the hotel bar.

Chip and John suggested they get another case of beer from the bar, and all go to the game room.

"Great idea. How about a game of cricket?" Lucas asked, knowing he and Topo were already warmed up.

During the height of summer, the hotel was always busy, even at midweek. This meant the bar was packed. Tonight, a local rock band played in the dining room. Center tables had been moved to make a dance floor area in front of the stage.

Until ski patrol and civilian employees came in from the street, there were only a few couples dancing. As the high-spirited locals rocked out, the band picked up its pace. At first, the hotel guests, including military people, did not know what to do about the crowd of partiers who invaded the dining room. After they saw the young locals laughing and having so much fun, everyone joined in.

Lucas, Shelley, Topo and Gabrielle danced to two popular rock songs. The young band did a good job, playing the Eagles' song "Take it Easy" and the Rolling Stones' "Brown Sugar." There were no empty chairs in the room, so Lucas and the other 3 headed toward the bar.

They edged their way through the crowd to a door on the left side of the bar, and they went downstairs. The game room was busy, but not too crowded. Most hotel guests were not aware of the game room. Employees had claimed it for their own use, so it was not advertised to hotel guests. At least, not by any of them.

Chip and John were playing darts. When they saw Lucas and Topo, they waived them over and challenged them to a game.

"How about a game of cricket?" Topo asked.

Looking at Shelley, Lucas shrugged as if to say, *"Is it okay?"*

"Go ahead," said Shelley. "It appears you have a little rivalry here. Gabrielle and I will see if we can play a game of pool. When I was in Santa Monica, I played a lot of pool."

Lucas had not planned on spending 4 hours there. However, the group chose to hold a small round robin tournament with co-ed teams competing against each other. The winners would get a case of beer. It was the best way to get everyone involved.

They all got together and agreed on a format for their tournament: Every team would play 1 match at every sport. The tournament would include 301 Darts, Table Tennis, Foosball and 8-Ball Pool. The team with the most wins would get the beer. In case of a tie, there would be a playoff to determine the winning team.

There were 4 couples who wanted to play. Other people went back to the bar. Everyone laughed and had fun as they moved around the room, playing different matches. Lucas and Shelley started out against John and Gayle, the cute brunette waitress. Chip played with Rosie, the talkative, perky Scottish gal who worked as a maid.

When he worked at NATO Officers Club, Lucas played foosball daily. Tonight, he was feeling it, no matter which game he played. His concentration was great, and Shelley was right there with him. They won easily, playing against the other couples, until they lost to John Reilly and Gayle at 8-Ball Pool.

Finally, John and Gayle won the tournament, best 2 out of 3 games in 8-Ball Pool against Topo and Gabrielle.

After the tournament, everybody was drinking their beer and talking. Chip challenged Lucas to a game of Table Tennis. They agreed on playing to 21 points, and they had to win by 2 points.

When Lucas eked out a win, 27 to 25, Chip told him, "I'll see you on the tennis court." They both laughed, but the competitive spirit between them was obvious.

The ladies showed the same spirit. Shelley and Gayle seemed to be well-matched in athletic ability. All the ladies were coordinated, but Shelley and Gayle were a notch above, at least in these bar games.

It was 3 a.m. when they finished the mini-tournament, and everyone wanted to raid the kitchen. Lucas, being head chef with the keys to get in, led the way. When they got to the kitchen, Heinz Ostler, the pastry chef, came out of the bakery to see what was going on.

When Herr Ostler noticed they were all a little messed up, he said, "Sinnlos betrunken." Then, he went back into the bakery.

Looking at Gabrielle, Lucas asked, "What did he say?"

"It means something like hopelessly drunk," she replied.

Everyone laughed and followed Lucas to the walk-in refrigerator.

For a few minutes, Lucas looked around in the refrigerator while the others were standing outside the door, trying to look in. Topo held the plastic strips in place across the doorway to keep cold air inside.

"Okay. Have you all had a Reuben sandwich?" asked Lucas.

Everyone said, "Yes," except Topo, Gabrielle and Rosie.

"Gabrielle, please ask Herr Ostler if he wants to join us," said Lucas. She agreed and went to the bakery.

Lucas grabbed things and handed them to whoever would take them and put them on the kitchen work table.

After he set up his *mis en place* (things in place). Lucas announced, "Everyone must have a beer with this sandwich."

John and Chip went to the employees' beer-vending machine. When they got back, Lucas had assembled the sandwiches, and he was putting them on the flat grill to toast the bread. While John and Chip passed beers around, Lucas explained what made these sandwiches different.

"The original Rueben sandwich is made with corned beef, Swiss cheese, sauerkraut and Russian dressing, grilled between slices of rye bread," said Lucas. "For this German-style Reuben, I used corned beef and Russian dressing with Tilsiter cheese, our own Bavarian sauerkraut, sliced pickle and pumpernickel bread."

"Russian dressing is different from thousand island?" asked Shelley.

"Yes," replied Lucas. "Russian dressing is made with mayonnaise, ketchup, Worcestershire sauce, a little horseradish, fresh cracked and cayenne peppers. Thousand island dressing is made with mayonnaise, ketchup, garlic, chili sauce, minced onion, sweet pickle relish, grated hard-boiled egg and ground pepper."

As Lucas was cutting the sandwiches, Herr Ostler and Gabrielle came in. She carried dessert plates, and Ostler set a chocolate cake on the table. Gabrielle described it as a *Schokolade Himbeertorte*, made with Guylian Chocolate, chocolate ganache and homemade raspberry jam. Everyone oohed and aahed over the beautiful cake.

Chip handed Herr Ostler a Wieninger beer, then he smiled, raised his beer above his head and said, "Prost." Everyone repeated, "Prost," and they all stood around the work table, eating, drinking and laughing about what a long eventful day, night and now morning it had been.

When they finished cleaning and had everything put away, the kitchen door opened.

In walked CID Officer Robinson. He asked, abruptly, "What are you guys doing here? This kitchen is supposed to be closed."

"It's an early staff meeting to plan a future event," said Lucas.

"At four o'clock in the morning?" asked Robinson.

"We are all too busy during the day, so we have to make the time when we can," replied Lucas.

Robinson looked sideways at Lucas, but he let it go. Then, he said, "While I have you all here, I want information. A man who came from the U.S. is looking for his brother. I know about Gary's connection with Bruno, but does anyone else know Bruno Castignoli, where he might be, where he was going, or anything about him?"

Since no one answered Robinson, Lucas spoke up. “Did you say Bruno’s brother is here?”.

“Yes,” said Robinson. “When I first saw him, I thought it was Bruno, but I learned he is Bruno’s brother. His name is Enrico Castignoli, and he came here from Long Island, New York.

“There is one more issue. You should advise all employees and staff to keep an eye out for anything suspicious. The military is on alert. We expect the RAF to retaliate for the capture of their leaders.”

Then, Robinson went out the way he came in.

John looked at Lucas and said, “Let me guess—you and the CID guy are not best friends.”

“We’ve had our differences in the past year,” he replied.

“I heard you broke his arm at ‘The Hof’ in B’gaden,” said Chip.

“Yeah, I didn’t mean to hurt him,” said Lucas. “He was drunk and obnoxious, so I guess I overreacted. Lately, he seems to have backed off. I think military police are busy, worrying about the terrorists.”

As everyone was leaving, Lucas thought about Enrico: *He must be the guy I saw at Hintertux Glacier when Shelley and I were in the lodge, eating lunch. I must talk to the other four about this.*

CHAPTER 39

Chiemsee Bakery

Since the hotel was booked solid, Bob Clarkson was hesitant to let Lucas and Shelley leave on August 12th to attend the Austrian Grand Prix for three days, but they promised to leave their departments in good shape. They really wanted to get away; both knew the hotel must have smooth operations during their absence.

They also agreed to work for 2 weeks without a day off, upon their return from Austria. The Summer Olympics would begin at the end of August in Munich which is close to Chiemsee.

Lucas called his friends in Garmisch to see if they could attend the Grand Prix. He hoped Eric, Sabine and Sonya would come to the race. He knew they would have fun, but he also wanted them all to be on the same page, just in case Enrico or the police came around to ask more questions about Bruno's disappearance. When Lucas spoke with Eric, he learned Enrico was all over Bavaria, asking if anyone had seen his brother.

The hotel and kitchen were busy, so days went by fast. During most of their afternoon breaks, Lucas played volleyball with Shelley, Gabrielle, Topo, Chip, John, Gayle and Rosie. Sometimes, ski patrol guys brought a case of beer and played with them. When tennis courts were available, Lucas and Topo practiced hitting balls. If Chip was around, Lucas noticed Chip watching them. Lucas wanted to challenge Chip to a tennis match, but he needed to practice more and be in good tennis shape. For now, he thought it could wait until after the Olympics.

On August 11, Lucas, Shelley, Topo and Gabrielle were all ready to leave the next day, go to the race and enjoy three days off.

Lucas could not bring himself to use a box of brownie mix from the commissary. Herr Ostler, the pastry chef, had given him a recipe and agreed to meet him in the bakery after lunch today. However, Lucas had not told Ostler his plan to add 8 grams of Colombian Black hashish to the recipe. In advance, Lucas made hashish butter: He mixed powdered hashish into unsalted butter, heated it for 1 hour, strained it and let it cool to become a solid form, then wrapped it in foil.

Since Lucas had become the head chef, Herr Ostler was friendlier toward him, and Ostler spoke excellent English when he wanted to. While traveling from country to country, Lucas discovered this was common throughout Europe. He took a case of Wieninger beer to the bakery and met with Herr Ostler. After they got the ingredients together for the brownies, Lucas pulled out the hashish butter, unwrapped it, showed it to Herr Ostler, and told him what he planned to do with it.

"What is it for?" Herr Ostler asked.

"With this ingredient, you eat a brownie, or maybe only half of a brownie, and you will get 'high' as if you smoked it," replied Lucas. "Have you ever smoked marijuana or hashish, Herr Ostler?"

"Let's use first names," he replied. "May I call you Lucas?"

"Of course," said Lucas.

"Then, please call me Heinz. I have never smoked marijuana or hashish. I've heard it makes you paranoid."

"Heinz, do you smoke cigarettes?" asked Lucas.

"I do sometimes, but only after work in the afternoon and before I go to bed," he replied. "I retire at six or seven in the evening because I'm at work by three thirty each morning."

"Well, smoking marijuana or hashish is like smoking a cigarette, except it also makes you 'high' which feels good," said Lucas.

Reaching in his backpack, he took out his hash pipe and said, "Here, just take a couple of hits. Then, you can see what you think."

Heinz took 2 hits on the pipe and coughed a little.

Lucas opened Wieninger beers and handed 1 to Heinz. It was time to make hashish-cherry-cheesecake brownies. Lucas wanted to layer the brownies, and Heinz came up with a workable recipe. First, Lucas lined a rectangular baking pan with parchment paper. He combined 5 cups of sugar with 2 cups of his hashish butter, added 2 tablespoons of vanilla extract and 8 eggs, then whisked the mixture well. Next, he added 2 cups of cocoa, 3 cups of all-purpose flour, plus 1 teaspoon of salt, and he stirred it well. Then, he spread 1/2 of the brownie mixture in the pan he had lined with parchment paper.

To make cheesecake, Lucas used 40 ounces of cream cheese, 4 eggs, 1 tablespoon vanilla extract, 1 cup of sugar, plus 3 tablespoons flour, and he mixed it until smooth. He folded in the cherries which Heinz had macerated in Kirshwasser (cherry liqueur), then spread the cheesecake over the brownie mixture in the baking pan. Last, using a pastry bag, Lucas piped the remaining brownie mixture on top of the cherry cheesecake. The pan went into the over to bake for 40 minutes.

Opening 2 more beers, Lucas handed 1 to Heinz and asked, "Heinz, what did you do and where were you during the war?"

"I was a pastry chef at the Berchtesgadener Hof," he replied.

"No kidding," said Lucas. "You worked with Anton Held then."

"Yah," he said. "We were fortunate. The Nazis enjoyed fine dining. In those days, 'The Hof' was packed with Nazi officers."

"When Herr Held took me and a few friends on a tour of 'The Hof,' he told us stories about Hitler and the Nazis. I'll bet you also have stories of those times in Berchtesgaden," said Lucas.

"Yah," he replied. "My sister Anna was a food server and one of twenty-two maids at Hitler's Berghof. She saw things first hand. The staff and guests were made to understand the importance of secrecy. They could not talk about daily routines, events or people who were there. The rule was don't see anything, don't hear anything and don't say anything about the Berghof. Gretl was one of Eva's Braun's sisters. My sister was Gretl's roommate, and they were close friends. Although they had sworn not to talk about things there, gossip still got passed around, and my sister always confided in me."

"Did she talk about Hitler's behavior at the Berghof? Was he the raving maniac we see on film?" asked Lucas.

Heinz smiled. "My sister went to work at the Berghof in nineteen thirty-six after it got remodeled and expanded. She told me Hitler was very proud of the Berghof when he completed the remodel. He used to brag: the place was his, built with his own money which he earned from his book, *Mein Kampf* (My Struggle). Construction in Obersalzberg continued even after the Berghof was finished. The whole area was fenced off, so the Hitler worshippers could not get close for a sighting of him. When the weather was good, he would sometimes walk along the inside of the fence at the base of the hill to greet big crowds who waited for a glimpse of their Fuhrer. People came every day from all over Bavaria."

"Do you know what people did at the Berghof? Was it a party atmosphere? Did they talk about politics and the war?" asked Lucas.

"The Berghof was like a small resort hotel with a full staff of cooks, housekeepers, servants, gardeners and domestic workers," he replied. "The staff and guests at the Berghof were all tied to Hitler's schedule, his routine and his moods. Apparently, Hitler needed people around him. He would become moody or depressed when he had to be alone. Anna told me Hitler seemed to be in a good mood, most the time, and he relaxed while he was there.

"However, Hitler changed toward the end of the war. His doctor, Theodor Morell, administered powerful drugs to keep Hitler going. Anna said Hitler would sleep late, sometimes until noon, and he didn't have a lot of energy in those days."

"My friend who lives in Seefeld told me her grandfather, a Dr. Bloch, was the Hitler family physician when Hitler was young. Someone told me Hitler had a personal doctor who was with him for a long time. I did not get his name. Do you know who he was?" asked Lucas.

"It was Dr. Karl Brandt," he replied. "His fiancée, Anni Rehborn, was a record-holding swimmer. She met Hitler before she met Dr. Brandt. When Anni and Dr. Brandt joined the Nazi Party, Hitler invited them to the Berghof. They were driving near Reit im Winkl at the Austrian and German border, following a car which got into an accident. Young Doctor Brandt took the injured driver to the hospital in nearby Traunstein, and he operated on the man to repair a serious head injury. The driver was one of Hitler's closest aides, Wilhelm Bruckner, a Nazi from Munich. He had been involved in Hitler's famous Beer Hall Putsch which failed and resulted in prison time for Hitler and Bruckner."

The timer went off for the brownies. After letting them cool, Lucas cut them into small squares. He asked Heinz, "Don't you think we should try these to see how strong they are?"

"I think it is a good idea, but they smell funny," he replied.

Lucas smiled. "Maybe we should eat only half of a piece, and we'll see what happens." Then, he added, "Since I've never eaten hashish or marijuana, I don't really know what to expect."

He cut one of the hash brownies in half. After eating his half, Lucas said, "They taste so good I want more, but I'd better wait and see." He grabbed 2 more beers, handed 1 to Heinz, took 1 for himself and said, "Prost. Now, Heinz, please finish your story of Dr. Brandt."

Heinz paused for a few seconds, then said, "Hitler was so impressed, when Dr. Brandt saved Bruckner's life, he appointed the doctor to be his personal physician. Brandt was with Hitler on trips and always nearby in case of any medical emergency, involving the Fuhrer. Dr. Brandt and his wife even rented a hotel suite near the Berghof. Hitler and several people from his Berghof inner circle, attended the wedding of Dr. Brandt and Anni in Berlin. Several years later, Hitler appointed Brandt the Reich Commissioner for Sanitation and Health."

"What about this Dr. Morell—what type of drugs was he giving to Hitler?" asked Lucas.

"At first, he only treated Hitler for stomach and eczema problems," he replied. "Later, when the Nazis were losing the war, and the country was invaded and bombed, Dr. Morell gave him stronger drugs. There was also an assassination attempt at the Wolf's Lair."

"Yeah, I have only heard a little about the Wolf's Lair," said Lucas. "Where was it and what happened there?"

"The *Wolfsschanze* (Wolf's Lair) was Eastern Nazi Headquarters," he said. "It was a large, well-guarded military complex where Hitler spent a lot of time with top Nazi Officials. The complex was protected so well, it took ten years after the war to clear off more than fifty thousand land mines which surrounded the complex. At its peak, about two thousand people lived and worked at the Wolf's Lair. They installed a nearby airfield and railway lines. Within the complex, buildings were camouflaged with bushes, grass and artificial trees which were planted on the flat roofs. Camouflage netting was also erected between the buildings and the surrounding forest. From the air, the installation appeared to be a dense forest area.

"There were three *Sperrkreis* (Security Zones). The first one housed the Führer's big bunker, centered in the complex. It was made of steel-reinforced concrete, two-meters thick. The next zone was housing for Nazi Officers and key personnel. Sperrkreis Zone 3 was the outer ring of security, serving as the main defense for the two inner-zones. The Führer Begleit Brigade (FBB), a special security unit of the Wehrmacht, manned the guard houses, watchtowers and checkpoints which were also defended by critical land mines.

"Hitler had a great fear of the complex being bombed by the Allies, but only a few planes ever flew over. Still, he was concerned; he had the whole bunker system refortified in the spring of nineteen forty-four. Although the bombing never happened, the Soviet Army was closing in, and Hitler departed on the twentieth of November. Lucas, stop to think about it. The Wolfsschanze existed for three and a half years. Hitler spent two years there, and the Russians were within fifteen kilometers (9.3 mi) when Hitler left it for the last time."

"Who attempted the assassination at Wolf's Lair?" asked Lucas.

"I read there were four attempts on Hitler's life before nineteen thirty-three," he replied. "Then, after he came to power, there were ten more attempts. The incident at Wolfsschanze occurred during a strategic conference on July twentieth, nineteen forty-four. Hitler and many of his officers were attending. Colonel Count von Stauffenberg led the attempt which was a part of a plan called Operation Valkyrie."

Heinz explained, "Stauffenberg was there with several aides and had a bomb in his briefcase, but there were last-minute changes for the meeting place and time. I think it was too hot in the bunker, so they moved it to a building above ground. Stauffenberg set a timer and placed the bomb next to a leg of the conference table where everyone sat. Then, Stauffenberg excused himself for a fake telephone call. He and his accomplices left in a vehicle and made it past several checkpoints before the bomb exploded. The impact of the bomb injured Hitler's right leg, and he suffered ear damage. Twenty people were injured, many had ear damage, and there were four deaths."

"What happened to Stauffenberg and his group?" Lucas asked.

"After the blast occurred, Stauffenberg *geblufft hat* (bluffed) their way through more auto checkpoints, and they flew to Berlin," he said. "When they landed, Hitler's SS took them into custody. Soon after, they were all executed. The SS arrested over seven thousand people who they thought were involved; they executed about five thousand of those.

"I won't talk about everything which happened before people realized Hitler was still alive. Stauffenberg assumed he was dead, but he was wrong. There was a lot of confusion and scrambling in Berlin. My sister said Hitler became dependent on amphetamines and cocaine Dr. Morell gave him for those injuries."

"How many doctors did Hitler have?" asked Lucas.

"Well," he said, "besides Dr. Bloch, Dr. Brandt and Dr. Morell, there was another doctor who traveled with Hitler for a while, but he stayed in Berlin most of the time. I do not remember his name. Dr. Morell often got opinions from renowned doctors and professors, in matters concerning Hitler's health."

"Where did this Dr. Morell come from?" asked Lucas.

"Hitler's photographer, Heinrich Hoffman, knew Doctor Morell," he replied. "Hitler had lost his chauffeur, Julius Schreck, around the same time. When Hoffman became ill, Hitler worried about losing him since Hoffman was a close friend. So, Hitler sent his private plane to Berlin, and it brought Doctor Morell back to treat Hoffman in Munich.

"After Morell cured Hoffman, Hitler wanted the doctor to treat him for a serious rash on his legs, stomach pains and loss of appetite. When Doctor Morell cured Hitler, he was welcomed into the Berghof inner circle, as a private physician. Morell also became Eva's doctor, but she complained about his body odor, as did everyone."

"Hitler could have used a dietician, a fitness trainer and a good supply of dope instead of pills and injections," said Lucas.

"Maybe, but his physical endurance seemed to be amazing," said Heinz. "At large parties and events, such as big parades and marches, he stood with his right arm outstretched for hours on end."

Lucas excused himself and went to the restroom. The kitchen was empty since everyone was on an afternoon break.

As Lucas walked, he thought about Heinz Ostler: *Heinz is a chubby guy, about five foot nine and around sixty years old. He has a dark complexion and brown eyes. Heinz rarely talks to people, but now he is talking like an auctioneer because he is "high." Herr Bucherl did the same thing when he smoked hashish for the first time.*

When Lucas got back to the kitchen, Fritz, the sous chef, came in to work the evening shift and said, "Gruss Gott, Lucas. Wie gehts?"

"Gut, danke. I'll be in the bakery with Herr Ostler," Lucas replied.

Feeling the effects of the brownie, Lucas wanted to get back and see how Heinz was doing. When he arrived at the bakery, he saw Heinz stirring something over a single burner stove.

"How are you feeling Heinz?" asked Lucas.

Heinz paused, thought about it for a few seconds, and said, "I feel good, danke schoen. I am heating goulash soup, and I have some fresh brotchen. Are you hungry, Lucas?"

"Since you brought it up, I'm starving," he replied.

They both laughed, and Heinz continued to tell his story of Hitler's Berghof, "Anna said when Hitler was in a good mood, he was a lot of fun. He enjoyed all of Wagner's music, but his favorite song was 'Moonlight Sonata' by Beethoven. His favorite movies were *Metropolis* and *King Kong.* He also liked animation and cartoons."

"I never heard of *Metropolis.* When was it made?" asked Lucas.

"It was a science fiction movie, made in nineteen twenty-seven," he replied. "Using complicated methods to film the movie, they placed mirrors into elaborate sets which were amazing. Making the movie cost five million Deutschmarks, and the film company finished right before they ran out of money. The creator was Fritz Lang. His wife was a big supporter of the Nazi Party. Hitler and Joseph Goebbels loved the film even though Lang was Jewish. When Goebbels and Hitler offered to make him and honorary Aryan, Lang asked how they could do it. Goebbels told him the party decides who is Jewish and who is not. Lang must not have liked their offer. He left for Paris the same night."

For some reason, this struck Lucas as funny. He laughed, and then Heinz started laughing.

"It's not really so funny, you know," said Lucas.

"Oh, I know it's not funny," he replied. But he continued laughing until he said, "Now, I'm starving."

While Heinz served goulash soup and brotchen, he continued talking, "I read about Lang. He got inspired to make *Metropolis* when he saw the skyline of New York City. His wife wrote the novel, then they both wrote the screenplay. After they finished the movie, the actors told the press Lang was a real slave driver. Many of the huge cast got bruised and battered during the filming. I understand some of the roles involved life-threatening scenes. They used thirty-five thousand people as extras while making the film which took over a year and a half to complete. The movie is two-and-a-half hours long."

"With Hitler in Berlin, then later at the Eastern Front, what went on at the Berghof while he was gone? Oh, wait. Didn't Eva attempt suicide a few times when he was ignoring her?" asked Lucas.

"Yah.," said Heinz. "Some people know the story. After Eva's second attempt, when she swallowed sleeping pills, Hitler's attitude changed toward her. He bought Eva and her sister, Gretl, a house in a very nice area of Munich. When he was away, he also allowed her to have friends and family visit at the Berghof."

"Did your sister witness open affection between Hitler and Eva," asked Lucas, "when they were at the Berghof?"

"I'm sure you have heard, Hitler always said he was married to Germany because the good of the country came first for him," said Heinz. "When Eva lived at the Berghof, she shared two bedrooms and two bathrooms with Hitler, like she was his wife, but the public had no knowledge of it. Anna told me Hitler would sometimes hold Eva's hand. He kissed ladies' hands, but Eva's was the only hand he held. They always drove to the Berghof in separate cars. It seemed strange to everyone because they would go upstairs together for the night."

"I understand Eva was a good athlete, a skier, gymnast and swimmer. Did they do things together at the Berghof?" asked Lucas.

"Anna said Eva only wanted to hear popular music, and Hitler only enjoyed classical music; however, Hitler and Bormann both listened to pop music with Eva," he replied. "Sometimes they played table tennis, and Eva would let Hitler win.

"Hitler hired Arthur, everyone called him Willi, and his wife Frieda Kannenberg. Willi was Hitler's butler and much more. He was a trained chef and a good musician who entertained Hitler and Eva, along with Berghof guests.

"What instrument did Willi play?" Lucas asked.

Heinz chuckled. "He played the accordion, and Hitler would sing along to his favorite song, 'Who's Afraid of the Big Bad Wolf.' They first met at Kannenberg's Bierstube in Berlin, and Hitler liked him right away. Willi was a happy, talented and funny man. Willi and Frieda worked at the Berghof from nineteen thirty-three to the end of the war in nineteen forty-five."

"What else did Hitler and Eva do together?" asked Lucas.

"Hitler and Eva would play rummy, and they went for walks with the dogs," he replied. "In the winter, they often had snow fights. I think Hitler loved to tease Eva."

He added, "Anna told me the only time she heard them argue about anything, it was because of her smoking. Hitler also did not want her to drink whiskey, but Champagne or wine were acceptable. Hitler didn't drink much at all."

"How did they address each other?" asked Lucas.

"It would depend on who was nearby," he said. "I understand Hitler had many nicknames for her. He called her Evi, Patscherl and Schnacksi."

Lucas looked at him with an odd expression, and Heinz said, "Oh, he used those names in private. He called her Fräulein Braun, and she called him Mein Fuhrer in public. When they thought they were alone, she called him Adolph or Adi. Anna said the sound in the Berghof carried so well, you could hear whispering from across the room. Hitler could relax there, he felt as if he was the host and head of the household. He considered it his real home. Hitler enjoyed ladies nearby, all the time. He not only had adults around the Berghof, he also invited children to visit."

Lucas smiled. "Who were all the ladies? Do you know?"

"The wives of Bormann, Speer and Goering came to visit often, plus Eva's sister and their girlfriends," he replied.

"What did Eva do when Hitler was away so much?" asked Lucas.

"She had her sister and girlfriends around," he replied. "They would often go skiing at the Zugspitze near Garmisch-Partenkirchen. Eva was athletic. She enjoyed gymnastics, swimming in nearby lakes and hiking on mountain trails around Obersalzberg. At the Berghof, Eva always snapped photos or recorded video movies. I understand she sold some of those to her old boss, Herr Hoffman."

After both finished eating soup and brotchen, they gathered the dishes and put them in the sink.

Heinz asked, "Are you still hungry?"

"Yes. It's the dope," said Lucas. "Do you have Danish pastries?"

"Yah, and I'm also hungry," he replied. "He went to the walk-in, came out with 2 pecan rolls, and put them in the oven to warm.

Opening 2 more Wieninger beers, Lucas asked, "Heinz, when did you start working at the Berchtesgadener Hof?"

"When the Nazis bought the hotel in nineteen thirty-nine, it was the Grand Hotel Auguste Victoria. The Nazis remodeled and renamed it. I came to work when the hotel reopened as the Berchtesgadener Hof in nineteen forty-one," he replied.

"Did they have a grand opening?" asked Lucas. "And did you get to meet any of the Nazi leaders?"

"Oh, yah. Hitler, Bormann and Party Treasurer Schwarz were all there, plus Eva Braun, Gretl and Hermann Fegelein," he replied. "We had many famous guests while the Nazis were in charge: The Duke and Duchess of Windsor, British Prime Minister Chamberlain, high-ranking military officers such as Goebbels, Himmler and von Ribbentrop."

"I heard Fegelein was a playboy," said Lucas. "Is it true?"

"Yah, he liked the ladies," he replied. "Gruppenführer Fegelein spent a lot of time in the bar at 'The Hof,' drinking with Bormann and others who were part of Hitler's inner circle.

"I would sit at the end of the bar where I saw and overheard things. Also, the bartender was my friend. He told me stories about interesting things he saw happen and things he overheard."

"Who lived at 'The Hof' during the war?" asked Lucas.

"Hitler's Doctor Morell did for a while. He moved down from the Berghof, when he became ill with throat and heart problems in the spring of nineteen forty-four," he replied. "He thought the lower altitude would help him. Sometimes, Morell came into the bakery, got a pastry and spoke to me. He loved to eat when he felt good, but he was very ill, so he spent most of his time in the hotel room.

"Morell would go up to the Berghof and give Hitler injections, but then he returned to the hotel and left Hitler in the care of his assistant. Morrell did not like the altitude at the Berghof. It is fifteen hundred meters above the hotel. There was also heavy vapor, produced by Nazi smokescreen generators, used to hide the Berghof from the view of allied airplanes. Morell told me the vapors affected his breathing.

"At the Berghof, people talked about how fast Hitler's health seemed to improve since Morell was not around very much. Later, at the end of the war, Morell stayed with Hitler in the Berlin bunker until Hitler got upset with the doctor. He told Morrell to take off his uniform and sent him out of the bunker. The doctor returned to Munich in late April of nineteen forty-five. Then, he spent time in the custody of the American military until he died in nineteen forty-eight.

"Hitler's sister Paula also lived at the Berchtesgadener Hof for a period of time, as did Angela Raubal who was their half-sister and the mother of Geli Raubal."

He asked Lucas, "Do you know the story about Hitler and Geli Raubal, and the story of her death?"

"I know she was his niece and supposedly his lover," he replied. "I heard stories about her being Hitler's one true love; and there are several versions of how she died, or how they found her dead."

"Well, you have summed it up about Geli," he said. "Her mother, Angela, went to work for Hitler as a housekeeper. I heard she left her job at the Berghof, due to her intense hatred of Eva Braun."

"What happened to Angela?" asked Lucas.

"She got married and moved to Northern Germany," he replied.

"Do you know what became of Paula?" Lucas asked.

"Wolf was Hitler's favorite alias, and he told her to use the name," he said. "After the war, Paula Wolf stayed in Berchtesgaden and lived in a tiny apartment until she died in nineteen sixty. She was buried under the name of Paula Hitler. Her grave is across the river at Bergfriedhof (mountain grave yard) near the Berchtesgadener Hof."

"Did Paula ever get married?" Lucas asked Heinz.

"No," he replied. "Paula asked Hitler, only once, if she could marry. She had met an officer named Jekelius, and she claimed to be in love. Hitler told her no and sent Jekelius to the Eastern Front. Jekelius died there after being captured by the Soviets."

"I've heard Hitler's personality was different at the Berghof," said Lucas. "Do you know what he did when he was there?"

"He was active there until he began to lose the war," he said. "Then, he stayed awake until two or three a.m. and did not get out of bed until noon or later. Some people say Hitler slept through the allied invasion of Normandy while a German tank battalion waited for his orders."

Both Lucas and Heinz cracked up. They laughed so hard, they had tears running down their faces.

Heinz settled down, and then he continued his story, "I think it was quiet when Hitler was around the Berghof. He was there about one third of his time as German Chancellor.

"During the war, food for the rest of the country was being rationed. But they always had plenty of food at the Berghof. Hitler ate special vegetarian meals, prepared by Willi, his personal chef. Luncheon guests, secretaries, Eva Braun, her sister and friends gathered in the living room until dinner was announced. Then, they joined Hitler in the lavish dining room. Hitler would greet each lady by kissing her hand, and Eva always sat on his left. My sister praised Eva Braun for her pleasant personality and her kindness to the help."

"Did she say what dinner conversations were about?" asked Lucas.

"Hitler enjoyed playing host," he replied. "But he dominated the conversations. He told stories of his younger days, and he often spoke about his vegetarian diet. Hitler would tease the guests who ate meat. He thought meat was unhealthy because of the unsanitary conditions in the *schlachthof* (slaughterhouse). His reported love of animals was another reason he did not eat meat. My sister Anna and the other servers all knew of Hitler's eating habits. The only meat dish which Anna saw him eat was Leberkloesse (liver dumplings)."

"Besides being a vegetarian, I heard he did not drink alcohol or smoke," said Lucas. "Why do you think he made those choices?"

"I think Hitler avoided alcohol to keep his mind clear," he replied. "He was determined to accomplish his goals and lead Germany to greatness.

According to Anna, he would have a beer with his dinner, occasionally. He hated smoking. Both Eva Braun and her sister smoked. When he found out, he got so upset, Eva had to hide her smoking from him. I think Hitler was in great shape until the assassination attempt at Wolfsschanze."

"You say Hitler's health was good before the attempt. Did he exercise at all?" asked Lucas.

"I heard he walked daily from the Berghof to a teahaus (teahouse) which he designed and had built in Mooslahnerkopf woods," he said. "It was a thirty-minute walk on a winding path, going through a meadow into the woods. He was usually with a group of military officers or visiting dignitary. Sometimes, Eva and others would walk with him.

"At the teahaus, he would drink tea, eat a pastry and maybe doze off for a while. Below the teahaus, Hitler had a small terrace built with a wooden bench to sit on. For safety, there was a log railing which did not obstruct the view. From there, he enjoyed a scenic overlook of Salzburg and the mountains beyond. On clear days he could see all the way to the Salzburg Castle. The teahaus was relaxing for Hitler compared with the Chancellery in Berlin where he did not go outside.

"Dr. Morell said when Hitler got stressed and overworked, or the war wasn't going well, he was more likely to become ill."

"Living in bunkers would not help his health, either," said Lucas.

"When the war turned to the advantage of the Allies, Hitler spent most of his time in bunkers," he said, "either at the Wolfsschanze in East Prussia, or at the Berlin bunker which was under the Chancellery Garden. He must have developed a bunker mentality of feeling safe, and he had solitude in which to work."

"Did he ever just socialize for fun at the Berghof?" asked Lucas.

"In nice weather, he joined the others for social time on the large upper terrace before dinner," he replied. "Hitler enjoyed talking to the many children of his associates and friends. In the summer, Hitler mingled with local children who came to the Berghof for a 'Fun Fair.' They ate cakes, fruit and other sweets. They also got to play with the dogs. Many children even got rides in Hitler's private airplane which he kept at the landing strip near the Berghof. Hitler loved to show off, so he gave all guests, the children and the adults, a tour of the kennels where he bred his fine German Shepherds."

"Heinz, do you know the difference between German Shepherds and Alsatian Dogs?" asked Lucas.

"Yah, I asked my friend who is a dog breeder the same question," he said. "He told me the British created the name of the Alsatian Dog during the last war. They did not want to use the German name because they were so hateful of the Germans. However, I read they are again using German Shepherd as the name of the breed.

"Hitler's German Shepherd, Blondi, went with him everywhere. He spoiled her with her own handler and caretaker. She slept in a wood box at the foot of his bed. In his train car, she also got to sleep with him. Some people believe Hitler killed his beloved dog after she gave birth to a batch of puppies at the Berlin bunker. They say he used Blondi to test the poison which he and Eva would use to commit suicide."

"Didn't Eva Braun also have dogs?" asked Lucas.

"Eva had two Scottish Terriers," he replied. "Hitler didn't like them much, and he referred to them as 'Handfeger' (hand brushes). My sister said Eva didn't like Hitler's dog either, and she would even kick Blondi when Hitler was not looking."

"How would you describe a typical afternoon there?" Lucas asked.

"When they returned from the teahaus, they had a few hours of relaxation, and Hitler usually went to his rooms," he replied. "Bormann often spent the time in a young secretary's room; it was no secret."

"And, a typical evening?" asked Lucas.

"Dinner was always at eight p.m. Hitler chose the dinner menu while he had breakfast," he replied. "All meals served to his guests were feinschmecker (gourmet), German specialties, prepared by his right-hand man, Willi Kannenberg, as were his vegetarian dishes.

"After dinner they would adjourn to the great hall which converted to a movie theater where they watched German or American films. Sometimes he and Eva would play cards, or he would sit and watch the fire burn in the big marble fireplace, or he would doze off.

"Most evenings, his monotonous monologues put others to sleep. Those went on until Eva could take no more. Then, she said, 'Gute nacht,' went upstairs and waited for him to join her. They would end most evenings alone in Hitler's study where he drank tea while she sipped sparkling wine.

"My sister told me the nights she worked late were the most boring times at the Berghof."

"Heinz, I must go back to work and check on things in the kitchen," said Lucas. "It has been great talking to you. Thank you for sharing your stories about the Berghof and the Berchtesgadener Hof. I'll take the brownies to my place, so nobody will eat one by mistake."

While Heinz and Lucas were talking, they had cleaned the bakery. Both enjoyed spending time with each other; and since they got "high" together, they now shared a special bond.

"Are you okay? You should not drive for a while," said Lucas.

"I think I'll go talk with Gunther in the bar and have a beer. Danke schoen, Lucas, for the hashish and good discussion," said Heinz.

Lucas felt so good, he worked with the cooks in the hotel kitchen. Everyone joked around with Topo and the waitresses. When the dinner service was over, all the cooks wished Lucas and Topo a safe drive and a fun trip. Lucas and Topo were glad to be leaving the next morning. They looked forward to seeing the Grand Prix race in Austria.

When Lucas closed his office in the kitchen, he picked up the tray of brownies and wrapped it in extra foil, not wanting to leave a trail of hashish aroma as he walked past the bar and through the lounge.

The hotel lounge was full of people, including a large group which came for a Pentecostal Retreat.

On his way out, Lucas peeked in the bar. Heinz was standing at the bar, talking a mile a minute, and he was laughing between words.

It is rather amazing to see him be so sociable, thought Lucas, *because it is rare to hear Heinz speak when he is at work.*

CHAPTER 40

Österreichring: The Grand Prix

A few days earlier, Lucas told Eric everyone should meet in the Annex parking lot across the autobahn from Lake Chiemsee Hotel, by 9 a.m. this Saturday morning.

Lucas walked out to the van, carrying the pan of brownies which he had made with Heinz. Sonya came up behind him while he was bent over, putting the pan into the food cabinet. A little startled, he turned and Sonya looked concerned.

"Wait until you see who is with Olivia," she said.

"Hi Sonya. Okay, please tell me. Who's she with?" asked Lucas.

"Bruno has a brother who is now in Garmisch. He looks like Bruno and he is dating Olivia," she replied. "They are coming to the race together in Olivia's van which Bob Ostergaard sold her. I wanted to warn you, so you won't look shocked when you meet him."

"He must be the guy who I saw skiing at Hintertux," said Lucas. "Wow! This could become uncomfortable. Are you here alone?"

"Gino came with me. You know Gino—He is already reorganizing my van," she replied. They both laughed.

Lucas said, "This trip will be fun. Who else is coming?"

"Gino said he counted 7 vans including yours," she replied.

"Here come Topo and Gabrielle," said Lucas. "Hey, Sonya, please take Gabrielle aside and warn her about Bruno's brother."

Lucas helped Topo put bags and ski gear into the van while Sonya told Gabrielle about Enrico. Lucas was a little concerned, having heard Bruno's brother would be joining them.

When he went upstairs to help Shelley with her bags, Lucas heard the other 5 "Shifty Sales" VW vans pull in the parking lot at 9:05 a.m. He and Shelley looked out of their apartment window and saw the group, all now out of their vans, talking and laughing.

Lucas laughed and shook his head, seeing the size of this fun-loving group in the parking lot below.

"This is going to be quite an adventure, Lucas. I hope we all live through it," said Shelley.

Looking at her, he asked, "What do you mean?"

"It looks like a pretty wild group," she replied.

"It looks like a lot of fun to me," he said. "Let's get going."

Downstairs, Shelley and Lucas greeted George and Judann, their two best friends who are now a couple. George is working as a coach and math teacher at the American School in Garmisch, and he bought a royal blue VW van from Bob Ostergaard. Bob seems to sell as many old rusty vans as he can find and fix up.

In this group, Lucas was the only person who was driving a new van, and he had put quite a few miles on it since he got it last year.

When he said hello to Eric and Sabine, Eric whispered to Lucas, "I guess you and Gabrielle heard who is going with us?"

Lucas whispered back, "Yeah, Sonya got here first, and she let us know. Why don't the five of us get together and talk this weekend, away from the group?"

"I think it's a good idea," said Eric. "Enrico is asking everyone about Bruno. He is trying to get a lead on where his brother went. So, I'm sure he will want to talk to you."

"Okay with me. I know nothing," said Lucas. "Let's get on the road. We have a three-hour drive ahead."

Topo and Gabrielle climbed into the back of Lucas' van. As they got settled, Gino knocked on the side door. Gabrielle opened the door, and Gino climbed in the back. He took a seat at the table, pulled out his hash pipe, lit the pipe, took a big hit and passed it to Shelley. Then, the pipe went to Topo, Gabrielle and Lucas.

Lucas took one hit and said, "No more for me, now. I'm driving."

"When did driving ever stop you?" asked Shelley. "Everyone laughed and thanked Gino who was handing a cassette tape to Shelley.

"Listen to this new album by Jim Croce," said Gino. "I think you'll enjoy it, and I'll see you at the Österreichring (racetrack)."

Bob Ostergaard and his girlfriend, Maggie, led the group out of the parking lot, under the autobahn, made a left turn, then straight for half a mile, made 2 more left turns, and then headed southeast toward Berchtesgaden. Streaming onto the autobahn, this parade of bright-colored, vintage VW vans was quite a sight. Bob Ostergaard had used rollers and spray cans to paint the vans various colors, using whatever cheap paint he could find. Lucas' cream-colored van stood out, only because of the professional paint job.

Following Ostergaard's red van, George and Judann were in the royal blue van, followed by Eric and Sabine in a tan-colored van. Right behind them was an orange van, driven by Regan Stone, with the Australian lady, Ashleigh, in his passenger seat. Next in line, Gino and Sonya followed in her dark blue Ford Transit Van. Trailing them was Ashleigh's Australian friend, Olivia, driving an emerald-green VW van, and Bruno's brother, Enrico, in her passenger's seat. Shelley, Topo and Gabrielle rode with Lucas, and his van was at the end of the motorcade.

"Who is the guy with Olivia?" asked Topo.

"His name is Enrico," replied Lucas. "He's looking for his brother, an Italian who used to work as a bartender in Garmisch. His brother seems to have left Garmisch, but nobody knows where he went."

"I heard about an Italian bartender who beat up a few women. Is he the brother you're talking about?" asked Topo.

"Yeah. He's the one," said Lucas.

Since Gabrielle was present, Lucas did not want to discuss Enrico and Olivia. Before Topo moved to Chiemsee and got involved with Gabrielle, Topo and Olivia were a couple.

Changing the subject, Lucas asked over his shoulder, "Hey, Topo. Would you open Wieninger beers for all of us?"

While Topo passed out beers, Lucas said, "We will be driving near Teisendorf where the Wieninger Brewery is. Eric and I were lucky enough to go there with the Chef from the Berchtesgadener Hof. We toured the brewery and had a great lunch. They also gave us as much Wieninger beer as we could drink. It is my favorite beer now."

"Are we ready to hear the tape Gino gave us?" asked Shelley.

"What is the name of the album?" asked Gabrielle.

"*You Don't Mess Around with Jim,* by Jim Croce," she replied.

"Let's hear it," said Gabrielle.

Shelley pushed in the tape as Topo raised his bottle of Wieninger beer and said, "Prost. Here's to Jim."

The first song was the title song on the album, and they were inspired by rousing words in the chorus sections. They played the song over, and all sang the chorus, joining the voice of Jim Croce and ending with the title words, "You Don't Mess Around with Jim."

"Slim was a tough dude," said Topo. "Can we hear the rest of the album now?" Everyone listened to the 30-minute album and loved it.

Lucas thought: *Hearing Jim Croce sing about "big and dumb" in the title song made me think of Bruno*. He chuckled.

Shelley noticed his smirk and asked, "What's so funny, Lucas?"

"It was a funny story," he replied. "I think it's a great album. I wonder if he wrote all of those songs."

"I'll bet Gino can answer your question," said Shelley. "Jim Croce seems to have it together. I like his style, the music and the lyrics in this album. I think 'Time in a Bottle' is my favorite. A beautiful love song always makes my heart beat a little faster."

"Where did this singer come from?" asked Topo.

"I don't know where he came from, but I get the impression he wrote these songs about his own life experiences, those told to him by others, or those he observed," replied Gabrielle.

"Maybe Gino can tell us more about this Jim Croce," said Lucas. "I'll be sure to ask him. I really like the album."

"I heard 'American Pie' the other day," said Gabrielle. "Can anyone explain the lyrics? I don't know what the song is about."

"Someone told me the lines about *the day the music died* refer to the plane crash which killed The Big Bopper, Ritchie Valens and Buddy Holly," said Lucas. "The lyrics are also about the Rolling Stones, The Beatles, Bob Dylan and Elvis. I am sure other people and other events are hidden in the lyrics. Gino probably knows all about it."

Still driving in Germany, the Austrian border was about half a mile away when they crossed the Saalach River. At the border station, an Austrian border guard glanced inside Bob Ostergaard's van, looked at Bob's paperwork and said something to him. Then, the guard waived everyone through, and people in the vans waived back to him. He stood there, holding what appeared to be a liquor bottle in a paper bag, as the parade of colorful vans passed by.

"It helps to be friendly and confident when crossing borders," said Topo. "Bribery also helps."

"I've been in the same situation," said Lucas. "I keep a full bottle of whiskey in this van, always ready for the border guards."

A few miles further, Lucas said, "We are going through Salzburg, now, but we don't have time to stop on this trip. I want to come back and explore it." He pointed toward a structure, off to his left. "You can see Hohensalzburg Castle, the huge fortress on the hilltop."

Everyone looked at the castle, as the van wound along the autobahn, passing by fertile farmlands which were dotted with grazing cows.

"Has anyone been to Salzburg?" asked Lucas.

Gabrielle and Topo chimed, "No."

"It would be a fun trip," said Shelley.

"I've read about things to see and do around Salzburg," said Lucas. "We should make it a three-day trip when we come back."

Shelley spoke to Gabrielle and Topo, "We met a couple when we skied at Hintertux. They live in Salzburg and will meet us this afternoon at the Österreichring in Spielberg. I imagine they can tell us all about this area and the fortress which overlooks the city."

Neil Young's new album, *Harvest*, was playing, and they listened to a great song, "Heart of Gold." They passed the small community of Gois near the Salzburg airport, and then they passed by the turnoff for the Schloss Hellbrunn near the Salzburg Zoo.

Several miles further, Shelley was looking out the window of the van and said, "Oh, we are near Hallein. One of our hotel maids is from there. She told me about a tour which takes you inside the salt mine, and you can ride down a long, steep, wooden slide."

They spent the next half an hour listening to music and enjoying the countryside. Lucas followed the parade of vans, driving across the Salzach River at Speckleiten, then turning south through Wenger, Weissenbach, Lacher and Steghof. At Bischofshofen, they turned east for a half hour and drove through Schladming, a narrow valley with houses on hillsides which led to several ski slopes. The Eastern Alps extended all the way to Graz. When they got to Sankt Michael im Obersteiermark, they took the highway going southwest. Along the way, they drove by many villages, including Sankt Stephan ob Leoben, Sankt Marein bei Knittelfeld and Sankt Margarethen bei Knittelfeld.

Topo felt prompted to say, "This must be Catholic territory around here. All these towns are named after saints."

Most of the villages had ski lifts, going up the mountains. They passed through Kobenz where a church steeple towered over all the other buildings. After Kobenz, they drove another 15 minutes and followed Ostergaard who made a right turn off the main highway, then a left turn, onto Spielbergerstrasse. Going past the main entrance of the racetrack, they turned right into the campground.

Sabine, being Austrian, negotiated with campground management and got them a prime spot, alongside a stream and bordered by a group of shade trees. They stopped the vans in a somewhat isolated area with a line of trees. Gino directed traffic, as the vans parked in a semi-circle, following the shape of the forest and facing an open meadow. The campsite looked prismatic with all the bright-colored vans (painted and sold by Ostergaard). As far as he could, Lucas parked away from Olivia and Bruno's brother, Enrico.

Topo and Gabrielle placed their tent next to the stream and behind Lucas' van. Scott and Faye Williams had arrived earlier, riding on their BMW motorcycle, and their tent was further up-stream. While others were setting up tents, Lucas and Shelley still had an hour before they would meet Otto and Bertha at the entrance to the pit area. So, they went over to talk with Gino and Sonya.

"This place is great, and it's right next to the racetrack," said Gino. "Since we can walk there, we don't have to move the vans."

Gino motioned for the other 3 to follow him, and he walked around Sonya's van. They went down to the stream and found a secluded spot by a group of Austrian Pine trees. Gino smiled, pulled out his hash pipe and filled it. He said, "Let's get this party started off right."

Taking a hit and passing the pipe back to Gino, Lucas said, "I made cherry-cheesecake brownies, using eight grams of Topo's Colombian Black hashish. Herr Ostler and I each tried a half of one yesterday. Believe me, I needed no more. If anyone wants to try some, the brownies are at the van, and I suggest starting with a half piece."

Ostergaard, Maggie, Olivia and Enrico left the campground to look at farms in the area and find old rusty VW vans for Bob to buy.

"Enrico knows about auto mechanics, and he has been hanging out with Bob at his 'Shifty Sales' VW van business," said Gino.

This worked for Lucas because he wanted to avoid contact with Enrico and avoid answering questions about Bruno if possible. Lucas had not been introduced to Enrico yet, and he was not looking forward to it. Hanging out with Bob would keep Enrico occupied.

Except for the people who left to look for vans with Ostergaard, the group gathered around Lucas' van. He set up a portable table, cut the brownie squares in half-pieces, placed those in paper confection cups and served them with a shot of Jägermeister. Standing beside Lucas, Gabrielle handed each person a bottle of Wieninger beer. This personal service brought cheers from the others.

Topo asked those around the table, "Have any of you ever eaten food containing hashish or marijuana?"

Lucas, George, Sabine and Sonya all claimed they had.

Shelley was the first to say, "These are delicious."

Everyone echoed her comment, and they all toasted the chef with a simultaneous, "Prost."

"It's too bad you didn't make some without hashish because I will want more of these," said Shelley. "They taste like a cheesecake."

Lucas wrapped 4 brownie halves and put them in his pocket.

Regan and Ashleigh did not eat any of the brownies, but they went with the group. If anyone got arrested or got in serious trouble, Regan could help them because he was a recent graduate of law school. However, Lucas hoped Regan's lawyer skills would not be needed.

With 18 people in their group, they started a 15-minute walk on a path through the trees, going to the entrance at the Österreichring.

This large group reminded Lucas of his trip to Cervenia with Olivia, George and Ashleigh. Now in Austria, they were together again, all with different partners, and all still friends, laughing and having fun.

Except for Enrico, Sonya, Scott and Faye, the friends who came to play this weekend had partied and skied together before in Cervenia. Some of them had slept in their vans, parked in a lot near the bottom of the cable cars which took them to the Plateau Rosa Glacier.

Once they were at the Österreichring and inside the main gate, Lucas spotted Otto at the entrance to the pit area. Otto saw Lucas first, and he was waving both arms. It was a hot day, and the asphalt on the track appeared to have steam coming off it. The weather reminded Lucas of summers in his hometown, Fresno, California. Temperatures there were often over 100 F, sometimes over 110 F.

Otto and Bertha dressed in traditional Bavarian clothes. Otto wore lederhosen, suspenders, calf-length plaid socks and an Alpine hat with a chamois feather in the hatband. Bertha was wearing a blue and white checkered dirndl and a white blouse.

After greeting each other with hugs, Lucas introduced the other smiling AFRC employees. People in their group had on shorts and tank tops or blouses, plus an assortment of hats. Lucas wore an Alpini hat, the one he got when they worked as extras in the *Snow Job* movie while they were skiing in Cervenia. The group had teased Lucas about stealing the hat from the movie set, but Lucas said he just forgot to turn it in.

Otto and Bertha saved a large table, but the group needed to find more chairs before they all got seated. Everyone went to the beer counter for half-liter glasses of Gosser beer, then returned to the table and sat under the shade of umbrellas. They were on a grassy area near a group of trees and close to a concession stand where rows of chickens were roasting on spits in upright ovens and smelling great.

Race cars were on the track, so they had to speak loudly. Everyone was excited, all talking at once. Otto asked how many of the group had been to a Grand Prix race before. Only Sabine, Gino and Sonya said they had. Then, Otto told them a little about this race and this racetrack.

Lucas pulled out a brownie and unwrapped it. He showed Otto and Bertha the 2 halves and said, "Eating this brownie will affect you the same as smoking hashish. Knowing the right amount to eat gets a little tricky. I tested this at Chiemsee with our pastry chef, and one half is plenty to begin with. This group ate our halves about thirty minutes ago. Eating hashish gets into your system slower than smoking it. This will take forty-five minutes to an hour for you feel the full effects. Do you want to try it?"

"Yes, please!" replied Bertha. "We had a fun experience when we smoked some with you at the Hintertux Glacier."

Otto and Bertha each ate half a brownie and complemented Lucas on the taste. They both wanted more, but Lucas said, "Later, after we see what happens. Since this is your first experience, digesting hashish, I think we should be cautious."

Over the roaring sound of race cars on the track, Otto spoke loudly, "There was a small three-kilometer track at the Zeltweg Airport where a Formula One race took place in nineteen sixty-four, but the track was too rough, so it was the only race at the track. In nineteen seventy, this track held its first Austrian Formula One Grand Prix race. It became one of the fastest racetracks on the Formula One circuit."

"Who won the first Grand Prix race?" asked George.

"Belgium's Jacky Ickx won," replied Otto. "Austria's Jochen Rindt had started in the pole position, but he dropped out at twenty-one laps with a blown engine. Weeks later, he died while qualifying at the Italian Grand Prix in Monza, Italy. A statue of Rindt stands in the central public area of this track. Having won by twenty points over England's Jack Brabham, Rindt was honored as the World Driving Champion."

"Otto, I know you are an avid race fan," said Lucas. "I think I'll stick close to you during the race, so I can learn what's going on."

"Do they have open restrooms and concession stands around the entire track?" Topo asked Otto.

"Yes. They should all be open for this big crowd," he replied.

"Does anyone want to walk around the track?" asked Topo.

Lucas wanted to talk with Otto about auto racing and about Salzburg where he and Bertha lived. Lucas, Shelley, Eric, Sabine, Gino and Sonya stayed at their table with Otto and Bertha. The other 12 got fresh beers and took off, planning to walk 5.911 kilometers (3.67 miles) around the racetrack, all laughing and talking.

"I don't know about the rest of you, but the heat, the noise and the smell of fuel is affecting me," said Eric. "How about going back to our campsite where we can sit by the cool stream under a shade tree?"

Everyone agreed, finished their beers and headed toward the gate. As Lucas passed the concession stand where chickens were roasting on spits, he said, "I have to come back and get some chicken later. Otto, where are you staying? Are you in the campground?"

"Yah," Otto replied. "We're in a German-made Ford Transit van, towing a nineteen seventy Eriba Puck Camper trailer. The camper has plenty of storage space which is great for our ski stuff, and it gives us more room to move around in when we stay in campgrounds."

"We have talked about going to see Salzburg, and I wonder if you might give us advice about what to do and see there," said Shelley.

"Of course," said Bertha. "Salzburg is the fourth largest city in Austria. It is famous for Mozart, The Sound of Music, the salt mines, underground lakes and the Augustiner Braustubl which is the biggest and best beer hall in all of Austria."

"Yah," said Otto. "Augustiner is one of the best and purest beers in the world. There are four halls which each hold about two hundred people, and three stuberl (small rooms). It has an indoor seating area of fifteen hundred square meters, and an outdoor area to accommodate another fourteen hundred people. The beer is the best I have ever tasted. It is brewed by Benedictine monks and served in steins (stone jugs) which hang in cupboards. You select a stein, rinse your stein, get in line, pay for your stein, and then get your beer drawn from wooden kegs. It is also cheaper than buying it at the Oktoberfest in Munich."

"We'll put it at the top of our list to do in Salzburg," said Lucas.

"The salt mine tour also sounds fun," said Shelley.

"Lucas, you might enjoy seeing the oldest restaurant in Europe, located inside the walls of St. Peter's Arch Abbey," said Bertha. "It was built around the ninth century and might be the oldest restaurant in the world. They call it Stiftskeller St. Peter, and their menu is quite impressive. If my memory is correct, the owners claim Christopher Columbus, Mozart and Faust dined there."

"Recent visitors to Salzburg include your President Nixon, Secretary of State Kissinger and our own Kurt Waldheim who is the Secretary General of the United Nations," said Otto. "Also, the American movie, *The Salzburg Connection*, was filmed in Salzburg and should come out in theaters soon. It is about people looking for Nazi treasure in a local lake. I can't wait to see it."

Gino spoke up, "You mentioned Kurt Waldheim. I read he was a Nazi intelligence officer during World War Two, and he might have taken part in mass executions."

"I have heard the same thing about Waldheim, but he has denied it," said Otto. "He said he was wounded in action at the Eastern Front in nineteen forty-two, and claimed he saw no further action during the war. I heard he was a member of the Sturmabteilung (SA), the paramilitary force known as The Brownshirts. He almost became our president in a close race, last year, but he lost to Franz Jonas of the Socialist party. Waldheim was representing the Independent Party."

"I understand it's quite common for ex-Nazi members to assume key positions in the German Government," said Lucas.

"The Baader-Meinhof Gang claimed one of their reasons for terrorist attacks was to oppose former Nazis in government," said Bertha.

"I think they had a very long list of grievances against the German government," replied Gino.

Changing the subject, Lucas said, “Man, it is hot here.” He looked at Otto and Bertha and asked, “Why don’t you show us your caravan before we get settled in the shade?”

The group followed Otto and Bertha to their campsite in a grassy meadow. They called the 1970 Eriba Puck Camper a touring caravan. To Lucas, it looked like the rear half of a VW van.

The camper had 2 wheels, large rectangular side windows, a larger rear window, and a small front window. It also had a pop-up roof. The top half of the camper was white, and the bottom half was navy blue, matching their German Ford Transit Van which towed the camper.

Looking inside, Lucas saw blue and white gingham curtains on all the windows. The interior was blonde wood with white trim. There was room for 6 to sit at the table. It dropped down to form either 2 single beds or 1 double bed. The inside of their camper was like the back of Lucas’ Westphalia VW van, except the area in his van was smaller.

Lucas thought: *When Shelley and I go to Greece, it would be great to have one of these for the extra space.*

The group walked across the grassy meadow to their own campsite. Since the campground was filling up, Lucas was glad to be on a site which was somewhat isolated. They were a short distance from the main section of the campground, and they could not have picked a better location for a racetrack. Pine forests and rolling green hills with cows scattered on the hillsides, surrounded the track and campground.

With no clouds in the sky, this sunny day was steaming hot. Those present were 8 of the 20-person group. They grabbed folding chairs and got comfortable next to the stream and in the shade.

“Now, this is more like it!” said Eric.

“Are all of you Americans?” asked Bertha.

“Let’s see…” said Shelley. “Sabine is an Austrian, living in Seefeld. Sonya comes from Garmisch. Her mother is German, and her father is American. Topo came from Argentina. Gabrielle is from Hanover, Germany. Olivia and Ashleigh are from Australia. Maggie is English. I think everyone else in this group is from the United States.”

“Oh, and you all work for the American military,” said Bertha.

“Does everyone feel as good as I do?” asked Gino, grinning.

“Whoa! I’m feeling it now. Strong stuff!” said Eric.

When he asked if anyone wanted a beer, everyone said, “Yes.”

Lucas saw an opportunity. He went to get beer with Eric, and Sonya followed them. At Lucas’ van, they talked quietly, and he asked Eric about his knowledge of Bruno’s brother.

Eric said, “Enrico has been asking around and talking to everyone who might have known his brother. He plays basketball at the gym, and he seems to be a nice, quiet guy. When he asked me about his brother, I told him nobody seems to know where Bruno went."

Lucas wondered if CID Robinson would tell more people he was from Long Beach. He did not think Robinson was stupid enough to tell Enrico about his connection with Bruno, Jodie and Inga. After Robinson told Bruno about Lucas, it cost Inga her life. However, Robinson did not know it also cost Bruno his life.

Lucas, Eric and Sonya carried beers down to the others and got settled in their chairs by the stream.

Shelley announced, "I forgot to tell all of you, Karen Tyler and Jeff are coming here tonight after work. They will both play guitar and sing if we want them to. She does Joni Mitchell songs, he does James Taylor, and they are fantastic."

"Where are they from?" asked George.

"Karen is from Portland, Oregon. Jeff is from Missouri," she replied. "I think they both spent time at Big Sur, and they were both at the Rolling Stones' Altamont fiasco."

"It will be a fun evening, and Bob brought firewood," said Gino.

"I guess the firewood is for effect because we sure don't need it for warmth," said Lucas.

Meanwhile, Topo pulled out his hash pipe, lit it, took a drag and passed it to Lucas. He got a hit and passed it on.

"How did you hide your stash, crossing the border?" asked Lucas.

"I've crossed many borders with hashish, and I haven't been caught yet, but my method is a secret," replied Topo. "So, let's enjoy it."

"How is everybody feeling?" asked Eric.

"I am a little concerned about eating hashish in food because I don't know the effects I will get or the amount I should eat," said Sonya. "I only know it is slower for digestion than fast-acting inhalation."

"It does sneak up on you," said Shelley. "After eating it earlier and now smoking it, I feel great."

Gino shared his opinion, "The brownie experience is like taking a fun trip. Things look brighter and my mind seems to expand. But everything seems slower and funnier with a hint of paranoia mixed in. I prefer smoking because I feel more in control. Although, when you ingest it as a group, everything is funnier."

Everyone laughed, as they realized they were experiencing the same things, and they all seemed to relax.

"I am starving!" said Eric, and everyone laughed again.

Shelley asked Gino, "We were wondering what the song 'American Pie' is all about. I have the tape in the van. Would you explain the lyrics to us later if you can?"

Gino agreed and said he had a cassette player at the campsite.

"Shelley and I brought snacks," said Lucas. "If we're all ready to go back to the campsite, I will put out the food."

Everyone was hungry. So, the group grabbed their chairs and headed back to the campsite. Gino went to get his cassette player, and Shelley went to get her tape of the song "American Pie."

Gino returned with his cassette player, a bottle of Jägermeister, and a stack of eight shot glasses which he was juggling. Everyone laughed at the sight of 5'6" Gino, fumbling and trying not to drop anything. With Eric's help, Gino put things down, set up the shot glasses and poured.

Working on a portable card table, Lucas put out some food. He had previously made a special item: a wheel of brie cheese he topped with caramelized onions and wrapped in puff pastry, decorated on top with small pastry flowers and baked to a golden-brown color. Lucas cut wedges from the pastry-wrapped brie and set those on a plate. He put out a bowl of pink-colored pickled eggs, and some sliced Bavarian pretzels which Heinz Ostler had made for the group. In anticipation of the munchies, Lucas also displayed a big tray of cookies: 2 dozen chocolate chip and 2 dozen oatmeal-raisin.

They all dug into the food and got settled in a semi-circle of chairs. Facing the stream, they could hear the racetrack noise beyond the trees. While eating and drinking beer, they carried on conversations, and everyone was talking at once.

Otto got very talkative when he was "high." Lucas recalled how hashish affected Heinz and Bucherl in the same way.

Since Shelley finished eating, she asked, "Do you want to listen to the song first? Then, we can try to figure out what it is all about?"

Everyone agreed, and Gino passed around the song lyrics, typed on 2 pages. He said, "A while back, I thought I had this song figured out, so I typed out the lyrics. This will help us follow along with the song, and then we can all give our interpretations."

After Bertha giggled, she said, "I'm not sure I needed to smoke the hashish." She took a bite of the brie en croute, and asked, "Sehr gute, Lucas. Did you make the pastry?"

"No. Our pastry chef made it," he replied. "He was also kind enough to supply me with some puff pastry which I can use when I need it for other things, such as Beef Wellington or a vol-au-vent."

Shelley played the tape, and they all listened to "American Pie."

"Okay. Let's talk about 'American Pie' now," said Gino. "The song is eight and a half minutes long, covering the period from nineteen fifty-nine to nineteen seventy, but it was about three different decades of changes in popular music.

"We will start with his first verse. I believe it reflects Don McLean, thinking back to his youth when rock 'n' roll impressed him. It was the new music in the fifties. It is obvious, he loved music, it made him feel happy, and he thought about becoming a singer. As a young teenager in the late fifties, he had a newspaper route. I think, the words, *February* and *widowed bride*, point to February third, nineteen fifty-nine, when the plane crashed with Buddy Holly, Ritchie Valens and The Big Bopper. Delivering papers, McLean must have read the headlines which said Buddy Holly's wife was pregnant and all those musicians died. McLean felt the loss of those great musicians. Holly was twenty-two, J. P. Richards, known as The Big Bopper, was twenty-eight, and Ritchie Valens was only seventeen years old.

"There is a story about Holly being tired of dirty laundry and being on the road in tour buses. He wanted to get home fast, so he chartered a small plane which took off in bad weather with an inexperienced pilot. The plane crashed, killing all four people on board, instantly."

"I read country singer Waylon Jennings gave up his seat on the flight which crashed and killed the three musicians," said Eric. "I also read the guitarist Tommy Allsup flipped a coin and lost to Ritchie Valens. I would say Allsup won by not getting on the flight."

"Yeah," said George. "I read about Buddy Holly who kidded Waylon Jennings for having to take the bus, and Jennings said he hoped the plane would crash. Of course, he was joking around."

"Imagine living with that for the rest of your life!" said Lucas.

It was ironic for Jennings, thought Lucas. *But it reminds me of my discomfort, living with Bruno's memory while trying to forget about it. And now, his look-alike brother shows up.*

"Next is the chorus which relates to McLean's take of the fifties," said Gino. "It was a post-war period of prosperity, and wealth in the country was shared. Americans got a slice of the pie as they married, raised children and bought essentials: automobiles, homes and furniture. Do you guys remember the Chevrolet commercial by Dinah Shore, *See the USA in your Chevrolet?* Those lyrics refer to a levee."

Otto was not interested in the group discussion of "American Pie." He was holding court with Sabine and Bertha. Sonya listened to their conversations, one in German and one in English, until she said, "This is driving me crazy. Can I get anyone a beer?"

Everyone said, "Yes!"

"Thank you, Sonya," said Lucas. "You know where they are in my van, so please help yourself."

Gino continued, "There are different explanations for each line of the song. Here's another slant on the chorus: McLean would drive his love to the levee for romance; but February third, nineteen fifty-nine was the day she broke up with him, so he felt empty. In this case, McLean would have dealt with two tragedies on the same day. One would be the plane crash, and the other would be breaking up with his girlfriend who was a beauty contestant. A friend of mine told me McLean's hometown of Purchase, New York, is near a town named Levee, New York. Also, there is a bar named The Levee in the same area which could have had an influence on the song.

"My theory is this: The Levee bar was popular, but closed its doors, forcing people to go elsewhere. And there is a town called Rye about six miles from McLean's hometown in in New York. Therefore, if people were drinking in Rye, New York, the song lyrics would mean… *drinking whiskey in Rye* instead of… *whiskey and rye*."

"Hey, Gino. How is it you know so much about the entertainment business?" asked Sabine.

"I was a movie and television director in Los Angeles before I came to Europe for a sabbatical," he replied. "While I'm here, I want to experience Europe the right way—as all of you are doing."

"Will you return to the same line of work?" asked Shelley.

"Oh, maybe after I get tired of this," he said. With a big smile, Gino raised his beer, and they all joined him in saying, "Prost."

Everyone who ate Lucas' hash brownies and smoked Topo's hash pipe was feeling the effects now. Otto was talking a mile a minute. He spoke German to whoever would listen. Sonya came back with beers for another, "Prost," and conversation about the song began again.

"A different theory about the levee involved murders of three civil rights workers in Mississippi," said Lucas. "In nineteen sixty-four, they were all students in their early twenties: one Jewish, one black and one white. The students wanted blacks to register as voters and people to boycott businesses which showed prejudice against blacks. Klu Klux Klan members went looking for the students, and some police officers were in the Klan group. They couldn't find the student civil rights workers, so the Klan burned down a church which had supported the students. When the students returned to the site of the church, police arrested the three students, took them to a secluded spot, maybe on the levee, then shot and buried them nearby."

"I remember the trial of those Klansmen, including police officers," said Eric. "They got off with light sentences, also one leader got off with no punishment. It was an all-white jury, and I think the judge was a member of the Klan."

"Okay, back to the end of the chorus," said Gino. "I think it was McLean's way of imagining the last moments of Buddy Holly, Ritchie

Valens and The Big Bopper. It also might relate to Holly's hit song 'That'll Be the Day' since each of them knew they would die, right before they crashed."

Shelley chimed in, "They were not the only persons who were lost to the music industry around the same time. Remember, Elvis was drafted into the Army, Little Richard switched to Gospel music, and the great Chuck Berry was arrested for having sex with a prostitute."

They all laughed out loud at the comment about Chuck Berry.

Gino, forever the organizer, said, "We'd better move on because we are only at the first chorus and there are six verses.

"In verse two, McLean was still a teen, and feelings of young love, mixed with religious beliefs, are all influenced by music. 'The Book of Love' was a hit song by the Monotones in nineteen fifty-seven. McLean might have been referring to the song. But I think this verse is all about McLean's love for rock 'n' roll, plus rhythm and blues, his vision of the mood in America, and his being an average lonely teenager who was in love with someone he couldn't have."

Shelley said, "He may have seen a girl who he liked, dancing with someone else at a sock hop where everyone takes off their shoes. The *pink carnation* could relate to the song by Marty Robbins. 'White Sports Coat and a Pink Carnation' was popular with teenagers. It was about a young guy at a dance without his girl."

"In verse three, *ten years* refers to the decade after the fatal plane crash. The sixties had rebellious youth and mass refusal of conventional values, as opposed to the fifties," said Gino. "The words *Rollin' Stone* were a song title on a Muddy Waters' nineteen-fifty-blues album. Muddy Waters claimed Brian Jones used their song title when he named his group The Rolling Stones (a slight variation). They had a raunchy look, wearing long hair and funky clothes, but they were rolling in green (raking in money). Music changed a lot in those ten years."

"I know this next one," said Shelley. "The *jester* was Bob Dylan who sang for the King and Queen of England, wearing the leather jacket he wore on his album cover. It was like James Dean's jacket in the movie *Rebel without a Cause*. I think the word *voice* refers to Dylan's style of singing which reflects dialog of people talking the way we do."

"Sounds good," said Gino. "In the next two lines, I believe the *king* and *thorny crown* refer to Elvis, the King of Rock 'n' Roll who got drafted into the Army; Dylan, the *jester*, then became the number one performer. In the court of public opinion, everyone knew Elvis got displaced while he served his country.

"Now…" Gino added, "… we come to *Lennon* and *Marx* which I think had to do with John Lennon's socialist leanings. *The quartet* was about the Beatles' last concert at Candlestick Park in San Francisco. Also, singing *dirges* would be funeral songs. These songs were for the Kennedys (John and Robert) plus Martin Luther King. They were all assassinated in the mid-sixties."

"The words *helter skelter* must refer to Charles Manson murders in nineteen sixty-nine," said Shelley. "I read about Manson. He was so strung out on acid, he thought the Beatles songs 'Helter Skelter' and 'Revolution Nine' were telling him a race war would happen soon, and he should commit those murders."

"After *helter skelter*, the words *birds* and a *fallout shelter* relate to a member of The Byrds rock group who got busted for pot and went to rehab," said Gino. "Back then, a *fallout shelter* was slang for drug rehab. The Byrds hit song 'Eight Miles High' was the first psychedelic rock song banned on U.S. radio because it's all about drug use. The band members denied it, saying the song was about their plane flight from the U.S. to London. However, one of the band members got arrested for possession of marijuana, and they admitted they were 'high' when they wrote the song. The U.S. ban hurt sales of the song, and it never made it to the top ten. Then, the group switched from rock music to country music which was their downfall. Now, who wants to give the next few lines a try?"

"Okay, I'll give it a go," said Lucas. "I see a *forward pass*, the *jester*, *half-time air,* and no chance to *dance*. In keeping with the Beatles theme, I think their concert tours in nineteen sixty-six were plagued with a lot of problems. The Beatles did not want to perform in the cold and fog at windy Candlestick Park in San Francisco, but they honored a contract to play there. They started the show late, and the crowd was so loud, the Beatles couldn't hear themselves sing. So, the concert only lasted about half an hour, thus no one got to dance. It was their last concert."

"Yeah. The *jester* again refers to Bob Dylan who was laid up in a cast for nine months after a motorcycle accident," said Gino. "The end of verse four is about others' attempts to *take the field,* and it asks what got *revealed*, relating to many groups who tried to grab the Beatles so-called *crown*. Although they disbanded after their last concert, the Beatles music remained extremely popular."

Eric felt the effects of hashish when he said, "What if the *players* were political activists who tried to make social change and wanted to gain control by demonstrating in the streets, like they did at Kent State and at the Democratic National Convention in Chicago? The *players* would have been turned back by the *sergeants*, being the law enforcement, such as Chicago Police who would not give up their ground, thus they *refused to yield*. The *sweet perfume* could be the smell of marijuana in the air at Kent

State in Ohio, or at Candlestick Park in San Francisco, or in Chicago, or anywhere else."

Holding his hash pipe in the air, Gino said, "It could even be right here at the Österreichring." He smiled, lit the pipe and passed it on.

Lucas considered the words *players* and *sergeants* in other context: *It could be German players who took the field. The Baader-Meinhof Gang are in prison now because their leaders refused to yield.*

Speaking to the group, Lucas said, "So far, I think this whole song is a complicated analogy about McLean's personal interpretation of the fifties and sixties. In verse five, he has a whole generation *in one place*, *lost* and unable to start over. This could describe Woodstock in nineteen sixty-nine. There was a generation of people who were lost on drugs, not to mention all those who were lost in the Vietnam War, either missing in action or killed in action."

"Couldn't it also mean the government focused too much on the space program, so they did not give enough attention and funding to earthly maintenance or environmental issues?" asked Shelley.

"Well, there's an interesting slant on it," said Gino.

"Yes. In which case, it could also mean there would be no going back if there was a nuclear war," said Lucas. "It would be the ultimate sacrifice if we didn't protect ourselves and our environment."

"Yeah," said Gino. "However, the rest of this verse seems to point to the nineteen sixty-nine Altamont Free Rock Festival in California. Did any of you happen to be there?"

Eric, Sabine, Lucas and Shelley all shook their heads.

"I believe Karen Tyler and her friend Jeff were there," said Shelley. "We can ask them tonight when they come to play guitar for us. Karen is from California, and she lived in Big Sur for a while."

"In the next line, I believe *Jack Flash* refers to the song 'Jumping Jack Flash' by The Rolling Stones," said Lucas. "The song came out after the Stones suffered a difficult period. They had experimented with acid and psychedelic music as heard in the Stones' album titled *Their Satanic Majesties Request* which did not do well for them. Critics thought the Stones were emulating the Beatles' album which was titled *Sgt. Pepper's Lonely Hearts Club Band*. So, the Stones struggled while returning to their own musical roots to crush the *fire* and *Satan's spell*. And McLean's use of the words *fists of rage* is evidence of his dislike for Mick Jagger."

"Weren't the Hells Angels involved with Altamont, and the whole thing went south? Didn't someone get killed?" asked Lucas.

"Let's ask Shelley's friends tonight," said Gino.

"I read three hundred thousand people were there. Big-name musicians performed, including Jefferson Airplane and Crosby, Stills, Nash and

Young. The Rolling Stones were the last act. The Grateful Dead were scheduled, but they never played, due to the violence. The concert was first set to take place at Golden Gate Park in San Francisco; however, it fell through. At the last minute, they got booked at the Altamont Speedway, but the organizers did not arrange for proper security. After the event, Grace Slick of Jefferson Airplane said it was peculiar, and the vibes were bad."

"Well, what happened at the concert, Gino? What was the violence about?" asked Shelley.

"I read a concert organizer asked the Hells Angels Motorcycle Club to keep fans from coming onto the stage; and they agreed to do it for a five-hundred-dollar-value of free beer," replied Gino. "They drank beer all day and got involved in fistfights. Later in the evening, it got very unruly. Hells Angels used sawed off pool cues and motorcycle chains to keep rowdy fans off the stage. An eighteen-year-old guy was 'high' on meth and pulled a gun. One of the Hells Angels stabbed him to death before he could shoot anyone."

Gino continued interpreting song lyrics, "The *flames* were all the bonfires around the area of the speedway, and *sacrificial rite* refers to the deaths which occurred. There was a stabbing, a drowning and an overdose. Many people claim it was the end of the hippie era."

"Yeah, all the hippies went to Ibiza and Formentera," said Lucas. "They got thrown off the islands while we were there."

Gino laughed, then said, "Right! You, George and I were there. None of us looked like hippies, so they let us stay."

Lucas thought: *I'm glad Gino did not mention Gabrielle being with me in Formentera. I do not want to explain it to Shelley.*

"Moving right along, now we're on the last verse," said Gino. "For the *girl* McLean is singing about, the only person I can think of is Janice Joplin who sang the blues. She died by a drug overdose in a Hollywood hotel last October."

"The *sacred store* must be a record store," said Eric. "I think the *music wouldn't play* because record stores no longer had listening booths or headsets to sample music. Over the years, music formats also changed from records to eight tracks, and then to cassettes."

"Who has ideas about what follows next?" asked Gino.

"After great thought," said Lucas, "I would say the middle of verse six is about war protests. Demonstrators would be *the children* in the streets; *lovers cried* would be the war widows and mothers; and *poets dreamed* would be the artists who wrote protest songs, such as those we have heard by Bob Dylan and other songwriters."

"Yeah. I agree," said Gino. "I remember Bob Dylan singing about the Vietnam War, the slaughter of children, widows crying and poets writing songs about it."

"I have a take on the broken *church bells*," said Eric. "Since I was raised as a Catholic, I remember when the Vatican assembled all the bishops and created the Second Vatican Council in nineteen sixty-two; they modernized church practices based on liberal goals of Pope John. Under Pope Paul, those practices were reversed in nineteen sixty-five. We know McLean is catholic, so I think the broken *church bells* may refer to the change in the Catholic Church."

"At the end of the verse, *the three men* could be Holly, Valens and The Big Bopper on *the last train* when they died," said Gino.

"It could also mean John Kennedy, Martin Luther King and Robert Kennedy who were all shot and killed in the sixties," said Lucas.

"Okay. We're done!" said Gino. "I don't know about the rest of you, but eating roast chicken from the racetrack sounds fantastic."

Hearing what Gino just said, Otto spoke up, "In Bavaria, we call it *brathendl* (whole roasted chicken). Right now, I think I could eat a whole chicken myself."

Eric, always the big eater, finished off the last pickled egg and the remaining wedge of brie en croute.

As the group finished their beers, Lucas put snack stuff away and locked the van. They all took off, walking back toward the racetrack. Along the path, trees shaded them from the late afternoon sunlight. They stopped at a beer tent near the main entrance, and Lucas looked to see if he could spot their other friends. It was so crowded and loud with the Bavarian rock music and people singing, they decided to stand in line at the food stand, buy roast chicken and pommes frites, take the food with them and walk back to their campsite.

When they had their food and were ready to leave, the other 12 AFRC people showed up. They were happy, but tired after their walk around the track. Regan Stone had his guitar, hanging over his shoulder. Today, he sang funny songs which he composed as he went along, and he wore a cowboy hat, living up to his nickname, Tex.

Then, out of nowhere, Jordan Lewis and Dennis appeared at the food stand. Everyone around them was laughing. Dennis, the homosexual Australian waiter, was always in character, being Dennis the 'flaming fag.' Lewis, the bouncer for The Grill, was doing his imitation of Dennis, only with a German accent.

With everyone back at the campground, there were 22 in the group. It was getting dark, so Bob Ostergaard, Maggie, Olivia and Enrico built a campfire in an open area. They all grabbed beers and chairs, then made a big circle around the fire, well away from the fire's heat. Everyone was starving, and the group got quiet, as they all ate brathendl, pommes frites, pretzels and curly white radishes.

After their meal, Lucas handed out hash brownies, cut in half. He reminded everyone what was in the brownies and what they could expect; they would feel the effects in 40 to 60 minutes; and they should only eat one-half, unless they were accustomed to eating hashish.

"You're with friends, so feel free to try one or not," said Lucas.

Everyone took a piece, except Regan and Enrico. When Lucas offered one to Enrico, Olivia introduced them, and they shook hands. This was the first time Lucas saw him up close. Enrico had a strong resemblance to Bruno, but Enrico was a much softer version.

Enrico said to Lucas, "A military policeman told me you were from Long Beach, California, and you knew my brother Bruno. I came here to look for him. Do you have any information which might help me locate him? I have found no clues although I have spoken to many people. No one has seen him for several months, and no one seems to know where he might have gone."

"I am actually from Fresno, California. I lived in Long Beach for several years, but I didn't know Bruno in Long Beach," replied Lucas. "The first time I met him was playing basketball at the Garmisch gym. We both worked at NATO Officers Club for a brief time, but I haven't seen or heard anything about him since then."

"Maybe I will try one of those brownies," said Enrico. "All of you are having so much fun. I don't want to feel left out."

People around the campfire applauded when they saw Enrico take the brownie. Otto announced to the group, "The fireworks will start in an hour." This brought more applause and a loud, "Prost."

They had all brought beer with them: Wieninger from the Chiemsee area, and Augustiner Bräu from the Garmisch area. As usual, a bottle of Jägermeister was being passed around. Regan (Tex) Stone played his guitar and sang funny, country songs.

Karen and Jeff arrived with their guitars. They received a warm welcome and got introduced to everyone at the campsite.

About 40 minutes after eating brownies, Lucas noticed the group was very gabby, and some people seemed off-balance when they stood and walked. He knew it could be due to the hash, or the beers.

Topo followed Lucas to his van. Lucas handed him a beer, and Topo said, "Hey Lucas, this is a great party. It is like being in Garmisch at The Grill, only we're outdoors with all the same crazy people."

Lucas stood there, watching the AFRC group who sat around the campfire. When Topo said, "… the same crazy people," Lucas thought: *It is great to be here in this campground, talking to Topo and watching all these good people who are having fun together. While Regan Stone is still playing guitar by the fire, Karen Tyler and Jeff are over to the side, tuning their guitars under a tree. I can hear Bavarian rock music, coming from the racetrack's outdoor theater and...*

His thought was interrupted when Topo said, "Lucas, I must tell you, I'll be leaving after the Olympics and going home to Argentina."

Hearing Topo's news stunned Lucas.

Eric, Gabrielle, Sabine and Shelley walked over and joined them.

Shelley put her arms around Lucas, gave him a big kiss and asked, "Are you going to come sit and watch the fireworks with me?"

"I think I'm in shock, Shelley," he replied. "Topo just told me he is going back to Argentina after the Olympics."

"Yes, I know," she replied. "Gabrielle cried when he told her."

"I'm sure it is difficult for her," said Lucas.

"Gabrielle told me she loves working at the hotel, and she is staying," said Shelley. "I am sure she will find someone else. You have never had trouble hooking up around AFRC, have you?"

Trying to ignore Shelley's question, he said, "I think I'll stand here and watch the fireworks. Right now, I'm too wound up to sit. Will you watch them with me from here?"

Shelley put her arms around Lucas and said, "Anywhere."

Lucas turned and asked, "How will you be traveling, Topo?"

"I'll be going by train to Lisbon, Portugal," he replied. "Then, I will try to get hired on a large sailing ship, going to the Bahamas. From there, I will make my way to South America, and I will get to Bariloche in Patagonia where my brother is now."

"Didn't you tell me there are Nazi connections in Bariloche, and it has a climate similar to Bavaria?" asked Lucas.

"Yes. We talked about it in Oberammergau, the night of the AFRC bar games," said Topo. "Oh, Lucas, I'm sorry to mention it."

"The bar games were fun. The rest, I try to put aside," he replied.

"I got a letter from my brother," said Topo. "The father of one of his close friends purchased a property with a big house, and my brother will stay there and do his research. Many people suspect this house is where Hitler lived after he escaped from Berlin."

Lucas got excited and said, "Are you kidding me? Does anyone have proof? Who bought the property? Does he know Hitler survived? Was he alive and living there after the war?"

"Whoa, slow down! I will tell you what I know," replied Topo.

Over the sound of fireworks which just started blasting, Lucas said, "I think it will have to wait until after the fireworks."

As Shelley leaned against him, Lucas put his arm around her and pulled her close. Everyone stopped talking, singing or whatever they were doing. Watching the spectacular show, a hypnotizing fireworks display seemed to shoot a million stars into the sky.

Following the fireworks, Lucas wanted Topo to tell him more about Bariloche, and he wanted to hear the story of Hitler's possible escape from Berlin. Karen and Jeff kept the group entertained, singing Joni Mitchell and James Taylor songs while they played their guitars.

Lucas, Shelley, Topo, Gabrielle, Eric and Sabine moved their chairs away from the fire. They sat by Lucas' van, so they could talk.

Since Eric and Sabine had not heard yet, Lucas said, "Topo gave me some sad news. He is leaving us to go searching for Hitler in Patagonia. Anyway, Topo, you tell them."

"It will be hard to leave this paradise," said Topo. "But my brother invited me to join him. His best friend's father bought a property near Bariloche. It has a big house, surrounded by dense forest on three sides and a large glacial lake in front of the house with a dock. They suspect this house is where Hitler lived after escaping from Germany. My brother is a journalist. He can now visit the secluded property to do more research on the subject."

"I read about it. What's the name of the house?" asked Eric.

"They call the house Residencia Inalco," replied Topo. "My brother kept me informed of his progress as he searched the history of the house and the grounds. It is on Nahuel Huapi Lake in a remote mountain area of Patagonia. Many Nazi refugees settled nearby in Bariloche. The area has the Alpine setting which is much like Bavaria."

"I thought there was proof of Hitler and Eva Braun's suicide. Is there any proof of Hitler escaping to Argentina?" asked Shelley.

"I've been to Bariloche to ski with my friend Raphael, several times. Believe me, there are many Nazis in the area," replied Topo.

"For example," he said, "I heard of a man named Erich Priebke who is known to have slaughtered many innocent Italian citizens in Rome, but he escaped conviction. He has been in Bariloche since nineteen forty-nine; he was the director of the German School of Bariloche for many years; and he has a delicatessen in Bariloche. I've walked past it, but I never went inside."

"Why have so many Nazis been able to live there, out in the open, without being charged for their war crimes?" asked Shelley.

"By the year nineteen hundred, most of Bariloche was a settlement of German immigrants," he replied. "After the war, between four thousand to five thousand Nazi war criminals escaped from Germany, and they settled in Argentina, thanks to Juan Perón. His friendship and business dealings with Germany and Nazis are well known. My brother said Perón sold ten thousand blank Argentine passports to a group called Odessa before the end of the war. Odessa's mission was to protect men of the Nazi SS, in case Germany got defeated."

"At the end of the war in nineteen forty-five, how would Hitler have been able to escape from his bunker in Berlin?" asked Sabine.

"There are different theories about how he could have escaped," said Topo. "Two burned bodies were found at the bunker, but they were not Hitler and Eva. So, the most logical conclusion is they escaped."

"Maybe they used Fegelein's body. I heard they executed and buried him in the Chancellery Garden, right at the end," said Lucas.

"As my brother told it," said Topo, "they walked in a secret tunnel to the airport, or a temporary runway, and flew out of Germany, maybe to Denmark, but more likely to Italy since people say the Vatican helped Nazis escape, using Vatican passports. Then, they went on to Spain where the Franco government was also sympathetic to the Nazis. From a Spanish port, they traveled by submarine to their destination on the southeast Argentina coast. Afterward, I imagine Perón protected them; and Hitler lived out his life in a setting much like the Berghof in Obersalzberg.

"The house, Residencia Inalco, got sold by José Rafael Trozzo, a banker who did business with Nazis in the area."

"Well then, what became of Hitler and Eva?" asked Gabrielle.

"My brother says Hitler lived his final days at the plush Eden Hotel in La Falda," said Topo. "It is seventeen hundred kilometers (1000 miles) north of Bariloche. Hitler was good friends with the hotel owners, Ida and Walter Eichhorn. They had visited Hitler in Germany, several times. He gave them a new Mercedes—the first Mercedes in Argentina. According to this story, Hitler was seventy-three years old when he died in nineteen sixty-two."

"So, does anyone know what happened to Eva?" asked Shelley.

"According to stories, Eva and Hitler had two daughters," said Topo. "Some people believe they separated, Eva kept the girls, and she moved to Neuquén which is five hundred kilometers (310 miles) north of Inalco. If this is true, I can imagine she wanted the girls to have a normal life, as much as possible. My brother wants to find out more and maybe write a book about it."

Karen and Jeff quit playing music, and all the activity around the campfire stopped. A moment later, Karen, Jeff and Regan played their guitars together and sang, "Tiptoe Through the Tulips…"

Lucas knew what was coming. He yelled, "Oh no! Not again!"

Out came Dennis to do his "Flaming A" dance, wearing a G-string. He was singing and skipping to the music. Toilet paper was stuck in the crack of his ass and streaming behind him. When he got to the fire, he lit the end of the toilet paper, dropped it behind him and pranced around the fire, moving back and forth between the people in chairs. By now, everyone was singing along with the music. Those who had not seen it before were stunned, but most of the group had seen it last year at the Thanksgiving dinner in Garmisch. As the toilet paper came close to burning his butt, Dennis pranced away. When he returned, fully dressed, he received a standing ovation.

Dennis responded, "Thank you all for tolerating me this past year. I believe fate was in my favor when I crashed my penny-farthing bicycle and broke my arm. The delay allowed me to join, work and play with you, the greatest people I've met on my long journey. For those of you who don't know about my journey, I started in London and planned to end my trip in my home city of Sydney, Australia. After being hit by a car on Fern Pass, I settled in Garmisch, working as a waiter and having the time of my life. I'm all healed now, and I will go on my way next month."

Karin and Jeff played their guitars and sang other songs. Gino and George got out of their chairs and joined the group at Lucas' van.

"This makes two good people who are leaving us," said Shelley. She looked at Lucas and added, "I wonder who will be next."

As George was joining them, he asked, "Next what?"

"Shelley wonders which of our friends will be next to leave after Topo and Dennis," explained Lucas.

"Yeah, it's funny you should mention it," replied George. "Judann and I are planning to go back to 'The States' and have a big wedding at her parent's ranch in Kentucky."

"It seems as if you just got here. Congratulations!" said Lucas.

"I had a great time, but I want to go back and find more challenging work," said George. "I've got the ski bug, now more than ever, so I may look somewhere around Lake Tahoe for a coaching job."

"Now, we are losing four people and still counting," said Shelley. Looking at Lucas, she asked, "Should I be hungry, already?"

Lucas shouted out to the group over by the fire, "Is anybody else getting hungry? We brought stuff from the hotel kitchen, and I believe Scott brought more food from the American School kitchen."

Since people were hungry, Lucas started making Béarnaise sauce to serve with beef filet bites and asparagus. He sat on the floor of the van, leaning over his Coleman stove which was on the fold-down table. As he observed the activity of people in front of him, he was also stirring butter into the egg yolks, for a nice smooth emulsion.

The musicians had stopped playing. And now, everyone mingled at Lucas' van, much like the times when a party ends up in the kitchen.

Shelley played the Jim Croce cassette and helped transfer items to the portable table where Lucas would display and serve the food.

Considering they were in a campsite, Lucas laid out a very nice spread. He put out trays of lemon herb chicken and green asparagus; plus 12-inch metal skewers with 3 square pieces of beef filet on each, ready for people to cook on the campfire grate. He also offered a choice of Béarnaise sauce or roasted garlic aioli for dipping.

Scott had long submarine sandwiches, made with sliced bratwurst, sauerkraut, sweet mustard and Munster cheese. He cut those into 2-inch slices. His wife, Faye, brought potato salad which she made.

When Enrico come over and started a conversation with Lucas, it caught him by surprise.

"How long have you been with AFRC, Lucas?" he asked.

"One full and eventful year, as of next month," Lucas replied.

"The friendliness of your group amazes me," he said.

"What do you do for a living?" asked Lucas.

"I'm an attorney for my father and the family," he replied.

"Where do you live, Enrico?" asked Lucas.

"My place is in Long Island near my family home," he replied.

"How long are you planning to stay in Garmisch?" Lucas asked.

"If I had the choice, I would stay in Bavaria," he replied. "I'm having too much fun to even think about going home now. But, in my family, we don't get to leave or quit our job. They expect me to stay with the family for life. I am only here because my father told me to find my brother. This is not something I wanted to do. I never got along with Bruno, and I've never liked him because he is a bad person who enjoys hurting people, including women."

"Well, I'm glad to hear you're having fun," said Lucas. "I feel the same about Bavaria. The people here are great and very friendly."

After he thanked Lucas for bringing and preparing the food, Enrico excused himself and went to get some.

Gino, Scott and Topo were passing their hash pipes around. As always, a bottle of Jägermeister also got passed and shared. The group had swollen to 24 boisterous partiers, adding to the other noise in the campground and music from the racetrack. It sounded as if it was one huge festivity.

Scott came over and joined Lucas. Sitting on the floor of Lucas' van with the sliding door open, they watched people huddling around the fire and cooking skewers of meat. Some had finished eating. Everyone in their group was talking, joking and laughing.

Out of nowhere, Lucas said, "Gemütlichkeit."

Scott asked, "What?"

"Otto said it means coziness, a sense of belonging and well-being in a social setting," Lucas explained. "Looking at our campsite made me think of it. This is a diverse group of people who all seem to bond and have fun together. Seeing this makes me wonder what we will do after we leave here. We are already losing several people. Topo, George, Judann and Dennis all said they're leaving."

"Lucas, those hash brownies were out of this world," said Scott. "I made chocolate chip cookies with hashish. Since people ate brownies and smoked hash, I'm not sure when I should put them out. Meanwhile..." Scott lit his hash pipe, took a hit and passed it to him.

"When I cross borders, I don't bring hash to smoke," said Lucas.

"You know Faye and I travel often to Spain and back on our bike," he replied. "They have never searched us at the border."

"Not worth the risk for me," said Lucas.

"We only carry a small amount with us, so I don't think they could charge us with trafficking," he replied. "If they did, Spain's penalty is now from three to six years in prison."

"I hope you never get caught," said Lucas. "Hey Scott, were you in Berkeley during the student protests?"

Faye and Shelley joined them as Scott said, "Yes, I was. Those protests were about three controversial topics in nineteen sixty-four: The Civil Rights Movement, the Free Speech Movement and the Vietnam War. Leaders in politics overreacted, law enforcement did not handle those situations well, and the forceful tactics they used were unnecessary."

Next, Gino, Sonya, Topo and Gabrielle came to Lucas' van.

"Lucas, you always amaze me with the spreads of food you produce, no matter where or when it is," said Sonya.

"Thank you," he replied. "I would add, it always tastes better when we don't have to pay for it." Glancing at Sonya and Gabrielle, Lucas noticed they were both smiling.

Lucas thought about the great meals he cooked for the RAF group: *RAF members won't be getting meals like those while they are in prison. It makes me sad to know they all gave up their freedom. And, what for? What did it all accomplish?*

People were wandering back to the card table and filling their plates.

"Scott, do we want to put out those cookies now?" asked Faye.

"Ooh, cookies! What kind?" Shelley asked.

"I made chocolate-chip-hashish cookies, late last night when no one was around in the school kitchen," replied Scott.

"You'd better watch out for snoopy CID Robinson," said Lucas.

"You might as well put them out. This will probably be an all-night party anyway," said Gino.

Otto and Bertha seemed to be having a great time, and Bertha wanted to entertain everyone. She spoke loudly for all to hear.

"There are different types of governments in the world:

Socialism—

You have two cows
Give both cows to the government
And they might give you some milk;

Fascism…

You have two cows
You give all the milk to the government
And the government sells it;

Nazism…

You have two cows
The government shoots you
And takes both cows;

Anarchism…

You have two cows
Shoot the government agent
And steal another cow;

Capitalism…

You have two cows
Sell one cow
And buy a bull;

Surrealism…

You have two panda bears
The government pays for surfing lessons."

The group enjoyed Bertha's rendition, and she got warm applause.

Looking around the campground, Lucas said "Austrians sure know how to party. There are no signs of this night slowing down."

After he and Shelley finished putting things away, they walked to the camp facilities and took a shower, wanting to beat the morning rush.

At about 3 a.m., their campsite party was over for now.

Lucas and Shelley were the last couple to close a van door. Since they ate one of Scott's special cookies, they were still wound up as they got settled in the van. Lying on top of the covers because it was still hot, both felt fresh and clean. He only had on tennis shorts, and she was wearing a bra and panties. This was all the incentive Lucas needed. They rocked the van for a while, and then both slept well.

Mid-morning, noise from the race and heat from the sun drove them out of the van, somewhat ready for race day at the Österreichring.

CHAPTER 41
Österreichring: Day 2

Overall, the group was slow to move on this race day morning. Lucas and Shelley began the day sitting on the floor of the van with the sliding door open and their legs dangling over the side.

Feeling sort of rough, Lucas reached over to the food cabinet, took out a hash brownie, cut it in half, handed one half to Shelley and said, "This should fix us and kick-start our morning."

Next, reaching behind him, he took two Wieninger beers out of the cooler, opened them and handed one to Shelley.

"Perfect. Thank you. What's for breakfast, Lucas?" she asked.

"I've got it covered," he replied. "How does smoked salmon, bagels and cream cheese with capers sound? We also have a pear and blueberry cobbler with crème fraiche, plus banana nut bread."

"Well, we had better get started. You know what happens when we bring food out," she said.

"Gino told people to bring their own breakfast food, plus some to share if they wanted to. So, we will see what happens," said Lucas.

To start his day, Scott Williams walked around their campsite and offered his friends a chocolate-chip-hashish cookie. It would help dull the pain of over-indulgence which occurred only a few hours ago.

Gino suggested it would be fun if each person picked a driver from their country of origin and cheered for that driver.

Half of the group are Americans who would cheer for Peter Revson, the only American driver in the race. Since Gino had researched the driver's backgrounds, he passed some information on to them, "Revson is the heir of Revlon Cosmetics. He had some success driving in the Indianapolis Five Hundred races and finished fifth as a newcomer. Last year, he finished second after starting on the pole."

The Austrians, Otto, Bertha and Sabine would cheer for Niki Lauda, the young driver from Vienna.

Gabrielle and Sonya would follow Rolf Stommelen from Siegen, Germany, who finished third in the first Formula One race held at this Österreichring in 1970.

Topo would be rooting for Argentinean, Carlos Reutemann.

There were 2 Australian drivers in this race: Tim Schenken finished third here last year. David Walker had never raced at this track; and he drove his first Formula One race at the Dutch Grand Prix last year. So, Ashleigh, Olivia and Dennis decided they would be *klatschen* (clapping) for Schenken.

The lovely English lady, Maggie, would cheer for Jackie Stewart.

Gino read aloud from a program which he had in his back pocket, *"Jackie Stewart, the British Formula One driver, was born in Scotland. He has won sixteen Formula One races in the last four years and has been on the podium twenty-two times in the same period."*

This Formula One Race was Lucas' first auto race. He had seen a few destruction derbies when he was young and had watched his crazy older brother, Gene, out on a dirt track in Madera, California, trying to wreck anyone who got in his way. Gene's driving career ended when officials barred him from the derby track.

Otto and Bertha led them all to a great spot for watching the race. It was on a corner, looking down the track to the start/finish line. Drivers came uphill toward this corner from the start line, reaching speeds up to 180 mph on the straightaway.

Otto described the spot as a very fast right turn, known as the Hella Licht Kurve which means *lights out* or something similar. From here, drivers went down a gentle slope which curved right, then left, then straightened out. They reached speeds up to 180 mph again, then they slowed to 55 mph at a sharp right-hand curve. On the next straightaway, they reached speeds up to 178 mph, followed by a sweeping left-hand curve which they took at 100 mph. Then, it was an uphill climb at 175 mph to the last turn, known as the Joshua Rindt Kurve, where they slowed to 105 mph. On the final, long straightaway, the drivers went over 180 mph across the finish line.

Lucas felt the race was very exciting. The whining sounds of engines and high speeds, mixed with the smell of fuel and rubber. At one point, seeing into the pit area, he noticed the drivers' glamorous wives and girlfriends were jumping with excitement and cheering for their man. Race car drivers all seem to have a rock star status. It made Lucas think about the RAF members who were known as Celebrity Terrorists.

If they happened to see their chosen drivers go by, people in their group were shouting and cheering. Then, the drivers settled into their positions, and the cars got spread out, going around the course.

Lucas was studying the people in his group. Shelley came over, kissed him on the cheek and said, "You appear to be in a trance."

“Oh, I’m sorry,” he said. “I was thinking about what will happen to each of our friends after they leave Bavaria and the AFRC.”

“After eating the brownie and one of Scott’s cookies, I’m not sure I can handle the conversation now,” she replied. “But I think Judann and George will get married and raise a bunch of kids in California.”

“Okay, I’ll agree with your prediction,” said Lucas.

“I’m starving. Can we go get some beer and food?” she asked.

Walking toward the concession stands, Lucas said, “Well, we know Topo is going back to Argentina where his brother is a journalist. Topo is too intelligent to be a drug dealer for the rest of his life. I could see him owning a sports bar in a place like Bariloche, Argentina.”

“I think Gabrielle will stay in Chiemsee for a while,” she replied, “She loves the pace of life in Bavaria, and she enjoys it more than the hustle and bustle in the big city of Hanover where she came from.”

“Yeah, I see her point,” said Lucas. “Having lived in the Los Angeles area, and then coming here, this is something else. You know, Scott Williams is a U.C. Berkeley graduate. He is now running the American School lunch program in Garmisch. I think Scott could get into politics. He gets so concerned about the unfair policies of the political right. I think Faye will be a grammar school teacher.”

When they arrived at the concessions area, they were both laughing at the bold predictions which they were making about their friends. Lucas looked at the menu, posted above the food stand window, and said, “I will have Wiener Schnitzel, potato salad and a half-liter bottle of Gosser beer.”

“I want a bratwurst, potato salad, brötchen and beer,” said Shelley.

They got their food and looked for a place to sit. Then, they heard someone call out, “Lucas, Shelley, over here!”

Both turned and saw George and Judann, holding plates of food and waiving at them from a table which a family of 8 was vacating.

Seated at the table, Shelley asked, “Did you feel the effects of the cookies and brownies, as much as I did?” Judann giggled.

“Look at us,” said George. “While the great race is going on, we’re all sitting here with the munchies.” Everyone laughed.

“As we stood in line and waited for our food, we tried to imagine what each person in our group here will do after they leave the AFRC,” said Shelley. “We already know you two are going back to get married and get settled in ‘The States.’ George, we think you will get a head coaching job at a University. But we had not yet gotten to you, Judann. Maybe you can help us out.”

“I want to be a travel agent in Southern California,” said Judann. “After much discussion, we plan to get settled there.”

"You know Gino is from Miami, and he's been traveling a while," said Lucas. "I'm pretty sure, Gino will get back in the movie industry. If he does, he will be moving to Southern California. Sonya plans to stay in Garmisch. She will take over The Last Chance when her mother retires."

Lucas heard Eric's deep voice say, "You know there's a race on?"

Then, he saw Eric, Sabine, Olivia and Enrico approaching, each holding a plate of food and a bottle of Gosser beer.

"Hunger and thirst won over speed and danger," said George.

Seeing Olivia and Enrico together made Lucas think of Bruno: *I'm glad I didn't tell Olivia about my connection with Bruno when I traveled with her. Now, she's dating Enrico. While he is looking for his brother, Bruno is wasting away at the bottom of a canyon.*

Sabine, Shelley and her friend Judann were in deep conversation. George sat across from Eric, and they were talking-trash to each other about their athletic skills. They both had impressive skills. George was known nation-wide as a great volleyball player, and Eric had pitched for a national, collegiate-champion baseball team. When they were all in Cervenia, Lucas had to pull them apart to end what had started as a friendly, macho wrestling match, then became a little too heated. Now, since they had both been intimate with Sabine, there could be more fuel on the fire. However, it was a year ago in Gomagoi, Italy, when George was with Sabine, and Lucas connected with Inga.

Today, Eric told George how he beat the Austrian arm-wrestling champion in St. Johann; and George was macho enough to think he could take Eric in arm wrestling. After Eric embarrassed him by slamming his hand to the hard-wooden table, George would not let go of Eric's hand, and he pulled Eric off the bench onto the ground. This time, it took both Lucas and Enrico to intervene and pull them apart.

Lucas hated to see these guys fighting. He knew George for several years in Long Beach, and they traveled together. After George went back to California, Lucas became good friends with Eric. It was several months before George returned to Garmisch with Judy and Deanna, the Canadian ladies who now work at "The Hof" in Berchtesgaden.

Maybe it's a good thing George is going back to California because Garmisch is not a very big town, thought Lucas.

They joined the rest of the group to watch the end of the race. Brazilian driver, Emerson Fittipaldi, the formula-one-point's leader, won the 54-lap race after battling with British driver Jackie Stewart who fell back and finished 7th. Fittipaldi raced in Car Number 31, his Lotus backup, instead of Car Number 20 which he drove in qualifying. He had driven both cars during practice, earned the pole position, then chose his spare car for the win. New Zealand's Denny Hulme drove a McLaren and finished 2nd.

His teammate from the U.S., Peter Revson, finished 3rd. American followers in AFRC gave him a big cheer.

After the race, the group took their time leaving since there would be a big traffic jam for a while. They all gathered back at the campsite and hung around until the traffic thinned out.

Lucas had time to talk to Olivia for a few minutes, and she said Enrico was a gentleman who treated her like a queen. Olivia claimed most men in Australia were very crude, by comparison. Enrico wanted to stay in Garmisch because his father was so controlling and demanding of him; it was a relief for him to get away and relax. Lucas asked about Enrico's search for his brother. Olivia told him Enrico did not care about his brother; they never got along; and he would rather not find his brother since Bruno enjoys being mean and hurting people.

Talking quietly at his van, Lucas told Shelley, "Olivia said Enrico wants to stay and work in Garmisch, but not look for his brother."

"I guess we can say they are a couple now. However, I wonder how it will end up," she replied.

"I could see them going to Australia together," said Lucas. "It would sure put more distance from his father's control. You know, Shelley, everything I've heard about the Castignoli family points to them being a mafia family in Long Island, New York."

"You don't want to get on the wrong side of them," she replied.

"Do you think anything permanent will come out of the Regan Stone and Ashleigh match up?" she asked.

"My guess would be no," he replied. "I've had several conversations with Regan, one-on-one. With all his wealth and background, he seems to live the life of a Texas playboy."

"What about Eric and Sabine?" she asked.

"They are two of my favorite people in the world," he replied. "Eric told me he and Mike Harker are heading to Athens in two weeks. Eric is taking his van, and Harker will ride his motorcycle.

"Harker is set to be a waterski instructor, working at Club Med in Glyfada Beach. Eric expressed a desire to work on a private yacht and sail across the Atlantic to the Bahamas. Then again, he could change his mind about going—or he could go and come back—or go elsewhere. A while ago, he said he wants to go back to Montana and get into the mining business. He is a tough one to figure out. I don't see Sabine going anywhere; she has the best job and lives in such a great place. If they do stay together, Eric will have to make the commitment to live here."

"Tell me about Bob Ostergaard and Maggie," said Shelley.

"Bob will be a millionaire, by the time he is thirty years old," he replied. "Bob works so hard and never seems to get tired. He is always reading financial pages and talking about schemes to make more money. I don't think he will settle down with anybody until he gets his ducks in a row. He has a degree in Marine Biology, but I don't think he plans to do anything with it."

"Okay. We are only left with Shelley and Lucas," she said.

Lucas smiled, took her hand and said, "An easy prediction, if Shelley still wants to go to Greece after the Olympics and the hotel's summer rush are over. Beyond Greece, our plans are open. It might be nice to work at 'The Hof' and ski in Berchtesgaden for the coming winter."

Shelley got excited, threw her arms around Lucas' neck and gave him a big kiss on the lips. It got the attention of other people.

George hollered over, "What are you two up to?"

"Lucas and I are going to Greece!" shouted Shelley.

The rest of the group gave Lucas and Shelley a good cheer.

"Great! You will love Greece," said Gino. "Now, we all have to get back to work in Bavaria, so we'd better get moving."

Karen Tyler and Jeff needed a ride back to Chiemsee. The people they came with had gone on to Vienna. Lucas offered, "If you will play music during the drive back, you can ride in my van."

Lucas drove, and Shelley sat in the front passenger seat. The bed was folded up, so Karen and Jeff sat at the table, facing the front of the van, with Topo and Gabrielle at the table, facing them.

Entertaining the group, Karen played songs from a new Joni Mitchell album, *Blue*. Lucas had heard Karen sing Joni Mitchell songs, several times at Chiemsee, either outdoors or in the movie theater. It was a completely different experience in the confined space of the van.

Lucas and Shelley were both touched by the song "California." They looked at each other and smiled.

They were right behind Eric in the caravan of AFRC vans. Lucas was still feeling the effects of the weekend, so he had to be careful and pay attention, driving in heavy traffic with a long line of cars, vans, campers, motorcycles and trucks.

Resting between songs, Karen talked about her youth, Joni Mitchell and Big Sur. Karen told them how she came to learn Joni Mitchell songs, and how she learned to play the guitar. She grew up in Portland, Oregon. Her father taught her to play guitar and sing. He was fond of country and western songs. At twenty years old, she found her way to the Haight Ashbury district in San Francisco. Then, she met a group of people who took her south to see the Big Sur Folk Festival.

"I heard about it. Who performed? Was Dylan there?" asked Topo.

"No, he wasn't there," said Karen. "He wouldn't go to Woodstock either. Crosby, Stills, Nash and Young were fantastic. Neil Young sang,

'Down by the River' and Joan Baez opened the festival with 'I Shall Be Released' which is a Dylan song. Joni Mitchell did her own song, 'Woodstock.' Her title was odd because she did not attend Woodstock. Even then, Joni's music was different. It was how she tuned her guitar and how she used her right hand, not to strum the guitar, but to stroke the strings, like an artist would use a paintbrush. A friend told me Joni bought a dulcimer from a lady who made them in Big Sur. I never spoke with Joni, but I saw her around with her boyfriend, Graham Nash. I found out she went to Europe with the dulcimer and a flute last year, leaving her guitar at home. On the *Blue* album, you can hear her play guitar, dulcimer and piano."

"What is a dulcimer? Is it a type of guitar?" asked Gabrielle.

"The Big Sur lady shapes them like a coffin with only three strings. You set it on your lap and play it, using a quill," she replied.

"Where did Joni go in Europe? Is she still here?" asked Topo.

"I heard she lived in a place called Matala on the island of Crete," she replied. "When Joni first arrived, she lived with another lady in a cinder-block hut on the beach. The lady met a soldier at the Mermaid Bar, and they ran off somewhere. Then, Joni met a guy who she wrote about in her song 'Carey.' He was a cook in a Matala restaurant, and Joni moved into Carey's cave. These caves are on the side of a sandstone cliff, overlooking a wide beach cove."

"Why did Joni Mitchell go to Crete?" asked Gabrielle.

"I guess, it was to get over her breakup with Graham Nash," she replied. "He is British, and Joni Mitchell first met him in Canada at a concert where he was playing with the Hollies. Later, they got together at David Crosby's house in LA. I heard there was a constant party with lots of people at his house. Crosby was the ultimate partier—He always had the best dope and great music because musicians hung out there, along with plenty of young women in skimpy outfits, or naked. So, there was also plenty of sex. When Graham Nash got there, he claimed he had found Hippie Paradise.

"Graham Nash enjoyed the Hollies' success for a while, but they split up. Then, Stephen Stills parted ways with Buffalo Springfield. At the time, his cocaine use was out of control."

"Did Joni Mitchell use drugs much?" asked Lucas.

"I heard she preferred to smoke cigarettes and drink coffee, but most of her musician friends did plenty of drugs," she replied. "When Nash arrived in Los Angeles, Joni took him to her house in Laurel Canyon. She had been with David Crosby before she met Nash, but Nash captured her heart. She saw no future with Crosby, his harem of young women, and his wild lifestyle. It was rather crazy time in the music industry. A lot of the musicians were changing groups and romantic partners. Before she got together with Nash, Joni was also with James Taylor for a while. Her house became a hangout for musicians and songwriters who shared their songs with each other and allowed different artists to record them. When Nash broke up with Joni, she came to Europe to recuperate and mend. After she left Crete, she went to Formentera where she worked on finishing the *Blue* album."

Lucas checked his rearview mirror and caught a wink from Gabrielle. Neither had told people about their time together in Formentera. Traffic slowed down, and Lucas saw the border in front of their caravan.

"Here's the border," said Lucas. "Get your passports ready."

The line of vans, a motorcycle and a Nazi-era Mercedes sedan stopped at the German side of the border. Sonya and Sabine got out and spoke to German border guards. A patrolman walked along the line of vans, telling people the guards would check passports and look inside vans.

When guards checked passports of the people in Lucas' van, Jeff told them he must have lost his passport, or maybe it was stolen. It was not in his backpack. One border guard took Jeff to the office while other guards finished their search.

Going through Lucas' van, a guard checked the food cabinet and saw a plate of cherry-cheesecake brownies. He said, "Ach, ein kuchen."

Gabrielle spoke German and told him they were taking the dessert to a party in Bernau. Thus, he did not ask for a piece.

Guards finished with passports and searches, but Lucas had to pull his van over to the side. The rest of their caravan headed to Garmisch. After a long wait, a guard came and spoke in German with Gabrielle.

When the guard returned to his office, she explained what he told her. "Our new friend, Karen's music partner, has been arrested. It seems he had escaped from Bernau prison which is across the autobahn from Chiemsee Hotel. Jeff was doing time on a drug charge. The strange part of the story is he walked from the prison, went under the autobahn to the AFRC gas station and got a job there, three months ago."

"I wondered why he was so quiet at the Austrian border. I guess he didn't want to be asked for his passport," said Shelley.

"Thanks to Bob, one border guard had a bottle of whiskey or something when they waived the rest of our caravan through," said Lucas.

"Yeah, it's good to keep a bottle of whiskey handy," said Karen.

"Whiskey may help with a small amount of dope for personal use, but trafficking to sell is a different deal. That is scary," said Topo.

Everyone looked at Topo as if they did not know what he was talking about. He said, "Oh, I mean the part about crossing borders with illegal drugs, and then going to prison is scary."

"Jeff said nothing to me about it," said Karen. "I wonder how long he intended to stay and work at Chiemsee without a passport."

"It was stupid to try crossing a border with no ID," said Shelley.

"He didn't want to come," said Karen. "I guess I talked him into it. Now, since I'm a solo again, I think this song will be appropriate."

She sang "Both Sides Now" which is on Joni Mitchell's 1969 *Clouds* album. Then, she sang the upbeat "Big Yellow Taxi" from *Ladies of the Canyon,* an album Joni Mitchell released in 1970.

Karen sang the whole *Clouds* album, and Lucas loved every song. Joni Mitchell has a new fan. Lucas planned to buy the *Clouds* album, knowing he would listen to it, many times over.

Right now, we have Karen in person, but she could be Joni Mitchell in disguise, thought Lucas. *She sounds exactly like Joni.*

"I think Joni Mitchell and Stephen Stills are two pure geniuses from the Laurel Canyon group," said Karen.

Shelley had grown up in the Los Angeles area, and she asked Karen, "What about Laurel Canyon?"

"I mentioned Joni Mitchell had a house in Laurel Canyon. It became a hangout for young musicians in the late sixties," she replied. "Joni may have helped Crosby, Stills and Nash get together. Yet, in another story, Mama Cass introduced them to each other. In truth, they all wrote songs and passed them around. For example, Judy Collins also sang 'Both Sides Now' which was a big hit for her."

"I read Stephen Stills was in a mental institution during the mid-sixties. Do you know anything about it?" asked Topo.

"I know everyone says Stephen Stills is a pure genius which can be related to mental issues," she replied. "He did spend time in a hospital when he started writing songs. I heard he was a head case, temperamental and egotistical, but he was a talented man. He and Judy Collins were an item in the late sixties, and he wrote about her in 'Suite: Judy Blue Eyes.' It was a great song on *Crosby, Stills and Nash,* their first album."

"I also read Stills was with Rita Coolidge," said Topo.

"Yes. Then, Graham Nash stole Rita Coolidge from Stills," she said. "It caused their group to breakup in 1970, for a while. Rock stars pass around songs the same way they pass around sex partners."

"Karen, how do you know so much about the personal lives of these musicians?" asked Gabrielle.

"I hang out with musicians," she replied. "We always seem to know what everyone in our craft is doing: where they are, what they are working on, what drugs they use and who they are sleeping with."

Back in Chiemsee, Lucas stopped at the Ranch House to drop off Topo and Gabrielle. Before they got out of the van, Lucas asked them, "Did you have a good time at the races?"

Topo and Gabrielle looked at each other, and she said, "I think so." Everyone laughed.

On the drive over to the Park Hotel, Lucas asked, "While you've been in Europe, have you been able to travel much, Karen?"

"Yes," she replied. "London, Paris, Berlin, Frankfurt and here."

"Where is the next place you want to go?" he asked.

"When I save enough money, I will go to Ibiza and Formentera to work on some of my own songs and style," she replied. "I thought about going to Matala where Joni Mitchell had lived on the island of Crete, but I understand Matala is on the south side of the island, and it's very difficult to get there."

"How did you get together with Jeff?" asked Shelley.

"When he heard me play guitar and sing, he approached me," she said. "He said he played James Taylor songs, but he didn't have a guitar, or enough money to buy one. I thought it might be fun to play together, so we got a cheap guitar from a ski patrol guy who was going back to 'The States.' Then, I helped Jeff with his guitar playing. His prior escape from prison is a complete surprise."

"Well, it's good to know he wasn't a serial killer," said Lucas.

When they arrived at the Park Hotel, Lucas and Shelley exchanged hugs with Karen, and then she went her own way.

Glad to be home and in their apartment, Lucas and Shelley got a good night's sleep. The next morning, they both returned to work.

The second half of August was busy; days were eventful, and time flew by. The hotel was booked solid until after the Olympic Games. Those would be held August 26 to September 11 at locations in and around Munich, a 1-hour drive northwest of Lake Chiemsee.

Bob Clarkson wanted to have a barbecue for the employees. Lucas, Chip and Topo wanted to have a tennis tournament. If they could get enough players involved, both events could happen on the same day.

Lucas had played doubles, switching partners between Topo, Chip and John Riley. However, Lucas was a singles player at heart, and he had not gone head-to-head with Chip on the tennis court, yet.

Chip was the hotel's tennis instructor during the summer, and Lucas looked forward to competing against him again. The next time they played, it would not be a bar game. Tennis was Chip's sport and Chip's court, but he had never played against Lucas' singles game.

CHAPTER 42

Munich Olympics 1972

Hotel staff and employees planned to have the barbecue and tennis tournament on the same day, along with beach volleyball, horseshoes and a miniature golf contest. Lucas, Bob Clarkson, Shelley, Topo, Chip and John Reilly organized the events. The barbecue and other activities would take place on Saturday, the 9th of September.

The 2-week period before the Olympics were crazy for Lucas, and the kitchen was running at maximum production. The Olympic Games would take place in Munich, straight up the autobahn. Lucas planned ahead, and the cooks prepared things they could make in advance, such as potato croquettes, veal cordon bleu, pork schnitzel and twice-baked potatoes. Those items were frozen and ready for hotel guests who would be coming for the Olympics.

Lucas worked split shifts during the Olympic Games. He practiced tennis on his afternoon breaks, then he worked through the busy dinner services until 10:00 p.m.

Shelley located a large television, and it was set up in the hotel lounge to show the Olympic Games. At the end of each night, Lucas, Topo, Shelley, Gabrielle, hotel guests, ski patrol and other employees could watch highlights of each day's events on the big TV.

After a long day at work, Lucas joined Shelley, Gabrielle and Topo in the lounge to see highlights of the Olympics' opening day.

Watching clips of the opening ceremonies, Lucas noticed most of the Germans were on one side of the room, and English-speaking people were seated on the other side. Then, he realized it may be due to the language difference. For anyone with questions, Gabrielle was often around, translating what the German announcers were saying on TV. Today, she explained the German motto: *Die Heiteren Spiele* (The Cheerful Games). She also pointed out the *Bright Sun* logo, and the Olympic mascot, *Waldi* (the dachshund).

The next day was Sunday, the 27th of August, and two gold medals were awarded for shooting and weightlifting competitions. On Monday, Olympic games continued with swimming, gymnastics and diving.

Lucas looked forward to seeing Olympic basketball and volleyball games on television. He also wanted to see the track and field events which came later in the week.

As American employees watched events and results, they naturally rooted for the U.S. teams against the rest of the world. Trash talk and friendly rivalry began between the American employees and ski patrol on one side and the German employees with friends who were all cheering against the Americans on the other side.

Gabrielle followed Olympic news by watching TV and reading the newspaper. Each day, she passed the most interesting news on to Lucas. He did not have time to read or watch TV, except to catch highlights after work around 10 p.m.

Several hotel employees and ski patrol drove to Munich and watched the Olympic events in person. When they returned, Lucas asked about security at the games. They all said there were no obvious signs of police or military, and no weapons were seen.

Lucas wondered if remaining RAF members might try to disrupt the games, or if they might try to free their leaders who now sat in prison. He thought: *Planners for the Olympics must know what they're doing. They cannot be just wishing for "Happy Games" to occur.*

Opening and closing ceremonies, track and field, the soccer final, gymnastics, handball, hockey, swimming, volleyball, field hockey and boxing events would take place within the Olympic Village in Munich. Other events, such as yachting, were on the North Sea around the port of Kiel. The soccer matches were being held in Nuremberg, Regensburg, Passau and Ingolstadt, all within a 2-hour drive of Munich. Canoeing and handball would happen in Augsburg, Ulm, Goppingen and Boblingen, northwest of Munich near Stuttgart.

During the first week of Olympic competition, there were several disputes. At the end of the Skeet Shooting event, 3 medalists had the same score, thus a shoot-off was held. The final shoot-off was between a Russian and the West German shooter, Konrad Wirnhier. To the delight of German spectators in the hotel lounge, their competitor hit all 25 targets and won the gold medal.

Next, a Russian skeet shooter, the 1971 world champion, disagreed on the judges' ruling for 1 of his targets, and he walked off the field. He was penalized 3 birds, and it caused him to not make a 4-way tie. Therefore, he finished 9th.

Nightly rivalry increased between the U.S. fans and the German fans as time went by in the Chiemsee Hotel Lounge. After one week: The West German team had won gold medals in skeet, the men's cycling team pursuit, the men's javelin throw and the men's coxed four rowing. For track and field, they won gold medals in the women's long jump, the women's 800 meters and the women's high jump. They also won a gold medal in the men's 50-kilometer walk, a gold medal in the men's javelin throw, plus a silver medal in the women's pentathlon. The United States won medals in the women's 800 meters, the women's long jump, the men's 50 kilometers walk and the women's high jump.

After having issues with equipment, the U.S. got silver and bronze medals in the men's pole vault. A few weeks before the Olympics, the Olympic Committee ruled against two athletes: American Bob Seagren and Kjell Isaksson from Sweden. They were using illegal poles which contained carbon fiber. Four days before competition began, the ruling was reversed. Then, on August 31, only one day before competition, officials reinstated the ban and confiscated poles from American and Swedish athletes. As a result, they had to use poles which they had never trained with. Wolfgang Nordwig, an East German, won the gold. For the U.S., Bob Seagren won the silver, and Jan Johnson won the bronze. Isaksson failed to make the final round. He was disgusted with the officials. So, he handed his pole, the one they forced him to compete with, to the president of the Olympic Federation. This was the first time an American did not win a gold medal for the men's pole vault during the prior sixteen Olympics.

The United States team won gold medals for swimming in the men's 200-meter breaststroke, the women's 200-meter backstroke, the men's 1500-meter freestyle, the women's 200-meter butterfly and the men's 100-meter butterfly, plus a world record for Mark Spitz.

Track and field had one of the most exciting races Lucas had ever seen. Lucas and everyone else in the lounge, including the Germans, cheered their heads off when Dave Wottle, wearing a golf cap, used his long arms and legs to come from 10-yards-behind all 7 runners. At the end, he caught up with 2 Kenyan runners, passed both, and then edged out the Russian runner who had fallen right at the tape. Wottle took the gold medal in the 800-meter race. A West German runner finished 4th. After 1 week, the U.S. had 11 gold medals, and West Germany had 8 gold medals.

Ever since he entered the restaurant business, Lucas had limited time for television, but he enjoyed watching highlights of Olympic Games, especially the track and field events.

The men's 10,000 meters was a great race. Finland's Lasse Viren came back after a fall when he got tangled with Mohammed Gammoudi who was from Tunisia. They both recovered, but Gammoudi dropped out after 2 more laps. Then, Viren took the lead at 6,000 meters, never looked back, finished 1st and set a new world record.

Tuesday morning, September 5th, was the 10th day of Olympic competition. Lucas was in his office, working on the hotel's grocery order. Gabrielle and Shelley burst in, and they were very upset.

"Arab terrorists have kidnapped several Israeli Olympic athletes," said Shelley. "They demanded the release of Arab prisoners in Israel, plus release of RAF leaders, Andreas Baader and Ulrike Meinhof."

"They didn't mention Gudrun Ensslin?" asked Lucas.

"Not on the news broadcast I heard," replied Gabrielle.

"According to news reports," said Shelley, "one athlete escaped from an apartment in the Olympic Village, and the terrorists killed one of the Israeli coaches."

"If they want to get the RAF leaders out of prison, then remaining members or sympathizers of the RAF must be helping the terrorists with this kidnapping, one way or another," said Lucas.

"It would make sense," said Gabrielle. "RAF assistance to help free Arab prisoners would be the obvious reason for terrorists to include Andreas and Ulrike in their plan. However, I doubt it will happen. Andreas causes more damage, every time he gets released."

"How did the kidnappers get into the village?" asked Lucas.

"A newscaster said they climbed over an obscure section of a chain-link fence," replied Gabrielle. "Athletes used the same area of fence to sneak in and out of the village and to access the women's quarters. I guess there were no guards around at four thirty in the morning."

"The television stations are setting their cameras throughout the Olympic Village," said Shelley. "This is all we know so far. Right now, everything seems to be quiet there. We will let you know when something else happens."

Lucas, Chip and John Riley developed the plan for The First AFRC Chiemsee Tennis Tournament which included 8 men and 8 women.

Only half of the 16 players came from American decent, yet all work in American military facilities. The Armed Forces Recreation Center (AFRC) employs people from around the world. It's obvious when you see their list of players, and Lucas thought it was interesting.

Men from Chiemsee: Lucas, Chip and John Riley (Americans) and Topo (Argentinean). From Berchtesgaden: Gerhardt Grassl (German). From Garmisch: George, Eric and John Ferrell (Americans).

Women playing from Chiemsee: Shelley (American) and Gabrielle (German). From Berchtesgaden: Judy and Deanna (Canadians who both work at the Berchtesgadener Hof). From Garmisch: Sonya (American father and German mother). From Seefeld: Sabine (an Austrian ski instructor). From the Garmisch area: Olivia and Ashleigh (Australians).

Bob Ostergaard and Jordan Lewis were in town to work on 2 VW vans which Bob had purchased at a farm in nearby Frasdorf.

They brought Dennis and his penny-farthing bicycle. After a year in Garmisch, his broken arm had healed. Dennis did not want to miss watching the Olympic festivities and watching his friends play in the AFRC games at Chiemsee. Last month, during the group camp-out at the Austrian Grand Prix, Dennis announced he was leaving soon. Everyone agreed, they would miss the homosexual waiter from Australia. He was likeable, funny and entertaining. Dennis will take off from Chiemsee on his way to Sydney Australia, riding his penny-farthing bicycle. This will complete a ride he began in London which got interrupted when a car hit him and his bicycle on Fern Pass near Garmisch.

Various games for the AFRC tournament would take place over a five-day period, starting on Tuesday, September 5th, and ending with the women's and men's tennis finals on Saturday, September 9th. Right after their final match, employees would have a pig roast and barbecue.

On the evening of September 9th, people would gather in the hotel lounge to watch the final game of the Olympic Basketball Tournament.

Lucas would wear many hats this week at work, while he supervised the hotel kitchen and prepared for the AFRC Barbecue; even more if he made it to the finals of the AFRC Tennis Tournament. He looked forward to having a fun day and seeing his friends, the people who he had met since his arrival in Bavaria over a year ago.

Tennis games got scheduled according to AFRC players' availability during the week and their opponents' mutual convenience, with the last four competitors playing in final matches on Saturday.

The American School in Garmisch was closed for a week, so George had time off work. He could enjoy all the activities, and he loved the new beach volleyball court. Although Lucas was busy, it was fun to have his old buddy from Long Beach around. Judann also had the week off from her waitress job at the Sheridan Hotel. Shelley and Judann were very good friends, and they enjoyed spending time together.

At tennis, Lucas is more of a reactive player, than a strategic player. He goes out and plays as hard as he can on every shot. He had worked on his strokes and his service game. At this point, he felt confident in every one of his shots, including his accurate serve, his overpowering topspin forehand and his two-handed backhand which is even more overpowering.

The most talented guys who also have a great mindset are the best. Lucas knows he has all the shots. Now, his mindset is important because he knows all these guys are great athletes. He does not yet know how good they are as tennis players, except for Chip. From what Lucas had seen, Chip would be the overall favorite to win.

In the past, playing tennis against George, Lucas had won easily. George concentrated on other sports, and volleyball was his favorite. But now, George claimed he had been playing tennis at the Garmisch gymnasium against one of the other teachers who was a great player. So, Lucas would not hold back any effort against his friend George who is an all-around athlete. They play their 1st game at 2:30 p.m. on Tuesday, September 5th.

Lucas was using the Jack Kramer Wilson Pro Staff Racket which millions of other people like. Chip had a brand-new metal racket, the Wilson T2000, which Jimmy Connors endorsed as a young, upcoming tennis professional. Lucas felt comfortable with the Pro Staff although he wanted to try out the new metal one in the future. For now, he would stick with the Pro Staff.

He had not played on a grass tennis court. Lucas read it is slippery and the fastest surface; but the ball does not bounce as high, and the bounce was sometimes unpredictable. Since he had been playing on clay, he found it is a slower surface, and the speed of the ball favored baseline players, like himself. Lucas uses heavy topspin on both forehand and backhand shots. This allows him to make those cross-court, angle shots which are difficult or impossible to return. Lucas' court speed (from his basketball play) allows him to cover most of the drop shots which players try against him when they see he is a baseline player. He will hit the ball deep, and he can hit either line with pace, both backhand and forehand.

The highest number of players use hard courts which are the most neutral. On asphalt and concrete courts, the ball travels faster than on clay, but slower than on grass, plus the bounce is predictable. A hard-court surface is also forgiving to all types of players, including those who are baseliners and those who serve and volley.

Lucas found he could use the slide on clay as a defensive move when going for a shot. As an offensive move, the slide was useless because he had to plant his back foot and keep it solid to gain the power he used in his strokes.

As he had done daily for the last two weeks during afternoon breaks, Lucas headed toward the tennis court.

Today, he will play against George Bennett, his longtime friend; and this is the 1st round of the hotel tournament. George's expertise is in volleyball, baseball and skiing. On the clay tennis court, George would have to adjust fast. The hardwood floor at the Garmisch gym was a lot different from the clay surfaces at Lake Chiemsee Hotel.

Lucas knew he could dominate him on the tennis court, but he thought George would play his best game. However, George never got ahead in the match. Lucas took him easily, scoring 6-2 and 6-3.

They both headed to the bar where they each grabbed a beer. Then, Lucas and George joined Shelley and Gabrielle who were watching the Olympics on television with other employees and a few ski patrol guys, returning from a day's work.

Being the final week of the Olympics, this would be the last big weekend for business until ski season started. On the news, there was already talk about officials canceling the rest of the Olympic Games because of the kidnapping and killing of Israeli athletes.

Gabrielle filled them in on what took place during the time Lucas was at work and while he and George were playing tennis.

"About four thirty this morning," she said, "several men, dressed in tracksuits, climbed over a section of chain-link fence. They were helped by some American athletes who were climbing the fence. Inside the building, one of the terrorists fought with a wrestling coach; another wrestler escaped, and he believes the coach got shot and killed."

Pointing to the TV, Gabrielle added, "Look, you can see the officers with machine guns, wearing sweat suits and crawling into different positions outside the building. This news coverage is the only problem with the sneak attack by police. Since it is being shown on television, it can also be seen by the terrorists. It's ludicrous!"

"Don't the police know they are being watched by the kidnappers? Who are these guys, anyway?" asked George.

"A man on the news said they are border police in civilian clothes, but they are carrying Walther MP machine guns," replied Gabrielle. "West Germany has no special law enforcement branch for terrorism, even though they have had the Baader-Meinhof Gang to deal with for several years. Officials claim the kidnappers have AK-47s."

"Gabrielle, what guns did the RAF favor?" asked Lucas.

"Andreas said he thought the Heckler & Koch MP5 assault rifle was a little better than the Walther," she replied. "They are both made in West Germany, so you know the engineering is excellent."

They all agreed with her comment about German engineering.

"Oh, now the police are climbing off the building, and they're leaving the scene," said Gabrielle.

"I'd bet they learned the kidnappers are watching," said George.

Lucas had to work, so he headed toward the kitchen. He peeked into the bar and saw the Canadian ladies, Judy and Deanna, there with Gerhardt Grassl. They all came from the Berchtesgadener Hof. Grassl was a sous chef, and the ladies were waitresses at "The Hof."

Lucas smiled, joined them, and they exchanged warm hugs. He said, "Welcome to Chiemsee. I missed you guys at the Austrian Grand Prix."

"We had to work," said Grassl. "Someone had to keep AFRC going while all of you were off partying."

"Well, Grassl, we party here every day," he replied. They laughed, and Lucas added, "I'm so glad you are playing in our tennis tournament. Do you know when and who you are playing?"

"I'm playing Shelley at three p.m. tomorrow," said Judy.

Lucas tried not to show any reaction to this bit of news, considering his history with Judy and his current relationship with Shelley.

He looked at Deanna and asked, "Who will you play?"

"I drew Sabine, Eric's girlfriend from Seefeld," she replied.

Grassl said, "I play against Topo, your head waiter from Argentina, at two thirty tomorrow."

"I'll try to get out and watch some of you play," said Lucas. "But I am busy preparing for Saturday while I keep the kitchen running daily. In fact, I must get back to work now. Have fun here, and I'll see all of you later tonight."

Lucas wondered if Judy and Deanna had a joint romance going with Grassl because he always sees those 3 together. The ladies look happy and they seem to be having fun.

Lucas fondly remembered meeting Judy and Deanna, shortly after he and George arrived in Europe. They all met at Camping Baciccia in Italy. Together, the 4 of them traveled to the French Riviera and to Barcelona, Spain. From there, the ladies booked a flight and returned to Canada. Within 30 days, George flew home to Long Beach. After 5 months, he surprised Lucas and showed up in Oberammergau with the same Canadian ladies. It was quite unexpected, and it was like seeing family again. They all took a short trip to ski at Zell am See. On the way back, they stopped in Berchtesgaden where they skied and partied with Grassl.

After a busy night in the kitchen, Lucas made his way to the lounge. It was 10:30 p.m., and he wanted to see what was happening with the hostage situation at the Olympic Village. When he walked into the lounge, everyone was crowded around the television set.

Lucas saw Topo standing in the back. He walked over, stood beside him and asked, "Did you just get here, Topo?"

"I've been here about five minutes," he replied. "Gabrielle and Shelley were here, but they went into the bar to get beers. The bar is packed, so they may be gone a while."

"Let's find the ladies and go to the employees' beer machine," said Lucas. "Then, we can take our beers outside and talk."

They found the ladies in the crowded bar, still waiting to order drinks. Shelley and Gabrielle joined the guys, and they all headed to the employees' beer machine.

When they got outside, it was a beautiful fall evening. Each were glad they wore windbreakers when they felt the wind, blowing off the lake and making ripples in the otherwise calm water. The skies were clear, and a crescent moon shined above them. Topo lit his hash pipe, took a hit and passed it on.

Gabrielle gave them a news update on the hostage situation. "This afternoon, two hostages, identified as a fencing coach and a shooting coach, were seen at a window. They were talking with German officials until a kidnapper hit one hostage in the head with the butt of an AK Forty-Seven. It's a Russian-made assault rifle which the PLO favors. We saw it all happen on the television.

"Around 6 p.m., the terrorists demanded transportation to Cairo, and the German officials agreed. The kidnappers planned to walk with the hostages from the garage to some helicopters, two hundred meters away. The officials had set an ambush, but they were noisy and gave themselves away, thus spooking the kidnappers. The terrorists then requested a bus to drive them over to the helicopters. A short while ago, their request was granted. Now, I think they are in the air and on their way to the airport. Unless authorities have set another ambush or have a rescue plan., they will arrive and board a plane to Cairo. Let's go back to the lounge and see what's going on."

The crowd had thinned out a little around the television. A mixture of employees, several ski patrol and a few hotel guests were still there. Over half of the civilian employees who work for the American military are German, and the rest are all different nationalities.

Someone said gunshots were fired at the German airfield. As they tried to figure out what was going on with the hostages, they heard conflicting reports from the news media.

These deadly events occurred in Munich and at Fürstenfeldbruck Air Base. During the afternoon, Olympic Games had been suspended, so the hostage situation was very serious.

At the hotel, however, there was a party atmosphere which always seemed to take place, at least everywhere Lucas went in Bavaria.

Looking at Lucas, Shelley asked, "Is anyone else getting hungry?"

He noticed the others were looking at him, expecting to follow his lead. Lucas said, "Okay, let's go to the kitchen."

Lucas had a leftover piece of medium-rare, grilled beef tenderloin. He decided to make some of Chef Anton Held's creation, Sauvignon Steak hor d'oeuvres. Topo sliced rounds of a baguette, buttered them, and then toasted the rounds under the kitchen salamander. Lucas prepared sweet onions, sautéing them slowly until the onions' natural sugars were caramelized for a rich golden-brown color. Next, he heated slices of tenderloin under the salamander, placed the meat onto the baguette rounds, added the caramelized onion and topped them with a Sauvignon sauce. Shelley and Gabrielle fried some Kartoffelpuffer (German potato pancakes) which Lucas had prepared earlier. To go with the puffers, his friends had a choice of toppings: homemade apple sauce, or homemade crème fraiche.

They went into the bakery and sat around the baker's table to eat. Everyone in the room was delighted, and they all moaned with pleasure after the first bite.

"This is Chef Held's signature hors d'oeuvre and his original sauce," said Lucas. "I'm glad he shared the recipe with me."

"I sure will miss these midnight snacks," said Topo. "What is in this sauce? I love it."

"This sauce is made with bell pepper, onion, garlic, pimiento, finely diced salami, a strong cheddar cheese, Cabernet Sauvignon wine and brandy," he replied. "The sauce only coats the top of the meat, but you must put a napkin underneath to catch the juicy drippings."

"Lucas, I know you made this crème fraiche. How did you make it?" asked Gabrielle.

"I mixed one and a half cups heavy whipping cream with a quarter cup of buttermilk, poured it into a sterile jar, covered and shook it," he replied. "I let it sit at room temperature overnight until it thickened, and then I put it in the refrigerator. It will keep for about a week."

The others could not hide their sad expressions when Lucas asked, "When do you plan to leave, Topo?"

"I leave for Argentina one week from today, right after the Olympics are over," he replied. "My brother, the journalist who moved to Bariloche, Patagonia, sent me an update on his research of Nazis who live or have lived in South America. At the end of World War Two, it appears Hitler gave Bormann orders to hide much of their loot and priceless artwork in various places around Bavaria and Austria. I'm going to check it out myself. Then, I will let Lucas know where the treasure is, and he can go get it. Simple, huh?"

"Hold on, give me a minute," said Lucas. He went to his office and brought back 4 shot glasses with a half-full bottle of Jägermeister.

Lucas filled each shot glass, handed one to each of his friends, raised his shot glass and said, "Here is to treasure hunting in Bavaria!"

"Okay, you guys can laugh now," said Topo, "but I have his letter, right here in my backpack."

Removing it from a large envelope, Topo waived his brother's letter in the air. "My brother wrote about gathering this information from Nazis who escaped Germany and live in the Bariloche area. The terrain and climate there are the same as in Southern Bavaria. The first place he mentions is a Polish town, Walbrzych. Before nineteen forty-five, the town was called Waldenburg, but after the Soviets gave the town's governing powers to Poland, they changed it to Walbrzych which is a Polish name. There are stories of a train, hidden underground there; it is full of gold, silver, artwork and maybe the Amber Room."

"Why does he think the train is hidden there?" asked Shelley.

Lucas interrupted, "Topo, if you will excuse me, I think I can answer Shelley's question. When I skied in Kaprun and Zell am See, I met a guy who was from the same Polish town. He told me his brother worked as a miner and spent his whole adult life looking for a Nazi train which is hidden in an underground tunnel complex, built by the Nazis. Older miners told him they saw German soldiers in his town, pushing a train into a tunnel during the spring of nineteen forty-five."

"Wow, Lucas!" said Topo. "Thank you. Your information about the train is new to me. My brother says Nazi officials escaped to Argentina and took loot with them. Things they couldn't take, they hid in Southern Bavaria and Northern Austria which covers the area between Garmisch and Neuschwanstein Castle, plus Lake Toplitz area, east of Salzburg. We drove near there when we went to the Austrian Grand Prix, but the lake is in the mountains. His letter has two potential sites: Lake Walchensee, southwest of here near Garmisch, and Lake Luenersee in Austria, west of Munich near the Swiss border. There are also reports of loot being hidden around our own Lake Chiemsee."

Lucas smiled. "Shelley and I will be traveling to Greece and beyond. We plan to be gone for two months, or more, depending on how long she can put up with me. By the time we get back, Topo, you'll be well-established in Bariloche, and you can let us know what you learned about hidden Nazi treasure and the house in… what was the name of the place where Hitler's house might be?"

"The house is called Inalco. It is near Bariloche where many resettled Nazis are living," said Topo.

"Why did you decide to go to Greece?" Gabrielle asked Lucas.

"Shelley and I want to see Europe, and we think traveling in a van will be the most fun way to go," he replied. "Eric got me thinking about Greece. He told me he was driving his van to Athens while Mike Harker follows on his motorcycle. I don't know who else is going, but Mike always has one or more young ladies, hanging around. Mike has a job with Club Med as a waterski instructor at Glyfada Beach, a 30-minute drive south of Athens. After he spends some time in Greece, Eric wants to find work on a large, private sailing ship and cross the Atlantic to the Bahamas. When Shelley and I get to Athens, we'll try to find them."

“Let’s clean up, here. Then, we can go see what is happening with the hostages,” Shelley suggested.

When they got back inside the lobby, Joe, the desk clerk, told them he heard the latest news, moments ago; the hostage situation had been resolved, and the hostages were safe.

“This is good news, now let’s go get some sleep,” said Shelley. “My crew knows I plan to sleep in and start late tomorrow because we are all working seven days this week, right?”

“Your plan sounds good to me,” replied Lucas.

It was after midnight, yet a few people were watching news in the lounge. Lucas, Topo and their ladies were tired, so they all walked to the Park Hotel where Shelley and Lucas said goodnight.

Gabrielle and Topo kept walking, past the Farm House to the Ranch House where they lived with Gretchen, a little Yorkshire Terrier. Their bottom-floor apartment was across from the marina and boathouse

Lucas and Shelley slept in until 10 a.m. They showered together which led them back to bed for some morning delight before heading off to work, both energized and ready. When they were climbing the front steps of the hotel, they met George and Judann coming down.

“Sad news, they called it The Munich Massacre,” said George.

Looking surprised, Lucas asked, “What? Massacre?”

“Oh, you don’t know!” said George. “Come on, you need to see this on television. They keep showing it over and over.”

George led them inside to the lounge where people were watching the television. He asked if he could change the channel to find a news clip of Jim McKay’s statement. It was first shown at about 3:30 a.m.

After 5 minutes of searching, he found a station, showing the clip. They all watched in amazement, as the Olympic announcer reported, “We’ve just gotten the final word. When I was a kid, my father used to say our greatest hopes and our worst fears are seldom realized. Our worst fears have been realized tonight. They have now said that there were eleven hostages. Two were killed in their rooms…. Nine others were killed at the airport tonight. They’re all gone.”

Everyone was speechless and shocked, hearing the news.

Lucas and Shelley both had to work. So, they agreed to meet George after lunch to watch AFRC tournament games at the tennis courts.

At 2:15 p.m., George was waiting at the beer machine when Lucas arrived and said, “How did you know I would be here?”

“Be serious, Lucas,” replied George. “Remember when we worked together in Frankfurt?”

“It seems like such a long time ago,” he replied. “You’re right. On all our breaks, we went to the beer machine first.”

When they got to the tennis courts, Shelley was leading in her match against Judy. She won the first set 6-4 and was ahead in the second set 4-3. Both ladies had been playing on clay courts—Judy played at the Berchtesgadener Hof, and Shelley played here at Chiemsee. These ladies were good athletes, and it was obvious. Shelley had played year-round when she lived in sunny, Southern California. Judy spent her winter time on the slopes in Banff, Canada, so she was not able to play as much. Shelley won the last 2 games for a 6-4, 6-3 victory. She would move on to play Sabine who beat Deanna, the other Canadian lady, in a close match 6-3, 4-6 and 7-5.

As he watched Shelley and Judy hug at the net, Lucas realized Shelley was the only American lady in the tournament.

Eric was playing against John Riley on the other court. Eric was a big, strong Swede from Minnesota who could hit a golf ball over 300 yards. He spent most of the summer playing golf in the daytime and tending bar in the evening at NATO Officers Club where Lucas worked last winter. Eric was a baseball player in college. He could hit a tennis ball very hard, but he also hit some wild. Recently, Eric played tennis on an indoor court in Garmisch, but he had never been on a clay court. This was John's home court, so he won easily 6-2, 6-2.

Topo and Grassl had played in the morning. When Lucas heard about it, he was sorry he missed it. George watched their match, and he told Lucas, "Both those guys played hard and really smacked the ball. Grassl won in three sets, 8-6, 4-6 and 7-5."

Shelley came and joined them. Lucas said, "Let's find Judann, and then George can tell us what happened with the hostages."

"Why don't we walk to the Ranch House to see if Topo and Gabrielle are around," replied Shelley. "I want to play with their cute Yorkie, Gretchen. She is the smartest dog I have ever seen."

"Where did she come from?" asked George.

"One of the desk clerks, Mike Flanigan, went to Morocco, so Topo and Gabrielle volunteered to keep her," she replied.

Lucas went out to the employees' beer machine and bought 6 beers. He put them in his backpack, went to the hotel entrance, and met his friends who were watching a military family of six play miniature golf in front of the hotel.

As they walked toward the Ranch House, George began telling them what had occurred during the early morning hours at the Fürstenfeldbruck Air Base near Munich.

"I went to sleep last night believing the hostages were safe, based on a newscast report I watched around midnight," said George. "This morning on TV, they showed a newspaper headline: *The Olympic Hostages are all safe, following a gun battle.*"

"Where did the story come from, George?" asked Lucas.

"A German government spokesman announced the terrorists were all killed, and the Israelis were safe," he replied. "We know now, however, it was nearly the opposite."

Topo and Gabrielle had a table and chairs set out under a Yew tree in front of the Ranch House. They had a great view, looking out over the lake, studded with sailboats, and it was a beautiful, clear afternoon.

Gretchen, their little Yorkie, was excited to see people, but she never jumped on you when she greeted you. She pranced around your feet until you acknowledged her with a pet, or a pat on the head.

Lucas reached in his backpack and pulled out 2 Wieninger beers which he handed to Topo and Gabrielle. Then he gave beers to Shelley, George and Judann. Topo reached in his backpack which was on the grass by his feet. He pulled out his hash pipe, lit it, took a hit and passed it on.

"Topo, I heard about your tennis match with Grassl this morning. It must have been fun, huh?" asked Lucas.

"You know, both of us grew up playing on clay courts," he replied. "This clay is a little different, but it plays about the same. We had a fun, even match. Grassl is tall, and his serve bounces high which threw me off a little. His forehand is so strong, I served to his backhand. It kept me in the match, but he is a great player. He plays Chip next, and even Chip better watch out for Grassl."

"Gabrielle, you played Ashleigh, the Australian lady. How did your match go?" asked Shelley.

"She was too good for me, despite my practicing here on the clay," she replied. "Ashleigh told me she has played on clay since she was old enough to hold a racket. However, she grew up near Melbourne where clay courts are known as *ant bed courts*."

"Are you talking about a bed of ants?" Judann asked.

Gabrielle said, "Well, not exactly. Ashleigh explained it to me. Until recently, most of the tennis courts in Australia were made with loam soil, crushed granite, or ant bed over a bed of ash.

"She had watched them construct the courts where she used to play. The property owner went out to the bush, filled the back of his *Ute* with ant hills, and took them to the chosen court location. He dropped them off the back of the Ute to break them up, then smashed them and crushed them by driving the Ute back and forth over the top. He watered them, let them dry, and drove the Ute over them again to pulverize the clay. In those days, it was a labor-intensive process."

“Well, I should hope they have streamlined the process, nowadays. Oh, what is a Ute?” asked Lucas.

“I asked Ashleigh the same question,” she replied. “It’s a utility vehicle with an open cargo area in back, similar to a pickup truck.”

“George, please finish telling us about the hostages,” said Shelley.

“From what I saw on television and read in the paper, the Germans are embarrassed by how the rescue attempt went down,” he replied.

“Yeah, why did they fail so badly?” asked Topo.

George explained, “The authorities’ first plan never happened. They had sharpshooters ready to take down the kidnappers when they walked two hundred meters from the garage to the helicopters.

“Meanwhile, the Palestinian leader and others had AK Forty-Sevens pointed at three hostages. The sharpshooters gave themselves away when one was heard crawling behind a vehicle which prompted the Palestinian leader to demand a bus. German authorities provided a bus to transport the kidnappers and their hostages the distance of two hundred meters. Then, the helicopters took off, carrying all of them, and it landed at the German airfield about ten thirty.”

Gabrielle had gone into the house for a few minutes. When she returned, she had 6 bottles of Wieninger beer and passed them out to everyone. She and Topo had the beer delivered to their front door for the same price as it was in the beer machine, 70 pfennigs per bottle.

“What did I miss?” asked Gabrielle.

“I’m not sure I know the exact details, but this is my understanding of what I heard and read,” said George. “They tried to deceive the kidnappers right away because Cairo refused to get involved. A Boeing Seven Twenty-Seven jet waited on the tarmac at Fürstenfeldbruck, a NATO Airbase. Two military Bell UH 1 helicopters transported the terrorists and the hostages to the airbase while German authorities were following in a third helicopter.”

After he took a drink of his Wieninger beer, George said, “We don’t have this beer in Garmisch. I drink Munich beer, sometimes Augustiner, Paulaner or Spaten, but I think I like this better.”

Then, he went on with the news, “The Germans set an ambush at the airbase, using five snipers. They placed three on the control tower roof, one hidden at ground level, and the fifth one behind a service truck. They had sixteen German officers dressed as flight crew inside the Boeing Seven Twenty-Seven. However, they did not have proper uniforms. The officers thought the terrorists might know they were not crew members, so they left the plane before the helicopters arrived without telling their command. The officers figured it was suicide to attempt the pretense of being flight crew.”

After another sip of his beer, George said, "I guess the authorities didn't have an accurate count of the kidnappers. It turned out, there were eight kidnappers, but only five snipers at the NATO Airbase. Two of the kidnappers got to the plane while the others guarded the hostages and helicopter pilots. They found the plane empty, realized it was a trap and ran back to the helicopters. From the reports I heard, the police sharpshooters opened fire first, and they killed two of the Palestinians. The helicopter pilots managed to escape. The terrorists took cover, went behind the helicopters and refused to move."

"Didn't they bring in some kind of tank?" asked Topo.

"Authorities expected to receive armored personnel carriers, but they thought of it too late and had problems with delivery," he replied. "The carriers got stuck in traffic and didn't arrive until midnight."

"What about the hostages? Where were they?" asked Judann.

"Four hostages were tied up in one helicopter, and five were tied up in the other," he replied. "When the armored carriers got there, one terrorist opened fire with a machine gun, killing four hostages, then he threw a grenade in the helicopter which exploded with the bodies inside. Another terrorist shot the last five hostages in the other helicopter."

"Did any policemen get shot?" asked Shelley.

"Based on what I read in the *International Herald*, one officer was killed by stray gunfire inside the airport building," he replied. "The Palestinians had shot out the tower lights, so visibility was poor; and a sniper on the ground was in the line of fire. He got hit with a bullet, shot by a sniper on the roof, but he survived."

"Didn't the police capture some kidnappers?" asked Judann.

"Three terrorists are alive; two had gunshot wounds, one was not injured, and all three were captured," he replied. "Another terrorist escaped briefly, but he was killed during a shoot-out at a nearby parking lot around 1:30 a.m. It was all over. Eleven hostages were dead."

"It was a rough… what, twenty hours?" said Topo.

"It didn't turn out well at all," said Lucas. "The only positive I can see is the Germans refused to bow down to the terrorists. But German authorities sure looked bad for their sloppy handling of the situation, resulting in the deaths of eleven Jewish hostages. What was the final death count, overall?"

"In the end," replied George, "there were seventeen people who died: six Israeli coaches, five Israeli athletes, five of the eight terrorists, and one West German Police Officer. I heard the attackers were a PLO terrorist group who call themselves *Black September*."

"What's going on in the Olympics, now?" asked Topo.

"Today, they are having a special ceremony for the dead Israelis," replied George. "Afterward, there will only be competition in fencing and weightlifting. Tomorrow, the games are expected to be back in full swing. They have seven track and field events scheduled, plus the women's volleyball finals."

"How is the Chiemsee Tennis Tournament going?" asked Judann.

"We just posted results of the tournament, so far," replied Lucas. "You can see the list in the hotel lounge. There are four matches left.

"Tomorrow, Shelley will play Sabine in the morning. Then, Olivia and Ashleigh will play against each other.

"I play John Riley in the afternoon, following Chip against Grassl who are going at it in the morning.

"On Saturday, all four winners play on."

AFRC CHIEMSEE TENNIS TOURNAMENT

MEN:

Round 1	Round 2	Finalists	Champion
Chip			
	Chip		
John Ferrell			
		______	
Topo			
	Grassl		
Grassl			
			______
John Riley			
	John Riley		
Eric			
		______	
Lucas			
	Lucas		
George			

WOMEN:

Round 1	Round 2	Finalists	Champion
Judy			
	Shelley		
Shelley			
		______	
Deanna			
	Sabine		
Sabine			
			______
Olivia			
	Olivia		
Sonya			
		______	
Ashleigh			
	Ashleigh		
Gabrielle			

CHAPTER 43

The "Happy Games"

There was no reason to hang around Wednesday night after work. Most people were still trying to process what happened to the "Happy Games." This was the motto American civilian employees were using for the Olympics before the horrific terrorist events began.

Lucas brought a nice dinner home: filet mignon with Madera sauce, dauphine potatoes and red cabbage.

Shelley surprised Lucas. When he opened the front door, she came out of the bedroom, dressed in a sexy bra and brief panties underneath a sheer see-through robe.

She greeted Lucas with a lingering kiss. Then, he set the dinners on the table and went to the shower. Dinner no longer seemed important. He did have his priorities.

On Thursday, September 7, after a full 8 hours of uninterrupted sleep, Lucas and Shelley awoke energized and ready for a big day. It was the 12th day of Olympic competition.

Shelley went downstairs to her office.

Lucas rode his Peugeot bicycle underneath the autobahn and over to the loading dock behind the kitchen where he locked his bike. He went to the beer machine and bought 3 beers: one for Fritz, one for Schmechtig and one for himself. Then, he was off to work.

After lunch, Lucas pulled tennis stuff out of his office locker. He got dressed and walked to the tennis courts, ready to play 2 out of 3 sets with John Riley.

John was already there, hitting balls with Eric. Shelley and Sabine were playing on the other court.

"Have you worn him out for me?" Lucas asked Eric.

"Watch out Lucas, John is hitting the ball very well," he replied.

Lucas walked out on his court, waiving to Shelley while the ladies switched sides on their court. Shelley yelled over to them, "Sabine won the first set 6-4, and I'm ahead in the second set 4-2. Have a good match, you guys."

"I watched Chip and Grassl play during the last set of their match, this morning," said Eric. "It took three sets, but Chip won, 7-5. Since the ladies played at the same time, I watched the end of their match. It was amazing to see Olivia and Ashleigh compete. They grew up playing against each other in Melbourne."

"Who won the ladies match this morning?" asked Lucas.

"Olivia won, 6-3, 6-4," he replied. "I think she is a little stronger with her service game. It will be interesting to see how she plays next, against the winner of this match between Shelley and Sabine."

Lucas started his match against John, the same way he did in any match, hitting sideline shots with pace down the sidelines, using both his forehand and his two-handed backhand with lots of topspin. Lucas knew if he focused on watching the ball go all the way into his racket, each of his strokes were automatic, including his serve. It was not the fastest serve, but he could usually put it where he wanted to. He and John always had fun, no matter what they were doing. When they could arrange their work schedules, they got together to drink beer, play in the game room, or sail on the lake. Lucas won the match 6-2, 6-3.

Lucas would meet his sports rival, Chip, in the men's final game of the hotel tournament on Saturday. So far, he and Chip had matching skills in all the sports they had played together. Although Lucas had never seen Chip ski, Lucas was sure Chip would be a lot better skier because he was on ski patrol, and he skied every day.

The Olympics were on again, and evenings in the lounge got crowded with ski patrol, hotel employees and hotel guests. The rivalry between the Americans and the Germans was spirited, but friendly.

Lucas loved track and field events. In high school, he went to all the track and field meets unless he was busy playing baseball or basketball. He remembered watching Bob Mathias and Rafer Johnson, running on the Fresno High School track. Both athletes were Olympic Decathlon Champions. Bob was from Tulare, and Rafer grew up in Kingsburg. Those are small towns in Central California.

In last week's Olympics, Lasse Viren fell in the Men's 10,000 Meter Race, but he got up, finished first and set a new world record.

Today, the Olympics had seven track and field finals.

In the Men's 400 Meter Run, Americans finished 1st and 2nd. The bronze medal was won by a Kenyan, and the West German runners finished out of the medals, placing 5th and 7th.

In the Men's 5,000 Meter Race: Finland's Lasse Viren took the gold. Steve Prefontaine, a great American runner from Oregon, finished 4th. A West German runner finished 6th.

Running for the United States, Rod Milburn won the Men's 110 Meter Hurdles for the gold and set a new world record at 13.24.

A lady from East Germany won the Women's 200 Meter Race, and an Australian lady took the silver medal which brought cheers from the Australian employees. A West German lady finished 6th. There were no Americans running in this final race.

When a West German runner finished second in the Women's 400 Meters, Germans in the hotel lounge let out a loud cheer as they watched her beat Kathy Hammond, the bronze medal winner who was from the United States. The West Germans cheered again when their equestrian team finished second to the Russian team in Team Dressage. Lucas noticed the rivalry between German and U.S. fans in the room was a little more intense this evening.

The Americans suffered embarrassment when Vincent Matthews and Wayne Collett, both medal winners, protested at the podium. During the U.S. National Anthem, they unbuttoned their sweat suits, smirked at the stands, slouched and acted badly, showing disrespect to the anthem.

Poking Lucas to get his attention, George pointed to the TV when highlights of the Women's Volleyball Finals came on. The Soviet Union beat Japan, winning 3 games to 2. West Germany finished 8th.

"What about a U.S. women's volleyball team? Do we have one?" Lucas asked George.

"Our women's team did not qualify for this Olympics, but we have some very talented young players who are coming up. So, watch out for our nineteen seventy-six team," he replied. Since George was a skilled volleyball player and coach, his predictions were usually accurate.

Referring to women's volleyball in the Olympics today, George said, "I saw the final match between the Soviets and Japanese women. It lasted over two-and-a-half hours. They played an intense game and had twenty-four service changes before a single point was scored.

"In the match between North and South Korea, the North Korean team won the bronze medal easily, three games to none. It was the first medal a team from North Korea ever won in the Olympics."

On Friday, September 8, Lucas spent most of the day in the kitchen or his office, preparing for Saturdays' events at Lake Chiemsee Hotel: Final matches of the AFRC Chiemsee Tennis Tournament would start Saturday morning; various other competitions would take place during the day; hotel employees, ski patrol and invited guests would enjoy a pig roast and barbecue on Saturday afternoon.

Saturday will also be next-to-the-last day of Olympic competition. Teams from the United States and Soviet Union will play Olympic Basketball for the gold, Saturday night, the 9th of September.

By Friday afternoon, Ski patrol guys had placed picnic tables for the barbecue near the pit. The pig would be roasted in the same pit they used last June for the Hawaiian luau.

Friday evening, Lucas worked late to be sure everything was ready for the next day. After he finished in the kitchen, he saw the bar was packed with hotel guests. Lucas went back to the beer machine, got 2 beers and went to the lounge. He wanted to see if Shelley or his friends were there and learn what was happening at the "Happy Games."

The hotel lounge had its usual mixture of civilian workers, ski patrol, German employees and a few hotel guests. Most guests were in the bar, or they were dancing in the dining room where a local band was playing. Lucas did not see Gabrielle, Topo or Shelley, but George spotted Lucas and came over to where he was standing. They were behind a big group of people, all crowded around the TV set.

"Lucas, do you have any dope on you?" asked George.

When Lucas nodded, George said, "Let's go outside. These guys are getting on my nerves."

"What guys, George?" asked Lucas.

"Oh, the German employees are in a really foul mood," he replied. "I think they're embarrassed about how the hostage situation went down, and there has been some bickering with other employees."

They walked out, went to the water's edge and sat on the wall next to the Chiemsee Mermaid. Lucas pulled out his hash pipe, handed it to George and lit it for him. George took a long hit, held his breath, exhaled and said, "This is more like it, nice and peaceful."

All they could hear was the sound of water, splashing softly against the lakeshore wall, and band music, coming from the dining room.

"In the Men's Decathlon, the top German athlete fell over a hurdle during the one-hundred-and-ten-meter race," said George. "It put him out of the competition, so Russians got the gold and silver medals. A Pole got the bronze; an American athlete, Jeff Bennett, finished fourth; and another American, Bruce Jenner, finished tenth. The Germans got upset again today when their soccer team got knocked out of the tournament by East Germany, three to two."

"What would the medal counts be if East and West Germany were the same team?" asked Lucas.

"Good question," he replied. "We can check the totals at the end of the Olympics and find the answer. I think we've covered the events of today. Tomorrow is a big day with eight track and field finals."

After he and George finished their beers, Lucas went to the dock and got his bike. He rode back under the autobahn to the Park Hotel, locked his bike and went upstairs.

When he walked in the door, Shelley was setting the table. She had grilled some chicken, and made macaroni salad, plus fresh asparagus. "I waited for you to get home, so we can eat together," she said.

Lucas had not eaten since breakfast. Now, after smoking hashish with George, he realized how hungry he was. After dinner, they went to bed for a good night's sleep. Tomorrow, they both needed to be ready for a big day at the Rastaus am Chiemsee.

On his way to work in the morning, Lucas rode his bike to the barbecue area. Brad, a ski patrol guy, was taking care of the pig roast and already setting up the pit. Lucas told Brad to send someone over when he needed supplies from the kitchen. Bob Clarkson, the hotel manager, would cook beef brisket, barbecue chicken, hamburgers and hot dogs on the big charcoal grill. Side dishes and desserts were all prepped and would come from the kitchen.

Besides the roasted pig and other grilled or spit-roasted meats, people will have a choice of Texas style Pinto Beans, Red Potato Salad, Creamy Cole Slaw, Corn Casserole and Spicy Shrimp Pasta Salad, plus Corn Bread and Apple Pie a la mode.

The barbecue area is behind the tennis courts and near the volleyball court. Gunther had tapped a keg of Wieninger beer, so there are lots of people around. Everyone is playing volleyball or drinking beer and listening to music. Karen Tyler and 2 ski patrol guys are playing their guitars and singing by the pit where the pig is roasting.

The 4 remaining tennis players, 2 men and 2 women, would play at the same time because none of them wanted to be the center of attention. As finalists, they simply wanted to compete. Lucas watched Shelley (his roommate, lover and friend) serve first against Olivia (his ex-traveling partner, ex-lover and friend).

Lucas loved to joke around and have fun playing. His match against Chip would give the winner bragging rights in the AFRC game world. While it would be a game between friends, he was sure both he and Chip would play all out on every point.

Lucas knew if he watched the ball go all the way into his racket, he could play well against Chip. He must use willpower, concentrate on each play and only focus on the ball.

Chip is talented, and he has a great mindset in competition. The jury is still out on whether Lucas has the same capabilities.

Lucas took up tennis 3 years ago as a serious sport. He played and worked on his game at the same public tennis courts which Billie Jean King used in Long Beach, California. At the time, her name was Billie Jean Moffitt. Last June, Lucas read about her younger brother, Randy

Moffitt. He got called up from the minor leagues, as a relief pitcher for the San Francisco Giants Baseball Team.

Lucas took to tennis as he did any other sport—he played and practiced until he became as good as he thought he could be, then he played and practiced more.

This was his "moment of truth" against a very good player. While the women are playing the best 2 out of 3 sets, the men are playing the best 3 out of 5 sets to win. Chip won the racket spin to have first serve. Chip was a lefty, so Lucas would have to adjust quickly. A left-handed opponent was a rarity for him.

FINALS: AFRC CHIEMSEE TENNIS TOURNAMENT

MEN:

Round 1	Round 2	Finalists	Champion
Chip			
	Chip		
John Ferrell			
		Chip	
Topo			
	Grassl		
Grassl			
			____________
John Riley			
	John Riley		
Eric			
		Lucas	
Lucas			
	Lucas		
George			

WOMEN:

Round 1	Round 2	Finalists	Champion
Judy			
	Shelley		
Shelley			
		Shelley	
Deanna			
	Sabine		
Sabine			
			____________
Olivia			
	Olivia		
Sonya			
		Olivia	
Ashleigh			
	Ashleigh		
Gabrielle			

THE MATCH

Chip served to Lucas' backhand. They exchanged both forehand and backhand volleys until Lucas sent a cross-court, 2-handed backhand. It made Chip hustle to the net where he hit a forehand down the line and out of Lucas' reach for the first point. Chip served again, and they both played to the other's backhand until Chip hit one down the middle. Lucas returned it with a powerful forehand, past a lunging Chip and out of his reach, landing inside the service line for 15 all.

Those 2 points set the tone for a hard-fought first set. Chip led 5 games to 4 and served for the set. Lucas saved 2 set points, using his spectacular cross-court backhands. Then, he was short, and the ball went into the net, allowing Chip to win the set. It was 6 games to 4.

Topo and George sat behind the fence, drank keg beer and watched both matches at the same time. While Lucas and Chip changed sides, George yelled over to Lucas, "Shelley won with 6-3 in the first set, and she is playing well."

The men's second set began. Lucas hit his shots with good topspin and went ahead in the set, 4 games to 1. Chip went to the net and broke Lucas' serve with a hard topspin forehand, tying the score, 4-4. To complete his comeback, Chip won the next 2 games which won the set. If Chip won the following set, he would become the champion.

Lucas thought he had his "back to the wall" and needed a turnaround: *This will take all my concentration and focus. I must watch the ball and keep my shots deep. I must stay in the game until I can find a way to win. Like the great Yogi Berra said, "It ain't over 'til it's over."*

They stayed on serve for the whole third set until Lucas finally broke serve, going in on his deep shots and using power shots with topspin to win the third set, 8 games to 6. Now, Chip had a 2 set to 1 lead.

Between sets, George told the guys, "Olivia won the second set, 6-2 against Shelley, and the ladies are beginning their 3rd set."

In the men's 4th set, Lucas and Chip held serve to 4-4. Chip held again and took a lead, 5 games to 4. He got ahead 30-15 in the next game with Lucas serving. Lucas put away a cross-court forehand for 30-30. He hit 2 more cross-court forehands, both winners, and tied the score at 5 apiece. Then, both held serve for 6 games all. After 2 miraculous saves by Chip, 1 at the net and 1 with a lob, Lucas put away another forehand down the line which made it 7 games to 6 in his favor. In the next game, Lucas got behind, love-30, but he rallied with a spectacular backhand down the line which fell in on the corner to take the set, 8 games to 6. This took them to a fifth set in the match.

The men's tennis match got a little attention from the crowd of beer-drinking employees, ski patrol and a few hotel guests who had wandered by. Watching the match, people howled and cheered.

Lucas blocked out everything, except his game. The task at hand was to focus on the ball. Lucas' first serve took a high bounce into Chip's forehand, allowing Chip to crush it with topspin. It was out of Lucas' backhand reach, making the score 15-0 for Chip.

Next point, Lucas hit a deep serve; Chip had a weak return; Lucas went to the net, and he put away a backhand volley for 15 all. After several spectacular shots and saves, Chip won the next point with an easy volley at the net. Lucas served to Chip's backhand and followed with his own winning volley at the net. Lucas scored on another weak return by Chip to make it 30-30.

Lucas got the better of a face-to-face volleying contest for a 40-30 lead. After a lunging volley by Lucas, Chip came in on his serve return and put the next one away which made it deuce for the game. After long rallies, Lucas won the next 2 points and the game. Both players took a break when Lucas was ahead in the fifth set, 1-0.

Playing again, Chip made it 1-1, using a backhand shot down the line which went past Lucas who had rushed the net. After they split the following 2 games, Lucas held his serve for a lead of 3 games to 2.

Chip came right back to win his serve and even the score at 3 games apiece. Lucas won his serve to take a 4 to 3 lead. Chip crushed an overhead for a winner at the net, and it was 4 to 4.

In the next 4 games, they both held serve to make it 6-6. Lucas won his serve again by keeping the ball deep which allowed him to come toward the net with a good view of the whole court. He hit the ball for an easy win and a 7 to 6 game lead.

Chip bounced back and won his serve with great play at the net. It was 7 games each, and Lucas was serving.

Chip got the first 2 points of the next game by hustling to the net and putting his shot down the line for 15-0, then putting away another overhead shot on a return which Lucas lunged for and lobbed up. It was 30-love for Chip.

Lucas hit each shot to Chip's backhand until he won the point, going to the net and hitting cross-court with his 2-handed backhand, making it 30-15 for Chip. Chip hit a blazing backhand just out of Lucas' reach which made the score 40-15.

In this hard-pressed situation, Lucas served and kept moving in on each shot he hit. Finally, he got the point with a forehand right to Chip's feet which made the score 40-30. Lucas hit a shot long over the baseline, and Chip took the lead 8 games to 7.

Lucas called time out. While he tightened his shoelace, he thought: *I must grit my teeth, hang in there and find a way to win, even though I'm not playing my best tennis.*

Lucas got the first point in the 64th game of the match, and he led 15-0. Chip evened the score with a deep serve and volley for 15 all. Another deep serve to Lucas' backhand with a weak return allowed Chip to get to the net and put away another volley.

It was 30-15. They each got a point which made it 40-30 for Chip. Chip served to Lucas' 2-handed backhand, and Lucas put such great topspin on it, Chip had no chance getting to it. It was now deuce.

Chip smashed a very hard serve to Lucas forehand, and Lucas could only tip the ball with his racket frame.

It is now Chip's add, and he is serving for the match. Chip's serve went down the middle. Lucas returned the ball down the middle without much on it, and Chip returned with good pace to Lucas' forehand.

Then, Lucas did the one thing he considered his downfall in tennis. He took his eye off the ball. Consequently, Lucas hit the ball into the net and lost the match.

Meeting and hugging at the net, Chip said, "Great match, Lucas. We must do this again, sometime."

"This time next year sounds good!" replied Lucas.

John Riley walked over and handed each of them a cup of keg beer. George, John Ferrell, Shelley, Topo, Eric, Sabine, Judann and Gabrielle were all there, telling them what a great match they had played.

A short while later, Lucas and Shelley headed to their place for a break before both went back to work. On the way, they talked about their games in the tournament.

"How did your match go, Shelley?" he asked. "I was focused on my game when I realized you weren't playing anymore."

"I started off great with two aces in the first game," she replied. "Next, I broke her serve, held on and won, 6 to 3. Then, Olivia seemed to elevate her game, the way you did after losing your first two sets. She won the next two sets, 6-4 and 6-4."

"For me, it's a matter of focus," he said. "If I watch the ball go into my racket, I know I can make the shots."

He stopped speaking for a moment and thought of how he could explain his feelings about competition sports to Shelley.

"I love it when those competitive juices start flowing," he said. "I hit a few winners in tennis, or I make a few baskets in basketball—then, I get into a zone and feel invincible."

"Do you think people are born with a competitive spirit, or can it be learned?" she asked.

"You know, I love winning, but I can take losing," he replied. "Most of all, I love to play. The match with Chip was the most fun of any match I have ever played, even though I lost. I don't think about it as losing; I either win the game, or I learn from it and want to raise the level of my game. Competing against a player like Chip is intense—it's a war, even if it's only a game of darts."

As they got close to the Park Hotel, Shelley spotted 2 guys who were working on the rear end of a VW van. They were close to the apartment building, but in a remote area behind the gas station.

"Do I see Bob Ostergaard from Garmisch?" she asked.

"Yes, you do, and Regan Stone is with him," he replied. "I think they are putting a new engine in the van. Let's go talk to them for a minute. Then, I want to hit the shower before I go back to work."

Poking him in his side, she said, "A shower sounds like fun."

Lucas winked and said, "Since you mentioned it, yes it does!"

Bob and Regan saw them coming and stopped what they were doing. "Y'all win your tennis matches today?" asked Regan.

Shelley answered, "No, but we will be back."

"That's the spirit! Will you be watching the Olympic Basketball Final between the U.S. and Russia, tonight?" asked Bob.

"Yes. We plan to watch it after work," replied Lucas. "Hey, Regan, I heard you are leaving to go back home. Is it true?"

"Yes. It is time to get back to the real world," he replied. "For me, it's law and cattle in Texas."

"After we finish and sell these vans, I'm going to California. I plan to research options for a railroad salvage business there," said Bob.

"It sounds right down your alley!" said Lucas. Bob smiled.

Shelley tugged on Lucas' shirtsleeve, and he said, "We'll see you guys later, during the big game in the lounge."

Their adrenaline levels were still high after their tennis matches. This afternoon, Lucas and Shelley both felt their lovemaking was off the charts. Going back to work, they held hands and walked toward the lakeside hotel with a spring in their steps.

"Lucas, let's talk about our trip to Greece. Are you planning to come back here with me afterward?" asked Shelley.

"I hope we will return together," he replied. "What do you think about skiing this winter in Berchtesgaden?"

Shelley looked surprised and said, "I thought we would come back to Chiemsee. Bob Clarkson said he would hold our jobs here."

"I love it here, but Berchtesgaden is so beautiful," said Lucas. "We would have a new area to ski and explore. Also, it would be educational for me to work with Grassl, Chef Held and Chef Drummer."

“What would I do? What if they don’t have a job for me? Where will we live?” she asked.

“Whoa!” he replied. “With your many talents, I’m sure they would invent a job for you if they didn’t already have one. We can get a room and live rent-free on the top floor of the hotel. Other hotel employees are housed there. Let’s think about it. We don’t have to decide anything until we return from Greece or points beyond.”

Shelley agreed. They had plenty of time to talk about this later.

Back at work, Lucas first went to check on the kitchen. Shelley went to check on the maids and her other staff workers.

Helping the kitchen staff, Lucas worked through the initial rush for dinner. Most of the hotel guests ate early because they wanted to watch the Olympics on television this evening.

When the kitchen rush was over, Lucas went out to the employee’s barbecue area on the far side of the tennis courts. From a distance, he could see a large group of people had gathered there. He knew many of his friends would be in the group.

Lucas went to the beer keg, filled a plastic cup with Wieninger beer and spotted Shelley. She waived him over to the picnic tables which their group had pushed together.

When he gave Shelley a kiss on the cheek, it prompted her to give him a naughty look which she sometimes does. Lucas sat between Shelley and George who was next to his lady friend, Judann.

“George is filling us in on the Olympic games,” said Shelley.

With a glance at Shelley and a hint of a smile, Lucas said, “Yeah, I’ve been so busy today, I have heard nothing about the games.”

“Then, I’m your man. I’ve been watching all day, off and on,” said George. “By the way, this is a great barbecue with fun people.”

“Have you eaten anything?” Shelley asked Lucas.

“I had a sandwich before I set up the dinner service,” he replied.

“While you talk with George and Judann, I will get you a plate of food and some apple pie a la mode,” she told him.

“Thanks,” said Lucas. “George, tell me the shooting has stopped.”

“I know you don’t mean this type of shooting, but since you mentioned it,” said George, “the shooting competition in the games was exciting because Americans were up against North Korean and Russian players. Both of those competitions were very close.

“In the Fifty Meter Rifle Prone Shooting, there was a dispute over some final scores because Americans thought the American shooter had won the competition. After officials reviewed it, the North Korean got five hundred ninety-nine points for the gold medal; and the American got five hundred ninety-eight points for the silver. A Romanian got the bronze medal. This was the first time a North Korean athlete had ever competed in the Summer Olympic Games."

"It was not the first controversy with these Olympics officials, and some of their rulings have been questionable," said Lucas.

"You're right," said George. "The same thing happened in the Three Hundred Meter Free Rifle Shooting. Their ruling benefited the American, a shooter named Lones Wigger. The Russian thought he had won, but officials recounted the score and gave Lones the Gold."

"What type of name is Lones Wigger?" asked Lucas.

"I presume it is the same type as Regan Stone," he replied.

"Is Lones a millionaire-cowboy-lawyer from Texas?" asked Lucas.

"No, he's a sharp-shooting soldier from Montana who ran an Army Sniper School in Vietnam last year," he said. "This is his third time at the Olympics. He has a room full of medals, trophies and world records."

"Were there any track and field events, today?" asked Lucas.

"Yes. An American, Brian Oldfield, used a new shot-put method: he spins like a discus thrower, but stays inside the circle boundary," he said. "I messed around with the discus and shot put. I even tried the hammer throw and javelin. So, I still have an interest in the field events."

"Well, how did he do?" Lucas asked George.

"Oldfield finished sixth," he replied. "Television announcers said he is a character, has his own style of dressing, has long hair, sometimes has a beard, and he even smokes cigarettes on the field. They also said he is an exceptional all-around athlete.

"Brian Oldfield scored five thousand seven hundred and fifty points in decathlon competition last year at the Ohio State Relays. The world record is over eight thousand points, but his score was still excellent. He high-jumped six feet-six inches, ran the one hundred meters in ten-point-five seconds and ran the forty-yard dash in four-point-three seconds. I think it's amazing—all of this was done by a guy who is six feet five and weighs two hundred seventy-five pounds."

"I thought I was a sports nut!" said Lucas. "You are full of info."

"I love all sports," he replied. "You play a lot of sports, Lucas."

"Action games, too," said Lucas. "At a party, or a gathering of people, I get bored with small talk and sitting around. So, if there's an option to play darts, a game of pool or even horseshoes, I'll be up and at it. Here is a Plato quote, 'You can discover more about a person in an hour of play than in a year of conversation.' I remember it from school."

"On Men's Olympic Volleyball Teams, neither team for the U.S. or West Germany have anything to brag about," said George.

"The U.S. has no team in these Olympics. Right?" asked Lucas.

"Correct. The U.S. Men's Volleyball Team did not qualify," he replied. "West Germany only won their last game, and it was against Tunisia for eleventh place in a twelve-team tournament."

"It seems strange, the U.S. invented volleyball, and we don't even have a team in the Olympics this year," said Lucas.

"Volleyball was invented in eighteen ninety-five," he replied, "by William Morgan, a YMCA Director of Physical Education. His idea combined aspects of handball and tennis for a new game to be played indoors. Basketball was catching on and becoming popular, but he wanted a game for people with less athletic sports ability to enjoy and participate in. Morgan called the game Mintonette."

"How did the name Volleyball come about?" asked Lucas.

"I imagine someone watched a game and noticed there was a lot of volleying with the ball, thus Volleyball was dubbed," he replied. "It was an American demonstration sport at the Summer Olympics of nineteen twenty-four in Paris, France. The other countries caught on to the sport in quick order. Here, the U.S. team cannot even qualify to play. It's not only strange, it's ironic!"

"I believe Johnny Weissmuller, known as Tarzan, won three gold medals in swimming and a bronze in water polo during the Olympic Games in nineteen twenty-four," said Lucas.

George looked at Lucas, shook his head and said, "Good knowledge, smart ass! Here comes your food."

Shelley returned with an overflowing plate of food and another cup of beer for Lucas. While Lucas was eating, he and George continued their conversation about basketball in general and the big game which would start in an hour.

"Only three players on the U.S. Olympics Basketball Team have any international experience," said George. "Bill Walton, the great player from UCLA, decided not to play."

"It's odd, there are no UCLA players on this U.S. team," said Lucas. "Under Coach John Wooden, they won thirty games with no losses and won the national championship again for the sixth straight year."

"Do you remember Ed Ratleff, the player from Long Beach State? Jerry Tarkanian recruited him in nineteen seventy, and Ratleff led the team to the final eight last year in the NCAA Basketball Tournament against UCLA." said George.

"Yes," replied Lucas. "Tarkanian had great teams at Long Beach State, and I had season tickets. It was an exciting time in Long Beach. I watched the UCLA versus Long Beach State game on television. They gave UCLA a battle, but lost fifty-seven to fifty-five after Ratleff fouled out on a controversial call. No team has ever been closer to beating UCLA in the university division tournament. It was at the Regional Finals in Salt Lake City on March twentieth, nineteen seventy-one."

"UCLA did lose a game to Notre Dame last year," said George. "It's unusual for a John Wooden team to even lose one game in a season.

"On this U.S. Olympic Team, Ed Ratleff is a guard. He is six foot six. They also have two seven-footers and some good college players: Doug Collins from Illinois State, and Jim Brewer from Minnesota. But, none of these guys have experience in international play."

Lucas had finished eating, and it was time for everyone to go see the big game in the hotel lounge. Their large group of 18 went together: Lucas, Shelley, George, Judann, Topo, Gabrielle, Eric, Sabine, Sonya, Bob Ostergaard, Regan Stone, Grassl, Judy, Deanna, Olivia, Ashleigh, Jordan Lewis and Dennis.

At 6'1", Lucas is one of the shortest guys in this group. Lewis is 6'5", and his size is intimidating as the bouncer for the International Bar and Grill. Ostergaard is 6'5". Eric is 6'3". Grassl is 6'4". Regan Stone is 6'2". George and Topo are both 6'1". Each of these guys have athletic builds, and they all play sports year-round.

When they got to the lounge, the big guys stood behind people who sat in folding chairs. The television was against the wall on the window side of the lounge. Chairs were 3 rows deep around the television. Everyone was watching the highlights of this day's Olympic events. Glass paneled doors were closed. They led outside to a walkway along the lake. Glass paneling extended to the ceiling and gave light, coming from a full moon and reflecting off the water. Everyone in the room was talking, all at once. There were a few military families in the room, but most of the crowd was young GIs, ski patrol, young German employees and some friends.

Lucas stood back and studied the mood of room. It was obvious who the Germans were cheering for in this game. They only cheered when the Russian players were announced, right before the start of the game. American fans fell into the rivalry and cheered for the U.S. players when the U.S. team got announced. Most of the people had been drinking beer all day, maybe some schnapps too, and they were getting loud.

Shelley and the other ladies wanted to go to the game room, so they excused themselves.

"You didn't get enough competition today?" Lucas asked Shelley.

"No," she replied. "Maybe I'll be able to win at darts or pool."

"You are a winner in my book," he said.

"Thank you, Lucas. I'll see you later," she replied.

The big game was set to start in 15 minutes.

Lucas, Topo and George went outside on the deck, passed the hash pipe around and smoked it.

"Does anyone know the differences between rules we have in the U.S. and the International Basketball Rules?" asked Lucas.

"I teach this stuff to my young students, so I think I can answer your question," replied George. "A man named James Naismith who coached a football team in Springfield, Massachusetts, invented the game of basketball to play indoors during the snowy winter months. He established thirteen basic rules for the game."

"How high off of the floor were the baskets set?" asked Topo.

"Dr. Naismith put the baskets at ten feet, and they are still ten feet," he replied. "International Rules have one difference which stands out: once the ball hits the rim, it is fair game. In the NCAA Rules—there is an invisible cylinder above the rim. If any part of the ball is in the cylinder or touching the rim, and you touch the ball, it is a *goaltending* call, and the basket counts, even if it did not go in. In International Rules—once it hits the rim, anyone can swat it away. Also, there is no defensive three seconds in the restricted area, so a player can *camp* under the basket on offense or defense. I imagine the smaller floor dimensions also make a difference in play."

"Let's hope our American team has played enough games, using International Rules and this different court size, to be ready for this game. The veteran team of Russians have played many more games under these rules," said Lucas.

The game had begun before they got back, and all the seats were taken. They joined Lewis, Ostergaard, Eric, Grassl, Regan and Dennis, standing behind the Germans who sat on the right and other people who found seats on the left.

OLYMPIC BASKETBALL FINAL - IN PROGRESS:

Lucas was standing in the center. He could see the television screen, but everyone was talking, so he could not hear the play-by-play of the game. As he watched, he was left to his own thoughts about how this competition was going down: *Both teams are cold early. The Russians pass the ball around to use up the clock. The U.S. turns over the ball. Russia took advantage with an easy lay-up, got fouled, made the free throw, and now leads 3-0. Next, a sloppy pass by Henderson, plus a steal and lay-up for Russia. After 3 minutes of play, it's 5-0. U.S. made 1 of 2 free throws for 5-1. They trade baskets, and the Russians are ahead at 9-5. A jumper by Alexander Belov for 11-5. Goaltending by a Russian, and it's 11-7. A Sergei Belov jumper makes it 13-7. Another U.S. turnover and a Sergei Belov jump shot for 15-7. A U.S. follow shot by Jim Brewer makes it 15 to 9.*

Standing next to Lucas, George said, "Since nineteen thirty-six when basketball first came into the Olympics in Berlin, the U.S. has won all sixty-three games in prior Olympics for seven gold medals in a row. This U.S. team is the youngest and tallest team they've had. Now, after winning their first eight games in Munich, they must pick up the pace of this game. Otherwise, they will be in trouble."

After a timeout, Lucas goes back to his thoughts, watching the game: *Russia inbounds the ball, but nobody guards Sergei Belov. He sinks a 17-foot jumper for a 17-9 Russia lead. U.S. turns it over again without getting a shot on a weak pass. Sergei Belov makes a beautiful feed to Alexander Belov under the basket for an easy lay-up and 19 to 9 lead. Ed Ratleff misses a short jumper, and Russia gets the rebound. Dwight Jones tips a lob under the basket to Ed Ratleff who elbows the Russian guarding him. Ed gets called on an offensive foul. Next, he intercepts a Russian pass, but throws the ball away, out of bounds. The U.S. team can't get anything going in the center since the Russians are clogging the middle. There is no 3 second rule here, and it's a disadvantage for the U.S. players who use the 3 second rule in America.*

In the lounge, younger Germans got verbal and gloated over Russian dominance of the game, so far. The U.S. fans had nothing to cheer about yet, and the Americans were not displaying a good offense against this experienced Russian team.

Lucas watches: *Jim Brewer hit a 12-foot jump shot. The score is 19-11 for Russia. Sergei Belov makes a long jumper for his 12th point and a 21 to 11 advantage. Henderson makes a lay-up on a give-and-go from Ratleff, and the score is 21 to 13. After both teams missed several shots, Tom Henderson gets free under the basket, and he makes a lay-up. The score is 21-15. On a rare Russian turnover, Henderson makes a short jumper, and it's 21-17. Then, Ed Ratliff's jump shot puts the U.S. within 2 points at 21 to 19.*

The U.S. team is showing a little sign of life and American fans have something to cheer about. But the Russians come back with a free throw and a lay-up, bringing the score to 24-19. They exchange turnovers on long passes, and then Alexander Belov gets a too-easy short jumper for 26-19. The U.S. scores on a put back of Doug Collins' 19-foot shot. It is 26 to 21, with 58 seconds left in the first half. Dwight Jones misses a short jump shot at the buzzer. The score remains 26 to 21 as the half ends.

"Man! The first half went fast," George said to Lucas.

"Yeah," he replied. "They play twenty-minute halves, as opposed to the four ten-minute quarters we had in the Long Beach City League; and I thought those games flew by. Sometimes, it felt like I just got warmed up and into the game when it would be over."

Topo motioned for Lucas and George to go outside, so they turned and followed him toward the bar. The bar was crowded, and they did not want to wait in line for beer. Instead, they headed for the employees' beer machine. On the way, they looked in on the dance floor. A local rock band was playing the Byrd's song "Mr. Tambourine Man." Lucas could not believe his eyes. He saw 3 couples dancing on top of the tables in the dining room.

"Those ski patrol guys sure know how to have a good time!" Lucas exclaimed to his friends.

"Yeah… with a nice following of young ladies," said George.

They got 3 bottles of Wieninger beer from the employees' machine, sat on the cement dock behind the kitchen, and passed Topo's hashish pipe back and forth.

"If the U.S. team doesn't quicken their defense and get a few breaks, such as steals and rebounds, they will lose this game," said Lucas. "They are playing the Russian's style of play. What they need to do is plain old hustle, move without the ball and move the ball faster. They are just going through the motions. I want to scream at them, 'Pick up the pace!' "

"I agree with you," said Topo. "This kind of basketball is not very much fun to watch, either."

"Both teams won their other eight games quite easily," said George. "The United States' closest game was against Brazil when the U.S. won sixty-one to fifty-four. Russia's closest game was against Yugoslavia. Russia won by seven points, seventy-four to sixty-seven."

"The U.S. coach, Hank Iba, has been Head Basketball Coach at Oklahoma State for thirty-six years," said Lucas. "The first seven years, he also coached baseball. Iba coaches a methodical, grind-it-out, boring offense, but he is known as a defensive-minded coach. He developed the *floating man-to-man defense* which many teams are using."

"You're right, Lucas. If the U.S. keeps playing the Russian style of play, they could be in trouble," said George.

"Topo, you are leaving this week? Where are you going?" George asked, turning toward him.

"I'm heading to Spain and Portugal," he replied. "I plan to work on a large sailboat and cruise across the Atlantic to the Bahamas. Then, I'll make my way to Patagonia where my brother is. What about you, George? Do you know when you and Judann will leave?"

"I plan to work at the American School in Garmisch until December. We want to be in California by Christmas," replied George.

"In two weeks, Shelley and I will be in Garmisch to get the van serviced at the dealership," said Lucas. "We want to see our friends before we head for Yugoslavia, Greece and who knows where else."

"Judann and I talked about coming back here after the wedding, but it's not yet decided, so we will see," said George.

"Does Judann want to start a family?" asked Topo.

"Oh yeah, and I would love to have children!" replied George. "I'm around older ones, most of time, teaching and coaching them."

"Gabrielle and I had such a great time this summer, we have talked about her coming to Argentina," said Topo. "Like you said, we will see. It's a long way off. Now, let's go watch the second half."

Back in the lounge, they took their places, standing in back. People seated in the separate cheering sections were still in the partying mood, but the trash talk was a little louder between opposing fans. Lucas could not hear anything from the television, and he asked George if he knew who the play-by-play announcers were.

"Frank Gifford who is in the Football Hall of Fame, and Bill Russell who is in the Basketball Hall of Fame," replied George.

"With those slow-talkers, a ho-hum game is perfect for them," said Lucas. "I sure hope the teams will play faster in the second half."

SECOND HALF - OLYMPIC BASKETBALL FINAL:

The game had begun. Lucas still could not hear it on the television, but he watched and followed it play-by-play: *Doug Collins dribbles to his left and hits a bank shot off the glass, making the score 33 to 27. After a Collin's foul, Sergei Belov makes 1 of 2 free throws for 34 to 27. Dwight Jones also makes 1 of 2 free throws for a 34 to 28 score. Next, Jones, the leading scorer for the U.S. team during these Olympics, and Mishako Kohia, a Russian forward who rarely plays, are both thrown out of the game for fighting over a rebound. Then, they started fighting for real.*

"Did you see the guy who elbowed Jones in the head on the rebound?" asked George. "I would have pushed him or hit him too. They didn't even call a foul on it."

"Maybe they put him in to provoke Jones," said Lucas.

Lucas' attention went back to the game: *On a jump ball, Alexander Belov elbows Jim Brewer in the face. Brewer goes down on the court in pain, and he gets taken out of the game.*

"This game is not going well," said George. "It's too rough."

Lucas noticed the Germans, seated in front of him, were being obnoxious while supporting the Russian team. There was a lot of banter in the room between the Germans and supporters of the U.S. team.

Back to the game: *Russia inserts a new player with a long name. He hits a long jump shot, and the score is 36-28. Sergei Belov makes another wide-open shot, and it's 38-28. Then Ed Ratleff takes the defender inside and makes a difficult shot. Now the score is 38 to 30. There is a Russian turnover on a double dribble. Jim Brewer comes back in the game and scores, going around a screen for a jumper. The Russian lead is now 38 to 32. Russia misses, U.S. gets the rebound, and Mike Bantom sinks a jump hook in the lane, cutting the lead to 38-34. The two teams exchange baskets, and the score jumps to 44-38. There are just over 4 minutes left to play.*

The U.S. looks to pick up the pace and Kevin Joyce makes a scooping lay-up for a 44 to 40 score. The Russians make another turnover when Belov dribbles the ball off his foot. Kevin Joyce gets open at the free throw line and sinks it. The U.S. team closes within 2. The U.S. picks up their defense and uses a full court press. A Russian misses 2 free throws.

"Now, it's really getting rough out there," said George.

Lucas goes back to the game: *Joyce misses a jumper. Russia makes 1 of 2 free throws and still leads with 47 to 44. Brewer misses a long shot, Russia gets the rebound, and Ratleff fouls Paulauskas who makes both free throws. Then, Kevin Joyce gets another bucket from beyond the free throw line, cutting the lead to 3 again, with 1:50 left on the clock. Doug Collins makes 2 free throws, and the score is 47 to 46. Another Russian player who has a long name sinks 1 of 2 free throws. It is 48 to 46, with 1:24 left in the game. U.S. misses a shot and Mike Bantom fouls out. With 55 seconds left, the U.S. is trailing by 2. Sergei Belov makes 1 of 2 free throws, and it's 49 to 46.*

Jim Forbes hits a long jump shot. The U.S. now trails only by 1. Seven-footer Tom McMillan is in the game, blocking a Belov lay-up. Doug Collins gets the rebound, dribbles to his left, and then flies in the air; but, as he releases the ball, he gets hit and knocked to the floor. He lands behind the basket, falls into the basket support pad, and he seems to be unconscious for a moment. With help, he gets up, and he looks dazed. He shoots 2 free throws and makes both, putting the U.S. in the lead for the first time in the game. It's 50 to 49.

There are 3 seconds left on the game clock. The Russians throw the ball in. The player with the ball takes 2 dribbles and stops before the center line because a man jumps out of the stands, shouting something. The referee waives to stop play, with only 1 second showing on the game clock. The American players are running and yelling at the officials. Everyone on the court seems to be confused about what is going on. The referees are talking to the man who jumped down out of the stands. An announcer says the man is an official.

Finally, they clear the court of fans who had strayed onto the court. The referee orders a 3-second reset on the clock and hands the ball to the Russian player who stands out of bounds under his own basket.

The Americans have a 7-footer guarding the inbound player who throws an overhead pass to a Russian player. The Russian heaves a pass down court, it hits the backboard and bounces away. The game is over. Now, U.S. players are hugging and celebrating on the court.

U.S. fans let out a roar in the lounge, and they shout trash talk at the Germans. Then, someone yelled, "Wait! What's going on?"

Everything got quiet. Lucas could not believe what was happening: *The official who was in the stands is now on the court again, telling the referees to put 3 seconds back on the clock.*

Lucas and George were both stunned.

Someone close to the television set shouted out what he had heard, "The announcer said the clock was set at 50 seconds in error on the last play instead of 3 seconds. So, they will play it over."

"This gives the Russians a third chance, with 3 seconds left on the clock. Or, maybe the officials will keep giving them the ball until they make the shot," said George. He shook his head.

Lucas watches the impossible happen: *Tom McMillan, a seven-foot U.S. player, goes to guard the inbound player, and the referee motions for him to move back. This gives the Russian player an opening. From under his own basket, he throws the ball in and makes it all the way to Alexander Belov, his teammate who is under the U.S. basket. Belov out-leaps two U.S. defenders, and he controls the ball. As the defenders fall to the court, Belov lays it in for a Russian victory.*

In the lounge, everyone is stunned.

The U.S. supporters are pissed off. After cheering for the Russian team, the Germans let the Americans have it, yelling trash talk. Within moments, the Germans were gloating about the Americans losing to the Russians, but the Americans insisted it was a farce because officials decided the winner.

Lucas and his guys wanted to find the ladies, so they headed toward the bar and game room. Looking in the crowded bar, they saw none of their ladies. Going toward the stairs which lead down to the game room, they heard a big commotion which was happening in the lounge.

Most of the guys returned to the lounge, but Lucas stopped at the door. He was disturbed by what he saw; and if the situation was not so serious, he would have laughed out loud at the scene. In front of the television set, there were about 10 guys, trying to hurt each other. Most of them got tangled in chairs, then fell and wrestled on the floor.

One guy stood, grabbed a chair and raised it over his head, right in front of Jordan Lewis, the bouncer from Garmisch. Lewis grabbed the chair away from the guy before he could do any harm with it.

Then, Lewis turned and spoke to his group of Americans, "I guess it's time to break this up before somebody gets hurt." Several of his biggest friends were ready to join Lewis and put a stop to the fight.

Fritz, the 55-year-old sous chef, walked over next to Lucas. Fritz was a boxer in his younger days, and he was built like a fireplug. When he saw there was a fight, he started to move toward the scuffle.

Lucas put his arm around Fritz's chest to stop him, and said, "Fritz, we are the old guys—we should not get into this. We have to work with these young guys, and they've had too much to drink today."

As Lewis and his big friends started disrupting the fight, people heard a loud gun shot, and everyone in the room froze. Lucas spotted Gunther, the bartender who had a smoking gun in his hand and his arm still pointed out an open door, aimed toward the lake.

Gunther shouted at everyone, "The world has seen enough fighting between Germans and Americans; and this is the most stupid reason of all, a basketball game against Russia. It has been a long day. Now, it is time to break this up."

Quietly, Gunther turned and went back to work behind the bar.

Shelley and the ladies were still in the game room. Topo and a few of the guys had joined them to watch the ladies finish their games. The rest of the guys arrived, sharing stories of the fight in the lounge and how Gunther put a stop to it. He was the "hero" of the evening.

While everyone was talking, Lucas got Eric, Sabine, Gabrielle and Sonya aside. They all left the game room. While Lucas went to his office and got his hash pipe from his backpack, the others grabbed beers from the beer machine. Then, they all took a walk down the road toward the dock and boathouse.

"I know I said it before, but let's hope this is the last time we discuss this subject. I want us to have closure on it. Does anybody know what is happening with Enrico?" asked Lucas.

"He and Olivia are still together, and he seems happy," said Eric.

Sabine agreed with Eric, and Gabrielle had no comment.

"He does not seem anxious to find his brother," said Lucas.

"I think he has stopped asking about Bruno," replied Sonya. "He sure is a lot friendlier than his brother. But he resembles Bruno, and it gives me the creeps, sometimes."

"Okay. He appears to be doing his own thing," said Lucas.

The others nodded.

He added, "I also want to thank all of you for coming this weekend. It was great to see you, and it sure was eventful! In two weeks, Shelley and I will be in Garmisch. We plan to party at The Grill and The Last Chance before we go on our vacation."

"You want a vacation from this paradise?" asked Gabrielle.

Lucas laughed. Then, he said, "We will come back to this paradise, but we want to see how people live in other parts of the world. Traveling by van is a great way to explore new areas. We'll get to know the local people by eating in their restaurants, drinking with them, listening to their stories, playing sports and rolling around in the dirt with them."

Everyone laughed and headed back inside. They gathered with their friends in the game room for a short while. Then, everyone went to their respective beds for a good night's sleep.

CHAPTER 44

Return to Garmisch

The next morning, Sunday breakfast service was extremely busy at the hotel, and Lucas jumped in to help the cooks. When things slowed down, he joined his Garmisch friends for brunch in the dining room.

Lucas got seated and ordered a vegetable omelette with home fries, wheat toast, strawberry jam and a Wieninger beer. All the guys were excited as they talked about playing a small tournament of doubles-volleyball this afternoon.

Most hotel guests would leave today. Business would be slow because summer was ending, and the hotel would be quiet until it snows.

The Garmisch and Berchtesgaden people stayed to play volleyball, drink beer and enjoy a beautiful day at Chiemsee before they all went home. It was an hour-and-a-half drive to Garmisch and an hour drive in the opposite direction to Berchtesgaden. Of course, it depends on who is driving and what type of vehicle they are in.

The guys paired up teams for an impromptu volleyball tournament. Lucas and George wanted to play together, but their friends objected because most had seen them play and knew how they dominated games. They both learned to play on Southern California beaches: Seal Beach, Redondo, Hermosa, Huntington and Manhattan Beach.

Lucas will play with Grassl who is 6'4". His volleyball skills are unknown, and he only claimed to have played some indoor volleyball. George will play with Bob Ostergaard who is 6'5". His game skills are also unknown. Bob was always busy with his van business, so he did not have time for other activities. Eric will play with Regan, and both are great athletes. Lucas knew the abilities of Chip and John. As a pair, they have an advantage since they have played together a lot.

The group planned to play a round-robin tournament, meaning 2-man teams will play each other once. To speed things up, games will end at 11 points. The team with the most wins will be the tournament winner. In case of a tie, the last 2 teams will play one more game to 15 points. They all agreed to meet at the sand volleyball court at 2 p.m.

Arriving at the court, guys were surprised to see their ladies. Some had folding chairs and others had blankets on the grass around the court.

Earlier, Lucas put together a large hoagie sandwich, made on a loaf of French bread with Westphalia ham, Muenster cheese, pickles, tomato and lettuce. He sliced the hoagie, then made coleslaw and some cookies.

Gunther, the bartender, sent a case of beer with Shelley; and she set up a card table for the snacks, disposable plates, forks and napkins.

The tournament got started. First up, George and Bob played Chip and John. George was by far the best player, but Chip and John together seemed to even out the teams. Chip and John jumped out ahead, 6 to 1, and they held on to win, 11 to 9.

Lucas had only seen Grassl play bar sports, not volleyball. When he set Grassl for a kill, Grassl smashed it cross-court, landing 3 feet inside the end-line rope, and Lucas was surprised. Although Eric and Regan are great athletes, they were not ready for what Grassl and Lucas threw at them. Eric and Regan got beaten, 11 to 6.

While Chip and John played against Eric and Regan. Lucas and Grassl sat out and joined George who was telling other spectators about the last day of Olympic competitions.

"For the Men's Fifteen Hundred Meter Run, known as the Metric Mile, the world record holder, American Jim Ryan, tripped on another runner's foot in a qualifying race. So, he didn't get to run in the final," said George. "Ryan also holds world records in the eight-hundred-and-eighty-yard run, indoors and outdoors, plus the fifteen hundred meters, indoors and outdoors. Anyway, a Finnish runner won the race.

"The American team had another disappointment in the Men's Five Thousand Meter Run when Steve Prefontaine faded to fourth, out of the medals, after he led the first fifteen hundred meters. Prefontaine was bragging before the race. He thought he would win because he set the American record during Olympic trials. However, Finland's Lasse Viren was the winner.

"Viren had already won the Men's Ten Thousand Meter Run after he got tangled with another runner and fell; he recovered, won the race by seven meters and set a new world record."

On the volleyball court, Eric and Regan's athletic skills kept them in the game, but they had not played much beach volleyball. Chip and John played together all summer, so they won the game, 11-8.

Now, Lucas and Grassl were up against George and Bob who had lost their first game, but started off well in this game. They won the first 3 points with hard kills by George. Then, Lucas gave Grassl 2 perfect sets, and Grassl put them away, 1 down the middle of the court and 1 down the sideline, both winners. Next, Lucas dug out a hard kill by George, and

Grassl gave him a decent set which he smashed down the middle and hit the end rope for a 3 to 3 tie. They battled back and forth, drawing the attention of a crowd which had gathered around the court. The score was 11 to 11 when Lucas hit a jump serve, and it hit the sideline, just out of George's diving reach. Now, Lucas and Grassl were in the lead, 12 to 11. When George went to block Grassl's kill, Grassl dinked it over his head, and the ball fell to the sand, untouched. Lucas and Grassl won the game, and they were still undefeated.

Next, George and Bob played Eric and Regan. They often played basketball with and against each other at the gym in Garmisch, so it was a spirited game. Since George was hurting from the loss to Lucas and Grassl, he stepped up his game. His hard smashes were too much for Eric and Regan by 11 to 5.

Returning to the sidelines with a beer in hand, George continued telling Lucas and others his summary of the last day of Olympic events.

"The finish of the Men's Marathon was amazing, and Frank Shorter, an American athlete, won the gold medal," said George. "It was a big deal since no American had won an Olympic marathon, in sixty-four years. Frank Shorter was the lead runner when he entered the stadium. Strangely, the crowd was booing, but not at Shorter. An imposter had gotten on the track and had run into the stadium, wearing a tracksuit. People started cheering the imposter until they realized the hoax, and officials escorted him off the track. When Shorter appeared, the crowd was still booing at the imposter. It did not stop Shorter from winning, but he must have wondered, at first, if the boos were for him."

"Do you know who the imposter was?" asked Lucas.

George shook his head. He did not know; but Gabrielle said, "He is a German student, named Norbert Sudhaus."

"Well, he may be an imposter, but he put his name in Olympic history, even if it was for being a jerk," said Lucas.

"Please, tell us what else happened today, George," said Gabrielle.

"The sprints were a catastrophe for Americans," he replied. "In the Men's One Hundred Meter Run, two American threats, Eddie Hart and Rey Robinson, missed their starting times for the quarter-finals, and they got eliminated. Valeriy Borzov, a Russian, won The Men's One Hundred Meter Run and the Men's Two Hundred Meter Run. Renate Stecher won both women's sprints for East Germany.

"To top things off, the U.S. team did not have enough sprinters for the last running event, the Men's Four Hundred Meter Relay. Kenya got an unexpected gold medal in the relay, edging out Great Britain.

"When the U.S. withdrew from the final relay, their team was short three men. During an earlier event, the Men's Four Hundred Meter Run,

John Smith went down with a torn hamstring, and he could not finish. Then, Vince Mathews, a gold medal winner, and Wayne Collett, a silver medal winner, staged a protest during the medal ceremony, and the International Olympic Committee banned them from competition."

Lucas and Grassl got back on the volleyball court to play against Chip and John. Lucas' quickness on the court allowed Grassl to go to the net. When Chip went up for a kill, Grassl blocked several shots. This frustrated them since most of John's sets were on the money.

When John tried to dink the ball, Lucas anticipated it and covered the spot where the ball was going. Lucas would dig it out, Grassl would set the ball to him, and he would put it away, usually down the center, but occasionally down the sides or cross-court. Lucas and Grassl had an 8 to 4 lead, but Lucas missed a shot down the line, and Chip got a few by Grassl's block. With Chip's determination and winning mind set, he and John had tied the game. It was 10 to 10. Both Lucas and Grassl hit their kills with authority, but Chip and John dug everything out. Neither team could get the 2-point advantage to win the game.

A sizable group of beer-drinking spectators got more boisterous with every shot. The score was now 17 all, and Lucas surprised Chip when he went forward and blocked Chip's kill. Grassl had stayed back this time. Chip got fooled, and the ball fell to the sand at his feet. It was Lucas' serve for the game. He hit his best jump serve with downspin, and John could not get under it. At last, Lucas had a payback for losing to Chip on the tennis court.

When Chip and Lucas shook hands under the net, Chip said, "Well, Lucas, down to the wire again. I can't wait for the next opportunity to play against you, no matter what game or what sport it is."

"Yeah, Chip. I'll be looking forward to our next match. But it will have to wait while I go to Greece for a much-needed vacation," he replied.

"Lucas, you're in paradise. Why go on vacation?" asked John who had joined them on the court. Lucas grinned, and the guys chuckled.

George was still hurting a bit, having lost at his best sport, volleyball. However, he joined them and said, "Great game, you guys. I'll be waiting to get my revenge. For now, we must head to Garmisch, and I must get back to work at the school tomorrow."

Lucas hugged his Long Beach buddy and said, "Shelley and I will see you when we come to Garmisch in two weeks. I look forward to seeing everyone, at least those who are still around. So many of our friends are leaving and heading back to the real world."

A group of spectators started playing Jungle Ball on the volleyball court with about 10 players on each side. They were all laughing and drinking beer under clear skies with plenty of late afternoon sunshine.

Lucas, Shelley, Topo and Gabrielle got beers, went to the lounge and settled into chairs around the television set. With only a few other employees and two families in the room, they all came to watch closing ceremonies of the Munich Olympics. It was a much quieter group in the lounge on this Sunday evening.

Television announcers were going over highlights and stories about the last day of the games. Lucas was always a statistics guy, so he watched and listened with interest.

The announcer spoke, "Mark Spitz set an Olympic record, winning seven gold medals in world-record times. However, he did not stick around to celebrate. Officials feared for his safety because he is Jewish, so he left Munich as soon as he finished his events.

"Handball returned to these Olympics after being absent since nineteen thirty-six. Archery returned for the first time since nineteen twenty. Canoe Slalom made its first Olympic appearance. Olga Korbut, a Soviet gymnast, won three gold medals. American wrestler, Dan Gable, won the gold medal without giving up a single point, something no other Olympic wrestler had ever done.

"The American Basketball team lost for the first time and refused to accept the silver medal. Americans claimed there was cheating which involved multiple and deliberate timekeeping errors at the end of their game with the Soviet Union."

When medal counts were posted on the television screen, Lucas said, "Look at the counts. If you combine the two German teams, East and West Germany, they have more total medals than the Soviet Union who ended with ninety-nine medals: fifty gold, twenty-seven silver and twenty-two bronze. The combined scores of the German teams would be one hundred and six medals: thirty-three gold, thirty-four silver and thirty-nine bronze. The U.S. team got ninety-four medals: thirty-three gold, thirty-one silver and thirty bronze."

During closing comments, the television announcer said, "Hundreds of journalists, from around the world, covered the Munich Olympics. The Black September assault and murder of Israeli athletes was, in fact, the first time that a terror attack got reported and broadcast live. We will always remember these Munich Olympics which began as *Games of Peace and Joy*. This was an opportunity for the government of West Germany to make amends for an offensive Nazi image which is always connected to the Berlin Olympics of nineteen thirty-six. Regrettably, these Munich Olympics ended as *Games of Terror and Tragedy*."

Saddened by the horrible truth, Shelley and Lucas left the lounge.

When they walked back to his office in the hotel kitchen, Lucas found a notice on his desk. The Health and Sanitation Department scheduled an inspection of the kitchen; it would take place in one week. This meant a lot of cleaning must be done between now and then.

When Lucas told Shelley about the inspection, she said, "It would be a good setting for an all-night party, cleaning the kitchen."

"Why didn't I think of it? What a great way to get the kitchen sparkling clean. Who shall we invite?" asked Lucas.

"Anybody who is crazy enough to come do it," she replied.

"Okay," he said. "I'll provide the beer and hashish, and we'll have AFRC provide the food."

Lucas made sure the kitchen employees knew a big inspection was coming up. They would be deep cleaning and organizing until the day of the inspection. This gave them 6 days to work on the kitchen.

Lucas phoned his good friend Eric at NATO Officers Club and asked if he was available for the kitchen cleaning party. Eric said he had 2 days off at the end of the week. He would come, and he would bring Sabine if she wanted to join him.

The special cleaning crew included Lucas, Shelley, Gabrielle, Topo, Eric and Sabine. Also, Heinz Ostler, the pastry chef, Herr Schmechtig from the pantry, and Fritz, the sous chef, would all stay to join the party for a few hours after work.

Lucas set out 2 cases of Wieninger beer and offered his hash pipe to anyone who wanted to indulge. Heinz had smoked and ingested hashish when he and Lucas made hash brownies for the Austrian Grand Prix, so he agreed to smoke the hash pipe without hesitation. Since Fritz had been drinking beer all day, anyway, he smoked it too. Lucas thought Fritz was a nice guy who was trusting and kind. He also loved to have fun.

Fritz and his wife had invited Shelley and Lucas over to their house for dinner and drinks. They spent the night communicating in German which Shelley handled better than Lucas, but they all had a fun evening.

For the kitchen cleaning party, Lucas and Fritz set out tapas which they prepared. Lucas' favorite was lamb meat balls. They had sliced bratwurst and Weisswurst, sweet onion rings, goulash soup and brotchen. Argentine empanadas with a beef filling were served, in honor of Topo's departure. Heinz Ostler added fresh cakes and pastries which he made.

Since the staff had done extra cleaning during the week, the hotel kitchen was clean. However, the goal was to get to every square inch of the kitchen spotless.

Lucas hid the table-mounted can openers and other small items which might need resurfacing or refurbishing. Inspectors wrote citations for unsanitary can openers most often. Looking in the storeroom, he found a new can opener which was still in the box. He put it on a counter, so an inspector would not ask where the can opener was. Lucas wanted to minimize the number of utensils and equipment items, so there would be no clutter anywhere in the kitchen areas. All the extra stuff was now well-hidden in the air-raid shelter.

To set a lively mood, Sabine brought a mixture of Tyrolean music and popular rock music on cassette tapes. After smoking some of Topo's Black Colombian hashish and drinking beer, the whole crew got into a cleaning groove and worked hard. Some people labored to the point of overkill, polishing the same spot 5 times.

Around 2 a.m., everyone took a break. Lucas was delighted when he saw Herr Schmechtig and Herr Ostler together, sitting side by side in front of Herr Schmechtig's work table, talking, laughing, drinking beer and eating. According to Fritz, they had not spoken for several years and always played mean tricks on each other.

For Topo, this was a going away party, of sorts. He would be leaving in 2 days and be on his way to Portugal.

Herr Schmechtig felt frisky tonight. When a young lady came into his view, he hollered out his favorite line, "Hallo Baby, ein bisschen (a little) lieben (loving) maybe?" If the food-service shutters were open during the day shift, he often used this line as the maids paraded by the kitchen, wearing their green uniforms.

At some point, Herr Schmechtig went to the restroom, but he never came back. Shelley went to look for him and found him asleep on a couch in the lounge. Lucas said he would take him to his room when it was time to go. Herr Schmechtig lived in the Annex building next to the Park Hotel where Lucas and Shelley lived.

After they finished cleaning and Lucas was positive the kitchen was spotless, he thanked everyone. Then, he and Eric put Herr Schmechtig into Eric's van and took him to the Annex. Herr Schmechtig felt light, like he was under 100 pounds, so Lucas picked him up, put him over his shoulder, and carried him up the stairs. Being able to do so amazed Lucas. He thanked Eric and would check on Herr Schmechtig later.

Lucas stopped at the apartment for a quick shower. He put on a new chef's coat with black slacks, all well-pressed, and he arrived 10 minutes early for the sanitation inspection in the kitchen.

Shelley came in with Bob Clarkson and the inspectors, 1 woman and 2 men, all dressed in military uniforms. Bob introduced Lucas, and they followed the inspectors, each with a clipboard, around the kitchen. None of them said a word, and their expressions did not change while they did a thorough search for any infractions.

When the inspection was finished, they thanked Lucas and Shelley, and then walked away with Bob, going toward his office.

Shelley and Lucas were both exhausted, but Lucas wanted to stick around and learn how the kitchen scored. Shelley told him she would see him later, and she went to their apartment.

While he waited for inspection results, Lucas sat in his office and did some paperwork. Suddenly, Bob Clarkson burst into his office.

"This is amazing, Lucas, you got one hundred percent," said Bob.

"No, Bob. We all got one hundred percent," said Lucas.

"Okay," he replied, "but it's the first one hundred percent score in AFRC history. Hell, it could even be the first one hundred percent in all of USAREUR (United States Army Europe)."

"It's great news, and it was a fun, team effort," replied Lucas. "You know, it is not difficult to get a high score if you know what the inspectors look for, and you have good people who are willing to do great work."

After a tearful goodbye to Topo at the station in Prien, Topo got on the train and headed for Mannheim, Germany. From there, he would continue to Paris, then go south to the Spanish border.

The next 2 weeks went quick. Lucas and Shelley spent their spare time organizing and packing the van for their trip to Greece.

In a deal they made with Chip, they left their skis and bicycles with him, and they took the volleyball net and volleyball. They promised to bring the stuff back by April. However, Lucas joked with Chip, as he said, "We will really try to be back by summer."

Things at the hotel were slow, and a lot of the employees were taking vacations. Many of the ski patrol were heading home to "The States." Others were taking "European Outs" from the military.

Gabrielle continued working and stayed in the Ranch House with Gretchen to keep her company. Karen Tyler left Chiemsee and went to Formentera where she would play guitar, sing and write music.

Bob Clarkson wrote very complimentary letters of recommendation for Lucas and Shelley. He hoped they would come back to Chiemsee. Right then, Lucas could not think too far ahead.

The morning of their departure, Lucas and Shelley had breakfast in Hitler's round dining room. As they enjoyed the view, looking out at Lake Chiemsee, Gabrielle rushed in. She was very upset and crying.

"A Spanish lawyer phoned and left me a message: Topo was arrested for drug possession at the French/Spanish border in Hendaye," she said. "He offered no further information."

After consoling Gabrielle and they all hugged and said goodbye.

Lucas and Shelley pulled out of the hotel parking lot, headed for Garmisch with heavy hearts. However, Lucas was optimistic, so he tried to think of something positive about Topo's situation.

“I think Topo’s father is a government official in Argentina,” he said to Shelley. “I hope he can pull some strings to get Topo released.” When she did not respond, he added, “This sure cures me of any notions about carrying drugs across borders. I told you about Ty Harden, the actor I met in Los Boliches. He also learned the hard way by getting arrested.”

“I’m sorry,” she replied. “My mind is occupied with other things. Tell me again why Topo is returning to Argentina?”

“Topo went to visit his brother, a journalist who moved to Argentina where the climate and landscape are similar to Bavaria,” replied Lucas. “He lives in the city of Bariloche in Patagonia which is in the southern part of Argentina. His brother is doing extensive research about ex-Nazis who settled in the area, and he hopes to determine if Hitler and Eva faked their suicides, then escaped from Germany and went to live there.”

“Okay, now I remember. Topo told us about his brother’s research,” she said. “The stories we’ve heard, from people who met Hitler in Bavaria, have all been educational; and everyone had a different story to tell.”

“Yes, I agree,” he said. “I have enjoyed listening to Gunther and Heinz Ostler in Chiemsee, also Chef Held in Berchtesgaden. They all have personal stories and experiences about Hitler and the Nazi era.”

Shelley put a Crosby, Stills and Nash tape into the cassette player, and she said, “Last night, the theater showed the movie *Catch 22.* While I waited in the bar for you to get off work, a few of us discussed the movie. Since you oversee the food department for AFRC, someone mentioned Milo Minderbinder, a character in the movie who was in a situation like yours, except Milo had no scruples.”

“Well, what did this character do? Milo… who?” he asked.

“The movie character’s name is Milo Minderbinder,” she replied. “He is the mess officer who bends the rules to suit his personal desires. Someone said you reminded them of this Minderbinder character, except you do not bend the rules for your own benefit; you bend them for the benefit of your coworkers and fellow AFRC members. Anyway, I think you should watch the movie or read the book. Let’s see if we can find a copy of the book and take it with us to Greece.”

“I may take advantage of my position as Head Chef,” he said, “to help create a positive, friendly atmosphere for employees, and for the guests to have a better hotel experience. I think it’s worth the extra cost to have a fun-first attitude for special employee functions. Bob Clarkson approved and supported those. I can’t speak for others involved, but I worked my ass off, had a great experience and formed relationships which I will never forget. We were all part of one big family with everyone living, working and partying in the same hotel.”

He took a minute to think about Shelley’s suggestion.

"The movie sounds like a crazy story. I think I want to read the book before I see the movie though. Did the story take place during the Second World War?" he asked.

"Yes, it did. I believe it was in Italy," she replied.

"It was a different era and situation. This is not wartime, although it is still the same old military," he said.

"I don't think you resemble the Minderbinder character at all," she replied. "As far as spending goes, you see a lot of waste in government and military spending from a civilian perspective. A pig barbecue, held for hotel employees, would not be too far off an appropriate budget. However, twenty people raiding the kitchen, late at night or early in the morning—might be pushing it." They both laughed.

Listening to *Crosby, Stills and Nash,* Shelley said, "This was their first album. Karen Tyler said Stills wrote 'Suite: Judy Blue Eyes' as a love song for Judy Collins, an American folk singer who was his ex-girlfriend. Karen also told us a lot about their backgrounds: Before going to Joni Mitchell's house in Laurel Canyon, David Crosby and Stephen Stills, both Americans, were notorious partiers. Crosby played with The Byrds. Stills was with Neil Young and helped form Buffalo Springfield. Graham Nash is British, and he played with The Hollies."

"I read about the group. They broke up because of Stephen Stills' alcohol and cocaine abuse in the summer of nineteen seventy," said Lucas. "I think they made another album together and had a few more public appearances, but they went separate ways."

"Lucas, do you think it is possible Hitler and Eva Braun escaped to Argentina, as Topo suggested?" she asked.

"Yes, I think it's possible," he replied. "The bodies, discovered at the Berlin bunker, may not have been theirs. The Russians found them and were secretive about the remains. After Topo told me about his brother's research in Patagonia, I thought about it, plus all the different things which people have told me and things I've read. A lot of Nazis escaped capture and went to South America. There were many Hitler supporters and top Nazi officers in Argentina. So, why not?"

"I am still curious about the women in Hitler's life," said Shelley. "By his count, Gunther claimed there were eight women who were intimate with Hitler and either committed or attempted suicide."

"I spoke to several Germans about it," he replied. "Heinz Ostler and I put together a timeline for Hitler's presumed love life.

"Sabine's Jewish grandfather was the Hitler family doctor. Hitler was fond of him and protected him during the war even though he was Jewish. Sabine told me a story about Hitler having a crush on a Jewish girl when he was sixteen, but he was too shy to talk to her.

"Maria Reiter was his first real romance, or so I've been told. She was seventeen when Hitler courted her. He got busy and ignored her which made her depressed, and she tried to hang herself. It was during the late twenties when Hitler was thirty-seven. Sabine said Maria also went by Mimi or Mitzi, she is married now, and she lives in Seefeld.

"In nineteen thirty-one, Geli Raubal, daughter of Hitler's half-sister, Angela Raubal, allegedly shot and killed herself in Hitler's apartment with Hitler's gun while he was out of town. We know Eva Braun was next, and she attempted suicide twice, once with a gunshot, and then a bottle of pills. Her attempts failed. But, in the end, she and Hitler committed suicide in the Berlin bunker."

"Or, they escaped to Argentina," said Shelley. They laughed.

"That is a whole different story," said Lucas. "We will have to wait until Topo gets out of prison to pursue it. Eva's first attempt was in nineteen thirty-two, and the other was in nineteen thirty-five. There were several other women, not well-known. In nineteen thirty-nine, Unity Mitford died of a self-inflicted gunshot wound, using a pistol Hitler had given her for protection. She was a British socialite who got depressed because England had declared war on Germany. In nineteen forty-two, Frau Inga Ley committed suicide because of her alleged addiction to drugs and the burden of being married to her boring husband. Apparently, Hitler admired her. All these stories seem a little strange, but most odd was a story I read about Renate Muller, an actress who Hitler also admired very much. She refused to make propaganda films for the Nazis; and when some SS officers pressured her, she threw herself out a window."

"I read a story which was strange, too," said Shelley. "It was about Martha Dodd, the daughter of the American Ambassador to Germany. While the Dodd family was living in Berlin, she became infatuated with Hitler and the Nazis. But, when she realized how brutal the Nazis became, she tried to commit suicide by slitting her wrist. Her attempt failed, and she is still alive."

"Let's see… we named seven," he said. "The last lover on the list is Suzi Liptauer. She had a relationship with Hitler for a while in Munich. before he became Chancellor. I remember Gunther saying Hitler was quite the ladies' man around Munich before nineteen thirty-three, and the women chased him. Suzi Liptauer realized Hitler would not marry her, and he was seeing other women, so she took her own life."

"Who knows, there may be others," she replied.

She is right about others, thought Lucas. *Much like I don't know if Bruno beat and murdered other women who I don't know about.*

"Lucas, you told me we won't be taking any hashish across borders. Won't you miss it?" she asked.

"One of the great things about marijuana is you don't get a physical addiction," he replied. "It's a shame people think marijuana is dangerous. As I've said before, it has many uses, depending on the strain of the plant you are using. There is a reason marijuana has been around for centuries. Although it became illegal, it keeps coming back. Up to this point, the only thing I see wrong with marijuana is it being illegal."

"If you had to choose, would you take beer or pot?" she asked.

"No brainer. I would choose pot over beer, anytime," he replied. "There are lots of downsides to drinking beer. Hangovers, belly fat and bloating. Beer is much more dangerous to your health, and it's very hard on the stomach. Pot makes me feel the way I want to feel while I still maintain control; and I have no symptoms of damage to my health or any bad lingering effects."

They drove into Garmisch, went straight to the VW dealer and left the van for service. It would be ready for pick up by late afternoon.

George had the day off, so he and Judann picked them up and took them to the PX. Lucas and Shelley shopped for things they would need on their trip to Greece.

Next, they all went to The Last Chance for lunch. Lucas was glad to see Sonya working; she seemed happy and over Bruno. The restaurant was quiet since the afternoon and evening ski patrol crowd had not arrived yet. George entertained the others with stories of local news and what their Garmisch friends were doing.

"Nobody knows for sure, but there is talk about Casa Carioca," said George. "Management may have caused the fire to cover up evidence; they embezzled millions of dollars from the business, putting fictitious employees on the books. Officials arrested the major who had overseen management. They found him in Switzerland. It's too bad we never got to see Casa Carioca before it burned down."

"I understand it was a spectacular place, and a lot of celebrities spent evenings there under the stars," said Judann.

"It had a sliding roof which opened for dining," said George. "They catered to royalty and celebrities, such as the King of Greece, Elizabeth Taylor and Richard Burton."

George's news is interesting, thought Lucas. *Until now, I believed the RAF gang had something to do with burning Casa Carioca.*

Sitting in The Last Chance, everyone drank Pschorr beers.

Lucas recalled the time he was here with Eric, Olivia and Ashleigh when he had eaten excellent Sauerbraten and spaetzle. So, he ordered it again, today.

Shelley and Judann ordered Jäger Hühnerschnitzel (chicken breasts in a white wine, mushroom cream sauce).

George selected Schmankerl Topf (beef and pork medallions, topped with a hunter's sauce, served with spaetzle and vegetables).

When Lucas asked who had left, of the people they know, George said, "It would be easier to tell you who is still here: Scott and Faye, Judann and me. Many of our friends went to California, including Ostergaard who plans to check out a railroad salvage idea. He can start a new company with the money he made here in his 'Shifty Sales' business, restoring rusted-out VW vans."

"What about Eric and Mike Harker?" asked Lucas.

George said, "They took off for Athens with two young Grill Queens. Eric was driving his van, and Harker followed on his motorcycle. Now, before you jump to conclusions, Eric swore the ladies were with Harker, and he was only giving them a ride."

"The ladies do seem to flock around Mike Harker, so Eric's story is believable… But, not very," said Lucas. Their friends laughed.

George said, "Yeah, and Regan Stone broke ladies' hearts around here when he left. He is headed home to practice law and raise cattle in Texas. I think you know Dennis, the waiter and fire dancer, is gone; so is Jordan Lewis, the bouncer."

"What about Gino and John Ferrell?" asked Lucas.

"John left after the Olympics. He headed for Southern California. Gino left two days ago, also headed to California. Gino hopes to get back into the movie or television business," replied George.

He added, "Oh, I forgot, Olivia and Ashleigh are around. Enrico and Olivia are still dating. Ashleigh has a broken heart since Regan left."

"AFRC seems to be a revolving door for European travelers," said Judann. "They work a while, then move on. The German employees are steadfast. They aren't going anywhere since this is their home."

"I have loved working with the Germans," said Lucas. "They are so friendly and very informative about history and life in Bavaria."

They split the check, left The Last Chance and went to get Lucas' van. George and Lucas planned to be at the gym by 6 p.m. George said he expected Scott to join them; he did not know who else would be there although Enrico usually plays.

After Lucas and Shelley checked into the Eibsee Hotel, George and Judann came to their room. While the guys went to play basketball, the ladies stayed at the hotel.

George and Lucas got to the gym before anyone else was on the court. While they warmed up, Enrico came in and joined them. Scott Williams was the next to arrive.

Then, 2 guys came in. Lucas had met and talked to them at The Grill. One guy, a ski patrolman named Terry, was about Lucas' size. He had blonde hair and light skin with some freckles across his nose. The other guy was 2 inches taller and thinner. He had a weather-beaten face which is common for people who spend most of their days outdoors. Everyone called him Kinky. Nobody knew his real name. He played guitar with a local band at night, and he was a ski instructor during the day.

With 6 guys ready to play, Lucas, George and Scott challenged the others to a half-court game of 3 on 3. They would play to 20 points, and you had to win by 4 points. Also, they would play *Winners' Outs*: If you make a basket, you can continue to inbound the ball until the other team gets a rebound, misses a shot or takes the ball away. On change of possession, you must take the ball back out and inbound it from the half-court line.

Lucas made his free throw to see who got the ball first. He passed the ball in to George who passed to Scott. Trying to dribble through 2 players, going toward the basket, Scott lost the ball out of bounds.

This is not a good start, thought Lucas. And it did not get better.

Each time Scott got the ball, he dribbled around and lost the ball, or he tried to pass and got intercepted. Their team fell behind, 14 to 6.

Lucas whispered to George, "Let's not pass the ball to Scott anymore. You and I can beat these guys with ease."

Scott remained on the court, but Lucas and George played a two-man game. Using a lot of screens and rolls to the basket, they cut the score, now 16 to 12. Lucas hit 2 outside shots to tie the score, but Scott lost his man, and Kinky made an easy lay-up. It was 18 to 16, in favor of Enrico's team. George inbounded the ball to Lucas, but Terry was all over him with defense. George set a screen and Lucas dribbled to his left, putting him at the top of the key about 18 feet from the basket. Enrico moved to double-team Lucas, leaving Scott all alone under the basket. So, Lucas bounced a pass to him, and Scott made an easy lay-up, tying the score, 18 to 18.

George was ready to pass the ball back in to Lucas. Enrico shouted, "Wait!" Then, he walked away, going toward the locker room.

Lucas turned around and saw 2 very large Italian men in dark suits, standing inside the main entrance next to the locker room. Enrico spoke with them, and they all went into the locker room.

To stay warm, the other 5 players shot hoops while they waited for Enrico to come back and finish the game. It was now tied.

They stopped when Enrico came out of the locker room, dressed in street clothes, carrying his gym bag. The 2 Italians were behind him.

Seeing this, Lucas headed toward the entrance and shouted to Enrico, "Where are you going? Can't we finish the game?"

"I'm sorry," he said. "I have to go back to Long Island. I want to stay, but you don't know my father!" Then, he left with the 2 goons.

"I guess we will have to settle for a tie," said George.

"Well, a tie means I'm still undefeated in this gym," said Lucas.

With Enrico leaving, I hope the case on Bruno Castignoli is closed, thought Lucas. *Tonight, I'll tell Sonya. We can call Gabrielle and Sabine. If I catch up with Eric in Athens, I will tell him in person.*

Lucas and George showered and got dressed. They told Scott they would meet him and Faye at The Grill, later in the evening.

They headed back to the Eibsee Hotel where they planned to have a nice dinner in the dining room with their ladies.

A young, attractive hostess escorted the couples to a window table. They had a great view of Lake Eibsee. The water shimmered under a full moon, and the Zugspitze cast a shadow on the water.

George ordered the New York Steak with Green Peppercorn Sauce and Baked Potato. Lucas and Shelley both wanted Filet Mignon with Béarnaise Sauce and Chateau Potatoes (hand-turned, olive-shaped potatoes, browned in clarified butter), and Judann went for Sauerbraten with Red Cabbage and Kartoffelpuffer (potato pancakes). They were all drinking Augustiner beer which the dining room had on draft.

"George, you told me Enrico left the gym during your game this evening. What was happened?" asked Judann.

George told the ladies about Enrico and his sudden departure with the 2 big Italian guys in suits.

"When we were at the Grand Prix, Enrico told me the Castignoli family lives in Long Island, and he can't ever leave the family business. I'll let you draw your own conclusions," said Lucas.

Maybe the search for Bruno Castignoli is over, thought Lucas. *I sure wouldn't want those two goons coming after me. The event with Bruno was unfortunate. Yet, the "Seefeld Five" have a special bond, since they handled the situation. We all joked about our nickname after the fact.*

"I wonder what Enrico will do with the vintage Black Mercedes he bought from Jordan Lewis." said Judann.

"I think it looks like a Nazi vehicle!" said Lucas.

"I doubt if Olivia even knows Enrico left," said Shelley. "She'll be upset when she finds out. We may see her at The Grill tonight. It's a good thing her friend Ashleigh is still here, although she is down in the dumps because Regan left."

"You're not hashish across borders, are you?" George asked Lucas.

"There is no way," he replied. "I shivered when I heard about Topo. One of the great things about marijuana is no withdrawal symptoms. At least, I have experienced none. I would much rather take an ounce of hashish to Greece instead of two cases of Wieninger beer which are in the van. Since pot is illegal, it's not worth the risk."

"Lucas, if you had to choose between marijuana and beer, which one would you choose?" asked George.

Shelley spoke up, "It's a good question, George. Coming to Garmisch, this morning, I asked Lucas the same thing."

"If I had to choose, it would be pot," Lucas said without hesitation. "It does exactly what I want. It gets me 'high' as advertised. Nobody says, 'Hey, do you want to get low?' In my experience, smoking good Sativa hashish, such as Topo's Colombian Black, gives me more energy, focus and creativity while doing whatever I do. I know everybody is different, and various strains of marijuana are different. So, while they all make you feel good, each strain will give you a different 'high.'

"Marijuana is a complex drug which we still know little about, even though it has been around for centuries. It has served a good purpose in many ways over the years, including medicinal benefits. Authorities make it illegal, based on opposition from various entities: religious and political organizations, companies selling alcohol and tobacco, and pharmaceutical companies. We are aware of the dangers of beer and alcoholic drinks. But, do we know about any dangers of marijuana, or what they might be?"

Lucas took a sip of beer and added, "For now, I am not even going to talk about the sexual advantages of the plant."

Everyone at the table sheepishly acknowledged his last statement, based on their own personal experience.

"I guess you learned a lot of this stuff about pot from Topo, huh?" Judann asked Lucas.

He replied, "Yes, from Topo and from David, a guy I went to high school with. George and I ran into him on the ferry to Tangiers. I also learned a lot from Stu, one of my young dishwashers in California, who turned me on to pot. He was fresh out of high school and grew marijuana in his backyard. When police came looking for a burglar in his area, Stu got busted. I helped his case get dismissed because I knew one of the policemen who made the arrest. The policeman was a good friend of mine, and he always had grass for himself. He would confiscate it during a traffic stop, but he would not turn in all the evidence."

Cops are into everything, thought Lucas. *Mike Fletcher told me about Bruno being in Garmisch. He suggested George and I work in Frankfurt, get military ID cards and travel before going to Garmisch. It worked fine, until Robinson found me last year, and confiscated my military ID.*

"So, tell us your agenda for the trip," said Judann.

Lucas looked at Shelley. In unison, both said, "What agenda?"

"Our only plan is a drive along the coast of Yugoslavia, get to Greece, then make our way to Athens and beyond," said Lucas.

“Do you think you will have any problems, traveling through a communist country, such as Tito’s Yugoslavia?” asked George.

“No. I’m sure they are used to many tourists who travel through their country to get to Greece,” replied Lucas.

“I read this is one of best times to go there because the busy tourist season is over,” said Shelley.

“Won’t it be hard with both of you living in the van for such a long time?” asked Judann.

Looking at George, Lucas replied, “While we traveled, George and I got a hotel room when we needed one.”

“Since last April, we saved our paychecks for this trip. We had no real living expenses at Chiemsee. So, now we can live it up!” said Shelley.

“I’m sure every day will be an adventure,” said George. “It will be great, seeing new places. I read they had a bad smallpox epidemic in Kosovo. Will you be going through Kosovo Province?”

“Yes,” replied Lucas. “Driving to Greece, we have to go through Kosovo because we must go around Albania. Besides being another communist country, Albania hardly ever issues visas to tourists. It’s fine with me since I have no desire to go there.”

“The epidemic was last March, anyway,” said George. “I think they had it under control by May.”

They shared apple strudel and black forest cake, each had a shot of Jägermeister, and they headed for the International Bar and Grill.

In the parking lot at The Grill, they sat in Lucas’ van and smoked a bowl of hashish.

When Lucas, Shelley, George and Judann walked into the bar, it was empty and quiet, except for cassette music, coming from the speakers. Neil Young was singing “Heart of Gold.” They got a table close to the bar and near the dance floor. Lucas went to get beers at the bar.

It seemed strange when he did not see Gino or John Ferrell behind the bar. Lucas recognized the new bartender, Steve, because they had met in Cervenia. Eric and Steve knew each other in Minnesota; they traveled to Europe together. Steve told Lucas he was living in Biberwier, Austria, a 1-hour drive southeast. He ran out of money and heard about the opening here. Since he had not seen Eric for a while, Steve was disappointed to learn Eric left for Greece, and he missed him by only a few days.

Lucas was still at the bar when Sonya walked in. Scott and Faye Williams were right behind her. He turned back to Steve and said, “You’d better give me a pitcher of beer, three more glasses and a bigger tray!”

When Lucas brought beers to the table, he mentioned his talk with Steve, “The bartender, Steve, is a friend of Eric’s. Steve has been living in Biberwier. I read they have the longest T-bar lift in Europe.”

"I've been on the lift many times," said Sonya. "It is very long and steep at the top. By the time you get there, you must rest before skiing. If you fell off the lift, you might slide down the hill."

George said, "I remember driving by Biberwier on Fern Pass when Lucas and I went skiing in Gomagoi."

"Are we the only ones left of our group of friends?" asked Sonya.

"Sabine is still in Seefeld, and Gabrielle stayed in Chiemsee," Lucas replied. "The others are scattered: John, Gino and Bob went to California. Eric has gone to Greece. Regan Stone went back to Texas. Dennis is riding his fancy bicycle to Australia. Enrico got escorted back to Long Island."

"Olivia and Ashleigh are still here, but they both lost their boyfriends and may go back home to Australia," said Judann.

Shelley asked about the 2 Canadian ladies who were with Grassl, and Lucas said, "They are still in Berchtesgaden, as far as I know."

"We plan to spend a few days in Salzburg, where we hope to see Bertha and Otto who you all met at the Grand Prix race," said Shelley.

Lucas and George went to the bar. While they waited for drinks, who should come through the doorway? None other than Lucas' old foe, CID Officer Robinson, and he was with a young Army Lieutenant.

The men walked over to Lucas, and Robinson said, "Hello, Gary. Meet Lieutenant Braun, the new Director of Hotel Operations for AFRC."

No one shook hands, but Lieutenant Braun spoke up, "I've gone over food costs and expenditures for the hotels. Your food costs at Chiemsee and Oberammergau were out of line and way too high compared with the other AFRC facilities. Let's get a table in back and discuss this."

Lucas grabbed his beer and said to George, "I won't be long."

Seated at the back of the bar and away from speakers, Lucas could barely hear a song he liked. It was "A Horse with No Name" which was recorded by a group called America.

"Mr. Gary, I want to know why your spending was so far out of line compared with the other hotels?" Lieutenant Braun asked.

"Well, the Head Chef left Chiemsee before the summer rush began, and I got thrown into a hotel emergency in the kitchen," he replied. "I did my job to the best of my ability, and with the Olympics being close by, it was the busiest summer in the hotel's history. We had several employee functions during the summer too. I can honestly say the group morale with our employees could not have been any better."

"Someone will have to answer to this," said the lieutenant.

"I just gave you my answer!" he exclaimed.

"We mean this might be a criminal offense," said Robinson.

“I have done nothing illegal,” he replied. “I did not steal or commit any crime. Everything I did at work is public knowledge and had the approval of my superiors.”

“Gary, you have been on the fence between legal and illegal since you got here,” said Robinson.

“That I deny!” he said with emphasis. “But, if I was on the fence, I had good balance and did not fall the wrong way.”

“Gary,” said Robinson, “one of these days you’ll cross the line…”

Robinson was interrupted when Lucas stood and said, “I don’t mean to be rude. But rather than sit here and discuss my future with you, I plan to go live it as it happens. Auf wiedersehen.”

“Hold on,” said Braun. “What should we do about this?”

“I don’t know about you, but I’m going to Greece,” he replied.

Braun and Robinson stood there with their mouths open, watching Lucas take Shelley by the hand to join their friends who were walking out the door to the parking lot. As the door closed, Robinson yelled out to Lucas, “Don’t forget to turn in your ID card and green license plates—and watch out for terrorists!”

Walking down the front steps of The Grill, Lucas thought: *I wonder what he meant by his last comment.*

Shelley asked, “Lucas, do you plan to turn in your license plates and military ID card?”

“Are you kidding me?” he replied. “There are military bases in Italy, Spain and Greece, including the island of Crete. We want to keep those options open. Sometimes it’s nice to get a hamburger, shoot a game of pool or go see an American movie. Also, we will pay a decent price for gasoline at military bases.”

“Who was the lieutenant with Robinson?” she asked.

“He is a brand-new lieutenant, handling AFRC Hotel Operations,” said Lucas. “This may be his first assignment, coming out of school, and I don’t think he knows about ‘Catch 22’ yet.”

Shelley laughed. On the way to the van, she said, “Lucas, you never told me why you came to Europe.”

Lucas gazed at Shelley for a moment, and then he replied, “I have always loved the adventure of seeing new places. Let’s go travel!”

"A good traveler has no fixed plans and is not intent on arriving."

Lao Tzu

Author's Note

High in the Bavarian Alps is the fascinating story of travels, experiences and unique friendships woven around Lucas Gary, the protagonist. His activities involve extreme lifestyles of the early 1970s in an American military playground—the beautiful, fairy-tale setting of the Bavarian Alps in Germany and Austria.

Lucas works as a chef for the Armed Forces Recreation Center (AFRC). He meets some interesting characters who come from around the world; many are civilian employees, and others are military personnel. Since he loves being a chef, the story offers information about food, cooking, tasting various cuisines, and dining in historic locations.

I never thought much about writing a book or being an author. I just started writing and this novel emerged, forty-four chapters later.

If you like historical fiction, you will love this novel. Having spent a lot of time in Europe, I traveled to most of the areas mentioned in this book. I like history and did extensive research to support the events in the story. However, it appears that I don't mind breaking a few rules and coloring outside the lines, literally and figuratively.

I often think about the days when young adults, myself included, were so involved with sex, drugs, and rock 'n' roll in the 60s and 70s. My most memorable experiences happened in Bavaria with new friends who sought answers to the same questions. It was a fun and wild adventure!

www.ingramcontent.com/pod-product-compliance
Lightning Source LLC
Chambersburg PA
CBHW060546310726
48982CB00009B/1392/J

* 9 7 8 0 9 9 9 7 5 5 2 0 4 *